I0788192

SHADOW FAE

BOOKS 12 - 15

DEMONS OF FIRE & NIGHT

C.N. CRAWFORD

COURT OF SHADOWS

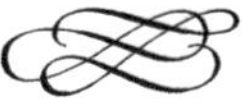

SHADOW FAE—BOOK ONE

For my son James, whose vivid imagination created the concept of Ruadan.

CHAPTER 1

The vampire bared his fangs, and I knew we'd both be dead by the end of the night if I didn't get him out of here. I leapt over the bar with the speed of a hurricane wind, hurtling toward him. I slammed my fist into his skull—once, twice, three times. He staggered back, then collapsed. He'd fallen so easily I almost didn't feel a sense of victory, but I grinned down at him anyway. The colored lights of the bar stained his porcelain skin red.

I *had* to get him out of here.

I tried to project a calm I didn't feel. "Like I said," I purred, "a guy like you would be more comfortable in a hipster joint with arcade games and herbal cocktails. You can talk about synthwave or whatever there. Move along. *Now.*" I may have screamed the last word. A sense of urgency was taking over.

It was at that point, I realized that everyone in the bar had stopped talking and were all staring at me over their pints. A pop song crackled through the speakers, and the neon sign in the window flickered on and off. Otherwise, silence shrouded us.

Easy, Arianna. Easy. I stood over the fallen vampire, holding up my hands. "Nothing to see here, folks! Just an ordinary Friday night kerfuffle."

I loosed a long sigh. Two thin hawthorn stakes jutted from my messy bun, ready for the vampire's heart, but I restrained myself. My boss would flip his shit if he saw me beating up customers—again. And I definitely wasn't supposed to kill people—even if they were undead—in front of a crowd. Rufus frowned upon things like that in his establishment.

You can take the girl out of the gladiator arena....

It was just unfortunate that the vampire had made the serious error of trying to bite me.

As soon as this guy had stumbled into our bar, I'd known he was trouble. In fact, I'd immediately assessed three important things about him.

One, his luxurious Viking beard had told me he was a hipster—not to mention his neon clothing, reminiscent of children's wear in the early 1980s. Whenever guys dressed like him decided to slum it in the Spread Eagle, it usually went down badly with the regulars.

Two, his staggering gait and furrowed brow had told me that he was a mean, sloppy drunk. Given the exceptional alcohol tolerance levels of vampires, he must have drunk his weight in craft beers tonight.

Three, and worst of all, he was a supernatural.

I cocked my head at him as he lay on the floor. He *might* even be old enough that the medieval Norseman beard was actually authentic. Supernaturals like him—like me—were outlawed these days. We had to fly under the radar if we wanted to live. Too bad this one was too stupid to keep a low profile. Four years of executions and assassinations, and this fucker had just brazenly walked into our bar, flashing his fangs around.

As the patrons turned back to their pint glasses, pretending to ignore us, I frowned at the hipster-vampire. Dazed, he still lay on the beer-stained floor, but he'd managed to push himself up onto his elbows. The undead bastards didn't stay down for long. His pale eyes were trained on me, possibly recognizing my own magic.

Ciara, my oldest friend, crept over to us, her brown eyes wide. Her hand was clamped over her grin. I could tell she was stopping just short of clapping her hands. "Oh my goodness, Arianna. You punched him. Do you see his fangs?" She had a sweet but unfortunate tendency to idolize supernaturals, like we were some kind of celebrities. After all, there weren't many of us around these days. "A real, live vampire," she whispered, pointing at him.

"I can hear you," the vamp slurred, now rising to his feet. He staggered closer. "Little girl."

"I need to get him out of here," I muttered. And I had to do it without using any of my magic. You never knew who was watching, ready to turn you in.

Now, my new Viking friend's gaze was locked on Ciara. Red flashed in his eyes. He was after blood tonight, and she was clearly an easier target than me. It didn't help that she was wearing a T-shirt featuring a male model with fangs poking from pouty lips. She gods-damned loved vampires.

"I know your game, little girl." The vampire licked his fangs, swaying on his feet. "You read your little books about teenagers falling in love with thousand-year-old vamps. Our skin is supposed to sparkle like a unicorn's arse, right? And you all get a happy ending. Wrong. Those books are crap. Come with me, and I'll teach you about reading real literature. Hemingway, Kerouac, Bukowski—"

His monologue was cut off by the sight of the thin stake I'd pulled out of my hair. I twirled it between my fingers, and the vampire seemed hypnotized by the movement.

I smiled at him. "Now that you're quiet, let's get one thing straight. I will not have you slandering romance books in my bar." Technically, it wasn't my bar, but that was beside the point. This arsehole thought he was going to feed on Ciara. And moreover, I would not tolerate anyone banging on about Bukowski. "I'd like to just get back to the shots of Johnny Walker I was drinking before you came in, and I don't want to have to keep punching you. I'd prefer not to get your blood on my new miniskirt. So run along. I'm pretty sure an ironic meth-trailer-themed bar just opened up a few blocks away." I leaned closer, arching an eyebrow. "It seems more your scene."

Despite the arse-kicking I'd just given him and the stake in my hand, he seemed unfazed.

He stumbled toward Ciara. "I think I'd be more comfortable if your friend came with me."

I gave him a hard shove, and he staggered back.

The door swung open, and a second vamp came in—this one in a visor, a handlebar mustache, and a pink bow tie. Had someone told them we had a sale on ukuleles or something?

I had to get them out of here. The last thing I wanted was for the Spread Eagle to attract the spell-slayers' attention for harboring supernaturals.

I flashed the two vamps a dark smile. "No supernaturals allowed in here. No supernaturals allowed *anywhere*. Those are the rules. You've got ten seconds to leave this bar," I said sweetly, while calculating all the ways I could kill them. "Or I might start getting angry. And you don't want that to happen."

Viking Vamp snorted, then his irises flared with red. The air seemed to thin around us. "And what the fuck are you, pretty thing? You're not human."

My blood chilled. I couldn't let anyone overhear him saying that.

He snatched a whisky bottle—my whisky bottle—from the bar, his movements lightning fast. Then, he jabbed a finger in my face. "You're not supposed to be here, either. I think I just might tell the spell-slayers on you. Tick tock. Your time is running out, pretty lady. But give me a look at those gorgeous tits of yours and I might keep your secret."

Rage surged. And then, as I registered the word "spell-slayers," dread slithered up my spine.

Okay. I was done being nice. Now he had to die.

There was only one thing in London scarier than me, and that was the spell-slayers. The fae assassins haunted London's streets in dark cloaks, blending into the night sky like smoke. They terrorized humans and magical creatures alike, ruling the city with the points of their blades, silently slaughtering in the shadows. No one was supposed to look them in the eye, or speak to them, or breathe in their direction. But we all owed them a tithe from our paychecks. Protection money, they called it. They were no better than a magical mafia. In short, they were the worst. I hated them and feared them in equal measure.

I narrowed my eyes at the vamps. "You want me to believe you're brave enough to attract the attention of the spell-slayers? And risk your own necks? Bollocks. You're supposed to be locked up in a magical realm with all the other supernaturals, not roaming London's streets. I'm now four seconds away from dragging you outside and staking you."

Truth was, I'd stake them whether or not they left willingly. I couldn't risk them turning me in.

I didn't really have time for too many mental calculations, because the next thing I knew, Viking Vamp was lunging for Ciara again, fangs bared.

Fast—maybe faster than I should have—I pivoted around him, pointing my stake at his neck. I wasn't supposed to move too quickly; humans were slow and sluggish. But the sight of him attacking Ciara sent my blood racing, and instinct kicked in.

I pressed the stake against his jugular. Then, I stood on my tiptoes, whispering into his ear. "I know a stake to the neck won't kill you. But I will make it hurt when I jam it into your throat and wiggle it round. Then I'll kill you."

Something sharp jabbed into my back, stopping me in my tracks. A quick glance over my shoulder told me that his friend, Visor Vamp, was holding a knife to my back.

"Drop the stake, darling!" said Visor Vamp.

Baleros's third law of power: Always let your enemy underestimate you.

I dropped the stake. I held up my hands as if I were surrendering, adding in a bit of trembling for good measure.

Then, when I felt the point of the knife retreat a little, I pivoted, slamming my elbow into his nose. I brought up my knee into his crotch—three brutal cracks to the groin. Vamps might not be alive, but they were still sensitive in the usual places. As he bent forward, I twisted his arm, forcing him to the ground. I snatched the knife from his hand at the same time. Then, I pointed it at his neck.

My lips curled in a mocking smile. "You still want to play?"

Now, at last, the vamps had the good sense to look scared. Apart from a warbling pop song, the room had gone silent again.

Viking Vamp held up his hands. "We'll leave."

I pulled the blade away from the other's neck. As he straightened, he leaned in close, breathing in my ear. "The spell-slayers will be coming for you."

At that, an icy tendril of dread coiled through my chest.

I watched as the two vamps skulked out of the bar.

I jammed my hand into the pocket of my miniskirt, and I pulled out a lollipop. Cherry, with gum in the center. Nothing like crystalized sugar to calm the nerves. I popped it in my mouth, staring at the door.

Ciara grinned. "Well geez Louise, this has been a heck of an evening." She'd lived in the UK for at least ten years now and still hadn't lost her thick American accent. "I haven't been this excited since my Aunt Starlene drew a clown on my bedroom wall to ease my loneliness."

"It's not over." There'd been something too cocky about those vamps, and their parting shot had told me everything I needed to know. I'd heard of some supernaturals acting as informants to the spell-slayers. Supernatural narcs. Maybe that was how these two idiots had managed to stay alive, biting humans like Ciara with impunity. "Can you cover the bar while I'm out?"

"No problem."

I had a pair of vampires to kill.

CHAPTER 2

I snatched my stake off the floor, then my backpack. I never went anywhere without it. My bug-out bag had everything I might need in an emergency: a headlamp, a lighter with aerosolized deodorant for smelling nice or lighting things on fire, medical supplies, a water bottle, cherry lip gloss, fresh knickers, a shortwave radio, ropes, assorted lollipops, duct tape, and a shitload of knives. Never say I wasn't prepared.

The door creaked as I pushed through it into the night air. A sooty bridge arched over the Spread Eagle, where pigeons made their home in the shadows. They cooed above me.

I tossed my lollipop in a rubbish bin. I didn't like to kill things with sweets in my mouth.

Shivering a little in the misty air, I scanned the dark streets under the bridge until I saw movement. The two vamps were moving toward the Tower—the seat of spell-slayer power. I wouldn't let them get any closer to its walls.

I trailed behind them over the damp, cobbled road, moving silently. A light rain misted over my skin, curling my lavender hair.

Quickening my pace, I drew the hawthorn stakes from my hair, holding one in each hand like a pair of daggers. My pulse raced, heart quickening with the thrill of the hunt. I had them in my sights, and I wasn't letting them get anywhere.

When I'd come up behind them, I crooned, "Hey, vamps."

They whirled, and I slammed my stakes into their hearts. And just like that, the fight was over.

Baleros's sixth law of power: Crush your enemies mercilessly.

Their eyes went wide, but within seconds, they had crumbled to piles of ash on the pavement. Rain dampened their blackened remains.

I pulled my stakes from the ash and wiped them off with a tissue from my bag. As I did, I lifted my eyes to the medieval fortress before me. Once, it had simply been known as the Tower of London. Now, people called it the Institute. It was the one place the spell-slayers hadn't outlawed magic. Even from here, I could see its walls and towers brimming with sorcery. Pale blue light streamed from the stony spires into the skies, and a moat of golden light surrounded the entire structure.

The spell-slayers claimed they'd outlawed magic to keep the peace. They said that the apocalyptic wars twenty years ago—the ones between angels, fae, and demons—were forever at risk of erupting again. They said all supernaturals should remain segregated and locked in magical realms. Apparently, only the fae nobility were capable and worthy of remaining neutral among the human world. Everyone else was an animal, you see.

But I knew how the spell-slayers really thought. Magic was power, and they wanted it all for themselves. I hated them with an intensity that rivaled the brilliance of their gleaming spires.

I turned, walking back to the Spread Eagle. As I did, I tucked the hawthorn stakes back into my hair. I'd rid myself of that threat quickly enough. So why did I still feel that eerie sense of dread hanging over me?

When I slipped back into the bar, I found that another grim hush had overtaken the place, and my heart started to race.

I scanned the room until I figured out why.

When my gaze landed on a fae male in the corner, my blood began roaring in my ears.

I glimpsed a sweep of black hair under his cowl. The neon lights of the bar flashed over olive skin and vibrant green eyes. His broad shoulders took up half the booth, and an opening in his cloak revealed leather armor underneath. I had no doubt that every inch of his body was muscled and strapped with weapons. He held himself with a preternatural stillness, gazing at me like a snake about to strike. My stomach dropped.

Fae nobility, and a spell-slayer. Like so many of his kind, he was shockingly beautiful and terrifying at the same time. Under his stare, I felt uncharacteristically self-conscious in my bargain-basement miniskirt that was just a little too short. Of course, spell-slayers like him wanted everyone else to feel like crap. They lived to dominate and terrify. They'd mastered messing with people's heads.

And right now, I was certain he'd come for me, even if I'd tried to be careful.

If I turned and ran now, it would confirm my guilt, and he'd be after me instantly.

My gaze slid to the bar, where Ciara was trying to act natural, although her hands were shaking as she pulled a pint.

Rufus, our boss, now stood by her side. The presence of the spell-slayers had unnerved him, too, and I could see sweat droplets beading at the edges of his graying hair. Ciara and Rufus weren't even supernaturals, and the slayer still scared the crap out of them.

Rufus met my gaze, his eyes flicking wide open. The strained look on his face said, *Get the hell over here. Now.*

Swallowing hard, I crossed to him. I watched as he pulled our most expensive bottle of wine—which, let's be honest, was something he'd picked up from Tesco, simply labeled *French Red Wine.* Staring across the bar at the spell-slayer, he poured a glass.

I cast a quick glance at myself in the mirror behind Rufus. Straight eyebrows, high cheekbones, amber eyes. The only thing that might have marked me as a supernatural was the pale lavender shade of my hair, but plenty of humans dyed their hair bright colors these days.

My fae canines and pointed ears only emerged when I thought my life was in danger, which didn't happen often. In other words, I could pass for human. Maybe he'd come for the vampires, instead?

"Take these over to him," whispered Rufus. "Tell him it's our best wine. Tell him it's on the house. Tell him we'll give him money. Tell him—" His eyes suddenly narrowed. "You didn't happen to see anything unusual tonight, did you?" He was still pouring the wine, and it spilled over the rim, pooling on the bar like blood.

I loosed a long sigh. I often found Rufus staring at the blank walls in his office, listlessly licking his yogurt spoon over and over. I honestly had no idea how someone like him had survived the apocalypse at all.

"Nothing unusual." I gently took the bottle from his hand. Might as well not give the guy a complete heart attack.

"Don't look him in the eyes," Rufus hissed, his eyes wide.

My gaze flicked back to the spell-slayer, and my stomach leapt as I realized his eyes were still on me. My throat went dry. There was no way in hell I was bringing him wine.

I was quickly realizing there was no way out of this situation without fighting a spell-slayer. And I knew only too well how vicious they could be.

"Actually, Rufus … I'm not feeling so well."

"You what?" He sounded incredulous.

"Lady stuff."

"Oh." He fell silent. Apparently, that topic was more terrifying than the spell slayer.

"Gotta run. I'll see you tomorrow." I cast a quick glance at Ciara as I headed for the door. She was the only one around who knew I was a demi-fae. Baleros—my former gladiator master—had once assigned her to tend to my wounds between matches in the arena. Ciara and I had slept in the same cage for years. She knew my dreams and my nightmares. She knew why the scent of roses made me sick. She knew almost everything about me.

Almost.

As soon as I'd slipped outside into the damp air, I shoved my hand into my bug-out bag, rummaging around until I found my iron knife, sheathed in leather. I hated having to use iron. It was poisonous to fae like me, but it was the only way to hurt a spell-slayer.

Then, I pulled out my mobile and called Ciara.

"Arianna," she answered immediately, whispering into the phone. "He's still here. And now there's another one, with violet eyes. I've heard of him. He's the one they call the Wraith. He moves like wind in the night and slaughters silently in the shadows. I think he's the Devil himself."

"Very reassuring, thanks." She was always saying weird shit about the Devil. Pretty sure it was an American thing. Whatever the case, this was not wonderful news. "Just tell me when they're leaving."

"The Devil wears many faces," she hissed.

"I know. Just simmer down, friend. Look, I might have to fight them both. Just text me when they leave."

"Wait. Wait. If you make it home alive, put cat pee in front of your door, mixed with old cabbage."

"Is that supposed to ward off fae nobility?"

"Dunno, but Aunt Starlene put it outside our trailer to keep the police away after she threw an alligator at someone in a McDonald's parking lot. And she set bear traps." She scratched her cheek. "Also, she might have shot them, so … that could have actually been the part that kept them out of our trailer."

"Thanks, Ciara. Gotta go." I shoved my mobile back in my pocket.

Dread bloomed in my chest.

Baleros's ninth law of power: Don't attack unless you're certain you can win.

I'd been trained by a spell-slayer. I knew how they fought.

As a gladiator, I'd often fought multiple opponents at once, taking them out within minutes. I had been the only female gladiator, and my stage name had been the Amazon Terror. The amount of blood I'd spilled had been more than enough to appease the crowds, and Baleros, because he was a complete prick, had fashioned special armor that emphasized my boobs. I'd been quite the attraction.

But spell-slayers were different than anyone I'd fought in the arena. They were ancient, disciplined, with centuries of exquisite training far beyond my own. My chances of winning in a fight against two of them were a little lower than my chances of sprouting wings and flying off to freedom. Before I flung my knife at them, I'd wait to see if they attacked first.

My phone buzzed, and I pulled it out to read the text.

They're leaving.

Adrenaline raced through my blood, and I dodged into an alleyway. It's not like I could really hide, though. Fae trackers like them would be able to smell me.

I quickened my pace, but I'd only gone a few steps before the hairs on the back of my neck stood on end. I could feel them watching me, and my pulse started racing out of control. A cold sweat dampened my brow.

How had they gotten here so fast?

I gripped the hilt of the knife hard, and I whirled.

A pit opened in my stomach at the sight of two cloaked spell-slayers standing just behind me. Frigid panic rippled up my spine.

CHAPTER 3

The green-eyed one from the bar stepped closer, his gaze flicking up and down my body, as if he were assessing my worth. I felt goosebumps rise on my skin.

But it was the other one who stopped my heart. Menacing shadows curled off him, like smoke from a funeral pyre. He was taller than the other, his shoulders broad and no doubt thickly muscled under his cloak. He gripped a dagger, red with blood that dripped onto the pavement. Drops of blood glistened on his cloak. Darkness breathed around him like a living thing, and I held my breath.

It was hard to look at him—the more I focused my eyes, the less distinct he seemed. The most salient thing about him was his piercing, violet eyes, which raised the hair on the back of my neck.

I took a step back. His magic was powerful—and unusual for a fae.

As they stared at me, I was mentally calculating the chances of taking them both on. It wasn't good, and worse, even if I managed to survive, it would mean the end of my life as I knew it. A fugitive permanently on the run from the spell-slayers.

"Hello, gents." I aimed for a casual tone, but it came out sounding strained.

"Hello, Arianna," said the one with green eyes.

My heart skipped a beat. He knew my name.

I licked my lips. "And to whom do I have the pleasure of speaking?"

"Aengus, Knight of the Shadow Fae."

The other one—the Wraith—said nothing.

Don't attack unless you're certain you can win.

The Wraith shifted, and I lost sight of him until he reappeared on the opposite side of Aengus. For a moment, the wind picked up his cowl, and I caught a better view of his eyes. His gaze held no emotion, just a cold detachment. And yet somehow, his glare slid through my bones. I felt like a pinned butterfly under his stare, completely helpless.

He shifted again, appearing on the other side of Aengus once more, before going completely still. Eerily still.

Whoever he was, he moved with a lethal, otherworldly grace. A shiver danced up my spine. He'd come out tonight for one reason and one reason only: to kill.

The Wraith's unnerving stillness ignited the most ancient parts of my brain with primal fear. Even if I couldn't see his face, his lethality was apparent. For the first time in years, real terror clenched my chest. I gripped my iron knife tighter.

I didn't see him coming, didn't catch the tensing of muscles that normally signaled an oncoming attack. Just the whoosh of wind, a blur of black, and the Wraith slammed my wrist against the brick wall behind me. The force felt like he'd cracked my bones, and I dropped the knife. He kicked it away, and it spun off down the alleyway.

So. This was going well so far.

The Wraith flickered away from me again, now behind Aengus.

Bollocks. The other knives were packed deep within my bug-out bag, and now all I had access to were the hawthorn stakes in my hair. Hawthorn wouldn't kill them, but jammed in the right places, it would certainly slow them down. In the future, I'd be strapping iron knives all over myself.

Assuming I got out of here alive.

Aengus stared at me. "Arianna," he said. "You're a demi-fae. You're supposed to be in a fae realm, but you're not. You should have submitted to our laws long ago. Do you know what we do to outlaws like you?"

My blood ran cold. "What makes you say that I'm fae?" I asked.

"We can smell our kind." Aengus's brow furrowed. "If you can be considered our kind at all. Your fae scent isn't noble, even if it is alluring."

My entire body had gone rigid with tension, and I reviewed all my combat lessons in hyper-speed. "Two on one isn't really a fair fight, is it?"

A half-smile curled Aengus's beautiful lips. "Who said anything about fairness?"

That was all the warning I got before he lunged for me. In the next moment, his hand was around my neck, but I slammed my forearm into his, knocking his hand off my throat.

Baleros's fourth law of power: Always anticipate your enemy's actions.

My gaze darted to the Wraith, and I realized I had absolutely no idea how to predict his actions, because what the hell?

But Aengus was clearer. By the tensing of his muscles, I knew he was about to strike again.

He swung for me. Despite his speed, I managed to catch his fist in my palm. I twisted his arm, then gripped him by the back of his hair, driving his face down hard into my knee. *Crack.*

Crush your enemies completely.

I yanked out a stake, ready to plunge it into his back, but he was up again within moments.

Unusually strong, even for a fae.

His fist slammed me hard in the jaw, dizzying me. It had been a long time since I'd taken a hard hit, and I was out of practice.

Still, I recovered fast enough. Before he got the chance to hit me again, I thrust my stake hard into his neck. Blood spurted. It wasn't iron, so it wouldn't kill him, but he wouldn't be getting up any time soon.

I pulled the second stake from my hair, ready to take on the Wraith.

Except—he wasn't there anymore. I didn't even see him moving for me, I just felt the force of his body twisting my arm, spinning me in the other direction. He slammed me into the wall of the alley. The cold stone bit into my cheek. He had me completely pinned, his powerful body pressing against mine. Before, I'd sensed something like indifference from him. Now, given the ferocity of his grip, it was a little more like cold-blooded wrath. Firm muscles pressed against me, completely rooting me in place.

I wasn't used to *anyone* being able to dominate me, and hot fury—mixed with fear—gripped me. Maybe the Wraith really *was* the Devil himself.

This was it. Baleros had no rule to describe this situation, because I was never supposed to let myself get pinned like this in the first place. My mind raced wildly as I waited for the pain that would usher me into the afterlife.

But instead of an iron blade severing my jugular, I felt the searing pain of magic at the nape of my neck.

Then, the force of his body disappeared.

When I whirled around again, both fae were gone. I stared only at the shadowy, cobbled street. I put my hand to my heart, catching my breath. And as I did, I realized I was clutching a piece of paper. I wasn't even clear how I'd gotten the paper, but as I unfolded it—with shaking hands—I found a note inscribed in unexpectedly feminine looping letters.

We will return for you. You will join the Shadow Fae, or you will die on the execution block.

What in the name of seven hells?

Exhaustion burned through me. They'd left me alive, and I'd survived the fight—but I had no idea why. Fear scratched at the back of my mind. Somehow, the mystery of whatever they had planned for me was more unnerving than the idea of death itself.

I crossed out of the alleyway, shaking all over.

The sight of the Institute's blazing spires sent a shiver of admiration up my spine. I hated my reaction to the place. It was a symbol of oppression, of domination and conquest, and I couldn't help but be awed by the vibrant display of magic.

And now—for reasons I couldn't fathom—they wanted me to join them behind its walls.

CHAPTER 4

I woke curled in a ball on top of a pile of laundry and lollipop wrappers, certain I'd just snapped out of a terrible nightmare. It was still night, and a quick glance at my phone told me I'd only been asleep for a half hour. In fact, I was still wearing my rumpled miniskirt.

I rubbed my eyes, flicking on my phone's light.

It took me nearly a full minute to remember what had happened earlier, and then it all came crashing down on me like a storm wave. The vampires, the spell-slayers. The disturbing and unfamiliar feeling of being helpless, my body pinned against a wall. The threat that I could either join them or die.

Something about the night—maybe the magical spell they'd applied to my neck—had exhausted me so much that I'd just collapsed as soon as I'd returned home to my East London shithole, completely disoriented.

I scurried over to my bug-out bag, rifling through my last medical supplies and road flares until I found an iron knife with a leather sheath. I strapped the sheath around my thigh.

Now, adrenaline pumped in my veins, and I yanked open the door, heading for the communal bathroom. Rufus didn't pay me much, and until I saved up, I was squatting with ten other people in an abandoned apartment.

I shared the bathroom with all my house-mates, including a fifty-year-old man who called himself Uncle Darrell and a woman who permanently wore a bathing cap and asked anyone within earshot if she could borrow hand lotion. I donated a bottle to her at least once a week, though I'd rather pull out my own teeth than learn what she did with it.

At the end of the hall, I slammed through the door into the bathroom. I tried to ignore Uncle Darrell, who was hanging out in a towel and flip-flops on the edge of the bathtub. I often found him here in the middle of the night.

"Have I ever told you what I do on the weekends?" he began.

Please don't.

"I connect to the power of the earth," he went on. "Bury my manhood in the fresh forest soil."

Vomit. "How about we don't have this discussion?"

"My shaman says it's gotta be the whole ballsack and not just the shaft. It's quite the commitment, going out into nature."

"Could you not just use a potted plant in the comfort of your own living room?" No idea why I was prolonging this conversation.

He scratched his chin. "I'm not sure that would work, but I'll try it."

Again—how had these people survived an apocalypse?

I rummaged around in the cabinet below the sink, while Uncle Darrell relayed the mild embarrassment he'd felt when a badger caught him balls-deep in Mother Earth. At last, I found a hand mirror, and I pulled it out.

I turned around, using it to look at the back of my neck. And there, glowing on my spine, was a faint, golden rune—a fae mark that I couldn't read.

My hands shook as I dropped the mirror on the side of the sink. I didn't know exactly what it meant, but if I had to guess, the spell-slayers would use it to track me, and it might explain my weird fatigue. So, the Wraith hadn't been kidding when he'd said I'd have to join them or die.

I wouldn't give them the chance.

"You ain't listening, are ya'?" yelled Uncle Darrell.

"Scrotum. Dirt. Got it."

I raced back to my dark room. My heart thumping, I slammed through the door.

My emergency backpack lay by the door, and I frantically unzipped it. I retrieved the headlamp, clamping it on my head.

Then, I found my sharpest knife. I was quickly developing a plan. I'd cut off the tracking mark, then I'd escape London. Maybe I'd go to Edinburgh, take on a new identity, dye my hair black or something.

Kneeling on the floor, I pulled the silver dagger from my bag, and I brought it to the skin on the back of my neck, pressing the blade into my nape.

"I wouldn't do that if I were you." Cold fear shot through my blood. I knew that voice—the lilting aristocratic fae accent. A voice from my most violent nightmares. And the sweet scent of rosewater— a smell from my nightmares.

I didn't think this day could actually get any worse.

I turned, and the light from my headlamp beamed over a man I'd hoped never to see again. Already, I was shaking at the sight of him. How had he even gotten in here?

Of course, he'd once been a spell-slayer, too. He knew how to move in the shadows.

Even though he was a member of the fae nobility, he'd cultivated a scruffy look. Baggy woolen trousers with thick navy and white stripes, a handlebar mustache, a bit of stubble. Pink cheeks, and eyes a deep copper, flecked with gold. He looked like an impoverished Victorian clown, but I knew the truth. He was actually a noble fae who viewed himself as king of the miscreants. Lord of the monsters. He'd created a world for himself where he was treated like an emperor. Like a god, even.

It was all part of his act. He wanted everyone outside the arena to underestimate him. I'd never make that mistake—which is why I didn't try to jam my knife into his eye socket right then and there.

"What are you doing here?" I spat out. The bastard already haunted my thoughts. Now he'd invaded my room?

He shrugged. "I've been watching you, of course. I'd never let anyone as valuable as you out of my sight. A delicate beauty and a ruthless killer in one perfect package. The Amazon Terror. I've missed you terribly."

My jaw clenched. He was already getting to me. "I'm not a ruthless killer anymore. Those days ended when the spell-slayers shut down your arena."

He arched his eyebrows. "Not ruthless? Then what did you do to those two poor vampires?"

I fell silent. I had no desire to engage with his mind games. He obviously wanted something, and I just needed him to get to the point.

He frowned at the mess in my tiny room. "Well, it certainly appears that you've made the most of your life since you left my care. Impressive what you've done with the place. And I very much like the look of you in a headlamp."

I narrowed my eyes, still gripping the knife. "Funny," I purred. "I must have missed out on a few housekeeping lessons when I was living on a dirt floor underground. The conditions in my cage never seemed to bother you. In fact, I thought you liked me surrounded by filth. Keep the monsters in their place, right?"

Okay. He was definitely getting to me. Of course he was. He was Baleros.

"What do you want?" I barked, eager to get this over with.

"I have a task for you," he said.

I took a deep breath to calm myself. I wouldn't let him see that he was rattling me.

"Why would I do anything for you?" I pressed the point of my knife to my fingertip, twirling it. "How about I stab you in the throat instead, then run your body full of iron nails?"

"I don't think so, Arianna." His face still betrayed no emotion. "You know better than to attack someone who would slaughter you within moments. But I must say, I'm surprised you're not living with Ciara. Wouldn't she be safer in your company?"

My stomach dropped. Why was he bringing up Ciara? He didn't give a shit about Ciara. As my helper, she'd been a servant to a slave—the lowest of the low. I was surprised he even knew her name.

"My dear Arianna," he said. "I know you've internalized all my laws. All of them apart from the second one: Caring for others makes you weak. You have a pathetic tendency to grow attached to anyone who shows you the smallest bit of kindness."

My blood turned to ice, and my legs started shaking. I could no longer control my voice. "What have you done with Ciara?" Fury snapped through my nerve endings. It was taking every ounce of my restraint not to lunge for him right now. "What do you want from me?"

He rose, towering over me. Then, he pulled out a mobile phone. He swiped the screen, and an image came up—Ciara, tied to a chair in a bare room. At the sight of her, icy dread tightened its grip around my heart.

A light shone on her, and tears streamed down her face. She looked like she was screaming, rattling the chair in her panic, but a gag bound her mouth. Her vampire shirt was torn at the shoulder, as if she'd struggled.

Rage shook me.

Baleros shoved the phone back into his pocket. "She's in my care until you get me what I want."

"What the fuck do you want?" I gritted out through clenched teeth.

"Something called the World Key."

Wrath spiraled in my mind. "The *what?*"

"You met a few spell-slayers tonight, didn't you? Of course, they recruit anyone who fights well enough. I knew you'd fight well, my little monster."

Understanding crashed into me like a freezing wave. "You turned me in, didn't you?"

A slow shrug. "I need you to join their ranks. I need the World Key, and the Institute has it. Those two slayers you met marked you, didn't they? They're going to recruit you. And you're going to go with them willingly. Find the key and steal it for me. A spell-slayer known as Ruadan possesses it. It's a simple task."

It was taking everything in my power not to attack him right now. "You set me up. You set all of this up."

My rage didn't faze him. "If you don't give the key to me within two weeks, I will feed sweet little Ciara to my dragon. When you have it, send a message through one of the Tower's ravens. I'll come find you."

He didn't have a dragon, but that was beside the point. He'd kill Ciara brutally, and he'd send me the photos. I knew that much.

Violence simmered in my blood, and I gritted my teeth. "What do you want this key for?"

He cocked his head, studying me. "A state of chaos is like unmolded clay, ready to be shaped by our wills. Anarchy is the opportunity to remake the world the way we want it."

I was in no mood for his lessons now. "Just don't do anything to Ciara, and I'll get you your bloody key."

He wagged a finger in my face. "But do not cross me, my Amazon Terror. I have eyes within the Institute, and if you betray me, I will destroy Ciara. Then you will die with the knowledge that you killed her."

I'd get him his key. But as soon as Ciara was safe, I'd find a way to kill him. The more power a man like him had, the worse the world would be.

CHAPTER 5

*J*locked the door to my room from the inside and dropped to the floor, trembling. I picked up my phone to dial Ciara's number, but it went straight to voicemail.

How had Baleros reacted so quickly after the spell-slayers had found me? How had he even known about it?

While my mind was whirling over all the possibilities, a powerful force slammed against the door. Another hit, and the wood splintered, fracturing into my room. I leapt to my feet. On the other side of the broken door stood Aengus and the Wraith, the latter's body shrouded in tendrils of darkness. Having just decimated my door, the Wraith pulled back his fist.

My stomach curdled again. There was something entirely unnerving about the shadows surrounding him. They writhed like ghostly serpents, sending chills rippling over my skin.

"You really could have just knocked like a normal person," I said, composing myself.

The Wraith didn't answer. He just reached through the broken wood to turn the doorknob. His cold, violet gaze promised savagery if I crossed him. In short, we were off to a wonderful start.

As he stepped into the room, Aengus gave a slow shrug. "Apologies. Something seems to have made him uneasy. He doesn't speak, so his motives are anyone's guess."

Oh, lovely. A voiceless, psychotic fae who I'm pretty sure wants to gut me.

Aengus frowned at me. "What in the name of the gods are you wearing on your head? Is this a gutter fae accessory?"

"It's a headlamp. It's practical. Our electricity doesn't work so well. And if you're trying to irritate me by calling me a gutter fae, it won't work. I've been called far worse by better people."

The Wraith sniffed the air like an animal scenting prey. When his eyes met mine again, he snarled. For one terrible moment, I was certain he was going to rip my head off. Then, he backed away again, and I loosed the breath I'd been holding.

I narrowed my eyes at Aengus. "I stabbed you in the neck. Even if it wasn't iron, how did you recover so fast?"

He shoved his hands in his pockets, amusement curling his lips. "Ah, but you're a gutter fae. The Mor like us aren't quite so easily defeated."

I let him see my dramatic eye roll. The Mor were an ancient race of the fae. I didn't know much about them, but I was quickly getting the impression that their arrogance and snobbery vastly outweighed the allure of their beauty.

"Right. Sounds like a load of bollocks," I said. "I'm going to hazard a guess that you have exceptionally skilled healers in your pretty little palace. The noble Mor must need them a lot, considering you managed to get stabbed while ganging up on a solitary female gutter fae."

Aengus shrugged. "Your appearance threw me off, and I didn't want to hurt you. I don't enjoy killing beautiful women."

I nodded. "You're good with murdering the ugly ones, though, right? Aren't you the gentleman."

"Since you're apparently so perceptive, Arianna, do you know why we're here?"

I touched the back of my neck. "I found a mark you left. Honestly, it was pretty hard to miss." I couldn't tell him the information Baleros had passed on to me, so I had to act natural. Or, as natural as one could act after two fae warriors busted down the door to your room and insulted your headlamp. "And your chatty friend left a note about joining you. You'll have to fill me in on the rest."

"The Shadow Fae have decided to recruit you as a novice. If you can survive the first trial," he continued, "you'll be matched with one of six knights as your mentor."

"Matched?"

"You'll spend day and night with your mentor, learning to be…." He gestured at my room. "Better than you are now."

I cocked my head. "Quite the intense relationship."

"Arianna." His silky voice caressed my skin. "Living with us is surely a step up from how you're living now."

He was insulting me, but his voice promised seduction, and somehow, I forgot to take offense. Pretty men were annoying that way.

And maybe he had a point. A musty smell hung heavily over my apartment—if it could even be called an apartment. It was a single room, with a hot plate where I cooked my dinner and a tiny sink. I had no bed. I slept on the floor—a relic of my old gladiator days.

I blinked at the mess around me. Crisp wrappers, an empty bottle of Jack, some of my dirty clothes. Cleaning wasn't really my forte. But that's what happens when you spend six years in a cage, I guess.

I crossed my arms. "Considering I'm a gutter fae slob—why exactly would you recruit me?"

He took another step closer, and he leaned down to whisper. "As you pointed out, you managed to stab me." His voice warmed the shell of my ear. "Normally, I'd never let a female get that close to me unless we were engaged in a more enjoyable activity."

I took a step away from him. Was he here to recruit me, or seduce me?

"You will compete with the other novices," he continued. "And probably die. But if you don't, you will be given the chance to become a Knight of the Shadow Fae, like us."

"A Knight of the Shadow Fae? Is that what you call yourselves? Everyone else says 'spell-slayer.'"

"We don't like that term."

"Of course not," I said. "It sounds unpleasant. What if I say no?"

Aengus quirked a smile. "Then you'll die, obviously. You're an outlaw. You have no rights."

"I'm not sure I like my options."

Surprise flickered in Aengus's green eyes. "We normally don't even bother with your type, but it was *his* idea. I'm not sure why. My companion here typically hates fae like you."

"Fae like me? You mean, someone with an actual personality?"

"No," said Aengus. "From what we've seen, you're a rule-breaking, impulsive slob prone to heavy drinking and undignified bar brawls. Your entire existence literally serves no purpose."

"I feel like there might have been an insult somewhere in there, but I can't quite put my finger on it."

"You're being given a chance at greatness, to live in a fortress and eat the food of knights, and you'd prefer to live like an animal, in a room covered in empty bottles and crisp packets?"

"Animals don't eat crisps or drink from bottles." I narrowed my eyes to deliver my final, stinging retort. "Animals don't even have hands."

"Quite clever for someone wearing a headlamp because they couldn't pay their bills."

"You play your cards right, I might get you your own headlamp someday. If you could see in the dark, maybe you could avoid the stakes flying at your neck."

This was all for show. For Ciara's sake, I was going with them no matter what, but it would perhaps raise suspicions if I just gave in without putting up a bit of a fight. After all, I was clearly an undignified, bar-brawling slob whose life served no purpose, and it might look a little suspect if I suddenly cared about achieving greatness.

I nodded at the Wraith. Shadows writhed around him. "And you're telling me I could end up roommates with Good Time Charlie over here?"

A slow shrug. "It's a possibility."

A distinctly unpleasant possibility, but Ciara's life was at stake.

"Why did you let me come back here at all? Why not just take me from the street?"

"We need permission from Grand Master Savus before any outsiders can pass through our gates, and we knew you wouldn't be going far with the fatigue spell placed on you."

"Okay. So I room with you or die. I get it. What happens now?"

"Now, you come with us. If you can pass the threshold outside the Institute, you become a novice."

"The threshold? You mean the glowing moat thing?"

"Enough questions," said Aengus. "It's time to go."

I cast a nervous glance at the Wraith, whose cowl covered most of his face. Still, I could tell by the rigid set of his shoulders that tension gripped him. I couldn't tell if that was from the state of my room, my status as a gutter fae, or if he'd had the misfortune to encounter Uncle Darrell and his ballsack anecdotes on the way in here. But whatever the case, the feel of his keenly intelligent eyes on me raised goose-bumps on my skin. I was pretty sure he didn't miss much.

I was supposed to steal a key from one of these guys. What would someone like the Wraith do if one of his enemies stole something important from him? I didn't imagine it would be pretty.

Thinking of Ciara locked up in a cell somewhere, I knew I didn't have a choice. Ciara wasn't a warrior. She'd been raised in some back-water American hellhole by an aunt who beat the crap out of her, and I'm pretty sure she'd never once fought back. After we'd escaped our underground life with Baleros, Ciara had saved up to buy a set of soft toys that she placed around her bed at night for safety. She had one called Mr. Huggins that she cuddled whenever she had nightmares.

Now, she'd found herself stuck in a real life nightmare, and no amount of soft toy protectors would get her out of it.

I snatched my bug-out bag off the floor.

"You won't be needing your things," said Aengus. "The Institute will provide everything you need."

My jaw tightened. "I take this everywhere."

With a lightning-fast reflex, the Wraith snatched it from me. He rifled through it. Then, he plucked out each knife from the bag and shoved it back at me. At least I had my emergency supplies and my lollipops. And duct tape, should things get really interesting with my roommate.

Most importantly, I still had the iron knife strapped to my thigh.

I scanned the room, grabbing a bottle of Jack on my way out the door. No way in hell was I leaving that behind.

CHAPTER 6

We approached the Institute, and I sucked in a deep breath.

What knowledge did they keep behind their ancient stone walls? What magical secrets and ancient teachings?

I pushed a strand of damp hair out of my eyes, staring up at the medieval tower as we moved closer.

After the angelic apocalypse decades ago, the world had descended into a dark period known as the Anarchy. Fae, demons, and humans battled to fill the power vacuum. In the end, humans agreed to let the fae nobility—these arseholes—act as enforcers. They were supposed to keep the peace. All other supernaturals were locked in magical realms.

And now? I'd find out exactly what secrets they'd been hoarding behind their walls.

We drew closer to the Institute. Its beaming spires and moat illuminated our bodies with blue and gold. The ancient stone walls loomed above the Thames. A bridge spanned the moat of light, leading to a stone gatehouse with two stout towers.

A fortress, one that had stood here for over a thousand years, a symbol of human achievement and conquest—and now the fae had taken it over. They'd made it their own. When the humans had cut a deal with the Shadow Fae, had they realized they'd be submitting to them?

I couldn't help but wonder about what magical knowledge lurked behind those walls now that they'd turned it into the Institute. Whatever it was, I wanted it for myself. The spell-slayers were right—magic *was* power.

Weirdly, my stomach started rumbling with hunger. It was hardly the time to think about food, but I couldn't stop thinking about the lollipops in my backpack. I fought the nearly overwhelming impulse to pull them out now. I needed to act at least a *little* cool in front of the slayers.

My two new friends flanked me, and Aengus slid his green eyes to me. "Ruadan and I will cross the bridge. When we get to the other side, you set out for the gatehouse, too."

I froze. Oh, *bollocks*. The Wraith was Ruadan? The person I was supposed to steal a key from?

I swallowed hard. "Why doesn't Ruadan talk?"

Shadows slid around Ruadan, and I glanced at his hands—powerful hands that could crush a man's windpipe within seconds. This would not be easy.

I'd never hated Baleros more than I did at that moment.

"Don't worry about why he doesn't speak," said Aengus. "Just worry about staying alive in the next ten minutes. Have a look over the bridge as you start to cross. Your headlamp should illuminate things for you. Most recruits don't make it past the threshold."

I'd faced death often enough, and I gave him a shrug. "I'm not most recruits."

"Your cockiness is going to get you killed some day."

I flashed him a charming smile. "It hasn't yet. Now, are you going to give me a clue about what to expect?"

"No."

Of course not. That would be helpful.

Without another word, he and Ruadan turned and began crossing the bridge. Amber light from the moat gilded the two spell-slayers. I hated them for it, but the bastards looked like a pair of warrior gods as they crossed the bridge, swords slung over their backs.

And here I was, shivering in my crappy clothes and headlamp, clutching my weird bug-out bag of lollipops. *Delicious lollipops.* For reasons I couldn't explain, I *really* wanted them right now. Why the hells was I so hungry? I'd eaten an entire pizza for dinner.

Aengus and Ruadan reached the other side of the bridge, and they stood in the shadow of the gatehouse, just in front of a wooden door.

Tension rippled over me. I didn't like facing unknown enemies. Being unprepared was an enormous disadvantage. Whatever foe I was about to face, he was probably used to fighting fae like me, and I didn't yet know how he operated.

Slowly, I began crossing the bridge. As I did, I felt the magical light washing over my skin in a rush of euphoric tingles. It felt like sunshine after a long winter, mixed with peppermint oil. If it hadn't been for my hunger, I would have felt perfect.

A tug at my chest compelled me to look down at the moat. The white circle of illumination from my headlamp pierced the river of golden light, and some of that euphoria dissolved. Under the golden magic, vibrant green grass grew around bones. Skulls, femurs, ribs … so *that* was what Aengus meant. What had happened to these recruits? When I strained my eyes, I thought I saw the faintest hints of green smudged on the skulls' teeth.…

A shuffling behind me turned my head, and I whirled to find a pathetic creature standing on the bridge. A skeletal, cloaked figure, with tangled white hair poking from his hood. He looked half dead, his cheeks hollow, lips thin. Strangely, something green and pulpy was smeared across the lower half of his face, like someone had mashed up plants and rubbed it over his mouth.

I'd been expecting someone monstrous—a fae giant, maybe a creature with one eye and a giant wooden club. I'd fought men like that before. I'd never fought a creature who looked like he already had one foot in the grave. I almost felt sorry for him.

But Baleros had taught me well, and I knew better than to underestimate my opponents, even if they looked like death. After all, anyone I'd fought in the arena had found themselves facing off against a petite, lavender-haired girl. Most had underestimated me. And they'd all lost.

Mentally, I reviewed Baleros's lessons.

Assess surroundings. Learn weaknesses.

The figure stepped closer, and the hunger in the pit of my stomach intensified. I clutched my gut, suddenly ravenous, my mouth watering. Images danced in my head of pies, sandwiches—even Ciara's weird American spray cheese. My stomach rumbled. Why the hells was I thinking about food right now? I was supposed to be evaluating my opponent, and I was thinking of gods-damned spray cheese.

I frowned at him as he took a step closer, and I felt as if a yawning void were opening up between my ribs. I'd never been this ravenous before. Even when Baleros had taken my food away for a week at a time, and I was sure the ravening hunger would drive me mad, it hadn't been this intense. Maybe the grass would fill me….

Another step closer. I clutched my stomach, unable to think about anything but the piercing desire to fill my stomach with grass.

But—grass? What in the seven hells?

That's when I understood his power. I'd seen the stains on the teeth of the skulls. Like the Horseman of Famine who'd once walked this earth, this fae inspired a feeling of starvation in a person. And then, a compulsive desire to eat moat grass. That's how the other recruits had died, chewing ravenously until their bodies gave out, drained of life.

I sniffed the air, catching the faintest hint of moss on him. He was a fae, like me. That meant he was particularly vulnerable to iron. Good thing I had the iron knife with me. I slid it out of the sheath on my leg. Ruadan really should have been more thorough.

I gritted my teeth, pushing the hunger out of my mind, and lunged for the creature. He dodged out of my way. Just a swirl of steam and a hiss of air, and he'd evaded my blade, reappearing on my other side.

Hunger gnawed at my gut.

I pivoted, lunging again, faster this time. But once again, he slipped away with just a hiss of air.

So he was fast, and the feeling of starvation was getting worse. Now, I could think of almost nothing except filling my belly with grass.

Focus, Arianna. Kill. Clearly, I couldn't defeat him through speed. I had to get him to let down his guard. I had to lure him to me.

Some fae—the worst kind—fed off the pain of others. If this one fed off hunger, I'd let him feast from me.

I went very still, forcing myself not to move even as I felt desperate need to fill my belly. As the sharp, gaping pain in my stomach intensified, I knew he was getting closer.

Oh gods, I needed to throw myself into the moat, to stuff my mouth with grass and chew and chew until the hunger didn't hurt me anymore. I needed to fill my belly so desperately…. The grass was calling to me. The grass would fill me. Drool pooled in my mouth.

But I knew that way lay madness. If I jumped into the moat, I'd never make it out.

Assess weaknesses….

With each sharpening pain in my stomach, I was drawing him closer. This one fed off other people's hunger, but he was also driven by his own cravings.

Exploit the weaknesses.

Maybe I had a bit of an advantage over some of the other novices who'd fought him. I was used to this feeling. When Baleros had grown angry with me—if I hadn't earned him as much money as I was supposed to, or if I'd talked back—he'd lock me in a metal box. I'd go a full week with nothing but water. And the only way I hadn't lost my mind was that I'd retreated to my fantasy world, one I dreamt about at night: a bedroom in a palace, with one wall open to the air. A roaring river carved through a verdant valley below the window, where honeysuckle bloomed all around me. And curling over the floral scents in the air, the sweet smell of apples….

I had no idea where the image had come from, but my fantasy world often seemed more vivid to me than the real world. Right now, I could almost taste the bread—

A sharp stab of hunger ripped me in two. I sniffed the air. He was close enough, and I opened my eyes.

Go in for the kill.

This time, my blade was in his chest before he had a chance to dodge away.

The creature's body began to crack and desiccate before my eyes, his skin flaking off. He crumbled to dust before me, until nothing remained but his cloak.

The hunger receded from my belly, and I slid the knife back into its sheath.

When I crossed to the other side of the bridge, Ruadan and Aengus were waiting for me, lurking in the shadows before a wooden door.

"You survived," said Aengus.

Ruadan moved for me—so fast I didn't have the chance to react—and in the next moment, he was pressing me up against the stone wall. His forearm dug into my chest, and he bared his canines in a ferocious snarl. Panic tightened my lungs.

His cowl had fallen, and for the first time, his features came into focus. White-blond hair hung over his shoulders. Even in the moonlight, his skin looked golden, and shadows molded the striking planes of his face. If it weren't for the malice etched across his features, he'd actually be exquisitely beautiful.

He snarled, and the sound reverberated through my gut. Panic dug its claws into my chest.

By the shadows sliding in his eyes, I knew, then, he was part demon.

"What?" I spit out, horrified to realize that my legs were shaking. "I did what I was supposed to do."

He smelled like a pine forest. And something else, too. The scent of seared air after lightning strikes—the smell of a powerful, dark magic.

His response was a hand up my skirt. He ripped the leather sheath off my thigh, and the force of it stung my skin.

Releasing me, he took my only weapon from me.

He glared at me for a moment, boxing me in to the stone wall. The wind toyed with his pale blond hair.

I let out a slow, shaky breath. "Usually I save up-the-skirt action for a third date, but since you've got such a sparkling personality…."

He simply pulled the cowl over his head, then pushed through the ancient wooden door. Stalking away from us, he disappeared into the shadows of the Institute's grounds.

Nice, friendly people here.

I suppressed a shudder. I'd fought many monsters in my time, but Ruadan was different. He ignited a primal sense of fear, stirring instincts far older than language. If I stole from him, I'd have two choices. Find a way to kill him, or spend the rest of my life hiding from him.

It would no longer just be Baleros haunting my nightmares. The Wraith would lurk there, too.

When we crossed through the gateway, we remained in the open air. Under a canopy of stars, I walked over the cobbled ground by Aengus's side. I had a general idea that two concentric, U-shaped walls formed the outermost fortifications of the Institute's grounds, and that we were walking between them. But I didn't have the full layout, yet.

As we walked, ancient stone walls loomed over either side of the path. My headlamp bounced over dark, narrow windows in the towering stone around us. Moss and vines grew all around.

I loosed a long breath, reviewing my situation. Ruadan had taken my knife, but it wasn't the end of the world. Baleros had taught me to turn the world around me into weapons. Furniture, brooms, glass bottles—all sort of objects could be used to maim or kill. I'd never be truly without a weapon.

As we walked, Aengus cast me a sharp glance. "You look ridiculous with that thing on your head."

"At least I can see." I bit my lip. "So, that was an interesting test. How many of those creatures do you sacrifice for your trials? And how do people kill them if we're not supposed to have weapons?"

"The gorta?" Aengus slid his gaze to me. "We've only sacrificed one so far. You weren't supposed to kill him. You were simply supposed to withstand the hunger and then walk on. You were the one who decided that the trial involved death. Now we have to get a new one, which will be a right pain in the arse."

Awkward. "Well, it involved death for all those recruits whose bones now decorate the moat. I wasn't about to let myself become one of them."

"Has anyone ever told you that you have a ruthless side?"

I flashed him my sweetest smile. *Oh, you have no idea.*

"Where did you learn to fight?" he asked, his eyes narrowing. "You look young for someone so skilled."

"I learned underground." And that was all the answer he was getting.

"I guess that explains the headlamp."

"Where are you taking me now?"

"To your temporary lodgings."

"And after tonight, I could end up with you or Ruadan?" I may have injected a bit of venom into his name, but he had seriously annoyed me so far.

"There are four other knights as well. I take it you don't like Ruadan."

"I'd call him interpersonally challenged, what with all the shadows and glaring and busting through doors. Not to mention the inexplicable silence. And he stole my knife."

"I see. He's got a personality problem, and yet you celebrated your invitation into our Institution by slaughtering our only gatekeeper."

"Are you still banging on about that?" I asked. "I thought we'd moved on."

"Eorleoch was four hundred eighty-three years old."

"The bones in his moat suggested he wasn't exactly the nicest of gents, so if you're trying to make me feel guilty, it won't work."

"He had four children."

"Stop."

"And a pet rabbit."

I snarled at Aengus. "You should have been more specific about the task if you didn't want me to kill him."

Still in the open air, he was leading me north. Silence hung heavily over the old fortress. We passed by several towers until, at last, Aengus paused under an archway. On either side of the archway's openings, a portcullis was raised partway, giving it the appearance of a gaping mouth with iron teeth.

As Aengus pulled a skeleton key from his pocket, I ran my fingertips over the rough stone walls. "Why do I feel like a prisoner here?" I asked.

"Because you are. If you attempt to escape, we will sever your head with an iron ax."

"Nice."

The door creaked open into a dark stairwell lit by a few candles. Inside, the air was musty. Golden runes glowed on the walls, and while I couldn't read the ancient fae language, I had a feeling that the runes provided a type of magical security. No one would be going in or out of the Tower unnoticed. Still, it was beautiful. Among the runes, honeysuckle grew all over the walls, and the ropes of plants seemed to move and shift like giant snakes.

I followed Aengus up several stories of crooked stairs.

We crossed into a cramped stone hallway. Silvery light streamed in through the windows.

"Hang on." I needed to get my bearings. I peered out the window to my left. From here, I had a view of the Institute's interior. A riot of vibrant wildflowers dappled long grasses beneath us. With this view, I confirmed my theory about the layout—we were standing within one of the U-shaped stone walls surrounding the Tower Green. And in the center of the Tower Green stood a pale, castle-like building with peaked turrets. Blooming flowers twined its ragstone walls. I thought it might be the oldest part of the Institute.

"Come on," said Aengus.

"Just a sec." I crossed to the other side. From that window, I could see the city of London spread out like a sea of twinkling jewels. Twenty-five years ago—when the four Horsemen had roamed the earth—this would have all been darkness. Apocalypse. Anarchy. And now, everything had returned like it once had been—except with the added horror of the spell-slayers.

I'd once read that the Great Fire in 1666 had completely destroyed most of London. The seventeenth century architects had planned to build a new world—one with wide, modern boulevards and straight roads that actually made sense. While they were making their plans, London's residents just went back and built everything the way it was, sticking to the crooked, winding, and completely nonsensical street patterns they'd been using forever. It was the same thing after the Anarchy. Everything just resumed the way it had been before the angelic apocalypse. Same bars, same food, same technology. Even the same brands and shops.

"I won't wait any longer." Aengus had already moved on, and he stood before one of the doors farther down the hallway.

I sighed, crossing to him. When I reached him, he was turning a key in the lock.

"Are you going to tell me what happens next? What our next trial is?" I asked.

"I'm sure Melusine will fill you in." Was that a hint of mockery in his tone? "But you might want to turn off that headlamp if you don't want to wake her."

I wasn't going to give him the satisfaction of asking him what he meant, but I flicked off my headlamp all the same. The door swung open into darkness, and he motioned for me to enter.

I stepped inside the room, sniffing the air. It smelled a bit of flowers, moss—and something like the damp mud of a riverbed.

The door slammed behind me. A stream of moonlight filtered through a slim window onto a figure—someone sitting bolt upright on a bed. I could just about make out feminine curves and long hair.

I dropped my bug-out bag by the door.

A pair of eyes snapped open, but her expression didn't change. "Oh. A roommate," she said. "They said I wouldn't have a roommate. Guess they were wrong. Training begins in the morning. You've got a wrinkled shirt. Recruited from the streets, weren't you? I see rumpled clothes, and I think 'not a volunteer.' I put two and two together. I get it. You were forced into competing here. A rogue. An outlaw. A ne'er-do-well. I'm not judging. But me? I prefer to follow the rules. You can follow the rules and still be a fun person. I like to think that I'm a kidder. You know, really funny."

Oh, gods. So *this* was Melusine.

"The rest are volunteers like me," she went on. "But they're large, muscular men. That's fine. That's their thing. I see muscles, I think strength. My strength is magic. When we get to the trials that require magic, I will be in my element. Personally, I'm here because of my superior intellect—"

It was at that point I mentally calculated the probability of convincing Aengus to give me a new room. I put the chances of him caring about my comfort just slightly above the likelihood of spontaneously combusting in the night but lower than the chances of randomly getting pecked to death by the Tower's ravens.

I decided to just stay where I was. And in any case, she was already telling me things I probably needed to know. Things like—we were supposed to know magic. And that would be a little problem for me, since I didn't know the first thing about magic.

"My mother *wanted* me to leave Maremount," Melusine continued in a matter-of-fact tone. "She said to me, you never found yourself a suitable husband. Not my fault none of the men could see what a good wife I'd be. I can make four kinds of bread. Corn bread, oat bread—"

I cleared my throat. "It's the middle of the night. Why are you sitting up in bed?"

"—and corn-oat bread, and also a second kind of corn bread with slightly more eggs. Did you ask some kind of question?"

"Why are you awake?"

"I have trained my sleep cycles. I can get twelve hours' worth of sleep in one hour. I don't like to waste time. It's like the old saying goes, even the fae will die someday, so you should never sleep."

"That's not a—never mind. I'm just going to go to sleep on the floor, and we'll catch up tomorrow."

"The floor. Interesting. I see floor-sleeping, I see a backpack you don't need—probably full of emergency items you can't part with—I think traumatic history. Ready to flee at any moment. Keep all your stuff with you. Get attached to items and not people if you can help it, keep your stuff close and expect the worst. I put two and two together."

Gods save me.

I couldn't see much in the darkness, just the dark contours of parallel beds and a dresser against the wall.

I pulled off my boots and stumbled over to one of the darkened corners of the room. I curled up on the floor, finding that a lush carpet covered it, soft against my cheeks. It smelled of the earth, of home.

Melusine was still lauding her intellectual powers as I let my eyes shut. Images swam in my mind—of Ciara, tied to the chair, a gag in her mouth.

Despite the horror of what lay within my skull, it turned out, Melusine's monologues were actually very good for drifting off to.

* * *

I WOKE with sunlight streaming into the room, and a vague memory of Melusine trying to wake me. I couldn't remember what she'd said exactly, but it was probably something like, *It's morning now. I always get up early, myself, because it's the best time to have an amazing sense of humor and make four kinds of corn bread.*

Normally, I was a light sleeper, but the magical spell Ruadan had slammed me with was still sapping my energy. I sat up, rubbing my eyes, and I got a clear view of my surroundings for the first time.

I hadn't actually been sleeping on a carpet at all. Thick, lush moss covered the floor, and honeysuckle climbed the stone walls. Wildflowers grew from the ceiling—bluebells, yellow wood-sorrel, and lavender orchids. The beds looked as if they'd been hewn from enormous oak trunks, with branches sprouting into the air around them.

The fae had *really* taken over in here since the apocalypse.

I rose, still wearing yesterday's rumpled clothes, and padded over the mossy ground to an archway leading into another room.

I found a bathroom, but one like I'd never seen. A stone tub rose from the floor itself, like a natural feature that had always been there, and hot spring water bubbled in it. Ferns surrounded it, and pearly sunlight poured in through the window. Enormous, gnarled stags' antlers grew from the ceiling, and water trickled into a rocky sink.

But most importantly, in this bathroom, I wouldn't be getting lectures about the joys of a freshly buried scrotum. In the peace and quiet here, I wanted nothing more than to take a warm bath, but I knew I was already late for—whatever I was supposed to be doing this morning. Possibly learning about magic.

Back in the bedroom, a leaded window looked out onto the Tower Green. Morning light washed over a fireplace, carved wooden furniture, and wooden sconces that grew from the walls.

Given all the wood and candles, I could only hope that some of the glowing runes on the wall managed fire safety.

As I scanned the room, I noticed a handwritten note on my bed.

Tried to wake you. Come to the Great Hall. Cailleach Tower.

Yep, I was definitely late. Not a great start. Slovenly, captured in the streets, terminally late: I was definitely well on my way to achieving Baleros's law about getting the enemy to underestimate you.

CHAPTER 8

My stomach rumbled as I pulled my lavender hair into a bun. I could only hope they'd feed us here. In the meantime, I decided to feast on a grape lollipop from my bug-out bag.

I rushed into the hallway, blinking at the bright light that streamed in through diamond-paned windows. Judging by the angle, it was already past seven.

With my backpack slung over my shoulder, I hurried down the stairs, then pushed through the door into the floral Tower Green.

Which one was the Cailleach Tower? It's not like they'd given me a map, and there were towers all over the place. I was pretty sure Cailleach was a fae name, but I'd never learned much of the ancient language.

I scanned the structures before me, referring to my own mental map of the place. The Institute was made of two concentric rings of stone walls—bordered by the river on one side. But embedded in those stone walls were dozens of towers. Cailleach Tower could be any of them.

Even without an actual map, I was lucky enough to have a powerful sense of smell—stronger even than most full-blooded fae. I sniffed the air. Through the floral scents, I picked up a riverbed smell. That was Melusine's scent, I thought.

I tracked it through the bluebells. The scent was leading me to the largest structure—the gleaming white castle within the fortress walls.

When I reached the enormous wooden door at the structure's base, I pushed it hard. It groaned open to reveal a carpet of vibrant moss spanning a long corridor. I followed it until I reached what I could only assume was the Great Hall.

A wooden floor and rough-hewn wood beams supported the ceiling. A long banquet table spanned the hall, and five other novices sat around it. The room smelled of rich food, and my stomach rumbled. As I crossed toward the table, they all stared at me.

It was at this point, I wished I'd forgone the lollipop, and I popped it out of my mouth, certain my lips had been stained bright purple.

Light filtered through tall windows onto the laden banquet table. The rich scent of baked pudding filled the air. My mouth watered.

It didn't take me long to figure out which one was Melusine, considering she was the only other woman in there. At night, I'd only seen a silhouette. In the daylight, I could see that she had blue hair cascading over rich copper skin. She sat on her own, with a few chairs between her and the men.

The other four were fae males, each of them staring at me with a combination of desire and hatred. I was still wearing my crumpled miniskirt from the night before. Contrary to what Aengus had promised, the Institute had *not* provided us with everything we needed. Not to mention the fact that I was pretty sure I stank of Jack Daniels.

The four fae males looked like purebreds, with pointed ears and elongated canines—which they were already baring at me. Of course they were. Most males from the fae realms treated women as servants, and if you weren't from one of the noble classes, you were basically a sex slave.

And yet....

Baleros's fourteenth law of power: Form bonds with unlikely allies.

I didn't think any of the fae males would be eager to ally with me yet—particularly given the fact that they were all snarling at me. But I decided to take control of the situation, anyway.

"I'm Arianna. Fellow novice."

One of the males had vibrant orange hair, wreathed with oak leaves. He'd pinned his black clothing with a golden brooch, shaped like a scythe. His family's emblem, I imagined. He nodded, nearly imperceptibly. "Maddan, Carver of Enemies, son of King Locrinus of the House of the Golden Sickle."

A prince, then.

"Fintan," said one with bluish skin and waves of green hair threaded with seaweed. "Slaughterer of the Feeble, Son of Og, House of Allod."

I knew his kind—they lived in the ocean and ate humans, apart from the livers, for some reason. Apparently, that particular organ was unclean.

Another wore his long, raven hair slicked back, and dark tattoos snaked over his pale skin. I'd mentally labeled him *Goth Fae.*

He narrowed his dark eyes. "Bran, Slayer of Foe, son of Deurbel, House of—"

But the rest of the conversation was cut short by a loud growl from the fourth fae—one whose claws now dug into the table. He was enormous, with shaggy brown hair, a silver breastplate, and a metal helmet shaped with hounds' ears. He wore a tunic of black fur. I had a feeling he was a barguest—a ferocious fae that could transform into a black hound.

His horned metal helmet was nearly falling off his head with his fury, and his fiery eyes were locked on me. I wasn't sure if he hated me for being female, a gutter fae, or if he gave everyone that sort of greeting.

Fine. I didn't really care who his dad was, and I'd just be calling him Dog Boy.

As the barguest's growl died down, a hush fell over the room.

Maddan—the prince—sniffed the air, his lip curling. "You're not a noble Mor, or I'd know of you. No wonder it smells like a gutter fae in here. Female, as well. The knights must be getting desperate."

"A gutter fae," Bran repeated. He sniffed the air, too. Not very creative, this one. "You reek like the bottom of a whiskey bottle."

I cocked my head. "You say that like it's a bad thing."

The barguest growled. "The gutter females in my kingdom are whores. I use them. When I finish, they beg for a coin or two, and I squeeze their throats till they go quiet again."

Change of plan. I was not making alliances with these twats at any point. In fact, I was going to kill Dog Boy. Somehow during these trials, I'd be running a blade through his chest.

"Agreed." Sea Monster narrowed his eyes at me. "Where I come from, women like that are used for sport, and then discarded."

"Where you come from?" I crossed my arms. "A trawler's net, was it?"

"Once," continued Maddan, drumming his fingertips on the table, "only noble males were allowed in the Institutes. Now they've opened their doors to any old gutter whores. It's almost enough to make me reconsider my choice to come here."

I cocked my head. There was only one reason noble males like this came here, and it wasn't exactly by choice. "But you don't have any other options, do you? Your older brother will inherit your father's title, and you're shit out of luck." I leaned on the table, looking him right in the eye. "Now you ask yourself why the knights would allow a gutter fae female outlaw in here. And a demi-fae, at that. One with a shady history like myself. Why would they break with tradition? Maybe, just maybe, it's because they know I'm exceptionally skilled at killing." I nodded at Melusine. "And maybe Melusine over there has some skills of her own. You'd better hope you get the chance to crawl back home in disgrace, but I think your chances of surviving are slim."

All four fae males snarled, baring their canines again. And while they got on with that asinine display, I mentally calculated how I could maim all of them in the next thirty seconds. The barguest would be first—I'd use his own knife in his throat. I'd kick Sea Monster in his head, then throw his knife into his chest. By then, the other two would be reacting. Bran would get a shard of ceramic plate in his neck, and Maddan—I think I'd kick Maddan half to death on the wood floor.

I folded my arms, smiling at the mental image. "Anyhoo, nice to meet you all. I'd better eat before I get cranky."

I crossed to Melusine, who'd ignored the entire encounter. Given that she'd chosen to sit a few seats away from the males, I was starting to give credence to her whole "superior intellect" claims. Best to avoid those arseholes all together.

Now, she was focusing completely on cutting up her food and eating it with remarkable efficiency. If I were going to make any allies here, she seemed like the most reasonable starting point. I dropped my backpack on the floor and pulled out a chair across from her, my mouth watering again at the rich smell of the fae food.

Of all the supernatural creatures, the fae in particular were known for their cooking. Before me lay a plate of strawberries, bread pudding, and apples drizzled with honey.

Maybe being a novice of the Shadow Fae wasn't the worst thing in the world.

Melusine kept her eyes on her food as she ate. "We'll be matched this morning."

"Matched?" I asked.

"Yes. We'll find out which knight will be training us. They're all highly skilled. Obviously, I wouldn't want to be matched with Ruadan."

The buttery bread pudding melted in my mouth. "And why is that?"

"He doesn't speak, which would make training with him difficult, and I heard he killed his last two novices. Snapped their necks. After they fell, he severed their heads with an iron blade."

My stomach clenched. This certainly wasn't getting any better. *Hang in there, Ciara.*

CHAPTER 9

I blinked in surprise. "He's silent and he kills his novices," I murmured. "Those are good reasons to avoid him."

She sliced a strawberry in half. "I told you. Superior intellect."

"Any idea why Ruadan doesn't talk?"

"Vow of silence, I heard. He won't speak until he's killed … someone. He's just really into killing, I think."

"No idea who it is?"

She cocked her head. "Have you heard the rumors that two Horsemen of the apocalypse remain alive? In magical realms. Death and Conquest. I think Ruadan wants to kill them, and their offspring. I mean, everyone knows angels don't belong on earth, and they caused all this. All the wars. The death."

"Oh." A silence fell over us. "I don't think I ever told you my name. I'm Arianna."

"I'm Melusine. I'm not good with people."

"You and me both." I leaned in closer, whispering, "Since you obviously know a lot of stuff about things, what else can you tell me about the Shadow Fae?"

"There are Shadow Fae Institutes all over the world, but this is one of the oldest." Melusine speared her fork into two strawberry slices. "The Grand Master of the London Institute is incredibly powerful. In fact, he controls mist. He has an entire army he can summon from fog, though I've never seen it. He acquired it by slaughtering the last Grand Master. It gets passed on, like an heirloom."

"A mist army. That sounds a bit ominous."

"All the Shadow Fae have a kill list."

"Any idea who's on the list? Besides the Horsemen and the angels?"

"Nope. I expect our mentors will tell us." She looked at my plate, frowning. "You have one less strawberry than everyone else." She speared a strawberry on her plate, then deposited it on mine. Then, she returned to cutting up her strawberries into pieces.

I was beginning to find Melusine oddly endearing. "So, this match you mentioned. How do we—?"

The clacking of heels over the floor cut my sentence short, and I turned to see a fae male stalking into the room. By the mist curling around his body, I knew this was the Grand Master. His white hair was pulled back, and a silver crown gleamed from his head. His clothes were trim and tidy, and he wore a bow and arrow strapped over his back. I wasn't entirely sure how he managed to use the bow, because one of his arms was missing—replaced with a silver replica.

His body glowed with pale light, and I could feel the power he exuded rippling through the room. He wore a silver brooch shaped like a horse pinned to his cloak. But most disconcertingly, in his good hand, he carried what appeared to be a human skull—at least, I thought it was human. It had been fashioned into a sort of drinking cup with silver flourishes, and mist twined around it. He took a sip from it as he prowled over the floor.

Suddenly, I'd lost my interest in the food.

He raised his skull cup into the air. "Novices of the Shadow Fae! I am Grand Master Savus. You have volunteered in the hopes of joining our esteemed ranks." His pale eyes landed on me. "*Most* of you have volunteered. Now, there are those outside these walls who call us spell-slayers. But we do not view our role as killing. We view it as protecting and as sacrificing. Shadow Fae serve the Old Gods. Gods who draw strength from sacrifices. We have always accommodated the gods with fresh blood. We have likewise protected the fae from demonic enemies, and we continue to enforce law and order today by slaying monsters who no longer belong here."

At this point, the six Shadow Fae Knights strode into the room, all of them wearing cloaks in different colors. Aengus wore green, Ruadan wore black, and the rest wore vibrant nature colors, like the orange of turning leaves and the pale blue of a lake under the sky. Like most high fae nobility, the six males were beautiful.

In the daylight, I could see Ruadan's features better. Sunlight washed over the chiseled planes of his face and stunning golden skin. Dark magic—demon magic—seeped into the air around him. He wasn't just a fae. He was a mongrel, like me. He must have been half demon. Whatever he was, a dark power rippled off him. Even from a distance, I could sense it snaking over my skin in a dangerous caress.

His violet eyes sparkled with cold silver, and when his gaze slid to me, a shiver danced up my neck.

"Here, at the Institute," Savus continued, "some of you will die during your trials. In fact, only one of you will gain a place among us as a knight. The rest of you will be returned from whence you came." His gaze landed on me. "Or executed, naturally."

Someone tapped my shoulder, and I jumped. Maddan—prick that he was—had moved into the chair behind me. "They're going to kill you," he whispered. "When you fail them."

I bit my lip. Apparently, in addition to finding the World Key, I had to actually take the trials seriously, or they'd execute me.

Good thing surviving trials was something I'd grown accustomed to.

"If you do survive to become one of us," Savus continued, "you will perfect the traditions of the Shadow Fae. You will learn the arts of warfare, magic, and espionage. You will learn to draw power from the earth."

Oh, please *tell me that doesn't involve scrotal burying.*

I glanced at the four males, who sat with their chests puffed. They were eating this up. *Desperate* to become knights.

"The mentor and novice relationship is a divine one," the Grand Master continued. "Among the Shadow Fae, it is known as *anathra*, the sacred bond between a teacher and a student."

I swallowed hard. Baleros had been a Knight of the Shadow Fae, and he'd been my teacher in the arena. Considering he'd kept me in a cage, I'm not sure he'd viewed our bond as sacred, but the fucker had certainly got in my head.

Savus's silver arm shone in the morning light. "Novices and their mentors will be doing everything together. You will train together. You will eat together, sleep together. You may travel to other realms together to learn the art of combat."

My ears pricked up at that. *Traveling to other realms.* Is that what the World Key unlocked?

That was exactly the sort of power-mad shit I'd expect from Baleros. He'd thrived during the anarchic years after the apocalypse. He had every incentive to unleash chaos again, and the best way to do that was to unlock the magical realms. Shadow demons, fire demons, storm demons, fae—all would flood the world once more, fighting for supremacy. And Baleros knew how to profit off chaos.

Savus lifted the skull. "You will begin your trials tomorrow. Your mentors should train you, and with any luck, you will survive the first trial." He smiled. "And now, you will be matched with your mentors, and you will form the bond of the *anathra*. Please understand that we do not choose these matches. The Old Gods choose for us."

I looked around the room, scanning the possible mentors. The knights stood rod-straight. For just a moment, Aengus shot me a half-smile. If it weren't for Ruadan and the World Key, I'd be hoping for him right now.

As I stared at the knights, silver magic snaked around the recruits. It brushed over my skin in a cool rush of tingles, raising the hair on the back of my neck. The power felt immense. It smelled of the ancient fae forest—of oaks and moss, lichen and rich, fertile soil—and darker things, like bones and blood. I closed my eyes, breathing in deeply. *Home.*

Across from me, Melusine yelped, and my eyes snapped open. She was clutching her arm, staring at it, wide-eyed. She beamed, looking up. "Aengus!" she read.

His green eyes gleaming, Aengus crossed to her, and he led her out of the room.

I scanned the other knights, my breath quickening. Ruadan's magic whirled around him, darkening his form and making him indistinct. Despite the fact that I needed the World Key from him, I *really* didn't want to spend any more time with him.

I shot a glance at the other recruits, and Maddan leaned closer to me. "You'd better hope you don't get the Wraith. He slaughters his novices."

I simply snarled at him in response. They already viewed me as gutter fae trash, so I didn't see the point in trying to act dignified around them. Let the fuckers underestimate me.

In any case, I *needed* to get paired with the Wraith, even if he had the unfortunate tendency to kill his novices. He had exactly what I wanted.

Bran—the goth one—straightened, lifting up his sleeve. Then, he read the name. "Eifion."

A knight in a crimson cloak lowered his cowl. Olive leaves wreathed his dark hair, and he solemnly crossed to Bran.

The two of them crossed out of the hall, footfalls echoing off the high ceiling.

I breathed in deeply, and a hot pain seared my forearm—like the magic that had branded my neck. I smelled burning skin. I pulled up my sleeve, and my pulse raced. I was both scared and delighted by what I found.

There—tattooed in black on my forearm—was the word *Ruadan.*

I looked up to meet his gaze.

But instead of walking over to me as the others had, he shot me a look of pure disgust.

Then, he turned and stalked out of the room, his shadowy magic trailing behind him.

For Ciara's sake, I needed to be matched with him, but my chest clenched all the same.

The other novices snickered behind me.

"What a shocking surprise," said Maddan. "Even your mentor wants nothing to do with you."

CHAPTER 10

efore running off in search of Ruadan, I returned to the beautiful room I'd shared with Melusine for a hot bath.

Now, I wanted to stay in the warm, bubbling bath forever. It smelled of wildflowers and moss in here. *Home.*

When I sank deeper into the warmth, a vision bloomed in my mind—my dream palace, with the river and the sweet scent of apples. I felt safe there.

Steam curled around me.

Sadly, I was supposed to leave this lovely room. The Old Gods had decided that I should sleep in the same room as a silent assassin who slaughtered his novices, and who was I to argue with gods?

I dried myself off, my gaze roaming over the scars that marred my arms, my abdomen. My chest, too. Basically, my skin was a wreck, but I was proud of it. Every inch of jagged, raised flesh was proof of my ability to survive. There was a crooked scar below my belly button, where a vampire had stabbed me with a sword. A deep divot by my collarbone where a hellhound had impaled me with a spear. My arms, covered in grooves and ridges from a hundred sword fights. And most importantly—the deep scar on the inside of my right wrist where

Baleros had branded me with his symbol. As soon as I'd escaped the arena, I'd cut the brand off.

If I'd been human, many of these wounds would have killed me.

I wrapped the towel around myself and gazed at my face in the steamy mirror. The hot bath had pinkened my cheeks, and the water had slicked my long eyelashes into black peaks. My amber eyes looked bright in the late morning light.

At least my gladiator opponents had left my face unmarked.

I knew a woman was never supposed to admit when she thought she was beautiful. It was a mortal sin. Everyone hates a woman who likes how she looks, and women are especially reviled if they're flawed and still have the balls to feel beautiful. Covered in scars, not the right shape, wrong hair—whatever. You're supposed to feel bad about it. So I just kept my thoughts about it to myself. I was scarred; I was beautiful, and I didn't need to know what anyone else thought about the matter.

Baleros's eighth law of power: Conceal your true intentions.

Considering I had nothing else to wear yet, I'd managed to wash my clothes in the bathtub. Then, I'd hung them out the window to dry in the sun, but they were still damp when I pulled them on. The fabric clung to my skin.

I crossed into the mossy bedroom one last time, already dreading having to hunt down Ruadan.

On the way out the door, I threw my bug-out bag over my shoulder. Ruadan had taken all my knives from me, so if he tried to murder me in my sleep, I'd be at a *slight* disadvantage. But he'd left me with the lighter and aerosolized deodorant. I guess makeshift flamethrowers weren't one of the ancient fae traditions.

As I hurried down the stairs, I wondered who Baleros's "eyes" were in the Institute. And why hadn't he asked them to steal the World Key for him? Why did he need me to do it?

I crossed outside into the bright air. On the lush, wildflower-covered green, I sniffed the air. The scents of bluebells, orchids, and fresh grass overwhelmed me. But layered under those—pine. Ruadan's scent. I started moving, my pulse already racing at the thought of seeing the Wraith again. I tracked his smell across the green, and it grew more powerful as I walked. The sunlight warmed my skin.

At last, the scent of pine led me to a circular tower with thin arrow slits and diamond-paned windows at the top. It stood near a low stone gate that opened to the river. I was pretty sure that long ago, human monarchs had ferried traitors through it, from the Thames into the Tower. Once through the gate, they'd never taste freedom again.

Right now, I felt a strong sense of kinship with those poor souls.

I circled the tower's base until I found a black, studded door, and I pushed through it into a stark stairwell.

As I climbed the winding stairs, I reviewed my mission. I had to stay focused on the World Key, without ever giving away my true intentions. I needed Ruadan to let down his guard around me, which right now seemed like it would be nearly impossible.

How would I earn the trust of the demonic assassin, someone so hell-bent on slaughtering his enemies that he wouldn't speak until he'd achieved the task?

My footsteps echoed off the stone tower walls.

Baleros's tenth law of power: Always think three steps ahead.

Once I'd stolen from the Wraith, what the fuck was my exit strategy?

I didn't have one. Even if I managed to kill Ruadan before I made it out of here, in itself a difficult task, I'd then find myself with the entire Order of Shadow Fae hunting me down to the ends of the earth until they meted out a gruesome death.

At this point, I was deeply regretting having never learned the ancient fae art of glamour. Though maybe even that wouldn't help protect me as a fugitive on the run from the Shadow Fae.

I swallowed hard, following Ruadan's masculine scent down a long, vaulted hallway. Maybe I could steal the World Key without anyone here noticing it was me.

What if I found a way to pin the crime on the prince? Two birds, one stone.

Baleros's eleventh law of power: Use the destruction of your enemies to achieve your own goals.

At last, the scent of pine led me to a door at the end of the hall. I sucked in a deep breath, then knocked. After a moment, Ruadan pulled it open. He glared down at me, silver flashing in his eyes.

For the first time, I saw him without his cloak on. He wore knives strapped to his waist, and a sword on his back. His shirt hugged his body, which looked thickly corded with muscle. I could see a few scars on the exposed skin of his wrists. Every inch of him was a warrior, and I got the sense that he was old. I wondered how many battles he'd fought over the centuries, how many lives he'd taken. It was hard not to feel small and vulnerable as I stood in front of him—a feeling I was not at all accustomed to.

Coldness gleamed in his eyes, and the vicious glare he was giving me slid right through my bones. No wonder the Shadow Fae terrified everyone.

I loosed a breath, trying desperately to ignore the instinct that told me to run away from him as fast as I could. "Looks like we're matched. I can see by the look on your face that you're as thrilled as I am."

That look kept me rooted in place, and I willed my breathing to slow down. I tried to imagine my frantic heart beating a little slower. I had to gain control.

He pulled the door open wider, and I crossed into the room. Ruadan's room was more sparsely decorated than the one I'd slept in last night. A perfect match for his effervescent personality.

There was no moss on this floor—just stark, gray stone. And in here, no flowers grew. Instead, flecks of jet-black rocks gleamed in the stone walls. His bed seemed to rise from the stone floor itself, as if the ancient flagstones had sprouted a resting spot just for him. Likewise, a small stone table seemed to grow from the floor, along with seats surrounding it.

The fae had altered so much of this place with their nature magic. Truthfully, it was all more beautiful than anything I'd ever seen. Even this bleak design.

A bureau stood on one side of the room—and on the other, Ruadan's arsenal hung on the wall: axes, swords, crossbows, knives…. Ruadan had about forty-seven different ways to kill people in here.

I let out a low whistle. "Well, Ruadan, love what you've done with the place. Charming and quaint as fuck."

He simply stared at me. A phantom wind whispered into the room, toying with a lock of his pale blond hair. I felt a pulse of his dark magic ripple over me, rushing over my skin in cold, electric tingles. My back arched at the raw power, pulse racing out of control. I willed myself to calm down again, breathing more slowly, and it took me a moment to compose myself.

I pointed at the bed. "I notice there's only one bed."

His posture was rigid. When I'd first met him, he'd projected a detached disinterest. Now, he stared at me with a sort of disturbing, intense curiosity, like I was an alien species he wanted to eviscerate and study. I couldn't say it was a *warm* look.

Good. I just wanted him to get the hell out of the room, so I could search it from top to bottom. The World Key might be in here. Perhaps I could use his distaste for me to drive him out of here.

I slipped out of my boots, then sauntered over to his bed. I sat on the edge, and I unzipped my bug-out bag. I rifled past matches, candles, and chocolate bars until I found a bottle of Jack buried at the bottom.

Aengus had said I wasn't the sort of recruit Ruadan would like— that he hated slobs, drunks, fuck-ups, bar-brawlers, wastes of space…. Maybe that was the best way to get a little alone time in here.

It was also possible that I was *really* good at finding excuses to justify drinking alcohol.

In any case, I took a sip of bourbon, reveling in the warm tingle down my throat. Then, another, longer sip.

I handed it to Ruadan, wiping the back of my hand across my mouth. "Here. I think maybe you could use some of this. You've obviously got your knickers in a twist about something, and this might help."

Strands of his dark magic lashed the air around him. Then, he pivoted, stalking out of the room.

Beautifully done, Arianna. Let no one say that the ability to piss people off wasn't within my skill set.

And now, I had a World Key to find. I wanted to get Ciara the hell out of that room.

CHAPTER 11

I started with the stark, black bureau. I rolled open the drawers, finding row after row of tidy black and gray clothing. Trousers, sweaters, even underwear. Finding nothing on the first round, I went through it a second time, slipping my fingers into pockets, checking the edges of the drawers. Touching everything, basically. As I worked, adrenaline raced through my blood. I was all too aware of what could happen if Ruadan caught me doing this. The threat of execution hung over me like a … well, like an executioner's sword.

Once I'd completely cleared the bureau, I moved over to Ruadan's bed. It smelled of him, and I found the scent disturbingly pleasing. I pulled down the sheets, slid my hand into the pillowcases. I scoured every inch of that thing before putting it all together exactly as it had been. And at every moment, I was painfully aware that Ruadan could bust into the room. Or more likely, waft into the room like smoke so that I wouldn't notice him until his hands were around my throat, ready to snap my neck. I worked as quickly as I could.

I wasn't a tidy person, but I knew *how* to clean. It was just that I didn't normally expend the effort, because honestly, who cares? I stepped back, scanning the bed to make sure it looked exactly as it had when I'd come in. Looked perfect to me.

Then, I surveyed the room once more. The only other pieces of furniture in the entire place were the rough stone table and a black desk that stood under one of the windows. But the desk didn't have drawers, just a few blank pieces of paper on top, and a pen.

Still, something about the placement of the desk seemed odd. Everything in this room was so symmetrical, so tidy. But the desk stood unevenly between the two windows—too far to the right.

I crossed to the desk, and I got down on my hands, crawling under it. I craned my neck to look up. Nothing. Then, I scanned the stone beneath the desk. At first, I found only a smooth expanse of flagstone. But after a moment, I noticed something irregular about one of the squares—a smaller square was inset into it.

Now, my pulse was racing wildly. Could this be what I was looking for? I was on my hands and knees under a desk, in a position that had no graceful explanation or exit plan. But I had to find out what he was hiding....

I pried open the small stone, my heart hammering. But what I found wasn't a key. No, it was a small piece of parchment.

My heart raced out of control as I pulled it out. I sucked in a sharp breath, reading through a list of names—

Adonis

Kratos

They were two of the horsemen—Death and War.

A number of other angelic names ran down the list. Refugees and fugitives from the war decades ago. Then, another name that made my heart leap out of my chest.

Baleros.

I hadn't found his key. I'd found his kill list.

It was about that moment that I became aware of a disturbing feeling of hairs standing on my nape, and goosebumps rising on my skin. I hadn't heard Ruadan come in, but I could feel him looking at me. Generally, I was very good at hearing footfalls and heartbeats, breaths moving closer behind me. But he was the gods-damned Wraith, and he didn't give anything away.

I swallowed hard, painfully aware of how I looked right now. On my hands and knees beneath his desk, in a skirt that was already too short, my pink knickers probably hanging out, and *clearly* reading his kill list. I loosed a long breath, shoving the kill list back into place.

I had a terrible feeling my name would be on there soon.

Then, I slid the stone panel back into position.

With my pulse racing, I backed out from under his desk, my mouth dry. When I turned to look at him, his violet eyes had darkened to pure black.

Oh, *shit.* That was generally the signal that a demon was about to rip your head off.

My knees felt a little weak. "I dropped a coin. It rolled away. Oh well."

Smoky magic carved the air around him, and he shifted in a blur of black to his bed. He lifted his pillowcase, sniffing it. He looked at me, snarling.

Oh, hells. He could smell me all over his bed.

In another blur of black, he was at his dresser, sniffing the air.

At this point, there was really no purpose in denying that I'd searched his entire room. So I started backing up toward the door. "I just wanted to know who I'd be living with. You'd do the same."

My gaze flicked to his arsenal of weapons, but I already knew I couldn't move as fast as he could. He'd be there before I landed my first step. Instead, I continued to back toward the door. His fury spooled out of his body in dark magic, like spirals of ink sliding through water, darkening everything around him. I opened the door behind me, keeping my eyes on him as I stood in his doorway.

When Ruadan growled, my stomach dropped. He lunged for me, picking me up by my ribcage. The next thing I knew, I was landing flat on my arse on the stone floor.

He'd literally thrown me out of his room. *Hard.* Just a moment later, he hurled my bug-out bag at me, and I raised my arm to block it from hitting me in the head.

"I want my whiskey back!" I yelled as he slammed the door.

He hurled the whiskey bottle at me, and I caught it easily.

And thus began the first day of our beautiful *anathra* relationship.

* * *

SINCE RUADAN HAD THROWN me out of his room, I spent the rest of the afternoon searching the Institute's grounds.

I'd learned that half the rooms were barred by ill-tempered ogres. Granted, I was pretty sure I'd managed to charm one of them—a beer guzzler who'd nicknamed me *Viscountess von Tittington* and kept trying to get me to sit in his lap. I suspected anyone with boobs could charm him, to be honest. Already, he'd told where I could find the Institute's library, and I was now on my way up a hidden spiral staircase, lured by the scent of old books.

At the top of the stairwell, an ancient fae guarded the entrance. Her white hair cascaded down a midnight blue cloak, flecked with stars. A high ceiling arched above us, as tall as a medieval cathedral's. I didn't think this had been here at all when the humans had controlled it, but I loved the addition. Just like the librarian's cloak, it had been decorated with silver stars, moons, and constellations dappling midnight-blue paint.

I peered past the librarian. Glowing balls of light hung in the air, illuminating shelves crammed with ancient tomes. The stacks spanned two stories. Flowering vines grew between the books, and the air smelled of honeysuckle. I could have sworn the vines were moving. Gods, this place was amazing.

The librarian peered at me over the rims of her crescent-shaped glasses. "A novice, are you?" she trilled from behind a wooden podium.

"Yes. Freshly recruited. I'm looking for…." I couldn't exactly come right out and say I was looking for the World Key. "Information about magical realms. I understand the role of the knights is to keep supernaturals in their worlds, using death as a deterrent. And I wanted to read more about the locked worlds."

A whirring sound filled the air as the librarian turned, gliding over the stone floor. It was at this point I realized she was on a sort of wooden Segway with silver wheels, powered by fae magic. It hovered gracefully in the air. Gods-damn, I *really* wanted one of those.

"This way," she chimed.

I followed her into the library, my gaze roaming over the towers of books that reached high up to the vaulted ceiling above us. A flicker of movement in the corner of my eye turned my head, and I caught sight of a large pair of cream-colored moths, fluttering around the books' spines. Their wings looked like ancient paper, and their rapid wing strokes raised dust clouds. Around us, dust motes hung suspended in the air, caught in the light.

"Aren't moths bad for books?"

"Those are the library moths," she said in a tone that suggested I was an idiot. Surely everyone knew about library moths. "They dust the books."

It was at this point, I realized the glowing balls of light were, in fact, giant glowworms. They hung curled up and suspended from the ceiling by thin threads of silk.

This place was a gods-damned orgy of magical knowledge. Magic Segways, towers of books, isolation from other people—I wondered if there was any way I could persuade the Shadow Fae that I should work here instead of becoming a knight. All I asked for in return was the World Key. Killing people was starting to get old, anyway.

She led me to a corner of the library, where pale light shone through steeply peaked windows, breaking through iron-gray clouds. It looked like a storm was about to hit us.

"Here we are," she said. "Magical realms."

The Segway whirred, and she abruptly zoomed up another story. She pulled out a book, blew a cloud of shimmering dust off it. Then, she plunged back down to the ground at an alarming speed, before screeching to a halt an inch above the floor.

Pretty sure my librarian friend had a bit of a risk-taking side. I liked her already.

A flash of light illuminated us. Then, thunder boomed, rumbling over the horizon so loudly it rattled the bookshelves.

Staring at me over the rims of her glasses, she said, "You'll find everything you need to know in there about the magical realms. Maremount, Acidale, Loukomourie, Lilinor ... all of them. It's merely an introductory guide. Once you finish with that" —she waved a hand at the stacks of books— "you can delve deeper with some of the other, more detailed books."

"Can I stay in here as long as I want?"

She shrugged. "Suit yourself." And with that, she zoomed away, her white hair flying behind her.

I sighed. She just might be the coolest person I'd ever met.

I began flipping through the ancient pages, skimming one world after another. The vampire realms, the witch realms, fae realms ... none of this was really helping, because none mentioned a World Key.

I paused only at a world labeled Emain—a one-page entry with hardly any information, apart from the words, *Mythical Headquarters of the Shadow Fae*. The top of the page briefly described it as a legendary Shadow Fae world, one that probably didn't exist at all. Apparently, many fae dreamt of it, but no one credible had ever been there.

Still, the pictures had my attention—a palace with columns that overlooked a rocky valley, its slopes dotted with apple trees. I brushed my fingertips over the brittle paper. It looked almost exactly like the palace of my dreams.

* * *

IN THE LIBRARY, I dug into my bug-out bag. I worked my way through chocolate bars, lollipops, and my emergency water supply over several hours. It wasn't like the fae used card catalogues or digital databases, and this was a serious time investment. They just lumped everything vaguely related in one section, and Segway Lady remembered it all.

By the time I actually found something referencing The World

Key, night had fallen. The glowworms weren't cutting it in this corner of the library, and I flicked on my headlamp.

I held a large black book in my hand, its spine engraved with the silver words *Protectors of the Realms.* Just the sort of pompous shit that the spell-slayers loved. Sorry—*Knights of the Shadow Fae.*

Unsurprisingly, the book was about them. I halfheartedly scanned the contents, until my blood began to race a little at the sight of the words *World Key.*

I began reading as fast as I could. Apparently, there were six fae Institutes, each populated mostly by noble Mor. Orders of Shadow Fae, Fire Fae, Storm Fae—and so on. Each Order had appointed a *seneschal*—a keeper of the World Key that locked up the magical realms. That, I supposed, was Ruadan. But where did he keep—?

My thought was interrupted by a powerful hand snatching the book out of my grasp.

Crikey.

My mouth went dry, and I looked up into the glacial gaze of Ruadan. Had he seen what I was reading?

CHAPTER 12

I frowned at him. "Gods below. Where did you come from?"

It had fallen so silent I could hear the moths flapping their wings. Shadows darkened the air around him.

"That's right," I said. "You're the Wraith, and you don't speak or engage in the common courtesy of having audible footsteps."

I traced my fingertips over the book spines nearby. Assuming he'd seen what I was reading, I had to find some way to explain it. "Since you didn't seem eager to train me and apparently are fine with leaving me to be executed, I thought I could at least learn about the Institute. I was just learning about the structure and all that, but you snatched my book away. So, are you going to teach me things, or do I have to keep reading?"

He wasn't giving the book back. He just stood there with that unnatural stillness, shadows seeping into the air around him. It's a good thing I had my headlamp on, or the billowing darkness would actually make it hard to see.

"Aren't we supposed to have a magical bond of some kind?" I continued. "Our anathra? I think I may find myself at a disadvantage for tomorrow's trial if I have no idea what it is. Everyone else is preparing for it today. Don't you have any sense of duty?"

He nodded brusquely at the exit, then turned to stalk out of the library. Given his general shittiness with communication, I had to guess that he wanted me to follow him, but I wasn't entirely sure. I could only stare at the two swords on his back as I followed him, wondering if one of them was destined for my throat.

Outside, the thunderstorm had returned, and a loud clap boomed over the Institute. Walking just behind Ruadan, I followed him across the overgrown Tower Green. He paused only to pull the headlamp off my head and toss it into the grass. I picked it up and shoved it back in my bag, then hurried after him. As we walked, the skies opened up, unleashing a torrent of cold rain on us.

I hugged myself, shivering as we walked. Where was he taking me, exactly? I didn't feel great about our little stroll together.

Maybe it was the human history of the place—a Tower Green where monarchs had once burned and decapitated queens, lords, and priests for treason—but I couldn't escape the feeling that he was leading me to my execution. I willed my heart rate to calm, gritting my teeth. I wasn't going down without a fight, and I needed to keep my wits about me.

He led me into a dark passage that cut through one of the ancient tower walls. As we walked through the darkened tunnel, I scanned my surroundings in case I needed a weapon. But I could hardly see anything in here.

Ruadan was more at ease in the darkness than I was, and I wanted to turn my headlamp back on.

"I don't suppose you'll tell me where we're going?"

The response was a glare from cold, violet eyes that pierced the darkness. But in the next moment, the passage opened up into a misty cemetery. All around us, stone graves jutted from the ground at odd angles, like the rotting posts of an old pier.

Fog curled around the graves. As we walked deeper into the cemetery, I read the names on some of the stones.

Lord Aubrey de Vere
Edward Plantagenet, Earl of Warwick
Mark Smeaton

Margaret Pole, Countess of Salisbury
Queen Anne Boleyn

That's where I paused, staring at her ornate headstone, engraved with an elaborate *AB* insignia. It was the first name I recognized, and I knew her story. Beheaded on the Tower Green for the crimes of incest and adultery—or, more accurately, for the heinous crime of continuing to exist after the king had fallen out of love with her.

These were humans who'd been executed here once, long ago. As traitors, they would have been buried in unmarked graves, so I had no idea what this place was.

I wasn't entirely sure what was going on here, but some magic was at work. Perhaps, while the humans had ignored their traitorous dead, the fae had honored them in their own secret burials, in a cemetery cloaked by fae glamour.

I loosed a long breath. It was a place of death, but hopefully not of execution.

"So, what are we doing here?" I asked.

I honestly had no idea why I kept asking him questions.

Ruadan loomed over me. When he reached behind his back to draw a sword, fear raced up my spine. It took me a moment to realize he was handing it to me by the hilt. Razor sharp, its blade gleamed with rain drops.

I gripped it, already feeling more comfortable. As the Amazon Terror, sword fighting had been my particular speciality.

I flexed my fingers on the hilt. "Please tell me this is training for tomorrow and not that we're supposed to fight each other to death right now."

His response was a curt nod.

Okay. Good. We were making beautiful progress in our anathra relationship already.

Lightning cracked the sky above us, illuminating Ruadan's masculine features, tendrils of dark magic, and the rigid set of his jaw. He drew his sword from the sheath at his back. His violet glare cut right through me, and he stood with that eerie, animal stillness—a viper about to strike its prey. The only things moving around him were his hair and his shadow magic.

I gripped my sword, readying my feet into a fighting stance. A gust of wind whipped at my skirt.

Ruadan narrowed his eyes at me, and the ice there slid right through me. In the next moment, he was lunging fast as the lightning cracking the darkness.

My instincts—and training—took over, and I parried. Our swords clashed, and we circled each other, movements fluid like dancers. The only sounds were our feet on the graveyard moss and our blades clanging against each other. A vicious slash from Ruadan, but I pivoted, avoiding his blade. His speed dizzied me, but somehow, it felt as though we could each predict the other's moves. Still, he just kept speeding up, until my breath grew ragged in my lungs. If we kept up this pace, I'd get sloppy.

"Are you training me?" I grunted. "Or trying to kill me?"

He swung for me again, at the speed of a storm wind.

Baleros's sixteenth law of power: Use the element of surprise.

Low to the ground, I slashed for his legs—not aiming to slice them, mind you. I'm not a complete monster. I just wanted to throw him off balance. It didn't work. He leapt up into the air, avoiding my strike. I sprang to my feet again, and the ferocity of our training intensified in a storm of clashing steel and rushing air.

Now I was getting a handle on his speed, and I let my fae side take over as I dodged him and attacked with grace. As we fought, a dark smile curled my lips. My blood sang with the ancient beauty of warfare. It had been a long time since I'd been able to fight anyone who could keep up with me, and my heart thundered in my chest. Rain poured down hard, slicking my hair to my face. Was there anything more perfect than a beautiful fight?

I started driving him back toward one of the monuments. I'd pin him there, point my sword at his throat. Maybe, just maybe, the Amazon Terror was a match for the Wraith.

Dominate. Crush your enemies completely.

Lightning flashed, and when I caught the amused curl of his lips, my stomach lurched.

I'd seen my fair share of combat expressions, and this one read, *I've been fucking with you.*

How was it possible? No one *ever* beat me with a blade. Aengus's warning that my cockiness would be the death of me rang in the back of my skull, irritating me to no end. I gritted my teeth, trying to focus solely on Ruadan. He was driving me backwards, now, cornering me between his sword and the willow tree behind me. Exactly the strategy I'd been trying to use. My blade sparked against his in the darkness, and I took another step back. I was losing ground to him at an alarming rate, but he just moved so breathtakingly fast, so precisely....

I hated losing. I gods-damn hated it.

He fought with a brutal, efficient ferocity that I couldn't match. I'd never faced a man like him in the gladiator ring because a man like him would never let himself get caught in the first place. As I took another step back, a brief flash of self-hatred pierced my chest, so sharp it took my breath away. But in the next moment, it had dissipated.

At last, he had me pinned against the willow tree. With a violent slash, he knocked the sword from my hand. It fell in the dirt, and he thrust the point of his sword at my neck.

Had he just *Balerosed* me? Lulled me into thinking he was weaker and slower than he was so I'd let down my guard? I think he had. And now, he'd pinned me here. I was completely defenseless.

A deep rage roiled in me. I hated being dominated, hated being proven inadequate, and I had to bite down hard on the urge to scream obscenities at him. That wasn't a graceful way to lose. And in any case, I wasn't one to give up so easily. Maybe I wasn't completely defenseless. After all, swords weren't the only tools around us.

Use the environment to your advantage.

Adrenaline snapped through my nerve endings. I channeled my strength, then leapt up, grabbing a tree branch that hung over me. I ignored the sharp sting of Ruadan's blade as it grazed my abdomen, and I gripped the branch. Then, I swung my legs, kicking Ruadan hard in the head. He staggered back.

As I dropped down, he was already bringing the blade of his sword up toward my neck. But I'd anticipated that, and I leaned away from it, thrusting his sword hand away from me. With my free hand, I punched him hard in the chin, using all the force I could muster. Then, I slammed my foot into his gut. When he doubled over, I kicked him in the face again, but he was still gripping his sword.

He straightened. His eyes darkened, and he dropped his sword of his own accord. Somehow, the gesture scared me more than if he'd brandished it at me. Like he'd just been fucking around before, and now he meant business. When he snarled, I had the disturbing feeling that he was about to prove a point—the point being that he could kick my arse without a weapon.

I swung for his face again—but this time, he caught my fist in his hand. Twisting my arm, he whirled me around and slammed me hard into the tree trunk. I didn't give him too much time before I brought my elbow back, hard, into his gut—one, two, three times. He loosened his grip on me.

I dodged around him and started raining punches on him, but he blocked every blow. His arms moved in a blur of speed, and he didn't even look like he was breaking a sweat. The only sign that I'd gotten to him was the terrifying darkness of his eyes, like I was looking into the void itself.

My breath was coming in short gasps, and I was getting frantic, now. I swung wildly. He ducked. And when he came up again, he punched me brutally hard in the shoulder. A jolt of pain shot through my arm, and I spun from the force, facing the tree.

The next thing I knew, he was gripping my hair with one hand, while his other hand was on my chin, his muscled body pressed against mine. He'd worked me into the perfect angle to snap my neck, and I was completely powerless in his grip. Then, I felt the brush of his canines against my throat. Pure fae domination. I shuddered at the feel of those teeth on my skin. My knees went weak, and I nearly fell.

My pulse raced wildly, my heart slamming against my ribs. I

gasped for air. But he wasn't moving, wasn't breaking my spine. I had the feeling he wanted me to cry mercy or something.

I had to remind myself that this was supposed to be training, not a fight to the death. Had I learned something from this exercise? Primarily, not to fight someone known as the Wraith.

"Okay," I gritted out. "You've made your point. You're very strong and manly, and I'm not a match for you. Yet."

Slowly, he released me. I pushed my soaking-wet hair off my face.

Oh, I was in deep, deep over my head with this one.

CHAPTER 13

*I*n the rain, I followed him back to his room in silence. I had no idea what he thought of my prospects in tomorrow's trial. I had to stay alive long enough to find the World Key.

Stay alive, find the key, save Ciara. That was my mission. And after that, I'd have to figure out how to adjust to life as a fugitive. I had a horrible feeling Ciara and I could end up living literally underground again.

By the time we reached Ruadan's room, I was shivering in the drafty castle air. My damp clothing clung to my body. I pulled off my backpack, and my stomach rumbled loudly, practically competing with the thunder. I gripped my belly. "I haven't eaten since breakfast."

Ruadan was doing that thing again where he went completely still and just stared at me, and I was starting to feel just a *little* weird about it.

When I looked down at myself, I realized that the freezing rain had hardened my nipples under my shirt.

That didn't increase my sense of comfort, and I folded my arms in front of my chest. "I'm freezing. I don't suppose you have a bath? And some dry clothes?"

He crossed to the black dresser and opened one of the drawers that I'd rifled through earlier. He pulled out a black tunic—just about ten sizes too large for me—and handed it to me. Then, he nodded at an archway that led into another room. It had no door on it, so … that was awkward. Then again, Ruadan had so far shown no sexual interest in me whatsoever.

I raised my eyebrows. "I'm going to hazard a guess that when they started this whole anathra thing, only men were involved."

He nodded, and I crossed into the bathroom. Like the rest of his room, the bathroom was sparsely decorated with sleek, dark stone studded with gleaming black rocks. A stone tub jutted from the floor —as if it had grown from it. Steaming spring water bubbled in it.

I peeled off the cold, sodden clothes that stuck to my body. Goosebumps covered my skin, and my teeth chattered.

I stepped into the bubbling water, the heat nearly scalding me, turning my skin pink. Still, it soothed my muscles. Sinking into the bath, I snatched a bar of soap from the side of the tub. I scrubbed my skin, luxuriating in the heat. Then, I soaped up my hair, and dunked my head under to wash it. The soap smelled like lavender. Funny. I hadn't taken Ruadan for a floral soap guy.

I really didn't know anything about him, except that he was a frustratingly skilled fighter, kind of a murdery dick, and obnoxiously beautiful. Oh, and he wanted to kill the man who'd sent me here. From what I'd seen, he had immensely powerful arms—

I clenched my fists, rebuking myself for musing too long about his appearance. I wasn't going to luxuriate here, naked in the man's tub, thinking about his beauty.

I rose, and the water dripped down my skin in warm rivulets. I toweled off, my mind flashing with the disturbing memory of Ruadan's teeth at my throat.

I pulled on his tunic, and it skimmed over my bare skin, reaching to midway down my thighs. My legs had suffered less damage than my torso. I only had a few brutal scars on my right thigh from an irritating dragon shifter who'd briefly pinned me in the arena.

When I crossed back into Ruadan's bedroom, my mouth started watering. On the jagged stone table in the corner of his room sat a warm meat pie, and steam curled from its crust. It smelled of rosemary, potatoes, and steak. *Perfection.*

Fae pies were simply the best thing in the world, and my stomach rumbled loudly again, much to my embarrassment.

I glanced at Ruadan, who still wore his wet clothes. He gestured at the table, and I grinned at the confirmation that it was for me.

Before sitting down, I snatched my bottle of whiskey out of my backpack and plonked it down on the stone table. I took my seat and drained a glass of water before filling the bottom of the glass with whiskey.

I lifted the bottle to Ruadan. "Care for a dram?"

His violet eyes bored into me.

I took a sip. "Ruadan, your attitude is harshing my mellow."

I cut into my pie. As I ate, I relished every rich mouthful. Whoever had made this had used just the right amount of butter. After six years in Baleros's care, I would never again take food for granted. For every single meal, Baleros had fed us his version of porridge—cold milk mixed with raw oats and a can of beans. Three times a week, we'd get limes so we didn't get scurvy. Nutritionally, it wasn't the worst thing, but it definitely hadn't lit my world on fire.

When I was about halfway through my pie, I glanced over at Ruadan, watching as he peeled off his wet shirt. My eyes roamed over his golden, thickly corded body. Like on me, scars lined his skin. He probably could have healed them if he'd wanted to, but didn't want the unlined skin of a scholar. A single, stark tattoo cut across the center of his back—a rune in the ancient fae language.

When he started to take off his trousers, I quickly focused on my pie again. He obviously wasn't shy about being naked in front of me, and it confirmed for me again that he had no sexual interest in me. I was just one of the guys, an irritating novice warrior he'd been saddled with. But I had functioning eyes and he was stunning, so I couldn't really treat him with the same indifference.

When he'd dressed again, he crossed the room to me, and sat across from me at the stone table. His pale golden hair framed his perfect cheekbones.

My belly was now full, and I leaned back in my chair. "I guess I didn't do so well in our training. Do you have any insight for me?"

He simply shook his head.

I was starting to get frustrated. "That's it? This is how you train someone?"

To my surprise, he reached into his trousers and pulled out a scrap of paper and a pencil. He started writing, the scratching of his pencil filling the silence.

When he finished, he handed me the piece of paper. There, in his looping script, he'd written

You are spoiled and defiant, and a ruthless criminal. You are undisciplined, angry, impulsive, and you fight like a gutter fae.

I snarled at him. "I *am* a gutter fae."

He pointed at the note, and I kept reading.

But you don't need my help for the sword fighting trial. Your skill far exceeds the other novices and some of the knights. Just take care to wipe the smug grin off your face, because it signals when you're about to strike.

"Fair enough."

Then, he pulled my piece of paper from me, writing:

Who trained you?

Conceal your true nature.

I shrugged. "It's just something I've always been good at. Must be in the gutter fae blood."

He narrowed his eyes at me. He clearly didn't believe me, and something like cold fury burned in his gaze. Baleros had once fought with him. How well did they know each other?

I folded up the paper. Since we were actually talking now, in a way, maybe I could bring up the topic of the World Key.

I took a sip of my whiskey. "I've heard some of the trials might happen in different realms. I thought the magical realms were all locked up these days."

He folded his arms. Shadows pooled on the floor around him.

"I know you can communicate now. You just did. You've got an obstinate streak."

He leaned closer, and his cold gaze swept down my body, examining me closely. When his gaze brushed past the thick scars on my thigh, his body tensed.

He shifted, kneeling down in front of me for a closer look at my scar. For some reason, it had piqued his interest. In the next moment, his powerful hands were on my thigh, fingers running over the ridge. I nearly gasped at the unexpected gentleness of his touch.

His brow furrowed. I felt acutely aware of the warm feel of his fingers, his breath warming my skin. He seemed intensely focused on the scar—not in a weird, scar-fetishist way. Just clinically curious. In fact, he was inching up the fabric a little higher for a better look. I tensed, painfully conscious of the fact that I wasn't wearing anything at all under the tunic.

I was starting to get the impression that he had no idea what effect he had on women, which, frustratingly, only made him more attractive. Maybe he was comfortable being naked in front of me, but I wasn't on the same page as him.

His hands inched up just a little higher, and I clamped down hard on them.

He looked startled, as if he'd just been undertaking some kind of scientific investigation and I'd stopped him. Then, he pulled away from me.

I grabbed the edge of the tunic, pulling it down again. I was pretty sure my cheeks had gone bright pink.

He pulled out his pencil and paper again, scrawling.

Where did you get those scars?

"Bar fight," I lied. "Someone threw me through a window after I called him a slack-jawed wank-stain."

Ruadan's expression cleared, as if he should have known all along that I was just an ordinary bar-brawler. He almost looked relieved.

"What happens tomorrow, exactly? Just straightforward sword fighting?"

Another scribble on his paper.

You will travel to another realm. You will fight the other novices, but also demons.

My pulse sped up. *Another realm.* "And how do we get there?" I asked.

His expression shuttered again, and he rose, crossing to his bed. It seemed he knew the World Key was a hot commodity, and if I pushed any harder right now, I risked alienating him completely.

He crawled into his bed and blew into the air. The lights in the candles instantly flickered out, and darkness shrouded the room. How did he do that? That definitely wasn't a fae trick.

Still wearing his tunic, I crossed to a corner of the room and curled up on the floor. The cold stone bit into my bare skin. Okay, so he'd got me a pie, but he wasn't about to stretch as far as giving me a blanket. I understood that he operated with a sort of stark efficiency. He was supposed to keep me alive, and I'd be rubbish in a sword fight if I didn't eat anything. But my physical comfort really had no bearing on the matter, so cold stone was fine for sleeping.

It didn't matter. I was used to sleeping on cold stone, even if I was shivering. In the cage where I'd lived, Ciara and I would tell each other stories every night before bed. Stories about magic, about heroes, about women leading armies to destroy the men who'd oppressed them. Stories about a made-up goddess we called Ciari-anna, who slaughtered the grotesque war gods who tried to enslave her. Stories of women who gutted the men who abused them. Lying on the floor, I quietly muttered one of those stories under my breath —the one about Ciarianna burning a warlord to death. Oddly enough, the gruesome details soothed me.

When I slept, I dreamt of Ciara, sleeping by my side, one arm wrapped around me to keep me from shivering.

CHAPTER 14

The next evening at dusk, we walked out onto the Tower
Green. Ruddy sunlight pierced the clouds, staining the sky
with hues of violet and amber.

The novices had lined up, with our mentors lingering nearby. We
stood on a cobbled square at the apex of a hill.

As soon as we'd arrived at our meeting spot, Melusine had leaned
over to me to whisper, "This is where they used to kill people." Given
the look of glee on her face, I had the impression that she stopped just
short of clapping with delight.

I touched the leather strap on my chest. That morning, Ruadan
had presented me with a whole pile of neatly folded clothes: lots of
black leather, fitted shirts, and a few dresses. Weirdly, it also included
underwear that somehow fit me perfectly, as if he'd taken in my exact
measurements. I wasn't sure if he'd picked out the clothing, or
someone else. But whoever had selected it had decided I'd look best in
sheer black bras and underwear, so that was interesting.

And more importantly, he'd selected one of his own swords for me
to use—a longsword of Celtic steel, etched with fae runes.

I glanced at the other novices.

Maddan—he of the golden scythe—sniffed the air when we made eye contact, and his lip curled with disgust.

Evening sunlight glinted off Dog Boy's helmet, and he snarled at me. Why was I supposed to be the disgusting one? The barguest literally turned into an animal who probably licked his own balls, and no one seemed to mind.

Goth Fae was looking straight ahead, the wind toying with his black hair, and the Sea Monster licked his teeth. I swear to the gods I saw droplets of blood on his canines, and I had to wonder if he'd even bothered to leave the liver behind or if he'd just consumed the entire person.

Ravens swooped overhead, cawing mournfully. Even they'd been altered by fae magic. They looked larger than they should be, with glittering black wings. They carried tiny, curled up pieces of parchment in their talons.

Dew dappled the grass, and a heavy mist curled around us.

I glanced at Melusine, who shot me a strained smile. When I looked up and down her body, I could see that she was shaking. Why had they even recruited this poor girl? She must have some hidden skill I didn't know about. It made me more determined to form an alliance with her.

Form bonds with unlikely allies.

As we stood on the cobbles, the mist only thickened further, swirling about us until I could no longer see anyone around me. I heard the sound of footsteps clacking over stone.

"Seneschal." It was Grand Master Savus's voice, and I straightened.

I felt someone brush past me, and I smelled the scent of pine, a flash of pale hair through the mist. Ruadan was their seneschal, the keeper of their keys, and it was probably supposed to be some sort of secret.

I took a tentative step forward, hoping for a better view of the key within all the fog, but Savus's voice stopped me.

"Stay in line, novices."

I froze. This was the closest I'd come to the World Key, as far as I knew. Part of me simply wanted to draw my sword, attack Ruadan, and run off with it. But as he'd demonstrated last night, I wouldn't make it out of that encounter alive.

"Novices!" Savus's voice penetrated the mist. "You are about to enter another realm, one where nothing protects you but your own skill. Some of you may not make it out alive. Your task is to kill as many demons as you can. These demons have been given to us as sacrificial gifts from the shadow realm. They are prisoners in this world." He paused before uttering the final words of his warning. "Because they were too deviant even for demonkind."

A burst of cold magic rippled over my skin, surging through my blood. My back arched at the power. Then, the mist began to thin. When it retreated fully, I found that we were still standing on the Tower Green. Except, this time, it looked like the Tower Green of old. Vines and wildflowers no longer covered the walls. Where the cobbled square had been a few minutes ago, now stood a forbidding wooden scaffold—an execution site.

I glanced at the other novices. Each of them had already drawn their swords, and they scanned the green. An eerie silence hung over us like a funeral pall. If I was going to survive the execution block, I'd have to outcompete the other novices. I had to kill as many demons as possible.

Just as soon as I could find them. Black studded doors blocked most of the entrances to the towers. Were there demons lurking behind them?

I sniffed the air, scenting something unfamiliar. Not fae, no. It smelled cold and musty, like the bottom of a grave. That was where I needed to go.

I glanced at the other novices, who were still hanging around the cobbled area.

At least, until the barguest unleashed a wild, bestial roar, charging for one of the towers. As he did, a white-horned demon burst through a door, dressed in silver armor. I watched as the barguest fought him with brutal swings of his sword. I took just a moment to analyze his form. He had a powerful swing, capable of slicing through a tree trunk, but his technique was a little uncontrolled, and he kept leaving himself open on the right side.

Still, sloppy or not, he was about to slaughter the demon, which meant he was one demon closer to winning than I was.

I sniffed the air again, catching the grave-like scent. I unsheathed my sword, following the smell across the green to one of the towers. I broke into a sprint before any of the other novices caught on that I had a lead.

I kicked through the wooden door into a stairwell, then crept inside, my sword raised. In here, the scent of rot grew stronger, and I followed it up the narrow stairs. Halfway up the tower, the stairwell opened into a great hall—one filled with around a dozen people dressed in gem-studded costumes. A banquet table spanned one side. A melodious song floated in the air.

My jaw dropped. This wasn't the slaughter-fest I'd expected. No, this was a lavish Tudor ball, and the guests wore beautiful masks: swans, butterflies, flowers…. Between balconies above us, vibrant silk swathes spanned the ceiling, flecked with pearls and gems. Jeweled fabric lined the walls, too.

If I didn't have demon killing on the agenda right now, I'd drop my sword and start digging into the meat and potatoes laid out on the table. The Tudors were damned good at throwing parties.

But who, exactly, was I supposed to fight? They didn't even look like demons.

As I stalked into the room, the chatter died down, quiet enough that I could hear my own footsteps and the clashing of swords outside. A roar from the barguest outside pierced the windows. Everyone stared at me.

As the crowd parted for me, a new figure emerged. There, at the other end of the hall, a woman glided toward me. She wore a green silk dress, studded with pearls, and her black hair had been pulled back tightly into a cap. On top of her cap sat a demure silver crown. Was she a queen?

Something about her dark eyes was particularly alluring, and her delicately curved figure gave the impression that she was about to burst out of her gown. She wore a beautiful pearl necklace around her delicate throat. The only thing a bit off about her was the sixth finger on her right hand. Still, my body tingled at the sight of her. In fact, I wanted to touch her.

So *she* was the demon.

An evil queen, perhaps. A warped, demonic, witchy version of Anne Boleyn?

She lifted a graceful hand. "Have you come to join us?" Her voice sounded alluring, an invitation I couldn't resist. I gripped my sword harder. I couldn't bring myself to just swing for her. For one thing, she hadn't attacked, and for another, she was giving me a seductive pout. I kind of wanted to be her friend or give her a hug or something….

I swallowed hard. "I'm looking for a demon."

Her lip curved in a graceful smile, and her eyelashes fluttered. "A demon?" she trilled.

Around her, the small crowd burst into delicate laughter.

Okay, this was really not going as planned. I'd frankly be *much* more comfortable if I'd busted into a room of naked men hacking into each other with swords. That probably said something disturbing about me, but it wasn't the time to dwell on personal flaws.

The witch glided closer again, her body undulating with seductive grace. The faintest hints of dark magic curled around her. A succubus?

My eyes flicked around the room, and I started to think that everyone in here was in her thrall, lured in by her spell. She was drawing me in, too, and I had to resist her.

I lifted my sword, ready to strike, except I couldn't quite bring myself to do it. I needed a different demon to slaughter.

As I stared at her, the woman's ears lengthened into those of a doe, her dark eyes widening. "Touch me not," she whispered, a delicate hand reaching for me.

I could almost hear her heart beating from here, and I was torn by competing impulses to hug her and kill her.

Then, she broke into a run through the hall—but it only lasted a moment before an arrow pierced her neck. One of the revelers had shot her—a bearded man in a ruff with a sort of beret on his head. His eyes sparked with wild flames.

I gritted my teeth. *He* had a weapon. He had demon eyes. He could die. He nocked an arrow, aiming it now at me, and he fired. I managed to deflect the arrow with my sword.

Definitely okay with killing him. While he was trying to nock another arrow, I lunged for him. I carved through his bow with my sword, then drove it through his chest. Bellows erupted around me. Now, flames gleamed in all the guests' eyes. I was starting to realize I'd misinterpreted the whole situation when I'd first arrived.

I was in a hell world of some kind, and the seductive woman was their victim. Because of course she was—that was how the world worked. Ciarianna would not put up with that shit.

I pivoted, ready to take on the next demon. But at the sound of swords being drawn from their sheaths, adrenaline blazed through my nerves. I'd apparently taken on a crowd of eleven men. I sheathed my sword, a hint of panic whispering in my skull.

Baleros's twelfth law of power: Know when you're outnumbered.

CHAPTER 15

I leapt into the air, snatching one of the swathes of fabric. I climbed up, hand over hand, until I reached the mezzanine level, and I swung into one of the balconies. I scanned my surroundings, my gaze quickly landing on a stairwell. I could make a fast exit, but I needed to take out as many as possible on the way out.

My gaze flicked over the lanterns burning brightly in the balcony. Maybe a little fire would help direct things my way.

Baleros's fifteenth law of power: Always use your surroundings.

My pulse racing, I pulled one of the lanterns off its mount and hurled it down to the lower level. The oil ignited, causing a small explosion that lit the fabric on the walls.

I sprinted for the stairwell, then thundered down the stairs, my sword drawn. As the demonic guests began to run for the exit, fleeing the smoke and flames, I drove my sword into them, one by one. In their panic, none of them were prepared for me, and I hacked into them, slaughtering the first two down the stairs. The rest turned and ran back into the burning building.

Smoke filled the air, now, and I turned to flee the tower before the whole thing burned down. When I reached the lower level, the silver-crowned queen raced past me. My jaw dropped. She'd come to life again.

It seemed she'd been condemned to a hell world where she was fated to die over and over again. What crime had she committed? Seduction, probably. In worlds ruled by men, that in itself was some kind of unforgivable witchcraft.

I was dimly aware of the other novices fighting demons around me, but my attention was on the queen, who stood in the grass. Blood spattered her green gown.

From behind her, a hulking, beastly demon burst through one of the iron-studded doors. His body was that of a giant man, bedecked in the robes and furs of a king, and his eyes glistened like white pearls. But his face was leonine, and he had a mane of ginger hair. A golden crown gleamed on top of his head. So, she was the queen, and here we had our king.

My pulse raced at the sight of him, and part of my brain screamed that I needed to run, fast.

I stared as he flicked his wrist, severing the woman's head from her body.

Another demon I'll happily slaughter.

As I ran for him, my sword drawn, he unsheathed his own longsword. He roared, and our blades clashed, steel against steel. His strikes held an immense power, and I struggled to keep my balance.

He roared again, and a powerful blow crashed into my sword. I stumbled for a moment, losing my footing, and he lunged for me, swinging wildly. Regaining my composure, I nimbly dodged back, but he caught me with the tip of his sword, drawing blood from my abdomen. I gripped my gut, my heart thundering.

Oh, shit. I was losing control of this situation.

He slashed for me again, and I dodged. This time, he just nicked me in the hip. A hot stab of pain shot through me.

I clenched my jaw. I needed to get control here.

I gripped my sword hard, striking for him. He parried, again and again, but his size also slowed him down. Now, a familiar strength and surety coursed through me. I knew exactly how to angle my blade, exactly where each step should fall, until I was driving him back into a wall. Power—my legacy, my heritage—suffused my limbs. Still, I took care to wipe the smug look off my face, just as Ruadan had instructed.

I could see that my opponent's form was growing sloppier the longer it went on. I suppressed a smile as he retreated toward one of the tower walls. I *really* liked defeating enemies who were much larger than I was. There was just something about the look of disbelief on their faces….

When he stumbled, I seized the moment and lunged for him, thrusting my sword into his heart. His milky eyes widened in horror, and I pulled out my glistening, red blade.

I'd been injured—pretty badly—but my gladiator training had conditioned me to survive a fight by blocking out pain. Adrenaline raced through me, numbing the agony I should have felt.

Once I slaughtered him, a loud bell began to toll, and a roaring noise rumbled off the stone walls. Streams of demons began bursting through the black wooden doors, racing onto the green, swords and axes raised. They wore jeweled clothing and velvet caps, and many had black wings and talons. My stomach dropped at the sight of them.

It seemed that killing the demon-king in this world was a bit of a faux-pas. In fact, the demons were all bellowing something that sounded like *treason, treason, treason!*

Just as I was contemplating the logistics of fighting off an entire horde of Tudor-era demons, a small whirlpool of water bloomed by the cobbled square.

That was our exit out of here. Already, Maddan and the barguest were abandoning their posts, leaping into the water. Not the *worst* idea in the world. Clearly, the knights had been watching us, deciding when they needed to intervene.

My gaze darted, and I caught a glimpse of a crowd of demons closing in on Goth Fae—Bran, his name was. So much for being a Slayer of Foes. I winced at the sight of his body getting hacked by brutal Tudor swords. He fell to the ground, and his blood stained the grass.

But before I abandoned ship completely, I surveyed the battleground until my gaze landed on Melusine. Two rangy demons in lacy ruffs were boxing her in. I couldn't let them just slaughter her. I raced for them, sword drawn.

As soon as I reached them, I carved my sword into the first demon, slicing through his gut. Then, I whirled, cutting my blade through the other's neck. Blood arced through the air.

"Get to the portal!" I shouted.

I glanced back at the woman in the green dress, who'd come to life again—reunited with her head. Gods-damn it. I couldn't just leave her here, either.

I had just one more task before I left this realm….

Danger was closing in around me, and my canines began lengthening as my fae form took over. Still, I ran for the woman in the green dress, moving as fast as a hurricane, dodging my demonic attackers. Pure power imbued my limbs.

When I reached her, I grabbed her arm. She was shrieking, hysterical, but I dragged her along with me. I used my free arm to fend off attackers with my sword. We reached the portal, and I shoved her into the whirlpool, pivoting one last time to drive my sword into a demon.

Then, I leapt into the portal, and the icy water enveloped me.

The portal sucked me in deeper, drawing me further under. I brushed past the queen's silky dress, and I wrapped an arm around her so I could drag her out with me when the time came. I wasn't sure exactly why, but apparently I'd made it my job to be her protector, and she was coming back to my world with me.

As we sank deeper into the portal, my lungs began to burn, until at last I felt the downward tug relenting. I kicked my legs to bring us up swiftly to the surface. Light began to pierce the water, growing brighter until we breached the surface. I hoisted myself over the stone lip of the portal. Then, I dragged the queen out.

I hauled both our arses out of the water, soaking wet.

On my knees, I struggled to catch my breath. From the ground, I looked up into the face of Grand Master Savus. He looked perplexed, his silver eyebrows furrowed. A splashing noise behind me turned my head. A velvet-capped, black-winged demon was trying to hoist himself from the portal. Instinctively, I swung for him, severing his head from his body. His blood stained the portal red.

As all the adrenaline left my veins, pain slammed into me, and I felt the deep gashes that had been carved into my hip and my abdomen. I realized that my blood was pouring down my body, mingling with the water.

Grand Master Savus cocked his head. "You're a demi-fae. What is your other half?"

I swallowed hard. I'd been hoping that wouldn't come up, but he must have realized that my strength exceeded that of even a noble, full-blooded fae. "I don't know," I lied. "I was an orphan."

With a swirl of dark magic, the portal began closing up in front of us.

Grand Master Savus glared at the queen, who was sobbing hysterically on the cobbles. "You brought something back with you."

I gripped my stomach, trying to block out the pain tearing through my side. "Sorry about that. She didn't belong there. Those demons were twats."

Swirls of mist poured off Savus, skimming over my skin like some kind of warning. "Well, you successfully slaughtered more demons than any other novice, so I will grant you a bit of leeway."

Melusine crossed to me, grabbing my elbow to help me up. "Why did you kill the demons surrounding me? The other novices are trying to thin the competition, and you decided to keep me in it."

I grimaced, holding my waist. "You gave me a strawberry. Also, we have a greater chance of lasting if we work together."

She nodded. "Oh. I see. It's strategic. I'm not good with a sword, but I can be useful, too."

I believed her.

The three other novices stood on the cobbles, bodies dripping with water. The goth had been killed, but the other males remained. I narrowed my eyes at them.

One down, three to go.

It took me a minute to pick out Ruadan, but he was there, standing behind the recruits. Shadowy magic cloaked him.

But from within his cloud of dark magic, his violet eyes burned with curiosity. I hadn't just surprised the other recruits. I'd surprised him, too.

CHAPTER 16

I sat on the cold floor of Ruadan's room, holding my side. I'd tried to stitch myself up a little bit. Since I didn't know any magic, I couldn't heal myself the way the other recruits would.

In the gladiator ring, the masters had allowed some types of magic —fireballs, electrical pulses, anything that didn't require words. For the most part, gladiators were suspicious of anything that involved language. They liked pointy things and magic that went boom, but they weren't exactly the thinking types.

I sighed. It was probably for the best that way. Someone like me probably shouldn't have access to powerful magic, because gods knew what I'd do with it.

So instead of using magic to heal myself, I'd spent the last twenty minutes gritting my teeth and stitching my skin together with a needle and thread—something I'd done many times before. Sadly, I had to use up some of my whiskey to clean the wounds on my belly and my hip.

The wounds still didn't feel quite right, though, and I only had to hope that the next trial would involve a bit less slicing.

Grimacing, I pierced the final piece of skin with the needle, then tied off the thread. I cut it and collapsed against Ruadan's rocky bed.

Exhaustion ate at me, and I was trembling a little from the pain. Just as my eyes were drifting closed, the door creaked open.

Ruadan glided into the room. His very presence seemed to darken the space around him, the air frosting about us, candles flickering in their sconces.

I shuddered at the sight of him, until he pulled down his dark cowl. Then, my gaze roamed over the stark perfection of his face. The irritating bastard had a way of mesmerizing me.

Given that the gods had blessed him with such overwhelming beauty, it was a shame he always cloaked it with his hood and dark magic. But of course, a man like Ruadan wasn't the type to indulge in trivial things like enjoying life at all.

Aengus pushed through the door behind him, and it creaked on its hinges.

"Where have you two been?" I asked.

Aengus's lips curled in a wry smile. "Trying to figure out what to do with the queen you brought into our fortress."

"Who is she?" I asked, still gripping my side.

Aengus shrugged. "Calls herself Nan Bullen. She's a bit of a diva."

"She's pretty," I pointed out. "Maybe she'll make a charming wife for one of the knights."

Aengus arched an eyebrow. "Has no one told you? Knights of the Shadow Fae are not allowed to take wives. Or lovers. Or anything enjoyable."

I glanced at Ruadan, who'd taken one of his knives off the wall to sharpen it. "I can see why Ruadan fits in so well here, then. He hates fun. He's happiest brooding in his room, sharpening his blades. He takes brooding breaks just to scowl at a bottle of whiskey and glare at anyone with the audacity to smile."

"I hadn't expected you to get to know him so quickly." Aengus frowned at a bra I'd hung from the doorknob, then picked it up by the strap with one finger. "I like what you've done with his room. I'm sure Ruadan loves the feminine touch."

Now that he mentioned it, I realized I'd left items of clothing strewn all over the place. My brain seemed to edit out my own mess until someone pointed it out to me.

"Doorknobs are made for hanging bras," I countered. "It's one of their important functions. Anyway, how is Melusine doing?"

"Alive, thanks to you." He frowned. "Why did you stop to save the queen?"

I shrugged. "Because unpredictability is an asset."

Aengus nodded slowly, his green eyes glimmering, but I had the sense that he didn't believe me. "And Melusine? Why did you save her?"

"She gave me a strawberry." I surprised myself with the truth.

I guess I *did* like her. I almost groaned at the realization that Baleros knew everything about me. Anyone showing me a tiny scrap of kindness would win my undying loyalty. He knew I'd been desperate for friendship in my cage, that the ruthless Amazon Terror lapped up kindness like a kitten drinking milk. Some sweets tossed on the floor every now and then, and he'd earned my devotion.

I'd escaped the cage, but I wasn't sure I'd ever escape him. I was his slave, even now.

The horror of my realization washed over me. Baleros didn't just think three steps ahead. He thought three hundred steps ahead. Years ago, when he'd noticed my tendency to become attached, he'd given me Ciara. Not because he wanted me to be comfortable—but because he could use her someday as leverage. Like he was doing now. Ciara was just a pawn to him, and always had been.

I shook with anger.

"Are you okay?" asked Aengus.

Ruadan, too, had paused his knife sharpening to stare at me.

"Fine," I said through gritted teeth.

All this only proved Baleros's first—and most important—law of power: *Get in your enemy's head. Knowing someone well gives you power over them.*

Breathe in, breathe out. "Where is Melusine? How is she?"

"Sword fighting isn't her strength, really, but magic is."

I traced my fingertips over my waist. "I was worried about that. Magic. We don't need to know it by any chance, do we?"

Ruadan looked up, raising his eyebrows.

"I can't really do it," I said. "I don't suppose we have a magic-based trial coming up?"

Aengus's features darkened. "Let's just say you two had better start training, then."

My stomach tightened. "I can't just kill things with swords?"

Aengus and Ruadan both shook their heads simultaneously.

"All fae have magic," said Aengus. "You just have to learn how to channel it. Not to mention whatever your other half is."

Oh, friend, you do not want me to unleash my other half. I loosed a long, slow breath. "Fae nobility train with magic from the age of four. How am I supposed to compete with that?"

Aengus shrugged. "You just have to survive." He nodded at Ruadan. "He's half-demon. None of us knows what your other half is, exactly. But the combination of fae and something else can be powerful, just like it is for Ruadan. His magic is more powerful than that of any knight here, including the Grand Master's. You couldn't have been matched with a better person to train you. You see? The Old Gods know what they're doing."

"Except that Ruadan hates me and he can't explain things to me in words."

Ruadan folded his arms, leaning back to glare at me.

"You are talking about him like he's not here," said Aengus. "He's silent, not deaf."

"Right. Sorry."

"And he doesn't hate you. He just doesn't … respect you."

"That's lovely. Cheers."

"Because of the alcohol, and the bar-brawling, and general pointlessness of your existence, and—"

I held up a hand. "Yeah, we've been over it. He wrote it down for me. It was pretty much the one thing he wanted to communicate." I frowned. "So why did you both choose me to come here?"

Aengus shrugged. "Because of how you fight. That's it. You're fast, clever, and ruthless. We could tell that before you even stabbed me in the neck. And we were right to choose you, because no novice before managed to slaughter the King of Mammon." Aengus rubbed at his throat, as if remembering the pain I'd caused him. "Anyway, I have to get back to Melusine. Good luck with your magical learning."

Tendrils of dark magic slid through the air around Ruadan. He stared at me, still sharpening his knife. Aengus wasn't kidding that his magic was strong. It was coiling over my skin right now, raising my hair and making my back arch. A memory burned in my mind—his hand gripping my hair, his teeth on my throat.

The combination of his knife-sharpening and coils of magic was deeply unsettling. I tried not to think about the fact that he'd snapped the necks of his last two novices. I never wanted to be on his bad side.

Too bad I didn't have a choice.

Cold dread spread through my veins. When I'd brought up the World Key before, he'd closed off. He didn't trust me one bit, which was a problem. Ruadan wasn't going to let down his guard at all around me.

I hugged my side, wincing a little. "Can we get some sleep now? It's been a long day, and I need this to heal."

Ruadan frowned, dropping his knife onto the stone table. Then, he rose, crossing to me.

He extended a hand to me, and surprise sparked in my chest. An unexpectedly friendly gesture. I took his hand and rose, and he walked me over to his bed. Then he gestured for me to sit down. I sat on the edge of his bed. The mattress was firm and unforgiving, because it was Ruadan's, and of course it was.

To my increasing surprise, he knelt before me.

Things did not get any less surprising when he began to pull up my shirt.

"Whoa!" I stopped him, tugging on the hem. "What are you doing?"

He cut me a sharp look. I'd irritated him again. Wasn't hard to do.

He pulled another small piece of paper and a pencil out of his trousers, and he started writing again. Then, he thrust the paper at me.

You need to heal.

"That's where sleep comes in."

He shook his head.

"You have healing powers, I suppose." Given all the shadows and darkness that whirled around him, it wasn't surprising. Shadow demons were known for their healing skills. Demons of death, demons of sleep, demons of easing the pain. They were like the opiates of the demon world, addictive and lethal at the same time.

I didn't want him to see the scars that slashed across my body—my hips, my belly, really every part of me that I'd covered up. Then, I could no longer pass off the lie about the bar fights. Once he saw my scars, he'd know that I'd been a slave, one forced to fight.

If he thought I was ruthless just because I'd stabbed Aengus in the neck, he'd have a whole new definition of the word once he understood I was the Amazon Terror. That I'd slaughtered thousands to survive. Only the most brutal killers survived the arena.

And more—he'd know the worst thing about me: that I was the sort of sloppy, careless person who'd allowed myself to be captured in the first place. That I'd allowed someone to control me for years. Knowledge was power, and I didn't need Ruadan learning that much about me.

My stomach clenched, and I shook my head. "No," I said quietly.

I didn't know why, but I felt tears stinging my eyes as I stood up. For some insane reason, I really wanted his approval. Why? I didn't even like him, but I already yearned for his respect. Possibly because I knew I'd never get it.

I lay down on the cold stone floor and curled up, ready to sleep. The stone chilled my skin, and I shivered.

Ruadan crossed to his bed, and he blew into the air. Darkness blanketed the room.

As I closed my eyes, loneliness carved through me, so sharp it blocked out the pain of my wounds.

CHAPTER 17

The next day, The Wraith and I stood at the perimeter of a stone hall. Through thin arrow slits in the walls, light blazed, illuminating Ruadan's smoky magic. Given our slight communication difficulties, I wasn't entirely clear what sort of magic we'd be practicing today. I only hoped it didn't involve memorizing Angelic spells, because that wasn't my strong suit. And I *definitely* didn't want to have shamanic sexual relations with a potted plant, if that was on the agenda.

I dropped my backpack on the floor. I'd brought my whiskey with me just in case I needed a bit of Dutch courage, but I'd try to keep it capped.

Ruadan wasn't wearing his cloak today—just fitted, dark, woolen clothes that sculpted his body.

As I stood against the wall, he crossed into the center of the room, his back to me. My body tingled, heart racing as his magic thrummed through the room. I breathed in deeply as it pulsed through me in powerful waves.

As he worked his magic, he touched something around his neck. My pulse quickened. Was that the World Key?

I inched closer, silently. And yet even with my stealth, his body tensed. He flung up a hand, a signal to stop me from moving any closer. He still mistrusted me, and I had the disturbing sense that he could always predict my actions.

Frustration rippled through me, and my fingers clenched into fists. I was getting nowhere here. Ruadan had what I needed, but he wasn't letting me get anywhere near it.

Sometimes, when killing wasn't the answer, I was all out of ideas. But an impulsive attack wouldn't get me very far. He was too clever and too powerful to overcome. I needed to earn his trust, even if it killed me.

As shadows lashed the air around him, his powerful magic intensified, stroking my limbs like a brush of velvet. It heated my skin.

For a warrior who hated to enjoy himself, he sure could work a disturbingly pleasurable spell.

I stared as he unlocked a world, and a pool of water formed in the floor. It spiraled larger and larger until it formed a portal, at least six feet across. I backed away from it, suddenly a little nervous. I wasn't a huge fan of the unexpected unless I had a sword in my hands, and right now I just had my backpack of lollipops and duct tape.

Ruadan gestured for me to move away from the portal, and anticipation hung over the room.

As I took a step back, I stared at Ruadan's throat, searching for something that looked like a key. I couldn't see anything—not a necklace, nor a brooch. Where in the seven hells was he hiding it?

A splashing in the water interrupted my thoughts. Then, an enormous man hoisted himself out of the portal. No, not a man—a demon. One with leathery black wings that swooped down his back and tattoos that were whorled over his chiseled body and olive skin.

I wasn't sure what was more disturbing: the fact that he'd just crawled out of a portal in the stone floor, or the fact that he was stark naked. Like Ruadan, he seemed to think his nudity was unremarkable. He just stood before us with the water from the portal dripping down his powerful body, like *not a big deal, just crawled from another realm with my penis on display.*

His eyes were deep gray-blue, and I tried to focus on them, even if my gaze kept drifting downward as if of its own accord. It took me a moment to realize he was gripping something in his hand.

And another moment to realize he was just sort of staring at me, his brow furrowed. And that we had been standing like that for an awkwardly long time, part of which had involved me staring at his penis.

I cleared my throat. "I have no idea what I'm supposed to do now."

For a moment, only the dripping of water filled the silence.

Then, I nodded at Ruadan. "He doesn't talk. Please tell me that you do, or this will just stay really awkward. I mean, more than it already is."

"I'm Bael, Sword of Nyxobas of the Shadow Realm. Ruadan never mentioned you were a woman."

"I am, yes. He didn't mention that you'd be naked. Mentioning things isn't really his forte, as it happens."

Ruadan shot me a sharp look, his violet eyes sparking with silver. He was part shadow demon. Was he related to Bael?

"The Institute never recruited females in the past," said Bael.

I folded my arms. "Will this be a problem for you?"

"No." He nodded at Ruadan. "My old friend, here, has asked me to instruct you in our ways."

"In the ways of the shadow demons?" I bit my lip. "I guess your ways don't involve trousers."

"I will not sully the waters of Nyxobas, God of Night."

Sure, and I guess he doesn't mind your balls all over the place.

All I knew right now was that the demon standing before me exuded powerful magic that snaked off his body, mingling with Ruadan's. With the two of them in the same room, the power almost overwhelmed me. On top of that, the room had become freezing with shadow magic, and frost iced the stones.

Given that it was summer, I was wearing nothing but a short dress Ruadan had given me—black, cotton, with frankly more cleavage than I normally showed. But here, in a room suffused with powerful shadow magic, goosebumps rose on my skin, and my teeth began chattering.

I hugged myself. Right now, I was working really hard to keep my gaze on his eyes. "Okay. So what are we doing here?"

"The Institute of the Shadow Fae is tasked with keeping shadow demons in line. They are the fae ambassadors to our demon realm—the shadow realm."

"Okay, I'm with you. What's the next trial?"

"First, a little background. Centuries ago," he continued, "the God of Night exiled the incubi from his realm. All except his son. The God of Night loathes pleasure and the vices of the body, while the incubi feed off pleasure."

"He sounds like a good time," I said. "He and Ruadan would have the best parties."

A heavy hush fell over the room, so heavy I could hear my own heartbeat. Ruadan cut me a death stare, his violet eyes darkening. Clearly, I'd said something wrong.

"Moving swiftly on..." I prompted.

Bael straightened. "The Shadow Fae have been hunting exiled incubi for centuries. The incubi breed heavily, and their numbers keep growing. And now, a nest of incubi have turned up in East London. Your next trial—along with the other novices—will involve hunting the incubi. You need to send them to the shadow hell."

Hunting. I liked the sound of that. It sounded like I'd be able to use weapons. "And we need magic for that? Why not just use swords? Or arrows? Or broken bottles or whatever?"

Bael stared at me for a moment before answering. "You will use your sword. But the incubi are experts in shadow-leaping. That is the magical skill you must learn."

Interesting. "What's that, exactly?"

Instead of answering, Bael disappeared in a blur of dark magic, leaving behind only wisps of dark smoke. It took me a moment to realize that he'd reappeared behind me. Still naked as hell.

"That is shadow-leaping," he said. "Moving from one shadow to another."

I'd seen Ruadan do that. I'd never seen anyone in the arena who could shadow-leap. It brought me back to a previous thought that raked at my mind: a warrior who could shadow-leap never would have been enslaved by Baleros. I *wanted* this skill.

My jaw dropped. "You really think I can learn that?"

He lifted a pendant in his hand—a rock that glowed with stunning violet light. In fact, the color wasn't altogether different from the violet of Ruadan's eyes.

Bael handed it to me. "I've brought you a lumen crystal from the Shadow Realm. Put it on, and Ruadan will teach you how to absorb the magic so that you can use it to shadow-jump."

I reached for it, my legs shaking a little. I was torn between the temptation to possess powerful magic and the fear of what would happen if I did.

They didn't know what I really was….

As soon as I clasped the crystal in my palm, I felt its dark, seductive power thrumming over me. "What does this do?" I asked.

"It charges your body with night magic. You must learn to channel it correctly, let it become one with your body. And once you do, you can leap from one place to another by communing with the darkness of shadows. Ruadan will help you learn to channel the magic effectively. He will need to see how you're able to handle the magic before you go further. Use the stone in the floor to anchor your feet, so the magic doesn't overwhelm you."

"What if…." I sucked in a sharp breath. How did I ask this question? How did I name this fear?

What if a dark, powerful magic infused me? What if there were worse things in the world than incubi?

What if I was one of them?

I cleared my throat, trying again. "What if this magic doesn't mix well with me? I don't know what my other half is." That old lie. Stick as close to the truth as possible. "What if I flip out and just start slaughtering everyone?"

"You won't." Bael nodded at Ruadan. "There is no better teacher."

I frowned, casting a doubtful glance at Ruadan. Like Bael, he had the rigid posture of a warrior. But without speaking, how was he supposed to teach me anything?

Whatever the case, I wasn't about to argue with the enormous, naked man in front of me. I'd just take his word for it.

Without another word, Bael turned and plunged into the portal.

Ruadan crossed over to the dark whirlpool, shadows intensifying around him. His cool, shadowy magic buzzed over my skin. The smell of burnt air rose in the room, like a thunderstorm after lightning strikes. I stared as the watery portal closed up again, replaced by a simple flagstone floor.

Once again, I'd failed to get a glimpse of the World Key, and my stomach sank.

Ruadan turned back to me, and he pulled the crystal from my hands. Then, he reached behind my neck, his powerful magic caressing my skin from my thighs up to my breasts and raising goose-bumps over my arms. He clasped the necklace behind my nape.

As soon as he did, a rush of power flooded me, pooling in my chest and my belly like glacial waters. My back arched, and my mind went dark, until an image arose—

A field of fae corpses lay around me, skin blackening, turning gray....

I gasped at the wave of horror that washed over me.

Powerful hands clasped me by the waist, and the image dissipated. Ruadan had jumped, and he was standing behind me now, his powerful body pressed against mine. I slowed my breath, inhaling deeply. A thin sheen of sweat had bloomed on my skin, and my blood roared in my ears. But my mind was no longer flooded with disturbing memories.

Shadow magic curled from my fingertips. Somehow, with his touch, Ruadan was helping me channel that magic so that it didn't overwhelm my mind. It was as if his body helped to ground the magic in my mind. Now, with Ruadan's warm hands on my waist, his fingers over my hips, I could feel the shadow magic pulsing up my legs, skimming over my thighs.

But that disturbing image from the darkest depths of my memory still lingered, and another wave of shadow magic slammed into me.

My legs trembled. Even with Ruadan's help, I felt like my body was rejecting the shadow magic. I leaned back against his powerful form, my head tucked under his chin. Still, darkness clouded my mind once more. The next thing I knew, I was walking in those tall grasses, fae blood staining the soil....

Glaciers slid through my bones, wracking me with shivers. I was freezing from the inside out, teeth chattering.

Ruadan's arms slid tighter around me, encircling my waist. His embrace warmed me, and some of the shivering relented. He dispelled the disturbing memory from my mind.

Why was I thinking about those terrible memories now? I'd worked so hard to forget.

Heat radiated from Ruadan's powerful body into mine. When another surge of ice flooded my veins, Ruadan's hands shot up, and he unclasped the crystal from my neck. He stepped in front of me, his brow furrowed.

Tremors wracked me, and I hugged myself. "I know. It's not working."

He pulled out a piece of paper and wrote on it.

We're going to start from the bottom up. Use the stone to anchor you.

I frowned. "What?"

He shoved the paper and pencil back into his pocket. Then, he put his hands on my hips and guided me back against a wall, pressing on my shoulders until they were flat against the stone. Warming me with his touch, he cupped my chin. He guided my head back against the wall until my spine lined up completely with the stone. I looked up at him, meeting his violet gaze, breathing in the smell of pine. So easy to get taken in by his stark beauty, so easy to forget what he really was—a cold-blooded killer.

"Why did you slaughter your last two novices?" I asked.

His fingers tensed on my hips, and for just a moment, shadows slid through his eyes until they darkened to pitch. And *there* was the shadow demon, eyes the color of the darkest hell. Icy dread raked a claw up my spine. That question *really* pissed him off for some reason.

"Quite handy, isn't it?" I said. "Only speaking when you want to."

He seemed to gain some mastery over himself, his eyes shifting back to violet with silver flecks, and his muscles relaxed. I wasn't going to get an answer. Fine. I needed to remember that even if he was my mentor—and even if his magic felt delicious—I'd never be safe with him.

He grasped my hands in his, then turned my palms to face the wall. I understood the intent—I was supposed to keep as much of my body pressed firmly against the wall as possible, and use the contact with the stone wall to stabilize the magic. I splayed out my fingers over the stone.

Then, with his thumbs pressed into my hips, he straightened the small of my back against the wall. Ruadan's magic thrummed over my skin. Pressed against the wall, with my head tilted back, I felt strangely vulnerable before him.

Once again, he lifted the necklace. But this time, he clasped it around his own throat. It took me a moment to understand, but he was going to channel the power from his own body into mine, to act as sort of a conduit. That way, he could temper the intense torrent of magic. While I stood, pressed against the wall, he knelt before me.

For just a moment, I imagined that I was his queen, and he was my subject, and it gave me a little thrill. A smile curled my lips. But the feeling was quickly over when his fingertips met my ankles, sending an intense jolt of shadow magic into my blood.

When I peered down, I could actually *see* the tendrils of dark magic curling around my bare legs. Slowly, Ruadan brushed his fingers over my ankles, then further up my calves. Every stroke of his fingers brought a rush of powerful tingles. Channeled through Ruadan, the power no longer overwhelmed me. It felt like an intense electrical rush over my skin.

Breathing in deeply, I tuned into the solidity of the rock behind my back, pressing myself firmly against the wall. It *did* work as a sort of anchor, diffusing some of the power of the shadow magic. Ruadan traced his hands further up my legs toward the hem of my dress, and my breath quickened at the feel of his hands on my thighs, under the hem. I trembled, the magic growing a little more powerful now. He spread out his fingers over my bare thighs. His touch felt distractingly *good* on my body, and my breath hitched.

As I looked into his eyes, I couldn't help the rush of molten heat that swept through my belly. His hands moved higher. My skin was warming, and I started to feel an overwhelming urge to crush myself against him. There were reasons this was a bad idea, but my thoughts had become too muddled for coherent thoughts. The air felt charged between us. My pulse raced, my mind no longer filling with dark memories. Now—much to my horror—my body was responding to him in a different way.

I stared at his mouth, wondering what it would feel like to kiss him. Something flared in his eyes, too. Was that desire snaking off his torso?

As his hands moved over me, his gaze roamed down my body. Slow, appreciative—as if he were imagining what I looked like without my dress on. His gaze lingered over my breasts, definitely taking notice of my hardening nipples beneath the fabric. My chest flushed with desire and embarrassment. He definitely *knew* how turned on I was right now, and there was no way to hide it.

Whatever he was thinking, it was no longer the cold, clinical look he'd given me before. His magic thrummed up my legs.

When I licked my lips, his gaze flashed to my mouth. His nostrils flared, fingers tightening on my hips. I thought of his canines at my throat, and bizarrely, the thought made me groan. Heat swooped through my core. My mind was blazing with a vision: Ruadan, spinning me around, grazing his canines over my neck. He'd rip off my knickers and fill me until I shuddered beneath him. Wild need overtook me, an ache building between my thighs.

Gods help me, some primal fae instinct was taking over and I *wanted* him desperately, even if the thought horrified me. I imagined my naked body sliding against his, his fingers stroking between my legs while I climaxed.

I knew he felt my desire when his eyes began darkening again, his own animal instincts taking over.

Night magic poured into me from his fingertips, and he pressed in closer. A stroke of his thumb on my hips—up and down, up and down —told me this was no longer just about magic, and the little moan I emitted confirmed it for him. He leaned in closer, his breath warming my neck. I was drawing him into my orbit, too.

His powerful shadow magic followed his hands up to my waist, and an intoxicating power pulsed in my core. Against my will, my back arched. I had to fight hard to remember to keep my fingers splayed against the wall, that I wasn't supposed to grip him by the hair and pull his mouth to mine.

Hands. Pressed. Against. The wall.

A vein in Ruadan's neck throbbed.

He ran one of his hands up my body, stroking up my back. Then he fisted my hair, his touch almost rough. With a dominating grip, he tilted my neck back, exposing my throat. My heart raced out of control. When he pressed his mouth to my neck, I moaned. His magic was distinctly, overwhelmingly sexual, and it had an intense effect on me.

He couldn't be an incubus, could he? Incubi loved pleasure. It's just that … he really felt like an incubus right now.

His other hand stroked me under the cotton fabric of my dress. It moved higher up over my ribs, magic pulsing from his hands—

Then, he froze.

He jerked his hands away from me as if I'd burned him. He pulled away, and his magic snapped out of my body.

It was at that moment that reality came crashing down on me. *My scars.* They were all over my ribs. The jig was up. No bar fight stories could explain that carnage.

I tried to catch my breath, staring at him.

How could I have let him get so close? Knowledge over someone was power, and now he knew more about me than I'd intended. It was his stupid, pretty face, plus some kind of animalistic fae instincts urging me to mate with him. I wasn't thinking clearly anymore, wasn't being tactical. I needed a much uglier mentor to get through this.

I loosed a long breath. I didn't think he'd directly connect me to Baleros. There'd been plenty of gladiator masters. Baleros just happened to be the cruelest.

Ruadan started writing on his paper, and I already knew what it would say before he handed it over.

Your body is covered in scars.

I crossed my arms, completely disoriented by the sudden absence of magic from my body, and also by the fact that, a few seconds ago, I'd been desperate to pull my clothes off.

I wasn't sure why tears stung my eyes, but it only made the situation more embarrassing. I didn't want him to know I'd been captured. I blinked, mastering control of myself, over my voice, before I answered. "Yep. From the arena."

I didn't want him to know me. Now, he was already looking at me differently, his eyes shining with something like pity. Exactly what I'd been dreading. Gladiators may have been fearsome warriors, but ultimately, we were slaves.

"You don't need to feel sorry for me," I snapped. "I survived. I'm proud of my scars." Proud to have survived. Ashamed to have been captured in the first place.

He nodded, then I noticed his gaze sweeping up and down my body. I had the sense that he was reconsidering me in some way, but I wasn't quite sure how.

He nodded, then handed me another piece of paper.

I don't feel sorry for you. You're strong. Let's get back to training.

I loosed a slow breath. Good. That was over, and we could move on.

He gestured at the wall, and I understood I was supposed to back up against it again.

I pressed my legs, my spine, my fingers against the wall.

Ruadan began at my ankles once again. Working from the bottom up, his hands moved further up my legs—faster this time—and shadow magic surged along with his touch. A delicious, powerful magic tingled over my thighs, a hint of an electrical pulse that caressed me beneath my dress. His hands moved over my hips, my waist, leaving a rush of tingling magic in their wake. Night magic surged in my core. He brought his hands up further under my dress, his fingers just below my breasts.

Magic surged now, spilling from my ribs, out through my limbs, filling my fingertips, my toes, my head. Now, the magic felt like a part of me. Ruadan leaned in closer. He unclasped the necklace from his own neck.

His eyes locked on mine, pulsing with violet like the lumen crystal, and he secured it around my own neck.

Now, the power started to flood me again—darkness descending. But Ruadan wasn't leaving. His powerful body was pressed against me, eyes locked on mine.

His canines were bared, eyes darkening as a dark, primordial power filled us both. He leaned down, the side of his face brushing mine.

Night magic was an intoxicating rush. Before he knew what was happening, I found that my arms were around Ruadan's neck.

His hands slid around my thighs. I whispered his name. Now, his lips hovered just inches from mine. His sensual magic whispered through me, throbbing in my blood like a drug. He hoisted me up, his hands below my thighs, and I wrapped my legs around his waist. He pressed me against the wall, and a dark heat swooped through my belly. The desire definitely wasn't just coming from me. It crackled between us like an electric charge.

Night magic surged, and I felt at one with the dark, with the void, with the perfect silence of a midnight sky….

I stared into Ruadan's night-dark eyes, lost for a moment in the stark beauty of his features….

Baleros's seventeenth law of power: Never let an opportunity go to waste.

Then, a voice whispered in the back of my mind. Baleros's voice.

The World Key, the World Key, the World Key….

I had to see what was there. I reached for the collar of Ruadan's shirt, and I just started to tug it down….

Then, his body tensed, his eyes returning to violet. He lowered me again to the floor.

The piece of paper he handed me read,

Your body has been charged with night magic. We're done.

I was still catching my breath, aware of the embarrassing flush of my chest. "Is that how you train all your novices?" My voice came out a little sharp, and I wished I hadn't said anything at all.

He'd returned to his usual state—animal stillness, violet eyes that burned into me. He knew what I'd tried to do, that I'd been looking for the key.

I lifted the lumen crystal from my throat. "Fine. So what happens now? Are you going to teach me to shadow-run?"

A muscle twitched in his jaw. But instead of answering, he crossed out of the room.

I glared at the doorway after he left. He'd caught me trying to get a glimpse at the World Key, and now I was one step further away from earning his trust.

CHAPTER 19

I sauntered across the Tower Green, sipping from my whiskey bottle on the way. A floral breeze kissed my skin.

I understood that the Shadow Fae reviled pleasure, but no one had taken away my whiskey yet, so for now, at least, it was my only real friend here.

As I walked, my heart was still racing out of control from the earlier encounter. At this point, I was nearly positive that Ruadan was an incubus, even if he didn't act like one. Incubi inspired lust, and they fed off it, too.

I gritted my teeth, angry with myself for letting him catch me looking for his World Key. Now, he wouldn't let me get anywhere near him. How angry was he, exactly? And what the fuck was I even looking for?

I needed some time to think. Since it seemed like he was attracted to me, maybe I could seduce him? Would he trust me that way? I wasn't sure. I wasn't exactly a romance expert, and I didn't know how to recreate the lust we'd felt in the tower room. I needed some more inspiration.

Instead of heading back to our shared room, I was making my way to the library. I pushed through a door, then climbed the dank tower stairwell until I reached the enormous hall.

My favorite Segway-riding librarian peered at me over the moon-shaped rims of her glasses, and I gave her a wave.

"Is there a romance section?" I asked.

She shook her head. "No. I have my own collection, of course, but those are private. We *do* have a romantic histories section."

"Fine. Can you show me where that is?"

She pointed to a wall in the library that was partially overgrown with moon flowers.

I crossed to it, clutching the straps of my backpack. Here, glittering moths dusted the books' spines. I sat on the ground before the stack, and I found an old favorite—a love story about a young knight, sent to fetch a wife for his rich uncle. But during their journey home, the two of them drank love potions. They fell in love with each other instead.

I chewed on my lip. What I needed was a love potion. If he were completely under the thrall of lust magic, I could get a glimpse under his shirt. Maybe I could even get him to tell me the truth in the heat of the moment.

I closed the book in my lap. I had no idea how to make a love potion, and maybe I didn't need to rely on magic, anyway. The intensity I'd felt as we'd trained told me he wanted me without magic. Heat had crackled between us.

Seducing him was the best way to get to the World Key.

Despite the desire we'd both felt while training, I wasn't exactly a genius at seduction. I'd had a boyfriend before, but that had been the result of getting drunk in Rufus's bar, sleeping with a trumpet player, and then continuing to get drunk and sleep with the trumpet player until I realized we had absolutely nothing in common. Seduction was definitely not one of the skills taught at gladiator school. I'd literally spent my formative years in a cage. This was the sort of thing I'd have learned as a teenage girl if I hadn't been so busy stabbing people to death, and now I was completely behind the eight ball.

I rose and started crossing to the exit. What I really needed was a female friend….

Melusine didn't seem much like the seductive type, either, but she was a self-proclaimed genius.

I pushed through the door, heading out of the library into the glaring afternoon light.

As I crossed the Tower Green, I sniffed my way to Aengus's room, following Melusine's scent to a gleaming white tower.

Inside, I knocked on the door where her smell was the strongest. Melusine pulled it open. "Arianna. I wasn't expecting to see you here. I have been practicing three kinds of magic to prepare for our next trial."

"Oh, wow, that's very—"

"Shadow leaping, an explosion spell, and a second kind of explosion spell with more fire. What have you been practicing?"

I scratched my cheek. Talk about being behind the eight ball. "Not much yet. Is Aengus here?" I asked in a whisper.

"No." She opened the door further, motioning for me to enter.

Mahogany furniture ringed the room, and Aengus's bed looked as if it had been carved from a giant stag's antler. Here, a soft bed of moss grew on the floor, and a musky scent filled the room. I noticed right away that a second, smaller bed stood against one of the walls, and irritation simmered.

"You have a bed?" I snapped. "Ruadan didn't give me a bed."

She shrugged. "You sleep on the floor."

I folded my arms. "It would have been nice to have been offered one." I shook my head. "Sorry, I'm getting sidetracked."

"Are you here to ask about shadow-leaping?" She beamed. "You must have heard I'm very good at it."

"Um, not really. I was hoping you knew something about seduction."

She stared at me. "Do I seem like the type of person who would know anything about seduction?"

"Not particularly. Not at all, really. But you're the only woman here."

She cocked her head. "You *do* know that the knights are forbidden from taking on any lovers."

Conceal your true intentions.

I rolled my eyes. "Of course I know that. It's just that they're not forbidden from killing novices. And I thought—if I really need it someday—seducing Ruadan might be a reasonable protection against getting killed by him. You know, getting him to like me."

Her features cleared, and she eyed me dubiously. "I'm not sure if that makes sense."

"Obviously, it's not like we can have conversations," I pointed out. "Seduction is my only defense."

This seemed to convince her, and she nodded. "Yes. Of course. It's not the worst idea in the world." Her forehead creased as she thought about it. "You know, I don't think there's a lot to it. I don't think you have to do anything fancy. I think men just like naked women. And you're beautiful. I don't think it's more complicated than that."

"Really? So ... I should get naked?"

"I believe so. Men like bared breasts, especially." She frowned at my chest. "And yours are fairly large."

"I mean, you're not wrong, and men definitely like breasts, but...." It couldn't be that simple, could it? And yet, the more I thought about it, the more I thought this sounded completely accurate. "Okay, thanks."

"Sure. I'll see you tomorrow night for the trial."

"Of course." Unless I managed to seduce the key away from Ruadan before then.

* * *

I FOUND Ruadan in his room, engaging in his favorite, super pro-social activity: knife-sharpening. His blade glinted, and he didn't even bother to look up at me as I crossed into the room.

Melusine's suggestion about bare breasts had seemed totally sensible in her room. But now, as I stood before a fae-demon who'd murdered his last two novices, I couldn't quite figure out how to just casually throw off my clothes without it being weird. Granted, Ruadan and Bael were fine with being naked, but it wasn't normal to me. I loved my body and I felt beautiful, but that didn't mean I'd just casually strip off in front of people.

I ran my fingertips over my ribs, where I felt one of the ridges of my scars. He'd offered to heal me before, hadn't he? Maybe that would be a sufficient pretense. The thing was, I didn't want them healed. I liked myself exactly the way I was, and each scar was a victory. But I'd do anything for Ciara.

Ciarianna would rise again.

I glanced in the gleaming reflection of one of his axes. I looked pretty enough, I thought. I pinched my cheeks a little to make them pink.

Ruadan was still looking down at his knives as he sharpened them. I took a deep breath. I sat at the edge of his bed and pulled off my boots. Then pulled off my dress, dropping it on a pile of my other clothes. The cold fortress air whispered over my skin as I stood in the middle of his room, just in my sheer black bra and knickers.

Ruadan was still looking down at his knives, pretending I wasn't in the room at all. I looked down at myself, then traced my fingertips over the ridge of a scar by my hipbone. A hellhound had caught me with an ax. I'd killed him by bashing his skull in with a rock. I was much more at home with that sort of mission than with the sheer bra sort of mission.

The boobs were sexy. The legacy of death maybe wasn't so much. But the scars were mine, and I hated to part with them.

Still, I crossed to Ruadan, and he lifted his gaze. His body went completely rigid at the sight of me. Sharp tendrils of his magic sliced through the air, menacing and ferocious.

Shadows darkened his eyes. I couldn't exactly tell if he liked what he saw or if he wanted to murder me in that moment, but either way, I felt completely vulnerable standing before him. The intensity of his gaze hit me like a wave of powerful magic, and my breath caught in my throat.

I touched one of the scars by my ribs. "You said you could heal me. Can you heal my scars?"

A long moment passed, and he eyed me with that eerie stillness. Then, he shifted and started writing on his piece of paper.

I will heal your new wounds. Not the old ones.

"Why?"

Because they don't need to be healed.

He was right. The wounds from the King of Mammon were still raw, and they hurt whenever I coughed or sat up too fast. The rest were just superficial. They didn't need to be healed.

"Fine."

He held out a hand to me, beckoning me closer, and I closed the distance between us.

As I stood in front of him, he brushed his fingertips over the wound on my abdomen. He curled one hand around me and it rested on my lower back. With the other, he traced over my skin around the cut. I stared as dark magic curled from his fingertips over my skin, snaking over the reddened marks. I was acutely aware of the fact that, with him sitting down and me standing up, my breasts were about level with his head. I couldn't quite pinpoint it, but something about the studied intensity with which Ruadan ignored my breasts suggested to me that he was actually completely focused on them. Melusine had been right.

The dull ache in my abdomen subsided completely.

The other new wound marred my hip, and I tugged down the side of my knickers to expose it. His hand on my back tensed, his other reaching for my hip. Before he touched my skin, his hand tightened into a fist, as if he were restraining himself. I was *definitely* having an effect on him.

I'm not sure what compelled me to do it, but I took another step forward, then slid into his lap.

Being this close to him, heat built within me. Now, his eyes were locked on mine as he traced his fingertips over my hip, inside my knickers. His magic stroked my body.

Then, as soon as he'd healed my second scar, he pulled his hand away from me, and he straightened.

I understood that was my cue to get off his lap. Fine. Boobs or not, seduction was not part of my skill set. But I was certain he'd felt something, and I was making some progress to getting closer to his chest.

I crossed back to my dress and pulled it on over my head. "So, are you going to teach me to shadow-jump?"

No key yet. But I could learn a new skill while I was at it. After I stole from the Seneschal, shadow-leaping might come in *very* handy.

CHAPTER 20

By Ruadan's side, I walked down a cobbled road in East London. To our left, an overground train line loomed over a dark park. Apparently, this is where I was supposed to practice shadow-leaping.

Ruadan wore not one, but two swords strapped to his back, doubling his intimidation factor. As we'd moved through the streets of East London, terrified humans had fled from our path.

We crossed into the grassy park, and a flicker of movement caught my eye. It took me a moment to register that I was staring at a man's naked arse, thrusting into the earth. When he looked back at us, terror paled his features, and he scrambled to stand and pull up his trousers.

"Uncle Darrell?" I whispered under my breath.

Ruadan must have heard me, because he turned to raise his eyebrows at me. I stared at Uncle Darrell, who was now sprinting across the park away from us. For a moment, I contemplated telling Ruadan that if he ever wanted to commune with the earth, he needed to bury the whole ballsack, not just the shaft. But I thought better of it as soon as I remembered that he had no sense of humor whatsoever.

Moonlight silvered the park, and mist curled around a few sparse trees. Under the elevated train track, shadows pooled in dark arches.

Something about this place gave me the shivers, and I wanted to fill the silence.

"I've been here before," I said. "There's magic in this place."

We moved along a cobbled road that cut into the park. Dandelions dappled overgrown grasses. To our right stood brick walls that might be two centuries old. To our left, a rickety wooden house on stilts loomed over the train tracks—maybe a switching station at one time, long since abandoned. A small city farm stood on one side of the fields, complete with vegetable patches, chickens, goats, and a pig.

Acrid smoke rose from a burning car, probably stolen, abandoned in one of the Victorian train arches. "Not all magic comes from the gods or from spells," I said. "This is the magic of things that don't belong together. This is the magic of weird, forgotten places. Farms, burnt cars. Dandelions. Goats." I pointed to a tree, where sneakers dangled from the branches. Some crazy person had tied them there. "Shoes hanging like fruit from the boughs. See what I mean?"

Ruadan's eyes slid to me, and I thought I saw a sparkle of curiosity, but he was probably wondering if I'd lost my mind.

"I know," I said. "We have shadow-leaping to practice."

Ruadan pulled the glowing lumen stone from his pocket. Then, he stepped closer and clasped it around the back of my neck. His piney scent enveloped me.

As soon as the clasp shut, I felt that overwhelming rush of magical power. Darkness swam in my mind, but I managed to clamp down on my most disturbing thoughts.

Still, energy flooded me, and the coldness of the shadow void spilled through my veins and tendons like ink, freezing my bones. I stared up into Ruadan's cold, violet eyes. He didn't need a lumen stone at all, because this magic was part of him, as innate to him as walking was to me.

I tried channeling the magic, tried using the stones beneath me to ground it. And yet try as I might, it seemed as if a frozen void had opened up within my chest. An unending pit of ice. I'd mastered the power before, but now, my muscles started to seize up.

As soon as Ruadan put his hands on my waist, some of the panic began to subside.

I stared into his eyes, and I found the magic of night glimmering there.

Moonlight sculpted the perfect planes of his face. It unnerved me to have the full power of his gaze on me, but it excited me, too.

"Are you going to have to touch me every time I wear this lumen stone?" Sometimes I had a bad habit of nervously filling silence with chatter. "Because it might get weird when we're trying to fight the incubi and you have to keep sticking your hand up my dress."

No answer, of course. The coldness deepened within my chest.

Shut up, Arianna. Shut up.

I breathed in deeply, focusing on channeling the freezing magic throughout my body. Slowly, I started to absorb it and to disperse it more evenly.

Ruadan's eyes flared with silver. Once again, something was passing between us—an electrical charge, a pulsing, sexual energy. An intense ache burned through my body. He was *definitely* an incubus, and the heat of his sensual magic melted the coldness of the shadows within me.

He let out a low growl, fingers tightening on me. Then, with a move both quick and rough, he pulled me closer. He thrust his fingers into my hair and once more pulled my head back. His gaze pierced me.

This time, he crushed his lips against mine, and lust arced through me. His kiss was carnal, demanding. Heat shot through my belly as I responded to its unflinching ferocity. I opened my mouth, my tongue sliding against his.

The kiss deepened, growing wilder, and I ached for him. His grip on me tightened. Something about the intensity of the kiss made me feel like I was an answer to a question he'd been asking all his life.

His magic stroked my skin, licking between my legs, and hot ecstasy spiraled through me. I had no idea what was happening anymore, or how words worked, or what we were doing in the park. I just wanted more from him, wanted his tongue to swirl over my body.... Heat ignited in me, so powerful that it warmed the frigid pit in my chest. When he nipped my lower lip, my knees went weak, and I think I moaned.

But just as soon as it had begun, he pulled away from me. Of course, kissing was forbidden to a Shadow Fae. My breath was hitching in my throat, and I tried to slow my breathing even as my legs trembled.

He released his grip on me, and he took a step back, shadows snaking around him. Lust still flooded me. *Definitely* an incubus. I touched my lips, stunned that he'd kissed me at all.

My heart thundered against my ribs. *Play it off cool, Arianna. Play it off cool.*

"Not a big deal." I actually said those words out loud. "Just a kiss, whatever."

Like I said. When I was nervous, I tended to chatter.

If it was a tactic to help me control the magic, the kiss had worked. The coldness of the shadow magic no longer overwhelmed me. It surged along my skin, swirling through my muscles—an electric, crackling power. But I controlled it. The heat generated by Ruadan's lust magic had *definitely* countered the iciness of the shadow magic.

I looked down at my hands, at the soft wisps of dark magic that spiraled from my fingertips.

"You're an incubus, right?" I asked.

One nod confirmed my theory.

As an incubus, Ruadan controlled magic through sexual energy. That meant he could draw power from sexual energy, channel magic —heal from it, even. It also meant that he'd known exactly how turned on I'd been around him, which was slightly mortifying. Particularly since I had no idea whatsoever what he was thinking or feeling.

I folded my arms. "I thought incubi were supposed to enjoy them-selves. You don't speak, don't drink alcohol, don't have lovers because the Institute won't allow it. You must be very conflicted."

A low growl told me it was time to drop the subject.

With a few deep breaths, I managed to master some of my over-whelming desire, but that kiss had knocked the ground out from under me. I'd been about twenty seconds away from stripping my clothes off right here in this park—even after I'd seen what Uncle Darrell had done to defile the poor earth.

I glanced at my fingertips, transfixed by the smoky magic that curled from them.

To my surprise, Ruadan reached out and lifted my chin so that I was meeting his startling gaze. Then, he pointed to the farm—at a goat pen, in fact.

"Okay. You want me to jump into the goat pen?" Magic sizzled over my skin. Maybe Bael had been right, and Ruadan was an excellent mentor in his own weird, slightly insane way. After all, I now possessed powerful magic, and I was about to learn how to use it.

And yet…. "Before I jump into the goat pen, can we talk about the thing where you murdered two of your novices? Is that right, or was it just a rumor?"

When he started writing on the piece of paper again, I fully expected it to come back with some kind of denial.

Instead, what he handed back to me was simply the word:

Executed.

No other explanation. No excuses or context. Just a stark reminder of what was at stake here. If I failed to impress the Shadow Fae, I'd be executed. If I stole from them and ran off with the key, I'd be executed.

And yet if I didn't, Ciara would die.

While I was mulling over this shitty predicament, Ruadan touched my arm. He pointed once more at the farm, urging me to jump.

"Right. To the goat pen." I stared across the field, at the goats, unable to conceive how I could just shift myself over there. Bael had said that I would be jumping from one shadow to another by connecting to the shadow's darkness. Since it was nighttime, shadows surrounded us, but I wasn't exactly sure how to meld with them.

All I knew was that the first step would be to move away from Ruadan, whose masculine scent was distracting me.

I took a few steps away from him, breathing in the night air. I picked through the scents of burning rubber and leather from the car, the chicken coop, the grass, the pigpen, the goat fur, the old chicken bones someone had left out nearby … the dozens of other smells. I tuned in just to that burnt air smell. That was the smell of shadow magic.

I stared at the uneven wood of the goat pen, my gaze locked in on the pool of darkness in one corner.

Magic crackled over me, and coldness spilled through my blood. I let my mind go blank, filling with shadows. Mentally, I felt myself meld with the darkest corner of the pen. Then, I leapt.

I slammed into a wooden gate post and fell back on my arse in the mud.

The goat brayed. With a jolt, I realized the fucker was running for me, his bell ringing. As I jumped to my feet, he head-butted me, and I fell back again. A goat hoof trampled on my hand. For a fraction of a second, I considered punching him, but there was definitely something morally dubious about punching a goat in the face.

As I struggled to stand with the goat smashing into me, knocking me off balance, my gaze flicked back to the park. I let my mind fill with shadows, my sights locked on the dark point beneath an apple tree. I communed with that shadow, and the darkness within me connected to it. In the next moment, I was there, free from my goaty attacker.

Then, I focused on Ruadan. In the night, he appeared like a pool of ink, two vibrant violet eyes peering out from a void. Like a black hole, the Wraith sucked in light and trapped it within his sphere.

I tuned into his shadows, to the dizzying, icy power within them, and I jumped. I slammed into Ruadan, and it was like hitting a brick wall. I stumbled back, but this time, I managed to regain my balance.

I crossed my arms, glaring at him. "Did you know that goat would attack?"

Seriously. *No* idea why I kept asking him questions at this point.

Ruadan reached behind his back, drawing his two longswords. He handed one to me.

I grasped it by the hilt. I was *much* more comfortable with the sword than I was leaping around goats. But I was pretty sure I knew what Ruadan wanted me to do.

"You want me to fight you while we're shadow-leaping, right?" I asked.

Ruadan nodded.

I had to admit, the idea of mastering this skill was thrilling. This would be an astounding advantage in a fight against someone who couldn't use it. Only problem was, it depended on me having access to a lumen stone. Baleros didn't have one, and I was guessing they weren't easy to come by.

But since I was planning on stealing from Ruadan anyway, what was one more, little item?

CHAPTER 21

I didn't get too much time to contemplate my future heist, because a cold current of air whooshed beside me, and Ruadan was gone.

I scanned the darkness until my gaze landed on the cold glint of steel—Ruadan's sword, across the park. I tuned into his shadows, then leapt to him. Once again, I overshot the mark, slamming into his chest. I stumbled back again, and his hand gripped my waist for just a moment before he released me.

It was starting to become clear that I needed to focus on the shadows around Ruadan, or I'd keep overshooting and ramming into the stone wall of his chest.

Then, another cold whoosh of air, his sword glinting twenty feet away. This time, I jumped to the shadows two feet behind him and swung my sword. But once again, he'd anticipated my moves. He parried, blocking my strike, then jumped away.

Always anticipate your enemy's actions.

Ruadan continued to jump away, each time anticipating where I'd land just moments later. We shifted around, moving from the dark archways to the train tracks over the park. I nearly tumbled off the house on stilts before I regained my balance. We jumped again to an abandoned train station, then to the shoe tree.

Just like before, Ruadan kept demonstrating an uncanny ability to predict what I was about to do next. Almost as if we had been trained by the same person.

Had Baleros been Ruadan's mentor at one time?

I needed to surprise him. I'd improved my skill already. I was no longer slamming into his chest. Since we were using longswords, we needed to be a few feet apart to parry, and each time, I landed just the right distance from him, quickly assuming my fighting stance. But maybe I didn't have to use my weapon like a sword.

Ruadan leapt away, and I glimpsed his vibrant eyes in the darkness. I melded with the shadows just behind him. With a blur of speed, I brought my sword to his throat. It required standing on my tiptoes, pressed against him, which wasn't the most stable position.

I whispered, "Drop the sword, pretty boy."

Instead, he gripped my hand, pulling it down. Then, he ducked down to slip under my arm—a smooth, lightning-fast gesture.

Instantly, he was behind me, pinning my arms. I struggled against his grip for a moment. Then, I realized he was trying to communicate something to me.

He slid his hand down to my sword hand and pulled my weapon from me. Then, he handed me a dagger. A misericorde, to be precise. I wasn't quite as skilled with daggers as I was with a sword, which might have been why we'd started in familiar territory. But I'd used stiletto knives plenty, and this wasn't wildly different. Usually, misericordes were used for a final death stroke to a wounded gladiator—not for combat—but you could kill with it. Its name meant something like *act of mercy,* an end to suffering.

I stepped away from Ruadan's grasp and turned the dagger around in my hand. "Is this what we'll be using?" I asked.

He nodded.

"It's not the best weapon to fight with...." I frowned, thinking it over. If we were fighting incubi, we wouldn't be killing them. Incubi were immortal.

Slowly, understanding began to dawn. Hellhounds and other

reaping demons had special tools they used to reap souls for their gods—to send them to one of the seven hells. Enchanted pens, daggers, and other sharp objects created by the gods themselves.

We wouldn't be using daggers to assassinate, but to reap their souls. Once we stabbed an incubus, he'd be sent straight to the shadow hell—the void.

"A reaping dagger, right?"

Ruadan nodded.

"Please tell me we're practicing with fake ones."

He nodded again.

Good. That meant if we accidentally stabbed each other while we were practicing, we wouldn't end up in the shadow hell.

Before I could ask another question, Ruadan was off again, shadow-leaping to the abandoned tracks.

We jumped and whooshed all over the park, blocking each other's attacks. We whirled through the darkness, slowly getting to know each other's quirks. Ruadan had a certain rhythm to his movements, moving slowly then fast again, and I started to be able to anticipate his jumps. He was aggressive but controlled, striking diagonally, aiming for my shoulder each time. Occasionally, he'd arc around to the side. Either he was certain I'd parry each strike, or he felt *very* confident in his healing skills, because he didn't seem to be holding back.

Our pace sped up, and I moved like a lunar wind, skimming over the ground. The faster I moved, the more the magic started frosting my veins, and emptiness welled between my ribs. Apparently, there was a limit to how much shadow magic I could channel at one time, and my legs began trembling.

Baleros's thirteenth law of power. Don't let your opponent see your weaknesses. And never admit defeat.

The shadow magic sent my teeth chattering, but I didn't want to relent, not while Ruadan was still leaping from shadow to shadow, evading me. I needed to keep going, to prove to him I wasn't just a bar-brawling, whiskey-swilling waste of space.

Crush your enemy completely.

I let the shadow magic flood me, surging through my bones. As I flew across the park, emptiness billowed in my chest, and my mind flashed with images of a dirt floor, the bottom of a cage. Twelve dead fae by my feet, skin rotting, turning black....

The void was eating at me, and long-buried memories started to surface. Once, Baleros had given me a butterscotch sweet. I had been seventeen, far too old to be impressed by sweets, but I'd snatched it up from the dirt. I'd kept it with me in the cage, refusing to eat it.

You have a pathetic tendency to grow attached to anyone who shows you the smallest bit of kindness.

Baleros was right about me.

Cold fury erupted. I gritted my teeth, fighting to control the shadow power. I wanted blood. I wanted to win.

I had a vague sense that Ruadan wanted to stop, now, that the training was over, that I'd lost control of the magic, but Baleros's voice rang in my head.

Crush your enemy completely.

Our swords sparked like stars in the night sky until a blast of frosted air whipped around me. My skin felt like cracking ice.

I wanted to leap again, but I'd lost track of Ruadan. Then, two powerful arms clamped around my torso, pinning my own arms down, and Ruadan's muscled body pressed hard against me from behind.

His grip dominated me, and he squeezed my wrist hard until I dropped my dagger. It clanged against the stones.

At this point, I realized how violently I was shaking.

From behind me, Ruadan reached under my shirt and pressed his palm flat against my belly. Slowly, the flood of shadow magic began to even out again, and I slumped against him. Still, the surge of magic had depleted all of my energy, and my eyes were already starting to close.

Ruadan slipped an arm under my back, one under my legs as he lifted me.

And then, I rested my head on his powerful chest, and breathed in the scent of pine.

* * *

I WOKE on Ruadan's cold flagstone floor. Nectarine light poured in through the windows. Was it sunrise? No, the sun didn't hit this side of the building in the morning. I blinked. Sunset, then. I'd slept a very long time.

I reached for the pendant at my throat, only to realize someone had taken it off before laying me down.

I rubbed my eyes, and it took me a few seconds to realize that a blanket covered me. And a *pillow*—a gods-damned pillow lay on the floor.

I glanced across the room to find Ruadan dressing, strapping a series of knives to his waist.

Had he really given me a blanket and pillow? It was the first really kind thing he'd done for me. It was the first indication that he cared about my comfort beyond just seeing me survive as part of his duty. I lifted the blanket to my nose, breathing in the scent of pine.

I scanned the room. A pie stood on the table, steam curling from its crust, and my stomach rumbled. Had he got me food as well? Last night, when we'd trained in the park, a sort of battle fury had taken over me. Ruadan had been my enemy. But what if he wasn't? What if he actually liked me?

But as soon as I glanced at the arsenal on his wall once more, I froze. I was doing it again. My tendency to grow pathetically attached to anyone who showed me the smallest bit of kindness. Something sharp and cold pierced my chest.

Last night in the park, I'd felt completely overwhelmed by our kiss. It had ripped the world out from under my feet and left me in a free fall. But of course, it had just been part of the training, a way to get me to channel shadow magic. If Baleros had been able to channel magic that way, he would have. Now, I was letting Ruadan toy with my emotions.

Ruadan was being kind. And what had Baleros taught me about kindness? It gave a mentor power over their student. It made the recipient a slave.

Think about this carefully, Arianna. What had he done with his last two novices? He'd executed them. His own words. He'd execute me if he thought it necessary. As soon as Grand Master Savus gave the order, Ruadan would have my neck on the block, iron sword raised. He'd take my head clean off. He'd told me this much.

So what were the blanket and the pillow for?

He was Balerosing me, again. He fought like Baleros. He used my old master's moves. He'd trained with Baleros—maybe was even trained by Baleros. And this was my fucking butterscotch sweet, the pathetic trinket I'd cling onto at the bottom of a dirt cage. This was my strawberry. The smallest bit of kindness....

I rose, my legs shaking, picking up the blanket as I did.

"I don't need a fucking blanket," I shouted. "Or a pillow. Got it?"

Ruadan whirled.

"I sleep on the floor. I look after myself. That's how it's always been, and that's how it always will be. I don't need this fucking pillow." Anger flooded me, and I threw it at him. I knew how this worked. He'd throw me a few tokens, and I'd be his to control until it was time to lay my head on the chopping block. The betrayal would kill me before the blade ever did. I wouldn't let that happen. I wouldn't let myself die inside. "I don't need your fucking butterscotch sweets."

Ruadan's brow furrowed, surprise etched across his perfect features.

Point one to me, Baleros. Never let your enemy anticipate your actions. Ruadan had definitely not been expecting me to yell at him about butterscotch sweets.

"It's a metaphor," I explained. *Careful, Arianna. Careful.* I couldn't let him know how well I knew Baleros. Already, my rage was fizzling out. "Never mind. I just don't need a blanket. I can sleep on the floor, and please don't pretend to be nice to me because I know what you're doing."

Now, he looked irritated, and he pointed sharply at the pie, shadows whipping around him in savage arcs. Apparently, he'd heard my stomach rumble, and he'd assessed—correctly—that at least part of my fury had to do with my hunger.

I crossed to the table. "Thanks for the food. I understand that you need to keep me fed and to keep me from freezing to death."

I sat down at the stone table, my mouth already watering. Potato and leek pie with gravy this time. Gods below, I no longer cared if he was trying to manipulate me, I wanted to wrap him up in my arms for getting me this pie. It melted in my mouth, rich and buttery.

"So I slept all day," I said.

He nodded, then sat across from me, his enormous form looming over the table.

My limbs still ached. "I guess the shadow magic burned me out a little."

It was actually damned lucky I'd been paired with Ruadan. While all of the other novices had been training with magic since birth, I'd needed a part incubus to help me manage the full force of the magic. Someone to unfreeze me a little.

Ruadan pulled out a piece of paper, and he wrote:

While you're focused on crushing your opponent, you're letting the magic overwhelm you. Remember to ground the magic in the earth below you, so you don't burn out.

"I'll be fine." I took another bite of the pie. "So, when do we go after this nest of incubi?"

In a few hours.

I leaned back in my chair. I wasn't exactly ready for this, but I'd gone into battle unprepared before. And I'd lived.

I glanced at the pillow on the floor, and the feathers that had tumbled onto the stone. Somehow, the damn pillow—that little hint of kindness—scared me more than the incubi.

CHAPTER 22

nder one of the dark arches—in the same park where I'd practiced with Ruadan—I stood in a line of novices. We were waiting for Grand Master Savus's arrival to give us the reaping command. The burnt car from last night had stopped smoking and now stood, blackened, among the other rubbish in the archway—old fridges, a children's plastic shopping trolley. Newspapers, egg cartons, and abandoned sneakers lay strewn around our feet.

And Aengus had promised me a life of glamour among the Shadow Fae.

From what I understood, the incubus nest wasn't far from here. In fact, somewhere nearby, they'd taken over a nightclub.

Maddan narrowed his eyes at my skimpy clothing—a short skirt, a low-cut silk shirt, and no bra. "Whore," he whispered.

Fuckwit. I wasn't going to argue with him, because it served no purpose. He had no idea what he was in for, anyway.

The fae males had no gods-damned clue that they were at a distinct disadvantage for this trial. None of the males had any idea how nightclubs worked in the human realm. They'd never been to a bar, or stood outside trying to get into an exclusive nightclub by showing just the right amount of cleavage. They probably planned to simply waltz up to the door and demand entry. They'd concealed their pointed ears and left the oak leaves at home. But beyond that, they wouldn't fit in at all.

Melusine and I, on the other hand, were perfectly attired for the occasion. Our skimpy clothing was our ticket into the incubi's nightclub.

I brushed my fingertips over the misericorde reaping dagger concealed by my side.

If the fae males somehow managed to get into the club, the advantage would shift. Incubus lust magic only worked on females. Melusine and I could possibly end up wildly distracted.

In any case, the most important thing to remember for tonight's trial was that one stray prick of our daggers would mean an eternity in hell. If we accidentally stabbed ourselves, it was straight to the void forever. And that might explain why the males were a little bit jumpy this evening.

The barguest growled. "Once you get in the club, whores, and sniff that incubus magic, you'll be rutting like bitches in heat."

"Are you suggesting that I'm dog-like? You literally transform into a—" I sighed. "Never mind." Not even worth it. He was an idiot, and he probably wouldn't survive this task.

The barguest growled again, but the echoing of footfalls in the archway and the thickening of mist cut him short.

Grand Master Savus stepped out of the archway's shadows, and the novices went quiet. A steady stream of water droplets dripped from above.

I shoved my hand into my pocket, brushing my fingertips over the lumen crystal. Someday, when I was living as a fugitive, the crystal would be mine.

Savus prowled before us. "Tonight, you will be reaping souls in a crowded nightclub. We will be watching to see how you perform. Stealth, efficiency, and discretion will be noted. Commoners fear us, but we do not like to call attention to ourselves more than necessary. If humans become too afraid, they will grow restless. Agitated. Our fragile alliance will crumble. Humans can be so irrational. What's more, you are novices. You are not Knights of the Shadow Fae. You may not present yourselves as Knights of the Shadow Fae. Tonight, you will disguise yourselves as humans."

Savus steepled his fingers.

"You all have your lumen stones, yes? Please be aware that these are extremely valuable. Any novice who loses their lumen stone can expect to meet their end with the blade of an iron ax."

Crikey. I was starting to think the knights were a little overeager to get the iron axes out.

I clasped the necklace around the back of my neck, and my body surged with an icy jolt of shadow magic. Just as Ruadan had instructed, I used the stones beneath my feet to ground the power, channeling the magic evenly. I sucked in a deep, shaking breath as the power imbued my muscles and bones.

Savus crossed to the archway's opening, pointing to the street that lined the far end of the park. "Find the incubi's nightclub. Enter discreetly, posing as humans. Reap incubus souls. Remember—we kill in the shadows. And if you don't remain discreet, you will likely end up dead. We believe many incubi lurk in there, and they will slither from the shadows to slaughter you if they discover your presence. Don't cause a scene."

I shot a glance to the barguest, once again convinced he'd die before the night was over. I could not say the thought brought me distress.

"Wait until I issue the command," Savus cautioned.

Along with the shadow magic in my veins, adrenaline arced through my blood. When I glanced at the other novices, starlight seemed to spark in their eyes. The magic of Nyxobas pulsed through us, just as it did with Ruadan.

The barguest growled low under his breath. Shadows whipped violently around Maddan—the prince—tinging his auburn hair with darkness. A cold night wind rippled over my body, and I drew my dagger from its sheath.

By my side, Melusine was muttering to herself. *Enter silently, send them all to hell. Enter silently, send them all to hell. Enter silently, send them all to hell. Enter silently, send them all to hell.*

Her mumblings, combined with her sweet face, had a deeply unnerving affect.

I turned to Melusine, whispering audibly, "Maddan is probably going to do something stupid, like miss the goat pen altogether."

Melusine frowned, ready to argue with me that we *should* miss the goat pen, that the goat was a belligerent monster who'd slam us into the mud repeatedly, worse than the incubi. But I held up a finger to silence her. Understanding dawned on her features, and she laughed a little too loudly. "Haha. Yeah. He'd be just that stupid. Miss the goat pen."

I stared across the park, beyond the farm, where the streetlights twinkled. With the coldness of the shadow magic chilling me, I wanted their warmth. I longed for light right now.

"Now," said Savus. "Go forth and reap."

Shadows spilled through my blood like ink, and I mentally fused with the pool of darkness just before the goat pen. I jumped, zooming through the air and landing softly in the wet grass outside the fence.

The barguest hurled himself into the pen, landing just before the goat, who immediately slammed into him. Of course he was the stupidest one.

Melusine and I were already moving on, jumping beyond the farm, toward the yellow streetlights.

Savus hadn't told us where to find the nightclub, and that was part of the test. As we moved closer to the main street, I sniffed the air, tuning into the smell of electric magic. It was the lightning-storm smell of night magic and of incubi. As I jumped into a shadowy alleyway on the main street, I homed in on the shadow magic—powerful under the smell of beer, sweat, and rubbish.

Graffitti-covered walls lined either side of a narrow main street. With its streetlights and club signs, there were fewer shadows, but I found them behind a line of food trucks, and by zigzagging across the street into narrow alleyways.

Partygoers staggered down the road, some of them singing loudly.

I knew this neighborhood—it was one where everyone went to get completely hammered, and I was quickly realizing that we didn't need to worry about discretion too much. You could run down this street in a flaming squirrel costume and most people wouldn't notice.

As I moved, I smelled the mossy scent of fae, and I caught a glimpse of bright red swooping past me.

Dammit. Maddan was getting ahead of me. Oh well. Let him burn himself out. He wasn't getting into the club, and maybe I could just let him lead me to it.

I tracked his movements to a dark alleyway that cut between two Victorian brick buildings. The prince was right on target, because the scent of incubi grew stronger here. In fact, I could already feel their magic sweeping over my skin in a rush of tingles. Even outside the club, my body was heating. No wonder they'd attracted a long line of human females. It was starting to become clear to me that infiltrating a nest of incubi would be distracting as hell, but at least Ruadan wasn't lingering around, making it worse with his stupidly beautiful face.

In the alleyway, the humans chatted to each other and toyed with their cell phones. Despite the fact—or perhaps because of the fact— that no sign marked the entrance to the incubi's club, this was apparently the hottest spot in the city tonight.

Maddan strutted on in front of me, every inch the royal fae. He'd left his oak leaves home tonight, but with his rigid posture and imperious glare, he still looked like a weirdo among the humans.

Getting into the club wasn't as easy as just shadow-leaping inside. You had to see a spot in order to shadow-jump to it, and a brick wall blocked our entrance—not to mention the two bouncers built like brick shit-houses. We were disguised as humans, but even if we weren't, the bouncers might not care. In London, nightclub bouncers might be the single group of humans unafraid of spell-slayers.

I glanced behind me, relieved to find that Melusine had followed hot on my heels, spine straight to emphasize her boobs. The girl was smart, even if she literally couldn't use a sword to save her life.

The barguest and Sea Monster shoved past us. Already, I could see the bouncers scowling at them. No way in hell were these fae males getting inside the front entrance. Unless they wanted to slaughter some humans in front of a crowd, they'd be forced to skulk below-ground, trying to find a way in through the sewers.

I hung back a little, so the bouncers didn't think Melusine and I were with those three twats. From here, I couldn't quite hear what Maddan was saying, but I'm *sure* it was something totally normal and human sounding, like, "Maddan, Carver of Enemies, son of Wanktonius of the House of Knob-Endians."

Whatever he said, one of the bouncers was already shoving him in the chest. I could practically *see* the steam coming off Maddan. Right now, he was probably considering reaping this bouncer's soul and just rampaging into the club. Certainly, the barguest's hand was looking twitchy by his sheathed dagger. If only Savus hadn't cautioned us to work in the shadows....

"In the shadows," I whispered loudly.

The barguest turned, snarling. Already, they were fucking up the discretion thing, and I hoped Savus was seeing this.

I took a step closer, until I could hear what Maddan was saying, and just caught the end of, "probably full of whores anyway," before the bouncer landed a hard punch on his cheek.

All three fae males snarled, before finally mastering themselves. I grinned at them as they skulked past us, dismissed by the bouncers. That was one big "enter silently" fail.

I leaned over to Melusine, whispering, "Time to unleash the holy trinity of nightclub bouncer approval: blogging, boobs, and banging the DJ. Or, in my case, pretending to have banged the DJ."

She cocked her head, frowning, and blinked her large, brown eyes. She had no idea what I was talking about.

Not a big deal. She'd given me a strawberry, and now she was my plus-one.

I sauntered over to the bouncers, swaying my hips and twirling a strand of my lavender hair around my finger.

"Hey, guys." For reasons I couldn't quite explain, I adopted an American accent for this. Maybe Americans were just sexier somehow. "I'm writing a piece for the Hot Nights in London blog. I spoke to someone earlier about coming in to do a piece on your herbal gin and tonics."

I didn't have to research that one. Every bar in London—even the shitty one where I'd worked—was doing herbal gin and tonics. In our case, we basically mixed some cheap oregano with Tesco Dry Gin, but an incubus club probably used hothouse cucumbers, freshly farmed rosemary, and a dusting of gold on the rim.

One of the bouncers scowled at me. "You spoke to someone, you said? Who was it?"

"My friend Gary, the DJ. We're very, very close friends."

I actually *did* know of a DJ named Gary. I'd never met him, but he played every club in East London. He was something of a legend. "I know Gary" had basically become a password for entrance to any of Shoreditch's clubs.

"Everyone says they know Gary," countered the bouncer. "Why should I believe you?"

Shit. It was becoming harder these days.

"Yeah, but I *actually* know him. We're mates! He's tall, slouches a lot, wears baggy T-shirts, often smells like spliffs. He rambles about government conspiracies, and carries around a bag of records."

Pretty sure I was describing literally every DJ who had ever existed.

The bouncer squints at me as he considered my proposition. "He always wears fitted black T-shirts."

Okay. *Almost* every DJ.

"If you know him so well," the bouncer went on, "what's he calling himself these days?"

It just so happened that I knew the answer to this, since I'd prepared weeks ago to get into an exclusive club for a "clothes swapping and suds night." Don't ask. "He goes by Gary the Tall, sometimes," I said. "Also known as Glad Gary."

He narrowed his eyes, not budging.

"Most recently," I added, "He's adopted the moniker Glad the Impaler."

"All right. Go on then."

He unhooked the velvet rope, stepping aside.

And point one goes to the ladies.

Melusine smiled at me, and we crossed into a long hallway lit by glowing blue stones embedded into the walls. At the end of the hallway, a silver door blocked our way, carved with the sigil of the Night God: a circle with a dot in the middle—basically a giant tit—next to a crescent moon. These demons weren't even trying to hide their demonity. They were just throwing it in the knights' faces. I almost felt a sense of umbrage before I remembered I had no intention of actually becoming a knight.

Before I could grab the door handle, Melusine grabbed my arm. "Enter silently, send them to hell."

CHAPTER 23

$\mathcal{B}$efore I pushed through the engraved door, I peered at Melusine. "Are you ready for this?"

"Yes." She sucked in a deep breath. "It's just that I prepared my whole life for this. I've been practicing magic and Angelic spells since I was a little girl. Believe it or not, I don't have many friends. I used to draw faces and tape them to broom handles so I'd have someone at my birthday parties. I'm not good with people. I'm not even good with the broom people. At least three of them hated me, and I could never get them to eat the cake…. If I fail here, I have nothing to go home to." Her brow creased. "And if you fail, they'll execute you. We both have a lot to lose. But only one of us can get a spot. None of this is good news."

A deep, throbbing bass pulsed through the door.

My jaw tightened. This wasn't the best time for this discussion. "Look, Melusine. We just need to take this one step at a time. Today, we just need to survive and reap some souls. We'll figure out the rest tomorrow. We're both survivors. You survived extreme loneliness." And I survived the gladiator ring. "We'll both make it through this."

She nodded, and I pulled open the door into a scene of pure hedonism. The club wasn't what I expected. I'd been expecting flashing lights, a large dance floor. Instead, it looked like an enormous, Victorian opium den. Persian rugs covering the floors, dark wooden alcoves with pillows and chaise lounges, silky drapes, candle-lit chandeliers…. Fire hazards all over the place, but none of the people making out in the alcoves seemed to care.

A curving wooden stairwell swooped up to a mezzanine floor overhead. In the balconies above us, I caught glimpses of naked women straddling men, some lying beneath them. People were dancing lasciviously to the strange, pulsating music, crackling from an old phonograph. Gary stood behind it in his fitted black T-shirt, rifling through a crate of albums.

So far, I saw humans everywhere, but I could feel the magic of the incubi all around us. Incubi's magic was twofold—they both fed off female sexual energy and could stimulate it. If the males ever made it in here, they'd have a huge advantage over us.

Still, it wouldn't be too hard to go unnoticed, because *no one* would be paying attention to us. They had far more interesting things to focus on.

I breathed in deeply, homing in on the scent of incubi. They were near, but not on this floor. I scanned the mezzanine, catching a glimpse of dark, leathery wings. *There.* With Melusine by my side, I crossed deeper into the club, trying to act casual while mentally tallying the incubi on the floor above.

My skin was growing hot, and I stared at a couple who lay on top of a table. The woman—a brunette with long legs—was straddling a powerfully built human man. His hands were sliding over her arse, and for just a moment, I gaped at them.

A smack to my arm pulled me out of my reverie. "Move silently, send them all to hell. *Now.*"

"Right."

I didn't have time to talk strategy with Melusine before she jumped away from me. For a few moments, I tracked her movements, impressed with her speed. So *that's* why they'd recruited her. She was brilliant with a lumen crystal.

Then, it was time to do some reaping of my own. I stalked into the shadows of an empty alcove, and I pulled my reaping dagger.

From there, I jumped into the shadows in the stairwell, whooshing up the stairs until I reached the mezzanine floor. From the upper level, I scanned the balconies. Silently, in the shadows, Melusine had already taken out two of the incubi. *Nicely done, girl.*

By the time the male novices got in here, there'd be nothing left for them. But I didn't have too much time to gloat about that thought, because I had souls to reap.

My gaze landed on an incubus in one of the balcony alcoves. He lay back on a chaise lounge, his leather wings swooping behind him. A red-haired woman lay on top of him, her body glowing and writhing. How was Melusine keeping the consorts silent?

She wasn't much of a killer, so she must've been using magic to knock them out. I didn't have those skills, but I did know how to choke a human out—just enough that she'd lose consciousness, but not enough that she'd die. My skillset was a little rougher than Melusine's.

Cold, electric magic whispered up my spine, and I jumped to a shadow in the alcove. The magic of lust was overpowering, heating up my core, and I struggled to focus. I took one step closer to the couple….

A wave of lust slammed into me. My pulse began racing, and I took a step back into the shadows, trying to master myself with slow breathing. I willed my heart rate to slow. Melusine was doing a lot better with this, but that girl was so tightly wound I wasn't sure she ever felt desire.

Either that, or she was thinking of her sad broom-people birthday parties. In fact, just the image of Melusine crying while trying to force a broom person to eat birthday cake was enough to drive the lustful thoughts right out of my mind.

I took another step forward and threw the dagger, landing it in the incubus's heart. Immediately after throwing it, I clamped my hand over the woman's mouth and pinched her nose shut.

She struggled against me, trying to scream. I let go as soon as she stopped struggling, and she slumped to the floor, unconscious. Her chest still rose and fell. Messier than whatever Melusine was doing, but it got the job done.

When I scanned the balcony again, I spotted another incubus—one I hadn't seen before. He was dancing, dressed in a long, velvet bathrobe. He had a thin, curly mustache and a glass of champagne in his hand. A naked woman sidled up to him, wrapping her arms around his neck.

Gods *damn,* these women were not making my job easy. They were just trying to have a good time, and I couldn't justify killing them. I had *some* kind of moral code, after all.

I waited until she pulled away from him, dancing on her own. She lifted her arms over her head and swayed her hips, eyes closed in ecstasy. Then, I summoned the shadow magic, that cold rush of power.

I jumped, landing just behind the woman. One hand over her mouth and nose, the other to throw the dagger. It landed in the incubus's throat, and he collapsed. *Say hello to Nyxobas for me.*

The woman was trying to elbow me in the stomach, and she got a few jabs in, but I held on tight until she stopped bucking, and she slid to the floor.

I breathed in deeply. We'd reaped a few incubi souls, but by the heat surging in my blood, I knew there were plenty more. We just had to find them. Only—we didn't have a ton of time before the women I'd smothered woke up, or someone stopped fucking long enough to notice all the bodies lying around the place.

I crossed out of the alcove into a dimly lit corridor of dark wood with doors inset into the walls. Candles flickered in sconces, casting dancing shadows over silky sheets and pillows strewn across the floor.

The farther I walked down the corridor, the more desire built in my body, and even my skimpy clothing felt too tight, too restrictive. That meant I was moving closer to the incubi.

Sensuality throbbed in my core, and my hips started to sway as I walked, nipples brushing against the silk of my top. I had an overwhelming urge to pull it off. I had to stop my hand from inching down between my thighs….

Arianna. Focus on finding the incubi in front of you.

Except, why did I feel like the waves of desire were coming from behind me, now?

I whirled, my dagger ready. But it wasn't incubi that I found.

No, it was the three fae douchebags, slinking around the dark corridors, their clothing sodden from the underground sewer system. Maddan stepped forward, violet light glowing between his fingertips. What the hell was that?

"You didn't leave any incubi for us to reap, did you? This is why females should not be allowed in the Institute. You've used your feminine wiles to your advantage."

I blinked. "Oh, I must have missed the part about how you needed special treatment because of your overwhelming incompetence, but it does make sense now that you mention it."

Maddan just cocked his head. "Where did you learn to fight as well as you do, gutter fae? You didn't learn to sword-fight in bars. There is something very *wrong* about you, and I'm going to find out what it is."

The deep thrum of incubus power felt overwhelming here, and I glanced at the violet magic pulsing between his fingers. What *was* that?

Right about now, I was wishing I'd armed myself with more than just the misericorde dagger. With a sword, I was pretty sure I could take on all three of them at once. But I could always jump—

Maddan took another step closer, and I surged with desire. What the hell? I felt like the incubi were all around me

"Have you heard of distillation?" asked Maddan, taking a step closer. "I refer to the distillation of magic, of course. It's something the noble Mor learn from a young age. But of course, you're not one of us."

Then, he hurled that ball of violet magic at me, and warmth spread through my chest.

CHAPTER 24

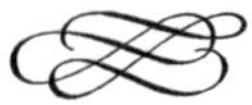

$\mathcal{I}$ couldn't quite focus on his words, because wild heat was building in my body, a ferocious need that made me want to run into the streets and hunt down Ruadan.

"'I've distilled incubus magic," Maddan went on. The barguest and Sea Monster flanked him. "I want to know your secrets, and this should get you to loosen up a little."

I had a vague sense that I needed to attack him, but I just couldn't think clearly. My legs were trembling with a raw, animal need.

In the next moment, Maddan's wet hand was around my throat, his face pressed down close to mine.

"Tell me your secrets, gutter fae, while I use you like I used the others of your kind."

Despite my disgust, a wave of aching need washed over me. He picked up my wrist—the one holding the dagger—and slammed it into the wall. Even as I knew he was hurting me, waves of pleasure washed through me at the force.

He was hiking up my dress, pressing me against the cold wood as I scrambled to remember what I was doing here, what my name was … anything at all. I dropped whatever was in my hand.

"Tell me where you come from," said Maddan. He ripped the lumen crystal from my neck, shoving it into his pocket.

As I stared into the calculating eyes of the fae prince, clarity came slamming back into me. Since the bastard had stolen my lumen crystal, I could no longer simply jump away.

I brought my knee up hard into his groin, and he doubled over. Then, I gripped his hair, bringing his head down hard onto my knee. Sea Monster lunged for me, and I smashed my elbow into his jaw with the full force of my strength.

So much for moving in the shadows. Any second now, the incubi were about to realize there were a bunch of fae brawling in one of their corridors, and that bodies littered their fuck den. But I was being attacked, three on one, and I had to neutralize these arseholes before I could get out of here.

The barguest growled, and I kicked him hard in the chest. He stumbled back into Sea Monster.

Crush your enemies completely.

At this point, I wanted them all dead. Savus had never instructed us not to kill the other novices, and I suspected he encouraged it.

Bloodlust surged—dark and hungry. I wanted the bodies of fallen fae lying at my feet once more, just like that day in the arena....

When Sea Monster swung for me, I ducked, then punched him in the crotch. He doubled over. As he did, I slammed my elbow into his kidney.

Lightning-fast, I clamped my hands hard on his head, and I twisted. The sharp crack of bone told me I'd snapped his neck, though only iron would kill him for good. A dark smile curled my lips. Death —this was what I was born for.

I whirled to take out Maddan. I hammered him with blows, one after another, bloodying his face, cracking his nose.

I was just starting to gain control of the fight when something pierced my ribs, cold as a glacier. The barguest had stabbed me.

A wave of dread pulled me under.

I looked down with horror at the reaping dagger jutting from my ribs. Emptiness pooled in my chest, a gnawing, glacial magic. I started shaking violently, my veins filling with ice.

And yet ... I hadn't been sent to the shadow hell, yet. Why not? What in the seven hells was happening?

The two remaining shadow fae stared at me. I could no longer control my body, couldn't lift my fist to punch them. Shivering convulsed me, and I hugged myself.

The two fae males gaped at me as my skin frosted over. I needed my lumen stone back.

The barguest bared his canines. "Why is she still here?"

"She should be in the shadow hell," Maddan spat, purple magic still flickering at his fingertips. "I told you there was something very wrong with her. Even the void is rejecting her."

I mastered enough control over my shaking hand to bring it to the dagger's hilt, and I pulled the blade out of me. But my teeth wouldn't stop chattering, and the coldness was spreading.

When I'd been with Ruadan in the park, he'd counteracted the iciness of the shadow magic with incubus lust.

What I needed was another hit of incubus magic to warm me up before I froze to death. Through chattering teeth, I managed, "You were so convinced you could seduce my secrets out of me. And yet even with incubus magic at your fingertips, you revolt me."

Rage flashed across Maddan's features, and he threw the ball of magic at me. It slammed into my chest. Now, warmth spread through my ribs and deep into my core, melting the intense chill of the shadow magic. Even as I shivered, desire started to blossom in my mind, and I thought of Ruadan kissing me.

As the barguest took a step closer, I felt my back arching, my eyes going dazed. I was trembling with need—but I was no longer freezing to death. For just a moment, I leaned back against a door, closing my eyes. The combination of shadow magic and desire dizzied me.

One of the fae males was yanking off my skirt, and I felt the cold whisper of air slipping over my skin.

I lifted my hands to push him away, mustering up just enough strength to punch him in the throat. It wasn't a hard punch, but I landed it squarely on his Adam's apple. He staggered back, snarling.

Then, a blur of black behind him, and the scent of pine….

I stared as Ruadan clamped his hands on the barguest's head. A glacial fury burned in Ruadan's dark eyes, his lip curled to expose his canines.

He didn't simply snap the barguest's neck. No, Ruadan clamped one arm around Dog Boy's jaw, the other around his shoulders, and he *tore*. He ripped the barguest's head right off. Blood sprayed all over the floor. Not the most discreet way to kill a man, but it looked like wrath had consumed him.

With a burst of shadows, Maddan shadow-jumped away.

Ruadan pulled an iron sword from his sheath, and he brought it down into the barguest's body. Then, he severed Sea Monster's head.

Both dead.

Tremors wracked me, a combination of the dagger's freezing magic and the distilled lust that still pulsed through my core.

I was trying desperately to focus while completely distracted by the feel of my silk shirt sliding against my bare breasts. My fingertips trailed down the front of my chest, and Ruadan's eyes watched the movement.

Ruadan rushed over to me, grabbing me around the waist so I didn't fall. I breathed in his masculine scent, and heat radiated from his body. Some part of me wanted to show him how much I ached for him, and my fingertips were inching their way into my knickers.

He lifted my chin to look into my eyes, demanding answers, and I blinked to clear my mind.

"Right." I leaned into his powerful chest, whispering, "The dagger. Maddan stabbed me with the reaping dagger. And they hit me with distilled incubus magic. They took my lumen crystal." I clutched at the fabric of Ruadan's shirt, trying to remain upright as my knees buckled. "Can you shadow-jump with me in your arms?"

He shook his head.

Shit. We'd have to get out of here the old-fashioned way. Walking. Except, I couldn't walk.

Ruadan gripped my waist, and the feel of his hands on me sent molten heat racing through my blood. Since he was an incubus, my desire was distracting him, too. His violet eyes were darkening to black, his animal side taking over. He snarled, his fingers gripping me harder, and he pushed me against the wood of the door behind me. I cupped his face, looking up into his eyes.

Then, a woman's scream ripped through the nightclub, and fear raked its claws into my chest.

We'd been discovered.

CHAPTER 25

$\mathcal{A}$ powerful force impacted Ruadan from behind—once, twice. My gaze flicked over his shoulder, and my heart sputtered. The incubi really *were* masters of shadow-leaping, and one of them was looming over Ruadan right now, leathery wings spread. His form had shifted, and talons now sprouted where his hands should be.

When Ruadan turned to face him, I caught a glimpse of the deep gashes carved into his shoulder.

"Eight fallen friends," hissed the incubus. "The work of the spell-slayers. You're one of us. Are you so disloyal to your kind?"

Ruadan drew his sword. In a blur of motion, he carved it through the incubus's shoulder, severing his body from collarbone to waist.

That's a hell of a sword.

But after the blow, Ruadan's body slumped. The wound gaped in his back, blood pouring out at an alarming rate.

Ruadan whirled, and his fae ears twitched. He sniffed the air. The scent of incubi hung heavily around us. Depending on how many we'd left alive, we could be just a few minutes from death.

Dizzying shadow and lust magic curled around my ribs, making my knees weak, and I slumped to the floor. Neither Ruadan or I were in great fighting form, now.

With a grunt, Ruadan scooped me up, and I wrapped my arms around his neck. He pulled open one of the doors, rushing me inside.

It wasn't even a full room—little more than a narrow booth. Thin chinks of light streamed inside flecking a wooden bench with the golden candlelight from outside. Ruadan sat, cradling me in his arms.

Despite the lust blazing from my body, the incubi probably had no idea how to pinpoint where I was, considering the entire joint was full of naked females writhing in ecstasy.

Ruadan frowned, lifting the hem of my shirt a little, and the brush of his fingertips sent a rush of hot tingles. It took me a moment to realize he was looking for the place where I'd been stabbed. Blood streamed from my wound, but it was a thin puncture, and it apparently hadn't pierced anything crucial. His forehead wrinkled.

"I know what you're thinking," I whispered, trying to fight my body's shuddering. "How does someone get stabbed with a reaping dagger and survive?"

His eyes met mine, and he nodded once.

"I have no idea." Ruadan's powerful energy rushed over my bare legs. "And I'm a little distracted right now."

He traced his fingertips over the wound, and his magic curled around it. Shadowy tendrils sank into my flesh, and I stared as the wound began healing over right before my eyes. The magic curled over my abdomen, smoothing my skin.

He met my gaze expectantly.

Right now, I felt acutely aware of every point of contact between our bodies, of his fingers on my upper thigh, of how close my mouth was to his neck. His primal magic charged the air. I could imagine him slipping his hands into my knickers, cupping between my legs while I writhed against him. I realized my own hand had crept into the hem of my knickers, and I flushed, yanking it out again.

Ruadan's posture was rigid, the unflinching gaze of a true soldier. And yet his eyes held that animal darkness.

I leaned in closer to Ruadan, whispering in his ear. "Is the plan to wait it out until the incubi are gone from this corridor?" I felt compelled to give his ear a nip, and his body tensed.

He nodded, still staring straight ahead.

It was a stupid plan. Incubi like Ruadan healed through sexual contact. I could be healing him right now. His body instinctively knew that, and he was practically glowing with pale, violet magic, already feeding off my desire. Even as he stared straight ahead, his arms tightened around me. One fingertip found its way to the hollow of my hip, stroking in lazy circles.

Then, he met my gaze, and the intensity of his dark eyes took me apart. Those slow, lazy circles on my hip made my breath hitch.

In his arms, breathing in the scent of his magic, a deep ache built within me—a wild, unfulfilled need, so powerful I wanted to beg him to ease it.

His attention was completely locked on me as he teased my hipbone, stirring my lust. A slow, pleasurable torture that left me panting. *More.*

I hooked my leg over him, sliding over his body so that I straddled him, and he stared into my eyes. Just minutes ago, I'd been freezing to death. Now, I felt as if warm honey were pooling in my body.

Seeming to lose control of himself, he snarled and clenched hard on my waist with one hand. His other slid up my back, the intense pressure making my spine arch against his palm. When his hand reached the shoulder of my silk shirt, he pulled it down, exposing my peaked breast. He leaned in to kiss me, his tongue flicking against mine. As his thumb brushed over my nipple, I moved my hips over him. Our kiss intensified, and I lost all sense of time and place.

Then, with a swift and rough movement, he lifted me up, pressing me hard against the wooden wall. My bare legs wrapped tightly around his waist. He pinned me to the wall, his gaze penetrating me.

I raked my fingernails down his back, wild animal need overtaking me. I couldn't remember how words worked anymore.

Already, I'd fed him more than enough lust to heal. But I wasn't done. I needed him to soothe my own ache. An electrical current was passing between us, and I was drawing strength from it, filling the empty void of the shadow magic. He leaned in, kissing me hungrily.

He crushed his mouth against mine with all the wild desperation of a last kiss.

I groaned into his mouth, threading my fingers into his hair.

His hand slipped into my knickers. I tilted back my head, writhing against him, moaning louder.

Then, he clamped a hand over my mouth, and I caught my breath. My mind snapped back into place.

Right. The incubi. I was getting too loud.

He pulled his hand from my mouth, then gave one last, heated kiss to my neck. But his muscles had tensed completely as he remembered the threat outside.

Slowly, his eyes shifted back to violet.

He lowered me to the ground and put a finger over his lips. My body slid against his, unfulfilled need ripping my mind apart. But even through my fog of desire I could understand that perhaps, in the middle of a battle with incubi, we had more important things to do than banging in a closet. Like, surviving.

Ruadan pulled a piece of paper out of his pocket and began writing.

Can you walk?

I could. In fact, Ruadan had filled me with so much of his magic that I felt ready to tear into a whole horde of incubi.

I pulled him close to whisper, "I just need my weapon back."

He pushed the door open an inch, peering out. Then, he grabbed me by the hand, and we slipped into the dark corridor. I snatched my dagger from the floor where I'd dropped it.

Shadows lashed the air around Ruadan, billowing until they ensconced us in darkness. His magic would help disguise us as we crept out of the nightclub.

At the end of the corridor, Ruadan pushed through an oak door into a dark stairwell, and we crept down the creaking stairs.

When we reached the bottom floor, the electrical smell of the incubi hit me like a wave. We'd emerged into a smoky room, one filled with glowing violet lights, ornate rugs, and silky pillows. It wasn't empty, but it seemed to be mostly naked women, who didn't notice us. They were too busy tending to themselves.

At least—until a ginger woman with extremely perky breasts pointed at Ruadan, a smile curling her lips. "This one is different. This one looks like a god. I want *him*."

An inexplicable sense of possessiveness snapped through me, and I nearly punched her. But Ruadan gripped my hand harder, pulling me toward the door.

Just before we reached it, a hissing noise turned my head. From behind, six incubi were closing in on us, brandishing swords and talons.

I needed to get one of their swords to even out the odds.

Already, Ruadan's sword was clashing with an incubus's. I locked my sights on one of the incubi—a blond demon closest to me—and hurled the blood-soaked reaping dagger. It landed in his chest. When he collapsed, I darted, snatching his sword from his limp hand.

I whirled, and my new sword clashed against a demon's.

Ruadan's magic filled me, imbuing me with strength. Now, I moved like a night wind: fast, silent, and cold. Ruadan cut his sword through another incubus, slicing him at the waist.

Two down, four to go.

I fought desperately, whirling and ducking as I parried the attacks of the incubi around me. Ruadan hacked through another demon. I grunted, just barely managing to fend them off as the fight wore on.

As I fought, blocking blow after blow, Ruadan's magic began to wear off. The reaping dagger hadn't sent me to hell, and yet I could feel the shadow hell living within me, blooming like a disease. My veins were icing over. I swung more wildly, just barely catching an incubus in the side.

From behind, pain sliced through my arm as an incubus ripped into it. Another lash of his talons ripped through my shoulder, tearing my flesh.

Ruadan pivoted, slicing his sword in a sharp arc through the incubus's neck. He picked up speed, a whirl of motion now.

I staggered back as iciness ripped through my bones. Shivering wildly, I collapsed onto the rug. Pain splintered my torso.

I *hated* being weak, but I couldn't fight the rising void within me. At least I wasn't in hell.

Yet.

I stared at Ruadan—a tornado of steel and dark magic, cutting into the incubi.

Glaciers were moving within my blood, and I couldn't keep my eyes open any longer. Arctic darkness enveloped me.

CHAPTER 26

I woke to something completely unfamiliar, so startling I
nearly screamed. Pillows, a mattress, a blanket.

Late afternoon light slanted into the room through diamond-
paned windows.

When I breathed in, scenting pine, I knew I was in Ruadan's bed. I
was still freezing, shaking hard, and my teeth chattered violently.

For the first time, I noticed another scent on him. Not pine, and
not shadow magic. *Apples.* I loved that smell.

A powerful arm hooked around me, pulling me close to bare skin.
A strand of white-blonde hair draped over my shoulder. I glanced
behind me.

Ruadan was trying to warm me, and heat radiated from his body
into mine. I was pretty sure he was also using a low dose of that
incubus magic to counteract the shadows. I nestled into him.

I ran my hand over my shoulder where the incubus had attacked
me with his talons. Already, the skin had smoothed over. Ruadan had
healed me. Now, his magic skimmed over my skin, caressing me. He
was using just enough incubus magic to keep the void from
consuming me from the inside out. Warm honey swept through my

core as his magic pulsed around me, and I had to restrain myself from rolling over and kissing him.

I closed my eyes, drifting off to sleep, and I dreamt I was back at the incubi's nest, back in that booth with Ruadan. His hand was fisted into my hair, tilting my head back, and his body pressed against mine. The night air and lust magic whispered over my bare legs, raising goosebumps.

He reached for my knickers, pulling them down. He spun me around so I faced the wall—

I woke to the sound of Ruadan groaning. Apparently, in my sleep, I'd pulled off my clothes. Even worse, I'd hooked my leg over him, and I may have been slightly rubbing against him. His own body was completely rigid, jaw clenched, with that "good soldier" look on his face like he was enduring something appalling.

Still, his fingers were clamped on my waist, and he wasn't pushing me away. In fact, his grip was growing tighter, almost pulling me closer. He was just … resisting.

I couldn't quite bring myself to unlock my body from his.

"I need to get out of here," I said. With a jolt, I realized I hadn't made any progress on finding the key.

Unless....

I glanced at his bare chest, and my pulse started racing. There, on his sternum, a fae rune glowed with silver light. My heart began to race. The key was part of his body.

I sucked in a sharp breath, and dread coiled through me. If that was the key, I might as well give up now, because I would not be hauling Ruadan's entire body to Baleros.

Shit. Shit. Shit.

I felt like I'd been punched in the gut. I pulled away from Ruadan, sitting up straight, the drafty air kissing my bare skin.

As soon as I moved away from Ruadan, I felt as if the void were ripping me apart from the inside out, and ice shuddered through me. My vision began darkening. I hadn't been sent to the void, but I hadn't escaped the effects of the dagger, either.

"I can't stay here." I mumbled. "I have to get out of here." I had to get to Ciara. Maybe I could just kill Baleros. Frigid magic iced my blood, and my teeth chattered.

Ruadan reached for me, pulling me in close until his warmth enveloped me. My breathing slowed again, my heartbeat calming. And as I drifted off, I started dreaming of the booth again, of hard kisses and arching backs....

* * *

THE COLD WOKE ME AGAIN, a bone-deep chill that had me scrambling to wrap myself in blankets. Through a darkening haze, I stared at Ruadan across the room. Thin slivers of moonlight streamed over the flagstones, and candles guttered in sconces, casting wavering light over Ruadan's bare chest.

Shivering, I stared at the glowing mark on his chest. I pulled the blankets more tightly around me, watching as Ruadan touched his tattoo. It glowed with a pale, silvery light, like starlight. Darkness spilled out from his body.

Shadows writhed around the room, then gathered over a spot in the flagstone floor. The tendrils of darkness whirled in wild eddies, until at last, the stones opened up and gave way to dark, glistening water. A portal of midnight waters flecked with starlight.

Ice slid through me. It *was* the key on his chest, and it was a part of him. Cold panic coiled around my heart. There was no way out of this.

I stared as a dark pool of water opened in the floor, its rippled surface glinting. The void gaped deeper in my chest, and I pulled the blanket around myself to cover my bare breasts. I had no idea where my clothes were at this point—probably crammed deep in the blankets. It seemed as though I couldn't bring myself to keep them on when I was around Ruadan and his particular brand of magic.

In any case, if Bael was about to come stark naked out of the water, he could hardly criticize my attire.

The cold was making my muscles seize up. Not just the cold, but that gnawing void, the painful emptiness....

I clenched my jaw, focusing on the World Key. I'd found it—what I'd been looking for all along. The only way to get it off Ruadan would be to kill him and cut it off him.

The void opened a bit larger in my chest, an emptiness so expansive it seemed like it was going to swallow me whole.

I have to kill Ruadan.

Dark shadows whipped about him, slicing through the air around his body. He'd let down his guard, and he seemed to trust me now. He'd let me into his bed, taken his shirt off in front of me. He was no longer hiding the World Key from me, as if I could be trusted.... He clearly didn't know me at all.

Baleros had turned me rotten through and through. Baleros had taught me to strike as soon as the enemy lowered his defenses. I could kill him in bed, take the skin from his chest—

Emptiness cut through me so sharply I thought I might die.

I stared as a beautiful man crawled out of the pool, his body dripping with water. His silver eyes had the cold sheen of moonlight, and dark curls framed his face.

The cold was making me convulse, and I fell back on the bed.

In another instant, Ruadan was by my side, scooping me into his lap. His magic stroked my skin, a velvety touch that warmed me. Had it been just a moment ago I'd been imagining how I'd kill him? Because right now, I was hugging him and leaning into his chest to breathe in the scent of pine. To say I felt conflicted was the understatement of the fucking year.

The silver-eyed one hovered over me, staring down with curiosity.

"Who are you?" I asked through chattering teeth.

"Caine." He looked at Ruadan. "You're telling me that someone stabbed her with a reaping dagger? One belonging to Nyxobas?"

How the fuck were they communicating? Ruadan wasn't speaking.

"And she's still alive?" Caine continued, incredulous. "What in the seven hells is she?"

If my nudity bothered him, he didn't show it. When I glimpsed the faint ghost of phantom wings behind him, I had the sense that he might be part incubus, too.

"All right," said Caine. "It seems as if part of the void is inside her. We can try to pull it out and absorb it. You'll need to send it back into the shadow realm using the World Key."

I was trying to tune into his words, although most of my thoughts were intensely focused on every place where Ruadan's body touched mine. His bare chest was heating my naked body, and I stared at the glowing fae rune at his throat.

I was having a hard time concentrating on anything except Ruadan's arms curling around me. It made it hard for me to think straight, and I wanted my mind back so I could start killing things again, like I was born to do.

But I could feel a wild, dark power trembling over my skin. The two gorgeous half-incubi closed their eyes. Now, the candles flickered in their sconces until they snuffed out, and the moonlight in the room began to dim. A thin frost spread over the stone floor, the bed—everything in the room but us. Glimmering shadows spilled from my body and whirled into Caine and Ruadan.

Even though cold seemed to be spreading within the room, my own body grew warmer. I closed my eyes, my mind whirling with cosmic visions—the birth of stars, the spinning of galaxies. A black hole, sucking in light. When I opened my eyes again, it looked to me as if the shadows in the room were breathing, like a bellows rhythmically expanding and contracting. My own breath moved in tune to the pulsing of the shadows.

In the darkness, in the hollow void of my chest, embers began to smolder, warming my ribs. I fell back into Ruadan's arms, closing my eyes, and I breathed in the scent of pine.

CHAPTER 27

When I opened my eyes again, Ruadan had left. I sat up, letting the sheets fall off me, until I noticed the shadows writhing in the corner of the room. A pair of silver eyes glowed from the darkness.

Once my eyes adjusted to the whorls of dark magic, I realized that Caine was sitting in the corner, drinking straight out of my whiskey bottle. A raven sat on his shoulder, its head cocked. Caine's clothes and hair were still damp from the portal.

The pool of starlit water still glimmered in the center of the room.

Caine sipped my whiskey. If he weren't so shockingly good-looking, the whole "lurking in the shadows, drinking whiskey while a naked woman sleeps" situation would be beyond creepy, but pretty blokes could get away with anything.

I snatched the sheets up, covering my breasts, but he didn't seem too bothered either way.

"You're still here," I said.

"Very observant. Ruadan did tell me you were clever, and you're not proving him wrong so far."

I arched an eyebrow. "He talks to you?"

"Not in words."

"Right. Of course. That makes total sense." I had no idea what he was talking about. It took me a moment to realize that I had now completely recovered from the reaping dagger. I no longer felt cold, or consumed with desire. "How did you fix me? How did you pull the shadow void from me?"

"The shadow void is already part of Ruadan and me. With our combined power, we were able to draw it into our bodies and absorb it. It doesn't hurt us."

I blinked. "What do you mean it's already part of you?"

Caine took another sip of my whiskey. "Nyxobas is our grandfather."

"Your grandfather is the god of night and shadows."

"Hence, Ruadan and I are demigods of the night."

I arched an eyebrow. "Wouldn't that make you a quarter—"

"Still considered demigods."

"Sure you are."

Caine narrowed his silver eyes, clearly irritated.

"So, what—you're brothers?" I asked.

"Half-brothers. He's even older than I am. I never knew he existed until after our father died."

"I'm sorry about your dad."

"Don't be. Our father deserved his death." Caine rose and slid the whiskey bottle across the stone table. "Thanks for the drink. My brother asked me to talk to you about something before I return to my realm."

"What?"

"The fae who tried to kill you still lives in this fortress."

Anger roiled in my chest. "Maddan? He should have been sent home in disgrace for fucking up our mission."

A slow shrug from Caine. "Grand Master Savus wouldn't allow it. He values ruthlessness, which is why you're here, as I understand it. And more importantly, the prince's father has been donating millions to the Institute." Caine held up a glowing, violet lumen crystal. "But while Ruadan was beating the living shit out of the fae boy, he pulled this off him. It should make it easier to defend yourself if he returns."

"Where is Ruadan?" I asked.

"Still petitioning Grand Master Savus for permission to execute the fae prince."

"Why does he want to execute him so badly?" Was he protective of me, or—?

"I think he just likes executing novices, to be honest. Particularly the rule-breaking kind."

"Of course. The Shadow Fae value ruthlessness." I let out a long, slow breath. Right. *Don't let this situation mess with your head, Arianna.* He wasn't trying to protect me. He just … liked executing novices.

Baleros's seventh law of power: Kill, or be killed.

There was no way out of the Institute without breaking several rules. I was going to end up on Ruadan's kill list, one way or another.

My chest tightened. Unless I took him out first.

Caine's eyes pierced me to the bone. "What are you? Why didn't the blade send you to the void?"

I shook my head. "I have no idea. I never knew my parents."

He stared at me for an uncomfortably long time. "You aren't as good a liar as you think you are."

My breath caught in my throat. Caine was starting to get under my skin. "You and your brother are both deeply unnerving, do you know that?"

"I have a charming side. Ruadan does not, as you might have noticed. Silently brooding, disapproving of alcohol, updating his kill list, executing people…. Those are his favorite pastimes."

"Mmm. Don't take this the wrong way, but I'd say you've kept your charming side well-hidden so far."

"You're not wearing any clothes. The effect of my charm would be overwhelming. Like a human learning the true names of the gods."

"Right." Gods below. The ego on this guy.

I took the lumen crystal from him, staring at the violet glow. It almost seemed like Ruadan cared about keeping me safe, but I knew better than to trust gestures of kindness. I had to find a way to kill him.

Even though the two incubi had pulled the void out of my body, coldness still washed through me.

When I looked up again, Caine was already crossing back to the portal. The raven fluttered off his shoulder and flew out the open window. Caine leapt into the water.

I shivered as Baleros's voice whispered in the darkest depths of my skull. *Neutralize all threats as quickly and efficiently as possible.*

Ruadan might be a demigod, but he'd let down his guard around me. He didn't see me as a threat, but that didn't mean he cared about me or anything ridiculous like that. It just meant he'd gotten sloppy while he waited to execute me. And tonight, while he slept in his comfortable bed, I had a threat to neutralize.

* * *

I still had half a bottle of whiskey left, and now was as good a time as any to drink it. I finally pulled on some clothes, and I sat by the cold, stone table. Night had begun to fall, and Ruadan hadn't yet returned.

I clasped the lumen crystal around my throat, and shadow magic shot through my blood. But now—after everything I'd endured with the reaping dagger—I could handle it easily.

My stomach rumbled, and I rifled through my bag for one of my lollipops. Somewhere, beneath the duct tape, flashlights, and bandages, I found an old protein bar, only partially eaten. I delved into it, ignoring its staleness.

I had to keep my energy up for tonight. You couldn't assassinate a demigod on an empty stomach. Not one of Baleros's laws, but it seemed like a good rule to live by.

I scanned the wall, my gaze roaming over Ruadan's collection of blades. I tried to push out the rising cold in my chest, that corrosive sense of emptiness. The voice in my head telling me not to do it.

Crush your enemies completely.

I needed two blades—one silver, to cut the tracking mark off the back of my neck. The other, iron, to drive into Ruadan's body when he slept. Either could be used to cut the World Key off him.

I hugged myself, shivering. Why did it feel as if the void hadn't completely left me?

A knock on the door pulled me out of my dark thoughts, and I whirled. I wasn't ready to face Ruadan yet, or look him in the eyes. My body tense, I crossed to the door and pulled it open.

Melusine stood beside Aengus. She was gripping a paper bag.

I exhaled a shaky breath as I looked at her. "Good. You're alive. So you have that advantage over two of our fellow novices."

Aengus leaned against the door frame. "What are you?"

I crossed my arms. "Alive. That's all that matters."

"What in the seven hells happened in there?" he asked. "Why did the others attack you? We were watching it all through a scrying mirror, but it was hard to see anything through the darkness."

Melusine tapped her fingernails on the doorframe. "He's been interrogating me, but I didn't see anything. I was too busy reaping."

My fingers clenched into fists. I was in here trying to plan a murder, and I didn't want to rehash our giant novice fuck-up. "Maddan and the others couldn't get into the club at first," I said. "They'd thought it would be an easy trial for them, that the ladies would be all hepped up on incubus magic and unable to think clearly. When they finally got inside and found that the girls were embarrassing them, they wanted to teach me a lesson. They were pissed I'd killed the king in our last trial, and they seemed to think I have some shady past—which, surprise, I do. After all, I'm just a gutter fae. But I know a knob-end when I see one, and the truth is, Maddan is no better than the bar-brawling demons who flip over tables every time they think they've been slighted by a chick. Rage rules their minds. Turned out, they were the ones who couldn't think clearly."

Baleros's fifth law of power: Don't let your emotions govern your decisions.

"But they're dead now," I went on. "All except Maddan."

"Idiots," spat Aengus.

Melusine thrust the paper bag at me. "You missed dinner. I brought you a steak pie."

I fought the urge to hug her. I didn't want to alert them that I might be on my way out of here soon. Instead, I just smiled. "Thanks, Melusine."

"See you at the trial tomorrow."

I nodded. I hadn't even known there was a trial tomorrow, but it wasn't like I needed to prepare. I'd be long gone by the time the sun rose—with Ruadan's blood on my hands.

CHAPTER 28

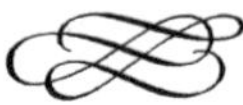

$\mathcal{I}$ lay curled up on the stone floor by Ruadan's bed, pretending to sleep. No blanket. No pillows.

I felt ice-cold, inside and out.

It must have been around midnight by the time he returned.

When he snatched the blanket off his bed to cover me with it, my breath caught in my chest. For just a brief moment, warmth sparked in my chest, my glacial resolve cracking....

Then, I extinguished it again. Like everyone said. I was ruthless. And the blanket was just another gods-damned butterscotch sweet.

I wasn't going to let my emotions rule me. I watched through a slit in my eyes as Ruadan pulled off his shirt. I swallowed hard, my gaze roaming over his perfect body. I practically sighed. What a waste of a beautiful man. I wished it could have been different. I wished I'd gotten to hear him speak, to learn his secrets....

Kill, or be killed.

I watched as he crawled into bed, my body seeming to grow colder as I contemplated what was coming next. For what seemed like ages, Ruadan lay in bed, staring up at the ceiling. His muscles looked tense, just as he had when I'd shared a bed with him.

At last, his eyes closed. I waited until his chest slowly rose and fell.

The dark pulsing of shadows that always surrounded him began to ebb, as if they, too, were falling asleep.

Silently, I reached underneath my body, where I'd hidden two blades. I had to act quickly. Every extra second was another second he could wake up and discover me.

I rose, my chest aching with a yawning emptiness.

This was it. This was who I was. A ruthless killer, but a survivor. Baleros might have been the worst person I'd ever met, but he'd taught me how to stay alive.

The lumen crystal glowed over my sternum, and I shadow-jumped. I landed on top of Ruadan, my arm raised, gripping the knife—

His violet eyes opened, and time seemed to slow down. I was hesitating, and hesitation meant death.

I twirled the knife and started to bring the hilt down hard—I could knock him out, then decide.

But as my hand descended, he caught my wrist. He snarled, baring his canines.

In a blur of night magic, he flipped me over, pinning me to the bed. The move took my breath away, and I stared up into his darkening eyes.

His animalistic side was coming out. If I didn't get out of this, I'd become executed novice number three within the next few moments.

Inwardly, I cursed myself for hesitating. I should have just stabbed him.

Was he hesitating, too? I wasn't going to wait around to find out. I thrust my hips upward, knocking him off balance, and I rolled, yanking one of my wrists free.

I didn't hesitate this time. Just as it had so many times before, a desperate, wild will to live consumed me. I slammed my fist again and again into Ruadan's face. Then, I snatched the silver blade off the bed.

I brought it down hard into his chest, piercing his heart.

Blood poured from the wound. I'd stopped his heart completely, and he wouldn't be getting up anytime soon. But as soon as someone pulled the weapon out, he'd start to recover.

I was shaking, trembling with the cold, and for just a moment, tears pierced my eyes. Panic was ripping through my mind. I'd failed.

I'd used the silver blade. Not iron. He'd have a hell of a hangover, but he'd live.

Apparently, I'd gone soft since he started giving me blankets and pillows, and I couldn't bring myself to end him. The first thing he'd do when he woke up would be to hunt me down and yet....

The fucking blanket. That stupid fucking blanket.

I was letting my emotions rule me, and it was a problem.

A hot tear spilled down my cheek, and I wiped it off with the back of my hand. I hated myself right now, my inability to do what needed to be done.

I started pacing the room, my mind racing.

Hesitation is death.

I hated Baleros with every fiber of my being, but his teachings had been my salvation. Without them, I'd be dead now.

Get in your enemy's head. Knowledge gives you power over a person.

And yet....

The fucker had become so deeply embedded in my head that I sometimes couldn't figure out where his ideas ended and mine began. Almost as if our minds had melded.

And that meant I knew how he thought, too.

Confuse your enemy by utilizing the unexpected.

My fingernails were piercing my palm, drawing blood, as I frantically tried to think of a way out of this.

Baleros claimed he had eyes within the Institute—that if I betrayed him, he'd kill Ciara. But that was just the kind of bullshit Baleros *would* say. If he truly had forces working for him here, then why didn't he know what the key was in the first place? If he'd known already it was a part of Ruadan's body, he would have sent me on a kill mission. He hadn't. He'd sent me to steal.

Of course Baleros had lied, because that's what he did.

I clenched my jaw tight. What if I could kill Baleros and save Ciara?

I had to find him first, but if I knew how he thought, I might be able to puzzle it out.

I glanced at Ruadan's body, relieved to find he wasn't moving.

What did Baleros believe about himself? He viewed himself as a sort of god among monsters. That was what he used to call us gladiators—the monsters. He liked to drive that word into us, until I'd believed it myself. Maybe I still believed it. Maybe that's why I'd just driven a knife into the chest of my new mentor.

Baleros had studied us, manipulating us all the time like a puppet master. But we scared him, too. There was some dead philosopher he used to quote. Something like "whoever fights monsters needs to watch out that he doesn't become a monster, too." Then something like, "When you gaze too long into the abyss, the abyss gazes back at you…."

"Well, fucker," I said out loud. "I'm gazing back at you. I know how you think."

Baleros's eighteenth law of power: When you achieve greatness, cling onto it with all your strength.

Baleros had thrived during the anarchic period between the apocalypse and the reconstruction. Practically singlehandedly, he'd rebuilt the old Roman gladiatorial ring under London's city streets. He'd employed a legion of slave masters, each of them making money off their fighters, but he'd pulled all the strings behind the scenes.

The Shadow Fae and the reconstruction ruined all that for him. All the gladiators—except me—were sent into the supernatural realms.

If I closed my eyes, I could envision Baleros, haunting the old amphitheater, looking regal and shabby at the same time. He'd mentally relive his glory days, when the monsters had treated him like the emperor he was supposed to be. Baleros had adopted the old Roman ways, encouraging his veneration. Within those stone walls, he felt not just like an emperor, but like a god.

I touched the lumen crystal at my throat.

I could shadow-jump, now. Baleros couldn't do that. I could take him.

I glanced at Ruadan again, my whole body trembling. His body was still as a grave. He looked completely dead, even though I knew he wasn't. Perhaps I could have convinced him to come with me if I hadn't stabbed him in the chest. But that would be a risk, too. Ruadan would be going on a kill mission. I was going on a rescue mission. Totally different objectives.

My mind whirled frantically, and I felt like I was coming undone. I willed my heart to slow down.

My plan was to get Ciara out of Baleros's clutches—ideally, to kill him, as well, but Ciara's rescue was the priority. Then, we'd have to flee London. Both of us would be living like fugitives, hiding from the Shadow Fae for the rest of our lives. There was no way out of that. We'd just have to get used to it, and eventually, maybe the Shadow Fae would forget about us.

Whatever the case, I had to get the fuck out of here, now. I honestly had no idea how long a demigod would stay down for. It wasn't like I'd fought them in the arena.

I was still shaking when I crossed to Ruadan's wall, and I pulled another knife from his arsenal. A silver blade, just like the one in his chest. But I had a different purpose for this one.

I brought it to the nape of my neck, where Ruadan had marked me with the tracking spell days ago.

Wincing, I carved the blade into my skin. I gritted my teeth as the pain speared my neck. Melusine would probably have a magical way to handle this, but all I had was brute force on my side.

At last, I'd cut it off. Blood dripped down my fingers, pooling on the floor.

If I didn't staunch the bleeding, Ruadan would be able to track me within moments of waking. Situations like this were exactly why I carried the bug-out bag with me. You never knew when you'd have to carve magical tattoos off your body. I pulled out a bottle of water, gauze, and my other medical supplies, and I washed the blood from my hands. I spread some antiseptic on the wound, grunting as it stung the open flesh. Then, I taped it tightly with thick layers of gauze. And one more layer of duct tape, for good measure.

When that was cleaned up, I pulled off my bloodied shirt, crumpling it in a ball. I pulled on a fresh black shirt.

Suitably cleaned up, I snatched a piece of paper out of my bag, along with a pen, and I hastily scrawled:

SORRY FOR STABBING YOU.

Then,

THANKS FOR THE BLANKET.

I cringed. That sounded sarcastic, like I was taunting him, but I actually meant it.

"Fucking butterscotch sweets," I grumbled, aware that I was sounding increasingly like a lunatic with every minute that passed.

In any case, writing pretty things wasn't my strength, and I didn't have time to obsess over the exact phrasing. I left the note by his side for when he woke up.

I crossed back to his arsenal, selecting the finest-looking sheath, and I tightened it around my waist. I picked up the iron knife from his bed and carefully slid it into the sheath. Even Baleros had a weakness. And as a fae, that weakness was iron.

I crossed to one of the windows and lifted it until the chilly night air spilled into the room. Shadows claimed the courtyard. Perfect for jumping.

I was pretty sure the halls were lined with magic that could track our every movement, and maybe it would set off alarms. Keeping to the Tower Green was safer. And with the lumen stone, I might be able to get out of here before any of the Shadow Fae got a chance to react.

Ruadan was the only incubus in here, the only one who could naturally shadow-jump. And I'd laid him out cold with his own silver knife. A twinge of guilt flickered through me, but I shoved it away again.

Glacial night magic whispered over my skin, surging in my blood. I gripped the straps of my bug-out bag. Living in a castle had been nice, but it was time for me to take my leave before someone killed me. I sucked in a shaky breath, stared down at a far corner of the courtyard, and I jumped.

CHAPTER 29

I moved like a lunar wind, jumping along the dark, cobbled alleys of the Tower. No bells rang, no alarms as I reached the final, outer wall. Thank fuck for that, because the gates were locked, and shadow-leaping wouldn't get me through them.

I scaled the rough stone wall, finding footholds and handholds in the jagged stones until I reached the top. Then, I hooked a leg over the top of the wall. From my perch, I stared out into the darkness beyond the tower.

I swallowed hard. A sense of loss pierced me for a moment.

I'd gone soft, that was all. And the longer I stayed in luxury, the easier I'd be to kill.

I stared across the paved expanse before me, focusing on the farthest dark point I could see. Shadow magic whispered up my spine and slid over my skin like a layer of frost. My cold breath iced the air. I jumped, my teeth chattering. I felt exhilarated and untethered at the same time.

From Tower Hill, I jumped through the shadows, moving further north. I rushed along what had once been the eastern edge of London's Roman wall, flying through the shadows. A gnawing pit had opened up in my chest, worsening the further I got from the Institute,

178

but I kept moving. I always had to keep moving. Rest meant death. Hesitation meant death.

When I reached Leadenhall, I took a left. In the middle of the night, in this ancient part of the city, no one lingered on the streets. And even if I happened to pass some drunk banker lost in the city, he'd feel nothing more than the whoosh of cold air as I slipped past him.

I wasn't a Shadow Fae, but I could kill in the shadows, now, too.

At last, I reached Guildhall. Thousands of years ago, the Romans had ruled the city. They'd built a wall, temples, an amphitheater. And they'd left their ruins deep underground.

Baleros had taken their foundations and built from them, creating his own empire. Once, when I hadn't performed like he'd wanted me to in the ring, he'd locked me up for a week with only water. When I got out, crazed with starvation, I'd called him evil. I'd wanted to see if he had any sense of shame. He'd told me that good and evil didn't mean anything anymore. He said that wasn't the way the world worked. He'd said empire-builders created their own realities, and that for men like him, it had always been that way.

In the shadows near Guildhall, I pulled the cover off a manhole, and I jumped down. I splashed in the water, landing hard. The remains of the ancient Walbrook River reached about mid-calf. Long ago—even before the Romans had come—the noble Mor made sacrifices here. Now, the Shadow Fae had found another way to appease the Old Gods: with the blood of the demons they assassinated.

Shivering—why the hells was I so cold?—I rammed my hand into my backpack and pulled out my headlamp. Rats scurried along the sides of the river. They didn't bother me. I'd spent enough time living with rats.

A circular, white glare from my headlamp bounced over the water and wet walls as I moved deeper through the river. The water froze my legs. It felt like gods-damned winter down here.

At last, I reached a fork where a narrow tunnel curved right. This would take me where I needed to go.

As I walked, shivers overtook me. I tried not to think about

Ruadan, but a mixture of guilt and fear clouded my thoughts. Honestly, you'd think I could pick one or the other. Either he was a ruthless killer who would probably execute me or he genuinely liked me, and … oh, who was I kidding? Even if he liked me, any rational person would slaughter someone who'd betrayed them that way. It was just the way of the world.

The water grew shallower as I walked, the splashing quieter, until the river petered out into a dull trickle. A few minutes later, I reached the end of the tunnel. A wooden door—painted green—was inset into the brick here. A padlock sealed it shut.

I reached into my bag, pulling out two bobby pins. I bent one of them into a pick, and the other into a lever. I slid them both into the keyhole, jiggling them around until I unlocked it.

Before I pushed through the door, I flicked off my headlamp. I tucked the lumen crystal inside my shirt, disguising it within my cleavage. No need to broadcast my shadow-leaping ability.

Always let your enemy underestimate you.

Holding my breath, I carefully inched the door open, relieved when darkness greeted me.

My relief was short-lived as the smell of the old gladiator ring hit me. The stones, the sand. The only thing missing was the metallic stench of blood, or the overpowering smell of sweat. It made me want to vomit.

I moved silently over the sand, sniffing the air. I didn't need my headlamp to find my way into the center of the ring.

The arena was so dark, so quiet, that for a moment, I wondered if I'd got it wrong. Maybe Baleros wasn't here at all. Maybe he'd never remain somewhere so obvious.

I sniffed. When I picked out his rosewater scent, my heart skipped a beat. He was here.

I pulled my iron knife from its sheath. Shadows were all around me, but I didn't yet know where to jump.

I sniffed the air again. Roses.

He was so close. I could almost hear him—

Iron clamped around my throat, and the back of my head slammed hard into a wooden stake behind me. Metal creaked, and my lungs burned. I was choking, and I couldn't even scream.

My vision swam with dots.

I already knew what this was—Baleros's garrote. I couldn't speak as he tightened it. This was how the Romans had killed their worst enemies—a humiliating death, not even fighting. Baleros had used it to keep us all in line.

A revelation hit me like a train. He'd been waiting for me.

Of course he had. He was Baleros, and he lived in my head.

He turned the garrote again, and the world slipped away from me.

* * *

I'D LOST CONSCIOUSNESS, but when I regained it, I was staring up into the face of my old master. He'd flicked on my headlamp, and it shone brightly over his features. His eyes crinkled at the corners—genuine delight.

I wasn't sure how long I'd been out, but my mouth felt like sandpaper, and the iron garrote seared my neck. Poison. The iron sapped my strength, and I wanted nothing more than to get it away from me.

I snarled at Baleros, and the fucker laughed.

As my vision slowly cleared, I took in the shapes around us. It took me a moment to realize we weren't alone. But it wasn't Ciara I found in the arena with us. It was an entire crowd of spectators, filling the stone seats. Excited murmurs rippled off the stone. What the fuck…?

Even more disturbing, a circle of archers lined the edge of the arena, each with a flaming arrow pointed right at me. A tendril of panic coiled through my chest.

I'd certainly gotten myself into a pickle.

"Arianna, my dear," said Baleros. "I was hoping you'd arrive."

I gritted my teeth. "How did you know I'd come for you?"

"I didn't, precisely. But I know how you think, and I prepared for all eventualities—one of them being your arrival in the arena. I thought, sometimes that girl does my bidding at first, then the naughty rebellious streak emerges, and she thinks she can take me on.

This was merely one of the possible outcomes, but I was prepared." An easy smile lit up his face. "Please forgive me for knocking you unconscious. I needed a bit of time to prepare. But I think you'll agree that the results are spectacular. One final fight for the Amazon Terror." He loosed a long sigh. "I thought you would have learned by now. You can never win."

My mind was foggy from dehydration and the iron burning me. I couldn't make sense of this. What the fuck was his endgame?

"I don't understand." I hated not understanding. Hated that he was always one step ahead. "Why did you send me after the key in the first place? Why not just drag me back into the ring if you wanted me to fight?"

He shrugged. "Because I wanted you to fight someone very hard to capture. You never lose. Now, you will."

Baleros stepped aside, and my world tilted. There, on the other side of the ring, stood Ruadan. The arena lights gilded his body, and he gripped a sword. His eyes had darkened to pure black, and his teeth were gritted with sheer, murderous rage.

I was supposed to fight him. "You wanted the Wraith to track me here so we could fight."

"No one can capture him. Not even me. I had to lure him to me. You were the bait."

"And you don't want the key? You just want a fight between us?" I didn't believe him. He was simply making the best of the situation, getting everything he could out of it. He wanted a fight *and* the key.

"I don't need the key," he said. "And now that I know what it is, that it's a part of him... It's too complicated. Look, I simply thought, why not make money one last time? Do you know how much people paid to see the Wraith take on the Amazon Terror?"

He was lying. I knew he wanted nothing more than to unleash anarchy once more. He was desperate for the key. Before Ruadan got the chance to jump away, before even the Wraith saw what was coming, Baleros would shoot his limbs full of iron arrows. Baleros still didn't know what the key looked like, but he'd try to torture the answer out of Ruadan. Just before he killed him.

My hands were at the iron garrote around my neck. "What if we simply don't fight each other?"

He opened his hands. "You don't have a choice, my little monster. Ruadan wants you dead. He can shadow-jump. You can't. You may not last long, unfortunately, but the crowd wants blood, and they'll have it." He frowned at me. "I like the headlamp on you. I think I'll leave it."

I could still feel the lumen crystal tucked in my cleavage, and a spark of hope lit in my chest. Inwardly, I smiled. Baleros had no idea that I had it on me.

I fought hard to keep the fear etched across my features. If he didn't know about my skills, he hadn't planned for them. That gave me an advantage.

"There is one way you can win." He scratched his cheek. "If you unleash that dark power within you. You know, the one that terrifies you. The one you can't control. I've seen you do things that no fae should be able to do."

My mind flashed with an image from my past, one I wanted to keep buried. Twelve dead fae lying at my feet, their bodies rotting before my eyes.

I clenched my jaw tighter. "You'd better hope I don't unleash that, Baleros. Because you'll die along with the rest of them."

He stroked the back of his fingertips along my cheeks, and I shuddered at his touch. There was a time when I would have welcomed it —any affection from him.

"My little monster, Arianna. A pretty, scarred little abomination." A sly smile. Charming, almost. "Arianna. But that's not your real name, is it?"

His words slid through my bones. If he told anyone….

I pushed the fear to the back of my mind. I had one more question for him. "How did you know I'd bring Ruadan here? How did you know I wouldn't kill him?"

A dark smile curled his lips. "Because you're pathetic, Arianna. When you're not busy murdering people, you're desperate for love. And all it would take was one tiny gesture of kindness to destroy your ability to think rationally. One little butterscotch sweet." He cocked his head, amusement dancing in his eyes. "What was it, Arianna? Some food? One of the lollipops you like so much?" He grinned at this like it was the funniest fucking thing he'd ever heard.

It was a blanket.

A wild rage roiled in my blood, so intense I thought I might explode and bring the world down with me, and the possibility was more real than I wanted to admit. "Someday, I will kill you. Slowly. And while you're dying, I will make you regret the day you pulled me off the streets of London. I am the Amazon Terror, and I will be your death." My voice was so cold, so full of wrath, that just for an instant, he flinched, and fear flickered across his face. It only took him a moment to compose himself.

He wasn't smiling anymore, and he stepped away from me. But the one little flash of fear had given me the insight I needed. Baleros had made himself into a god because he was afraid. He feared pain. And if he had enough power, he imagined he'd never have to feel anything that hurt.

If you stare into the abyss long enough, the abyss stares back at you.

He backed away from me, and he signaled to someone to open the garrote around my neck.

Then, Baleros turned to face the crowd, lifting his arms above his head like a circus ringmaster. "You've all heard of the fearsome skill of the Amazon Terror. She may look like a beautiful lavender-haired fae with tremendous breasts—"

He always mentioned the breasts in his preamble. The crowds loved breasts.

"—but she has left the bodies of countless warriors at her feet. She now faces the first enemy she may be unable to defeat. A spell-slayer. The Wraith. He moves in the shadows, slaughters silently. Ladies and gentlemen, I give you the fight you've all been waiting for!"

Someone handed me a bottle of water, and I chugged it down fast. My throat felt like a desert, and apparently Baleros wanted this battle to last a little longer than four seconds.

I stared across the sandy arena at Ruadan while the familiar proceedings began—the ancient customs marking the start of combat.

The licti—servants—carried a bundle of sticks with an ax. That was the fascia—it was supposed to represent Baleros's power. My guess was it was there to compensate for a super disappointing manhood.

Then, the frankly irritating trumpeters blared away. Last, a servant held aloft a bust of Baleros that everyone was supposed to cheer for.

The entire time, my gaze was locked on Ruadan. Inky shadows slid through his eyes, and darkness breathed around him. He stood firmly in place with that eerie, animal stillness, bar a lock of pale blond hair that floated on a breeze. A predator about to attack. The sight of him sent ice racing through my veins. The ancient part of my brain was already screaming at me to run. I'd fought many enemies, but none as terrifying as him.

Unlike Baleros, Ruadan probably realized I'd stolen the lumen crystal, which meant he wouldn't mess around. He could shadow-jump faster and more skillfully than I could.

I gripped my sword tighter, my mind whirling. We could stall, trying to find a way to get out of this together. If we teamed up, maybe we could both live.

Or, we could assume the other person was a monster and go for the kill right away. After all, he was the Wraith. And I'd just stabbed him in the chest. Ruthless monsters, both of us.

Sweat dampened my palms as my mind frantically spun in a million directions. To trust him or not to trust him....

One of the licti commanded us to raise our weapons and salute our master. I turned to Baleros—seated on the stony emperor's throne in the center of the audience. I raised my sword without thinking—an old habit.

As I lowered it again, I knew that, one way or another, it would be the last time I saluted my old master.

My heart pounded rhythmically in my chest, beating in time to the war drum that signaled the start of the fight. And with a final trumpet's blare, it was time for the carnage to begin.

CHAPTER 30

Time seemed to slow down, and I stared at Ruadan, at his terrifying stillness.

Tonight, I fight a demigod.

Neither of us moved. I wasn't sure I was even breathing. Ruadan just stared back at me, his eyes black as the void. Dread clamped bony fingers around my heart.

I calculated where he would land if he shadow-jumped, realizing that the glaring lights cast my silhouette in front of me, not behind. If I could try to stay facing this direction, it would help me know what was coming.

Conversely, Ruadan's shadow was behind him. *Maybe* I could jump behind him and end this now....

Battle fury was already trembling through my limbs, making my legs shake. Complete silence shrouded the arena.

And yet, I just kept standing there. Waiting. My blood roared in my ears, and tension rippled off the crowd as they grew restless.

Then, in a blur of black, Ruadan jumped—whirling through the air, just enough time for panic to steal my breath. He landed just in front of me. But instead of simply running his sword through me, he swung for me, aiming for the shoulder. Just like he always did.

I parried, our swords clashing, sparking in the air. We circled, swords slamming ferociously. I knew his rhythms, knew where he'd strike. And he knew mine. When I swung for him, he ducked, just like I knew he would. My sword whooshed over his head.

The audience bayed for blood.

From the ground, he swung for my legs, and I leapt into the air. Then, with a vicious strike, I snarled and slammed my sword into his blade so brutally that I knocked it from his hands. He jumped, landing in front of me, and clamped his hand hard around my throat, lifting me into the air. I dropped my sword, but I brought my knee up hard into his chin, his jaw cracking.

The crowd roared their approval.

He dropped me, and I slammed my fist into his stomach with all my might.

Good. With the swords out of the way. I might even get the chance to say something to him. Something like, *Baleros wants to kill you, so let's get out of this together. Sorry again for the stabbing.*

Ruadan was only down for a moment, and then his hands clamped down hard on my waist. He lifted me into the air, and the crowd screamed for death. Then, he threw me across the sandy pit, and I landed hard on my back. As I started to push myself up, his foot smashed into my ribs.

Well, he was giving them a good show, but I wasn't dead. That meant he was holding back.

Unless … unless he really just wanted to kick my arse all over the arena before he killed me.

I blocked out the pain wracking my body. From the ground, I lifted my hips, hitting him hard with a brutal side kick into his knee. Another kick, my heel slamming into the same knee. He faltered. When I jumped to my feet again, I stepped in close, planting one foot behind him. I swept his legs, and he slammed down onto his back.

I leapt onto him, straddling him, and I hammered him with punches—until he caught my fist. He snarled, canines bared, then started to crush my hand. With his iron grip, he twisted my arm until I shifted off him, landing face down in the dirt.

In the next moment, he was on top of me, a powerful arm hooked around my throat. He was going to choke me out.

He leaned in close.

Then, he whispered in my ear.

"I'm not going to kill you."

It was the first time I'd heard his voice, the rich, velvety timbre, and it sent my pulse racing.

I reached behind my head, grabbing at his arms, pretending like I was struggling. "I'm not going to kill you, either," I whispered. "But Baleros is. He wants the World Key."

I elbowed him hard in the face. Maybe we weren't going to kill each other, but we didn't want Baleros to catch on. I started to get up, and he pinned me down from the front this time, still straddling me.

Then, I thrust my pelvis up hard with all my force, knocking him off me. I scrambled up. Before I could even fully right myself, Ruadan hurtled into me. He knocked me hard to the ground, just managing to cushion the blow of my head against the floor with his hand. Quite the gentleman.

The crowd screamed, demanding a sacrifice.

Grandson of the Night God.

He was between my legs, and I stared up at his pure black eyes.

He controlled the shadows.

"Make it dark," I whispered. "I will find Baleros."

Without another word, frosted night magic burst from him, ripples of shadows that snuffed out the candles around us. I flicked off my headlamp as the shadows slid over the flaming arrows, dimming their flames until darkness reigned.

Screams erupted all over the arena.

Anarchy is the opportunity to remake the world the way we want it.

Baleros knew how to rule in chaos. And now, so did I. I knew this arena like the back of my hand.

In the darkness, I shadow-leapt to the emperor's seat before Baleros had a chance to escape. I sniffed the air. Roses. The scent that always made me sick.

I'd found him, and he had no idea I was here.

I gripped him by the collar, then reared back my arm, punching him over and over in the face with all my strength, so hard I was sure I was breaking my own fist. He caught one of my punches, but fury whipped through me, and I brought my knee up hard into his groin.

He'd never seen me coming. He'd had no idea Ruadan would give me the lumen crystal, or that we'd refuse to kill each other. Baleros had never prepared for this.

The man had spent years drilling all of his thoughts into my mind. He'd studied me, learning how I worked, anticipating everything I'd done. Knowing my weaknesses. I was his monster, and he controlled me.

But it was like he always said—if you stare too long into the abyss, the abyss stares back at you. He knew how I thought, and I knew how he thought, too.

I rammed my elbow into his face, and he moaned. "Ruadan…."

"I'm not Ruadan," I roared. "I'm the abyss, bitch!"

I'm not sure that made sense, and maybe I needed a better catch-phrase. But it felt right in the moment.

"Where's Ciara?" I screamed.

He tried to hit me, but I was blocking his blows. Then, I jabbed my fingers swiftly into his Adam's apple. He emitted a choking sound, unable to breathe, and I shadow-jumped behind him. I gripped his head—Ruadan-style—ready to snap his neck.

"Where's Ciara?" I shouted. "Do not make me rip out your spine, because I will, fucker."

Screams tore through the air around us, but Ruadan was keeping a tight control of the shadows. Darkness claimed the arena.

As soon as Baleros could speak again, he groaned, "Secret location."

"Where?" I roared.

"I brought her here tonight. Your cage," he choked out.

I snapped his neck, and he went down. Without iron in my hands, I couldn't kill him now. I had to leave for Ciara while I still could, but I hoped to hell that Ruadan would drive an iron sword through his heart.

I leapt through the darkness, the arena air rushing over my skin. Just before I rushed into the exit, I whirled to look behind me. A burst of light flashed in the arena as Ruadan's darkness receded for just a moment. It was just enough time to watch as Ruadan cut his sword through Baleros's neck. My heart leapt.

As Baleros's body fell, it erupted into flames, and the scent of charred flesh filled the air. *Dead.* My breath caught in my lungs.

I had no idea why his body had ignited. I only knew it was all over, although I almost couldn't believe it.

I spun, leaping through the tunnel again. Baleros might be dead, but he had dozens of lackeys working for him here.

Baleros's thirty-fourth law of power: never let down your guard.

My heart slammed against my ribs. Maybe his body was dead, but he'd be living on in my mind for a while.

I LEAPT THROUGH THE DARKNESS, knowing exactly where to find Ciara. I knew these tunnels intimately, and with the lumen crystal, it only took me a few seconds to get there. He'd brought her here tonight. What if I'd gone straight for the cages instead of into the arena? He wasn't worried, because he was convinced I'd act exactly as he'd predicted.

At last, I reached the damp cavern where I'd once lived. A flood of memories washed over me, the dank scent and dripping water making bile rise in my throat. I'd given six years of my life to this hole.

Dead. It was hard to wrap my mind around it. Baleros's presence was still a living thing in my mind.

At this point, I remembered I was still wearing my headlamp, and I flicked it on.

There, curled up in the bottom of the cage, was Ciara.

She sat up, squinting in the bright light, her face covered in dirt.

"Ciara! It's me."

"Arianna?" Dehydration had paled her lips and cheeks.

I pulled my homemade lock pick out of my pocket and jammed it into the lock. "I'm getting you out of here. Now." After a few seconds of fiddling, the lock clicked. With a racing pulse, I ripped off the padlock. "Baleros is dead."

"You killed him," she shrieked with joy, beaming.

"No. The Wraith did."

"I don't care who killed him, as long as he's dead." She blinked at the headlamp. "How the heck did you manage to find me?"

"The Wraith and I did the one thing Baleros never would have anticipated. Something he'd never begin to understand."

"What?"

"We trusted each other." I grabbed her hand. "Come on. We need to get out of here."

Baleros had never anticipated that Ruadan would trust me enough to give me the crystal. He'd never imagined we'd work together to survive, because that wasn't how Baleros thought.

I pulled Ciara along as we ran through the dark tunnel, our feet pounding hard over the dirt. Mentally, I calculated our next move.

Ruadan and I had worked together, but that didn't mean the Institute would forgive me for what I'd done. Did they know? Had someone found Ruadan and pulled the knife from his chest? I wasn't sticking around London long enough to find out. I had a pretty strong feeling I was on Grand Master Savus's shit list. Also known as his kill list.

I didn't think I'd exactly be welcome at the Institute at this point.

Ciara's breath heaved. "Where are we going?"

"We're getting out of London, Ciara. We're going into hiding."

At last, we reached the part of the tunnel where only a steel manhole cover blocked our exit. I hoisted Ciara up until she could push it to the side, and we hauled ourselves out into the London night.

Within minutes, we were disappearing into the night's shadows.

CHAPTER 31

I sat across from Ciara, in a dark corner of a pub in Edinburgh. The bar was indistinct, just like I wanted it to be. Ordinary wooden tables, an old carpet with wine stains, plain yellow walls. We'd spent twenty of our last pounds on haggis and neeps, which had been a mistake, because it was disgusting. Of course Ciara loved it.

In the past few days since we'd run from London, I'd made myself look as nondescript as possible. I wore a hood or wig to cover my lavender hair. I wore jeans and sneakers. I didn't make eye contact with anyone. No one had noticed us.

Problem was, we were running out of Ciara's money, fast.

Ciara leaned back in her chair, sipping her beer. "We have twenty-six pounds and thirteen pence left."

I swallowed hard. I still had the lumen crystal. It wouldn't be particularly difficult to steal from people. "I'll find us what we need."

She leaned in closer to me, whispering, "You said Baleros's headless body just caught on fire? He was a devil. I knew it."

"No doubt about that. I hope it hurt."

She shoved a forkful of haggis into her mouth, chewing thoughtfully, her gaze intent on her food. "Why did you run from Ruadan? I thought you said you worked together to kill Baleros."

I swirled the wine in my glass. "We did work together in that moment, to get out of that situation. To save both our lives. But I don't know what it means. Grand Master Savus calls the shots in the Institute, and I don't know what he thinks. I could be on a kill list. I stole from them. And I stabbed one of them. And the Shadow Fae really don't have a sense of humor about those kind of things."

"You took something from me." A rich, velvet voice sent ice racing through my blood.

It was a voice I'd heard before.

Only once before—in the arena.

My mouth went dry, and I turned to find Ruadan looming over us. His bright violet eyes looked striking against the gloom of the bar.

"Ruadan!" I tried to sound cheerful. "I was just talking about you."

He stared at me with that preternatural stillness. For just a moment, a chill rippled over me, but it was gone within an instant. If he'd wanted to kill me, he would have done it by now.

A hush fell over the bar as the humans began to realize a powerful fae warrior stood in their midst. So much for discretion.

"Why don't we talk outside?" I said.

He nodded once.

I ignored everyone's wide-eyed stares as we crossed outside. Clouds covered the moon tonight, and a light rain misted on the old, winding street. From where we stood, I could see all the way up to Edinburgh Castle, a gothic palace on jagged slopes.

"So. You want your crystal back?" I asked.

He pressed his hands against the wall, boxing me in. His glare cut right through me. Silver glinted in his eyes. "How did Baleros compel you to enter the Institute?"

Knowledge gives you power over a person. How much power did I want Ruadan to have? I supposed my life was already in his hands right now. How much worse could it get? Still, I'd leave out the key details.

"How did he get anyone to do anything?" I asked. "He had leverage. Nothing made me happier than to see you cut his head off."

A gust of wind whipped at his hair, and an eerie stillness overtook his body.

"Am I on the kill list?" I asked.

No answer. Just dark shadows whipping the air around him. The bastard had already broken his vow, but he preferred brooding in silence and generally trying to scare the crap out of people.

"I'm sorry I stabbed you," I added. "Honestly, *stabbed* sounds a bit dramatic. You're a demigod and a fae. I knew you'd live if I didn't use iron. I mean, for a minute I did consider...." I was nervously babbling, filling the silence with things that would get me in trouble. "You know what? Let's not dwell on what might have been. I'm alive. You're alive. Baleros is dead. Let's try to keep it that way."

Even though The Wraith stood before me, his magic crackling the air, I didn't feel threatened right now. I felt an overwhelming urge to close the distance between us, to press myself against his powerful chest. I took a step closer to him, breathing in. There—under the pine and the magic, the scent of apples. I loved that smell. I closed my eyes, inhaling again, and that's when I realized where I knew it from. It was the one from my dreams.

I frowned at him. "Have you ever heard of a place called Emain, by any chance?"

He cut me a sharp look, eyes darkening. "No."

The look in his eyes told me he was lying.

"You're not as good a liar as you think you are. What's the big deal about it? I've dreamt of it. One of the library books says dreaming of Emain is a fae thing. Also that it's the headquarters of all the Shadow Fae. You smell like my dreams." I cleared my throat. "Which sounds more like a pickup line than I'd intended."

His gaze flicked up and down my body, as if he were still considering something. "It's a myth. Don't speak of it again."

Right. Convincing. "So, am I on the kill list?" I asked again.

The cool breeze kissed my skin while his gaze bored into me.

At last, he said, "No. I don't think you are. I'm coming back for you. The Institute hasn't finished with you."

My chest unclenched, and I released the breath I'd been holding. "Are you going to tell me why you've suddenly become a chatty Cathy?"

"I can speak again because I've completed my mission."

I nodded slowly. "Killing Baleros?"

"In the arena, I thought you were going to do it. You left him alive. Why?"

I really wasn't used to the sound of him talking, and his voice was having a distracting effect on me. In fact, its richness seemed to skim over my skin and stroke my body in places I shouldn't be thinking about right now. No wonder he didn't talk.

A long silence stretched out between us. I wasn't sure I trusted him enough to tell him how much Ciara meant to me. "There was something else I had to do," was all I said.

Before I could ask another one of the hundreds of questions burning in my head, he turned, prowling off.

I watched as he stalked into Edinburgh's shadows, blending in with the night itself.

I touched my throat, realizing that he'd left me with the lumen stone. As he walked away, that faint scent of apples hung in the air, and I felt an unfamiliar sense of safety. Did the demonic Wraith actually make me feel safe now?

Surprise flickered in my chest as I realized I was looking forward to his return.

With a sharp pang, it made me think of something that hardly ever popped into my mind these days. A place I'd nearly forgotten on the dirt floor of Baleros's cages.

Home.

I pushed the thought away. Home was an impossibility, now, and I'd never find my way back. Now, Ciara was my home. When I crossed back into the pub and found that she'd saved half her disgusting haggis for me, warmth lit up my chest.

I beamed at her. "What are you smiling at?" she asked.

"You." I sat back down in my chair. "Giving me food. Sometimes a butterscotch sweet is a genuine gift."

"Right. I remember how obsessed you were with butterscotch sweets—that one you hung onto forever in the cage because you didn't want it to be gone. I need to get you a whole bag."

I shook my head. "I don't even like how it tastes. I don't like haggis, either. I just like that you gave it to me."

"You're a weird one, Arianna."

I reached into my bug-out bag, pushing the headlamp and duct tape out of the way until I found a grape lollipop, then I popped it into my mouth. "I don't know what you mean."

COURT OF DARKNESS

SHADOW FAE—BOOK TWO

CHAPTER 1

$\mathcal{I}$ had less than a minute before the dragon shifter found me in his bedroom. The rich bastard had a private lift that opened right into his hallway. Through his bedroom doorway, I could see the numbers ticking up as the lift rose from the lobby. *Two...three...*

If it reached forty-one, the jig was up.

Frantically, I scanned the room. I stood on the forty-first floor of a sleek skyscraper in the center of London. Wind whipped into the room from the open balcony door. Moonlight streamed in through the expansive windows, casting silvery light over tasteful gray and gold furniture. From here, the gleaming lights of London spread out below like glittering treasure.

Only problem was, I couldn't find the actual treasure, and that was the whole reason I'd come.

The lift's number ticked up. *Eight...nine...*

The white spotlight from my headlamp bounced all over the darkened room. Where the hells was he keeping his gold? All dragon shifters had gold. This one wasn't big on clutter, so it hadn't taken long to ransack his entire flat. Hunger gripped my stomach. Ciara and I were starving, and I was *not* leaving empty-handed. The great heroine Ciarianna would rise again.

My stomach rumbled. In the past week, we'd had nothing to eat but three tins of economy beans and two ice cream sandwiches. I could hardly think straight. I hadn't felt this hungry since I'd murdered the Institute's hunger fae.

Twelve...thirteen...

The bathroom. I hadn't fully investigated the bathroom yet, and he had a medicine cabinet I needed to rifle through. I rushed into the bathroom, flinging open the cabinet.

I blinked. Among the painkillers and some anti-anxiety medication, the shifter had filled his cabinet with Barbie dolls and plastic dinosaur figurines. Not to mention two tubs of Vaseline.

What in the world...?

I didn't dwell on it too long, because in the next second, I was crouching down to search under the sink. Toilet roll, cleaning products, an enormous vat of Vaseline. I mean, I supposed a dragon shifter's scales *would* get dry in the winter.

Twenty...twenty-one...

Under his bed. I hadn't yet searched under his bed. It was a stupid place to hide gold, but I hadn't found a sensible hiding place. Like a safe.

I knelt down and flung up the silver duvet. The white light from my headlamp beamed over a bunch of magazines.

I pulled one out, and my jaw dropped. First of all, in this day and age, who read porn in magazine form? And more importantly—where did one find magazines featuring women mating with men dressed as dinosaurs?

I mean, I supposed when you thought about it, maybe it made a strange sort of sense. Dragon-on-human porn would get old after a while, and he'd need to up the ante. One kink level up from dragons was obviously dinosaurs, and—

Twenty-nine...thirty...

Right. The gold. My wild hunger was making me get sidetracked. Still, I was taking one of these magazines with me because no one would ever believe—

On second thought, maybe I didn't really want to touch it. Thinking of all the Vaseline, I dropped it with a grimace.

Thirty-four...thirty-five...

I leapt up, scanning the room again. Now, adrenaline raced through my veins. I was out of time. I touched the lumen stone around my neck—on loan from the Wraith—and reassured myself that I still had a way out of here. Shadow-leaping came in *very* handy sometimes, even at six hundred feet in the air.

Then, my gaze landed on the one thing in the flat I hadn't yet searched. A potted orchid that stood on a mahogany table in his bedroom. A perfect hiding place.

Thirty-eight...thirty-nine...

I thrust my hand into the soil, and relief washed over me as my fingers came into contact with a smooth, metallic bar.

Bingo.

Forty-one.

The lift doors slid open just as I ripped the gold bar from the plant. Dirt flew all over the shifter's sleek gray sofa. I slid my bug-out bag off my shoulder and shoved the bar into it.

Now, I just needed to find a way out. Good thing I'd been practicing shadow-leaping. I touched the lumen stone, summoning its icy power as I rushed out onto the balcony.

Behind me, the dragon shifter roared, already transforming into his reptilian form. Scales were forming on his face and arms, but if he fully shifted in here, he'd break everything in the bloody flat. He was practically vibrating with the effort to restrain himself. Talons began to sprout from his fingertips.

I scrambled over the wooden table on his balcony, then climbed onto the short barrier of glass. Adrenaline raced through my veins as the view dizzied me. The lights of Spitalfields twinkled below me. Gods, this was high.

The shifter screamed something, but since he kept shifting and pulling back to his human form, it came out all garbled. Half-dragon speak. Something like *mablig blupart plucking skrill you!*

I stood on the glass barrier, the wind tearing at my hair, and my heart raced out of control. *Time to go.*

A blast of hot fire seared the air behind me, and I leapt off the balcony before I had a chance to properly choose my target.

I gripped hard to my backpack straps as I started falling, the wind whipping my hair into my face. My stomach lurched, and I started to regret several of the night's decisions.

Through the strands of my lavender hair, I spotted a dark corner of Wormwood Street. Mentally, I melded with its shadows, smelling the seared-air scent of the magic within all darkness. Then, I channeled my shadow magic. I leapt.

I slammed hard onto concrete, rolling over the ground with a grunt. Pretty sure the gold bar in my backpack left a dent in my spine.

The impact had rattled my bones. So, I was learning that shadow leaping when you're already falling at a high velocity only took *some* of the impact out of the fall. If I were human, I'd be dead now. But as a demi-fae, I escaped with a few fractures and a shitload of bruises.

My gaze flicked up the sleek skyscraper. Dragons could fly, but there was no way this guy was coming after me. Supernaturals had been completely outlawed for the past four years. Executions and assassinations meant the shifters had to lay low, disguise themselves completely. Which meant I could take his gold bar—

My thoughts were interrupted by the sight of a man's silhouette plunging off the balcony, just as I'd done. My pulse began to race. This wasn't what I'd expected.

The dragon shifter started to fall, his descent picking up pace, until —midair—black, scaly wings burst from his back.

Okay. Maybe I'd overestimated his intelligence. With a flagrant display of magic like this, he'd be dead within a day, never to defile his dinosaur figurines again.

In the air, he shifted completely, rearing back his head to eject a hot stream of fire into the midnight sky.

Oh boy. London hadn't seen a reptilian display like this in years.

I jumped up, eyeing the farthest point I could see on Wormwood Street. At this time of night, the streets were mercifully empty.

I summoned the icy shadow magic, channeling it throughout my limbs. Then, I melded with the dark pools of shadows under a pedestrian crossway. I began shadow-leaping through the financial district—past pharmacies and skyscrapers—using alleyways and the darkness beneath the trees lining the street. The wind rushed over my skin, and my heart hammered from the flight. I leapt into a medieval churchyard, melding with the shadows behind a crooked tomb. It was three in the morning, and I hardly passed anyone.

But while I raced through the city, moving like the wind through the trees, the dragon soared just above me, managing to track my path. His fire scalded the air. I glanced up, my blood roaring, as he started to dive for me.

With the magic igniting my body, I shadow-leapt across the street. I needed to hide from him, to go underground. Fortunately, I used to live under the streets, and I knew how to navigate subterranean London.

I leapt south, zooming closer to Guildhall, until I screeched to a halt by a manhole. Beneath this pavement flowed one of London's underground rivers.

A wild roar ripped through the skies as I glanced up, my heart skipping a beat, and saw the dragon dive-bombing for me.

With a grunt, I shifted the manhole cover. I jumped into the hole and dropped down into three feet of freezing, stinking water. From above, a blast of fire exploded through the manhole opening, singeing the hair on the back of my arms. With magic flowing through my body, I leapt away into the tunnel's darkness.

Underground, shadows reigned. Only the bouncing white light of my headlamp pierced the darkness.

The dragon's enormous body wouldn't be able to fit through the hole, and in his human form, he'd never catch up with me. Now, the tunnel was mine. I leapt through the darkness, the water growing higher and higher on my body, past my hips, my ribs, until it covered my head.

I dove deeper into the cold water, swimming under the surface.

Once underwater, I wasn't able to shadow-leap, and my lungs started to burn. My headlamp flickered out.

At this point, the dragon must be long gone. I could only hope he hadn't been clever enough to predict where I'd emerge out of the tunnel.

Just when I was certain my lungs were about to explode, thin streams of light pierced the water as the tunnel opened up into the Thames—London's largest river, no longer underground.

I kicked my feet as hard as I could, rushing up to the surface. I gasped, sucking in air. I scrambled for the stone embankment, then hoisted myself over the edge. A quick glance at the sky told me that the dragon hadn't caught up with me yet.

Unfortunately, a low iron fence blocked my path to the pavement. Iron would burn me if I touched it, though it wouldn't kill me.

Grimacing, I gripped the iron bars, wincing at the pain. Fast as I could, I climbed it, then leapt over the top. Exhausted, I flung myself down on the pavement. I rolled over on my back, my backpack bulky beneath my spine. I stared up at the night sky, catching my breath.

It took me a moment to get my bearings. I'd ended up just south of the river. Here, the street lamps cast amber light over an empty walkway and neat rows of trees. My little white sundress clung to my body.

It wasn't just the underwater swim that had exhausted me, but the overuse of shadow magic. My muscles buzzed and burned. Shadow magic wasn't native to my body like it was to Ruadan's. I could draw it from the lumen stone, but it tended to overwhelm me and wear me out. This must be what drug addicts felt like on a comedown.

On the pavement, I closed my eyes for just a moment, still gasping for air, when a familiar power brushed over my skin—a dark, sensual magic that raised goosebumps on my body.

When I opened my eyes, I was staring into the penetrating, violet gaze of Ruadan.

CHAPTER 2

Moonlight sculpted the perfect planes of his face. My heart thumped harder against my ribs.

I clasped my hand to my chest, staring up at him.

When I'd imagined running into Ruadan again, I hadn't pictured myself lying flat on my back in a dress soaked in dirty river water.

"Hi, Ruadan." The sight of him sent a rush of energy through my blood, but I feigned a casual tone. "What are you doing here skulking by the riverside?"

A gust of wind picked up his cloak. I glimpsed the armor that gleamed underneath, sculpting his body. His shadowy magic lashed the air around him, and a shiver rippled over my wet skin.

My stomach loudly rumbled, giving away my hunger. "You can calm down with your menacing display of magic." I pushed myself up, sitting upright. "You're already dressed like a medieval undertaker. The shadows are just intimidation overkill."

The wind rustled through the nearby leaves.

"Back to your silence, then. Even though you killed Baleros and completed your task." I pushed a lock of sodden lavender hair out of my eyes. "Did you know that dinosaur porn exists?"

So quiet it was almost inaudible, I heard a low growl rumble from Ruadan's chest, and the sound trembled through my gut.

The silence stretched on. Then, as I looked up at Ruadan, a wild roar rent the air. My body tensed, as a burst of flame cut across the sky. The dragon had found me, and he was dive-bombing again, unleashing his fire.

Ruadan unsheathed the sword on his back, whirling to face the dragon. An intense pulse of icy magic burst through the air, and violet magic danced over his sword.

As the dragon raced for us—only twenty feet away now—shadow-magic exploded from Ruadan's sword. It slammed into the dragon's chest, and ice frosted the creature's scales. Instantly, the dragon's flames were snuffed out. As it screeched to a stop on the pavement, Ruadan leapt. He swung his blade, and it carved into the dragon's neck. Blood arced into the air.

The dragon's head rolled onto the pavement, his dark eyes wide. The creature's body shuddered, then slumped to the ground with a loud *thud*. The two detached pieces—head and body—shifted back into their human form one final time.

When Ruadan turned back to me, cold fury had darkened his eyes. I couldn't say he looked particularly happy to see me.

I stood, my teeth chattering. I crossed my arms, wishing I'd worn something other than white for my little river swim. My dress looked completely transparent, and I felt vulnerable enough standing in front of Ruadan.

Ruadan crossed to a tree, just behind the dragon shifter's headless corpse. To my surprise, he knelt before the tree. He lifted his sword, and plunged it into the soil that surrounded the tree's base. He bowed his head, as if in prayer. His body glowed with violet light, and I breathed in his scent—apples and pine. It was a strangely seductive smell, one that curled around my shivering body, warming me from the inside out.

It took me a moment to figure out what he was doing, until I cast my mind back to Grand Master Savus's little history lesson. The Shadow Fae didn't think of themselves as assassins. They viewed themselves as servants of the old fae gods—gods who demanded sacrifices. In Ruadan's mind, the dragon's death had been a sacrifice—blood to feed the soil of those older than even the fae.

When he rose, the coldness in his eyes sent a shiver up my spine. They had gone completely dark.

Shadows in an incubus's eyes meant one of two things: he was turned on, or he wanted to kill someone. And unless I was way off about Ruadan's tastes, I didn't imagine that dragon decapitation got him in the mood.

I cleared my throat. "You said you'd find me, and now you have. Well done. Your tracking abilities are without parallel."

His silence never failed to unnerve me, and his low growl slid through my bones. As his eyes pierced me, a gust of wind toyed with his hair. His tightly coiled body language was that of an animal about to attack its prey.

I heaved a sigh. "How I've missed your sparkling personality." I touched the lumen stone at my neck. "I thought you could speak again, now that you killed Baleros."

Blood-chilling stillness from the Wraith. I was starting to get the impression he was annoyed that I'd been using the lumen stone to burgle gold.

"Look, I'm staying with my human friend, Ciara," I said. "She and I needed to eat. You said you'd be back for me, and that I wasn't finished at the Institute. But I had no idea when that would be. We spent a month in Scotland, unemployed and starving. I managed to find a bar job for one week, but my boss thought he could withhold my paycheck until I showed him my boobs. Naturally, I was forced to throw him through a window, after which point my employment was unceremoniously terminated. Which was absurd, frankly. Humans are so sensitive about scrapes and bruises."

The only sound around us was the rushing of the river behind me. The lethal look in Ruadan's eyes promised violence. Somehow, that was my cue to continue.

"So, we came back to London," I went on. "I mean, it's not like we could hide from the Shadow Fae, anyway. You know how to find me.

Rufus wouldn't hire us back. Do you know where we've been living?" I took a step closer, working up a bit of a temper. "In one of those burnt-out cars under the arches by that goat pen. That's right. Just off the park where Uncle Darrell makes sweet, sweet love to the earth—a sight that has greeted me every morning for the past three weeks. That image will be forever burned into my mind, the dawn light ruddying his arse cheeks as he thrusts gamely into the soil. I blame you for this memory."

I took another step closer, now jabbing him in the chest, which felt like poking a brick wall. "Before you wafted into my life in a puff of smoke, I had a job. I had a flat." I cocked my head. "I know. I know. I didn't have a fancy rock bed or black stones glittering in my walls like you have, but I had crisp packets on my floor. They were *my* crisp packets. My flat. My life. Now, I'm out of a job, out of a place to live. I've got no money. Do you know what I had for breakfast this morning? A half-eaten Egg McMuffin that a janitor threw out at Liverpool Street station. I'm *starving,* and so is Ciara."

I lifted the lumen stone. "But at least you left me with this. So what's the best way to get a shitload of money in one go? Shadow-leaping into a dragon-shifter's flat. One bar of gold, and Ciara and I are set for decades. You can hardly fault me for that. It was perfectly reasonable."

Ruadan loomed over me. His magic seemed to suck in the light from all around us, and flecks of starlight glinted in his eyes. It was hard to forget that he was a demigod—a god of the night.

He held out a black-gloved hand.

"Of course you want the gold. Because it's not enough to take my job, my flat, and my vaguely functioning life. You also have to take the gold bar that's rightfully mine by virtue of burglary."

"It belongs to the Institute."

"Interesting. So you can speak."

He held out his hand to me. "The gold."

"Fine." I jammed my hand into my sodden backpack. I'd find another, more subtle way to steal if I had to. "The Institute are a bunch of thieves, you know that?" Perhaps this wasn't the best night to go around accusing others of thievery, but irritation was simmering and I hadn't thought of a better insult. "You're the Mafia, just with swords and a pretense of sacrifice."

"I don't think you've fully absorbed the seriousness of your situation."

I blinked, still irritated. "No, I haven't absorbed anything whatsoever. Do you know why? Because you just stand there staring at me with your magic whipping all over the place and no words coming out of your mouth." I jabbed him in the torso again, my finger crooking at the steel in his chest. "If you want me to *absorb* things, you can tell them to me in words. I will accept writing on paper. Am I on the kill list now, or am I coming back to the Institute?"

He pivoted, already stalking off into the shadows. "You're coming with me."

Of course, that wasn't as many details as I'd hoped for, and I couldn't say the timing was ideal.

"Now?" I hurried after him, gripping the straps of my backpack. I pulled off my headlamp, which had broken underwater. "Where are we going?"

"The Institute. You're returning."

"I live with my friend Ciara now." I was giving too much away here. I was letting Ruadan know exactly how to get to me—the same way Baleros had. "I look after Ciara. She's waiting for me to come home with some kind of food. If she stays on her own, she's vulnerable. Honestly, we were just getting our lives back together."

A sweep of his eyes up and down my body gave me a hint of what he was thinking. Something along the lines of, *What do you mean you are getting your life together? You look like a drowned Victorian prostitute and you live in a burnt car.*

Or, I may have been projecting my own internal thoughts onto him. Hard to say.

He pivoted. "Let's not forget the reality of your situation. You stole from the Institute. You stabbed me—"

"I *did* apologize. In written form, and I believe verbally. You really need to move on."

"You failed to kill an enemy of the Institute when you had the chance. You used the Institute's lumen stone to steal gold from a dragon. Do you know what Grand Master Savus would do to you if he knew about that?"

"Decapitation with an iron sword?" He talked about that a lot.

"Worse." Shadows thickened around us, and the temperature dropped. My breath misted in front of my face at the chill in the air.

He took another step closer, and I shivered. "If you anger Grand Master Savus any further, the Shadow Fae will exalt you."

My eyebrows shot up. "Exalt? That doesn't sound bad. Exalt is a good thing, right?"

He shook his head. "In English, yes. I was using the Ancient Fae word. It's an execution method involving evisceration with burning iron instruments."

I winced. So I wasn't on the kill list, but it didn't sound like the situation was wonderful.

I let out a long, slow breath. Best not to piss him off more than I already had. "I get it. I'm sorry. I just had some responsibilities to take care of." Namely, Ciara. I didn't want to bang on about her though, in case I found the Institute using her as leverage, just as Baleros had.

His dark eyes lightened to violet once more, and his features softened, just a little. He stared at me for an uncomfortably long time before responding again. "I will send someone to collect your human."

He really did have a way with words.

He stalked off again, and I picked up my pace to follow after him.

"What happened to the trials after I left the Institute?"

"Training."

"For two months?" I asked, incredulous. I let out a sigh. "I guess it makes sense. Savus clearly has a favorite, doesn't he? He wants Maddan to win. Too bad extra training won't help that idiot."

Silence.

"I take it my return to the Institute won't be a warm welcome."

Silence.

"Can I kill Maddan during one of the trials?"

"Savus would likely exalt you if you did."

"That's the bad kind of exalting, right?"

"He'd send every Shadow Fae from every institute in the world after you." Ruadan's rich voice rumbled through my gut. "Not to mention his mist army."

I grimaced. "I heard about the mist army. Melusine said he acquired it by killing the last Grand Master."

"Yes. And the point is, Maddan's death would cost the Institute millions of pounds per year."

I frowned. "Seems that no matter what I do, Savus wants to kill me. Why is he allowing me back into the Institute at all?"

"Because the Old Gods demand it. Choosing new Shadow Fae is their role. It's up to the Grand Master to interpret their desires."

As we moved closer to the Institute, my breath caught at the sight of the gleaming spires, light beaming into the night sky.

I quirked a smile. I imagined it would *really* piss off some of the fae nobility if the Old Gods favored a gutter fae ex-gladiator like me.

CHAPTER 3

Trailing behind Ruadan, I crossed the threshold into a vaulted chamber within the Institute. Here, the ceiling arched high above us like the spine of a great beast. Floral vines climbed the stone, and moonlight shone in through peaked windows. I'd never been in this room before.

It was 3:30 in the morning, and the entire Institute had shown up to watch my return. A long stone aisle led to Grand Master Savus's throne, where the regal fae sat, a spindly silver crown gleaming on his head. A heavy mist curled around him, spooling from his fingertips. Guards flanked him on either side, each gripping an iron axe. My chest tightened at the sight of them.

The throne jutted from a stone floor, the back of it peaked like a second crown, glittering with dark jewels.

The other Shadow Fae lined the aisle. Aengus shot me a sharp look, his emerald eyes piercing—perhaps a bit irritated that I'd stabbed his friend.

But it wasn't just the knights in attendance. The two remaining novices stood there as well.

Maddan—that prick—was wearing a gold crown over his autumn leaves and ginger hair. Lest anyone forget, he was a prince. He'd royally screwed up our last mission, stabbed me with a reaping dagger, and attempted to send me to the void, but that was fine. His father was a king, after all, and he had a pretty crown.

Given that Ruadan was characteristically silent all the way over here, I had no idea what I was in store for now. I only knew that the smug look on Maddan's face meant it wouldn't be pretty.

I followed a few paces behind Ruadan, crossing closer to Grand Master Savus. A phantom wind whispered through the hall, bringing up goosebumps on my skin.

In fact, the only friendly face in this hall was Melusine's. She flicked a strand of blue hair out of her eyes, and flashed me a wary smile. She actually looked nervous for me. Also not a great sign.

When we were just five feet from the throne, Ruadan abruptly stopped.

Savus's eyes flashed, and he leaned forward. "Kneel." Venom laced his voice.

Baleros had enforced his authority in exactly the same way, in grand public displays. The sharp reminder of Baleros had my blood racing. That man loved nothing more than making a spectacle of his authority. Inwardly, my mind was raging. For just a moment, I envisioned myself ripping the spray deodorant and lighter out of my bug-out bag and greeting Grand Master Savus with a makeshift flamethrower.

But in a room full of Shadow Fae, the glory of that moment would not last long, and I suppressed the impulse. Most importantly, I needed to stay alive to make sure Ciara got fed. After all, Ruadan had promised someone would fetch my human, hadn't he?

My stomach rumbled as I knelt on the cold stone floor. I was freezing in my soaked dress.

"Novice." Savus's deep voice rang off the high ceilings. "I wanted to run your body full of iron nails, or perhaps give you some time in the iron maiden. We haven't exalted anyone in a while, and I was beginning to miss the spectacle of it."

My chest tightened. I hadn't expected hugs and margaritas, but this was a little bleaker than I'd anticipated.

"But your mentor persuaded me not to," he continued. "He explained that you went temporarily insane from the reaping dagger." For just a moment, his pale gaze flicked to Maddan. "And of course, your proximity to all the incubus magic drove you mad, and you found yourself wandering the streets of London, trying to satiate your lust—until Ruadan found you again."

That was what Ruadan had told them? I shot the Wraith a sharp look, but the shadows around him had thickened so intensely that I could hardly see him. Just his violet eyes in clouds of dark magic.

"Your mentor," Savus went on, "failed to control you."

For just a moment, I felt a twinge of guilt for getting Ruadan in trouble, before reminding myself that I did not care.

"More importantly," Savus's voice boomed over the hall, "you have made me question if allowing female novices was a mistake. Or perhaps allowing those of your social class. Maybe our predecessors had a good reason for excluding your kind." Ice laced his voice.

He was talking to me, but staring at Ruadan. Why? Did Savus have a problem with mongrels like us? I didn't entirely understand what the situation was, but given the tension crackling between the two male fae, I was starting to get the distinct impression that they were not on the same page.

Savus's gaze slid back to me, and he tapped his fingertips together.

"Because it seems that the Old Gods have favored you so far, we have removed you from the kill list. I put the trials on hold while you were away, communing with the Old Gods to divine their will. It seems they wanted your return. Assuming no one else stabs you with a reaping dagger, perhaps your skills could be of value to the Old Gods. If you can win the next three trials, I will continue to assume they favor you. If you fail any of the trials, then you will die a slow and painful death. Unfortunately, you have missed a bit of training. Oh well."

Maddan's eyes were fixed straight ahead, but his face was beaming. He was looking forward to my "slow and painful death." On my knees, I felt a hot flash of fury when I looked at him. He was a prince, and that meant he could get away with anything.

"However, the Institute does not tolerate insubordination. If you defy us, at some point, the favor of the Old Gods will turn against you. I had warned all the novices that you could not lose the lumen stone, or you would be executed with an iron axe. You chose to steal it from us." Something in his smile reminded me of a cat eyeing its prey. "I can hardly let you just waltz back in here to rejoin our ranks, can I?"

The stone floor bit into my knees as I knelt, and my fingers curled into fists. I wanted to say that I'd never asked for any of this. During the years when supernaturals were ferried off to the magical realms, I'd been locked in a cage. I'd emerged into a world where I was breaking the law just by existing.

Savus leaned back in his throne. "It's clear to me that you must be punished. Your new lodgings will be in the Palatial Room. If you are able to win every trial, we will reconsider your value, and perhaps you will even find a place here, after serving your penance. However, I find it hard to believe the Old Gods will favor you for long."

The Palatial Room? That didn't sound awful, but based on the delighted look on Maddan's face, I had to wonder what it meant.

I glanced at Ruadan. Even through the whorls of his dark magic, I could tell that his body had tensed.

General Savus lifted his skull cup. "Ruadan, please divest her of the lumen stone. We don't want her running away again, do we?"

Shadows billowed around Ruadan, and in the next moment, he was towering over me. His powerful hands clamped around my biceps, and he pulled me up from the floor—much more roughly than he needed to. Then, he reached for the lumen stone around my neck and yanked it off in a single, smooth motion.

When I glanced at Maddan and Melusine, I saw the violet stones gleaming around their necks.

This was, frankly, a load of shit. I was supposed to compete against the two other novices in the trials, without the benefit of a lumen stone. If I lost any of the trials, I'd be ripped apart with hot pincers.

I gritted my teeth. "This is a death sentence. Why drag it out?"

Savus nodded at one of the guards, and he started moving toward me with his axe.

My heart skipped a beat, and I held up my hand. "Wait! Okay. I'll do it. I'll join the trials without the lumen stone."

"I'm glad you came to your senses," said Savus. "Now, your mentor will escort you to your new lodgings. And Ruadan—along the way, please help our prisoner to understand the severity of her infractions."

Ruadan gripped my arm, but I jerked it away from him, shooting him a ferocious look. He hadn't said much on the way here, but I still felt misled. "What about Ciara? You told me you'd send for my human."

"Did he say that?" an icy rage burned in Savus's eyes. What the hells was going on between these two?

Ruadan was gripping my arm again, his fingers tightening on my bicep. "It was the only way the gutter fae would come willingly. The simplest way to get her here without causing a scene."

I stared at him, white-hot fury simmering in my chest. So I was just *the gutter fae* now? And he'd misled me about Ciara. "I should have used the iron knife," I hissed through gritted teeth.

I couldn't bring myself to leave Ciara on her own. But what leverage did I have here?

My gaze flicked between Ruadan and Savus. They'd brought me here for a reason, hadn't they? Ruadan could have easily killed me, but they needed me to compete in the trials. Apparently, the Old Gods demanded it.

Leverage. Something Baleros had taught me to identify in every situation.

I straightened, staring at Savus. "If you want me to compete in your trials, instead of simply slaughtering your little prince over there, you will need to bring Ciara to the Institute. My human. I need to know that she is safe and taken care of."

Savus narrowed his eyes. "Do you really think you're in a position to make demands?"

"You need something from me, don't you? So it would seem that I am."

Savus tapped his silver hand on the stony armrest of his throne, considering me. "Fine. She'll join you in the dungeons. Find a separate cell for the human."

My stomach churned, and I was quickly getting the impression that my grim life as a gladiator had returned. At least Ciara and I would be together.

Ciarianna would rise again.

CHAPTER 4

Ruadan dragged me down a dank set of stairs—dark stone faintly glistening in the candlelight. Down here, the dungeon air felt heavy with dirt and mildew.

Maybe it was my overactive imagination, but I thought I could hear the distant sounds of screaming. Was this where they tortured rogue supernaturals, or was someone just losing her mind in the darkness and isolation down there?

We reached a lower level, where fae guards stood within the shadows, iron swords and axes glinting in the faint light. They wore gloves to hold the hilts so that they wouldn't burn their hands—but one swing of those would be the end of me.

"When you said someone would fetch my human," I snarled, "you didn't mention she'd be imprisoned."

Ruadan said nothing.

"If I'd known these were the conditions," I said, "I'd have done my best to kill you. You're going to lock me in a cage. How very Baleros of you."

Ruadan jerked to a halt and turned to look at me. Shadows pooled in his eyes. Something about that comment was getting to him. And being who I was, I had an overwhelming impulse to stick the knife in further, to twist it a little. I had to know what enraged Ruadan.

Knowledge is power...

I was keenly aware that the guards were watching me, and that my time down here might be worse if I insulted one of their precious knights. And yet I couldn't quite restrain my desperate need to understand how he thought. What set him off? What were his limits? And most importantly, what was his deal with Baleros? Because that tension went *deep.*

"Very Baleros indeed," I said. "Dirt floor. A captive. Mind games. Sometimes you're nice to me. Sometimes you're throwing me into a medieval dungeon. Using kindness to manipulate. I think I've played this game before. Of course it makes sense. Baleros was one of you. You're all the same, I'm sure. Have you ever heard the theory that what people hate the most in others is what they hate in themselves? You are the mirror image of him."

Ruadan's fingers tightened on my bicep, and the chilling, demonic look on his features made ice run through my blood. But I wasn't done.

With my free hand, I tapped my lips. "He wasn't your father. He's not an incubus. So that means...he was your mentor."

A low growl from Ruadan confirmed my theory.

"Tell me, Ruadan. Did he ever keep you in the dungeons? Did he ever make you happy with little gifts? Sweets wouldn't do it for you, I'm sure. Praise, wasn't it? Did he give you praise every now and then to control you? Did he make you feel like he was your father and you needed his love, and then he turned on you?"

The guards were staring at us. Ruadan gripped my arm so tightly I thought he might break it. Then he started moving again, dragging me behind him. He picked up his pace, moving in a blur of speed, too fast for me to keep up without the lumen stone. I ran, but he was inhumanly fast. Soon my feet were dragging on the floor, my body bumping over the stone.

Was there a time when I thought Ruadan actually liked me? That he'd healed me and made me comfortable because he cared about how I felt? Obviously, I'd been an idiot.

Ruadan had been trained by Baleros, and the two men were probably more alike than I'd been willing to admit.

At the end of a passage, Ruadan flung open an iron-barred door. It creaked open to reveal a minuscule space.

My stomach dropped when I looked inside. This wasn't just a cage. This was *worse* than a cage. A cell too small to lie down in—one where I'd be stuck in a contorted position, crouching on the floor. *This* was the Palatial Room.

My breathing quickened. I didn't fear much, but tight spaces weren't my favorite. That was the legacy of six years in an underground tunnel—plus time locked in a box when Baleros wanted to punish me. I snarled at Ruadan, overcome by a desire to rip his pretty throat out.

He shoved me in, and my body slammed against the wall. I turned back to him, desperate to come up with a witty retort, something to let him know this wasn't getting to me. I wanted him to know that he couldn't affect me, that I felt no sense of betrayal, that I'd never expected anything from him in the first place. Except, tears stung my eyes, and my throat seemed to have closed.

I already felt the walls tightening in on me, and my mouth opened and closed without a single word on my tongue. His eyes had returned to their vibrant violet shade—no longer on the verge of killing. For the briefest of instants, I thought I saw a glimmer of sadness. Then, he slammed the cell door shut, and shadows consumed him as he stalked away.

I started to grip the bars, but as soon as I did, my fingertips burned. Of course. Iron.

My dress was still soaked from my little dip in the river, and I shivered. By the time I emerged from the Palatial Room for my next trial, I'd be completely filthy. Not to mention the fact that I had an unbelievable urge to pee, and the Palatial Room did not contain a toilet.

In the cramped space, my breath was coming in short, sharp bursts. It was only a few feet square, and I could hardly even sit. I definitely couldn't lie down, and I had to draw my knees up to my chest. At least I could see through the iron bars. Without that faint flicker of torchlight, I'd lose my mind.

But as I leaned back against the wall, I realized I was still wearing my bug-out bag. A smile started to curl my lips. Maybe I'd rattled Ruadan so much that he forgot to pull it off me.

My bag contained sweets, a now broken headlamp, lighters, soap, medical supplies, knives…and I had at least one bottle of water, which I could drink slowly to ration it. When I emptied it, I'd pee into it so I didn't have to sit in my own filth the whole time. Given that the door was iron, I wouldn't be able to get myself out of the cell, but I could improve my conditions at least a little.

Had Ruadan really overlooked that? I clenched my jaw.

Probably. I wasn't going to make the idiotic mistake again of thinking he'd been *nice* to me.

Still, I was pleased with his mistake. Maybe my time here wouldn't be so terrible, after all.

* * *

As Maddan stood before my cell, my mind went back to the time when I thought this wouldn't be so terrible. It seemed like days ago, but I had an awful feeling it had been something like twenty minutes. I was pretty familiar with how underground-cage time worked. Three days of underground-cage time was roughly twenty minutes in the real world. Hence, I was something like six thousand years old in cage years. Not sure of the exact math, as calculations weren't my strong point—particularly when sitting in a cell confronted by The Royal Fae Arsehole, and the unsettling sight of magic flicking between his fingertips.

Guards stood nearby. If Maddan murdered me right now, would they do anything to stop it? Probably not. After all, his father was a king and a benefactor, and it would save the Institute from the unpleasant possibility that the Old Gods might like me.

Maddan cocked his head, and red light gleamed between his fingers. At least he wasn't about to hit me with lust magic again, but I couldn't imagine the red magic would be pleasant.

CHAPTER 5

$\mathcal{A}$ dark smile curled Maddan's lips. "When I last saw you, you had the audacity to reject me. I slammed you with lust magic. Do you remember?"

Was there anything worse than a man who felt entitled to every woman he met? A man who would literally kill over a rejection? I thought of the iron knives in my bug-out bag. I could probably nail him with one right now.

Unfortunately for me, that would most definitely result in my death. I could kill him, yes, but there was no way out of this cell, and Savus had already made it clear that he mostly wanted to torment me a bit, then kill me in the most painful possible way.

So I would have to do something extremely difficult for me. Something that, had I ever seen a therapist, I would surely have been working on: not using violence as a way of getting out of every difficult situation.

Maddan cocked his head, the smug look on his face stoking my rage. "Am I right to understand that all the incubus magic drove you mad? That you roamed London's streets, satiating your lust in every filthy back alley until you wore yourself out?"

The story wasn't true, but I'd go with it anyway. He wanted denials, shame, and humiliation. He wouldn't get it.

"That's right. Every back alley. Lots of men." I looked at my fingers. Already, dirt had become encrusted under my nails. "I had a blast. Am I to understand that you're trying to make that sound like a bad thing? If your dead barguest friend had done the same, banging women all over London until he wore himself out, you'd have sung his praises. Don't you think?"

He cleared his throat, and I had the distinct impression that I'd taken the wind out of his sails. "You're still a whore."

I rolled my eyes. "Good one. And they say the royal fae have become stupid through centuries of inbreeding..."

The magic between his fingertips burned brighter. "You cannot talk to me like this, gutter fae. You try to humiliate me, over and over again."

And here we were at the crux of his problem. His giant ego. "You mean, when I kicked your arse at one trial after another, or when I said I found you repulsive?"

"A gutter fae, rejecting a prince..." he snarled.

He hurled the magic at me, and it slammed into me through the iron bars. Pain spread through my body, racking my bones. I started shaking, fingers wildly clutching at the stone walls, trying to manage the agony. My mind flashed to the knives in my bag, and I was doing everything in my power not to pull one out right then and throw it at him.

Don't kill the prince. Don't kill the prince. Don't kill the prince.

When I looked up at Maddan again, I was gritting my teeth. "What do you hope to accomplish here, prince? When the next trial comes up, they will be unleashing me on the world. And I might not be gentle when I take you down."

He didn't respond, just summoned another flash of red fire and threw it at me. I raised my arms to block it, but it slammed into my forearms, and the pain raced through my bones, my tendons, ripping me apart. I grunted, trying to keep myself from screaming. I didn't know what this magic was—if it was actually breaking my bones, or if it just delivered pain. Either way, by the time I got to the next trial, I may not be in the condition to take him down at all.

Another blast of his hellish magic tore through my body, and I could no longer think straight. The pain was splintering. A few disconnected thoughts flickered in my mind—Maddan is a prick… Ruadan is a prick…Savus is a prick… Nothing particularly useful or insightful.

With the final attack—one last burst of red magic—I fell back against the wall, and my world began to go dark.

* * *

I BREATHED in the scent of apples. I felt rough stone biting into my back where I leaned against the wall, and as I gasped for breath, I felt particles of dirt going into my lungs. But the air smelled different now. It smelled of the city of Emain, and in my mind's eye, I could see the apple trees dappling the mythical land's wild hills.

Pain racked my body, and I groaned. Gentle fingers lifted me from the stone until I was standing, my eyes still closed from fatigue. I slumped into a powerful body. Apples and pine.

My mouth had gone completely dry, and I licked my lips. "Who's there?" I asked, still half asleep, even though I knew by his scent it was Ruadan.

"It's me." He whispered so quietly, I almost didn't hear him.

My eyes snapped open, and I found myself staring at the dark contours of a shirt. Then, I looked up into violet eyes, bright in the darkness. His powerful arms held me up, and heat radiated from his body over my freezing skin. I hated the bastard, but despite myself, I wanted him to stay here with his arms wrapped around me, just for the warmth.

The Palatial Room offered barely enough space for two people to stand—especially given the size of Ruadan's broad shoulders. He pulled me closer to him, his muscled body pressing against me. I was dimly aware that I still stank of river water and piss, but I was too tired to care. In fact, I was glad Ruadan had to deal with the stench.

"Where's Ciara?" I asked in a whisper.

He leaned down, and his breath warmed the shell of my ear. "She's here. Two cells down. You must be quiet."

"Why are you here?" I whispered.

He put his finger over my lips, shushing me. Interesting. He didn't want the guards knowing he was in here.

I felt the warmth of his fingertips on the small of my back, and he traced up my spine. Healing magic pulsed in my body, comforting and soothing. One of his enormous hands encircled my waist. As much as I hated it, my skin was warming in response to his incubus magic.

His fingertips traced higher up my spine, and the pain flowed out of my body.

When his hand stroked down my back again, an unwelcome memory bloomed in my mind—me, naked in Ruadan's bed, writhing against him.

What the fuck was wrong with me? My body was in complete rebellion against my better judgment. It was the incubus magic.

Ruadan leaned down, whispering, "You need to survive."

Before I could look up into his eyes again, his cold magic pulsed over my body. Silently, he opened the iron gate, and disappeared into the prison's shadows. He was gone.

I leaned back against the rough wall, the stones cutting into my skin through my dress. My muscles and bones still ached, but not nearly as much as before. I slid down the stones, grimacing a bit.

The fucker hadn't even bothered to heal me all the way. He could have, but I supposed he needed to heal me just enough so I wouldn't expire before the trials. He wanted me punished as much as Savus did, but he also wanted to make sure I lived.

Crammed into the Palatial Room, I leaned back against the cell wall.

The dim torchlight wavered over something on the floor that made my heart leap in my chest.

A butterscotch sweet.

My mouth went dry. Baleros, my old gladiator master, had used a butterscotch to control me with a glimmer of kindness. But he was dead now.

Right?

For a moment, I wondered if it was real at all, or just my mind screwing with me. Then, I reached for it, picking it up with a shaking hand. I felt as if Baleros were fucking with me, except he was dead. Had Ruadan left this here? Why would he try to mess with me like that?

With a snarl, I threw the butterscotch out of my cell, between the bars.

It took a few minutes of deep breathing before I could relax myself, forcing my heartbeat to slow.

"Ciara?" I called out into the darkness, and my voice echoed off the rocks.

Only a faint dripping noise answered.

"Ciara?" I tried again.

"I'm here," she said. "You know, I think we were a little better off in Ciarianna Castle."

"In what?"

"The burnt-out car. I've started calling it Ciarianna Castle in my mind, even though I kept finding myself sleeping on eggshells and half-eaten chicken bones. But that seems like paradise now. Here, I have to sleep on bugs and dead mice, just like I did as a little girl. But I'm not going to let them get to me. I'm beating the system."

"How, exactly?"

"I'm not going to sleep on bugs, because I'm not going to sleep. I've been keeping myself awake by standing."

I held my head in my hands. "You need to get some sleep, Ciara. Human brains break if you don't sleep."

"That's a myth. Like, there are a lot of benefits to permanent wakefulness...you have more time for thinking, and you start to hear voices. Worst-case scenario, you get visual hallucinations, possibly permanent brain damage." Her voice echoed off the rocks.

"Ciara. I'm going to get us out of here."

"Or maybe I'll get us out of here," she said. "Did you know that the women in my family are legendary protectors? Fiery. Like demons. Family legend says my grandma came from a flaming pit under the Appalachian Mountains. Grandma McDougall was a fearsome woman. She caught squirrels for breakfast with her bare hands, snapped their necks. She wore gowns of raccoon fur and crowns of black locust leaves, and men trembled before her."

I wasn't entirely sure if this was an actual family legend or the product of her prison hallucinations.

"Well," I said, "maybe you'll get us out of here."

"The McDougalls protect people we love. So you'd better believe I won't let anything happen to you. When it comes down to it, I will protect you with everything I've got. I come from mountain fire."

"Okay, sweetie. Close your eyes."

"Ciarianna will rise again. And when she does, she will light her enemies on fire. She will glory in their screams and bathe in their ashes."

For a sweet woman who got excited about things like "bologna cake," Ciara could be remarkably macabre.

"Ciarianna will dance on their graves," I added.

"She will fashion flutes and other wind instruments out of their bones. And then she will celebrate their demise with a meal of Twinkies."

The dripping of water filled the silence. "You kind of frighten me sometimes, you know that, Ciara? Maybe just…settle down a little."

"You can't trust these people at the Institute. Ruadan is a pretty man with a face like a god, but you don't know jack about him."

"Oh, believe me. I know."

"Things aren't always what they seem. The devil wears many—"

The slamming of metal against metal cut her off. "Shut it, you two!" boomed a male voice. "Or I'll cut your tits off."

I gritted my teeth. When I got out of here, I was going to punch that guy in the dick.

"Ciara," I loudly whispered. "Ciarianna will rise again."

Time for me to rest a little. Slowing my breathing, I leaned my head against the sludgy rock, and then willed myself to sleep.

CHAPTER 6

I crouched in the cell. I had no idea how much time had passed. Two days, perhaps? I only knew that Maddan never returned, and that one of the guards had shoved water and gruel through the cell's trapdoor around four or five times.

But worst of all, every time I fell asleep, I'd wake to find another butterscotch in my cell. And each time I found one, I'd hurl it out from between the bars.

Somehow, I'd managed to sleep most of the time in the cell—dreaming of Emain the whole time. I did my best to ration out the sweets from my bag—lollipops, two chocolate bars, a bag of peppermints. Proper athlete stuff. I'd be in amazing shape by the time I had to fight anyone.

In the middle of a particularly delicious dream of Emain, one in which I was biting into a sweet apple, the sound of my name snapped me out of my sleep.

I woke, blinking in surprise at the sight of Melusine standing outside my cell.

She held a little bundle in her hands—something wrapped in cloth—and she shoved it through the cell bars, wincing as her hand brushed against the iron.

"""

"What are you doing here?" I asked.

"I brought you food. I see a dungeon, I think hunger. I put two and two together. I've got to tell you though, it was not easy getting in here. I had to give the guards a sleep potion, and they're already stirring."

I blinked, snatching up the little bundle. "I was starting to think everyone had forgotten about me."

She shook her head. "No one has. Maddan keeps talking about you. All the time. I think he's obsessed with you. When I hear someone talking about the same thing all the time, I think 'obsessed.' I put two and two together. Ruadan has been stalking around, snarling at everyone, like he wants to rip off everyone's head. I see black eyes on a demon, and I think 'anger.' I can't say why, but I think it has to do with you."

I shook my head. "What happens if Savus defies the Old Gods?"

"The Old Gods have blessed Savus with the silver crown that gives him power of the Institute. As long as he has their blessing, no one can take that thing off. No one can kill him or overthrow him, or challenge his power. The Old Gods bestow their blessing on novices. They make the choice, and the Grand Master is just supposed to interpret it. If you keep winning in the trials, it means the Old Gods favor you. If Savus gets rid of you, he'd be going against their will. He could lose the crown. Anyone could depose him. Ruadan especially. I see them snarling at each other, I think they're angry at each other. Competing like stags. Know what I mean?"

Ahh…so I had some serious leverage. Savus needed me to keep his power within the Institute. In fact, maybe the Old Gods would be my ticket out of the Palatial Room of Nightmares.

"This is extremely valuable information, Melusine. Maybe even my way out of here." A rock was digging into one of my shoulder blades, and I winced, rubbing the raw flesh. "I guess the 'Palatial Room' is something of a Shadow Fae joke."

She blinked at me. "Fae nobility don't make jokes. They're incapable of it. *Palatial* is actually an Ancient Fae word, translating to something in English like…" she scratched her cheek as she thought.

"The devil's arsecrack?" I offered.

"Festering dung-hole would be more accurate."

"I see. That is quite accurate."

Someone groaned farther down the hallway, and Melusine touched the violet lumen stone at her neck. "They're already waking. I've got to go."

"Wait!" I said, maybe a little too loud. I thrust the bundle of food back at her, grimacing at the sting from the iron bars. "Can you give this to Ciara?"

She nodded once and snatched the food from me. My stomach rumbled and my mouth watered at the scent of food, but at least I'd had a few sweets to sustain me. Ciara had nothing but gruel the whole time. Plus, I'd had the pleasure of dreaming of apples and baked bread.

Melusine frowned at the food, then nodded again. Shadows burst around her, and she disappeared.

Gods, I missed my lumen stone. If I ever got out of this prison alive, I'd be stealing it back.

I took a deep breath, my eyes already growing heavy. Why was I so tired?

"Ciara?" I called out.

"Yeah?"

"Are you okay there?"

"Someone just dropped off a package—"

"Shhhhh. I know." I desperately wanted to know what was in it. Chicken? Bread? I clutched my famished stomach. At this point, I'd start eating the gruel.

"I'm going to get us out of here," I promised.

I picked up another butterscotch from the dirt floor, and threw it out from between the bars.

"Ciara." I loosed a long breath. "I keep finding butterscotches." She would know what that meant.

"Who's leaving them? It's not *you-know-who*. He's dead, Arianna."

"I know. But I have no idea where they're coming from."

"Maybe Ruadan. Not sure that I trust the man. Not sure that I trust shadows and darkness." She was talking with her mouth full, and my stomach rumbled again. "The devil wears many faces."

"I know."

"I said that shadowy monster—"

Metal slammed against metal again, and a guard's voice barked, "What did I tell you?"

"Right. You'll cut our tits off," I said. Sometimes, men were the worst.

* * *

ROUGH HANDS JERKED me out of another dream of Emain.

Someone was yanking me up, and I blinked at the sight of the open cell door.

It took me a moment to realize that Ruadan had returned, and that he was dragging me out of my cell. He wasn't exactly gentle about it.

He dragged me past Ciara's cell, and I caught a quick glimpse of her slumbering against the wall, covered in crumbs. The sight warmed my heart.

I scrambled for balance, then elbowed him hard in the chest. "You don't have to drag me everywhere. Arsehole. I can walk."

"Your next trial begins soon," he said. "You'll need to be cleaned and fed if you're going to pass it."

"Cleaned and fed? You're making me sound like a farm animal."

"Well, no one knows what your other half is. It's entirely possible."

I glared at him. Was that a…joke? No. Fae nobility didn't make jokes. He was just a twat.

Still, I didn't *hate* the idea of taking a bath and eating a proper meal.

As I passed the guards, one of them sniffed the air, his lip curling in disgust. In cage years, I'd been in there for, I don't know, decades? But given the number of meals I'd received so far, I'd wager it had been something like three days. Three days during which my competition had been preparing, while I'd been eating lollipops for sustenance and getting my bones broken by magic.

Ruadan let go of my arm, and I started to wonder how difficult it would be to simply escape on the next task. Could Savus really hunt me down and exalt me? The hardest part would be getting Ciara out of here.

"What is the next trial, exactly?" I asked.

"You'll do fine."

"You didn't answer my question." I followed him up the narrow stairwell, my muscles burning. I'd been in a contorted position for far too long—not to mention the fact that I still hadn't fully healed from Maddan's magical assault. "I probably will do fine, but what is the task? If I screw anything up, I'll literally be torn to pieces."

"The next trial involves killing vampires using a stake. I'll be with you the entire time, so you won't be able to escape. Without the lumen stone, you are slow and sluggish."

Slow and sluggish? "Remember when you couldn't talk? I'm thinking fondly of those days."

I knew that I stank like the bottom of a sewer, but I was angry enough at Ruadan that I felt satisfied he had to deal with the stench.

When we reached the sunlight, it burned my eyes, and I lifted an arm to shield my vision. I sort of wanted to crawl into a coffin. So *this* is how vampires felt.

I blinked in the bright light as my eyes adjusted. "Are we going to your room?"

"You're not going anywhere near my room."

"Just because I put a little knife in your heart? Honestly. You're all making a big deal out of nothing." I shadowed my eyes as we crossed the flowery green. After the magical beating I'd taken, I could hardly keep up with Ruadan, and I walked with a limp. "Does anyone else know about…my time in the arena?"

"No."

Interesting. He wasn't entirely forthcoming with Grand Master Savus.

We reached the tower door, and Ruadan opened it into the stairwell.

My bones ached, and I glared at him. "You didn't heal me very well."

He shot me a sharp look, then gave a subtle shake of his head. He wanted me to drop it.

As Ruadan and I walked up the stairs, anger started to simmer in my chest. Ruadan had drastically misled me when he'd lured me here. "You never said anything about a prison cell. And I distinctly remember a promise that someone would fetch my human."

"The promise was honored," he said.

"But you threw her in a dungeon. She would have been better off where she was." Fury was rising now. I suppressed the urge to punch him hard in his beautiful face and mess it up a little. "You are no different than Baleros, who I'd vowed to kill. Are you so certain you'll outlive me?" The words exploded out of me, and I knew I was being incautious, but after days in the Palatial Room, I didn't have the best grip on self-restraint. Plus, my body still ached from Maddan's attack, and a wild hunger was making me feel a little crazy.

Ruadan simply fell silent, and he led me down the hall until we reached an oak door.

He pushed it open, revealing a sparse stone bathroom. Like the other bathrooms I'd seen at the Institute, the stone tub seemed to grow from the flagstone floor itself like a natural feature. The bath had already been filled. Ruddy sunlight streamed in through the window, blazing through the curls of steam that rose from the bathtub. While the bath itself looked inviting, I wasn't super thrilled at the sight of six armed fae guards standing around the room, staring at the tub. Were they going to watch me bathe?

"I'm supposed to bathe in here?" I asked.

"You will need to be clean for your next trial. You're going to infiltrate a vampire's den, and you'll need to blend in. The filth on your body would make it difficult." He raised his eyes to the guards. "Turn around."

"But sir," one of them began, "Savus has ordered—"

"Turn around." The cold fury in his voice brooked no argument. "And if I catch you looking at her, I will sever your head from your body before you can draw another breath."

CHAPTER 7

"Aren't you the gentleman," I said drily. "You leave me in a festering dung hole where my enemies can torture me within an inch of my life. But gods forbid anyone sees my nipples." Fae males were absurd. Possibly all males were absurd.

The shadows around Ruadan grew so thick, they seemed to suck all the air out of the room. With one last withering look, he turned away from me. With his back to me, he stood in the doorway, his large frame blocking my exit. Weapons glinted all over his body—knives strapped to his legs, the sword on his back. Every inch of him was equipped to kill, while I was about to strip myself completely naked. The balance of power was not in my favor here, if I wanted to cause trouble.

I surveyed the room. There wasn't much in here, except a short wooden table with some clothing and a towel.

I looked down at my dress. At one point, it had been white, but now dirt smeared the fabric—along with a few red smudges from what I thought were my sweets (or perhaps blood), and green stains that I thought might be from moss or mildew growing in the Palatial room. In short, I was absolutely disgusting.

I breathed in deeply, determined to convince Ruadan that none of this was getting to me. "Do I *have* to bathe? I've been a bit nostalgic for the old days." He knew what I meant, even if the guards didn't: my cage underground. "Right now, I smell like home. You know what I mean, don't you?"

"Undress."

I blinked. Even with his back to me, even in a room full of guards, there was definitely something unmistakably sensual about that word on his tongue. "Clean yourself. Then, you will eat."

Despite his commanding tone, his voice seemed to wrap itself around my body, stroking places I desperately needed to wash right now. But I pushed his allure out of my mind. He was a monster—a devil wearing a beautiful face—and he'd *exalt* me on a whim if it struck his fancy.

"It's unfortunate you had to take me out of my Palatial Room. I was having the most exquisite dreams in there." I pulled off my dress and tossed it on the stone floor, then stepped out of my underwear. The drafty castle air whispered over my skin. "But do you know? Every now and then I'd think of you, Ruadan, and what a lovely man you are. Am I getting that word right—*lovely?* My Ancient Fae is rusty. I'm looking for something that translates to 'violet-eyed psycho twat' in English."

He didn't answer, but his body looked tightly coiled, like he was about to explode. What was that about?

I cocked my head. It was the same tension that had gripped his body when I lay in bed with him. He was supposed to be celibate. As an incubus, it couldn't be easy for him to be this close to a naked woman. Is that what it was about?

Like a child poking a bug with a stick, I wanted to prod at that wound to see what would happen. "It feels good to get those filthy clothes off. I'm awfully dirty though, Ruadan. Perhaps you can help me bathe?"

His growl rumbled through my gut.

"It's just that there are some delicate places I can't quite reach on my own, and you're so good with your hands." I dipped one foot into the bath, sighing at the feel of warm water on my skin. "I do remember what your fingers felt like on my body when you healed me. I remember what it felt like when I was naked in bed with you, writhing—" I unleashed a long sigh. "Oh, that's right. You've taken a vow of celibacy. Never mind, then. How long has it been, anyway? Centuries? Is it true that Shadow Fae in other institutes are allowed to enjoy the pleasures of the flesh? Kissing, stroking, fucking up against the stone walls? Too bad you're in the one institute where none of that's allowed. Must be hard for an incubus. So to speak."

His magic thickened in the room, shadows darkening around him. I couldn't help but smile. I *was* getting to him, and it filled me with satisfaction.

Then, I stepped in, submerging myself completely in the stone tub. It felt amazing.

I pulled a bar of soap from the stone lip of the tub, and I began scrubbing some of the grime off my legs.

"If I become a knight, I'm not sure I'd be able to abide by that particular rule. The celibacy one. I suppose I could always pleasure myself in the bath."

"Stop talking," Ruadan snarled.

I smiled again as I ran the soap over my arms, watching the bath slowly fill with dirt from my body.

The fun in prodding at Ruadan was beginning to wear off, and I frowned as I washed myself. Why, exactly, were all the guards necessary? As Ruadan had so nicely pointed out, without a lumen stone on my body, I was slow and sluggish. There was no way in hells I could escape someone who could shadow-leap. Why did they need six guards here if Ruadan could easily guard me on his own?

Maybe it had to do with the animosity between Savus and Ruadan. Maybe the Grand Master didn't want us speaking to each other. Perhaps they weren't here to guard me, but to report on Ruadan. After all, he'd tried to keep it a secret when he'd healed me in the cell, hadn't he?

I ran the soap under my filthy fingernails, getting dirt all over the soap. Why had Ruadan left me with the lumen stone I'd stolen?

Even if he was simply a violet-eyed shadow twat, his behaviors were confusing and inconsistent. He left me alive, left me with a lumen stone, campaigned to spare my life...He even concealed my connection to Baleros from the Institute. Then he dragged me into a prison and left me there. He healed me, but only a little.

At this point, I had no idea how to predict his actions or motivations, and he was a complete cipher. I needed to speak to him alone—except it seemed Savus didn't want that to happen.

I turned on the tap to wash my lavender hair, and quickly lathered up my locks. Then I bent under the tap to rinse myself. The stream of water ran brown with all the filth from my body. When I'd completely scrubbed my skin and hair, I unplugged the drain, letting the filthy water drain out. Then, I rinsed my entire body with fresh water from the tap. I sniffed my bicep, inhaling the smell of lavender. Completely pristine.

Utterly naked, I crossed to Ruadan, and I touched his back, watching his muscles tense as if I'd burned him. "I'm getting dressed now."

I crossed to the table, my bare feet padding over the cold floor and leaving wet footprints.

As I pulled on the fresh underwear, I stared at Ruadan's enormous back. "Do I get to learn anything else about the trial before we begin? Do I need magic?"

"You won't need magic," Ruadan answered. "Just to kill vampires. This clan happens to be particularly ancient and powerful, but I trust your ability to kill."

"I want to go to the library," I said. I pulled a tight, black dress over my head, finding that it fit my body perfectly.

"Why the library?" he asked. "You don't have much time."

"It's how I prepare." I needed no preparation to kill vampires. I just wanted to be alone with Ruadan for a few moments if I could get them.

One of the guards shifted in place. "Sir, Grand Master Savus ordered us to remain with you and the gutter fae at all times."

"It's just a quick trip to the library," I protested.

"I will take you for a few moments," said Ruadan.

"Sir," the guard said, "I don't believe we're supposed to deviate from—"

With an explosion of shadow magic, Ruadan whirled and slammed his fist into the wall just by the guard's head. Bits of rock rained down, and Ruadan glared into his eyes.

"Then come with us," Ruadan snarled. "So you can report to your Master that you've done your job."

My gaze flicked to the floor, where urine pooled at the guard's feet.

I crossed my arms, staring at Ruadan. Savus was old, and lacked Ruadan's demonic night magic powers. If it weren't for the magical power of the Old Gods, Ruadan would clearly be the alpha fae. Savus better hope he didn't piss off those gods.

* * *

We crossed into the library, my heart already warming at the smell of books, and the sight of library moths dusting the shelves. Glow worms, suspended by silk from the ceiling, cast golden light over crooked shelves of books.

As we crossed between two stacks, I caught a glimpse of my favorite librarian hovering on her magical Segway. Her silver hair seemed to float around her as she moved up and down.

I cast a quick glance back at the guard who was trailing us, his eyes locked on me. His skin had paled, and he clearly looked terrified at the prospect of having to choose between infuriating Savus or Ruadan.

The librarian zoomed around a corner, then screeched to a halt. She peered down over her moon-shaped spectacles. "Can I help you?"

"I'm looking for nonfiction vampire books," I said. "And if you happen to have a paper and pencil, I'm hoping to take some notes."

She reached into the pocket of her shimmering blue dress, and pulled out a little lined notepad and a pencil. She handed them to me.

"Thank you."

"Follow me." She nodded curtly, then zoomed across the library to an enormous archway, its shelves crammed full of books. I picked up my pace, hurrying to catch up with her. I swear she'd become even speedier since the last time I saw her. Reckless, even.

Ruadan didn't utter a word as we walked, and the fae guard simply stomped along behind us.

The librarian hovered just above us, high in the archway. She peered down at us, then gestured at one of the walls.

"Vampires," she declared.

My gaze roamed up and down the ancient books, and I randomly pulled one from the shelf, titled *The Vampyre*.

I glanced back at the guard, who was staring at us, his blue eyes narrowed. The librarian whooshed over our heads at a speed that made my heart race. It was a wonder that woman didn't injure herself.

Standing next to Ruadan, I cracked open the book, and began jotting down my "notes." I needed some answers.

Why did you heal me, but only partway?

He pointed at what I was writing. "You've got that wrong. Let me do it."

He snatched the notepad and pencil from me.

You need to appear injured. Don't trust anyone.

I loosed a long, slow breath. I was still confused, and I snatched the pencil back.

Why do I need to appear injured?

I heard the guard take another step behind me, and I slammed the book shut before he could see what we'd been writing.

The guard cleared his throat. "The trial begins soon, sir. Savus will exalt me if I defy his orders."

We'd never gotten around to that feeding part, and my stomach rumbled. And all I'd learned was that Ruadan was hiding things from the other Shadow Fae.

CHAPTER 8

*W*e waited on a tiny street in London's Smithfield, illuminated by the amber glow of a streetlight. The air felt heavy and damp, as if rain were going to fall.

By ancient hospital walls, I stood between Melusine and Maddan. I smoothed out my clean black dress. On the way here, Ruadan had tossed me a chunk of stale bread. Better than nothing, I supposed. My bones and muscles still ached—but not nearly as much as they would if Ruadan hadn't healed me.

Maddan narrowed his eyes at me and growled. Considering what he'd done to me, he probably had no idea how I was standing at all.

I ignored him, instead focusing on my surroundings. Centuries ago, this had been a place of execution—the very place where William Wallace had died a horrific death, just outside a medieval hospital. The place also where Bloody Mary had burned the Protestants. Here, the scent of human death had mingled with the offal and refuse of the butchery trade.

We'd be bringing the death back to Smithfield in the form of another trial.

Seemed a perfect way to spend a Saturday night, I supposed. I wasn't entirely sure where we'd be going, but it was most likely the dark, medieval church on the other side of an ornate Tudor gate. It was the exact sort of creepy place a vampire would inhabit. They'd probably been in it for centuries.

Mist flowed over the ground, and the hair on my arms stood on end. The fog itself formed eerie shapes, as if it were alive—wolves, lions, grasping fingers. The sound of footfalls echoed off the stone. Then, Grand Master Savus crossed in front of us, his fingers steepled.

Thunder rumbled over the horizon, the boom skimming my skin.

Ruadan walked behind Savus, his dark magic tingeing the mist with shadows. Tonight, Ruadan was acting as my prison guard, making sure I didn't escape anywhere.

Savus's pale eyes bored into me. "You all know that you're supposed to silently enter and kill in the shadows. Do not do anything that calls attention to yourselves. Kill when no one is looking. As soon as the vampires learn that Shadow Fae have entered their lair, they will descend upon you and feast like vultures on a corpse."

I blinked innocently. "Anything attention-grabbing, like stabbing the other novices with a reaping dagger? Like hurling lust magic at them? That sort of thing?"

Savus didn't answer, but he continued glaring at me.

"Your task tonight is to enter their lair, and kill as many of the vampires as you can without the humans in their company realizing. This clan is at least five centuries old, and they believe London is their home. They are wrong. They should have fled for a magical realm years ago. We believe ten or fifteen vampires lurk in there. If you are capable of remaining in the shadows, you should be able to take them all on. If you are clumsy and expose your presence, you will all die."

I had a thin wooden stake jammed between my cleavage, which meant I had everything I needed to kill vampires. A simple hawthorn stake to the heart, and the vampires would be sent to the shadow void for all of eternity. Vampires weren't nearly as difficult to kill as Ruadan, and I'd killed plenty in the arena. The only tricky part would be the "stick to the shadows" directive. And maybe the first hurdle of getting into their lair.

In fact, I wasn't entirely sure how Savus expected me to get into the church. The others—including Ruadan—could simply shadow-leap wherever they wanted. I didn't have that advantage.

Still, my time in the arena had taught me how vampires thought. Most vampire males would welcome an innocent female, seeing us as fresh blood. All I had to do was knock and make sure they didn't notice the stake between my boobs, until it was too late.

My objectives tonight: kill vampires, find alone time with Ruadan so I could interrogate him before someone tried to throw me back in the filthy piss hole.

"Be warned," said Savus, "the vampires have been living in horrific, depraved conditions. What you find in there might be worse than you imagined."

For a moment, a shudder whispered up my spine, but I quickly mastered control of myself. How bad could it be? A bit of blood, some horrible skull decor? A severed head and some rotting limbs here and there? I'd practically grown up around carnage. It didn't scare me.

"Now." Something dark glinted in Savus's eyes. "Go out there and slaughter."

Melusine and Maddan were off before I took my first step, shadow-leaping away. The flicker of movement by the old Tudor church gate told me they were slipping beneath its ancient arches into the cemetery. Heading for the medieval church, just as I'd thought.

For a moment, I considered rushing after them as fast as I could limp on my hobbled legs, but I reconsidered. Their departure had been a little too hasty. None of us knew for certain that the vampires were in the old gothic church—it just *seemed* vampy.

I stepped out of the shadows of St. Bartholomew's Hospital. I sniffed the air. Given all the shadow magic pulsing around us from Ruadan and the other novices, I couldn't use that to pick up the scent of vampires.

Thunder boomed again, lightning cracking the sky.

The muscles barked in my legs, and I limped down a narrow road near the church, noting the street sign—Little Britain. A light rain began to fall, dampening my black dress.

I sniffed the air again. Now, another smell hung in the air—one faint, but distinct. The coppery smell of human blood. I smiled. *That's* how I would track the vampires, and it wasn't coming from the church. I sniffed again, moving further down the narrow road. As I walked, Ruadan's magic whispered over my skin from behind me.

Lucky for me, I didn't need to depend on speed. As the scent of blood intensified, I was increasingly sure that the others had gone in the wrong direction.

I glanced behind me, irritated to find that Savus was staring at Ruadan and me from the mouth of the narrow street. I wouldn't be able to speak to Ruadan with the Grand Master watching.

I limped onward, until the scent of blood led me to a pub, the facade painted with chipped brown and green paint. The place looked like a bit of a dump, with empty crates piled out front, and a few half-drunk pints.

I could hardly make out the pub's name. I looked closely and saw that the faint gold lettering above the door read *The Garlic and Cross.* Those things were not actually repellent to vampires, but maybe it was an in-joke. In any case, the scent told me I was in the right place.

Then, to my utter horror, I noticed the hand-drawn, grammatically incorrect sign on the door. It heralded something I hoped I'd never have to encounter, something I'd spent years avoiding.

Saturday! Open Mic Night. Comedian's. Singer's. Performance art. £5.

I swallowed hard. Savus had been right. This *was* more depraved than I'd anticipated.

And on top of it all, I had no money to get in. I'd been living in a bloody dungeon.

I glanced at Ruadan. "I don't suppose you have a fiver?"

"I'm not allowed to help you. If the Old Gods favor you, then you will be able to succeed in the trials no matter what obstacles lie in your path."

"What exactly is the point of you?" I snapped.

He narrowed his eyes, his dark magic lashing the air around him. "I'm the only thing keeping you alive."

"What do you mean?"

His gaze slid back to Savus, who was lingering nearby, and he fell silent again.

The rain had begun to fall harder, soaking my hair, and I hugged myself. I didn't suppose I could simply kill the doorman. Might create a bit of a spectacle.

No, I'd have to blag my way into the bar, because there was no way in hells I was volunteering as a performer.

Now, the rain was really pouring down, soaking my clothing.

Baleros's fifteenth law of power: Always use your surroundings.

I glanced across the street at another pub—The Crown and Two Chairmen. An idea started to form in my mind. I'd have to start there before I made my way into the vamp bar.

I ignored Ruadan's presence and pushed into the second pub. It was a Saturday night, and the place was completely full. Humans sat crammed around the old wooden tables, or lingered between them with pints. I could easily move unnoticed in here. I scanned the empty wineglasses and pints on the tables. Within moments, I was collecting them by the armful, acting like I worked in the place. If you appeared confident enough, no one questioned it.

When I'd stuffed my arms full of the glassware, I crept out into the rain with my stolen bounty.

Ruadan was waiting for me outside, his magic darkening the air. "What on Earth are you doing?"

"Finding a way in before Prince Fuckwit figures out what the hells he's doing." I let some rainwater fill the glasses, and then I dumped the remnants onto the street. Clean.

I snatched one of the old crates off the ground outside the pub— along with the pint glasses—and I crammed all the glassware into it. With a smile, I stood.

I pulled open the door to the pub to reveal a rickety stairwell, and Ruadan followed behind me.

I paused at the top of the stairs. As soon as the door creaked closed behind Ruadan, I turned to him. "Tell me what's going on. Why didn't you warn me about the prison cell?"

"I didn't know Savus was going to throw you in prison. And we don't have time to discuss this now. Savus will be watching us through a scrying mirror. I'm going to hide myself." His gaze sharpened. "Arianna, don't do anything stupid. You can't escape the Shadow Fae. Do you understand?"

"Yeah, I get it. I'm a prisoner. Understood."

Shadows bloomed around Ruadan, and he was gone without another word.

My jaw tightened, and I gripped my crate of glasses. Of course, Savus watched everything we did in the trials.

I limped down the creaking stairs, already cringing at the sound of stilted comedy booming through the club.

A human man sat at a desk at the bottom of the stairs, flicking through his mobile phone, utterly bored. When he saw me, he tapped his fingernails on the wood. "Five pounds, please, darling."

"Oh, I'm just here to deliver the glasses you wanted." I had once again lapsed into an American accent, which seemed to happen every time I wanted to blag my way into a nightclub. I honestly couldn't explain it.

He narrowed his eyes. "Someone asked for more glasses?"

If you acted confident enough, you could get away with anything.

"Yeah. The owner. Said you were running out." Standing tall, I began to step into the bar.

"Hang on," he grabbed my arm. "I'm the owner. What are you trying to pull?"

My jaw tightened.

Fuck it. Fuck it all to hells. I needed the Old Gods on my side, or I faced a grisly death.

I cleared my throat. "I meant to say, the glasses are part of my act. It's all…it's all part of my act. I'm here to perform."

CHAPTER 9

"*P*art of your act?" he repeated.

My pulse raced. "It's a glass-shattering act."

He stared at me. If I'd had a few more minutes to prepare, I probably would have come up with something a little more artistic than "glass-shattering." Maybe those people who make music with the rims of glasses, or maybe some kind of glass-related dance routine. But I was short on time, short on talent, and as usual, my first and most powerful instinct was simply to break things.

"It's totally a thing," I said in a voice suggesting that he was an idiot. "You haven't heard of glass shattering?" I crinkled my forehead. "It's huge in Brooklyn. You know, in New York. America." Overdoing it. Tone it down, Arianna.

He stroked his beard. "Of course I've heard of glass shattering." He nodded at the man on the stage—a pale-skinned fellow in a flouncy shirt. "After this prick is done, you're on. What's your name, darling?"

"Arianna."

The man on stage gripped his microphone. Long, black hair hung over his translucent skin, and I caught a flash of fangs. "So what's the deal with humans? My wife is human. I'm on my tenth human wife, you know what I mean? I marry them when they're twenty and they've got cute arses, and sixty years later, it's like I've married the Crypt Keeper."

The crowd groaned. The audience sat around small round tables, nursing drinks. Most looked human. A few people wore flouncy shirts with ruffled collars—a few even in Elizabethan ruffs and velvet suits. But without seeing their fangs or sniffing them up close, it was hard to get a handle on which were vamps and which were fang-hags.

I took another step inside, surveying the layout of the place. A curtain hung at the back of the pub, forming a sort of makeshift stage. Maybe I could stake this comedian arsehole behind it. The handy thing about killing vampires was that they didn't leave a body behind —just a discreet pile of ashes, easy to miss in the dark.

"My wife is crazy." He spoke into the mic, and the feedback pierced the air. "You know, she tries to eat all natural. No GMOs, no preservatives. Then she gets these fake tits and Botox. So it's all well and good for her to eat quinoa, but she's poisoning my dinner with chemicals, innit? I don't want to drink that shit. Disgusting."

I loved it when my victims made it easy for me to forego the guilt.

"What are you booing me for?" he yelled.

I had no idea where Ruadan was, except that he was probably watching me from a dark corner.

With my box of glasses, I stalked behind the curtain.

It smelled of old beer and piss back there, and there wasn't much room—just enough for a small card table, a folding chair, and a few saggy costumes hanging on a crooked clothing rack. A door stood open to a unisex loo.

I dropped my glasses on the table, listening to the comedian haranguing the crowd about his human wife's tits. I pulled the stake from my cleavage, ready for action. I slid it behind my back so he wouldn't notice it.

As the crowd fell silent again, the raven-haired vampire stepped behind the curtain. His gaze swept up and down my body, and he flicked his black hair out of his eyes.

He licked his fangs. "Hello there, darling. You look like a fine bit of crumpet. You all right?"

"I'm fantastic." I smiled at him, then whipped out the stake and rammed it into his heart before he could see what was coming. His eyes widened with shock, and then his body blackened and cracked.

He collapsed into a pile of ash, and it clouded the air a bit. I tried not to breathe it in, disturbed by the idea of inhaling vampire particles into my lungs. I coughed.

One down, fourteen to go. I kicked the pile under the table, then tucked the stake back into my cleavage.

That was easy.

From the stage, the emcee's voice boomed over the pub.

"And our next act, directly from New York City—the Big Apple— is Arianna, with the hot new trend of glass smashing!"

Before heading out to the stage, I grabbed one of the stained dresses on the clothes rack—some sort of a fairy costume with a tulle skirt. I ripped the bodice until I had a long strip of fabric, and I wrapped it around my knuckles.

I flicked my hair over my shoulder, plastering a smile on my face. It probably came off like something between "deranged children's TV presenter" and the rictus of a clown-obsessed serial killer before he slit your throat. I had no idea how to put on a show. At least, I didn't know how to put on a show devoid of blood and severed limbs.

Already, I could feel the crowd tensing, as if my presence alone were putting them on edge. I scanned the audience, trying to pick out the real vampires from their goth admirers. I noticed a few fangs, but most kept their mouths shut. A few clearly looked like performers: an elderly woman slumped near the front, dressed in a Little Bo Peep burlesque outfit, nursing a martini; a scarecrow with a bongo drum.

How to lure the vampires out of this crowd of humans...

A small stool stood on the makeshift stage, and I dropped my box of glasses onto it. Then, I leaned into the microphone. "Hello, London!" I said in my American accent, and feedback pierced my ears.

A heavy silence greeted me. Little Bo Peep snorted dismissively. All right, old woman. I'll show you how it's done.

I cleared my throat. "I'm here to...smash glasses."

I hadn't thought much about what this would entail, but I was trying to improvise.

I took a deep, shaky breath. *Gods below,* could I just go back to killing people already?

When I scanned the room again, I caught a glimpse of violet eyes burning from an alcove. No one seemed to notice Ruadan. When I'd first met him, I found it hard to focus on him at all, as if his entire body were a blur of magic. Now, he stood out to me like a beacon.

As Ruadan came into focus through the whorls of his dark magic, I caught a distinct curl of his lips. Was he *smiling?* I'd never seen him smile. It was almost enough to put me right off my glass-smashing routine.

I wrapped the fabric a little tighter around my knuckles, then lifted the first glass. I tossed it in the air, giving the throw a bit of dramatic spin. As gravity pulled the glass down again, I slammed my fist into it. Shards of glass rained around me. A few people in the audience screamed—men, I was pretty sure.

I grabbed the next glass—a wineglass—and tossed that. As it fell, I drove my fist into the stem. That one didn't smash quite as spectacularly in the air as the first one had, but it did shatter on the floor. The act was still living up to its name.

Still—clearly, the pint glasses were better. So for my next trick, I grabbed one of the pint glasses. Before I threw it into the air, I surveyed the room. A blur of movement tightened my stomach. It wasn't Ruadan —I could still see him lurking in one of the alcoves, though his body was now completely alert. That meant it was one of the other novices, already here and killing vamps. And I'd only slaughtered one, so far.

All the vampires' eyes were on me—the insane woman on the stage. I'd given the other novices the perfect distraction to kill while I was stuck up here.

Baleros's twentieth law of power: Bring your enemy to you.

I unwrapped the cloth from my knuckles, then tossed the next pint glass in the air. Bare-fisted, I punched through it, and glass shattered around me. A few people screamed again, but some also clapped, and I was starting to feel a bit proud of my show. More importantly, I had just a hint of blood on my knuckles, which meant the vampires would be homing in on my scent.

Once a vampire had his senses locked on someone's particular smell, he wanted to pursue it.

They wouldn't rush for me. No—vampires who lived among humans had learned to restrain their wildest impulses. A vampire scenting blood was sort of like a man hitting on a beautiful woman in a bar. Usually, they took turns, to have a go one at a time, instead of just all crowding around at once. They were competitive, but they had a sense of propriety about it. It was, after all, a seduction.

I lifted a wineglass, throwing it high in the air, and I smashed it perfectly this time. Glass rained around me, and a few shards cut into my skin.

The humans were cheering louder now, a few even whooping. If I ever made it out of the Institute alive, I could have a glittering career ahead of me.

One more glass—twirling into the air, catching in the golden lights —and I shattered it with my fist.

The audience roared their approval.

Now, blood streaked over my fist, and I raised my hand, waving it at the crowd. Blood dripped onto the stage. "Thank you, London! That's all for tonight!"

My good mood was dampened by the sight of Maddan's red hair, slinking in the shadows. I'd recognize his stupid, lumbering gait anywhere. But despite his awkward movements, he moved silently, like he was supposed to. Cloaked by shadows, he staked a vamp.

Prince Knob-end of the Wanktonians was showing me up, and I had to act fast.

At least the vampires had my scent now, which meant they'd pursue me. Through the crowd's cheers, I heard the owner bark something about "cleaning up that fucking mess," but I ignored him, slinking back to the loo behind the curtain.

When the vamps approached me, I had to slay them before any of them realized I was fae. I didn't want them to catch on that I was a spell-slayer before I had the chance to stake them.

I stepped into the loo and closed the door, readying my stake. Then, I inched open the door to peek outside.

It was only a few seconds before the first vampire prowled behind the curtain. He was tall and lean, with blond hair, spectacles, and a hint of stubble. In his Batman T-shirt and jeans, he nearly looked human—apart from the glowing red veins in his pupils.

He sniffed the air, and I flung open the door. I leaned against the doorframe, cocking a hip—trying to look seductive, and no doubt failing. I held the stake behind my back with one hand. "Why, hello there, young man," I drawled in my American accent.

"Hi." He smiled, showing off his fangs. "I'm Mike. Your act was very impressive. Perhaps we could—"

BAM. I slammed my stake into his chest, and his eyes flew open with shock. His body blackened, then crumbled into ash on the floor.

I frowned down at the pile. I almost felt bad about Mike. He actually seemed kind of nice, but the Old Gods must have their sacrificial blood.

In any case, he was properly dead now. I kicked the ashy pile to the side of the doorframe, sort of mashing it into the stained rug so no one would notice it.

I stepped out of the loo, closing the door behind me.

It was another twenty seconds before the next vampire rounded the corner—he looked about twenty-five, much shorter than the last. He wore a fedora and a beaded necklace.

Once more, I held the stake behind my back. It was amazing how easily male vamps would ignore a stake behind your back if you showed off some cleavage and stuck out your boobs a bit.

Fedora narrowed his eyes. "What happened to the other bloke? I thought I saw someone come back here."

I nodded at the closed door. "I wouldn't let him drink from me. He's in there, crying into his Batman T-shirt."

Fedora smirked. "Of course he is. But vampires shouldn't ask for permission. That's not how we operate. That's why they call me the Tamer of Women. I'm a legend—"

A stake to his chest cut off the rest of his seduction pitch. His skin cracked, desiccating before my eyes as it turned to ash. I coughed in a bit of charred vamp.

Three down. Now I needed to move outside before they started to realize the vamps weren't coming back from behind the curtain. If I could lure—

The sound of shrieking interrupted my thoughts.

"Spell-slayers!"

Oh, balls. We'd been discovered.

I peered around the corner, and my breath caught in my throat as I realized one of the other novices had cocked it up again.

How long until the vampires realized that I was one of the slayers, too?

I gripped my stake.

The scene was chaos—vampires attacking humans, flinging them against walls, snatching them by their shirt collars to sniff them. They were trying to hunt out the fae. Given my position in the pub, I'd have to fight my way through a mob of fae-hunting vampires to get out.

My heart raced, and I scanned the pub until my gaze landed on Ruadan. In a cloud of inky magic, his violet eyes burned bright. He beckoned me toward him, summoning me to leave the pub with him. But maybe this was my opportunity to make up for the time I'd lost while I'd been stuck smashing glasses on stage.

Baleros's twenty-second law of power: Chaos is the opportunity to remake the world into your vision.

CHAPTER 10

One of the other novices had already outed us, which meant we weren't in the shadows anymore. Might as well make the most of it, use this as my chance to prove the Old Gods really *did* favor me. Just like in the old arena, my ability to kill would give me leverage.

As I started into the fray, I felt a whoosh of magic by my side—cold power pulsing over my skin. Then, I felt the warmth of Ruadan's body behind me. He reached out, grabbing my arm that held the stake.

He leaned down, whispering, "We need to go before they turn on you." His piney, apple-tinged scent surrounded me. For a brief, insane moment I had an urge to lean back into the security of his powerful body. Something about my days alone in the prison had left me desperate for another person's touch.

Instead, I shook my head. If he thought I was afraid of a few vampires, he really didn't know me at all.

"I need to win this," I said. "I need to get out of the prison you're keeping Ciara and me in. Killing gives me leverage. That's just how it's always been."

I ripped my arm from his grip, elbowed him hard in the chest, and then leapt onto one of the tables. I was heading for a vampire who'd started punching a human woman in the face. I slammed my stake down hard through the vamp's back, piercing his heart. As he crumbled to ash, I yanked out the stake, ready for my next victim.

From below, a blonde female vamp pointed at me. She screamed, "Spell-slayer!"

She leapt high into the air, arms outstretched. I brought my stake up hard into her heart. She burst into a cloud of ash in the air, and I inhaled a puff of blackened vampire.

Now, three male vamps were prowling closer. Too many to stake at once. Still, I'd take them all out, one at a time. I jumped off the table. When the first vampire ran for me—a large male with a shaved head—I grabbed his arm, using his velocity to hurl him into one of his friends. The move sent both crashing to the floor, and I whirled to drive my stake into the third one's heart. I sucked in a bit more ash as he crumbled.

The remaining vampires in the pub moved in closer, and a familiar feeling arced through my limbs—the glorious battle fury of the arena. It was a cold, brutal sensation, but in a way, it felt like home.

I ducked and pivoted, fending them off with an avalanche of fists and elbows—the occasional kick to the face. Whenever the chance presented itself, I slammed my stake into a vampire's heart.

Even without the lumen stone, my speed picked up. Battle rage sharpened my senses. Dust and ash rained down around me. Forget performing—this is what I was made for.

My attacks stalled when a vampire surprised me by gripping me by the hair, yanking back my head. I bashed my elbow into his gut. He bent over, holding his stomach. I slammed my stake through his back.

From the corner of my vision, I glimpsed Melusine staking a vamp who was coming for me. We were working pretty well together.

But the attack had thrown me off, and another knocked me to the ground. He was pinning me, clamping down on my wrists, so I brought my knee up hard into his groin, loosening his grip. I grabbed him by the back of the hair, pulling him off me. He smelled of petrol.

As I did, I caught sight of something that sent a jolt of fear racing through my blood. On his wrist, he had a tattoo of a bundle of sticks

—the fascia. It was Baleros's symbol. My body began shaking. I knew that symbol well. Baleros had once burnt it into my wrist as a brand.

"Who are you?" I shrieked.

"He's coming for you." The vampire grinned. "He burns for you."

My heart thumped against my ribs, my mind racing. The butterscotch candies in my prison cell, the strange blaze of fire when he'd died…Baleros was never going to be easy to kill. Was it possible that he was alive?

I slammed my fist into the vampire's face over and over, until blood poured from his nose and mouth. "Where is he?" I screamed. Fury ripped through my mind. I was losing it.

The vampire's head lolled. "Who?"

I sat on top of him, my knees pressing into his chest, and I punched him again. He reeked of petrol…

"Where is Baleros?" I hit him again. "Is he alive?" Maybe I needed to hold back a little, or he wouldn't be able to answer any of my questions. I was about to break his jaw.

"Can't say." He tried to punch me, but I grabbed his fist.

I twisted his arm until I heard the snap of bone. I twisted it some more until the vampire screamed.

My gaze flicked up, just long enough to determine that Melusine was managing to keep the other vampires at bay with her shadow-leaping and staking routine. That was handy, because I needed answers from this fucker.

Pressing my knees into his chest, I held the stake up higher in the air.

"Tell me where he is."

"No."

"I'm not going to kill you now. This will be much worse."

I slammed the stake into his shoulder, pinning his body to the floor. Without a direct hit to the heart, it would hurt like hells, but it wouldn't kill him. He screamed again, the sound of agony piercing the air.

It took me a moment to realize the vampire was holding a lighter in one hand. Then it took another second to connect the lighter to the scent of petrol burning my nostrils.

The vamp brought the lighter to his lapel, and his body burst into flames. I leapt off him with a yelp, the flames already licking at my bare legs. A few embers burned on my dress, and I smacked them out with my hand. Luckily, the fabric was still damp.

And that's how a vampire commits suicide.

When his body had decayed into an ashy pile, silence fell over the pub. All of the vampires had turned into piles of ash on the floor, and the humans had all fled.

Unfortunately, Maddan was still here.

He glared at me, his lip curled. "What *are* you, gutter fae? How do you kill the way you do? What sort of nightmarish demon is your other half?"

I shrugged, slipping the ashy stake back into my cleavage. I was trying to act casual, but my entire body was shaking from what I'd just seen. *Is Baleros alive?*

I crossed to Maddan, narrowing my eyes at him. "What am I? I don't know, but it seems like the Old Gods don't have a problem with it. Seems like they sort of favor me. I killed at least ten vamps here tonight. What about you?"

I was beginning to *really* get into this "favored by the Old Gods" situation.

"There is only one spot," said Melusine. "If you win every trial, what does that mean for us?"

Maddan dusted off his expensive top. "It will never happen. Grand Master Savus would never allow a thieving, rule-breaking, criminal gutter whore to become a Shadow Fae." He raised his hand, and that bright red magic flickered between his fingertips. "Savus will keep you in a filthy cage until it's time to bring down the axe on your neck, or exalt you in the Institute. But before he does, I want to find out what this animal really is. I want to be the one to interrogate you."

He stepped closer, and my stomach tightened at the sight of the red magic. That stuff had *really* hurt. Still, I didn't want to give him the satisfaction of seeing fear on my face, so I schooled my features to calm.

I crossed my arms. "Is it just me, or are you a little creepy about your obsession with me?"

A dark smile curled his lips. "Should I visit you in your hole again? I did so enjoy seeing you crouching in filth, at my feet. It's the way it should be." He took a step closer. "I liked hearing you moan when I hurled my bone-ripping magic at you...almost as much as I liked hearing you moan when I hit you with the lust magic. What would happen if I used both at once? It would be fun to find out."

Violet magic pulsed between the fingers on his other hand.

"Stop it, Maddan," said Melusine. Green magic glowed from her fingertips. "I know seventeen types of attack spells. Fire magic, disease spells, pestilence spells, which are totally different..."

I gritted my teeth, tuning her out as she listed several types of disease. I glared at Maddan, who toyed with the glowing magic at his fingertips.

Ruadan had promised me the Grand Master would have my head if I killed him. And if I tried to escape, he'd send every Shadow Fae in the world after me. So what was I supposed to do? Just allow him to torture me?

I narrowed my eyes, mentally calculating the best ways to hurt him. Slam his head into the table, then into my knee. I'd kick him in the chest; he'd fall back. Then, I'd take my stake—

Maddan hurled his magic at me—both red and violet at the same time.

Magic slammed into me, and I felt as if my body were exploding. Pain shot through my limbs—but strangely enough, it felt pleasurable at the same time. Waves of ecstasy shot through my muscles. A strange, euphoric agony surged, until my entire body was trembling. I dropped my stake.

I was starting to get the feeling that Savus was keeping me in the Institute not because of the Old Gods, but simply because he had a sick desire to torment me.

When I lifted my eyes, I had the satisfaction of watching Melusine hurl her green magic at Maddan.

Before my very eyes, I stared as lesions began to open on his skin.

"Syphilis," Melusine declared with pride. "Brought to Europe in the fifteenth century by Columbus. Symptoms include: skin lesions, fever, hair loss, rotting skin…"

Maddan's screams drowned out the rest of her description.

Pain and euphoria still pulsed through me, racking my body. I had a hard time focusing on Maddan's torment.

The intense wave of dark magic over my skin told me that Ruadan was nearby.

"Novices." His voice was glacial. "We are done here."

He prowled under the flickering neon lights of the bar. His footfalls crunched over shattered glass, and his shadow magic snaked around him like ink through water. I didn't know when I'd get the chance, but I had to tell him about Baleros. I just couldn't do it in front of anyone else. Maybe—just maybe—Baleros was alive. And perhaps someone from the Institute had tipped him off about my location. My money was on Maddan, of course, but who the hells knew?

Ruadan was right. I couldn't trust anyone.

As the magic pulsed through my body, painful and sensual at the same time, I glanced at Ruadan.

I couldn't trust him either. But I was fairly certain he wanted Baleros to stay dead as much as I did.

CHAPTER 11

In Savus's throne room, I stood between Maddan and
Melusine. With his silver arm, Savus gripped a skull-
topped scepter.

My mind roiled with panicked thoughts about Baleros.

He's coming for you. He burns for you.

Ruadan stood behind us, his dark magic whispering over my body.

I cast a quick look at Maddan. Regrettably, the Institute's healers
had already fixed his little syphilis issue. The lesions and rotting nose
had already cleared up.

I had not been offered the benefit of healers, and no one here
seemed to care if my body still burned from Maddan's magic. Half
lust, half pain, and all distracting.

I felt acutely aware of Ruadan's presence just behind me, and some
insane impulse had me wanting to back up into his body and press
myself against him.

For one thing, the lust magic was still swooping through my core,
heating my body. For another, I instinctively knew that Ruadan could
heal the remnants of the pain eating at my bones and muscles. But I
held my ground, and I clenched my fists to avoid letting Maddan
catch on to how much he'd screwed with me.

I sucked in a deep breath.

He burns for you. What did it all mean?

On the throne before us, Savus's body glowed with pale, silver light.

"I asked you to kill within the shadows," he began, "and once again you failed. You slaughtered every vampire, true, but you terrified the humans at the same time. What is the explanation for this?"

From behind, Ruadan stepped forward, and I felt the power of his magic snaking up my spine. It licked at my body, taking away some of my pain.

"One of your novices got sloppy," said Ruadan, "staking a vampire in the open—just by the entrance. The other vampires saw the attack, and pandemonium erupted."

Savus lifted his eyebrow, glaring at me. "Which novice?"

"Prince Maddan."

I could see Savus's jaw visibly tighten, and he narrowed his eyes. That was not the answer he wanted. "Are you sure it was the prince?"

"Yes." A cold fury imbued that one little word. Ruadan didn't like being questioned.

Of course, if it weren't for the crown, *he* would be the alpha.

Grand Master Savus cocked his head. "Fine. Your novice did well enough, today. Bring her back to her cell."

I stepped forward, rage simmering in my chest. "I'm not doing that."

Savus's eyes flashed with fury, and wavering candlelight glinted off his silver crown. "You don't have a choice. Unless we decide that you are fit to become a knight, which is unlikely, you are our prisoner. It's the cell or your head on the execution block."

I looked down at my fingernails, feigning nonchalance. "You can't execute me. It's clear now that the Old Gods favor me. Once again, I killed more than the other novices. You keep trying to throw obstacles in my way, but it's not working. I have no lumen stone. I had no money. I was in a cell for days, getting hit with Maddan's bone-shattering magic. No proper food. And I *still* killed more vampires than they did. The Old Gods favor me, and you can't defy them. They're the ones who keep you on the throne."

Maddan's face reddened. "Perhaps they're just keeping the gutter whore alive as a joke?"

I crossed my arms, desperate to get out of here and to speak to Ruadan. There were a few holes burned into the fabric of my dress from the would-be-assassin's explosion. The vampire was a deranged psycho, but gods-damn, that man was committed. He'd gone out on his terms. He'd committed to his task—abduct me, or die trying.

I was going out on my own terms, too, even if it meant self-destructing.

I cocked a hip, the pleasant smile still warming my features. "If I have to stay in that prison, perhaps I'll sit out the next trial. And the next one. I simply won't participate. That's not what the Old Gods want, is it?"

"What if I simply kill you?" he hissed.

I shrugged. "Then kill me." I was calling his bluff. If he killed me, he'd lose that precious silver crown of his, and anyone would be able to overthrow him.

His jaw tightened. "Perhaps you don't value your life. If that's not a deterrent, how about I torture you?"

"You're already letting Maddan torture me in the prison. I don't see how it could get worse. Maybe you should have kept a leash on him if you wanted better leverage."

Savus's low growl reverberated through my gut. "What do you want?"

"I just want what the other novices have. A lumen stone. A proper room for Ciara and me to sleep in. Oh, and some of that amazing fae food. That's all I ask for. What every other novice has."

Grand Master Savus cut a sharp look at Ruadan. "Bring her to the Liorcan Tower. She may sleep in one of the servants' rooms. Her human will remain in a separate room. And please understand that our guards will be watching you at all times." He snarled. "No lumen stone. This is as far as I'm willing to bend before I rip your body to pieces."

Well, it was better than the devil's arsecrack, I supposed.

* * *

THROUGH AN ARCHED STONE HALLWAY, I walked by Ruadan's side. Candlelight danced over the hall, gilding his perfect features. He towered over me, casting me in his shadow.

Two guards trailed behind us, prepared to listen to anything we might say.

I couldn't quite explain the deep sense of betrayal I felt whenever I looked at him. After all—I'd betrayed *him*. I'd stabbed him, and run off with his precious lumen stone. But then we'd worked together to take down Baleros, and for some idiotic reason, I'd hoped it had meant something. I'd hoped for forgiveness.

A pit opened in the hollow of my stomach. He'd done a few nice things for me in the past—blankets, healing. Letting me keep the lumen stone. Allowing me to live. A pathetic part of me had desperately wanted to believe that he'd done those things because he'd cared.

Now that I'd returned to the Institute, I realized how stupid that was. He'd killed his last two novices. He'd lured me back here, only to throw me in a prison. He called me "gutter fae" instead of using my name. He'd left me to rot in the Palatial Room, healing me just enough so that I didn't die. He wanted me punished as much as Savus did.

My jaw tightened. When did I start giving a shit if anyone called me "gutter fae"? This wasn't like me. Something about him just got under my skin and drove me crazy.

Ruadan paused at a door, and it opened into a tiny room. This wasn't like the other rooms I'd seen. It was more like the size of a closet, with a single bed in the center. A plain, red rug lay on the stone floor near the bed.

I had no bath in here. Still, an archway opened into a tiny bathroom, so that was a step up from sleeping in my own filth.

I crossed into the bathroom, irritated to find that it was basically just a hole in the stone, with a bowl of water next to it for handwashing.

I breathed in deeply. The bedroom itself contained only two objects—the bed and the rug.

One of the guards—a broad-shouldered man with a long, aquiline nose and golden hair—crossed into the room. It took me a moment to recognize him, but he was the same guard I'd briefly charmed the last time I was at the Institute. He was the drunk one who'd nicknamed me *Viscountess von Tittington.* Creepy, but oddly endearing, and at least he didn't hate me.

Ruadan gestured at him. "Ealdun here will be your guard. He will remain in the room with you."

I stared at them. "In the room with me?"

Ealdun lifted his chin. "Grand Master Savus's orders." I noticed he wasn't calling me *Viscountess von Tittington* in front of Ruadan. In fact, he was making every effort not to look at me.

I shrugged. "Fine. Suit yourself. I hope you enjoy my singing, Ealdun, because I do love Taylor Swift."

"Enjoy the gutter fae," said Ruadan. He turned, stalking out the door in a blur of dark shadows.

I bit down hard on the urge to scream at him that he was a snobby twat. Truthfully, my heart tugged at his parting shot. I shoved my disappointment deep down inside, willing myself to forget about it.

I'd already known what he was like. I'd told myself that trusting him was a mistake—that he'd lead me to the execution block, and the betrayal would kill me before the blade ever did. I'd been right.

Fatigue pulsed through my body, and the cold stone floor was calling to me. When I wasn't sleeping in a festering dung hole, I slept on a stone floor.

I began singing—off key—as I pulled off my boots.

I took a little pleasure at the grimace on Ealdun's face as I sang. I had nothing to change into, so I curled up on the floor, still wearing my black dress. It was covered in rainwater, vampire ash, and my own blood. I *really* wanted a bath.

I was on the other side of the bed from Ealdun, shielded from his view on the stone floor. Maddan's magic still flickered through my veins—hot and cold, pleasure and pain, and the intensity overwhelmed me. I felt as if my body were clenching and unclenching, racing with sensations. My nipples chafed against the filthy fabric of my dress.

Even so, my eyes floated shut, and I tried to calm myself with thoughts of tree-dappled hills—just like the ones I'd dreamt about in the cell.

I didn't even notice as I drifted off to sleep.

I awoke to the scent of pine, and a warm hand on my back. Violet eyes pierced the darkness. A heavy rain hammered the windows outside. For just a moment, I wanted to wrap my arms around Ruadan, to let his warmth and his magic soothe me.

Then, rage and that sense of betrayal welled in my chest as I stared up at him. Humiliatingly, tears pricked my eyes, and I fought the urge to punch him in his beautiful face.

"How did you get in here?" I whispered.

He brushed his hand over my waist, pulling the remaining bone-shattering magic from my body. I sighed with relief, closing my eyes again for a moment.

Then, I met his gaze again. "Have you come to call me a gutter fae again?" As soon as the words were out of my mouth, I regretted them. I'd just let him know that his words had gotten to me, when I'd been trying to pretend that I didn't care.

Baleros's first law of power: Knowledge gives you control.

"Don't raise your voice too high," he whispered. He nodded at the other side of the room.

I peered over the bed, where I found Ealdun slumped on the floor, sleeping.

"What happened to him?" I asked in a whisper.

"I made him fall asleep. The same thing I've done to Maddan every night to keep him away from your cell."

"You've been putting Maddan to sleep? Why?"

Ruadan raised his perfect eyebrows. "Because I didn't want him to torture you anymore."

I took a deep breath. More confusion. "Why are you here?"

"I saw the vampire immolate himself. What happened?"

I sucked in a deep, shaky breath. "On his wrist, I caught a glimpse of Baleros's tattoo. He said, 'he's coming for you.' And 'he burns for you.' He works for Baleros. Not to mention the fact that…" I paused, not wanting to explain the whole butterscotch thing. "Someone was screwing with me when I was in the Palatial Room, tossing me little symbols of my relationship with Baleros. Is there any chance that monster could still be alive?"

Shadows flitted through Ruadan's eyes. "I can't entirely explain why his body ignited after I killed him. But I did kill him. Are you sure it was Baleros's symbol?"

I lifted the sleeve of my dress, showing him the brutal scar on the underside of my wrist. "Oh, I'd know his symbol anywhere. I had the same mark on my skin. Except, because I was a gladiator, it was a brand instead of a tattoo."

A powerful pulse of Ruadan's dark magic thrummed over my skin, and shadows pooled in his eyes. It seemed the topic of Baleros provoked some kind of primal rage in Ruadan.

"What happened to yours?"

"I cut it off, obviously. I didn't want to live with his brand."

"Why not?"

I gritted my teeth. "*Why not?* Are you insane? Because he's a monster who made me think I was a monster. I didn't want him to control me any more than he already does. I mean, any more than he did. I've always wanted him dead. What the hells do you think?" I willed my heartbeat to slow, realizing that I'd lost control of my emotions.

Ruadan's icy magic slid over my skin. "You say you wanted him dead, and yet you did his bidding, and you allowed him to live in the arena." Anger flickered in his violet eyes, and the ice had returned to his voice.

"Why do you hate him so much? Because he turned on the Shadow Fae?"

A sharp breath. "Something like that."

I could tell by the hesitation in his response that it wasn't the full answer. Moreover, I'd turned on the Institute of the Shadow Fae, and he hadn't killed me.

Whatever the case, Ruadan was hiding important things from me. He trusted me no more than I trusted him.

CHAPTER 13

"You haven't explained to me why you failed to kill him. I brought the darkness, like you asked." A ripple of dark magic thrummed over my skin. "But you didn't even try. Why?"

Knowledge gives you power over a person. How much power did I want Ruadan to have? I supposed he already knew I cared about Ciara, considering I'd insisted on bringing her here. He could already use her as leverage if he wanted.

"He took Ciara," I said. "He was holding her in a cage, and he was going to kill her. I didn't kill Baleros in the arena because I was there to save Ciara, and in the moment, I could only do one or the other. I didn't have an iron weapon, and I needed answers from him. As soon as I knew where she was, I went after her."

Silver glinted in his eyes, and his magic stroked the back of my neck. "You stabbed me to protect Ciara."

"Yes. I still think *stabbed* is a bit much. It didn't kill you. It was more like a…you know, like a setback, I'd call it."

"You setbacked me in the chest, with a knife," he said, with a straight face.

I almost wondered if that was a joke, but Melusine had warned me that the fae nobility were incapable of joking.

"Did you consider using iron?" he asked.

Only the rain filled the silence, until I added, "Let's not dwell on what might have been. I'm alive. You're alive. Let's move forward."

He cocked his head, studying me closely. I had the impression he was reconsidering something.

He reached for me, lifting my wrist, and he traced his fingertips over the scarred skin where I'd cut off Baleros's brand. The feel of his fingertips on my skin sent an unwelcome rush of tingles through my body. I had a hard time reconciling this gentle touch with the Ruadan who called me gutter fae and dragged me over stones.

"You hate Baleros." His intonation suggested this was some sort of revelation.

"Of course I hate him. He's been messing with my head since I was fourteen."

Shadows slid through Ruadan's eyes, and his fingers tensed on my skin. "That's how old you were when he enslaved you?"

"Yes."

I realized he was still holding my wrist, still tracing the scarred skin. Why did that scar fascinate him so much? Whatever the case, the feel of his gentle fingertips over such a vulnerable part of my body made my cheeks warm.

Gods-damned incubi.

"And you think Baleros could still be alive? That he sent an assassin after you?" He was leaning in closer, his velvety voice, now sensual, slipping around my skin like a caress.

What was with this guy? Were his hot and cold moods just another method of control?

I stared at the hypnotic swirl of his fingers over my skin. Somehow, I knew the truth deep within my bones. Baleros would never be easy to kill. "I think he's alive. I think he's working with someone from the Institute, someone who tried to screw with my mind in prison. Someone who tipped him off about the trial tonight. Obviously, my money is on Maddan, because he's one of the worst living creatures on Earth. But the vampire lit himself on fire before I got the chance to torture him for information, so that's just a guess."

Ruadan was gently pulling me closer by my wrist—the gesture almost protective. "You've got a guard in the room with you, and more outside the door. In theory, you're safe. But Baleros has sent his spies into the Institute before. It's not entirely outside the realm of possibility that some of the guards could be working for him."

"He's sent spies here? Into the Institute?"

"The last two novices I executed."

My eyes widened. "Oh." Slowly, understanding was beginning to dawn in my mind. "That's why you killed them."

"When I first saw you fight Aengus, I knew that Baleros had trained you. I considered killing you. Then, I thought maybe you would lead me to him."

I swallowed hard. "I get it. You thought I was a drunk, undisciplined gutter fae slob, but you still wanted me here to lead you to Baleros."

"Once I learned you'd been a gladiator, it changed things a little. Not the slob part, I still think that's true. But I understood you were not a spy. You were a slave."

My cheeks flushed. "Not a fan of that term."

"Baleros had ways of controlling his gladiators through mental torment. I started to think maybe you'd turn against him if given the chance. In the arena, you nearly did. Until you let him live."

"Is that why you've been…" I gestured into the air, unwilling to finish my sentence. There was no way in hells I was letting him know he'd *hurt my feelings.*

"What?"

It was embarrassing how much I'd wanted it all to be an act, and it really had nothing to do with anything. We had a common goal: kill Baleros. That was it. Were those *tears* stinging my eyes? Mortifying.

I turned away from him. *Caring about people is a liability.* "Never mind. You can fuck off now. You interrupted my sleep. And don't come back into my room without my permission. I don't need your unwelcome intrusions. Do you understand?"

He dropped my wrist, and my entire body suddenly felt cold.

I waited until I felt the whoosh of his shadowy magic over my skin.

When I turned back, Ruadan was gone. A pit opened in my chest, and I shivered. I lay back down on the cold stone floor and closed my eyes. But this time, dreams of Emain didn't enter my mind.

Instead, an old memory rose in my skull—one I'd long tried to forget. A field, rotten with fae bodies…

My eyes snapped open again, and I stared at the ceiling. Maybe I'd just stay awake tonight.

With Ruadan gone, I realized he'd left something behind for me—my bug-out bag. This time, there was no way it was an accident. He'd actually gone into the prison to fetch it for me.

Was he being *nice?*

I crushed the dangerous thought as soon as it entered my mind.

CHAPTER 14

*E*aldun poured me another measure of whiskey. I needed the drink, considering I'd been stuck in this tiny room for the past twenty-four hours. While the other novices had been training, I'd been locked in here with no one for company but my guard. Worse, he'd alternated with a much more unpleasant guard who tried to insist that I call him "Master."

I supposed it was part of my ongoing punishment, but I had no bath in here, and no clothes to change into. I was still wearing the ashy, blood-stained dress from the last trial, and I'd just stopped wearing underwear all together. I did my best to wash with the little bowl of water, while Ealdun repeatedly asked if he could help.

Unlike *Master,* Ealdun loved to chat. After one day, I knew that he never wanted to have children, that he liked thongs on a woman but women didn't wear them enough these days, and that he had night-mares about being smothered by mermaids' breasts—and also longed for such a death.

He wasn't the *worst* guard in the world, given that we had similar hobbies. Namely, whiskey and vulgarity.

Still, none of this was helping me get ready for the next trial. In fact, all the sitting around and drinking was basically the opposite of training for combat.

"I'm not sure I'm going to survive my next trial, Ealdun."

"Nonsense. Whiskey will fortify you. It's fortifying me. I've got a bit of a cold." Ealdun sniffed. "Whiskey's good for a cold."

I frowned. "Is it?"

He nodded. "Kills the bug, innit. Gets the bug drunk, and the bug dies of all the alcohol." He knocked back his shot. "They can't process alcohol, right? Bugs don't have the right sort of livers for it."

Ealdun really wasn't the brightest bulb, but I just nodded rather than arguing.

"My dog Scroton has a bit of whiskey every morning."

I stared at him. "First of all, you have a dog named Scroton? Please tell me that's an Ancient Fae word."

"It is, actually."

"What does it mean?"

He sipped his drink. "Scrotum."

"Right." Despite all the alcohol, tension gripped my entire body. As much as I enjoyed sitting around and drinking whiskey with idiots, a cloud of doom was hanging over me. I had to pass the next trial, or I faced a certain and excruciating death at the hands of Savus, or perhaps Ruadan. And what would happen to Ciara if I died? I wouldn't be here to protect her. I *had* to exploit every advantage I could.

So I poured Ealdun another shot. The man had a tolerance to rival Hannibal's elephants, and we were now on day two of my attempt to get him completely wankered.

I had a powerful buzz going on, but I'd only been drinking one shot for every three of his. Any more alcohol and I'd be unable to do anything.

I filled his glass to the top. "Best get that bug nice and drunk so he doesn't do any damage."

Ealdun mumbled under his breath, and he took another sip. He was muttering something about how there were two kinds of women:

those who took it up the bum, and those who did not, but I did my best to ignore his binary classification of the entire female gender.

When his head lolled, his eyes closed, and I knew I had my chance to sneak out of there.

Baleros's seventeenth law of power: Never let an opportunity go to waste.

I wanted to find Ruadan to learn what I could for my next trial. Ever since I'd told him, "Fuck off and don't come back in my room," I'd regretted it a bit. Yes, I'd been angry at him. He'd hurt my feelings, and I didn't want to let him do it again.

But this was bigger than hurt feelings. This was my survival. And whether or not I liked it, my life—and Ciara's—depended on Ruadan's help.

When Ealdun's snores began to echo off the stones, I crouched down on the floor.

It hadn't taken long for me to find the way that Ruadan had entered the room. After my temper had cooled, I'd simply lifted the rug.

He was the Wraith, yes, but he couldn't transport himself through material things like walls and windows. He'd actually just walked into the room—albeit in his silent and stealthy Wraith-like way.

While Ealdun snored, I pulled up the rug. Inset into the stone, lay a wooden trapdoor. I'd found it during the night, but I hadn't been able to risk lifting it without Ealdun noticing.

The trapdoor creaked, revealing a ladder that led down one level into darkness. A quick glance at Ealdun told me he was still asleep.

I jammed my hand into my bug-out bag, and pulled out my head-lamp. I flicked it on. After drying out, the trusty thing was working again.

With the light beaming from my head, I slipped into the hole, climbing down the ladder in my bare feet.

The dank tunnel air whispered over my bare thighs. At the bottom of the ladder, my feet hit wet, slimy rock. The white circle of light from my head illuminated glistening stone walls. Here, the air hung heavy with the smell of moss and mildew, and maybe a bit of fungus. I regretted not having slipped my boots on, but I'd been too tipsy to think of it.

Down here in the tunnel, I could feel myself stumbling. The combination of whiskey and the sludge on the floor made it hard to balance.

Still, I was starting to home in on the scent I'd been trying to track. Pine, a hint of apples. For whatever reason, Ruadan's smell now stood out to me among all the others.

Locked iron grates interrupted the ceiling in some places, and light pierced the cracks, flecking the stone floor.

At last, the scent of pine and apples grew more powerful, and I knew I was drawing closer to him. But when the sound of footfalls began echoing off the walls, my heart slammed against my ribs. I flicked off my headlamp, my muscles tensing. I wasn't alone down here. Who in the seven hells was that? I had nothing to use as a weapon, so I hoped I could take them with my bare hands.

Time for a quick retreat.

I whirled, breaking into a run on the slick floor. I nearly slipped a few times, but I righted myself. I hadn't gotten very far when a rush of cold magic slid over my skin—then, a powerful arm hooked around my waist.

When he pulled me closer, I slowed down long enough to breathe in the scent of pine. Ruadan's powerful arms enveloped me, and I felt strangely vulnerable in his grasp.

I willed my heartbeat to slow. "Ruadan. Fancy meeting you here."

I flicked my headlamp back on.

"Arianna. I was hoping you'd come for me." He was still holding on tight to me, his grip confusing me with its warmth and protectiveness. "I was just on my way to see you." His deep voice stroked my skin.

"Even after I forbade you from intruding?"

"Yes. Whether or not the intrusion is unwelcome, you need me to survive your next trial."

"Right. Well, that's why I came to find you, as it happens."

Ruadan loosened his grip on me, and he turned back in the other direction. "You reek of whiskey."

"That's not all I reek of. I'm hoping to take a bath in your room."

His thrilling magic snaked over my body.

Ruadan shook his head. "Savus can't know that I'm helping you."

"Why?"

Shadows lashed the air around him, sucking up all the light from my headlamp.

"The Grand Master must think that I hate you," Ruadan explained. "If he believes I favor you, he'll continue to find worse and worse ways to torment you."

I frowned. "I don't understand."

Ruadan shook his head. "He hates me, and he wants to crush anything and anyone that I might…favor. That's why I couldn't heal you fully—Maddan had to think you were still injured. It's why I've had to create a spectacle of derision for you. I need Savus to believe that it's real."

"Why does he hate you?"

His jaw tightened, and a heavy silence filled the room. For a moment, I was certain Ruadan had lapsed into his characteristic "vow of silence" trick, until he finally answered. "Grand Master Savus and I have a history. That's all."

That illuminated almost nothing, but what did I expect? It was Ruadan, after all.

I narrowed my eyes at him. "When you dragged me down the corridor and threw me in the Palatial Room, did you leave the backpack with me on purpose?"

"I rarely make mistakes."

"And when you called me 'gutter fae'—"

"It's important that the others think I'm disdainful of you, or things will become much worse for you."

I loosed a breath I'd been holding. Hearing that his cruelty had all been for show felt like a weight off my shoulders, and I hated that I cared so much.

"It'll be fine if I take a bath and change. I'll convince Ealdun that he got me the clothes I asked for. He won't remember a thing from tonight."

We reached a trapdoor, and Ruadan paused. He pushed on it, and it slammed open into his room. Then, he leaned down and grabbed me by the waist. He hoisted me up into the light.

My head was definitely swimming from the booze, and I toppled over a little, onto the stone floor. By the time Ruadan pulled himself inside, I'd managed to right myself, straightening my hair like I was totally composed.

Ruadan closed the door behind him. "You bypassed Ealdun."

"He drinks a lot. He's snoring over the table right now."

"That's why I chose him as your guard. He's terrible at his job. And as you might have guessed, I chose your room strategically."

"I don't suppose you have a change of clothes that would fit me?"

Ruadan crossed his arms, his body growing still. "You really risked coming here just for a bath?"

"No, I also want to learn about my next trial. I'd very much like to avoid that whole iron pincers situation."

His electrifying magic kissed my skin. "The next task will be difficult for you."

Great. "Fill me in while I'm bathing."

I'm not sure at which point I'd decided that I liked being naked around Ruadan—possibly it had been when I'd been in his bed, hepped-up on lust magic, and I'd felt the way his body had tensed. Then, there was the bath where his body had again become rigid with tension.

As far as I could tell, he lived to brood, and I liked ruining it for him.

So as I started across to the bathroom, I tugged up the hem of my dress, making sure he got a view of my bum. He might be a stronger fighter than I was, but his pent-up desire gave me some power over him, and I could practically *feel* his gaze drinking in my body as I pulled off the dress.

Completely naked, I let my hips sway a little as I crossed into the bathroom, and Ruadan's magic whispered over my skin, raising the hair on my nape. Ice frosted the air as a pulse of his magic billowed through the room, and my nipples hardened. A smile curled my lips.

I was *definitely* getting to him.

Once through the arched doorway, I tossed the dress on the floor next to the tub, which was already burbling with spring-fed warm water. Steam rose from the surface. I stepped into the hot bath, the water reddening my legs.

I slipped all the way in, closing my eyes. I didn't really want to have to leave here and listen to Ealdun's snoring all night, but I suppose I'd have to.

"Are you coming in?" I asked.

"While you bathe?" The torches in the room flickered on and off.

Ruadan crossed into the room, his movements as predatory as ever, and he refused to look at me. Then, his dark magic snaked through the air. It curled around the torch flames until it snuffed all the light from the room. With his entrance, he'd smothered every light particle.

I let out a long sigh. "Now I don't know where the soap is. You'll have to come over and help me."

"You're trying to tempt me. Is it just me, or do you thrive in chaos?"

"Chaos is an opportunity. Don't you know that? Anyway, I don't know what the problem is—oh that's right. The whole virginity thing. No wonder you get angry so easily."

"For the love of the gods." Irritation laced his voice. "I'm not a virgin. I've only been here fifteen years."

"Right. Just celibate. And why is it that you have to be celibate?"

"Grand Master Savus's orders."

"He's an arsehole."

"He believes self-denial encourages mental fortitude. Incidentally, that brings us to the next trial. You will need mental fortitude."

It was unfortunate that he couldn't see my eye roll in the dark. "I thought you said I'd be bad at it. I'm perfectly mentally strong."

"You lack discipline. You showed up drunk tonight, and within minutes you were also naked."

"I mean, yes..." The bath felt amazing, and I clumsily felt around the stone rim of the tub until my hand slid over the bar of soap.

"Naked and drunk. I can see why that would look bad on paper. In my defense, I have had a hell of a week."

"You solve most of your problems with violence. You were unable to withstand the gorta without slaughtering him. You stabbed—sorry —stopped my heart with a silver setback in my aorta."

Spring water burbled into the tub, pooling between my thighs. "Are we just pointing out each other's flaws now? Because as far as I can tell, you're a giant killjoy with no friends."

"You surround yourself by those weaker than you, because they can't control you, and you use them to distract you from things you'd rather forget."

I gritted my teeth, now furiously scrubbing at my arms with the soap. "Look, criticize it all you want, but I *did* pass the gorta trial." I inhaled deeply, willing my body to relax in the warm spring water. "So what is this trial, another hunger fae?"

"No. It's called a gwyllion. A female fae who came to London from Snowdonia. You will be asked to fetch something from her lair. And when you do, she will torment you with your worst fears and memories. Your mission will be to withstand the mental torture for as long as it lasts. You cannot run from her."

For once, I was quiet, soaping my body in silence. Unfortunately, Ruadan was right. I would not be good at that. This was not like killing vampires, and I did not welcome the idea of a Welsh mountain fae rooting around in my mind.

CHAPTER 15

"How do I prepare for it?" I asked, after a moment.

"The same way you prepare for anything," he said. "You practice."

Even in the warmth of the bath, my body was tensing. There were many things I'd rather not think about. I ran the soap over my legs, scrubbing harder, wearing the damn bar down to a nub. Still, I would show Ruadan that I had plenty of mental fortitude. "How?"

"I can help you summon your darkest memories."

"You can?"

"I'm a demigod of darkness."

"Oh, right." I splashed water over my shoulders, dreading what was to come. "Is that Ancient Fae for 'brooding killjoy with no friends'? Sounds like the same idea."

"Get out of the bath."

"You're very bossy, you know that?" Still, I complied with his orders, and I stood.

Water dripped down my naked body, and I squeezed out my hair into the tub. I hadn't planned ahead with a towel or anything like that, so my wet feet slapped against the stone floor. Maybe it was the whiskey, but I felt an overwhelming urge to move closer to Ruadan.

Barefoot, I crossed over to him until I was standing right next to his heat. Warmth radiated off his body onto my damp skin. I inched just a little closer, until my breasts brushed against his chest.

His magic rushed off him in a wave of power, flowing over my skin. Then—for just a moment—his fingers were on my waist. Instantly, my back arched.

I couldn't see him in the dark, but I looked up at him anyway.

With a low growl, he snatched his hand away. "Get dressed." His voice was curt, commanding.

A smile curled my lips. And because I was me, I inched just a little closer, pressing my body against his. His muscles completely tensed, and it was like standing pressed up against a stone wall. "But I don't have any clothes," I protested.

He pulled away from me, stalking out of the bathroom, taking his darkness with him. The shadows snapped back into his body as he prowled to his dresser. I stared at him from behind, frowning at his arms. He was wearing a black T-shirt, and red scars slashed across the back of his powerful biceps.

"What happened to your arms?" It must have been iron—the only substance he wouldn't heal from easily.

He didn't answer. Instead, he pulled open the drawer of his bureau.

"Someone attacked you with iron," I said. "How did they manage to get that close?"

He selected a black shirt from his drawer and held it out without looking at me.

Whatever had happened to him, I felt bad about it, so I'd stop tormenting him with my boobs for now. I crossed to him, grabbing the shirt from his hand, and I pulled it over my head. It reached about midway down my thighs. My wet hair dampened the shoulders. "Thanks. You can be helpful sometimes. When you're not locking me in dung holes and whatnot."

"We have work to do." He turned to me, silver glinting in his eyes. "Sit down. On the floor."

I did as instructed, planting my bottom on the cold flagstones. I hugged myself. Ruadan's room always felt a little colder than the rest of the Institute. That was his magic, I guess.

I gazed up at him. "I am at a disadvantage for this task. I think I have more terrible memories than most."

"You'll get through it."

I sucked in a deep breath. I didn't want to do this, but I wanted to prove to him that I could. Maybe I lacked discipline, but I wanted to impress Ruadan.

His magic began darkening the room, curling around the flickering candles and snaking over the rays of moonlight that beamed in from the windows. The shadows pulsed in and out, like the breath of a living thing.

Already, a pit was opening in my chest, and coldness seeped into my blood. I shivered, my teeth chattering. Ruadan's power washed over me, and my blood pounded in my ears.

I closed my eyes, listening to the sound of my own heartbeat. Then, darkness slammed into me, burying me alive. My heart raced, and I felt like I was suffocating, as if I needed to claw at the dirt above my head. I gasped, a gnawing void widening in my chest. Ruadan was killing me.

Then, light pierced the darkness—sun rays filtering through oak leaves, my heart pattering like a frightened rabbit. Oh gods, not this...

I wasn't really there. I needed to remember, this was just a memory. It wasn't real. Not anymore.

I was running barefoot over the mossy forest soil, my feet crunching on twigs. They'd come for us—the invaders from another land. He'd told me to run, but I couldn't just leave them there. I had to go back. Sweat dampened my skin, and my heart was racing out of control. I turned, heading back in the other direction. I pumped my arms hard, my breath coming in short, sharp gasps. Panic raked its claws through my heart. But the smell of blood, of death was growing stronger, filling my nostrils. I knew what I was about to find there. I didn't want to see it.

Anger rose in me. Why did I have to remember this? Why was Ruadan forcing me to relive this?

When I breached the clearing, horror slammed me in the chest. There, staining the fields in red, a legion of dead fae soldiers, fed the earth with their blood…

An ache built in my chest, cutting me so sharply I thought I might die. I had to stop this.

Fury erupted, and I lashed out with violence, my knuckles hitting flesh, striking and striking—

The illusion fell away from me as Ruadan caught my wrists.

My body was trembling, my legs ready to give way. My knuckles ached like I'd been punching walls. Ruadan stared down at me, his cold gaze slicing right through me. He didn't say a word, but he didn't need to. I knew what he was thinking—something along the lines of "you lack discipline."

I ripped my hands from his grasp and gritted my teeth. "Let's go again."

"Sit down." That irritating, commanding tone.

My body trembled as I took a seat on the floor again.

My chest was heaving, nostrils flared. Ruadan was only trying to prepare me, but right now, I wanted to setback Grand Master Savus right in the face. I could kill things. Assassins were supposed to kill things. So why did I need to revisit the horrible things from my past?

Once more, Ruadan's magic breathed darkness into the room, and the shadows slowly pulsed—in and out, in and out, the movement slow and hypnotic. I needed him to know that he was wrong, that I was perfectly disciplined. I was capable of controlling myself.

The air around me cooled, until my breath misted in front of my face. Then, the blanket of darkness smothered me, burying me underground. Panic surged, and I gasped for breath. A cool tongue of shadowy magic licked up my spine. My lungs felt heavy, the darkness all-encompassing.

Then, fire flashed before my eyes. A yawning void had opened within my chest, eating at me from the inside out. The arena's torches cast wavering light over the empty stone seats, the red dirt. There was no audience. A dark power vibrated through my body, trembling along my bones, and the sound of the ocean roared in my ears.

No audience. No, today Baleros had wanted me to train. It had been an experiment, really. What would happen if he set fourteen opponents against me? If there were enough people to fight me, could I be taken down?

I felt weightless, unmoored from the earth, as if I were floating in space. Now falling. Death coiled around me.

Horror slid through my gut as I stared down at what I'd done. Fourteen opponents lay dead at my feet, their skin turning black. Blood trickled from their mouths, their ears. I knew one of them, a fire demon named Elish. Baleros had kept him in a cage not far from mine. Once, when I'd been starving after a week in the metal box, he'd tried to pass over his bowl of gruel to me. It had tipped over in the dirt, but I hadn't forgotten the attempt.

I screamed within my own mind, the sound curling around the inside of my skull until I couldn't hear my own thoughts anymore.

I wouldn't have killed Elish if I could have helped it. But this was a power I couldn't control.

Sometimes I didn't mind killing, but this—this controlled me. Darkness had pooled in my mind, and then nothing but death.

All the breath had left my lungs.

A slow clap filled the arena, and Baleros crossed over the dirt.

"Arianna. I knew you were special, but I never imagined you possessed this level of evil. Now do you understand why you must be kept in a cage? Why a monster like you must be controlled?"

My fingers twitched, rage surging sharp and hot until it burned away the illusion. And there it was again—that terrible feeling of power trembling up my bones, the sound of the ocean roaring in my ears. A wild, uncontrollable force of destruction, threatening to break free.

Ruadan was standing there, staring down at me in his billowing cloud of shadow magic. Tendrils of magic snaked over his stupidly beautiful face. So calm, so controlled, his gaze was pure ice. Gritting my teeth, I willed my heartbeat to slow again. I needed to stay in control.

I rose on unsteady feet, and I crossed to Ruadan. Maybe he could see I was about to lose it, because he grabbed onto me, pulling me in close, and his soothing magic began stroking my skin, warming me. My breathing slowed, my heartbeat calmed as he pulled me in tight against him. He ran a hand down the back of my hair, soothing me, and his piney scent wrapped around me. For a moment, I almost had the urge to rest my head against his chest, to close my eyes.

Then, he leaned down and whispered in my ear. "What are you?"

I froze. I couldn't let him know.

I pulled away from him, staring at his face. "We're done now." My voice was so cold I nearly didn't recognize it. "You don't know what you're playing with. Don't come to my room again."

He didn't say a thing as I pulled up the wooden trapdoor in the floor. I dropped down into the darkness, my footfalls echoing.

I hurried away from him as fast as I could. Maybe he was right. Maybe I lacked discipline. For some reason, the thought of disappointing him made my chest clench. But the truth was, Ruadan had no idea what would happen if he pushed my limits too far, and I didn't need any more terrible memories to haunt my worst nightmares.

CHAPTER 16

$\mathcal{E}$aldun lay slumped over the table, his snores echoing off the stone walls. If it weren't for the line of guards stationed outside my room, I'd be able to escape.

Tonight, as requested, Ealdun had brought me a piece of paper and a pencil. I'd told him I needed it to play tic-tac-toe to kill the boredom.

Oddly enough, I'd started to think of him as a friend. He'd actually been a perfect gentleman, and he'd been delighted to have an audience for his interminable Scroton stories.

Ealdun's snores rang out as I crossed to the secret trapdoor. I pulled it up, and slid my legs into the hole, jumping down. I hit the damp stone floor with a soft thud.

After a few nights in my little room, I'd convinced Ealdun to fetch me some clothes. I now wore a pair of black leggings and a dark shirt. Much more respectable than the T-shirt and bare arse I'd been sporting for a few days.

This time in the tunnel, I wasn't heading for Ruadan, but for Ciara's room. I wasn't sure exactly where to find it, but I tuned into her smell—wildflowers and a bit of musk.

If I told the Shadow Fae that I wanted Ciara released, I'd be giving the game away. They'd guess my next move—that I was planning an escape to avoid my execution, and I wanted my friend out of here. I couldn't telegraph my actions that way. Instead, she needed to escape while I was *at* the trial, before they knew what was coming.

As I walked, I traced my fingertips over the damp wall.

Despite my warnings that he needed to leave me alone, Ruadan had returned one night after another. He'd slipped into the room while I slept, put my guard to sleep, then tried to convince me to practice my mental discipline skills. I kept telling him *no*.

I knew I was proving him right, that I was only demonstrating my lack of discipline, and a flash of fury lit me up. Still, I couldn't let myself completely lose control.

I understood that I had to face the gwyllion, and that it would be unpleasant. But the fact was, if Ruadan pushed me too far, he might end up dead. I wasn't willing to risk it.

Still, I didn't get much sleep those nights. My mind churned, over and over. If I failed this task, the Shadow Fae would kill me. Would Ruadan do it? I didn't want to kill him, but would he bring the blade down onto my throat? Would he demonstrate his mental fortitude by forcing himself to kill someone he liked? Assuming he even liked me at all. I really didn't know. Whatever the case, the thought of dying at Ruadan's hands never failed to send a sharp pang of sadness tearing through my chest.

Already, I'd explored the entire passageway. Unfortunately, the tunnels didn't offer any escape. Mossy stone walls bookended either side of the tunnel. Besides the door into my room, the only other door opened into Ruadan's room. Still, I could find a way to get a message to Ciara before we both busted out of here.

I traced my fingertips over the scar on my wrist. Once the Shadow Fae purges had closed down the arena, I'd cut Baleros's brand off the inside of my wrist. Ciara had been there to help me patch it up. She'd treated it with a human ointment called Bacitracin that I'd never seen before, then she'd patched it up with cotton bandages. It had healed a lot better than the wounds she'd treated below ground.

I breathed in the damp air. I liked it down here in the dank tunnels, and at least I didn't have Ruadan trying to torment me with brutal visions from my past. The tunnel seemed to go on forever, an immense labyrinth that wended through the castle.

It took about ten minutes before Ciara's particular smell grew stronger. I frowned when I reached her room. There was no trapdoor and no way for me to enter, but a metal grate was inset into the stone. I thought it might be the bathroom.

If I failed the trial, I'd go on the run again, straight away. I'd evade Ruadan for the rest of my life.

But what did that mean for Ciara? She'd be trapped here in the Institute. The Shadow Fae would use her as leverage.

And that meant I had to get her out of here now.

Below the locked grate to her room, I pulled out my pencil and paper, scribbling on it.

Ciara. I may have to go on the run after the next trial. You will need to leave here. I will find you in...

I chewed my lip, trying to think of a location. *Oxford. Near the University. Stay there until I find you. And destroy this message.*

Could I really escape Ruadan at all, even if I wanted to? I had a feeling his tracking skills were unparalleled.

I pushed my worries to the back of my skull and gently tapped the grate.

After a moment, Ciara's face appeared, her dark eyes wide. Without a word, I slid the paper through an opening in the grate.

She read it, then nodded at me. She disappeared for a second, then reappeared, scribbling something of her own. She thrust the piece of paper through the hole.

You can't run from them. Ruadan will find you.

Right. Ruadan was the devil. The devil wore many faces. I'd heard this before. But she didn't know my real fear—if I let them prod at the worst things in my mind, I might not be able to control who I killed.

I scribbled on the paper. *It may be our only option. I'll try to disguise my scent if I have to escape.*

My chest tightened at the thought of Ruadan hunting me down, an iron sword in his hand. I couldn't allow him to find me.

The betrayal would kill me before the blade ever did.

More furious scribbling from Ciara.

I don't trust any fae except you. When we get out of here, we will cele-brate with corn dogs, sloppy joes, and snow cones. I want to bathe in the blood of our enemies and fashion their skulls into battle drums. Are you with me?

I blinked at her message, beginning to think I was not the scarier friend in our pair.

Yes. I wrote back. *Skulls and corn dogs. Sounds like a good time. I have to go. Get ready to escape.*

I shoved the note through the grate, then turned, crossing back down the passage. Now, I needed to convince Ealdun to help me. All he had to do was incapacitate Ciara's guard, and she could sneak through a window into the darkness.

When I reached the light that pooled into the tunnel from my room, I leapt into the air, catching the edge of the opening. I hoisted myself up, and scrambled into the room. Quietly, I closed the trap door, then covered it with the rug.

Ealdun still slept on the table, his head partially propped up on his hand. A thin stream of drool trickled out of the corner of his mouth.

"Ealdun," I said quietly.

He snorted, his eyes still closed.

"Ealdun," I said a little louder.

He murmured something about nipples, still asleep.

"Ealdun!" I shouted, and I smacked the hand propping up his head.

He jolted awake, looking dazed for a moment and blinking in the light. His gormless expression almost had me feeling bad for hitting him.

"You fell asleep," I said.

He scowled at me. "I did not. I was meditating, innit."

"Right. Look, I won't tell anyone. But while we're on the topic of doing each other favors, I have a favor to ask of you."

"If you want me to free you, you can forget it right now. Savus scares the ever-loving shit out of me. And Ruadan is even worse. I'm not letting you loose on the world."

"Ealdun. We're friends, right?"

"I suppose so."

"I'd never ask you to risk your life like that. But I would ask you to maybe…find a way to distract or incapacitate Ciara's guard. She's only a human. And she's only here because I wanted her here. It's time for her to leave."

He frowned at me. "I don't know if this is a good idea."

"No one will blame you. They'll blame the guard who failed."

He scratched his cheek. "I never liked Drem, but…"

I let out a long sigh. "Look, if you help me, I know where you can find a mermaid in Cornwall. I will give you specific directions. She's often drunk on cider and she's not very picky. She's perfect for you."

He scratched his cheek, eyebrows raising. "A mermaid?"

"Yep. Huge rack."

"Sold. What do I need to do?"

"Just, you know, distract Drem until Ciara can get out the window and go off to the human world where she belongs."

Ealdun's eyes were just starting to drift closed again, when a knock sounded in the room. My body tensed.

Gods below. I'd made it back just in time for another trial.

Ealdun frowned at me. "Expecting someone?"

"Nope, but it's not as though anyone ever fills me in."

"Who is it?" Ealdun shouted.

"Ruadan." His voice permeated the door. "I'm here to collect the gutter fae prisoner."

I clenched my jaw. So we were back to that, were we?

I stared at Ealdun. "Will you do what I asked? Please?"

He rubbed his eyes. "I'll distract Drem. That's all I'm promising. His fault if she leaves, right?"

"Exactly."

Ealdun stood, then pulled open the door. Ruadan stood in the hallway wearing his cloak. Shadows slashed the air around him.

I crossed to the door, unwilling to meet Ruadan's gaze. I didn't need to see the disapproval there, after a week of me refusing to train with him.

We both knew the truth. I had no mental discipline.

"It's time for your next trial."

Ruddy afternoon sunlight streamed in through the ancient windowpanes in the hall. Like a living thing, Ruadan's magic did its best to smother it.

A shiver of dread snaked up my spine. "I'm ready," I lied.

But I wasn't moving. I stood in the doorway, a weight pressing on my chest.

I needed to make a run for it tonight, but I wasn't sure I could escape the Wraith if my life depended on it.

And the truth was, my life did depend on it.

CHAPTER 17

I clutched my bug-out bag, stalking along the pavement at dusk. The neon lights of a tattoo parlor flickered over a puddle.

For tonight's trial, Maddan had decided to wear a golden crown, since he had basically no idea how to appear normal in public. Like me, Melusine wore simple black clothes, tightly fitted. At least Maddan seemed to be ignoring me this evening.

Our mentors walked behind us as we trod the rain-slicked street in East London. Rain dampened my hair and clothes, but a few sun rays pierced the clouds. The sun was just beginning to set, casting lurid nectarine light over Brick Lane and staining the rain clouds with purple.

Even in the rain, a few people stood smoking outside some of the pubs and nightclubs, the collars of their coats pulled up high.

I turned, glancing back at Ruadan. Menace curled off him, and as we walked, humans scrambled out of the way.

Aengus walked with his hands in his pockets, his green eyes scanning everything around him.

Then, he narrowed his eyes at me. "Will you be stabbing any of us tonight, Arianna?"

"Keep talking, and I might," I muttered.

Maddan's mentor, a knight named Cronan, skulked behind him, his black hair falling in his eyes. He was giving me a death stare, too. Ever since my escape from the Institute, I wasn't the most popular person among the Shadow Fae.

I loosed a sigh, focusing on the street ahead of me. A mustached man in flannel stumbled out of a chicken shop, dropping the chicken bone in his hand when he caught a glimpse of Ruadan's eerie eyes and his enormous frame.

Nothing to see here, folks. Just a group of creepy-ass fae, stalking the streets on a Thursday night—one of us wearing a crown.

I hadn't expected to find a mountain fae in the center of East London's nightlife, but stranger things had happened. If I had to make a fast escape, I was lucky there were plenty of people around to mask my scent.

"Turn left," said Aengus.

We hurried across Commercial Street onto a narrow lane. A multi-story car park rose up to our right, its white metal fences giving it the appearance of a skeleton.

"This place reeks of humans," said Maddan. "What are we doing here?"

Aengus paused in front of the white barriers of the car park. As he did, its appearance began to shift. Now, a brick wall shimmered into view where the barriers had been.

A glamoured building in the center of East London.

As the glamour further thinned, a black storefront came into view. The setting sun pierced the shop's colored glass windows. Through the muddy hues of orange and purple, I could see a shop crammed with strange knick-knacks: stuffed hummingbirds in bell jars, an antelope's skull, a gaping-eyed doll with a red-lipped grin who was probably stealing my soul.

The gold lettering over the shop window read *Bronwen's.*

A gust of wind swept over the street, toying with a set of wind chimes. Honestly, I really preferred the vampires to this creepy place. When I glanced toward the main road, I saw a bleached-blond woman in a white dress wander toward the entrance to our street. Then, her brow furrowed as if she was confused, she pivoted, then walked away.

It seemed some sort of glamour stopped humans from walking down this street, as if they simply didn't see it.

I felt a tap on my shoulder, and I turned to see Melusine. She wore her blue hair in a messy bun on her head. "Yeah, I'm not too worried about this one. We go inside, she gets in our heads. We just stand there. What's the problem? I've had mental torture before. You know, one of my broom friends used to call me a loser. All the time. Just this high-pitched voice, shrieking at me. Sounded like my voice in a weird way."

Aengus stepped forward, tapping her arm. "This would be a good time to clear your thoughts, Melusine."

She ignored him. "Anyway, the point is, I have three ways of maintaining mental discipline. I take baths with small chunks of ice, I hold my breath as long as I can, and I also take baths with large chunks of ice."

"Very impressive." Was the test of mental torture starting early, or...?

"Maddan has a lot of mental fortitude, too," she went on. "Not because he's strong, but because he has no feelings."

I frowned. "Shit. That's actually a really good point."

"No feelings means no fear, right? I put two and two together. Now *you* have feelings. A lot of rage. Some fear. Some sadness. Mostly rage. I'm not so sure how this will go for you. I think you might crack."

You and me both. "Thanks for the vote of confidence."

She shrugged. "I tell it like I see it."

The clacking of boots on pavement caught my attention, and I turned to see Grand Master Savus stalking toward us, his silver arm glinting in the ruddy light. Mist curled around him, forming shapes as it moved—a snarling wolf, a writhing snake.

As he glared at me, he bared his canines. But when I looked at his crown, my chest began to warm. It looked *withered,* the silvery spindles wilting. It had lost its luster, turned now into a dull gray.

A smile curled my lips. The Old Gods were turning against him.

But *why?* Why in the seven hells would he risk all that power just to get me out of here? It didn't make sense. I understood he wanted Maddan because he came from a rich family, and I was just a gutter fae. But there had to be more to it than that.

Savus stopped in front of the colored glass windows, his crown sagging on his head.

"Novices," he said. "Tonight, you must withstand Bronwen's torment for as long as she delivers it. This is a test of discipline, of mental fortitude. Most of all, it requires that you are able to face yourself." His icy gaze fell on Melusine. "Melusine, you're first. Enter the shop. Endure the torment for as long as the gwyllion delivers it. You may not run away from her. Return with a deck of tarot cards. Hand them back to me."

She nodded, her expression resolute. The door chimed as she pulled it open. She slipped into the gloomy shop, the door creaking closed behind her.

I shifted on the darkening street. I had no idea what mental torture Melusine would be facing, but I was sure it had to do with her sad birthday parties—the ones where she tried to force her brooms to eat cake. Or, maybe something much darker lurked in her past.

After a few minutes, a keening noise wound through the streets, piercing me to the core. It took me a moment to recognize it as Melusine's voice, and a shudder danced up my spine.

Sounded a lot worse than a sad birthday.

Maddan stepped in front of me, smiling to show off his canines. He looked like he was about to start something. And why wouldn't he? Nothing could touch him. I wasn't supposed to kill him. Ruadan couldn't help me, or the Shadow Fae might think he cared for me. And as we all knew, caring about someone put them at risk.

A chill slithered over my skin as Maddan skulked around me, now standing behind my back. When he brushed my hair off my shoulder, I shuddered. While Melusine's screams continued to pierce the air, I closed my eyes, envisioning how I would kill Maddan someday. I wondered if I could punch right through the center of his chest and rip out his heart. If I did, would he live long enough to watch me throw it at him? That would be special.

His hand gripped my waist, and he leaned down. "What will the gwyllion stir up in your mind, gutter fae? The days you spent roaming the streets, desperately fucking—"

His sentence was cut off, and I whirled to see Ruadan lifting him in the air. With a ferocious snarl, the Wraith hurled Maddan at a parked car across the street. Maddan's body dented the car.

Then, Ruadan's cold, shadowy gaze slid to Grand Master Savus.

When I was a kid—back when I lived in the woods—I once watched two stags fighting for supremacy. A younger one and an older one, antlers locked, until the younger gored the old stag, piercing his neck with his antlers.

Ruadan's glare promised savagery, his magic lashing the air around him.

Tension rippled across the horizon, until at last Savus's crown began to slip, and he pushed it back up on his head.

He cleared his throat. "Get up, Maddan," was all he said.

The Old Gods were turning against Grand Master Savus. Had Ruadan just upended the hierarchy of the entire Institute?

I crossed my arms, a smile warming my face. "Are we allowed to beat Maddan now? This day is turning out better than I'd anticipated."

But already, my mood was darkening. The Old Gods might be turning against Grand Master Savus, but for now, he still held the power. If I failed this task, my life was still in his hands.

Maddan was cradling his arm, his face red. "My father is the king of Elfame," he said. "Do you know how much money he has given to the Institute?"

Before anyone had the chance to answer, Melusine slammed through the door, her face pale. Then, she collapsed into a heap on the pavement in front of the shop, her teeth chattering.

Gods below. A gnawing void opened in my chest.

"A failure," bellowed Grand Master Savus, nudging the crown up further on his head. "Her time with us is done. Aengus, take her away from here."

My stomach sank. At least she didn't face the threat of execution for a failure, as I did. She'd just be sent back to the broom people who hated her.

Savus lifted his silver arm, beckoning Maddan closer to the door. "Prince Maddan. Enter, please. Return to us with a golden apple."

Maddan sneered at Melusine's heaped form on the ground, then stepped over her and into the darkened shop.

CHAPTER 18

*A*engus crossed to Melusine, helping her up. Her entire body was shaking.

I inhaled deeply, listening for the sounds of Maddan's tormented screams.

Silence.

It was just as Melusine had said. Psychopaths didn't feel things. Maddan felt no guilt, no emotional pain. He was ruled only by a stark sense of self-preservation. The prince of Elfame was as empty as that creepy doll's vacant stare.

Just a few moments later, Maddan stepped out of the shop, gripping a gleaming apple in his hand.

Smiling, he tossed it in the air and caught it again. "I thought this task was supposed to be hard."

"Congratulations." I shot him a fake smile. "You have no soul. You must be so proud."

He handed the apple to Savus, then smirked at me. "Have fun."

"Arianna," Savus barked. "Go. Return with the gwyllion's teeth. Endure the torment in the shop for as long as she delivers it."

I sputtered. "Her *teeth?*"

"That's what I said." His tone suggested this was the most reasonable request in the world.

I narrowed my eyes at him. "Right. That's perfectly sensible. I'll pull out all her teeth and deliver them to you." Seven hells.

Still, that was my assignment, and I'd try to complete it.

I pulled open the door, and its chimes made me shiver.

Inside, thin rays of light streamed through the colored glass, illuminating rows of dolls and corked vials of colored powders and potions. Shelves towered over me on either side, and the warped wooden floor creaked under my feet.

A porcelain doll stared at me, half her head shorn, her mouth blood-red. She wore a dingy petticoat. I shivered at the sight of her. And when her jaw opened, my heart skipped a beat. She started to scream, and I clamped my hands over my ears. Bizarrely, it sounded like my own voice.

When her scream died down, I started moving deeper into the shop. From the ceiling, sagging teddy bears hung from hooks.

At the rear of the shop stood a woman in a green tracksuit, her back to me. Lavender hair—the same shade as mine—tumbled over her shoulders, and she had a cute figure. But when she turned to face me, my heart skipped a beat.

Amber eyes—the same shade as mine—stared out of a gaunt, haggard face.

I swallowed hard. How did one politely ask for a person's teeth?

"I need your teeth." Not like that, I was sure. "Let me rephrase that. Um, I must have the teeth from your head." Nope, that wasn't it either.

My fists clenched. I couldn't just attack her and yank her teeth out. She seemed like a harmless elderly woman, and I had some moral code. Plus, I was supposed to endure the mental torture first.

She grinned at me, displaying her long rows of teeth, and the hair on the back of my neck stood on end.

"Sorry, I'm not good with people," I went on. "I lived in a cage..." The rest of my sentence died out. Why was I telling her this? I had no idea what I was doing here.

My gaze flicked to the iron hooks hanging from the ceiling. *Good for killing.* No. No. I was not supposed to kill her.

My pulse started racing, and a cold sweat rose on my brow. "It's not important. Just, underground cage—"

A wall of black slammed into me, darkening my mind, and I fell to the ground, my knees hammering the wood. Darkness smothered me, spilling into my lungs like ink.

Then, a flash of light. I was running through the forest, barefoot. My heart was a hunted rabbit, and I knew what was coming. I didn't want to see it.

When I reached the edge of the wood, my blood roared in my ears.

It wasn't just the bodies of fae soldiers littering the ground. Not just the invaders.

My mother lay there, too, blood dripping from her mouth, a thin red line down her beautiful skin.

I have to get out of here. I have to run...

I turned, rushing for the portal as fast as I could. I'd leave home forever.

The image shifted. Hunger rippled through my stomach, and I rolled to the side, fingers in the dirt. After a week in the iron box, I was too weak to stand. Dirt was under my nails, in the cracks of the dried skin on my hands. It was in my mouth, my nostrils. It got everywhere.

Baleros stood over me. "My little monster. I think a week in the box did you good. Taught you your place. Creatures like you need to be controlled. You look like a sweet thing, but things aren't always what they seem. Do you understand?"

My mouth had gone completely dry. He hadn't given me enough water in the box. The hunger cut through me so deeply it didn't even feel like hunger anymore. It felt like a living thing eating me from the inside out. As I lay on the dirt, my legs shook. How much torment could an immortal body take?

"But you must be starving," said Baleros. "I brought my little monster a present."

He tossed the butterscotch sweet into the dirt of my cage. Starving, trembling. My fingers scrambling in the dirt. I grasped the butter-scotch, then clutched it to my chest.

Another wave of darkness pulled me under, and my mind flickered with the image of my mother, my screams piercing the air.

He killed her…

This wasn't real. It was just a memory. Gods below, I had to stop this.

All the air had left my lungs, and I was drowning in the memory.

My dirty fingers, desperately grasping for the sweet…

What sort of creature would do this to a person? What sort of malevolent being would force you to relive the worst moments of your life? A fae that fed off pain. A fae that should die.

The vision disappeared before my eyes, and I was back in the shop, staring into the gwyllion's aged face. She grinned, showing off her long teeth. "Baleros is coming for you. He's going to make you his again. He's going to make you crawl in the dirt for your little sweeties. Arianna. What a joke that is. That's not your real name, is it?" She was shrieking now, and I clamped my hands over my ears. "Not your real name! Things aren't always what they seem. Baleros knows that. Is that the real reason you want him dead? To keep your little secret? To keep him from telling people what a monster you really are?"

Blackness descended, claiming my mind. A hot flash of violence erupted in my brain, that familiar brutality that always lurked under the depths.

"Not your real name!" Her voice rang in my ears like a death knell. "Things aren't always what they seem."

I gasped, my vision clearing once more. I blinked at the iron hook in my hand. Blood dripped from the tip, and my stomach turned.

Then, slowly, my heartbeat slowed. My breathing slowed. I let the clear air fill my lungs.

When the haze of rage dissipated from my mind, I stared down at what I'd done.

The gwyllion lay on the floor. My throat tightened. It seemed that while she was tormenting me with my memories, I'd ripped one of the iron hooks from the ceiling, and I'd rammed it into her throat. Her blood had sprayed all over a collection of Victorian dolls. Apparently, I'd also smashed her mouth with the hook, because her broken teeth now lay on the floor next to her body. The gwyllion stared up at the ceiling, wide-eyed. Her hair was no longer purple, her eyes no longer amber. Both had shifted to a dull gray.

High-pitched screaming pierced my ears. "Not your real name! What a monster you really are!"

It took me a little while to realize it was that gods-damned creepy doll, shrieking in my own voice.

Oh, seven hells. I was supposed to withstand the mental torture for as long as she delivered it, and I'd killed her instead.

With a shaking hand, I grabbed her shattered teeth. I stared at them in my palm. Then, I stuffed them in my pocket. I didn't suppose the teeth alone would get me out of this situation.

The doll's screams had shifted to an accusation. "Killed her! Killed her!"

I looked down at my blood-soaked clothes. I'd done exactly what I *wasn't* supposed to do. I'd completely screwed up the task.

My heart began to slam against my ribs, and I scanned the shop's back wall, desperate for an exit. It was time to go on the run, wasn't it?

The doll's shrieks had died down.

Jars of preserved body parts stood on a table before a grubby window, and I grimaced at the sight of them.

I glanced back at the door. A silhouette loomed through the glass. It had gone too quiet in here. Was someone about to come in?

I rushed back to the screaming doll, lifting it by the torso. I felt a porcelain skeleton under its dress. The creepy thing blinked at me.

"Scream," I said.

The doll blinked again.

I let the darkness pool in me, the rage, the destruction. "Scream," I said again, my voice laced with cold fury.

The doll opened its red mouth and unleashed a shriek, a mimic of my own terror. I dropped it back on its shelf. Right now, I was just glad I'd had the foresight to get Ciara out of the Institute.

Adrenaline surged in my blood, and I could only hope that Ciara was already on her way to Oxford.

I climbed over the table, careful not to break any jars. Then I slid open the window, and it creaked up. At last, I'd pulled it open high enough to slip through. It opened onto a narrow London street, on the opposite side of the building from the other Shadow Fae. Night had fallen, giving me a little cover of darkness.

I'd found myself once again on the run, heading for one of London's rivers.

My sodden clothing dampened the seat in the narrow canal boat. I glanced up at the stars, breathing in the clear air as I steered the boat. In the dark, I cracked open another Budweiser—not my favorite beer, but it would have to do. I hadn't found any food in the boat, so the calories from the beer would have to fill me.

Rivers made it hard to track a person. While the creepy doll had screamed into the shop, mimicking my voice, I'd had just enough time to escape before the Shadow Fae noticed anything amiss. I'd run south to the Thames. Then, I'd let the river carry me east until I reached the River Lea.

From there, I'd swum north against the current, until I reached an abandoned canal boat.

Now, I was sitting in someone's boat, drinking their beer. I shoved my hand into my bug-out bag, desperate for food, but found only a few crumbs of sugar. I pulled out my headlamp and flicked it on. I needed to snatch a few hours of sleep.

Someone would likely report the boat stolen, which meant I'd have to abandon it, but it was working for me for now.

I knocked back the rest of my beer, then slowed the propeller as I reached a stony mooring point. Using the tiller, I slowly steered it in.

I had no idea where I was, but I'd been moving north of London for a few hours. Oak and maple trees lined the canal.

With the boat safely moored, I stepped off into the soft grass, my body aching from my long swim through the rivers. My muscles burned.

My wet clothes clung to my body. I lay down beneath an oak tree, and I closed my eyes. As sleep overtook me, I found myself walking through an apple grove, dressed in nothing but a short, silky dress—cream-colored. Moonlight silvered the leaves and fruit around me. A man stood at the other end of the orchard, dressed in a black cloak. I couldn't see his face, but his dark magic whipped the air around him, and violet eyes pierced the darkness. My skin began heating, breasts peaking under my silk dress. I could imagine how his hands would feel cupping between my legs.

As I crossed to him, my pulse raced, and I pulled off the dress…

* * *

WHEN I AWOKE, a wave of horror slammed into me. I was no longer in the park. Somehow—while I'd been sleeping—I'd returned to the Palatial Room. The rough stones bit into my back, and my bones ached.

What in the seven hells?

A layer of grime covered every inch of my skin and my damp, black clothing. How in the gods' names had I ended up *here*? I wanted to scream, but screaming would do me no good.

A guard stood directly across from me, chewing tobacco. He spat onto the sludgy ground. It was the guard who'd threatened to cut our tits off. The one I wanted to punch in the dick.

At this point, all I really knew was that it had not been a successful escape.

I swallowed hard, my mouth dry. When a shadow loomed over the cell, my heart sank. Ruadan's violet eyes burned in the gloom.

"Arianna."

"You threw me in the dung hole again," I snarled. "How did this even happen?"

"You ran. Did you really think you could outrun me?"

"Did you really think I wouldn't try? I'm facing my execution here."

He slid a key into the lock, and the door creaked open. "Come with me."

My legs were shaking as I stood, my stomach turning in flips. "Where are we going?"

"We're going to face Grand Master Savus. He believes you should die."

I clenched my teeth. It was just as I'd thought—the betrayal felt like a death blow. "You dragged me back here just to kill me. You could have just let me go," I hissed. "What difference would it make to you?"

As we walked up the stairs, he slid his gaze to me. "The Old Gods don't want you to die."

"But I failed the task. I thought I had to keep winning in order to demonstrate the approval of the Old Gods."

"Did you fail?"

I frowned as we moved up the stairs. "I slammed a hook into the gwyllion's throat while she was feasting on my worst memories."

We reached a metal gate at the top of the stairs, and Ruadan unlocked it. It swung open into a vaulted corridor.

"I noticed that," he said. "She is quite dead."

I had no idea what he was talking about. All I knew was that my heart was racing. Despite Ruadan's assurances, I felt as if I were on my way to my own execution.

My mind was flailing out of control, blood roaring. "How did I even end up here? I don't remember anything after I fell asleep under the tree. How did you find me? I traveled in the rivers."

"Your dreams."

"My dreams," I repeated. He had an amazing knack for answering things in a way that elucidated nothing.

"I can see them in my mind, and hear them. They vibrate, like a song, each with their own signature. If I tune into your dreams, they beckon me."

I'm not sure what horrified me more—the fact that he could track me so easily, or the fact that he might have witnessed my sex dream starring him. If I remembered correctly, we'd gotten to know each other really well up against the trunk of an apple tree.

"When you say you can see my dreams—"

"The orchard, yes." He kept his gaze straight ahead.

My cheeks burned. "That's very intrusive, do you know that? You shouldn't spy on people's dreams."

"It was a beautiful dream."

I snarled, my face heating. Suddenly, I'd forgotten about my possibly impending death. "That's not the point. The point is that it was mine. You shouldn't pry."

It wasn't until I realized that we'd entered Grand Master Savus's hall that I focused again.

On his throne of rock, Savus loomed over us. His crown looked even more withered, now a dark gray. The other mentors stood in the hall—along with Maddan. As the only remaining novice, he beamed with pride. His golden crown gleamed on his head. And here I was, literally covered in filth from the dung hole.

But Maddan wasn't the worst of my problems. A low, rocky slab rested on the floor by my feet. It took me a moment to recognize what it was—an execution block. At the sight of it, my hand began to twitch, and an icy chill licked up my spine.

Death is coming.

My heart beat like a war drum. I felt as if I were falling, my body becoming weightless. I felt unmoored, dropping through space. An icy wind gusted through my hair.

Savus nodded at one of his guards, who held an iron sword in the air. The guard crossed to Ruadan, who gripped the sword by the jeweled hilt. The world felt unsteady beneath my feet.

Would he execute me here?

Deep inside, I felt myself plummeting. My fingers twitched again, and a song of death sang in my veins. A yawning void opened within my chest, and a phantom wind tore at my hair. Weightless.

It's happening again. Death is coming.

They didn't know what I really was, that I'd be the one person to make it out of here alive.

"Kneel," Savus commanded. "You couldn't live with dignity, but perhaps you can die with it. Rest your neck on the block."

I wouldn't kneel for him again. I would kill him. My cold gaze slid to Maddan, who was staring at me expectantly, waiting to witness my death. In a few moments, he'd be lying on the floor, bleeding from the mouth.

I no longer felt as if I were on the earth at all, and I slid my gaze to Ruadan. "You betrayed me." My voice didn't quite sound like my own, and it scared even me.

But Ruadan's eyes weren't on me. No, he was still staring straight ahead, looking at Savus. Icy wind surged through my veins. I was plummeting in a void. Did they realize they were all about to die? It didn't seem that way.

"I don't know what you're giving me the sword for," said Ruadan. His voice was calm, subduing. "She completed the task, just as she was supposed to. Clearly, the Old Gods continue to favor her."

That was all it took to feel that I was back on the earth. The whisper of death left my mind, my feet meeting the stone floor with a lurch.

But what the hells was he talking about?

Ruadan looked at me, his powerful magic pulsing off his body. "You have the teeth, don't you, Arianna?"

I shoved my hand into my damn pocket, feeling the jagged, broken teeth. I'd nearly forgotten about them. "I do."

I pulled them out, showing them to Savus. My hand was shaking so hard I could barely keep them in my palm.

But as I held them out, the cogs in my mind began to turn. Maybe I *had* done what Savus had asked.

Endure the mental torment in the shop for as long as she delivers it.

Savus steepled his fingers, staring at Ruadan. "She slaughtered the gwyllion."

"She endured the mental torment for as long as the creature delivered it. She did exactly what was asked. She ceased enduring the torment when the gwyllion ceased to deliver it."

Savus now gripped the edge of his throne. His silver crown began to slide from his head, and he pushed it back up again. He gritted his teeth, his face paling. "That was not what I meant and you know it."

Ruadan's magic iced the room. "Look at your crown, Grand Master Savus. You know in your heart what the Old Gods want."

"Control her. Whip her. Beat her into obedience. Whatever it takes. Or you will no longer be welcome here at the Institute, Ruadan."

Ruadan straightened. He didn't answer, but his dark magic whipped at the air around him like a hurricane of shadows.

Maddan's face had gone bright red. When he turned to look at me, he held out his hands in a grip suggesting he was going to choke me to death. I'd welcome the chance to fight him hand-to-hand.

Maddan had no idea how close he had come to losing his life, just moments before. Death was a power I couldn't control, but I was starting to think it rose within me when I thought I was about to die.

Ruadan turned to walk out of the hall. I faintly heard the words on his lips as he leaned down to whisper to me, "You're staying with me, now."

CHAPTER 20

I sat at the stone table in Ruadan's room, dressed in one of his black shirts. Since Savus's crown had begun to wither, something had shifted between him and Savus. A change in the balance of power. But how long would that last?

I took another bite of the steak in front of me, the texture so soft it seemed to melt in my mouth. I leaned back in the chair, closing my eyes as I ate it. Gods, it tasted amazing.

As I finished the steak, a question burned in my mind, and I had to ask it. "Grand Master Savus's crown is literally wilting before our eyes. Could another Shadow Fae usurp his powers?"

"Without the approval of the Old Gods, we are no longer beholden to a magical hierarchy. Physically, I could kill him now. But there is another force keeping him in power, and the Shadow Fae High Council would not tolerate such an assassination. They would send knights from all across the world to dispatch the usurper."

I swirled the wine in my glass. "Even if the Old Gods strip him of his power?"

"We would need proof of wrongdoing. A crime, a betrayal of some sort. A semblance of a trial."

"You told me that you have a history with Grand Master Savus.

You said that Savus would want to crush anyone that you might favor just to get to you. That's why you were dragging me over the stones and calling me a gutter fae." It was a classic Baleros move—use others to get to your real target.

"That's right."

"Considering that your 'favor' resulted in bruises on my arse and far too much time in the Palatial Room, I think maybe you could shed a little light on that history."

A long silence stretched between us, heavy as wet soil.

Darkness consumed the light around him. "He is my mother's cousin. Fifteen years ago, she was killed. Savus blames me for failing to protect her. He loathes me."

The weight of his words pressed on my chest. "He blames you for your mother's death? That must be incredibly painful. Has he really said that to you?"

"In his own way."

"What an arsehole," I snapped, anger roiling. I wanted to snap Savus's little neck. After a few moments, I asked, "What happened to your mother?"

No response, just a flash of silver in his eyes. So...he didn't want to talk about it. Fair enough—I more than understood the desire to keep the past hidden. "Never mind. Neither of us want to dwell on the torment of our personal histories. We have that in common. Best to keep the nightmares locked in their cages." The wine tasted delicious, and I let the berry flavors roll over my tongue. "Incidentally, that's what Baleros used to say about me."

Ruadan had gone still as the stone walls. "You have a nightmarish side. You thrive in chaos."

"Well, haven't you heard? According to Baleros, chaos is an opportunity to remake the world the way you want it." I arched an eyebrow at him, my mind flickering with the memory of that execution block. Ruadan had no idea how close he'd been to death. "There's something I'm missing. Why is Grand Master Savus so eager to kill me that he's willing to let his crown and his power wither? It can't just be the convenience of having a fae prince among the Shadow Fae."

"You're right, and I don't know. His behavior is irrational. He's driven by a strange compulsion to hurt you and perhaps kill you."

I frowned. "When you captured me on the boat and brought me back to the Palatial Room, were you certain I'd survive? That you'd found a loophole?"

"I'm not sure what's driving Savus, but he is defying the will of the Old Gods. I will not let anyone kill you."

I loosed the breath I'd been holding. I wanted to ask if he was protecting me because of the will of the Old Gods or because he actually liked me, but I reminded myself that it didn't really matter. As long as he was helping to keep me alive, I didn't need to know his motives.

I frowned at him. "You really had to leave it to the last moment to let me know you weren't going to cut off my head? You could have explained that a bit better on the way up the stairs."

He didn't respond, lapsing back into his characteristic silence. I swirled the wine in my glass, glaring at him. "Oh, you've lost your voice again. It's a wonderful way of avoiding things."

"I suppose I could always avoid things with constant chatter, like you do."

I glared at him, overcome by a desire to rile him up.

I kicked off my shoes and let the T-shirt ride up as I put my feet on the chair. I felt his gaze sliding up my legs, drinking me in until he reached my face. I licked my lips, and his eyes caught the movement. "Didn't Savus say you were supposed to punish me? Whip me, I think?"

Shadows billowed around him, and his body became eerily still. Ruadan, of course, said nothing, but his entire body tensed.

"No?" I went on. "Maybe a light spanking until I learn my lesson?"

I was teasing him, but I could also feel my chest flushing at the mental image.

His violet eyes darkened, and I smiled at the sight. Then, he lunged forward, planting his hands on the chair, one on either side of my hips. I leaned back, looking up at him as his magic washed over me. He wasn't touching me, but he was still boxing me in, in total control.

His mouth hovered just inches from mine, his body practically vibrating with tension. His eyes were completely black as his demonic side took control. My knees slid open just a little, lips parting as heat swooped through my belly, and my pulse raced.

Then, he rose with a growl. He prowled away, with his hands clenched into fists.

"What happened to your human?" he asked, with his back to me. His voice had an edge to it. "She escaped from her room."

My good mood dampened as soon as I thought of Ciara. I could only hope she'd found a good place to hide out, and that maybe she could scrape together some food. "I guess her guard wasn't very good." *And that's all the information you're getting.*

I loosed a long breath, my pulse slowing again. "Ruadan. There's something I have to tell you. The gwyllion said something right before I killed her. She said Baleros was coming for me. That he wanted to make me his again. That's the second person now who said this. First the assassin, then the gwyllion. Plus, there were the sweets. I'm certain he's alive."

Ruadan's shadows seeped into the air around him like blood spilling into a field. "I believe he's still alive, too."

My chest tightened. "So why can't we track him? You hunted me down in a forest just by using my dreams. Why can't you track Baleros in the same way?"

"I've never been able to track him, to feel his dreams, or get into his mind. I've consulted with a fae elder, and I think I know what's happened."

"What?"

"We both saw his body ignite after I killed him. I think he may have sold his soul to the fire goddess."

"Emerazel?" I shook my head. "What would that mean?"

"The fire goddess is the ancient enemy of the god of night. That would explain why he's immune to my powers. It also would mean that he can't be killed. If he dies, the fire goddess revives him."

My jaw tightened, steeling my resolve. "There's a way to kill everyone. *Everyone.* And we will find a way to kill Baleros."

"We will. But first things first. You have another trial coming up. It's the final trial before a knight is chosen from the novices. And we both know what happens if you fail."

I knocked back the rest of my wine. I was getting a nice buzz going. "Right. What do I have to do?"

"What do you know about angels?"

I schooled my features to calm and poured myself another glass of wine. Talk about dredging up nightmares from the past. "The angels aren't on Earth anymore. So we don't need to worry about them. After the apocalypse, all the angels were exiled to the heavens. Driven off the earth forever. Everyone knows the story."

"Not exactly. Some of them have returned, and two of the horsemen of the apocalypse never left. After we kill Baleros, they're next on my list. They're a scourge upon this earth."

I stared at him, my unease growing. "What's the harm in a few angels on Earth? They're hardly wreaking destruction these days."

A chill rippled through the room, and candles flickered in their sconces. The ice in the air had my teeth chattering.

"It doesn't matter what they're doing *these days*." His deep, velvety voice had an edge of steel to it. "They're unnatural. They're responsible for everything that happened during the apocalypse. Millions of unnecessary deaths just to appease their egos. Men, women, children slaughtered across the globe. The angels—and worse, the horsemen—are the face of pure evil. They are death itself, and they must answer for their crimes."

I gripped the wineglass, ready to snap it. "Fine. So what's the mission? Hunt some angels?"

"Yes. A few cohorts of angels have returned to Earth. They're trying to learn to live as humans, to blend in. As you know, angels believe that humans are beasts. The angels have come to Earth to consort with humans in their most primitive, bestial state."

"In their most bestial state? What does that mean, exactly?" I asked.

"The task requires that you figure that out."

"And why, exactly, are they trying to live like primitive humans?"

"We think they're spies, possibly planning another apocalyptic assault on Earth. Except this time, they're disguising themselves. They've hidden their wings. They look like humans. They're trying to learn to behave like humans. We have to ferret them out before we find ourselves facing another apocalypse."

"If they're disguised, then how do you suggest that I pick out the humans from the angels?" I asked.

Ruadan lifted his hand. Purple light flickered between his fingertips, illuminating the beautiful planes of his face. "You know what happens if an angel indulges in earthly pleasure."

"He turns into a demon." A smile curled my lips. "I get it. I hit them with lust magic. The angels turn into demons. I kill them. Does that pretty much summarize it?"

"It's as simple as that. And I know you can kill. The hard part will be controlling the magic."

"But I still don't get a lumen stone?"

"Not until you become a knight. For now, you're considered a flight risk."

"Fine. So how do I distill this magical power?"

Ruadan pulled one of his swords off the wall. "We're leaving the Institute for this one. I don't want Maddan to know what we're planning."

He sheathed his sword, then turned his back to me. His magic rippled over my skin, and I stared as a portal opened in the floor—whirling dark waters flickered like starlight.

He turned to face me, and he gestured to the portal.

I jumped in, and the icy water rushed over my skin. As I sank deeper, it occurred to me that I didn't even ask him where we were going. I'd just simply jumped. Was I actually starting to trust him?

Ruadan's body plunged into the portal next to me, and we continued to sink, until at last, thin rays of moonlight pierced the water's surface. As my lungs burned, I kicked my legs, hurtling up toward the surface, faster and faster.

Then, the lip of a fountain came into view. I grasped on and hoisted myself up, catching my breath. Above me, water spilled from the mouth of a stone woman, splashing over the dark cobblestones. The air smelled intoxicating, heavy with sandalwood and jasmine.

Ruadan was already climbing from the fountain, his dark clothing dripping onto the cobblestones. "Lilinor, the vampire realm. We're safe. My half-brother Caine rules here with the king."

Ruadan's black shirt clung to my body like a second skin as I pulled myself over the lip of the fountain. We were standing on a narrow lane, where moonflowers and gardenias climbed the walls of rickety timber-framed buildings.

My gaze roamed upward, all the way to a crooked Gothic castle that loomed over the city. Amber lights burned in its narrow windows.

"Are we going up to that castle?" I asked.

Ruadan's damp, pale hair hung over his shoulders. "We don't need to go that far. We're going to practice in my friend's garden. It's nearby."

He began walking over the cobbles, and I followed behind him. We were heading for a grand house—it looked like a gabled Tudor mansion, with crisscrossing wood over white walls.

As we stood before the wooden door, Ruadan lifted the silver knocker, shaped like a hand. He knocked three times.

The clacking of footfalls penetrated the door. Then, it swung open. A buxom woman stood in the doorway, her dark hair piled high on her head. She wore a long lace gown. "Well if it isn't my favorite fae prince!"

I blinked at him. "Prince?" Prince of what?

"Get the hells inside," she said. Her accent was American—Southern, in fact. "I need to hang a damn towel over that fountain so you don't trail all that water inside next time. Ruining my good hardwood floors with all that portal water."

She opened the door wide into a hall of dark wood, with an enormous stone fireplace burning bright.

Ruadan gave a slight bow. "We were hoping to use—"

"Shhhhh." The woman lifted a finger to her lips. "Where are your manners? From a royal family like you are, and you don't even know how to introduce a woman. No wonder you can't find yourself a damn wife." She turned her sharp, dark eyes to me. "I don't suppose you're his lover. Our grand fae prince here never has a lady friend."

"No, ma'am," I said. I had no idea where the *ma'am* came from. It just came out.

She stuck her finger in Ruadan's chest. "You're such a gods-damn fool, a man looking like you, warm-blooded man like you, can't find yourself a damn lady friend. Brooding all over the place, vowing silence, scaring everyone away with all your damn shadows. Making the lights flicker out when you walk into a room. No sensible lady is gonna want to go on a date with you if you keep making lights flicker out. They'll be tripping all over the place, running into walls, burning their pancakes. Can't see a damn thing when you're around with your moods."

Ruadan opened his mouth again to speak, but she silenced him with another jab to his chest.

"Making the air all cold with your tempers. At least you're not doing that stupid vow of silence anymore. Good. You know what won't help you kill people? Being silent. Gets you nowhere. Doesn't help you get a lady friend either."

Her sharp eyes turned to me, and she looked me up and down, letting out a low whistle. Then, to my horror, she stepped closer and poked at one of my breasts. "Good solid girl like this, good ample bosoms that a man could lay his head on at night, and she's not your lover. Gods-damned fool. Grown man like you, making lights flicker off. Six hundred years, still not remarried. Damn shame."

At last, her tirade seemed to have died out, and Ruadan gestured to me. "Elise, this is—"

She raised her hands. "Now I know you were married before, but that was a long damn time ago. Time to move on."

I stared at Ruadan. Well, I was certainly learning more about him now than I had in weeks of living with him. A prince, previously married.

And most shocking of all—he *actually* had friends.

Still, this last bit about his former wife seemed to have irked him, and a coolness fell over the room—an actual chill that raised goose-bumps on my skin.

"Quit making my living room cold," shouted Elise. "What's the matter with you? Fool. That's what happens when you spend too much time celibate. Lose your temper over every damn thing, drive up everyone's heating bill with the cold air from your magic. No one wants to pay for that. No wonder you're still single."

Ruadan's body had stiffened, and he looked as if he were trying to restrain himself. Then, in a voice that was a little too smooth to be calm, he said, "This is my novice, Arianna, from London's Institute of the Shadow Fae. Arianna, this is Elise. She likes to go by Grandmother Elise. She's an old and dear friend."

"Grandmother?" I asked. "You don't…you don't look old enough to be a grandmother."

"I am two hundred seventy-eight years old. I have sired six generations of offspring." She beamed, apparently pleased with the introduction. When she smiled, her fangs glinted in the candlelight.

Ruadan narrowed his eyes at her windows. "You need to get light-blocking curtains on these windows, Elise. I've told you that before. You know what will happen if the sun rises and you've fallen asleep in the living room."

"Two hundred seventy-eight years old, and do you know how many times I've fallen asleep in the living room? Not once. Not once," she repeated.

"I'm coming back with curtains," he said, his voice a sharp command. "And I'm putting them up. Do not question me on this, Elise."

She rolled her eyes. "The prince makes an official decree. But you'd better not come in here with cheap curtains. Silk or nothing. Now what are y'all doing here? You need something to drink? I've got strawberry daiquiris, heavy on the rum."

"Yes." I smiled.

"No," Ruadan cut in. "But thank you. We're just hoping to borrow your orchard for some practice."

"You want to practice some of that Shadow Fae magic?" She turned and began walking through the hall, heading for an oak door at the back.

We followed her.

"Now what kind of magic are you going to be practicing, just so I know?" she asked. "You're not going to be blowing up my apple trees, are you? I take very good care of my apple trees."

"No, Grandma Elise. Just lust magic." He said this like it was no big deal. In the same tone that one might discuss having a ham sandwich for lunch. *Oh, you know, just going out into your garden to magically channel sexual arousal all over your plants. Nothing awkward.*

She whirled, arching an eyebrow at Ruadan. "Grown man like you with lust magic. No wife. It's a gods-damned waste is what it is. You know all that pent-up sexual energy is no good for you. Human men blow themselves up over a thing like that. It's not natural. Gets your insides all clogged up and angry. Vow of celibacy. Making you all crazy, making the rooms go cold." She jabbed him in the shoulder. "People need to get themselves some hibbly jibbly."

She yanked the door open, glaring intensely at both of us with this hibbly jibbly directive.

When we stepped outside, the night wind whispered over my wet skin, making me shiver. I breathed in the powerful scent of apples. The air here felt moist and heavy.

Grandma Elise closed the door behind us.

We moved deeper into the garden—if it could even be called a garden. It was more a large, walled orchard. A stone bench sat in the center of it all, engraved with vines.

"You never told me you were a prince." I folded my arms. "Prince of what, exactly?"

His violet eyes pierced the darkness. After a long moment, he finally answered, "Emain."

I breathed in deeply. "So it is real. The place I dream about. The place in the library book."

"It's real." The intoxicating breeze of Lilinor lifted strands of his blond hair. Apart from that, he'd gone completely still, shadows thickening around him. "It's where the Shadow Fae High Council resides. It's where Baleros trained me, and where Grand Master Savus once lived."

I sucked in a sharp breath. I'd never known a bloody thing about Baleros's past. Of course I hadn't. *Knowledge is power.* "Emain? That's where Baleros is from? *That's* where he mentored you?"

"A legion of Shadow Fae protects Emain. It's part of our mission to keep the land secret, to convince everyone it's a myth. The realm is home to precious metals that demons would love to exploit. The Shadow Fae of Emain are some of the fiercest assassins in the world, and our training is harsher than most. In our youth, we scale mountains and swim across oceans—all for the purpose of training to protect the realm. We sacrifice to the Old Gods, but our mission is also to assassinate enemies of Emain. We kill demon and fae invaders and those we believe are planning attacks on the city."

I moved closer to him, desperate to learn more. The night air rushed over me. I kicked off my shoes, and the grass felt soft under my feet.

But I wasn't relaxing. I was hunting for information on Baleros, and I was going after this knowledge like a foxhound scenting blood. "How did Baleros end up in London? Why did he leave Emain?"

"You're not going to let me get away with silence, are you?"

"You bet your life I won't." My fingers tightened into fists. I needed to know the truth about all of this.

"Baleros was my mentor in Emain hundreds of years ago, when I was young. He left Emain three centuries ago. He joined the London Institute, but he chafed against the authority of Grand Master Savus. Baleros fled the Institute in the 1800s, and he began trafficking stolen magical items. After the apocalypse, it wasn't enough for him. Fifteen years ago, he returned to Emain and tried to seize control of the realm. To become king. He slaughtered Queen Macha. Shot her through with iron arrows, burnt her body until nothing was recognizable except her crown." Shadows darkened his eyes, and the temperature around us cooled until my breath frosted in front of my face.

I'd moved closer to Ruadan, and his face had taken on a haunted quality. My chest ached for him, and I had the strongest urge to wrap my arms around him. "Queen Macha—your mother?"

"Yes. I was the one who found her in her room. But when Baleros realized none of the warriors supported his coup, he fled Emain. I vowed silence until I achieved his death. I joined the London Institute. Baleros was top of my kill list. But I could never track him, and now, I know why. The goddess of flames protects him. The ancient enemy of my grandfather."

I sucked in a deep breath. "And while you were hunting Baleros, he was keeping me below ground as a slave, less than a mile away from the Institute." I swallowed hard. "What was your mother like, before she died?"

"Strong. A warrior. She was small, but powerful. She rode a horse faster than anyone in the kingdom. She spoke sixteen languages and swore like a gutter tramp." He frowned. "No offense."

"I actually didn't take offense until you said 'no offense.' Anyway, your mum sounds brilliant." I hugged myself, chilly in my damp dress. "Why are you telling me about Emain if it's such a deep secret?"

"Because I know you'll keep it."

"I will." The idea that he trusted me sparked a bit of warmth inside. I fought the urge to ask him about his wife. Curiosity burned in me, but I'd seen how he reacted to Grandma Elise, driving up her heating bill with his coldness.

CHAPTER 22

"You will become a knight," Ruadan said. "The Old Gods desire it. You will live. And you will help me find Baleros. But first, you have to pass tomorrow's trial. You'll need to identify the angels and kill each one of them." He held out his palm, and a silver ring gleamed in his hand. It glowed faintly with violet light. "I've imbued this with my magic. You'll need to learn to channel it."

I picked up the ring from his palm and slid it onto my finger. As I did, a jolt of heat raced through my blood. I became acutely aware of Ruadan's T-shirt clinging to my body, my breasts peaking in the cold breeze. My mind flashed with a vivid memory of my dream about Ruadan. I wanted him to lose control of himself, to pin me up against a tree. Already, the blood was rushing out of my head and making it hard for me to think.

"You need to control it." His magic licked at my skin, stroking up the back of my spine like a silky fingertip, an invisible caress. "Not the other way around."

My pulse raced, my breathing quickening. "I'm perfectly in control." I stared at my fingertips, which now flickered with violet light. Without realizing what I was doing, I reached for Ruadan's sodden shirt. I pulled him close, and he stared down at me. He felt *warm*. I slid my hand up his powerful torso.

"Control it." His voice was a blade wrapped in silk, and it only made me want to touch him more.

I rested my head against his muscled chest, looking up at his perfect face. My fingers slid inside the hem of his shirt, over his muscled abs, and I heard him gasp, his muscles tensing. His skin was soft, with pure steel underneath. I ran my hand higher up his chest, feeling his muscles. He leaned down, his breath warming the shell of my ear. He wasn't pushing me away.

Fifteen years he'd been with London's Institute. Fifteen years since he'd had sex. He must be desperate for it.

When I closed my eyes, the scent of apples grew stronger. A vision rose in my mind of an orchard on a rocky slope—Emain. Someone had decorated the tree branches with candles that flickered in the darkness like stars, and a distant drum beat through my blood. I stalked through the trees, hunting...

Ruadan pulled my hand off his body, his grip like iron on my fingers.

I gritted my teeth, trying to gain control of myself. "What the hells was that vision?"

"What vision?" he asked.

"It was Emain, with candles in the trees, and a drumbeat."

A silence stretched out between us. "I think you saw one of my memories. It must be carried by the magic I gave you."

"You were hunting something."

"A woman. It was a fertility festival."

I shook my head, willing my body to cool down. "Right. You know most people just get drunk and watch TV, but I do like the candles and drums. I take it the Emain Shadow Fae were not celibate?"

"Fortunately, no."

It took me a moment to realize that I'd grabbed onto his shirt again and pulled him close, arching my neck to look up at him. Gods, I wanted to be there in Emain for that festival, to be hunted by

Ruadan, pulled down in the dewy grass. I wanted Ruadan's powerful hands to rip my clothes off while I writhed beneath him…

Through our damp clothes, his body warmed mine. I clenched my fists, still clutching his shirt, and I looked up into his eyes. He gripped my waist once more, and his heated gaze burned right into me. I felt an overwhelming urge to pull my wet T-shirt up higher. Darkness slid through his eyes as my arousal started to affect him, too. Even if he was supposed to be celibate, the incubus in him was responding.

When the chilly wind hit my thighs, raising goosebumps, I realized that I actually *had* inched the shirt up to my waist.

Now, I was desperate to kiss him, to feel his tongue sliding against mine. My pulse raced.

I wanted to get down on the damp ground with him, and…

Focus, Arianna.

I expected him to be annoyed, because so far, I was completely failing to effectively channel the magic. But I *had to* prove to him that I could do this. His faith in me was not misplaced.

I willed my heartbeat to slow, still staring into his eyes. And as I gazed up at him, I saw something new there. Something almost possessive. Or was it protective?

"How, exactly, do I control it?" I asked.

"It's the magic of life," he said, his voice an erotic rumble through my belly. "And the opposite of life—"

With an iron will, I forced myself to take a step back from him. "Death. You want me to think about death?"

"Fill yourself with darkness. It will help you control the power as it dampens the lust magic."

A dark smile curled my lips. "Oh, believe me. Death is something that comes naturally to me."

While the lust magic continued to heat up my body, I closed my eyes, summoning my worst memories of destruction: fae blood staining the soil, bodies lying at my feet in the arena. Vacant eyes. Hearts ripped, still beating, from bodies. Like ink spilling through water, the darkness pushed out some of the lust magic from my core, moving it to my extremities.

"There," said Ruadan, his voice wrapping around me like velvet. He traced his fingertip from my shoulder, down my arm, and tingles raced in its wake. "I can see it moving through your body, the way it should."

I took a deep breath, in control once more, and I stepped away to look at my hand. Violet magic throbbed at my fingertips.

"Good."

The approval in his eyes made me smile—at least for a moment, until I mentally excoriated myself for caring so much what he thought. I shouldn't want his approval as much as I did.

"Of course it's good." I stood tall. "The Amazon Terror is nothing less than amazing."

"That's a ridiculous name."

"Okay, *Wraith*."

"You'll notice I do not refer to myself in the third person. In any case, now you'll need to learn to hurl the magic at a target."

"Right."

"I'm going to move through the trees. Try to hit me with it."

"Won't you be overcome by an overwhelming desire for hibbly jibbly?"

He shook his head. "No. The magic comes from me. I'll be fine."

With a hissing sound, he disappeared, leaving only a whorl of shadows behind.

I tracked his movements through the trees, and he slowed to a normal walking pace. I looked down at the pulsing violet magic at the tips of my fingers, and I flung back my arm to try to hurl it at him. Except, on the back stroke, the magic flew off my fingertips. I watched as it soared through a glass window into Grandma Elise's house.

I sucked in a deep breath. Looked like she might be in for an interesting evening.

Once that burst of magic had left my body, the lust magic began surging again, heating my skin. Even from across the orchard, I could feel Ruadan's unmistakable masculine allure. I closed my eyes as I walked barefoot through the dewy grasses, breathing in the sensual scents of the orchard. The night air felt heavy, and the wet T-shirt slid against my bare legs. My breasts, too, seemed fuller in the shirt. If I took off all my clothes, could I tempt him to hunt me?

My gaze slid over every inch of Ruadan, the moonlight washing over his muscled body, his powerful arms. I could imagine the feel of his mouth on my throat, my bare legs wrapped around his waist. Molten heat surged, and my hardened nipples chafed against the wet shirt.

The rush of cold air over my bare thighs told me that once again I'd started hiking up my T-shirt. *Death. Blood, broken bodies, rotting flesh, vacant eyes.*

Darkness spooled out through my limbs, chasing away the sensual magic until it pulsed from my fingertips once again.

I lifted my hand, taking care to throw the magic faster this time. It hit Ruadan in the chest, his back arched, and a smile curled his lips. Then, magic surged through my blood once more, and erotic heat stroked over my skin, pooling between my legs.

I closed my eyes, letting my body fill with the dizzying weightlessness of death, until the darkness pushed the violet magic out to my extremities again.

"This time," said Ruadan, "when you throw it, try to toss it into the air and disperse it over the orchard."

"How do I do that?" I asked.

"It's all in the throw. Splay your fingers. Just practice."

I hurled the magic into the air, my body rocked by each burst. It took me four or five tries until I could flick my fingers in just the right way that the magic spread out, raining down over the orchard.

Ruadan prowled closer to me. When he was only a few feet away, I threw more violet magic at him. His back arched as it hit him. All at once, the magic recharged in my body, and heat arced through my core until I could think of nothing but how my naked body would feel sliding against his.

I grabbed him by the shirt, then pushed him down to the stone bench. Without entirely realizing what I was doing, I straddled him, my shirt riding up, exposing my panties. His fingers clamped around my waist, hungry and possessive. I leaned in to kiss him, my tongue licking his. My hips rocked against him.

The kiss deepened, and my breasts brushed against his chest. His fingers slid up my wet thighs, higher and higher, until he was gripping my bum. When I pulled away to look into his eyes, they'd turned completely black with the unrestrained lust of an incubus. His magic slid over my skin, stroking me all over.

He shoved his hand into my hair, and he pulled my head back, exposing my neck. His kiss seared my throat, and my back arched further. With his tight grip on my hair and my waist, he was in complete control of me now, and my body was on fire. My thighs clenched around him.

But something he'd said rang in the hollows of my mind. *Angels were never supposed to be on this earth...they are the face of true evil, and they must answer for their crimes. A scourge...*

My blood turned to ice, and I pulled away from him, jumping to my feet. I smoothed down my damp T-shirt, taking a long, slow breath. I forced my pulse to slow. "Let's not do that again." My voice sounded sharper than I wanted it to.

For just a moment, I thought I saw a flash of vulnerability in his eyes, and I felt the impact of it like a pang in my chest. Then, his gaze shuttered.

Now that I'd stood up, I was freezing.

"You're right," he said. "Of course. And it seems like you've mastered the skill we came here to practice." He rose, and his eyes faded from deep, animalistic black to their usual cold violet. He wasn't looking at me anymore. "Tomorrow, when the trial begins, you will need to hunt down the enclave of angels. Use the lust magic." Already, he was moving for the house, eyes straight ahead. He did not want to look at me at all. "You'll see the angels begin to transform before your very eyes. Then, you just need to slaughter them."

"I take it you don't think I need any extra lessons in slaughtering demons."

"I have no concerns about your ability to kill. Just make sure you get there before Maddan does. Don't leave anyone for him to slaughter. If you succeed in this trial, Grand Master Savus will have to accept that the Old Gods have chosen you. It will be over for Maddan, or Savus will lose his crown for good."

He pulled open the door to Grandmother Elise's house.

She stood in the center of the room in a cream bathrobe, her cheeks flushed. She took a sip of a pink cocktail, her cleavage on full display. She *really* didn't look like a grandmother.

She crossed to Ruadan, swishing her hips. "Big strong man like you, going to waste." She gripped him by the belt of his pants and pulled him closer. Her drink sloshed as he slammed into her. "I'll tell you what, Prince of Misery, I will ride you hard until I put a smile on that face." She nodded at me. "Your friend can come too. I'm not greedy. I will share."

He disengaged her hand from his trousers. "Thank you for your orchard, Grandmother Elise. I'll visit again soon to fix your curtains."

Ruadan ushered me toward the door with his hand on the small of my back, quickening his pace.

"I want more than just curtains when you get back here. Gods-damned waste," she muttered as we left.

CHAPTER 23

$\mathcal{M}$addan and I stood before the Institute's gates, and our mentors flanked us. At least His Royal Twattiness had the good sense to leave the crown behind. I wore a black dress and boots—the dress short enough that I could easily run.

For our angel-hunting mission, I wore a sword slung over my back —my favorite weapon. Ruadan's ring sat tucked in my pocket, and I was ready to slip it on when I found the angels. I was keeping it hidden for now. No need to let Maddan know what I had planned.

This time, we had to hunt down our targets on our own. All I knew was that the angels were trying to live like primitive humans to learn about human culture, and that they wanted to infiltrate our world again— covertly. But it wasn't much to go on. They could be hiding, disguised as humans, anywhere in London. I had no idea what to make of the whole "primitive" idea.

I glanced at Maddan again, and the violet lumen stone glowing around his neck. He'd be able to leap all over the city with that thing. Unfortunately, I was stuck moving around in much more mundane ways: walking or crammed between drunk, sweaty men on the Tube.

As I turned it over in my mind, mist roiled over the ground, bubbling like a cauldron brew. Footfalls echoed off the stone, and

Grand Master Savus shifted out of the shadows and into the moonlight. His silver crown gleamed on his head—now slightly restored. Apparently, his failure to execute me had him back in the Old Gods' favor.

"Tonight," he began, "You must act like real trackers, the way the Shadow Fae must track in real life. Somewhere, in the great city of London, the angels have made it their mission to learn the primitive ways of the human species. These angelic spies seek to live like primal human beasts, connecting themselves to the earth. They want to study the wild impulses of the human race."

I frowned, fairly certain they'd arrived several thousand years too late for that sort of caveman thing. Then again, if the Millwall football team lost, they might be in luck.

"We're not telling you the targets' location." Grand Master Savus's silver hair flitted in the breeze. "Your task is simple. Find the angels, and kill them." Then, Savus glared at me, his silver eyes glinting. "I will be watching your every move through my scrying mirror. Ruadan will follow you to make sure you don't attempt an escape. I'm sure you understand by now that you cannot escape him."

Nope. He finds me through my sex dreams.

The gate groaned open to a stony esplanade before the Institute. In a blur of dark shadows, Maddan was off, the wind whooshing past me as he dashed away. I had to hope that he had no idea what the hells he was doing.

Now, how to find the angels? I closed my eyes, letting my mind go blank for a moment.

Mentally, I reviewed what Savus had said. *Primitive. Primal. Beasts. Wild. Connected to the earth.*

As I rolled the words over and over, a seed of an idea took root in my mind, until I knew *exactly* where to start.

* * *

IN THE MILDEWED hall of my old squat, I knocked on Uncle Darrell's door. A shuffling noise sounded on the other side, and then the door creaked open.

As soon as I saw his face, I knew I'd made the right decision. He stood before me wearing a bicycle helmet with stag's horns duct-taped to either side. In addition to the antlers, he wore a wool poncho with no trousers, and about forty-seven crystal necklaces.

He beamed. "Arianna! What happened to you? Did you hear all the rumors that the spell-slayers got you? I told people, I said no—" His gaze darted to Ruadan, who stood behind me, and he fell silent.

Then, he dropped to his knees. "Oh ancient one! Oh masterful fae! Being of eternal light!"

"Darkness, really," I corrected him. "Never mind. Darrell, please stand up. We need your help."

As he rose, the tips of his antlers knocked into the top of the door-frame, and he winced, straightening them. "Took a lot of time to put this together," he muttered.

It smelled *heavily* of spliffs inside.

He brushed off his hands on his poncho. "What can I help you with, then?"

"I'm looking for a…some kind of primal, primitive event. I don't know what you'd call it. People acting like beasts? Connecting to the earth?"

"The midsummer festival. Yeah, I'm on my way now, actually. Men only to start, but we could use a real fae, like your friend here. You'll really connect to the earth; do you know what I mean?" His lip curled in a "hurts so good" face. "Feel Mother Nature's glorious embrace like a…" He grunted and made a cupping motion with his hands, and I tried not to imagine what the gesture was supposed to represent. "Do you know what I mean?"

Ruadan just stood there, his arms folded, darkening the hallway with his magic. The air misted in front of my face, and I thought of Grandma Elise complaining about her heating bill.

I scratched my cheek. "Yeah he's not into that so much. I think he'll be hanging back, actually. You said it was men only?"

He scrunched up his face. "It's sort of a man thing, you know? Recharging our testosterone from the earth's roots. Really reconnect to our balls." He raised his eyebrows at Ruadan, as if hoping for some sort of approval.

The lights in the hallway flickered on and off.

Darrell's antlers clacked against the doorframe. "So anyway, the idea is that the primal drumbeats will attract females, who will mate with us like beasts."

I nodded. "Right. Seems reasonable. Maybe I could just...be in the vicinity for when that happens."

He nodded enthusiastically, antlers wobbling. "Yeah. I like it. We will celebrate like the ancient primordial power of the earth. We'll populate her flesh with our seed. Right." He clapped his hands together. "Let's take the District Line. It'll bring us right there."

* * *

We rode the old, creaking Tube train across town. Ruadan sat at the far end of the car, cloaked in shadows, occasionally provoking screams from anyone who entered near him.

Uncle Darrell and I sat in the center of the car, and he pulled out his bongo drum to serenade me for the journey. Get me in the mood. I closed my eyes, trying to mentally summon a happier place, which—given the grim circumstances—included the Palatial Room.

As he drummed on the bongos, singing along, one of his helmet antlers caught on a silver pole. "Fucking hell. The way they make these bloody trains. Honestly." He shook his head at me, as if I were about to commiserate with him about the lack of consideration for helmet-antlers in the Tube's design.

At last, the train pulled up to Richmond Park station, the brakes screeching as it ground to a halt. Darrell snatched up his drum, with one hand on his helmet. The doors slid open, and Uncle Darrell carefully ducked to avoid catching his antlers on the ceiling on the way out. Ruadan slipped out another door, keeping his distance from us. I wasn't sure if that was mentor protocol, or just the sheer embarrassment of walking around in public with Uncle Darrell.

Darrell reached into his bag and pulled out a bottle. He unscrewed the top, then handed it to me. "Try it."

I took a sip, then immediately spit the rancid liquid onto the pavement. "Fucking hells. What is that?"

"Fermented goat milk. I make it myself."

I gagged, not entirely sure he even knew what "fermented" meant.

Through an open gate, we crossed into a dark, grassy park. I glanced behind me, catching a glimpse of Ruadan's bright violet eyes. He was still hanging back—just watching. Making sure I didn't escape.

"I'm afraid this is where I've got to leave you," said Darrell. "The men are gathering. Can you hear the drums? Can you feel the beat of primal life in your blood? We'll mate soon."

"So should I just wait a bit then?"

He shrugged. "Yeah, just give it a few minutes. Let the drums lure you."

One of his antlers started to sag, and he held it up with his hand as he turned and walked off in the darkness.

I closed my eyes, tuning into the distant sound of the drums. After giving him a few moments, I began following Darrell at a distance, while scanning the park for signs of Maddan. I sniffed the air. I couldn't smell the prince, but I smelled something new—the scent of iron. The metal of the angels.

I slid the silver ring onto my finger, and my back arched at the rush of magic through my body.

Time to watch some angels fall from grace.

CHAPTER 24

$\mathcal{I}$ walked barefoot over forest soil on my way through Richmond Park. Moonlight beamed over tall grasses. A distant drumbeat boomed in my gut, stirring my blood—but not for lust, as Darrell had hoped. No, I was in a fighting mood.

The drumbeat grew louder as I approached a clearing. Someone had tied ribbons from the trees surrounding the glade. Through the trunks, I caught a glimpse of a bonfire. I'd come to the right place.

I glanced down at the violet magic twisting between my fingertips.

Sheltered behind an oak, I peered through the trees into the clearing. There, men dressed in loincloths danced around the fire, Uncle Darrell among them. He wore bells on his ankles and wrists.

As I stared at them, footfalls crunched behind me. I whirled, shoving my glowing hand into my pocket. There, standing behind me, I found a man. His potbelly hung over his loincloth, and he'd painted his face with blue streaks. Moonlight shone on his bald scalp. By his smell, he was definitely human.

He pushed his spectacles up on his nose. "Oh, hello there. The, uh, the shaman said the drumbeat might attract mates. Primal thing, innit. Are you here to mate?"

"No, I'm not here to mate," I said quietly. There was no way in hells

I wanted to hit this guy with lust magic. This conversation had started off bad enough as it was.

"You are, actually." He leaned against the tree.

"Don't tell me what I think, fuckwit." My voice came out louder and angrier than I'd aimed for.

He held up his hands. "Sorry. I was told that what women really want is to be controlled and protected by an alpha. We went stag hunting tonight to connect to our primitive selves."

I brushed my fingertips over the strap on my chest, tempted to use my sword on him. This man was wasting my time.

"It's in the hormones," he went on. "Females like a man who can provide. I read a book about it. Men are supposed to plant their seed in a harem of younger females. It's biology, innit." He cleared his throat. "Unfortunately, turns out, a stag is very hard to shoot with a bow and arrow, so I can't say we caught one. Derek caught an arrow in the leg, and Kevin injured himself with the bowstring. Someone brought a goat, but it ran away before we could shoot it. The bloody thing ate our cheesy biscuits, too, and I'd really been looking forward to them."

I was still mentally ticking over the moral issues with just cutting off his head.

"Anyway, how do we proceed?" he went on. "I'm not entirely comfortable with human mating rituals. Should I buy you a sausage or another type of food item? A box of cereal? I could get you a kebab or something and then we could have some sex while I try to bite your neck from behind, like a lion?" He made his hands into claws.

I blinked. "You're not...human?" I could have sworn he was. He smelled human, and he seemed too feeble to be anything else.

A loud chortle. "Oh, I am! Of course. I just seriously don't know how normal human mating rituals work. I was told something about providing food and biting, to assert dominance."

I glanced back at the shamans. Uncle Darrell was gripping the stag's antlers on his head. "None of these people know how normal humans behave. You're learning from the wrong people." Which would make it all the more difficult to pick out the angels among them, unless I just rained the magic down on top of them.

Another human man lumbered behind him. This one had strapped cardboard to his arms, and he'd glued the cardboard with orange and yellow feathers. He wore a bird mask pushed up on his head, and he gnawed on a chicken wing. "Oh, heya, Martin. Did you lure a female for mating?'

Martin scratched his nose. "Yeah, I'm not sure she's going for it. I'm not really sure what's going wrong."

"Did you tell her about the lion-biting?" His friend frowned, perplexed. "And the kebab?"

Martin blinked. "I did, Gareth, yeah."

"I'm not going for it," I confirmed.

The bird man spread out his wings. "I'm actually a gladiator myself."

There was no way in hells this man was a gladiator. He'd die within seconds.

"In World of Warcraft," he added. "How'd you like to mate with a phoenix? Spiritually connect to the beginning and the end of the universe?"

I shook my head. "Birds don't have penises, so…"

His face fell. "They don't?"

"Only ducks, but…" I let the sentence trail off. I'd wasted enough time with these two. "You know what? Never mind. Also, sorry about this."

"About what?" asked Martin.

Rapid-fire, I slammed my fist twice into the side of Martin's head, knocking him unconscious. Bird-man started to emit a little yelp, but I pivoted, bashing his skull with my left hand.

The two human men fell to the ground, their chests still moving. Good enough.

I turned back to the clearing. With the ring on my finger, I summoned the lust magic until it crackled at my fingertips, pulsing with violet. I hurled it into the air, flicking my fingers at the end of the throw. The violet magic dispersed, spreading out over the festival.

Pure lust rained down on the men. Within moments, they were groaning, rubbing their chests. Uncle Darrell got down on the ground to defile the soil once again. Overhead, ravens circled us, wildly cawing.

Hiding behind the oak, I pulled my sword from its sheath, staring as some of the men began to transform. Dark, leathery wings sprouted from their backs. Their skin scaled over, reds and greens glistening in the moonlight. Claws and talons sprouted from their hands. Lightning cracked the sky, a flash of white light illuminating horns.

The breath left my lungs. I'd heard of angels falling, but I'd never seen it before. My lip curled. It was repulsive.

The Institute had been exactly right. Angels *were* trying to infiltrate the human race once again, an insidious attempt to start another apocalypse. I hadn't thought angels were much of a threat these days, but apparently they were. We had to let these celestial beings know that if they tried coming to Earth, they would all die like mortals.

Lightning speared the sky again, thunder rumbling. I scanned the crowd, counting the demons among them. Eight in total.

What I hadn't expected was for the demons to immediately turn on the humans, hungry for flesh. Their teeth and claws sunk into the humans' skin. Inwardly, I cursed Ruadan. Maybe this hadn't been the best plan. The pleasurable groans had turned to terrified screams.

In any case, I was about to dispatch all the fallen angels. And Maddan hadn't even arrived yet. Things were looking up for the Amazon Terror.

With my sword drawn, I rushed into the clearing.

As I did, a demon with iridescent skin and shimmering wings spotted me. He raced for me, dark magic spilling from his body, snarling as he ran.

I swung my sword in a controlled arc and struck it through his neck.

The scent of demon blood drew the others closer. Seven demons surrounded me, but at least they'd stopped ripping into the humans.

I sliced my blade through the air, pivoting rapidly to keep them at bay.

The human men were running away from the scene, shrieking. I caught a glimpse of Uncle Darrell pulling up his trousers as he tried to flee.

A demon clawed at me from behind, slashing into the flesh of my back. I whirled, bringing down my sword hard into his shoulder. I nearly cleaved his torso, but I couldn't quite drive it in deep enough. The fucker was still standing. Another vicious slash at my back, and I whirled again, driving my sword through the demon's heart.

Pain splintered my upper body, but I tried to block it out, to focus on the fight. I'd been outnumbered before, but six on one wasn't ideal. At least they didn't have weapons beyond their own claws.

My own primal instincts began to take over, my blood sparking with adrenaline. They'd come to Earth to witness primitive beasts, and I could show them what they wanted to see.

I had to move quickly, whirling as they lunged for me. I fended them off with parries from my sword. When teeth sank into my neck from behind, I nearly dropped my weapon, and blood pounded in my skull. Losing my sword would be death. Luckily, I managed to keep a tight grip on it, and I slammed my elbow hard into the demon's ribs. Then I kicked the next demon who was lunging for me.

Battle fury raced through my blood, my heartbeat slamming against my ribs. Strength imbued my limbs, as memories of my gladiator days whispered through my blood. The warrior in me was coming out to play. I was no longer Arianna. I was the Amazon Terror, steel and teeth, fists and rage. I didn't feel pain or fear, only cold fury. The demons were after my blood, and I'd fend them off with the tip of my blade.

My senses had tuned into the demons' smallest movements—their labored breaths, their grunts, the shifting of their feet, their wings beating the air. As they clawed at me, I had a mental map of their positions.

I thrust my sword through another demon's chest. *Five to one.*

A clawed hand raked at my back, deeper this time. I whirled. My sword carved right through his neck, blood spurting. *Four to one.*

If these had been archangels, I would've been screwed. Luckily, they were regular old angels.

I was breathing faster now, my heart racing. The demons had started screeching, frantic with a lust for death. One of them grabbed me by the hair, pulling my head back. His teeth clamped into my collarbone, and pain splintered my neck. I brought my foot up hard into his groin, then swung for the demons again, my action more wild this time.

I tightened my grip on the sword, trying to summon the battle fury that would give me energy, and would block out the pain. As blood poured from my body, my attacks grew clumsier. Dizziness clouded my mind.

CHAPTER 25

My mouth had gone dry. Blood loss? Somewhere, in the back of my mind, I was wondering what Ruadan would do if it looked like I was about to die. Would he intervene?

Sharp talons seared my side, and I swung again, slicing my sword right into the demon's ribs. I drove it through to his heart.

Three to one.

I was floundering, badly injured. I needed a new tactic to finish this fight. A quick scan of the surroundings didn't highlight anything I could use against them. But maybe distraction alone would help.

Baleros's sixteenth law of power: Use the element of surprise.

I shifted my sword to my left hand, summoning the lust magic with my right. I flung the violet magic into the air, and it rained down on us. As it hit me, my skin heated, and my mind flashed with images of Ruadan.

Gods damn it. I'd distracted myself, too.

Still, it had worked, and the demons stopped trying to kill me. I tried not to look at the unfortunate demonic bulges they were sporting in their trousers, and I attempted to block out the memory of how Ruadan had looked without a shirt on.

Death. Think of death.

Darkness pooled in my body, racing through my limbs like an opiate, pushing the lust magic out to my extremities.

Three distracted demons left to go. With a sharpened focus, I cut my sword into the first one, hacking off his head.

Six down.

I whirled, stabbing another in the chest. I drove my blade through his heart. When the last one lunged for me, I ran my sword through his abdomen. He fell, and I drew out my blade. Thick, sticky blood coated the steel, dripping onto the earth.

Eight down. Euphoria bubbled in my chest. I was going to be knighted, at last. I'd finally be safe.

With my opponents all dead, I gripped my side. They'd torn some of my flesh to shreds, ripping through old scars to make new ones.

I speared the earth with the sword, then knelt down in front of it. A sacrifice for the Old Gods, who seemed to favor me.

"Old Gods," I mumbled, dizzy from the blood loss. "This is for you. A sacrifice and whatnot. You're welcome."

A strong hand helped me up. I rose, practically falling, into Ruadan's chest. He steadied me.

"You did well." His rich voice soothed me.

I closed my eyes, leaning against him. "I'd say so. They're all dead. None left for Maddan."

Ruadan's body tensed, and when I looked up at his face, my pulse started to race. I could feel his heartbeat quickening through his shirt. His eyes had darkened, and he stared across the park.

The air cooled. Ruadan pulled away from me, letting me stand on my own. I gripped my side, where one of the demons had slashed into my flesh.

"What do you see?" I asked.

"Grand Master Savus is here, and he's not alone."

"To knight me, or what?"

"He should be knighting you. It was the final trial, and you clearly won. But the ceremony usually happens at the Institute."

Mist had grown thicker in the park, curling in steamy tendrils off the grass. Slowly, my eyes adjusted to the dark and the fog, and I shuddered at the sight of a small legion marching closer. Their silver armor shone in the moonlight, cowls pulled over their heads.

"Who are they?" I asked.

"That's the mist army." Ruadan stepped in front of me. The gesture would have annoyed me, except I was losing so much blood that I frankly needed the protection.

Savus stepped out from the mist, his silver hair tucked neatly beneath his crown—the metal now rotten and black. "Arrest her."

Ruadan's dark magic billowed from his body, tingeing the mist with darkness. The air around us grew so cold that the dew on the grass turned to crystallized frost. I hugged myself, shivering.

"Arrest her for what?" asked Ruadan. His deep voice held a threat of violence that slid right through my bones.

I gritted my teeth. Considering Grand Master Savus had brought an entire mist legion with him, we weren't going to fight our way out of this.

Savus's serene smile was like a single claw up my spine. And when I scanned the army behind him, my heart only beat faster. Fog pulsed around them, as if someone were blowing it through a bellows. Their eyes glowed with silver.

Savus tapped a leather-gloved hand against his silver fingertips. "The excuses about the reaping dagger. The lust magic driving her mad. That's not what happened." He cut a sharp look to Ruadan. "And you know it. You lied for her, didn't you? I already had you flogged once for failing to kill her like I'd asked. I knew you favored the gutter fae. Now, I've learned you lied to me. Your mother would be so disappointed. A traitor to the Shadow Fae. All because a pretty demi-fae caught your eye."

My body felt weak, and I faltered. Savus had asked Ruadan to kill me? I supposed that was one way to get around angering the Old Gods. Have someone else do your dirty work for you. But Ruadan had refused. In fact, he'd taken a flogging for me, and he hadn't even told me. I guess that explained the deep scars I'd seen on the back of his arms.

But if Ruadan hadn't told Savus about Baleros, who had?

Ruadan's dark magic snaked through the air. "Baleros was threatening her friend, and Arianna was trying to protect her. Our role is to protect, isn't it? That's what she was doing."

To the right of the mist army, another man was moving. The fog curled around his body. Except, he wasn't part of the army. By his red hair and glittering crown, I recognized him as Maddan.

"You can't turn on her now." Ruadan's voice boomed through the fog. "The Old Gods have chosen her. She successfully completed the task. She identified and slaughtered all the angels. Angel blood coats her sword. Look at the state of your crown."

Maddan crossed to Ruadan, his face beet-red. "Lies!" he shrieked. He'd dipped his sword in blood at some point, and it dripped off his blade. "I won the task by default. The incubus was helping her. Anyone could see that he was helping her. He gave her his magic. This is not the work of the Old Gods. This is the work of Ruadan. I killed an angel on my own, without the benefit of his help."

"You didn't kill a single angel," I shouted. "You weren't even here."

He lifted his sword. "You left one of them alive. I finished him."

Grand Master Savus straightened. "Perhaps the Old Gods do favor the demi-fae. But she came from Baleros, and we cannot trust her. Clearly, she cannot be a Shadow Fae. The Shadow Fae must trust one another, and she is a spy. We will keep her in the Palatial Room until we decide a further course of action."

Ruadan's dark magic roiled around him like a storm, and the temperature plummeted. His pale hair whipped around his head. "Who told you about Baleros?" he asked, in a tone that turned my own blood to ice.

"Arrest her," Savus repeated.

At his order, a line of mist soldiers began marching for me. Injured, I was too weak to fight them. Ruadan had no chance of slaughtering them all. And yet, for some insane reason, he decided to try. As the soldiers closed in around us, he drew his blade, moving like a hurricane wind. He was a blur of shadows and speed, furiously carving into shadow soldiers. But it didn't seem as if a blade could hurt them. With each attack of his sword, the soldiers dissipated like smoke.

When a new line of mist soldiers raised their bows, arrows nocked, my mind started to go blank. That familiar darkness—the weightlessness of falling—spilled through my blood.

I held it back the best I could. If I unleashed my true self, everyone would die—Ruadan included.

The archers launched their arrows, all aimed at Ruadan. He shadow-leapt, shifting position, but one of the arrows still slammed into his chest. He fell back to the earth.

My world tilted as I recognized the dark sheen of iron. An inch or two to the right, and it would have pierced his heart, killing him.

I stared at him, my own heart squeezing in my chest as the mist soldiers surrounded me. They gripped my arms, dragging me away from him. What would happen to him? He'd risen up against Savus—committed treason. Would they kill the prince of Emain?

Rough hands of mist pulled me down, smothering me, until my world went black.

CHAPTER 26

I woke to find myself back in the Palatial Room. This time, no one had thought to leave me with my bug-out bag. Rough stone bit into my back, and the stench nearly overpowered me. An irregular dripping noise echoed off the dungeon walls.

My wounds felt like they were ripping me apart. "I'm getting really irritated with this place," I muttered.

"Arianna?" Ruadan's voice wended through the dark, a velvety caress on my skin.

My chest unclenched at the sound of his voice. "Ruadan? Are you okay?"

"I've been better." His voice sounded strained.

"Did they get the iron out of your chest?"

"No. But it missed my heart."

I winced. The agony must be excruciating. In fact, it must be poisoning his blood even now.

"I don't suppose you can *Wraith* your way out of here," I said.

"Not with all the iron piercing me. I hardly have any magic left. How are your wounds?"

Someone had snuffed out all the candles, and I couldn't even see

346

my injuries in the darkness. But oh gods, I could feel them. Pain lashed me from all sides. "I've been better," I said. "The last time I was in here, I dreamt of…" I didn't want to say the word *Emain* in case a guard was listening in. "I dreamt of apple orchards on a rocky slope. I'm not sure how I slept so well in here. I slept the entire time." Only now was I starting to put the pieces together. As a demigod of the night, Ruadan had sleep magic at his fingertips. "That was you, wasn't it?"

He didn't answer, but now I was certain that it had been him. A prince of Emain, who'd sent me calming dreams so I could rest in this horrible place. "They were nice dreams," I added.

"When I was a boy, before I joined the Shadow Fae, I spent all day in that orchard. My brothers and I played soldiers, hunting each other with wooden swords."

"You have brothers other than Caine?"

"I had six. Three of them died."

Silence hung over us. "I'm sorry."

The uneven dripping grew louder. My mind was still whirling, reviewing everything that had happened. Grand Master Savus striding out of the mist. Maddan throwing a fit, insisting—despite all evidence—that he'd actually killed more angels than I had.

"We'll get out of here," said Ruadan quietly.

"How?"

"I'm still working on that."

"Who do you think told Savus about Baleros?" I asked.

"Do you have any idea where Ciara is?" he asked abruptly.

"I have no idea." My heart began to race. "Do you think Savus has her? What if he tortured it out of her?"

"Shh…" he said. "Save your energy. Panicking won't help her."

I wanted to slam my fist into the wall. Of course panicking wouldn't help, but what else could I do at this point? My breath was coming in short, sharp bursts, and my heart raced wildly. I rested my head in my hands, gritting my teeth so I wouldn't sob or scream.

"Your breathing sounds panicked."

I didn't answer him. I was too focused on trying not to scream with rage. I leaned back against the wall, sucking in a sharp breath as the jagged rocks pierced the wounds on my back.

"You're in a lot of pain," he said. "Hold on."

His dark magic whispered around my skin, and spirals of shadows wrapped around me, sliding over my skin. I sighed as his calming magic stroked my body, until I couldn't feel the pain anymore. I ran my fingertips over the skin on my side. He'd completely healed it.

His magic continued to caress my skin, calming my nerves, until my eyes drifted closed. His magic started to ebb, and yet sleep was claiming my mind. Once more, I dreamt of Emain.

* * *

When I woke, I couldn't feel his magic anymore.

"Ruadan?" I called out.

The only response was the uneven dripping of water.

Gods damn it. Had he gone unconscious, or had they dragged him out of the cell to kill him? I fought the urge to slam my fist into the wall. Breaking my hand wouldn't do any good.

Groaning, I stood in my cell. How long would Savus keep me in here? I gritted my teeth, my fingers twitching.

Ruadan had healed me, and with my body now strong, I felt an overwhelming urge to hurt the people who'd put us here. When I closed my eyes, I could envision myself punching Savus in the jaw, over and over, smashing that creepy grin off his face.

When I heard the murmuring of voices farther down the hall, and saw the flickering of warm light over the damp stone, my heart sped up. Footfalls moved closer over the stone.

Savus hadn't wanted to kill me, because it would put him at odds with the Old Gods. But he seemed to think he'd found a loophole by asking Ruadan to kill me. Let someone else take the fall for him. I imagined he hoped I'd simply start failing the trials, or perhaps that Maddan would properly kill me at some point. But Maddan was so amazingly incompetent that here I was, still alive. Ready to savage my enemies.

Still, I could now accept that there was no way Savus was allowing me into the Institute of the Shadow Fae. Old Gods or not, my invitation had been canceled.

As I stared through the bars, Maddan's smug face showed up outside my cell. He held a torch, and its warm light lit up his face from below, giving him a devilish look.

Ciara's voice rang in my mind. *The devil wears many faces.*

I imagined Maddan had been up in his room for days, dreaming of this moment in such a fevered state that he'd run out of tissues. Was he here to kill me?

"Arianna," he purred.

This time, it didn't look as if he'd brought any distilled magic with him.

My lip curled. "Maddan. You couldn't win the trials, so you've come here to kill me."

"No, I've just come to look at you in your filthy little cage." The bulge in his trousers confirmed my tissue theory. "Grand Master Savus won't let me kill you. It seems he has a plan for a public execution of you and Ruadan. I can't wait to see it."

"Why does he want us dead?"

He arched an eyebrow. "I'm not supposed to say."

I snorted. "As if you're privy to that information. There's no way he'd trust an incompetent idiot like you. You're just a pawn in all this. Not a real player."

"Bollocks." He spat. "I know plenty. You're leverage, just like Ruadan is."

I rolled my eyes dramatically. "Oh, sure. That makes sense." I prodded. "Leverage for what?"

"Baleros wants you dead. He wants both of you dead. He needs the World Key from Ruadan. You? I think he just hates you. Just like I do."

Rage slammed into me. I gripped the iron bars, ignoring the fact that they burned my skin, and I stared into Maddan's eyes. "Grand Master Savus is working with Baleros? Enemy of the Shadow Fae?"

So that's how Grand Master Savus knew about my connection to Baleros. Baleros had told him right out. Savus had been giving up my location all along, sending assassins to try to kill me during the trials. Why would they be working together—the leader of the Shadow Fae, and one of their greatest enemies? "Why?" I gritted out. "Why is Savus working with a traitor to the Shadow Fae?"

Maddan's mouth closed, his lips pressed into a thin line. It seemed he realized that he'd said too much.

"I'm not saying anything else. I'll see you again when it's time to kill you."

The world fell out from under my feet. I wasn't sure how I'd save Ruadan and myself, but I would. I wasn't going to let these creeps slaughter us.

Maddan cocked his head. "Do you know that I've always dreamed of having a little prisoner like you of my own? My father wouldn't let me have one. He says madness runs in our family line. And it does, you know. My grandfather's favorite courtier was his pet lion. He made him his Minister of Festivals. He used to feed the gutter fae to his lion, William. When I was a boy, I'd go to watch. I wanted some of the gutter fae slaves for my own." He closed his eyes, a smile curling his lips. "The females' clothes were often torn, just rags, so I could see their shameful parts."

I blinked. *Shameful parts?* "Can you go now? I prefer the sound of my own screaming in my mind."

"With your short little dress on, I can almost see your shameful parts."

"Oh my gods, *stop.*"

But he was still standing there. "Eventually, the gutter fae rose up and slaughtered my grandfather. My father became king. He had all sorts of ideas about keeping the gutter trash happy." He opened his eyes again, moving closer. "But I want one little gutter fae for my own. Just one." His cheeks were pink, his eyes glazed with fever. "Too bad you'll be dead soon. Still, I'll have the memory of you trapped in here."

My lips quirked in a smile. "Go on, then. Open this iron door. I'm right here for the taking."

If only I could get him to unlock the door, he'd be dead within moments…

He took a step back into the shadows. "I'm not that stupid. I'll have to admire you from here."

I closed my eyes, frustration rising. When I opened them again, he was gone.

Without Ruadan's help, I could no longer sleep on my own. I crouched against the rough wall in the Palatial Room, trying to think about Emain. Sadly, it seemed that I couldn't summon the vivid visions myself.

My heart rate quickened at the sound of footfalls moving down the hallway again.

Savus held a torch in his silver hand, and the light danced over his crown. Soft and black like rotten banana peels, it hung limp over his skull.

I glared at him, envisioning myself killing him. If I could get myself out of here, perhaps I could rip off his silver arm and batter him half to death with it...

I flashed him a charming smile. "How nice to see you. Where the fuck is Ruadan? If you kill him, I swear to the gods I will find a way to rip every inch of flesh off your body."

"Arianna. You don't need to worry. He's still alive. For now. And I won't be exalting you. However, I will behead the both of you with an iron sword." He pursed his lips. "Or at least I'll have Maddan do it for me."

My body shook with rage. "You're working with Baleros. You've been giving him my location all along." I narrowed my eyes. "Were you throwing butterscotch sweets in my cell for him? Seriously, what the hells?"

He sighed. "Baleros has been giving us instructions. He did say the sweets would upset you, but he never explained why."

I still didn't understand. What was Savus getting out of this? "How can you betray the Institute this way?"

He stared at me. Along with his sagging crown, his shoulders looked slumped, no longer the rod-straight posture of a Grand Master.

He arched an eyebrow. "I suppose Maddan was the one who told you about this. He can't keep his mouth shut." His hand shook—a tremor I'd never seen before. Something had broken him. "But you're going to die anyway, so I suppose it doesn't matter what you know."

I felt as if a weight pressed on my chest. "Why do you want Ruadan and me dead?"

Grand Master Savus flinched. Then, he tapped a shaking, gloved hand against his silver fingertips, eying me through the bars.

"Why?" I shouted again.

"I don't. Killing you means I forfeit my crown and my power." Mist billowed around him. He clenched his hand into a fist, his jaw tightening with rage. "But Baleros demands it, doesn't he? He wants the World Key, of course. And he wants you dead. I have to comply with his demands." His voice cracked. "I tried to resist. I tried to find a way around it. I deserve to be the Grand Master. But I find I'm quite unable to resist his demands."

"Why?" I gritted out. "What leverage does he have on you?" Baleros always had leverage.

Savus cocked his head. "After you and Ruadan nearly killed him in the arena, he sent me a message. It was the first time I'd heard from him in over a century. It seems he's been keeping a secret for fifteen years."

"Fifteen years." The time frame sounded familiar. "Fifteen years ago was when he invaded Emain. That's when he killed Queen Macha." As soon as the words were out of my mouth, I began putting the pieces together. Baleros would never be so stupid as to kill a queen. That wasn't his M.O. Sure, he could kill someone like me. He'd always been willing to sacrifice my life. No one important cared about me.

But a queen, on the other hand—what could he get for a queen? Baleros collected leverage years in advance of playing his hand. Just like he had with Ciara.

I stared at Savus. "Queen Macha isn't really dead, is she?" Ruadan had said that her body was unrecognizable.

His gaze clouded, shoulders slumping even more. "I thought she was. Until Baleros sent me one of her fingers, just after you went missing." His voice cracked. Now I was getting a hint of what had broken him. "I'd know it anywhere. The golden skin, the delicately tapered fingertips. The sheen on her nails. I was her loyal subject for centuries. I kissed the rings on those fingers, bent my knee. She was the greatest ruler Emain had ever known." He met my gaze, his eyes filled with pain. "Baleros has been keeping her hidden in an unknown location. Trapped by some sort of magic. I've been sending a few Shadow Fae on secretive missions to find her, but to no avail. I have had no choice," he said through gritted teeth.

My breath was coming in short, sharp bursts. "If Baleros has had the queen all along, why did he go through all the rigmarole of sending assassins into the Institute? Why not just—I don't know—get Ruadan to do his bidding, open up worlds in exchange for his mother's life?"

"He doesn't want to get anywhere near Ruadan, not without dozens of iron arrows pointed at the Wraith's body. Baleros is terrified of him. He waited as long as he could to play his trump card. He tried getting his lackeys to steal the World Key. He tried getting you to steal it. He feels that he's now out of options. He's using the best bargaining chip he has. The fingers of a queen we all love." His eyes glistened. "I tried to resist. The Old Gods chose Ruadan, and they chose you. I couldn't send the mist army after you, or the Old Gods would steal my power. I hoped there was another way. I hoped you'd die in a trial, or fail one."

"You really thought Maddan could beat me?"

He shrugged. "No, not really, but it was a hope. And while I kept you here in prison, delaying his requests, Baleros bade me to do things to torment you. Butterscotch sweets, locking you in a cell… But he grew impatient when I failed to kill you. He wanted his World Key. I never wanted to kill Ruadan. She'll be so angry with me. But Baleros sent me another one of her beautiful fingers. You see that I had no choice, don't you? There was no other choice."

He had a hungry look, and I got the impression that he actually wanted my approval for his decisions. Like he wanted me to agree that executing Ruadan and me was clearly the best course of action.

I gritted my teeth. I wasn't giving him the redemption he was looking for. "And you have no idea where he's keeping her?"

"Do you honestly think that I wouldn't rescue her if I knew where she was?" he shouted, his voice bellowing off the stones. His eyes flashed. For a moment, intense fury contorted his features, and I had a vision of the formidable man he must have been at one time. Then, his eyes dulled again.

The way he described the queen's fingers made me think he was more than a loyal subject.

"You're in love with Queen Macha," I said. "That's why Baleros could manipulate you so easily."

Savus's mist whipped around him. "She was supposed to marry me. Centuries ago, she was supposed to be mine. But I couldn't marry her after she sullied herself with that incubus, and after she gave birth to Ruadan. He was a mistake that ruined both our lives."

"Of course, I understand. Ruadan's entire existence is a slap in your face, isn't it? A living symbol of your life's ruination." My lip curled. "Is it really all Baleros's doing, or do you just want to correct this blight on your life?"

The mist thickened around Savus. "I am doing what I must to protect a queen of Emain. That is all."

I could tell by the shaking of his hands that I'd rattled him.

"Do you honestly think Queen Macha could love you after you kill her son? You can't erase a mistake when the mistake is a person's child."

Savus's face turned pink. "I resisted Baleros's demands for as long as I could. But Baleros will rip her apart! He will exalt her!"

"You could turn the mist army against *him*."

"The goddess of fire would simply revive him. He can't be killed."

"Everything can be killed," I snarled. "You really haven't tried. You're giving a monster like Baleros the power to control the portals? You really think that's a good idea? I don't think you understand. Queen Macha won't just be *angry*. She will *hate* you with every cell in her body. His mother will want you dead—"

He flicked his hand and mist slid over my mouth, solidifying into a gag. Furious, I screamed into it.

"You're right," he said. "I can't let her know that I gave the command." He tapped his fingertips together. "We'll do this in private. Maddan will strike the blows. He's been eager to do that. I'll blame it on him, then I'll have him killed as well. Queen Macha will be so pleased when I exalt him. I don't care if I anger his father. I'm willing to make that sacrifice. You see?" His eyes shone in the darkness, the terrifying gleam of a fanatic. "I am willing to make that sacrifice for my queen."

I shouted into my gag, my chest heaving.

He arched an eyebrow. "I know what you're thinking. It's a betrayal of the Institute. But the truth is, I'm making a sacrifice for the good of Emain." He tapped a finger against his lip, eying me warily. "You're dangerous. I'm going to need to subdue you."

He flicked his hand again, and the mist covered my nose so I couldn't breathe. As my lungs burned, I knew what he was doing. Smothering me, knocking me unconscious until I no longer posed the smallest of threats to him.

CHAPTER 28

I couldn't see much when I awoke—just the mist around me, and the contours of mist soldiers. A small cohort surrounded me, fog wafting off their silhouettes.

Even if I couldn't see much, I sure as shit could feel the iron garrote searing my throat. So *this* is where Baleros had learned about the iron garrote—apparently an Institute classic. Rope bound my wrists behind an iron stake, and the metal scalded my skin. My hands were crammed between the stake and a jagged stone wall.

The mist had been taken from my nose so I could breathe again, but it still gagged my mouth. A jagged edge of stone bit into my fingers, practically crushing them against the stake.

By the dim sound of dripping water and the heavy, mildewed feel of the air, I had the sense that we were in an underground space, one without open windows.

I'd tried to talk Savus out of a public execution. Instead, I'd given him the idea to secretly assassinate us.

"Arianna?" Ruadan's voice echoed off the stones.

I screamed into the damned mist gag, then I willed my heartbeat to slow, trying to think clearly.

As I surveyed the hall around me, I flexed my wrists. When I looked up, I could see the contours of the room. A high, mossy ceiling arched a hundred feet above us. No windows. It seemed to be an enormous underground hall, and iron torture devices hung from the stone above. Not a fitting place for the prince of Emain to die.

Then, torchlight tinged the mist with warm light, and footfalls clacked over the stone. From between the mist soldiers, Maddan stalked closer, a silver-hilted sword slung at his hip. I had no doubt the blade was iron, ready to dispatch us. My heart was a hunted animal.

I wanted to vomit into my gag. Frantically, I rotated my wrists back and forth to loosen the bindings. If I managed to free my hands —well, I'd still be shit out of luck, because iron pinned my neck to the stake. But with my hands free, maybe I could attack Maddan if he got close enough…or delay things until I thought of a better idea.

I grimaced, now shifting the ropes up and down against the jagged rock. Maybe I could saw through them.

Maddan bit his lip at the sight of me, his cheeks reddening. He stroked his fingertips over the silver hilt of his sword, up and down, up and down.

I shot a quick glance in the direction of Ruadan. As the mist shifted, I caught a glimpse of him. His arms were bound to a stake behind his spine, an iron garrote at his neck. All that iron around him would dampen his powers, sapping his strength.

Maddan unsheathed his sword, a smile curling his lips as he stared at me. "I'm glad you now understand the proper order of things." His gaze nervously slid to Ruadan, as if he were scared the incubus was about to break free and rip his head off.

"I never wanted to execute a prince," said Maddan. "It goes against everything I was raised to believe. But Grand Master Savus said that I had to. It's the only way I can become a Shadow Fae. The only way he'd let me slaughter the gutter trash. As you can see, I don't have a choice in this."

I glanced at Ruadan again. For once, no dark magic whipped around him, since the iron absorbed it all. He glared at Maddan, his eyes completely black. He didn't say a word, his animal stillness taking over. Was he just going to stand there, completely still, until the iron sword cut into his throat?

A grin spread on Maddan's face, as he seemed to forget Ruadan was in the room. He prowled closer to me, and my skin crawled.

Behind Maddan, the cohort of mist soldiers marched forward, armor glinting in the torchlight.

Panic started to crawl up my throat.

Maddan licked his lips. "I just want to savor this moment. A pretty little gutter fae, bound by iron." His voice was a groan. "All mine. I'll be thinking about this for a long time."

By the creepy-as-fuck leer on his face, I knew he'd forgotten about Ruadan altogether. I just focused on the small but rapid movements behind my back. *Up and down, up and down.*

Mist whirled around the room, snaking over the floor and curling around our bodies, rushing over the rough contours of the stone walls. I could hardly see the soldiers anymore—only Maddan in front of me. The mist was a mercy, concealing the subtle shake of my shoulders that might otherwise give away my attempt to saw through the rope.

Dimly, I could hear the faint, almost inaudible groan of metal coming from somewhere near Ruadan. What was he doing over there?

Maddan, the sick twat, looked all too thrilled with this situation. Maybe I could keep him distracted long enough to cut through the rope. I opened my eyes wide in a mimicry of terror and screamed into my gag.

Maddan groaned with pleasure. He couldn't possibly imagine that right now, I was thinking of how it would sound when the crack of his bone echoed off the stones.

Up and down, up and down.

I longed for anything to disrupt Savus's plans, to delay the point when the blade would hack into our throats…anything to give us time to figure a way out.

When Maddan clamped his hand on my waist, I nearly threw up. Instead, I distracted myself with images of his death. Let's see…an iron nail through the heart, one in his skull. *Up and down, up and down.*

The sword, of course, would be easiest—

At last, the final bit of rope snapped, and my hands burst free. I grabbed Maddan's head—one hand around the back, one on his jaw. I twisted, and the crack of bone sounded off the stone ceiling.

Maddan's body slumped to the ground with a dull thud, and I stared down at him, smiling under my gag.

Slowly, the fog began to part, and Savus stepped forward.

"You killed my executioner," he said. Then, a long sigh. "I suppose he's not fully dead. Until he recovers, I'll have to find another." He tutted. "Honestly. This is highly inconvenient."

Truthfully, I'd hoped for a bit more of a reaction than that.

Still, that faint, nearly imperceptible groan of metal…what *was* that?

Savus flicked his wrist, and the mist snaked around my hands, binding them from the front. Sadly, this was a binding I wouldn't be able to saw off.

Savus crossed out of the room, his footsteps clapping over the stone floor. But he'd left his soldiers behind to watch us, and their silver eyes burned through the fog.

* * *

I'm not sure how much time had passed by the time Savus returned with his new executioner. Pinned to an iron stake by a garrote that burned my throat, I was running on cage time. It had seemed like four hours, so it was probably about twenty minutes. Twenty minutes of silence broken only by the faint, nearly inaudible sound of groaning metal.

A new figure stalked into the room, dressed in a black cloak, a cowl over his head. He gripped an iron sword.

It took me a moment to realize the hands were not a man's, but were delicate, with a rich bronze color.

My heart galloped. *Melusine* was going to kill us? She wouldn't.

"They are enemies of the Institute," Savus's voice boomed off the damp stone walls. "Traitors working with one of our greatest enemies. I have reported them to the High Council of Emain, and we have received permission to execute. They are agents of Baleros. They are an insidious infection that will destroy the Institute from within… I have allowed them to live, and my crown has withered. We must correct this at once."

Melusine pulled down her cowl. She stepped closer, the mist coiling around her face. "Honestly, Grand Master Savus, I'm a little perplexed. Why do you want me to kill them?"

His low growl boomed through my gut. "As I said, they are enemies of the Institute. Traitors. If you do as you are asked, you will be inducted as one of the Shadow Fae. You will have proven yourself, and you can take Ruadan's spot. I know that's what you've always wanted—to be a Shadow Fae. Now, you'll no longer have to return home in disgrace. Isn't that what you want, Melusine? To be a hero? For your life to mean something? I know it was lonely for you back home. This is your chance. It's a matter of good and evil, as I'm sure you understand."

His voice had a soothing quality that snaked over my skin, almost convincing me that this was all a perfectly logical state of affairs. *Of course it made sense that we should die.*

Maddan shifted at my feet, gasping for breath, but his eyes hadn't yet opened. He groaned. When he awoke, he'd hack our heads off within moments. Even an idiot like him would know better than to screw around a second time.

Savus didn't want Queen Macha to know that he'd given the order. If I had to guess, his plan probably involved slaughtering Melusine right after she dispatched us.

I glanced at Ruadan, hoping to see a sign that he had a plan, that he was working on something, but he was completely still. Had he simply accepted his fate? He seemed like the kind who would try to go out with dignity or something asinine like that. I'd go out screaming and clawing at flesh, bellowing curses into the void.

Melusine wrinkled her nose, staring at me. "Thing I don't get,

Grand Master Savus, is why you came to get me and handed me this sword. Seems to me like you don't want to kill them yourself. Seems like you don't want your mist soldiers to kill them, either. I see Maddan here, lying on the floor, and that looks like a failed attempt at an execution to me. Then you come get me, try to get me to do it. I put two and two together. I may not be the strongest, but my intellectual capacities are fully intact. I can do six kinds of math. And what I see here is that you're looking for a loophole, trying not to anger the Old Gods by getting someone else to do your dirty work. Now—"

"Kill them!" Savus's voice boomed. "Or I'll turn the mist soldiers on you. You ungrateful wretch. I'll have them tear you limb from limb, and boil your flesh in heated iron. The Old Gods don't protect you."

Her face blanched as the mist soldiers began moving closer to her. Still gripping the iron sword, she held up her hands. "Now hang on. Hang on. Let's just think this through."

On the ground, Maddan shifted again, groaning.

The mist soldiers took another step closer to Melusine. Through the swirls of fog, I couldn't see the expression on her face, but when she spoke again, I could hear the tremor in her voice. "I'm just asking that we all think—"

Maddan leapt to his feet, and he snatched the sword from Melusine. He whirled, turning on me. As he moved closer through the fog, I could see the fury etched on his features.

Then, a loud groan of creaking metal. My gaze flicked to Ruadan. Through the mist, I could barely make out what he was doing. He was pulling the garrote apart with his bare hands. Even with all the iron around him, weakening his body, he was powerful enough to *bend* the metal. Never underestimate a demigod, apparently.

Joy bloomed in my heart at the sight of his garrote separating from the stake.

Maddan raised the sword, ready for a swing, and panic paused my heart for just a moment.

Then, the rumbling of the ground beneath us stopped Maddan's swing—an earthquake that shook through my bones.

CHAPTER 29

"What's going on?" Maddan shrieked, trying to keep his balance.

Stone began crumbling beneath my feet, the floor cracking. Through the cracks, I caught a glimpse of dark, churning waters, flecked with stars. Ruadan was opening a portal.

While Savus and Maddan shouted for the mist soldiers to attack, the world fell away under my feet, and I plunged into icy water.

As I sank deeper under the water, hot wrath simmered inside me. Someday, I'd quench my fury with blood. I wanted to kill Savus, Maddan, all of them…

In the cold waters, the mist around my arms and mouth began to dissolve. Unfortunately, I was still trapped to the damn stake by the iron garrote. Worse, the stake was connected to a large chunk of stone, and the whole thing was pulling me in deeper underwater, choking me as I sank into the portal. I flailed around, kicking in the water, but I couldn't move myself upwards. My lungs were on fire.

At last, a powerful arm looped around my waist.

I held my breath, sinking underwater, and I stared into Ruadan's violet eyes. Already, the presence of his magic and his body's warmth soothed me.

He reached for the garrote around my neck. Gritting his teeth, he pulled at it, bending the metal.

Nothing particularly clever, no magic. He was just unbelievably strong, even when the iron around him had dampened his powers.

Freed from the garrote, I kicked my legs, swimming for the surface. My lungs felt as if they might explode, but I stared with relief at the rays of light piercing the water. Hope began to bloom in my chest. Above us, I could see other bodies moving, kicking to the surface. Soldiers from the mist army must have fallen in. But as I swam, they began to dissolve in the icy water like sugar.

The iron sword—the one Maddan had been holding—drifted down, and I caught it by the hilt. Had Maddan fallen through as well? I hoped he had. I'd drive this weapon right through his throat.

Now, I saw only moon rays piercing the surface. If Maddan had pulled himself out of the water first, he'd probably be waiting for us at the portal's exit, ready to strike.

At last, I breached the surface. I gasped for breath, frantically scanning for signs of Maddan, but I saw only a dark orchard, and a starry sky arching high above us. I still gripped the sword. As I caught my breath, it took me a few moments to recognize that we'd emerged in a fountain. Unlike the fountain in Lilinor, this one looked natural—a small geyser spurting out of a rough, stone-rimmed pool. Water rained down from above.

I sucked in air to fill my lungs, and grasped onto the lip of the fountain. When I glanced behind me, I saw Ruadan climbing out of the water on the other side of the fountain.

Still gripping the sword, I followed suit. Exhausted, I flopped down on the wet soil. By the heavy scent of apples in the air—a smell that Ruadan carried with him—I had the sense that he'd brought us to Emain. But that wasn't my most pressing issue right now. I pushed myself up again, surveying the space around us.

First things first. Establish the existence of a threat.

"I think Maddan came through." I lifted the sword, still catching my breath. "Found this sinking in the water."

Ruadan sniffed the air. "I think you're right. But he was wearing the lumen stone. He must have leapt away from us."

"You don't sense him around us?"

"No, but we'll need to find him."

I inwardly cursed myself for my sluggishness, relative to Ruadan. If I hadn't been here, he could have shadow-leapt after Maddan. Instead, Ruadan was waiting for me.

"Bloody right we need to find him," I grumbled. "Let me have the honor of severing his head, please."

Ruadan's magic snaked over my skin, raising goosebumps. "Not yet. We need to capture Maddan as soon as we can and take him to Emain's High Council."

"Why?" I asked.

"Emain's High Council is the central seat of Shadow Fae power. We need their permission to execute Grand Master Savus. Without their approval, all the world's Shadow Fae will hunt us down."

"And why do we need Maddan for permission to kill Savus?" My wet black dress stuck to my body, and I hugged myself. I was still shaking from my brush with death. Disoriented, I struggled to focus.

Ruadan rubbed the back of his neck. "He'll be the evidence we'll submit at the trial. He's our witness."

At this point, it occurred to me that Ruadan still didn't know the truth behind what had just happened. With all the drama of being knocked unconscious and nearly executed, it had slipped my mind a bit. Ruadan still didn't know *why* Grand Master Savus was doing all this.

"Let's go," said Ruadan. "I've scented Maddan's path."

"Wait! There's something you should know."

Ruadan whirled, his shadows whipping around him.

I stared at him, at a loss for words. I wasn't great with tact, but this would pose a conundrum even for the most diplomatic and empathic of people. How did you tell someone that his mother wasn't actually dead, but his worst enemy had been holding her for years?

"Well, there's good news and there's bad news," I began. "I'll just get right to the point. I won't dance around it. At least, I think it's good news and bad news, according to Grand Master Savus. If he can be trusted. Can he be trusted? The point is, I'll just say it. Of course, he can't be trusted, though, he just tried to sever our heads…so, taking that with a grain of salt—"

Ruadan raised a hand. "Stop. What are you trying to tell me?"

I took a deep breath, marshaling a sense of calm. "Just before Grand Master Savus knocked me unconscious and dragged me to the execution chamber, we had a little chat. He claims that Baleros never really killed your mum, and that he's been holding her as a pawn for fifteen years. Waiting for a moment to use her. Grand Master Savus is in love with her, so he was doing Baleros's bidding by trying to kill us both in exchange for the queen."

Ruadan went completely still, his eyes dark as the night sky. A gust of wind toyed with his pale hair. At the sight of him—so predatory and still—a shudder crawled over my skin.

Might as well tell him everything, though.

"Savus said that Baleros sent two of your mother's fingers," I went on. "The Grand Master recognized them. That's why he was so desperate to act. He thought that getting others to kill for him was a loophole or something idiotic."

Near silence greeted me, just the sound of the wind rustling the trees, and crickets chirping in the distance.

"Maddan was in on it, too," I added. I wanted to make sure Ruadan hated him as much as I did, so that when we killed him, it would really hurt.

Ruadan's magic billowed so deeply around him, it looked like a blanket of darkness. The temperature dropped about twenty degrees, and my wet dress felt like it was going to freeze to my body. The air misted in front of my face as I breathed in and out.

"Could you stop with the ice?" I asked. Then, feeling tactless, I added. "Sorry about your mum. I mean, the fingers. Good that she might be alive, though, right?"

If one of our trials had involved tact, the Old Gods would have turned on me in seconds. I'd never have made it this far.

Then, switching to a more comfortable line of conversation, I added, "We will hunt down everyone who hurt her and rip their spines from their bodies, starting with Baleros. Even if the fire goddess revives him, we can still brutally punish him while he lives. Furthermore, I will beat Savus to death with his own silver arm." There. That was my best attempt at being comforting.

My teeth chattered, and some of the ice receded from the air.

At last, Ruadan spoke. "Where is she?"

"Savus said he doesn't know. He sent some Shadow Fae looking for her, and I expect he killed them, too, because he didn't want this secret getting out. After he told me, he sealed my mouth and prepared to have me executed. But we'll find her. I promise."

Shadows seeped into the air around Ruadan. "Savus has hated me for years."

"Right. I don't think it's because your mum died. I think it's because he's in love with her."

He nodded once, almost imperceptibly. "I see. He resents me."

I inhaled sharply, crossing closer to Ruadan. I stood so close to him that I could feel the heat radiating off his body. "He wanted you dead."

Ruadan's magic pulsed around him, floating on the breeze and seeping into the forest. His body was still as stone while the breeze whipped at his hair. At last, he spoke. "The plan remains essentially the same. We get permission to depose Grand Master Savus. We find out what he really knows through an interrogation. Then, we kill him. After he dies, we go after Baleros, and my mother."

"You still want to find Maddan?"

Ruadan nodded. "We will need him, yes. Grand Master Savus has reported us to the High Council as traitors. They won't take our word alone."

I shivered in the cold air, teeth chattering, until Ruadan pulled me tight against him. His body warmed mine until my teeth stopped chattering, and my muscles relaxed.

"Keep your eyes alert as we move through the forest," he said. "Rivers and streams run all around us. Here, the forest is full of fae who can lure you into insanity. There are gancanagh, who will seduce you until you lose your mind, and bean nighe, who will drag you under the water to your death. Fuathan live in the waters, protecting this realm from invaders. There are birdlike creatures, spirits of the unquiet dead who will swoop down and drive you insane. All are here to protect Emain from invaders. Sentinels of a sort."

"So we need to try to find out where Maddan went, before one of these monsters slaughters him. Maybe you should shadow-leap after him. He's not exactly the sort who would live long in any kind of dangerous situation."

"I'm not leaving you on your own."

I gripped the sword tighter. "You really think I can't handle the fae sentinels here?"

"I know you can fight them, but they're not ordinary opponents. The forests can be confusing, and they can muddle your mind. They can lead you astray."

"The sentinels wouldn't come after you, would they? You're not an invader."

"I am now. I've been away a long time. Just remember, Arianna. Here, things are not always as they seem."

We walked through the forest, and I moved as quickly as I could, trying to keep up with Ruadan. He didn't speak, but my pace must have frustrated him. I moved faster than an ordinary fae, but I couldn't shadow-leap.

We sniffed the air as we traveled, following Maddan's path. Given what I knew about him, he'd probably arrived in Emain, panicked, then blindly run off in a random direction with literally no plan.

As we walked, the apple orchards gave way to a thicker forest—oaks, elders, and rowans. Their boughs framed the starry night sky above us.

"Any idea where we're headed?" I asked after a while.

"Maddan doesn't know his way around Emain. It's an island, with a few cities on the eastern shore. The rest is wilderness, inhabited only by the most ancient fae. Fae so old they're practically part of the landscape. That's where he's heading."

"Have you ever been here before?"

"As part of the Shadow Fae training, we spent years out here. And my mother used to take me here. She's the one who taught me to track and to hunt."

Once again, I had the impression that his mum sounded brilliant. I wanted to say something reassuring, something like, "She sounds like the kind of woman who would be fine in captivity," but everything I could think of sounded flippant and callous instead of reassuring. And what did I know? Maybe someone like Ruadan, who'd spent years training in the wild, didn't need reassurance.

"What were your parents?" Ruadan said, abruptly.

It was sort of a strange way to phrase a question. Not "*who* were your parents." He wanted to know what my other half was.

"Your guess is as good as mine." I hated lying. I wasn't even a good liar. Still, I couldn't tell him the truth.

I wanted to change the subject before he could ask for more details. Details like, "Where did you come from? When did you last see your parents?" Things I wanted to avoid.

"You said that Grand Master Savus hated you for years," I said. "What did he do to you?"

As soon as I felt the air frost around me, saw the breath misting in front of my face, I knew that I'd struck a nerve of some kind. At least I'd succeeded in changing the subject. A rough gust of wind slid over us, and I silently cursed the cold.

After a minute, I was certain he didn't want to answer.

Then, he shot me a quick look, his eyes shining in the darkness. "You've seen the tattoo on my back?"

"Yes. The fae word? What does it mean?"

"The Shadow Fae of Emain are divided into cohorts, each named after a type of tree. My cohort was the Yew. I had two half-brothers in the cohort—my mother's sons. We were together for centuries, training in Emain, fighting and assassinating enemies of our realm."

Already a sense of dread was curling around my ribs. He'd said that his brothers had died.

"When I joined the London Institute," he went on, "Grand Master Savus sent me on a mission. He told me to employ my old cohort—we were called the Eburones. Men of the Yew. Grand Master Savus told us we were hunting down an angel, someone who never should have come to Earth."

My mouth went dry. "What happened?" With an iron nerve, I willed my voice to remain steady.

"I had to open a portal to another world. The angel was hidden there, living with his family. They lived as part of a little village, in fact. It confused me when I arrived and spotted the cottage—a wife with red hair. And a son. A young boy who ran away as soon as we arrived. I didn't understand. Angels can't have children. The pleasure they'd feel when siring a child would cause them to fall."

I could hardly breathe as he spoke. All the air had left my lungs.

"It wasn't an angel," he went on. "Not an ordinary one. It was the Horseman of Death. One of the architects of the apocalypse. Do you know what sort of destruction such a creature can wreak?"

My mind went numb. Oh yes. I knew. "What happened to your cohort?" I asked in a remarkably steady voice, but I already knew the answer.

"Dead. Every single one of them died before my eyes."

I exhaled slowly. "Why didn't you die?"

"I was the only one there with the blood of a demon-god. I'm nearly impossible to kill. Unfortunately, Death can't be killed either. But after what he did, he is on my list, and I will figure out a way to end him and his line. He killed almost everyone I loved. He was protecting his son, but he hit his wife in the crossfire. I remember seeing her lying in the dirt. He killed the other fae, too. The ones living with him. His son was the only one to get away."

My thoughts were racing out of control, and I willed my heartbeat to slow down. Ruadan could probably hear it. It would alert him that something was wrong. Only once I mastered control of myself did I speak again. "You want to kill his son?"

"Of course. Such a creature is monstrous. He'd be a grown man now. I just need to learn who he is."

My blood roared in my ears. "And Savus is the one who sent you on that mission."

"Yes. A part of me always wondered if he'd done it on purpose. Perhaps it hadn't just been a mistake. But maybe he'd known that Death lurked there.

A heavy silence fell over us. "I'm sorry you lost your cohort," I said at last. "And your half-brothers. Do you have any family left?"

"No. My younger sister inherited the throne, but that was it."

"If she's younger, why didn't you inherit the throne?" I asked. "Or what about Caine?"

"Bastard."

"Beg your pardon?"

"I was illegitimate. And Caine and I are related on my father's side. The city's elders debated the line of succession, but in the end, they chose Queen Brigantia. Fine with me. I'm more of a warrior than a prince."

"Your own sister won't believe you without proof?"

"She will, I think. But the High Council will not."

My mind still whirled back to everything Ruadan had told me earlier—the attack on the horseman, his entire cohort dying.

My skull roiled with images of dead fae, littering a field. I could almost smell the death...but just as soon as the scent of decay filled my nose, it dissipated, and I breathed in the smell of fresh bread. It reminded me of home. Home before Baleros had found me. Where raspberries grew all around us.

Now, the light seemed to grow brighter—shining silver moonlight that gleamed through the trees. As I walked, I could no longer see Ruadan, but it didn't bother me. I felt at peace.

A flicker of movement through the dark bushes caught my attention, and a new scent filled the air. The briny scent of the ocean. I closed my eyes, breathing it in. I licked my lips, tasting salt. Night cloaked my body like silk.

When I opened my eyes again, a handsome man was standing before me in the dark grove. His long, brown hair fell over his shoulders. He had full eyebrows, a neatly trimmed beard, and his clothing looked as if it had been made from the colors of the forest itself: rich greens and browns, a velvety texture. Pale smoke curled from an ivory pipe in his lips.

"Welcome," he said. He spoke in Ancient Fae—a language I'd never learned. And yet somehow, I could understand him. He stepped closer to me, his movements oddly silent. "Who walks before me with all the darkness and beauty of a cloudless, starry sky?" He took another step closer, and with a delicate stroke of his fingertip, he brushed a lock of my hair off my cheek. I shuddered at his touch.

"Your beauty is like the ocean," he purred, "stirring within me terror and ecstasy, an inexorable lure." His voice wrapped itself around my body, and I closed my eyes.

I hardly noticed myself dropping the sword to the soil. What did I need a sword for? Love was all around me.

"I will bathe you in morning dew." His fingertips were on my hips, stroking them in circles.

Where was I? I had no idea, and it didn't matter because nothing in the world mattered but the feel of his fingertips on my skin. Why was I wearing this stupid dress? The fae lived in nature. We weren't made to wear clothing.

As if hearing my thoughts, my new friend began inching up my dress. My skin started to heat.

I had a vague sense that I should be fighting him, that he was dangerous, but I couldn't bring myself to do it.

"When I'm around you," he went on, his honeyed voice licking at my skin, "a fevered heat blooms in me."

He pulled my dress off, and the heavy night wrapped itself around my bare skin. With an ecstatic shiver, I leaned back into his body. Hunger grew within me.

He stroked a hand down my skin, and my mind blazed with images of Ruadan—his golden skin, his powerful arms...

"Your breasts draw me in like the moon in Earth's orbit, the waves of your hair frame your face like the ocean frames the shore, and light radiates from your eyes—two perfect orbs like two moons."

This time, my body tensed at his voice. Was it just me, or was he a little bit of a knob? At this point, his metaphors were just confusing me, and he had at least three moons in that one.

Smoke curled from his white pipe, but I smelled something different in it. The scent of decay.

I pulled away from him, narrowing my eyes. Now, he looked a

little different. The pipe he smoked looked like a human rib, and a drop of blood shone at the corner of his lips.

I took a step back from him. What had happened to Ruadan? And where was my dress? So *this* was the gancanagh. Honestly, I'd expected better game than this from a legendary seducer. This guy sucked.

He reached for me, his dark eyes wide. Now, his cheekbones looked sharp, his features a little too hungry. "A wild storm rages within my breast, a ruthless tempest. You are Diana, and I am—"

"Fuck off." I scanned the ground, searching for my dress, my sword. As I reached for the iron, the gancanagh lunged for me, canines bared. His teeth sank into my neck, and he yanked down my bra as he bit me.

Just moments ago, I'd wanted his hands all over me. Now, I yearned for the feel of knuckles hammering bone. I reared back my arm and slammed my fist into his face, over and over. My knuckles sang as I broke the skin on his skull, and it felt glorious.

Blood streamed from my throat where he'd bitten me, but I ignored it, focusing instead on pounding his face.

He grabbed my throat, fingers tightening. From below, I brought my elbow up into his jaw, knocking him off. He staggered back, and I punched him hard in the throat.

Something glinted out of the corner of my eye—the dull gleam of an iron blade. I grabbed the silver hilt, and the gancanagh reached for one of my legs. Surprisingly strong, he yanked me to the ground, and I slammed down hard on my back. The sword fell from my fingers, and the gancanagh's hands were around my throat again, squeezing until I thought my larynx might crush my spine. My eyes bulged, and the creature leaned down, groaning as he licked my cheek.

I grabbed one of his wrists, then rotated my hips until I managed to knock him off. I rolled, shifting him off me. I pinned him to the ground with my knee over his throat.

I punched him—once, twice—until his eyes looked glazed. Then, I shifted off him to snatch my sword from the earth.

As he rose to lunge for me, I swung the sword through his neck.

Blood sprayed all over my bare skin, and his head rolled over the forest floor. With the fight finished, my pulse began to slow.

I looked down at myself. No bra or dress, covered in blood. I'm not sure I'd make a super convincing defendant when I showed up at the High Council to plead our case.

As I caught my breath, I spotted my black dress on the ground. I grabbed it. Grimacing, I used it to clean off the gancanagh's blood, leaving behind only a few streaks of red. With the cotton soaked in blood, I didn't want to put the dress back on. Instead, I crumpled it up and threw it next to the headless fae.

I'd have to ask for Ruadan's shirt.

Speaking of Ruadan, where the hells was he? The bastard thought he was going to protect me, and here I was getting attacked by creepy poets lurking in the bushes.

It took me a few moments to get my bearings, until I glimpsed the broken branches that marked my path back to the main trail. I pushed through the undergrowth, sticks scratching at my bare skin, until I found my way to the larger, clear path. I was wearing nothing but my knickers, but I held my hand over my breasts as I walked.

On the main path, I found not a single incubus. I considered yelling out for Ruadan, but decided I may not want to call any more attention to myself, particularly considering I was basically naked and reeking of ancient fae blood.

An alluring song floated through the tree boughs—a female voice. I sniffed the air, breathing in the scent of pine, a faint hint of apples. Ruadan was nearby. I spotted a few broken branches in the shrubs, and I sniffed the air again.

Well, well, well. Seems Ruadan got a bit distracted as well.

I cupped my breasts as I walked through the darkened forest, my feet crunching over the leaves, until the little path opened into a clearing. A sensual song floated through the night air, trembling over my skin. A sapphire pond glittered in the starlight, so beautiful I nearly missed the people standing by the lake's edge.

My chest tightened with irritation at the sight of Ruadan. Sirens dressed in sheer, gossamer dresses surrounded him, singing into his ears. Their wild berry-colored hair cascaded over delicate shoulders. The women—with very visible nipples—gripped his limbs, sliding their hands over his body. Pearly wings swooped down their backs, rhythmically beating the air.

Ruadan's eyes had turned black as the night sky, and he didn't seem to see me. The sirens' music lured me closer, their song a powerful tug in my chest.

I gripped the sword tighter. I ran my fingertips over the iron, using the pain to keep control of myself, even as the song seduced me. Ruadan's muscles tensed. With a grunt, he ripped himself away from the sirens. He whirled on them, snarling, canines bared. His dark magic poisoned the air, and the lake began to ice over. *Finally.*

The sirens' wings fluttered, feathers flying around as they scrambled away from him. Their beautiful song fragmented, the melodies falling apart. Then, they clambered back into the icy lake.

"Enjoying yourself, Ruadan?"

CHAPTER 31

*H*is head snapped toward me, eyes dark as pitch. "I was just leaving." His eyes slowly raked up and down my body. "Perhaps I could ask the same of you. It seems someone has divested you of your clothing."

"He's dead now. But it just seems like you were making a few friends."

His magic lashed the air around him as he stared at me. He went completely still, and I had the odd sensation that he was about to pounce on me like a wild animal.

After a moment of silence, he said. "You're wearing nothing but a few streaks of fae blood."

"Why are we still talking about that?" I snapped.

I crossed to the sirens, my eye on one with blue hair. Before she could escape me, I leaned down and gripped her arm *hard.* I pointed my sword at her. Chunks of ice floated around her, and her breath clouded the air. She blinked at me, pouting, her face a mask of innocence. I tried to ignore the fact that I'd now totally uncovered my breasts.

"I'm going to need your dress," I said. "Now."

She opened her mouth to sing, and my back started arching at the sound. "Stop it!" I yelled. "I will sing over you. And nobody wants that. It's not pretty. Also, in case I wasn't clear, this sword is made of iron and I will cut out your larynx."

Did I feel bad for stealing a woman's dress at swordpoint? Maybe a little, but I *really* needed it, and I'm sure she could find a new one.

She pouted for a moment, then held out her free arm. The other sirens swarmed around her, untying the ribbons from her arms and back. They peeled off the gossamer fabric, and her breasts bobbed in the water. She scowled at me as she handed me the dress.

I let go of her arm as I snatched the dress from her, and the sirens began humming again.

I shot Ruadan a sharp look, clutching the gossamer fabric to the front of my body. "Let's get away from them before they start singing again."

"I was just leaving them."

"Were you now? Looked like you were standing there while they rubbed their gossamer tits all over you."

After a long silence, he said, "There were five of them." Then, his gaze slid over my body again. "You haven't explained what happened to your clothing."

"I met the gancanagh."

"And he stole your dress." I heard a hint of snarl in his voice.

"Yes. Before I killed him. He talked a lot. You know what I like?"

He didn't respond, but I answered anyway. "Men who don't talk too much."

For just a moment, the corner of his lips twitched in a smile. "I'll take the sword while you put the dress on."

He took the sword from me and turned away. With his back to me, I slipped the dress on. It was a bizarre cut, with holes in the back and swaths of fabric meant to accommodate wings. A series of ribbons hung down the back.

Freezing lake water soaked the dress. With the sheer fabric, it didn't hide much, and I'm not sure it was worth the bother.

"Ruadan? Can you tie up the back?"

He didn't say a word, but within moments, I felt his fingers nimbly moving up my spine as he tied the ribbons.

I turned to face him, and I held my hand out for the sword. But he wasn't handing it to me. Instead, his eyes were on my body. I watched them shift from violet to the darkness of night, and his magic snaked over my body.

In the sheer dress, and without my sword, I felt strangely vulnerable under his dark gaze.

"Ruadan," I said. "We need to find Maddan."

His eyes cleared again. "I know."

He crossed to me and handed me the sword.

"I'm amazed Maddan didn't get pulled in by the siren women," I said. "Apparently, he has better self-control than you. But honestly, Ruadan, it's a good thing you were around to save me, just like you said."

"I was about to leave them," he reiterated, a hint of a growl in his voice.

I sniffed the air. "There. Do you smell him? We're still on the right track."

Ruadan's eyes were on the ground. He didn't say anything, but after a moment, I caught what he was looking at—footprints, about the right size for Maddan. Gripping the sword, I crossed onto the main path. I moved as quietly as I could through the underbrush.

After a few minutes, the trail cut into the thicker forest. Here, broken branches and footprints signaled Maddan's route. Here, too, his scent grew stronger.

The distant sound of chatter pricked up my ears, until we reached a clearing.

As soon as we did, hunger gripped my stomach. Silver moonlight washed over a long banquet table laden with the most elaborate feast I'd ever seen: fruit pies, roast pheasant, bowls of strawberries, an entire duck, bread, and butter. My mouth watered.

I nearly missed the sight of Maddan. He was rolling around in the dirt in only his underwear, his pale skin covered in cream and smeared berries. His face beamed ecstatically.

"What's going on?" I asked.

Ruadan held a finger to his lips, then quietly whispered, "The enchantment of the forest has lured him in. But it's likely to be a trap."

I'd never seen his bare feet before, but now that I could, I realized they were comically small. Practically the size of a child's feet.

My nose wrinkled in disgust. No wonder he had that weird, lumbering walk.

I was about to take another step closer, when Ruadan grabbed me by the waist. My muscles tensed.

This didn't seem like a particularly dangerous situation—apart from the enduring psychological horror of watching Maddan roll around in cream and mashed berries. But of course, here, things were not always as they seemed. If this was a trap, it was like a fae spider's web. But what sort of fae sentinel was trapping us?

The shrill cry of a bird pierced the canopy of trees, and I looked up through the boughs, catching the silhouette of a crow against the moon.

When I looked back at the table, one of the pies was shaking and trembling, the crust bulging. A sharp beak pierced its surface, and a black bird burst from it. In the air, the bird transformed into a warrior, clad in black. Her white-blond hair whipped around her head, and she drew a sword—an iron blade, just like mine. She was enormous, practically the same size as Ruadan, and the sight of her sent a jolt of dread through my chest. The iron spikes jutting from her black leather didn't really lessen the intimidation factor. Here I was, in a gossamer-lake-water dress.

Ruadan leaned in, whispering in my ear. "Do you have this?"

"Yes." Already, battle fury raced through my limbs, making my legs shake.

Without waiting, I rushed for her, and our swords clashed. Within moments, we were whirling around each other, iron hammering against iron.

Through the clanging of our swords, I heard more birds dive for us, screeching. Ruadan was unarmed, but I wasn't too worried about him.

My opponent thrust her sword at me, but she left herself open on the right side. I drove my blade between her ribs.

She fell to the earth, and I whirled to take on the other attackers—three of them. For just a moment, I stared at Ruadan, who was fighting bare-handed. He was a maelstrom of fury, a whorl of black shadows and canines tearing into flesh. He was managing to fend off three attackers at once.

I cocked my head, learning from him as he fought. With his speed, no one could get a blow in. I liked watching him fight, and I stared as he snapped a warrior's neck. Shadows whipped through the air, and he whirled again. I smiled at the sound of crunching bone when he slammed his fist into a warrior's face.

Maddan was still rolling around on the ground, oblivious to the violence around him. Before he got the chance to clear his mind, I reached down and snatched the lumen crystal off his throat. I clasped it around my neck, and shadow magic rushed through my limbs. After a dizzying moment, I managed to evenly channel it throughout my body.

I gripped the sword again, but when I turned back to Ruadan, it was clear he didn't need my help.

In another five seconds, all three warriors were lying on the earth. They weren't dead, but they wouldn't be getting up in the next few minutes. Good enough.

Maddan pushed himself up onto his elbows, blinking. When his gaze landed on Ruadan and me, his face paled. He scrambled to his feet, reaching for the lumen crystal around his neck. It took him a moment to realize he'd lost it.

"Maddan," I said. "How lovely to see you again. I love the new look. Seems like you're doing fantastic since we last met. When was that? Oh, that's right, it was just an hour or so ago when you were about to slice off my head with this iron sword." I lifted it.

Ruadan stepped closer—two fae princes squaring off, one of them considerably more intimidating than the other.

"You're coming with us." Venom laced Ruadan's voice.

"You can't kill me," he sputtered. "My father will send an entire army after you. Grand Master Savus will, too."

"You're coming with us to the High Council," Ruadan interrupted him. "Put your clothes on."

I frowned at his feet. "Do you wear extra-large shoes to hide the ridiculous size of your feet? How do you even manage to stand?"

His face reddened, and he fell silent. Without another word, he snatched his clothing off the ground, frantically dressing himself. He was shaking so much, he didn't bother trying to clean the cream off his body. "Where are you taking me?" he asked.

"The High Council of Emain."

Maddan blinked, pausing with his trousers halfway up his legs. "Emain? Why are we going to see the High Council?"

I swung the iron sword in the air, carving it in sharp arcs before lowering it again. I just wanted to remind him that we could easily kill him. "All we need is for you to tell them what happened. Tell them what Grand Master Savus asked of you, and that Baleros has the queen."

"That's it?"

The ground trembled beneath our feet, and cracks of water opened within the soil.

It took me a moment to realize what was happening, and that magical light glowed from around Ruadan's body.

The ground gave way to icy water, and I plunged down beneath the depths, still gripping the sword. I held my breath as the water enveloped me.

The prince of Emain was *really* starting to piss me off with his lack of warnings.

CHAPTER 32

The jolt of freezing water shocked me. As I sank deeper, a few thoughts whirled in my mind. One, apparently you could take a portal within worlds, and not just between them. And two, I owed Ruadan the shock of an ice water bath as he slept.

At last, pale light streamed onto the water's surface from above, and I kicked my legs hard, swimming past Maddan. The silver orb of the moon appeared, and my hand pierced the surface. Still clinging onto the iron sword, I looped one arm over the stone lip of the portal's edge, and I hoisted myself out, gasping.

Ruadan had already climbed out, and he stood, his body dripping with water. He was staring up at the castle that loomed above us.

I clambered out of the water onto soil. "A little warning would be nice," I grumbled.

But my attention was already turning to the palace itself. A rocky, mountainous slope rose above us. The castle seemed to grow from the slope itself—its turrets made of uneven rock. Narrow gaps in the rocks formed windows—chinks of pale light in its walls. Thick ropes of tree roots and vines wound around the castle walls.

Inset into the base of the castle was an ornately carved wooden door.

The splashing and gasping behind me told me that Maddan had arrived through the portal.

Maddan sucked in breath so sharply he almost sounded like an animal. Then, he grasped for the fountain's rim. Grunting, he pulled himself over the edge and flopped onto the soil.

"How do we get in?" I asked.

Ruadan was already moving for the carved door. I grabbed Maddan by the arm, yanking him off the ground and dragging him toward the door. Still barefoot, he stumbled after me on his ridiculous small feet.

"Why do you need me to report to the High Council?" he protested. "Do you want me to explain to them that you're traitors who worked for Baleros?"

"They've already heard that story," I said through gritted teeth. "You need to tell them the part about how Grand Master Savus is working with Baleros."

"And what if I don't tell them that?" Maddan sniffed.

Ruadan whirled, and the look on his face, the darkness in his eyes, slid right through my bones. Despite his beauty, Ruadan's was a face from nightmares.

"In Emain, we interrogate people through torture. It's not reliable, but it's an old tradition. I could break your bones," said Ruadan, "one by one. It would delight me to hear your shrieks echo off the ceiling. Or, you could simply tell them the truth, like I've asked."

Maddan swallowed hard. "Torture? Even royalty from other realms?"

"We do things our own way here," said Ruadan. He whirled again, moving for the door. As we approached it, my eyes roamed over the carvings. It looked like it was made of oak, probably thirty feet high. A craftsman had carved it with pictures of stags, curling leaves, trees, and an engraved hand in the center.

When Ruadan reached it, he leaned down to his boot. He unsheathed a silver dagger. Then, he slid the blade across his palm, drawing blood. He pressed his bloodied palm against the engraved hand.

The door groaned, slowly sliding open, the weight of it shaking dirt from the rocky walls above us. Slowly, the enormous door heaved open.

"Is that an Emain royalty benefit?" I asked.

"The castle knows my blood."

The door rumbled open, revealing towering stone ceilings. Oak roots seemed to grow into stone around us, and torchlight faintly illuminated a vaulted ceiling that peaked hundreds of feet above us.

While I was gaping at the hall, Ruadan had already moved ahead, his footfalls echoing off the high arches.

I gripped Maddan's arm tighter, still dragging him along on his baby feet.

As we marched, a low, sonorous bell began to toll. An alarm, perhaps? Whatever it was, Ruadan didn't seem bothered, and he simply stalked onward.

At the end of the long hall, another set of wooden doors loomed over us. When Ruadan reached them, he pressed his hand against the door again. The doors groaned open over the stone floor.

In this hall, silver moonlight streamed through tall windows onto an ivory marble floor. An empty stony throne sat at one end of the hall.

I tightened my grip on the sword, with a chill rippling over my skin. How exactly had we been able to wander in here so easily? Ruadan was royalty with special door-opening blood, but we'd been reported as traitors. It was like this castle had no real defenses.

And yet as soon as the thought passed through my head, shadows whispered over the floor, whorls of smoke. Phantoms? The shadows spun faster, until they materialized into solid forms.

The sentinels wore black leather—all males. By their canines and pointed ears, I could tell they were fae as well as phantoms. But most importantly, they'd surrounded us, and they were thrusting swords at us. Maddan yelped behind me.

For a moment, I wondered if we were supposed to fight them. Since Ruadan never told me anything in advance, I had no idea.

"Lower your sword to the floor," Ruadan said quietly.

At last, he was filling me in.

Ruadan straightened, and when he spoke, his voice boomed over the hall. I had no idea what he was saying, since he'd launched into Ancient Fae. The only word I understood within the stream of sounds was "Ruadan," so I could only imagine he was announcing his entire lineage, possibly dating back to the Bronze Age. Seemed to be a bit of a thing for fae nobility.

The phantom-fae continued to stare at us, bodies unmoving. The silver in their eyes pierced the gloom of the hall. Their heads were cocked at unnatural angles. A draft whipped through the hall, lifting locks of their hair.

They crowded in closer around us, towering over us, until I could see nothing but the sentinels and their gleaming blades.

It felt freezing in the hall, and I was still wearing nothing but the waterlogged, gossamer gown. I regretted not getting the chance to strip the armor off the bird-warriors before Ruadan had ripped the ground out from underneath us.

It seemed like ages before the sound of heels clacked over the hall, a staccato slap punctuating the air like gunshots. When silence descended, the phantom-guards fell away, still pointing their swords at us.

There, on the throne of rock, sat a woman in a sheer black gown that plunged to her navel. She crossed her long legs, and platinum hair cascaded over her shoulders. A black, spiky crown gleamed on her head.

On either side of her stood rows of fae draped in silver cloth. They wore crowns of rowan leaves with red berries. Presumably, they were the High Council, and their grumpy expressions told me they were not pleased to have been roused out of bed in the middle of the night.

Queen Brigantia—Ruadan's sister—looked oddly relaxed, considering a reported traitor and possible rival for the throne had just burst in here with an iron sword and two random, half-naked fae.

"Of all the things I could have imagined when my servant woke me at three in the morning, the last thing I would have expected was the sight of my brother arriving, dripping wet, with a barely clothed demi-fae and a small-footed prince from another land."

I was amazed that she recognized Maddan, but maybe all the fae royals knew each other.

The queen leaned forward. "What is this about you being a traitor? I'd only just received word from Grand Master Savus that you'd betrayed the Institute. He wanted permission to execute you. I said no, of course."

Ruadan straightened, his shadows darkening the air around him. He nodded at me. "Arianna is my novice. Prince Maddan is a traitor to the Institute and to Emain. I've brought him here to testify. Grand Master Savus has been compromised. He is working with Baleros, who is demanding my execution in exchange for the World Key. Baleros wants to open the worlds again, to unleash chaos and recreate his gladiatorial arenas."

The queen narrowed her violet eyes—the same shade as Ruadan's. "Why would Savus work with Baleros? Baleros slaughtered our mother."

"Baleros has figured out exactly how to control Savus," said Ruadan. "He claims that he has a very important hostage."

The queen's eyes widened. "Who?"

Ruadan spoke again in Ancient Fae, his voice booming off the walls. I had no idea what he was saying until he switched back to English. "Our mother."

The Fae High Council began murmuring to one another, while Queen Brigantia's eyes were locked entirely on her brother. She didn't move, her body taking on that strange, animal stillness Ruadan so often displayed.

A ghostly wind whipped through the hall, and the queen's pale hair danced around her head. "You found our mother's body in her bedchamber."

Ruadan's body was as still as his sister's. "She'd been burned beyond recognition. It may have been another victim. Alternately, Baleros may be lying. But the important part is that Grand Master

Savus believes Baleros, and he is now essentially an agent working for the traitor."

One of the High Council members stepped forward, her white hair piled high on her head. "You have a witness?"

Ruadan shoved Maddan forward. "He has been working with both Baleros and Grand Master Savus. Before I opened the portal, he was about to drive an iron sword through my throat. Arianna's as well."

The line of sentinels closed in around Maddan, swords pointed at him. Maddan's limbs were visibly shaking. "I was only acting as the Grand Master instructed," he protested. "He told me the Old Gods supported it, that once I did their bidding, I'd become one of the Shadow Fae."

The queen tapped her fingernails on the rocky throne. "There was a time when we were reluctant to torture royalty from other lands. It caused certain diplomatic problems, like wars. Invasions. But now, the worlds are locked. My brother is one of the few people with the power to open and close the portals. Your family cannot come for us. I'm afraid we must know the truth."

"It's all true!" Maddan shouted. "It's all true. Baleros has been sending Queen Macha's fingers to Grand Master Savus. Savus loves her. He only wanted to save her life."

The queen leaned back in her chair. "Torture him to make sure he's telling the truth."

Her logic made no sense whatsoever, and yet I was happy to jump in. I raised my hand. "Can I help with that?"

The queen nodded once.

I took a step closer to Maddan, and slammed my fist into his jaw. He tried blocking my blows with his forearms, but I dodged around them. I hit him in the ribs, the skull, cracking his nose. The sting on my knuckles felt glorious.

Then, I took a step back. Blood streamed from Maddan's nose.

The queen looked at him again, expectantly. "Well?"

Blood dripped down his hands. "Yes. It's exactly what I said before. Grand Master Savus was trying to save your mother by complying with Baleros's demands. He wants to steal the World Key from Ruadan's body."

The queen straightened. "So the leader of the Institute is no longer serving the Shadow Fae. Instead, he serves a traitor."

The High Council began arguing with one another, voices echoing off the ceiling. But they were speaking in Ancient Fae, and I had no idea what they were saying. After a minute, they seemed to come to some sort of a consensus, nodding and stepping back into their line.

The queen cocked her head. "Imprison the fae prince in the Institute. Assassinate Grand Master Savus. Assume control of London. Then, find Baleros. We will send word to the Shadow Fae institutes across the world. Report back to me, and do not waste any more time."

The sentinels closed in around Maddan, binding his arms behind his back. They clamped iron around his wrists.

The queen rose from her throne. "Aithmóre."

Ruadan repeated the fae word. Whatever it meant, the sound of it rumbled over my skin.

The sentinels stepped away, and Ruadan's body began to glow, his magic pulsing and rippling over my skin. As I felt the floor rumbling again, I prepared myself. When the first cracks appeared in the marble, I reached for the iron sword I'd dropped.

Churning waters appeared through the fissures, and the floor fell out from underneath us. I plunged into the icy water. The portal's watery depths enveloped me once more.

We had what we wanted—a directive to kill the Grand Master. But as I sank deeper into the portal, I had to wonder if Baleros was already one step ahead of us. It seemed he always was.

*W*arm light glimmered on the portal's watery surface, and I kicked my legs. I wasn't entirely sure where the portal would be opening until I reached the air. Gasping, I scrambled for the stony ledge. The smell of mildew, must, and an undercurrent of blood hit me like a wave.

Ruadan brought us to one of the empty torture rooms in the dungeons, which was smart. It was completely empty down here.

Given the mist army situation, the only way to kill Grand Master Savus would be through a stealth assassination—not exploding into the Tower Green in a hail of water and rock. Another benefit was the arsenal of weapons glinting from one of the rocky walls.

I climbed over the ledge, and Ruadan turned back to the portal. When Maddan's ginger hair breached the surface, Ruadan hauled his shackled body out of the water.

Lying on his side, Maddan coughed up water onto the stone.

Ruadan gripped him by the shoulders and began dragging him off to a cell in the other direction. Maddan's tiny bare feet left trails of water on the stone behind him.

My muscles tensed. I couldn't quite explain it, but something felt wrong in the air. The hair on my arms stood on end. Icy water dripped off my body, and I gripped the hilt of the sword, prowling slowly down the corridor, away from Ruadan.

I heard the sound of a cell door creaking, then slamming shut as Ruadan locked Maddan inside. The prince of Elfame was screaming something, his voice rattling with rage, but I blocked him out, trying to attune my senses to the Institute.

Faintly, Ruadan's footsteps sounded behind me, and I turned to him. "Something isn't right."

Ruadan gripped a broadsword that he'd pulled off the wall. "What do you sense?"

I bit my lip. I couldn't explain my sense of unease. "I don't know. Just—we need to be cautious."

His gaze flicked to the lumen stone at my neck. "Okay, but time is of the essence. The longer we spend here, the greater the chance we'll be discovered before we assassinate the Grand Master. Once we get to the Tower Green, I'm going to shadow-leap to Savus's chamber. I'll slaughter him within seconds. It will all be over."

I had complete faith in Ruadan's killing abilities, and yet as we climbed the dank stairwell, I couldn't shake the feeling that something was very wrong here at the Institute.

By the time we reached the top of the stairs, my chest was pounding.

Then, just before Ruadan pushed through the door to the Tower Green, it hit me like a fist to the gut.

The scent of roses.

Baleros's scent.

I gripped Ruadan's arm, pulling him back. On my tiptoes, I whispered into his ear, "He's here. Baleros is here."

Grand Master Savus had failed in his task of slaughtering Ruadan. Maybe Baleros thought he had to do the job himself.

Baleros's nineteenth law of power: Never send a servant to do the work of a king.

When Ruadan met my gaze, his eyes were as black as the void, and a chill slid through my bones. As we stood behind the oak door, mist curled under it, twining around us.

I frowned at the magical fog. Was Grand Master Savus deploying his mist army, or...

I gripped Ruadan's arm tighter, sliding the puzzle pieces together in my mind. "Do you really think Baleros would stick around here, facing the Grand Master's mist army in person? My old master doesn't face opponents he can't beat." My heart slammed against my ribs. "If Baleros is already here—"

My breath caught in my lungs, and I pulled open the door just a little, peering outside. My stomach sank at what I saw.

My old master—Baleros—prowled across the flowery green, a lumen stone glowing around his neck. The mist army surrounded him, fog lifting off of them in steamy tufts.

Panic climbed up my spine, and I closed the door again. As I did, another deep bell began to toll—just like the one in Emain.

"There's good news, and there's bad news," I whispered. "The good news, is we don't have to worry about killing Grand Master Savus. He's already dead. The bad news is that Baleros is now ten times more powerful than he was before, because he can shadow-leap and he's assumed control of the mist—"

A loud boom and the splintering of wood cut off the rest of my sentence. A battle-ax splintered the door, and mist began pooling inside.

"He controls the mist army," I said, completing my thought.

"Use the lumen stone," said Ruadan.

He didn't have to tell me twice. Without it, Baleros would corner us here in the dungeons. His mist army would slaughter us.

Through the shattering door, I glimpsed the darkened towers. I let my mind meld with the shadows across the green, and dark magic whispered through my blood.

I shadow-leapt outside, the wind whipping at my damp, half-naked body. I landed hard in a dark spot by a tower archway. Then, I whirled to find a small cohort of mist soldiers closing in on me. Just beyond them, I glimpsed Shadow Fae knights running out of the towers, swords raised. They were responding to the alarm, attacking the invaders.

Already, I'd lost track of Baleros, but I had a more pressing concern in the form of the ten mist soldiers closing in on me.

Shadow magic skimmed and buzzed over my skin, and I mentally bonded with the shadows behind them. I used the lumen stone to leap out of the circle of mist warriors. From behind them, I swung my sword into their backs. But instead of hitting flesh, it was like swiping through steam. How were we supposed to kill these guys?

My gaze flicked to Ruadan, who moved so fast I could barely track him. I saw only puffs of steam as my mentor carved his sword through the mist soldiers. Too bad the attacks didn't kill them. They simply wafted away like smoke, then solidified elsewhere in the green.

I shadow-leapt away from the mist soldiers, sniffing the air until I tuned into the scent of roses. The sickly-sweet scent dripped over the whole Institute. I could smell Baleros, but I couldn't see him.

Two mist soldiers ran for me. I whirled and leapt, my sword clashing against the mist soldiers' blades. Adrenaline blazed through my limbs as steel met steel. Still, every time I thrust my blade at them, it met only air. The fruitless attacks were throwing me off balance.

Everything could be killed. But how?

As I fought them, I kept scanning the Tower Green, searching for Baleros. I glimpsed the other Shadow Fae fighting the mist soldiers, but Baleros had hidden himself somewhere, letting his army do the work for him.

His absence was making me nervous. As usual, he was much more in control of this situation than Ruadan and I were. He knew where we were—and we had no idea where he'd gone.

I lunged into another mist soldier, my blade slicing steam. I'd worked up a sweat now, and I'd killed not a single soldier.

As cold sweat dripped down my gossamer gown, a fiery glow appeared through one of the Institute's arches. Baleros had committed his soul to the fire goddess. My heart thrummed. Was that him?

I had no doubt it was—my old master, about to unleash fiery hell on the Tower.

I summoned my shadow magic from the lumen stone, a cold burst of power. Then, I shadow-leapt closer to the archway. When I landed, I staggered back.

Baleros crossed through the archway, dragging someone with him. He was holding a knife to Ciara's throat. Of course the fucker had leverage.

His body glowed with orange light, and he was chanting a spell in the Angelic language. As he did, the sky blazed with searing light, fires in the heavens. It took me a moment to realize what he was doing.

With the fiery light he'd created in the sky above us, Baleros had burned out all the shadows. He'd made it impossible to shadow-leap anywhere.

My mind was a wild animal, ready to tear down everything in my path, but I had to move carefully, or Ciara would die. I froze, staring at Baleros, waiting to see what he'd demand of me. Drop my sword? Go with him? I'd do whatever he wanted to get Ciara away from him.

"What do you want from me?" I said through gritted teeth. "You have your leverage. What do you want?"

His lip curled. "Only to watch you suffer. You defied me. People need to learn there is a price for defiance."

Rage coursed through my body, and I went completely still.

Guilt gripped my heart. If it hadn't been for me, Ciara would never have been pulled into any of this. Baleros never would have brought her into the arena as my servant. He would never have brought her here.

My senses had become heightened. I felt the slither of mist over my skin, the distant heat of Baleros's glow. I felt the rush of Ruadan's shadow magic as he leapt over to us. I sensed the chilly, damp air of the mist soldiers closing in on us, their swords drawn.

I lifted my hand, signaling to Ruadan that he needed to be still. One false move, and Ciara was dead.

And yet my mind couldn't work out what to do next.

This wasn't leverage anymore. This was punishment.

Baleros was going to kill Ciara before my eyes.

"Watch your friend as she burns," said Baleros, and icy dread crashed into me.

For the briefest of moments, Baleros released Ciara, and she ran for me under the blazing light of the sky. Then, he hurled an enormous fireball at her body.

I stared, my mind reeling as she ignited, and her clothing and skin caught fire.

I started to run for her, desperate to stamp out the flames.

It took me a moment to realize she wasn't screaming, or writhing. Instead, she was simply transforming.

Great tendrils of red hair snaked around her head like flames. Her back arched, and her skin became ashy and cracked, with lava flowing beneath the fissured surface. But within the fire, she was *smiling*, her features ecstatic.

Behind her, Baleros's face looked as shocked as I felt. He hadn't seen this coming, either.

She grinned at me. "The devil wears many faces," she hissed.

I stared as the clothing burned off her body.

I hardly registered the darkness falling around us, the light receding from the sky.

Then, Ciara eyed me through the fires that licked around her body.

What in the hells…?

She took another step closer to me. "Arianna. Behind you."

I blinked, completely at a loss for words. When I felt a cold lick of steam at my neck, I whirled again to slash my sword. A mist soldier puffed into the air. To my right, Ruadan was trying to fend off another group of mist soldiers, his sword clanging.

I turned back to Ciara, my legs shaking. "What the fuck, Ciara? You look like a gods-damn demon. You *are* a gods-damn demon."

She pointed again. "Behind you."

I spun. A sharp arc of my blade slammed into a mist soldier, vaporizing him.

She looked down at her own blazing hands, fire curling from her skin. "I always thought the McDougall family legends were true." Then, she met my gaze, fire burning in her pupils. "Didn't I tell you I'd protect you if it came down to it? I told you my grandma was from the embers under a mountain, didn't I? I sensed something bad was about to happen. I could feel it behind my knees, like when a storm is coming. Baleros captured me, but I wasn't scared. A McDougall woman always gets out alive."

My jaw dropped open. *Things really aren't always what they seem.* "I thought you were human. What the hells are you?"

"I've been telling you and telling you. The devil wears many faces." Flames erupted from her eyes, and a long tongue of fire unfurled from her mouth.

I ducked, narrowly missing the flames.

Without another word, she leapt into the center of the mist army. Swaths of flames curled off her body, snaking around the soldiers. As the fiery magic touched their bodies, they hissed, evaporating like steam. The air felt heavy with water as Ciara's fire singed the mist soldiers. I stared at the steam curling up into the heavens. She was actually destroying them, when our blades couldn't.

Ciara really *was* protecting me, this creature forged in the fiery depths of a mountain. And all this time, I'd thought she was the one who needed me.

I didn't have much time to gape at this transformation. A battle still raged here at the Institute, while Baleros was fighting to slaughter the Wraith. Speaking of the Wraith, where had he gone?

While I'd been staring at Ciara, Baleros and Ruadan had both leapt away once more.

My old master's rosewater scent coiled through the air like a miasma, a smell that would forever make me sick. I desperately needed to end him, to rid my skull of his phantom presence. As long as he lived, Baleros would always be one step ahead of me, living in my mind, predicting my moves before I made them.

And worse, if he lived, Baleros would tell everyone the truth about me.

Frantically, I searched the green for Ruadan, for Baleros. And when I saw them, my heart stopped.

With dozens of mist soldiers surrounding him, Ruadan didn't see

Baleros shadow-leaping behind him. He didn't notice that Baleros was raising an iron sword.

I didn't think. I just leapt, fury erupting like a volcano. I needed Baleros's blood on my hands. I landed just behind Baleros with a hard thud. As he whirled, I thrust my iron blade into his heart, thrilled at the feel of my blade carving into his chest.

It took me a moment to feel the pain fracturing my own body… just a moment to realize that while I'd been stabbing Baleros, he'd thrust his sword into me at the same time.

The blood drained from my skull as I stared down at Baleros's iron sword protruding from my heart.

The world started to dim, and I heard Ruadan shouting my name as if from a great distance. His magic rippled over me, trying to pull me back from death.

Before I died, I had just enough time for a single thought to pass through my mind.

I always knew I'd die at the hand of Baleros.

CHAPTER 34

Darkness enveloped me, and I felt myself falling through space. Weightless, unmoored.

I plummeted for hours, tumbling through a void.

I'd always thought death would be peaceful, a long sleep. This was not peaceful. No, it was pure panic, endless regret, and sorrow that cut me to the marrow. I longed to feel the light on my skin again, to hear the sounds of birds calling, to skim my fingers over a lake's surface. I needed to wrap my arms around Ruadan, around Ciara. I needed answers from them, needed their stories completed in my mind. I yearned to breathe in the scent of Ruadan's neck as I lay under the blankets with him, limbs entangled.

Emptiness cut me to the bone.

I fell faster, wind tearing at my hair. When I'd been alive, this darkness, this death, had dwelled inside me like a cancer. I'd filled the void with chatter, with whiskey and blood. And I wanted those things now more than ever. And more. More. A wild hunger tore through me. I wanted to feel Ruadan's skin against mine, to skim my teeth over his neck, to run through a forest with brambles scratching my legs, and to swim through clear, cold waters.

I plunged ever downward—until a powerful set of arms caught me. I gasped, endlessly relieved to feel the solidity of another body.

Pale blue eyes blazed over me, flecked with gold. I'd know those eyes anywhere. Eyes that haunted my nightmares. *Death.*

He leaned down, breathing into my mouth, and warmth blossomed in my lungs.

* * *

I OPENED MY EYES, gasping. Pain racked my body, and I gripped my heart. A wound gaped in my chest. And yet…

I was alive. I'd come back to life.

If I could come back to life, that meant…

It took me a moment to realize someone was cradling me, and I looked up into Ruadan's black eyes. For a second, I took in the pain etched on his features. Then, the shock as he realized my eyes had opened.

I clutched my chest, gasping. Pain still coursed through my muscles, until Ruadan's magic slid over my skin. It soothed the hurt.

"How are you alive?" he asked, his voice rough and jagged.

I held my hand over the gaping wound in my chest, and I simply shook my head. I'd thought of him in death. Who could have imagined that my dying thoughts would turn to the Wraith? Things were definitely not always as they seemed.

"Never mind," said Ruadan. "Don't try to speak. You killed Baleros." The scent of burnt flesh filled the air, and smoke curled behind Ruadan's head. "The fire goddess will bring him back." Ruadan's pale hair caught in the wind, and he cocked his head, studying me closely with those black eyes. "He killed you. He drove an iron sword into your heart. You were dead."

I loosed a long breath. *Death is difficult to kill.*

He leaned down, and his breath warmed the shell of my ear. "What are you?"

A nightmare. I said nothing. I'd learned from the best.

His magic still whispered over my body, leaching away the pain. I wanted sleep more than anything. I rested my head against his powerful chest, and I closed my eyes.

* * *

I SAT before a mirror while Ciara did her best to smooth my hair over the back of my long gown. Silver chinks shimmered on the sheer fabric like stars, and its violet hue matched the lumen stone around my neck.

My oldest friend's skin looked normal again, but fire still licked in her eyes. Apparently, this was the new Ciara.

Moonlight streamed in through the windows. I had my own room now—one covered in wildflowers, with a bath of my own.

It had only been three days since Baleros had rammed an iron blade into my heart, and a deep scar still marred my chest. Ruadan's magic hadn't been able to fully heal the skin, but he'd mended everything inside me, knitting together arteries and muscles with his magic. Now, I felt only a dull ache in the center of my chest.

Ciara took a hairbrush to my hair, and I winced at the sharp tug of the bristles through my tangles.

I glanced at Ciara, whose red hair still snaked around her head.

"You never told me you were a demon," I said.

She shrugged. "I didn't know. Just kind of came out. I told you my grandma came from a volcano, didn't I?"

My lips twitched in a smile. "We'll make a formidable gods-damn team, you know that?"

"Ciarianna has risen again." She yanked at my hair, tugging my snarls into submission with the brutal hairbrush. "And now, you're about to be knighted as a Shadow Fae by Grand Master Ruadan. Are you ready for it?"

I stared at myself in the mirror. For just a moment, darkness flitted through my eyes, and weightlessness tugged at my chest. Then, my mind cleared. "I'm ready. Now, you'd better get the hells out of here before someone finds you."

"They still don't want me here?"

"No, Ciara. We're supposed to slaughter demons. That hasn't changed."

She blew a strand of her hair out of her eyes with a sigh. "Fine. Good luck with your knighthood. I'm coming back to check on you." She jabbed me in the ribs. "And we need to fatten you up. You're too thin." Then she crossed to the center of the room. Fire blazed around her, a small tornado of flames that consumed her body. When the fire burned out, she left nothing behind but a few ashes and the scent of smoke.

I coughed. I'd need to think of some way to explain the scent of burned flesh that the New Ciara left behind whenever she departed.

A knock sounded at my door, and I crossed to it. I pulled it open and smiled at the sight of Melusine. She still wore a violet lumen stone around her neck.

"Melusine!" I beamed. "Did you return just for the knighting ceremony?"

She nodded. "That, and I live here now. I wanted to come back, and I hear about this job opening and I think, *that's my chance*. Turns out, the librarian can't fly around so well anymore. Got a skull fracture in a Segway accident. So I show up and I say, you know what? I belong in the library, on account of my superior intellectual skills. I can read in over three languages. English, Ancient Fae, Modern Fae, and English written by Scottish people."

"Nice."

"Yeah, I'm pretty good at stuff."

I smoothed my hair over my shoulder. I felt oddly nervous for this ceremony, unaccustomed to this sort of attention. "Want to walk with me to the knighting?"

"Yeah, let's go." And without another word, she began stomping down the hallway.

I hurried to catch up with her.

As she crossed into the stairwell, she shot me a puzzled look. "Hey, why did it smell like smoke in your room?"

I cleared my throat. "I've been smoking."

She shook her head. "No, it did not smell like tobacco. It smelled like burnt flesh."

I traced my fingers over the stone walls as we descended, and I tried to think of a plausible lie. "I roasted a squirrel."

Nope. Nope. Not a good one.

"I heard a fire demon took out part of the mist army," she said, as we reached the bottom of the stairwell. "A friend of yours. Not supposed to be in this realm anymore though, is she? I put two and two together." Before pushing through the door, she stared at me for a long time. At last, she said, "Not my problem. I'm just the librarian."

She stepped out onto the night-dark Tower Green. Shadow magic pulsed around her body, and she leapt across the green to the white stone Cailleach Tower.

For a moment, my eyes flicked across the Green to the spot where Baleros had driven a blade through my heart. My breath caught in my lungs. That feeling of weightlessness whispered through my blood, dizzying me.

I faltered, then focused again on the feel of my feet on the stony earth, rooting me in place. I was here, my feet solidly on the ground. I was alive. *Breathe in. Breathe out.*

Then, I shadow-leapt to the entrance of the Cailleach Tower. The oak door stood open, and I crossed inside.

The silk gown brushed against my legs as I walked. I wasn't used to wearing such delicate fabrics, but I liked the way the dress draped over my body. Even better, I liked imagining what the new Grand Master's face would look like when he saw me in it.

I smiled to myself as I crossed into the Great Hall.

The last time I'd been in here, I'd been standing over an execution block, while Maddan smirked at me, awaiting my demise.

Aengus, Melusine, and the others lined either side of the hall, waiting to see me knighted.

Ruadan sat in the rocky throne on the dais, and a silver crown gleamed on his head.

Baleros might have the mist army, but Ruadan had the crown and the blessing of Emain. Now Ruadan ruled London's Institute of the Shadow Fae.

And just as I'd imagined, his eyes bored right into me, drinking in the sight of the thin, silky gown. A smile curled my lips. He might be the ruler here, but I had my own sort of power over him, and I wanted to see how far I could push that.

I'd never wanted to be a spell-slayer, never imagined myself as an enforcer of arbitrary laws. But now, as I walked deeper into the hall before Ruadan, a thrill washed over me.

Now I belonged somewhere.

Ruadan rose as I crossed to him, and he drew his sword. Just before the dais, I knelt on the stone floor. This time, I didn't mind kneeling.

Ruadan stood over me, speaking in Ancient Fae. I couldn't understand what he was saying, but as he spoke, starry magic whirled around me. For just a moment, I felt myself falling again, but I focused on the feel of my knees and shins on the stone floor.

As Ruadan tapped the sword on my shoulder, a crackling power imbued my muscles. At last, he commanded me to rise. I stood, looking into his violet eyes. I'm pretty sure I saw pride glinting there.

Then, he leaned down, whispering into my ear, "What are you, Arianna?"

I smiled at him, then turned to walk away.

Let's see how well The Wraith liked the silent treatment.

COURT OF NIGHT

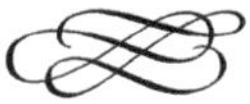

SHADOW FAE—BOOK THREE

For to those who have a little darkness inside.

Please join my facebook group if you would like to talk about books!

https://www.facebook.com/groups/cncrawford

CHAPTER 1

 stared at the gruesome offering, bile rising in my throat. Someone had nailed a human arm to one of the exterior doors of the Institute—driven the spike right through the palm, onto the wooden door.

It smelled like a fresh kill. Sticky blood oozed down the severed elbow, dripping onto the pavement. Frowning at it, I clutched the straps of my bug-out bag. Touching severed body parts wasn't my favorite way to spend the day.

And yet I had to move the thing, because behind the hand, a blank piece of paper hung on the door. A note, probably? Given the method of delivery, I could only assume it was important, and probably not something nice like a thank-you card.

Grimacing, I pulled at the nail. My stomach churned at the faint slithering sound it made, my hand brushing against the cold flesh. Thick blood coated the tips of my fingers. When I had pulled the nail all the way out, the arm fell to the pavement with a wet *thud*.

I snatched the paper and flipped it over, finding a letter scrawled in blood.

As I read its contents, my pulse pounded in my ears.

Arianna,

Tomorrow night, deliver Ruadan to me. He should wait for me outside the Institute's gate, unarmed and wearing iron cuffs. Fail, and London will suffer the Great Mortality once more. In case you think I don't possess that power, I've already started with a small population on the Isle of Dogs.

I'll wait till nine at night tomorrow, then everyone dies.

And Arianna, my darling. If you fail me, I'll let everyone know what you really are. How long will you survive, then?

Love,

Baleros

My stomach dropped, and my hands were shaking so hard I could barely rip the note into pieces.

No one could see this letter. No one.

Frantically, I tore bits off the paper. One piece after another, I shredded it.

I'll let everyone know what you really are.

Fear had gripped my throat. What if someone glued the scraps back together? I shifted my bug-out bag off my shoulders and rummaged around until I found a lighter.

Should have started with the burning.

Crouching on the ground, I brushed the bits of paper into a small pile over the stone, then held a flame over them. I had a hard time igniting them, and I burnt my thumb.

It wasn't enough that he'd stolen an *entire* mist army from the Institute. It wasn't enough that he'd imprisoned Ruadan's mother, the Queen of Emain. None of that was enough power for him. He had to have everything, didn't he? He had to have it all.

Baleros's twenty-third law of power: Use terror to control your subjects.

He knew me well enough to understand what would terrify me: the truth. What if Ruadan saw this?

I stuck my burnt finger in my mouth, sucking on it. Then, I leaned down again toward the small pile, igniting it from the top. A tendril of smoke curled around me.

Baleros might have a flair for the dramatic, but my old gladiator master did not make idle threats. If he said he was going to kill people, he meant it. If he said he'd reveal the truth about me, he meant that, too. He wanted the World Key on Ruadan's chest, and he wouldn't stop until he got it.

Pieces of paper stuck to my blood-smudged fingers. What, exactly, was the Great Mortality? Whatever it was, it didn't sound like a wonderful time. It sounded like a lot of death.

Still, I'd give up my own arm before I handed over Ruadan in chains. Not only had I grown attached to the giant, brooding demigod, but I wasn't about to present Baleros with all the power he wanted in the form of the World Key.

I exhaled. I had only a few more pieces to ignite, now, on the cobbles. I singed my fingers again and cursed under my breath.

"What the hells are you doing?" A deep voice sent my pulse racing.

Slowly, I turned to find Aengus glaring down at me. As one of the Institute's most powerful Knights, his steady, green gaze sometimes unnerved me. Plus, he didn't really like me.

"What's the problem?" I tried to keep my tone light. *Nothing to see here, folks.*

"You're crouching next to a severed human arm," he said. "Burning tiny scraps of paper. I'd venture to say it's not a typical way to spend a Tuesday morning."

I rose, trying to smile. *Stick as close to the truth as possible.* "I found a note along with the arm. I didn't want it to create more panic than necessary." The panic, in this case, was my own, but Aengus didn't need to know that. "The humans in this city have been freaking out for weeks," I added. "Baleros has been terrorizing London with his army. No reason to make them panic anymore."

"What did the note say?" He wasn't letting this point go.

"It was from Baleros, of course. We have until nine tomorrow night to hand over Ruadan in chains, or Baleros unleashes the Great Mortality. And apparently he already started on the Isle of Dogs."

"Bloody hells. If that's true, we need to contain that."

"I know." I clenched my jaw. "What exactly is the Great Mortality?"

"It's the plague that killed scores of people in Europe several times over. The Black Death, some people call it. How the hells is he capable of this magic?"

I nodded. "I have no idea. But you can put 'dying of the Plague' in your agenda book for tomorrow night unless we can kill Baleros between now and then."

He narrowed his eyes. "We once had a gorta here, guarding the gate, but you killed him. Do you know how hard it is to find a good gorta?"

"Quite hard, I imagine, or we'd already have one," I replied. "Why are we talking about this right now?"

"Because we have no gorta. No guard on duty. No witnesses. You burned the letter. Now, we have only your word to go on. How convenient for you."

Ever since I'd stabbed Ruadan and run off with the Institute's lumen crystal, Aengus had been a bit frosty. Apparently, he frowned on violent assault and theft.

I crushed the ashes into the cobbles with my foot. "I don't know what planet you're coming from, but I don't think there's anything convenient about dying from the Plague, Aengus."

And with that stinging rebuke, I strode through the Institute's blood-smeared door, leaving Aengus behind with the severed arm.

* * *

STANDING OUTSIDE THE SPREAD EAGLE, I took a long sip of Maker's Mark. Tension gripped my body. Pigeons cooed in the bridge that arched overhead, their calls slowly drowned out by the rumbling of a train.

A reckoning was coming to the great city of London—and I had my own personal reckoning in store. Baleros was the only one in London who knew the truth about me, and he'd hold it over my head as long as he was alive. Blackmail I couldn't ignore.

It had been twelve hours since I'd found the note. During that time, Ruadan had sent out most of the knights on a mission to hunt down Baleros. He'd kept only two behind: Aengus and me.

So far, no one had reported anything useful. All we had was bad news: the plague outbreak on the Isle of Dogs had been confirmed.

As far as we could tell, Baleros had been moving from one place to another, never staying in one spot long enough to get caught. The last place we'd tracked him to was an apartment in Barbican. He'd left only a half a pack of cigarettes and a box of cereal, and the cloaked knights had zoomed off after him to the next location.

In my case, tonight, I'd left the cloak at home. I was undercover in an ordinary pair of leggings and a sweater.

Once upon a time—like, two weeks ago—the Shadow Fae were the only ones wandering around London in cloaks. I mean, who else would do weird shit like that?

But now? There were these *other* cloaked people. Cloaked people who pushed people into oncoming trains, then jumped after them. In the Institute, someone had started calling them jackdaws because of their dark gray and black cloaks, and the name stuck.

Who were they? We didn't know. But the rest of London? They had a pretty good idea. They saw cloaks, they thought *Shadow Fae*. Simple as that.

In other words, someone was framing us, and I had a strong hunch it was Baleros. Maybe—just maybe—one of these jackdaws could take us to their leader.

I touched the lumen stone around my neck. A gift of magic from Ruadan—one that would help me move around fast if I found one of these cloaked men.

From the pub windows behind me, a piercing song floated through the glass. A woman was singing karaoke—or, more accurately, screaming it. Alanis Morissette, over and over.

I frowned at her through the fogging glass. *Bloody hells, woman. Just download a dating app and move on.*

Footfalls turned my head, and my heart sped up at the sight of Ruadan prowling toward me. Dark magic curled around him. The edges of his broad body seemed indistinct, like a photograph shot out of focus. But he still stood out to me, those violet eyes like a beacon in the night. Even with his fuzzy appearance, I felt acutely aware of every one of the thickly corded muscles under his dark clothes. Every movement of his called to me—the breathing, the purposeful gait—precise and focused under the fog of his magic.

As he stepped closer to me, he began to look sharper. The distant streetlights washed over his perfect face. His serene beauty belied the ruthlessness underneath. I sipped my drink.

When he reached me, he leaned against the wall. This close, his magic vibrated over my skin, making my toes curl. His magic was disturbingly addictive.

"Hello, Grand Master."

"What have you found?" No greetings, just right to the point.

"I haven't seen any of the jackdaws yet, but I will. They stick near the Institute, and they usually linger around this overpass. I'll see one soon."

"What did the note say?" Ruadan asked.

Oh. So he'd been speaking to Aengus. "I already told your mate. It said we needed to hand you over by tomorrow night, or Baleros will unleash the Great Mortality. That's the Plague."

"I know what it is. What *else* did the note say?"

I'd been hoping to skip over that part. I took another sip of the whiskey. "What makes you think it said something else?"

"You burnt it."

I was a terrible liar, so I decided to stick with a simple statement of fact. "You still don't trust me."

His dark magic stroked my skin, a subtle reminder of his overwhelming power. It had a primordial feel to it that made my spine straighten.

He took another step closer, his muscled form looming over me. "I can hear your heart race when you get nervous. And your cheeks flush."

I knew exactly how to throw Ruadan off.

I licked my lips. "How do you know that's nervousness and not lust?"

His muscles tensed.

I took one step closer, nearly touching him, and an electrical charge buzzed between our bodies. "You seem very in tune with my physiological reactions. There's something very appealing about that."

His eyes darkened. I shivered as his magic dragged the temperature down.

My jaw tightened. It didn't seem my flirting had worked to distract him. "Look, Baleros knows things about me. Things I don't want anyone else to find out. He's blackmailing me. We give you over, or he tells everyone. That's why I burnt it."

There it was—the truth. As much of it as I was willing to tell.

"What things?" His commanding tone set my teeth on edge.

Another sip of my whiskey, and I let the silence hang over us. Then, I narrowed my eyes. "Like you don't have your own secrets. You hardly speak. I'm sure there's plenty you haven't told me."

Ruadan looked away from me, his eyebrows furrowed. Then, he nodded. I was dead on with the "you have secrets, too" theory.

"Try to report back to me within an hour. If the jackdaws don't lead to anything, we'll track him another way."

Ruadan started to turn back to the Institute, but the pub door slammed open, and he froze. The heartbroken karaoke singer stumbled outside, and Ruadan turned to her. Rivulets of mascara ran down her face, and her lipstick had been smeared over her chin. She sloshed a bit of white wine out of her glass.

Ruadan stared at the drunk woman, who was singing quietly to herself. His eyes darkened, body going completely still.

I took another look at the woman. She was beautiful, sure. Big blue eyes, full lips, rosy cheeks. But apart from that, she seemed like an ordinary human—nothing remarkable or stare-worthy. She wiped a hand under her nose, then sniffled into her wineglass.

Ruadan's gaze was locked on her. A faint hint of violet glowed off him. His magic seemed to be intensifying, pulsing in delicious waves that skimmed over my skin.

Pleasurable as it felt, it seemed he'd forgotten all about me, his eyes black as voids. Then, he closed his eyes, breathing in deeply. Was he smelling her? What the hells was going on here?

<h1 style="text-align:center">CHAPTER 2</h1>

I crossed my arms. "You were saying I needed to report back," I said, my voice unnecessarily harsh.

The black snapped out of his eyes, and he turned his violet gaze to me. The air seemed to glow around him, and the drunk woman simply swayed, staring at him like she was transfixed.

"It's just like I said," I added. "We all have our secrets, don't we?" I turned to the woman. "Can you piss off, now? It's not safe out here. Shadow Fae all over the place." Was I being a bit territorial? Perhaps.

She nodded, her eyes still on Ruadan, then pulled open the pub door again and disappeared inside.

Before I could say another word to Ruadan, darkness billowed around him, and he was gone.

I surveyed the empty street. There hadn't been many humans around in the past few weeks. Not since Baleros had begun his recent reign of terror with his own growing army.

A couple rounded the corner—middle-aged, but dressed from head to toe in piercings and leather. As they walked, I tuned into their conversation.

"Should we really be out so close to the Institute?" the woman hissed. "The Shadow Fae might murder us."

There it was again. All it had taken was a few black cloaks to confuse the entire city of London.

The man glanced over his shoulders. "Keep it down, Lucy. They could be anywhere."

My plan was simple: find one of the cloaked buggers, then hurt him until I found out more. If my hunch was right, the jackdaws were connected to Baleros. We'd find him, imprison him, demand to know where Ruadan's mother was. Then we'd kill him.

Or, at least, that's how it would all work out in my head.

But things were never that easy, were they? And why weren't there any jackdaws around here tonight? It was like they were avoiding me. Or avoiding *something.*

I sniffed the air, and a faint, earthy scent hit me. Mossy and dank—a fae smell, but an unfamiliar one. Older than most fae, and a bit more coppery. It smelled of death. I slid my glass onto the windowsill. Maybe this was what they were avoiding.

I started walking north, and as I reached an empty intersection, a blur of movement sent my pulse racing. I turned, catching a glimpse of a woman crossing toward a narrow alleyway.

There she was—the fae I'd scented. She reeked of death.

Just before she disappeared into the alleyway, she turned to look at me. Immediately, I could tell I'd been right about the fae thing—long, metallic talons; rapid, animalistic movements. When her eyes met mine, my pulse quickened. Her skin was the color of bone, and a dress hugged her body, its leather the color of dried blood. Long, black hair hung down her back, and her eyes had the blue-gray hue of a murky lake. She opened her mouth, and for just a moment, a forked tongue snaked out. Then, she pivoted, marching onward.

I wasn't sure what was happening, but this was a lead worth chasing. An ancient, powerful fae like this one wasn't an everyday occurrence.

I pulled a knife out of my bug-out bag as I walked, wishing I'd come armed with a sword instead. It's just that swords tended to ruin the whole *ordinary human* undercover vibe.

I followed her through the alley, which opened up into another street.

When I reached the mouth of the alley, the fae turned back to look at me, murky eyes landing on my face. Across the street, three men in white football shirts were chanting a song, drunkenly stumbling into each other. One of them carried a pint that sloshed on the pavement.

The fae's attention darted back to them. She wasn't interested in me.

I stared as her form began to change, her skin scaling over. A sharp, knobbled spine protruded from the back of her dress.

My pulse raced faster. The men in the football shirts hadn't even noticed her. My fingers twitched on my knife hilt as I waited to see what she'd do next.

I had my answer when her shockingly long tongue shot out, lashing the three men across their faces. The attack left deep, red gashes in their skin, and the men staggered, shouting now.

I took a step closer. I didn't want to intervene yet—I wanted to find out exactly what she was.

The men seemed to be frozen in place. From fear, perhaps? Whatever it was, it didn't look as if they could move.

The lower half of the fae's body then shifted, elongating and growing scales, becoming a tail with a rattle that then slithered across the road toward the men.

I touched the lumen stone at my neck, then narrowed my focus to a single point near the fae, willing myself to summon its magic. Electric power crackled up my spine. I got ready to leap, and—

The fae's head whipped toward me, tongue lashing out. She struck me in the neck, ripping through the skin. As soon as her tongue made contact, my muscles began to seize up, body freezing. I stood immobilized as she turned her attention to the three men again. Her tail wrapped around them like a ribbon encircling a bunch of flowers. Their eyes went wide, faces red as she squeezed their chests. Garbled grunts rose from their throats. They couldn't breathe, and with each gasp, she seemed to tighten her grip even more.

She was squeezing the poor bastards to death. I tried opening my mouth to scream, but even my mouth was frozen, and I couldn't move my vocal cords. The only sounds in this deserted street were a low hissing rising from the ancient fae and the strangled gasps coming from the men. Gripped around the waist, they made a gruesome bouquet of humans, eyes popping.

The fae's body glowed as her tail constricted further around them. Dark veins shot through the men's skin—a poison from her tongue, perhaps?

With an iron will, I forced my neck muscles to move just a little, then my eyes. I looked down at my own body, nauseated to see dark toxins pulsing through my veins. I felt as if I were rotting from the inside out. Wrath pulsed along with the poison. What *right* did she have to do this to me?

When I forced my eyes up again, two of the three men had died—suffocated in her grasp. The third, horrifyingly, was being crushed against the corpses of his friends. I opened my mouth again to scream, and this time a tiny sound emerged from my throat—a little squeak. But what good did that do me? All I could do was stare as she crushed the breath out of the last man, his face now purple.

As soon as the life left his eyes, her tail slithered away from the rotten bouquet. She transformed back into her legged form.

I stood there, frozen, like an idiot.

I understood that she was a *fomoire,* a fae who fed off suffering. A living nightmare. In fact, that's where the word came from—nightmoire. If I hadn't been here, she'd probably have prolonged their suffering just to feed off it. But now she had a second target. Me, immobilized by her poison.

Her head swiveled back to me, body glowing with a pale blue light. She stalked closer, high heels clacking over the pavement. Her jerky gait reminded me of a fox walking on its hind legs, and she seemed like an animal wearing a human suit more than a fae.

I strained, desperate to grip the knife at my side, desperate to thrust it into her chest.

Three crushed humans, and me unable to move. This day was not going well for me. As she moved closer, I could see the pale, greenish tinge to her porcelain skin.

When she was just a few inches away from me, I braced, expecting her tail to come out again. To my surprise, she pulled a silver cigarette case from her pocket. She opened it and pulled out a smoke. She lit it, put it in her mouth, then offered the case to me. "Smoke?"

I could hardly say *no*, could I? I mean, I literally couldn't say anything at all.

She cocked her head, smiling. Then, she jammed a cigarette in my mouth, just between my gritted teeth. She lit it, and smoke curled into my eyes, making them water. I *hated* this woman.

"There," she trilled. "Now you look relaxed."

The cigarette fell out of my mouth, along with a thin stream of drool. Lovely evening I was having so far.

Right now, I pretty much wanted to rip her throat out with my bare hands, but the immobilization put a kink in that desire. Why wasn't she crushing me to death?

She blinked at me. "They were enjoying themselves. I had to make them suffer. You understand, don't you? You know what I am. I feed off pain." She leaned in closer, sniffing me. "But you were already suffering before I got to you."

Rage simmered. What was she talking about?

A smile curled her lips as she looked me up and down. "Guilt. Loneliness. Fear. Not of me—no. You're afraid of yourself. Afraid of people knowing the truth." She closed her eyes, breathing in. "It's lovely." When she opened her eyes again, her body was growing brighter. "It's all right, darling. I'm going to kill you, and then you don't have to worry anymore. I'm here to end your suffering."

Bitch, please.

I closed my eyes, summoning the darkness from within. Cold wrath flooded me. Yes, the snake lady was terrifying—but so was I.

CHAPTER 3

These beasts, crawling over the earth, acting like gods. She needs to learn her place.

The voice in my mind wasn't quite my own. It scared me, but I knew it would save me.

A blast of dark magic pulsed out of my body like a toxic cloud. It pounded through my blood, pushing out her poison.

Here it was—my dark side. The part of me I had to keep secret. I was the fury of the gods, and I had my own venom.

The darkness had exploded for just a few moments. Then, the magic had snapped back into me again. My body shook and nausea gripped my gut. I hunched over, vomiting up my whiskey onto the pavement.

Holy crap. Had that actually just happened? Had the real me nearly come out? Panic had such a tight grip on my mind that I nearly forgot about the fae.

I'd nearly lost control.

I looked at the ancient fae, who lay flat on her back—hurt, but still breathing. My little burst of dark magic had flattened her. More importantly, it had freed my muscles.

Fighting nausea, I twirled my knife, my sights locked on her.

I smiled. She hadn't seen this coming.

Her eyes opened wider. "What *are* you?"

Fury of the gods.

"I'm your worst nightmare." It came out in a voice I didn't recognize—many voices, in fact; a chorus of them, harmonizing with each other.

She narrowed her eyes at me, then pulled out another cigarette. With what seemed a great deal of effort, she rose to her feet.

Should I let her live?

"You and I are the same, darling," she said. "We're monsters. The only difference is that you're lying to yourself."

Nope. You don't get to live.

I lunged for her, slashing with my knife. She darted back, her movements bestial. Her tongue lashed out again, striking me in the side. Pain seared me, but her poisons didn't seep into me this time. She hit me again with her tongue, but this time, I cut into it with my blade. Dark blood stained the pavement.

Battle fury pulsed through my bones, and I lunged for her, ready to stab, to slice, to carve.

A rattle rose from her throat, and she darted away from me again, landing in a puddle of water with a splash. She was *fast*.

I lunged for her again, but she disappeared into the puddle. Her body vanished completely.

She left behind only the smell of moss and blood. I looked at the pile of human corpses, my stomach turning. It was only then I realized that my whole body was trembling, that the knife in my hand was shaking. I didn't feel in control of the death force in me, and I wanted to keep it locked up.

I let out a long, slow breath. I couldn't let my dark side come out—not completely.

I stared at the puddle of murky water, marshaling a sense of calm. One more night, and I still didn't have any answers.

I didn't know if that woman was directly connected to Baleros, but his chaos had allowed her to roam London's streets, feeding off death. I cocked my head, staring at the still puddle. Maybe now that

I'd rid the streets of her death-stench, I could find myself some jackdaws.

I shoved my hands into my pockets and turned to walk back toward The Spread Eagle.

The streets still looked empty, and I attuned my ears to the sound of footsteps. Ruadan had given me a time limit on this particular mission, and I had about a half hour left before I was supposed to report back to him. I was starting to think I'd be late.

It took me another twenty minutes before I found one of them, stalking down Fenchurch Street. The oldest part of the city, where humans had once made sacrifices to the river gods.

My pulse started to race as I turned to follow him, and I sheathed my knife again. He was heading south, toward The Spread Eagle. When he turned his head, I caught a hollow look in his eyes that made my blood run cold. He didn't seem to be taking things in, didn't notice me. He was human, but the expression in his eyes made me think he was staring at me from one of the hells itself. What had Baleros done to these men?

I picked up my pace, moving after him to close the gap. I shoved my hand into my pocket, then pulled out a grape lolly to pop in my mouth.

When the jackdaw turned left into a narrow alleyway—not far from the glowing spires of the Institute—I followed him into the passage.

His footsteps echoed off the brick walls. I quickened my pace, drawing my knife as I moved closer. Then, when I was within arm's reach, I grabbed him. In the next heartbeat, I had him pinned up against the wall, elbow to his chest, knife to his throat.

That wasn't hard. Not hard at all.

He stared at me, his eyes heavy-lidded. Bizarrely, he didn't look one bit scared. Beneath his cloak, he had pale skin and a hint of a beard.

"Who are you?" I barked, my lolly sticking out of my mouth.

He blinked down at me. "No one."

"What's your name, dimwit?"

His mouth opened and closed mutely. Then he said, "The Great Mortality is coming for us all."

And that confirmed my hunch. The jackdaws had been Baleros's work.

I pressed the blade a little harder, drawing a tiny bit of blood. "Let's just get down to brass tacks, shall we? Where do I find Baleros?"

His eyes widened—just enough to tell me that he recognized the name. Still, he didn't say anything. Why wasn't he scared of his clearly impending death?

I grabbed one of his wrists, slamming it against the wall. He grunted. The cloth slipped up his arm, and for a moment, my heart skipped a beat. There—burned into his skin—was a brand. But it wasn't Baleros's brand as I'd expected. No, this was the moon rising over a tower.

It was the symbol of the Institute. So it wasn't just the cloaks. Baleros had gone to serious lengths to frame us.

"That looks familiar," I muttered. Thing was, the Institute didn't brand people. *Baleros* branded people. I knew, because I'd once cut his brand off my own wrist.

I leaned in, sniffing the faint, electrical scent of magic. Nearly imperceptible, a dark aura glimmered around him. What sort of enchantment was this?

"Where is he?" I hissed. "Where is Baleros?"

The man simply shook his head. "Can't tell anyone, can I?"

I reared back my arm and slammed my fist into his chin, the bone cracking as I made contact. Now, his shattered jaw hung at an angle, already swelling.

When he met my gaze, I still saw no fear there. He just stared at me, a quiet desperation in his eyes.

"How is Baleros recruiting you people?" I demanded, rage and fear rising in my chest. I could already feel myself losing control. "I need answers. Where did he find you?"

"I used to be alive." His voice sounded haunted.

I narrowed my eyes at the pulsing vein in his neck. His skin was warm, and I could hear his heart beating from here. If there's one thing I knew, it was death. And this man was not dead.

"What the hells do you mean?" I shot back. "You're still alive."

"Nah, not anymore. My name used to be Alan. I was the manager of a small sales division. An insurance company. Not only was I alive, but I was known as a bit of a party animal, as it were. Organized company footie and barbecues. Fun and games."

Oh, gods. I wished he'd just talk about torture or something.

"That was me. Right laugh," he continued in his monotone. "Before I died, I wore a boa for a laugh, made jokes about bumming the other lads. I burned my knob by sticking it in the cheese dip, and—"

I punched him hard again in the jaw. It took me a moment to realize I had no strategic reason for hitting him just then, but I didn't want to hear anything else about his life.

"You would have been my type," he said. "Pretty face, completely insane, nice set of baps—"

I hit him again. His head lolled again, and his eyelids fluttered.

"What do you mean you're dead?" I snarled. "You're objectively not dead. It's not up for argument."

"I'm dead, innit?"

Idiot. At least this explained the jackdaws' fearlessness. If a man thought he was dead, he had nothing to fear.

He stared at me. "He promised me eternal life."

"Baleros?"

"I must keep his secrets. That's the rule."

"He's not going to give you eternal life. You're not dead. You're a fucking muppet, but you're not dead. Tell me about this Great Mortality. What's the plan?"

"The dead cannot die," he said in a flat voice, blood dripping from his chin, streaming from his broken nose.

It took me a moment to hear the dim beeping noise. Another second to notice his thumb on a button, the blinking lights at his waist. And a fraction of an instant to put together that this man was about to blow himself up, with me standing next to him.

I dove away from him, landing hard on the pavement just as the bomb went off. The explosion seared my back, and shrapnel pierced the skin at my waist. I didn't want to think too long about what the shrapnel was—probably bits of Alan's bones. The explosion had temporarily deafened me, and I clamped my hands over my ears to dampen the piercing ring.

Smoke billowed around me, and I turned back to look at the man formerly known as Alan. There was hardly anything left of him, just gristle and body parts spattered over the brick and pavement.

I coughed, wincing in pain, and pushed myself up onto my hands and knees. I blocked out the vague sense that I was inhaling Alan dust, and I rubbed the smoke and grit out of my eyes. As I did, something on the pavement caught my eye—a scrap of glittering gold and green.

I crawled over to it, grunting. I picked up the colored remnant, running my fingertips over its surface. It looked like a piece of a matchbox, and the fragment read *The Skull and Cr—*

The singed edges and heat told me it had come from Alan.

My hands were shaking, and dizziness clouded my mind as I forced myself up. The jackdaw situation was worse than I thought. Somehow, Baleros was convincing people they were already dead, that serving him was the key to their eternal salvation. Not only did he have the mist army, but he'd made himself a legion of fearless human slaves.

CHAPTER 4

I rose unsteadily, leaning against a brick wall as I tried to stay standing. I'd learned a few things. But not the big question of where I'd find Baleros.

One day till the world ends.

I gripped my side, using breathing to manage the pain. The explosion had burned some of my skin, and had lacerated my back and waist.

The mournful sound of church bells knelled over the city.

I hobbled to the mouth of the alley, staring out onto the empty, darkened street.

What was he doing with the jackdaws? If there was a single piece of philosophy that guided Baleros's actions, it was the idea that chaos was the opportunity to remake the world the way he wanted it. And he was doing a bang-up job of it so far.

Amidst the city's panic, only the Institute felt calm, our walls protected by a magical moat and a river.

I touched the lumen stone at my neck, working on summoning its shadow magic. Cold power flooded my limbs, igniting my muscles. Then, I shadow-leapt down the dark street. With the tower in view, I leapt again, landing hard just before the moat of light.

A shock of pain shot up my body as I touched down before the light. I'd mistimed it a bit, landed too hard, and I was sure at least some of my limbs had been bruised in the blast.

Catching my breath, I stepped onto the bridge that spanned the magical moat. Instantly, warmth flooded me, washing over my skin. It almost felt like the light was healing me.

As I crossed the stone bridge, hunger rose in my gut. In fact, the feeling of starvation overwhelmed me so much, it eclipsed the pain of my injuries. What the hells? I'd killed the hunger gorta that once guarded the Institute. Why was I feeling this famine now?

I could think only of filling my belly, and of gnawing on the sweet, sweet grass that grew below the moat.

Furious, I jammed my hand into my bug-out bag, and I pulled out a chocolate bar and my headlamp. I flicked my headlamp on, then unwrapped the chocolate, taking a huge bite.

A cloaked fae approached me, and I just caught a glimpse of his gaunt features under his hood.

"Who are you?" I barked, furious in my hunger.

"I'm the new gorta. They're paying me double the last fella. Just doing my bit."

My stomach rumbled wildly. I clutched it, nearly doubling over. I thought Aengus had said it was nearly impossible to get a gorta.

"How's it going, then?" He pointed at my stomach. "Does the ol' belly feel a bit hollow?"

"You're not supposed to strike me," I yelled, clutching my stomach. "I'm one of the Shadow Fae. I belong here."

Ah. Right. It was hard to get a *good* gorta.

"Just want to make sure the Grand Master feels he's getting his money's worth," he said. "I've got a family to feed. Not many of you going in and out. Not many of you here, in fact. Everyone's out looking for this bogeyman. Baleros, innit. Whole place is empty."

I straightened, looking him right in the eye. "I'm here, and I'm a knight. I belong here. Let me through." I pointed out beyond the moat of magic. "I'm bleeding all over the bridge right now, having done a night's work for the Institute, and the Grand Master wants to see me."

He shrugged. "Go on, then." He jumped off the bridge to the grassy moat below.

As soon as he did, the gnawing hunger disappeared from my ribs.

I wrapped up the rest of my chocolate bar and dropped it in my bag. Then, I flicked off my headlamp, passing through the gate into the old Tower itself. My body ached in places I didn't even want to think about, and fragments of bone were embedded deep within my flesh. I winced as I walked; blood poured from my sides.

We had one day left, and only a tiny scrap of paper to go on.

* * *

As I crossed into the great hall, my body hummed at the sight of Ruadan on his rocky throne. Somehow, he looked like he'd always belonged there, as if his prior absence from its jagged contours had been a terrible error. A silver crown gleamed on his head, and the wavering torchlight gilded his perfect features—the dark eyebrows, the aggressively beautiful planes of his face.

I was so intently focused on Ruadan, I nearly missed the king standing on the flagstones before him—and the woman by his side.

The same woman, in fact, who'd tried to kill me just a half hour ago. It was the serpent fae, smiling smugly in her red leather dress, long black hair tumbling gracefully over her shoulders. The only sign that she'd just been on a murdering binge was the glow of her body from feeding on their pain.

I limped into the room, my lip curling. "What's she doing here?"

Ruadan took in my injuries, and he tensed in his throne. His dark magic whooshed over the hall, suffocating some of the flames at the ends of the torches. For just a moment, shadows pooled in his eyes. "Are you okay?" His voice was quiet, but somehow seemed to fill the hall.

All eyes were on me, and I held my side as I walked, feeling as if I was trying to hold my body together. I'd gone a bit dizzy from the blood loss.

"I'm alive. I had some altercations." I nodded at the serpent woman. "In fact, I believe I met your friend here, earlier."

I wasn't going to mention the jackdaws in front of these strangers I didn't trust.

"How fascinating." The auburn-haired king failed to hide his irritation.

And who was *he?* Red magic glimmered and crackled around his body—not just a king, but a powerful magician.

The king turned back to Ruadan. "I don't care if you've taken him out of the dungeon. I want my son back. I am King Locrinus of Elfame, Carver of Enemies, House of the Golden Sickle, and I demand that you return Maddan to me."

Oh. Of course. He was the father of the Institute's least competent recruit, Maddan. And I suppose he wanted his son back.

Ruadan ignored the king, his eyes locked on me. He rose from his throne. "We need to speak. Privately."

The king huffed. "Honestly, what in the gods' names is this creature?"

"I'm Arianna, daughter of.... You know what? Let's not get into who sired whom. I already met Serpent Lady when she was crushing some humans to death, anyway."

As Ruadan crossed to me, he shot the serpent woman a look of such venom that I had to wonder if they had a history.

Ruadan stood over me, tugging up the edge of my shirt to inspect the damage. "How injured are you?"

"I might have bits of an insurance salesman lodged within my spleen."

"You're coming with me now."

Then, he scooped me up as if I didn't weigh a thing. His magic began snaking over my body, numbing the sharp pain and the burns. I rested my head on his chest, listening to his heartbeat.

Once we were through the archway, he whispered, "What happened?"

"First, I saw that serpent lady. The fomoire. She's vile."

Ruadan carried me up the stairs.

"Then, I found one of the jackdaws. They're definitely human, but they've been hit with a magical spell. Alan believed he was already dead. Hence, he didn't mind blowing himself up. I mean, what's the harm in blowing up when you're dead, right?"

I had a vague sense that I wasn't explaining this well, but the blood loss was starting to get to me. Leaning into Ruadan's chest, I closed my eyes.

"Everything is confusing right now, but Baleros has built himself a fearless army of humans. He's got himself a mist army, and now, an army of human suicide bombers."

At the top of the stairs, Ruadan crossed into a drafty hallway. Then, he kicked through a door. In the small, stone room, Aengus sat behind a desk, a spell book spread out in front of him.

The door slammed shut behind us.

"What's going on?" asked Aengus.

"Jackdaw bomb," I said. "They're working for Baleros, and they're now blowing themselves up."

Ruadan laid me on the desk, still cradling me against his chest.

"You're not giving that king Maddan, are you?" I asked. "Maddan's an enemy of the Institute. He's also a leaf-wearing, small-footed, dead-eyed mistake of a man."

"Quiet." Ruadan examined my waist.

"It's like the gods scrambled a person when they tried to make him."

"*Quiet.*"

Ruadan's healing magic skimmed my skin. As the pain began to seep out of my body, pleasure washed over me. Closing my eyes, I sank further against Ruadan's muscled chest, before I remembered that Aengus was watching.

I shifted on the desk, dangling my legs over the side. "Am I healed now?"

"Not exactly," he said. "I took the pain away and stopped the bleeding, but we've still got shrapnel to deal with."

I lifted a finger. "Wait. I forgot a key part of this whole situation. The jackdaws have been branded, like I was." I pointed to my wrist, where I'd cut off Baleros's brand. "But Baleros didn't brand them with his symbol. He's branded them with our symbol. He has convinced them that he will grant them eternal life as long as they do whatever he wants. I think he's going to let the Institute take the fall for his whole Great Mortality plan. He's turning the city against us."

Aengus scrubbed a hand over his chin, leaning back in his chair. "What do you think Baleros's end game is?"

"For now, the goal is to create chaos and pin the blame on us," I said. "He's trying to unsettle people. Have you seen the skulls and skeletons painted on the walls around here? He really *does* have a flair for the dramatic." I tapped my fingertip to my lips as I thought. "He had this theory that the best way to take over a kingdom was to prop up a tyrant. Then, you execute the tyrant publicly. You get to look like a hero, and you rule the kingdom. And I think that's what he's doing. He's making us into the tyrants."

Ruadan crossed his arms. "People are supposed to believe those little, dead-eyed humans are Shadow Fae?"

"If humans are scared enough, they'll believe anything." I looked up into Ruadan's eyes. "He still wants that World Key on your chest. Once Baleros decides he wants something, he never lets it go. He'll want to kill you, then take your key. I don't think you should leave the Institute."

Aengus snorted. "Good luck with that advice. The fastest way to get Ruadan out of a place is to tell him that he needs to stay locked within it."

Ruadan's eyes darkened. "I'm not staying locked in here. Nearly every knight in the Institute is out there searching for Baleros, and we will be, too. We don't rest until we find him. Baleros still has my mother imprisoned somewhere, and I'm not hiding behind these walls while others try to find her and stop the Plague."

I gripped the desk hard, my thoughts muddled. "I'll take care of it."

Ruadan shook his head *no,* then added, "You can't even stand up straight. You've lost too much blood, and you have no idea where to go next."

"The clue." I reached into my pocket. "I forgot the clue. A pub called The Skull and Crossbones. It was on the jackdaw." I didn't want this lead slipping away from me. "I think I should go there now."

"Not now." Ruadan's commanding tone rang throughout the room. "Aengus, make sure King Locrinus doesn't get into any trouble. Arianna's coming to my room."

I blinked. "What?"

He touched the small of my back, guiding me to the door. "Don't argue with me. Do you know what happens to a knight who argues with the Grand Master?" His soothing voice caressed my skin, but there was a hint of threat in it.

I followed him into the corridor, hurrying to keep up with his pace. My lip curled. "Disobeying the Grand Master? A light spanking?"

"In Emain, disobedient knights were tied naked to trees—"

"I like where you're going with this," I said.

"—they were fed meals of oatcakes and honey—"

"Literally none of this sounds bad."

"—and then wood-poppets would rise from the tree trunks and rip through their guts to get to the honey."

I winced. "That part sounds bad. What the fuck is a wood-poppet? You know what, never mind. Why are we going to your room?"

"Arianna, even if you can't feel it, you still have bits of … insurance salesman lodged in your organs."

I grimaced. "You make a good point."

"And I'm coming with you to the pub."

Obviously, I should not have told Ruadan that he needed to stay confined within the Tower, because he clearly had a contrary nature. He'd start banging on about wood-poppets again if I argued with him.

"I'm not being disobedient, but it makes no sense for you to come with me," I said. "You're the target, and Baleros can't get inside the Tower."

Dark magic snaked around him. Frost slicked the walls as we walked, and my teeth started chattering.

"You don't like feeling trapped in places, do you?" I said.

"No." His eyes were straight ahead, not meeting my gaze.

"Particularly by Baleros, I'm guessing."

He didn't respond. Baleros had been my master and Ruadan's mentor centuries ago, when Ruadan was just a young fae. I knew what kind of methods Baleros used to control people.

"Did he used to lock you in an iron box?" I felt like I was entering dangerous waters, but I wanted to know more about Ruadan.

"Rock," he said. "Underground river."

Silence fell over us as we walked, but Ruadan's quiet rage had sucked nearly all the light out of the hall.

I knew one thing for certain. Like me, Ruadan would never be at ease until Baleros was in the grave for good.

CHAPTER 5

I sat at the edge of Ruadan's bed, and he stood over me. We had less than a day to sort out this whole situation.

"Take off your shirt," said Ruadan.

I considered making a "buy a girl dinner" joke first, but it wasn't funny, and I smothered the impulse. I kept my mouth shut and pulled off my shirt.

Ruadan sucked in a sharp breath, and I looked down at myself, craning my neck to see my wounds. When I saw the damage, I groaned. I couldn't feel it anymore, but my back and sides had been shredded and burned.

"Lie down on your front," said Ruadan.

I did as he said, folding my arms beneath my chin. I closed my eyes, feeling only faint pressure as he cleaned the wounds, pulling out the shrapnel. Because of his magic, I felt no pain.

"Don't you have healers for this?" I asked.

"We do. But they're not as thorough as I am."

"I feel privileged to be treated by the Grand Master himself." I licked my lips, daring myself to ask the question really on my mind. "With Savus dead, are you keeping that whole virginity pledge?"

"It wasn't virginity."

"Whatever. Abstinence."

"As has always been the case, Knights of the Shadow Fae may not take lovers within the Institute. They may take lovers outside the Institute. Not that any of that is my top concern at this point."

Okay. That was a very formal way of saying "you and I will never be sleeping together, so get it out of your overheated mind."

Silence fell as he worked. Then, Ruadan said, "You died." It seemed Ruadan was not letting this little point go. "When Baleros was here, he thrust a sword into your heart. You thrust your sword into his. Both were made of iron. You both died. I know why Baleros came back to life. He pledged his soul to Emerazel, and she revives him. I do not know how you returned."

I let silence fall again. He hadn't actually asked a question, so I didn't bother answering it.

He tugged down the top of my skirt, working on the flesh over my hip.

I breathed in his smell—pine and apples. Weeks ago, I'd spent a few days naked in this bed, my body wrapped around his, writhing from an overdose of lust magic. And now, Ruadan's magic was rushing over me in tingling waves of pleasure. I couldn't see it, but I was sure my skin looked better already.

After a few more minutes of his delicious healing magic, he spoke again. "The wounds are cleaned and healed. Now tell me what you are."

Ruadan had a little habit of not answering questions that he didn't want to answer. A brilliant tactic in its simplicity. He just kept his mouth shut and that was that. I had another brilliant tactic up my sleeve. Instead of answering, I turned over onto my back, one hand slung over my breasts, but leaving one of my nipples in view as if by accident.

I blinked at him innocently. "What was the question?"

Black slammed into his eyes, his demonic form taking over. For just an instant, I caught a glimpse of phantom wings sweeping down from behind his shoulders. *Ahh ... there's the incubus.*

My breath caught in my throat. I'd never seen those before. Still, he hadn't fully shifted yet. If he did, I didn't imagine his incubus side had much self-restraint.

He planted his hands on either side of my head, boxing me in, and warmth pulsed through my belly. Slowly, he raked his gaze up and down my body, lingering on my bare breasts, swooping down my waist, my hips, between my legs. The look he was giving me was purely carnal, like he wanted to devour me completely.

Lightning-fast, he leaned down, his breath warming my neck. He inhaled deeply, growling in a low timbre that reverberated through my gut. My back started to arch, and I let my arm fall away from my breasts completely. I licked my lips, staring into his dark eyes. He gripped the sheets so tightly his muscles were shaking.

It took him a moment to master control of himself, until at last, his eyes returned to violet.

Damn.

He pushed himself up, turning away from me.

I let out a long, slow exhale, staring at his muscled back.

"Rest for an hour," he said. "Then, we're leaving for The Skull and Crossbones."

* * *

After about twenty minutes of resting, I hopped out of bed. I snatched a change of clothes out of my bug-out bag—a white button-down dress. It looked absurdly innocent—perfect for undercover missions, since the Shadow Fae never dressed in white.

I pulled it on and grabbed my bug-out bag. Then, I armed myself with one of the swords and sheaths from Ruadan's wall. I headed out to the courtyard.

Before leaving for a mission, I liked to spend a little time delving into research at the library—even more so now that my friend Melusine worked there.

Fully healed now, I moved rapidly up the stairs to the dim light of the library. There, I found Melusine perched on a ladder, nose in a book about unicorn shifters. A glow worm illuminated the air above her with golden light. She didn't seem to notice me stride in.

"Melusine."

She jumped, slamming the book shut. It took me a moment to recognize the flushed look on her face, and the heated look in her eyes, and to realize that Melusine had a bit of a thing for unicorn shifters. Interesting.

"I wasn't thinking about anything weird!" she blurted. "It says here in the literature that there's nothing wrong with someone reading a simple, educational book about muscular men growing hooves and a horn."

"Simmer down, Melusine. I just need some help learning about a particular type of magic."

She nodded, straightening her dress. "What can you tell me about this particular type of magic?"

"You ever heard of something where a human thinks he's dead, but he's not?"

"Like he's physically fine, but he's all screwed up in the head?"

"Yeah."

She scratched her head. "It sounds like psychomancy. It's a new type of magic, about a hundred years old. You know, when I hear about people thinking something that's not real, I think *delusions*. I put two and two together. Right? I once had a delusion that my brother's toy soldiers were trying to kill me with poison. But it was actually our cat. Do you know what I mean?"

Nope. "Sure. Yes."

She began leading me to an alcove in another corner of the library.

"What did you call it?" I asked. "Psycho-something?"

"The psychomancers were influenced by the human field of psychology. It's a fascinating field. I know at least several hundred things about it." She pushed her glasses up on her nose. "Some psychomancers are able to meddle with human minds in ways that mimic actual human delusions."

She pulled a book off a shelf and began paging through it,

humming to herself quietly as she did. At last, she stopped on a page, her face brightening.

"Here we go. Cotard Syndrome. Person thinks he's decaying, sometimes that he's in hell. Total shock to the system, really. It can be caused by brain damage." She shut the book. "Or, in this case, magic."

I crossed my arms. "It makes a weird sort of sense. The jackdaws are fearless, and Baleros is using them to frame us." I bit my lip. "And what can you tell me about the Black Death?"

"That one's easy. Humans ascribe it to a bacterium, but it was actually caused by magic. Legend says the Horseman of Death caused it."

My throat tightened. "What?"

"That's the legend. Big outbreaks in the sixth century, the fourteenth, the seventeenth. Streets filled with bodies, red crosses on the doors, stench of death everywhere. Real fun, you know? Tell you the truth, some *did* have real fun. Did you know that people reacted in two ways? They flogged themselves in the streets, or they fornicated everywhere."

I nodded. That actually made sense. From my experience, humans were obsessed with precisely two things: shagging and hating themselves for shagging.

"Whips and sexual relations all over the place," she added.

"I've been to a party like that."

Melusine shrugged. "I don't know a lot about romance, per se, but plague-infested London doesn't seem like a romantic setting to me. Bleeding neck buboes, red crosses on the doors, rats feasting on the dead. Is that something humans find sexually stimulating, like a man staring at an attractive brassiere in a catalogue? I've got no idea. That part's not in the literature. To be frank, I don't understand humans or people in general. But maybe they figured they had to make the most of their lives."

I nodded. "Okay, I get the idea."

"Why are you asking about the Plague?"

"Oh, um, maybe I should have led with that. We have less than a day until everyone in London gets the Plague and the world ends."

"Ah."

"I expected a bit more of a reaction."

She frowned. "I mean, the Plague sounds bad, but the world won't end."

"The world has ended before," I countered, vaguely aware of the absurdity of my argument.

"Not really, since we're still here."

"Right." I chewed my lip. "I see your point. Melusine, what the hells is a wood-poppet?"

"A wood-poppet? I've never heard of that."

Had Ruadan been messing with me?

A loud boom interrupted our conversation, and the floor beneath us shook. Books tumbled off the shelves, and I covered my head with my arms. "What the hells?" I shouted.

Melusine—cleverly—had immediately leapt to an archway, avoiding the falling books.

"Gods below," I grunted. I clutched the bookshelf as the floor stabilized. "That's the second explosion tonight."

"Someone's attacking the Institute," added Melusine, rather unnecessarily.

I pulled out my sword, summoning my shadow magic. It whispered through my veins, cold and electric. I began shadow-leaping, rushing through the air, down the stairs. I slammed through the Tower door, then shadow-leapt across the Tower Green. Smoke curled into the air from one of the Towers.

As I shadow-leapt, the wind whipped at my lavender hair. Blurs of movement whisked across the green as the other Knights of the Shadow Fae leapt into action, moving for the battlements.

I leapt up to the top of the tower walkway, slamming down hard on the stone. My heart hammered against my ribs as the smell of smoke thickened around me. From the inner wall, I leapt over the stony gap, my sword already drawn. I hurtled through the air to the exterior tower wall.

I landed on a walkway that loomed over the Thames. The golden moat beamed below. From the ground, dark smoke billowed into the night sky.

At the top of the barbican, I stared down at the gaping hole in the stone wall below me—and the ragged gap in the moat's golden light. Glittering red magic shimmered in the air. Two humans lay injured on the pavement—a man and a woman, clothing torn, bodies bloodied. Rubble littered the ground around them.

The wind tore at my hair, and I frantically scanned the dark river, looking for signs of our attacker. City lights glistened on the water, but I couldn't see anything resembling an assailant.

Ruadan landed next to me on the battlement, and he gripped the side of the wall as he looked out onto the river. His dark magic lashed the air around him.

Then, cold air whooshed past me as he leapt to the pavement below. Gripping my sword, I summoned my lumen stone's power and leapt down by his side, landing hard on the stony debris. The shock of the impact shot through my shins.

I turned to survey the damage. The explosion had ripped through the exterior wall into a sparsely furnished room.

"This is precisely where we'd been keeping Maddan," Ruadan growled. He whirled, scanning the horizon for the ginger prince. "He's gone. He shadow-leapt away."

"How?" I asked. "He didn't have a lumen crystal." But even as the words were out of my mouth, I was beginning to understand. "Baleros has one, though."

Ruadan reached out, skimming his fingertips over the glittering red magic.

My fists tightened. "How could he possibly break through the magical moat? I thought it was impenetrable."

"It is," said Ruadan. "From the outside."

Unfortunately for us, Maddan's father had been *inside* the fortress.

I scanned the debris, my gaze roaming over glistening pieces of flesh, a fragment of bone…. A passerby caught in the wrong place?

No.

A dark scrap in the rubble caught my eye. I reached down, picking up a tattered bit of black cloth. The coarse wool felt just like the fabric worn by the other jackdaw, edges singed.

"This was a coordinated attack," I said. "The king on the inside to pull down the moat, a jackdaw on the outside to blow himself up. Someone here at the right time to deliver the lumen stone. But why would Baleros care about Maddan?"

"He doesn't," said Ruadan. "You know how he thinks."

Baleros's twenty-fifth law of power: Divide and conquer.

"Of course," I said. "He's trying to sow division. It's hard to fight a battle on two fronts. If you get sidetracked by fighting the small-footed prince and his father, you'll be vulnerable. Don't let Baleros distract you."

Ruadan's magic iced the air around him until my breath frosted in front of my face. "His distractions won't work. We're staying focused on Baleros. I'll have our mages restore the moat."

I hugged myself. "How long will that take?"

"Could be a few days."

"Shit. He's leaving us vulnerable while we try to hunt him down. You've got the knights roaming all over London looking for him, and he wants you to call them back here to defend the Institute."

"I'm not doing that. The Institute can stay vulnerable. Right now, you and I are leaving for The Skull and Crossbones."

CHAPTER 6

$\mathcal{I}$n my little white dress, I gripped the straps of my bug-out bag as we skulked down Crutched Friars. The night air skimmed over my bare arms and legs, tension hunched my shoulders, and I kept looking behind me. At any moment, another jackdaw might run out of an alley to blow himself up.

We now had about twenty-one hours left until everyone died of the Plague.

"Gods, I want a whiskey," I muttered.

Ruadan let the comment hang in the air. One of these days, I was going to get him drunk, assuming that was even possible.

As we walked, he loomed over me, his silhouette indistinct. He was doing his *wraith* thing where you couldn't really see his outline.

I swallowed hard. Twenty-one hours until rotting bodies filled the streets, eaten by rats….

The hair stood up on my nape. Around the Institute, the roads were eerily empty tonight. These streets were thousands of years old, with strange names like Savage Gardens and Seething Lane. For thousands of years, the streets had teemed with people. Not now.

We walked down the long, curving road called Crutched Friars. These streets had been around the *first* time the Great Mortality had hit the city. What stories these streets would have to tell—ancient as Baleros. Older than the Wraith....

Shadows climbed the walls around us as Ruadan kept us hidden with his magic. What stories did *he* have to tell after all these centuries?

"How old are you, exactly?"

"What difference does it make? That has no bearing on Baleros."

"That vampire woman, Elise, said six hundred." I plowed right on. "Is that true?"

"Six-hundred ninety-six."

"That's bloody ancient. Surely you need to go to bed at seven-thirty, after a quiet night of soaking your feet and watching gardening shows."

He grunted.

I couldn't do the mental math, exactly, but I thought he was born sometime in the thirteen hundreds. "So you were around when the Great Mortality hit? The big one? The fourteenth century one?"

"Yes." His dark magic snaked over my skin. "It seemed as if the world was ending."

I swallowed hard. "How often did you leave Emain to come to London?"

"Once I escaped some of my training with Baleros, I was married here in London."

"How old were you when you joined the Shadow Fae?"

"I was raised among them from birth."

My blood stirred. A rare flash of openness from Ruadan, but these memories didn't seem like happy ones. Cold magic poured off him, rushing over my skin.

I should have left it there, should have heeded the warning—the air frosting, the shadows thickening. But I had to know more.

"What happened to your wife?"

"She died."

"How?" I'd missed some tact with my question, like telling him I was sorry for his loss.

"Killed by Adonis. Horseman of Death."

His words slid over my skin like cold rain. "Oh?"

"I'm almost positive, yes."

"But you're not entirely sure?"

"I'm certain that a monstrous creature like him doesn't belong on Earth."

"But aren't many of us monsters in our own way?"

He narrowed his eyes. "Along with the other horsemen, he created the apocalypse twenty-five years ago."

"But I thought he worked to stop it. He fought *against* the Horsemen of Pestilence and War. He tried to stop all the destruction. At least, that's what I heard."

"In the end, yes. But his very presence on Earth led to it. Without him, none of that would have happened. Not to mention the fact that he can still slaughter entire populations just by losing his temper. I think he was responsible for the Black Plague."

"But you don't *know* that he was."

"And he's probably responsible for this most recent plague in the Isle of Dogs. He is Death, and he has no place here."

I fell silent.

"I can hear your heart racing," Ruadan said quietly. "Why?"

"I'm just wary, that's all. There could be jackdaws with explosive vests in any of these alleyways. Anyway, my point was—Baleros seems to be drawing from the old days. The Plague stuff, the skeleton murals, the cloaks. You and Baleros were both alive then. I wasn't. What was London like in those days?"

"Is there a point to this?"

"We're undercover. We're supposed to be blending in. I'm not sure if you've ever spent time around normal people in your six hundred ninety-six years of life, but they do this thing called chitchat. They talk about the weather, or sports, or the mystery persons who stole their cheese at work."

He shot me a sharp look. "That's asinine."

I loosed a sigh. "Well, when we get into The Skull and Crossbones, how about you let me do the talking? We don't need Baleros tracking our movements, and you don't have a chance in seven hells of blending in. And anyway, that time period seems to interest Baleros. Maybe it's important. Maybe he liked his life back then."

Shadows snaked around us, and the silence stretched out for so long that I was certain the conversation was over. At last, he said, "London was full of death and beauty. Elegance and depravity." His gaze flicked to mine for a long moment, and I had the inexplicable sense he was talking about me. "An intoxicating combination."

A smile curled my lips. "More details, please."

"Murders, executions. Towering, spindly churches that reached for the heavens. Human heads on pikes. Pageants, maypoles. Claret and beer. A royal menagerie with lions and bears. On this road, a king marched his brother's mistress through the streets half-naked as penance for her sins. Her hair was golden in the sunlight. Those with strength ruled. Kings led their troops into battle. And most of all—chaos and death ruled the streets."

"Ah. And there's our answer. Chaos. What a glorious time for Baleros."

Captivated, I was about to push for more information, but Ruadan stopped walking. His violet eyes burned as he stared across the street. I turned, catching sight of what he was looking at.

A mural of black and ivory with splashes of red—skeletons dancing with kings, queens, and soldiers. And behind the skeletons lurked cloaked men. Jackdaws. No. Not jackdaws … I think they were … were they supposed to be us?

"There's another one of his murals," I muttered.

"The Great Mortality." Silver flashed in Ruadan's eyes. "Those pictures were everywhere once."

I scrubbed a hand over my mouth. "Could be a message for us. A reminder. We have just over a day to deliver you, or he unleashes the godsdamned Plague."

Ruadan cocked his head. "He already delivered that message. What else?"

I felt like I was being tested here. I closed my eyes for a moment, trying to get in Baleros's mind.

Baleros's twenty-fourth rule of power: Win their hearts by slaughtering their oppressor.

"Frightened people are easier to control. When the humans are scared enough, they'll turn on us. When Baleros kills you in a giant spectacle, they'll be thankful. It's quite brilliant, really."

"Brilliant," he repeated.

"I mean, he is very good at planning ahead."

Ruadan started walking again, fog and shadows curling around him, until he reached a blank brick wall. He halted, staring at it. It took me a moment to register the faint gleam of magic that shimmered over the wall. A glimmering red—the same color as the magic we'd seen at the Institute.

The wall was glamoured, and the magic belonged to King Locrinus.

Ruadan reached out, stroking his fingertips over the wall, and the glamour fell away. Now, we stood before a warped wooden door. Just above us, a pub sign creaked forlornly in the breeze—an ivory skull and crossbones on black paint.

Ruadan pushed through the door, into a pub where candlelight wavered over crooked stone walls and oak benches. The stone walls were hung with stags' antlers, skulls, and framed pages from alchemical texts.

Three humans sat at a table, dressed in black cloaks and star-flecked wizard hats. They hunched over tiny, pewter figurines and colored dice. A human man with long, blond hair in a ponytail rose, knocking over his chair. "I am Boradrion, Dark Fae Lord of Hellbania! I will smiteth mine porcine enemy with a roll of—" He rolled the die across the table.

A bearded man sighed loudly through his nose. "You rolled a natural one. The boar bites your dick off."

Boradrion's face reddened. "Methrior rocked the table with his meaty dwarf hands!" He slammed his fists on the table. "I need a re-roll. Dungeon Master Ethan, this is bollocks."

"What the hells," I muttered.

My heart sank. I'd kind of been hoping for a good fight, but I would not find that here. And yet ... *someone* with magic had glamoured the door. Maybe they were more powerful than they appeared.

It was at this point that Boradrion of the Ponytail realized we'd come in, and he pushed his glasses up on his nose. His face still looked pinched and red. "Who enters The Skull and Crossbones?"

Baleros's third law of power: Always let your enemy underestimate you.

I blinked. "Yeah, so, like, this door just kinda appeared in the wall? It was kind of weird." An American accent again. Always with the American accents. "And it looked like magic or something? And so we just came inside. You know what I mean? Do you guys have vodka and Red Bull?"

Boradrion glowered at me, then turned to his friend. "Gods *damn* it, Methrior. I told you the glamour wouldn't hold. You're a terrible mage."

Methrior scooted out from the booth, glowering through his spectacles. "I thought it was a solid spell," he said quietly. "King Locrinus helped me with it."

Did he, now? Quite the little alliance Maddan's father had formed with Baleros and his human idiot crew.

Still, no one had noticed Ruadan. With his Wraith fog around him, people just didn't see him.

I cocked my head. "You guys seem to know a lot about magic and stuff."

Methrior's chest puffed. "I'm being instructed by a real fae king."

The bearded man—Dungeon Master Ethan—strode up behind Methrior, wiggling his fingers. "He's not the only one. Watch this. *Ekkimu.*" Red light glowed from his fingertips, and he grinned.

Methrior grunted with disapproval. "Yes, but he's spent more time on me, because he has recognized my innate talent. I can do real attack spells now. Look." Methrior lifted his hand, staring at his fingertips. "*Baraqu!*"

Lightning shot from his fingertips, striking the ceiling. Instantly, the wood ignited, flames roaring above us.

Boradrion covered his head with his arms. "Put the fire out, you bloody donkey! I told you to stop doing that inside."

Coughing, Methrior called out, *"Malititu!"*

Water rushed down from the ceiling, quenching the fire. It soaked my hair and my clothing before petering out to a brown trickle. I stopped myself from kicking the living shite out of all of them.

With water dripping off me, I widened my eyes. "Amazing. How did you get a fae king to instruct you?"

"Something big is coming," said Boradrion. "A reckoning. Something that will change the world we know. And we're the foot soldiers. When the change comes, we will rule by his side."

Sure you will, fuckwit. I licked my lips, shivering a little in my sodden clothes. "What's coming, then?"

"The Great Mortality will come for us all. Death, the great leveler. Corpses will litter London's streets once more, bodies falling so fast there will be no time to bury the dead. Only those with magic will survive. Or those we take under our protection. You have but one more day to make the most of your existence before you begin to rot." He cocked his head, grinning. "Unless you want to join us as our serving wench. If you would like to come to my abode for cheese sandwiches and some sexual intercourse I would be happy to oblige."

The mage rolls a critical failure, no charisma modifier. The serving wench imagines ripping off his head at the neck.

I pouted. "But I thought a boar bit your dick off?" Wrong move, but I couldn't help myself.

His face reddened. "I assure you, everything is in working order."

"I'll think about it." *Or, more accurately, I'd sooner be buried in the earth up to my neck and pelted to death with twenty-sided dice.* I crossed my arms. "And while I'm thinking about that tempting possibility, can you tell me how the Great Mortality will come to London?"

CHAPTER 7

*B*oradrion's eyes shone. "*He* will bring it. And I am his soldier." His eyes widened, and he took a step closer. He pulled up his cowl, which got caught for a moment on his ponytail.

Now we were getting somewhere, and there was no doubt in my mind that he was talking about Baleros. "And where do we find him? If I wanted to serve him, too?"

Boradrion tapped his fingers on his arms, wrinkling his nose. "I'm not supposed to tell anyone that. Not even sexy wenches."

"Where is your leader?" Ruadan's voice rumbled through the room.

Boradrion's beady eyes shifted to Ruadan, his body tensing. "What the hells? I didn't notice that one, did you, Methrior? He's bloody enormous." He stepped closer, squinting as he tried to home in on Ruadan. "Are you.... Are you *fae*? Are you the Wraith?"

He'd just signed his own death warrant with that realization. Now, there was no way we could leave these three alive.

In a blur of black smoke, Ruadan shifted. Within the next heartbeat, he was gripping Boradrion by the throat, lifting him off the ground. "Tell us where we find Baleros, or I crush this one's throat."

Boradrion kicked helplessly at the air, his eyes bulging.

Methrior began chanting in Angelic, and a ball of fire glowed in his hand. Dungeon Master Ethan chanted right along with him.

Maybe we would be getting that fight after all.

"Edin Na Zu!" Methrior screeched, fiery magic blazing from his fingertips.

I pulled my dagger from its sheath just as Methrior screamed the final word of his spell—*Iddimu*--and red magic exploded from his body.

The magic slammed into my chest, and I lost control of the knife. I hit the ground hard, with a loud crack. The force of the magic had knocked the wind out of me. On the ground, I grimaced, fairly certain he'd cracked my ribs.

My gaze flicked to Ruadan across the pub, and it seemed like he'd taken the brunt of the attack. His body had cracked a stone wall.

I could feel his rage from here. In fact, his eyes had turned completely black. Shadows billowed around him, expanding and contracting like lungs. Ice frosted the air, the temperature breaking some of the glass bottles. Looking at Ruadan with his nightmarish face on was like looking into the void itself. And he hadn't even fully shifted yet. No, I was only seeing the phantom wings behind him.

"Methrior!" Boradrion yelped. "It's an incubus. Do you know what happens when an incubus loses control?"

My ears perked up. *I* didn't know what happened when an incubus lost control.

A low growl boomed around the room, and ice spread across the floor. Ruadan stared at Methrior and flicked his wrist. I gaped in fascinated horror as Methrior's body split in two, starting at the crown and splitting downward, the man screaming until his mouth and throat had been ripped apart. The other two humans began screaming, their hysteria deafening.

My blood boomed through my veins. Ruadan was more terrifying than I'd imagined.

And yet still, Ruadan seemed perfectly in control, his muscles tightly coiled. I'm not sure I even wanted to imagine what he'd look like out of control....

I grunted, willing myself to roll over on all fours. Pain shot through my ribs, but I kept my eye on Boradrion.

He clutched his throat, wincing. "Get them out of here," he rasped. His face reddened. "Dungeon Master Ethan, get them out of here!"

Ethan was trying to chant again, but I could tell he was stumbling over his words, panicking. The temperature in the room plummeted further, my breath misting in front of my face. Then, dark magic snaked across the room from Ruadan's fingertips. From the magical tendrils, thorny spikes dug into Boradrion's flesh.

Slowly, with pain splintering my ribs, I pushed myself up.

"Where is Baleros keeping Queen Macha?" Ruadan spoke quietly, but his voice seemed to boom around the room, echoing in my skull.

Blood dripped from Boradrion's punctured skin, the magical thorns digging in deeper. "I don't know where she is!" he shrieked. "Ethan! Ethan I will light your fucking dice on fire if you do not kill him!"

"Where is Baleros?" The quiet control in Ruadan's voice sent tremors up my spine.

Dungeon Master Ethan tried to chant, stuttering in a panic. His face had gone completely white. He had about four seconds before he just passed out.

I scrambled for my knife, wincing as I snatched it off the ground. At last, Ethan managed to summon a red ball of magic.

He tossed the ball of fire just as I leapt across the room. I touched down behind him and held the blade to his throat, nicking the skin just a little. The bastard was taller than me and the angle wasn't easy.

Electric magic crackled the air, and the hair began standing up on my nape. I couldn't fight with magic. All I could do was leap away and try to avoid it.

"We're done playing," I said sweetly. They were all going to die. "Tell us where to find your leader, or I'll make sure you suffer at the end."

I could feel Ethan's body trembling. Good. If he was scared, he'd do what I asked. "You don't understand," he stammered.

"Oh, I understand. If you don't give us the information we're looking for, I will gut you right here. I don't usually like to kill humans. It's not a fair fight. But you made a very bad choice when you decided to work for Baleros, so I won't feel bad."

"*Edin Na Zu!*" he shouted, and magic crackled up his spine, searing me.

I pulled my hand away, then lunged forward and stabbed him in the shoulder before he could continue the spell. He screamed.

"What did I tell you?" I shouted. His blood had spattered over my sodden clothes. "I told you I would hurt you. And you saw what Ruadan just did to your friend, didn't you? That was bloody terrifying. I think we can all agree on that point."

Ethan turned to me, his face pale, streaked with tears. "Stop hurting me!"

"I will. Just tell me where to find Baleros, and you can be on your way."

The sounds of Boradrion's screaming echoed off the walls. Still, no one was giving up their leader.

Ethan stammered, "*Edin Na—*"

I caught him in the left shoulder with the blade, and he fell to his knees, wailing. Why was he protecting Baleros with his life? These three didn't seem like the most loyal and courageous of men.

"Stop!" shrieked Ethan. "I don't know where he is. He has three generals. They're the only ones who know. One of them is meeting now—"

"Don't you tell her, Ethan!" Boradrion screamed. "You know what he'll do to us!"

Ethan sobbed, "*Edin Na—*"

I kicked him hard in the chest, and he fell backward onto the wood floor. Blood pooled around him.

"Where do I find the generals?"

"Meeting now. Skull and Crossbones…" he muttered.

"But *this* is The Skull and Crossbones…."

"*Edin Na Zu!*"

A ball of magic slammed into my thigh and pain rocketed up my hip. Another caught me in the side and agony danced up my spine. I landed hard on my back again, all the wind knocked out of me. Apparently, Dungeon Master Ethan was finding his mojo again in his last moments on earth.

"*Edin Na—*" Ethan bellowed.

Dark magic shot out of Ruadan's fingertips, winding around Ethan. It bound his arms to his body, lashing his skin with thorns of magic. They sliced deeper into the human's flesh, flaying him.

My stomach turned. I'd never seen Ruadan unleash his most terrifying abilities before, and I had a feeling this was only the tip of the iceberg.

"You're not going to win this battle," Ruadan growled. Frost and ice spread out over the floor, and my teeth chattered. Ruadan and his godsdamned rage ice.

"You don't understand!" Ethan sobbed. "Whatever you do to us, it won't be as bad as what *he* would do!"

Morbid curiosity got the better of me. "What would he do?"

"Unspeakable torture; bodies broken, flayed, then healed again. Over and over." Ethan's words were nearly incomprehensible in his panic. "Then, turned into jackdaws."

Ruadan cut me a sharp look, one that said "prepare yourself." Except I didn't know for what, which made the warning a bit pointless.

Before I could so much as grip the back of a chair, darkness descended, blooming from inside my mind until it coated my skull. Terror slammed into me like an oncoming train.

I'd been hit with a little dose of Ruadan's fear magic, and I wasn't good at withstanding it. Adrenaline shot along my veins, and the wood floor fell out from beneath my feet.

CHAPTER 8

My bare feet pounded the forest's soil, snapping twigs. The
scent of death filled the air. I knew what I'd see when I got
to the forest's edge. Bile rose in my throat as I peered out from behind an oak.

He'd done this. My father. He'd killed them all.

*I'd seen her red hair splayed out over the ground, the blood pouring from
my mum's mouth.*

Darkness washed over me like ink. He killed her.

No. No.... That's not what happened.

*This time, a new thought hammered in the back of my skull, a shrieking
staccato note I tried to block out.... The terrible truth I'd been running from.*

That's not what really happened.

Screaming pierced my mind, drowning out all other thoughts.

I was horrified to realize it was my own.

The vision cleared, and I found myself on the floor of the pub,
hunched over on my hands and knees. Nausea climbed up my throat,
and I vomited onto the hardwood floor, my entire body shaking. The
sickness had been rising in me for a while now, since I'd seen Ruadan
rip a man in two with just a flick of his wrist. The memory of my
mum's death had pushed me over the edge.

I'd stopped screaming, but the shrieks continued in my mind.

Luckily, there hadn't been much in my stomach, since I'd already puked once tonight. I scrubbed my hand across my mouth, more than a little mortified that Ruadan was here to watch me throw up from fear.

Had the humans spoken? Had they given up their master? I had no idea, because I'd been busy throwing up on the floorboards.

Thanks for that, Ruadan. Arsehole.

When I looked up again, the shrieking in my skull had started to fade.

"Three generals! Three generals!" Ethan shouted, nearly incoherent. "Look for The Skull and Crossbones!"

"Ethan, no!" shouted Boradrion. That's when I saw the tiny, red button dangling from his keychain.

"Bomb!" I shouted.

I didn't even see Ruadan move, just felt the force of him slam into me, then us hurtling across the room. The wooden door splintered into shards as our bodies made impact. At this point, it felt as if my ribs had been cracked in multiple places.

We crashed onto the ground outside just as the bomb went off, and my bones took another blow from the pavement.

Ruadan's heavy body covered me, practically crushing me. Heat from the explosion seared the sides of my arms, glass and wood raining all around us. I coughed onto the ground as the initial blast receded.

I gasped for breath. It took me a moment to realize the flames had disappeared completely—no sign of an explosion whatsoever. My chest heaved, and Ruadan slowly shifted his enormous weight off of me. When I craned my neck to look back at the pub, it wasn't destroyed as I had expected.

Wincing from my broken ribs, I stared at the wooden walls and glass windows—all completely intact once more. The only thing that looked different about it was the crackle of glittering red magic before the pub's dark facade.

Then, a hot shock of pain, a shard piercing my chest. It took me a moment to realize what had happened—that one of my broken ribs had punctured my lungs.

I gasped, momentarily unable to speak from the pain. Ruadan whirled back to face me, crouching down by my side. Agony speared my chest.

"Where does it hurt?" he asked.

"Ribs," I gritted out.

Ruadan's fingers slid over my damp dress, his magic already meandering up my chest. As it skimmed over my body, my muscles began to unclench, the pain ebbing from my bones. Strange that someone with such intense healing powers could also rip a man in two the way he had. Ruadan, demigod of the night, could be either the most beautiful dream or the most terrifying nightmare, depending on how he felt about you.

Which was exactly why I couldn't let my secret get out.

As the pain left me, I breathed out slowly, my mind flickering with the image of red hair spread out over dirt. That memory....

Anger started to simmer. What right did Ruadan have to screw with my mind like that?

"Better?" he asked, his violet eyes shining with genuine concern.

"Fine," I said, a hint of anger in my voice. "But we have to find the generals they were talking about."

I pushed myself up, my body groaning as I crossed to the pub door.

I pulled the door open, finding that the pub looked much as it had when we'd first come in. Except now, three human bodies lay on the floor—two of them surprisingly intact, considering the explosion they'd just endured. Only Methrior lay ripped apart, courtesy of my charming mentor.

I hurried over to Ethan and put my fingers to his throat to feel for a pulse. Nothing—no breath, no heart pumping.

Death came for them. Death will come for me.

I clamped my hands over my ears as if trying to drown out my own thoughts. Ruadan had *really* screwed with my mind.

Ruadan's eyes pierced the pub's gloom as he studied me. "What's wrong with you?"

"You shouldn't toy with people's heads and expect them to carry on like normal," I snapped. "You don't know what you're messing with." *I will kill you all....*

Ruadan had gone completely still. "No, I don't, because you haven't told me. What are you?"

This conversation had taken a dangerous turn. "I'm someone who's good at killing, Ruadan," I said grimly. "That's why you recruited me."

"I recruited you because I thought you'd lead me to Baleros," he corrected me, but his attention was already shifting somewhere else.

I leapt over the bar to where they kept the alcohol, eager for a little buzz to calm my nerves. I snatched a bottle of Johnnie Walker off the shelf and unscrewed the top. I drank straight from the bottle, the booze burning my throat deliciously as it went down.

When I looked back at Ruadan, his violet eyes pierced me to the core. "You will never defeat Baleros as long as you're running from yourself."

But Ruadan, my beauty, a sane person runs from a monster.

"Can we skip the psychoanalysis?" I took another sip of whiskey.

His gaze flicked to the wall above an old, stone fireplace.

"What were you looking at?" I came out from behind the bar and glanced in the same direction.

There, on top of the pub's fireplace, sat a skull and crossbones. Three skulls, in fact, grinning and gaping-eyed. Bizarrely, one of them wore a victory wreath. The text beneath the skulls read *Mors mihi lucrum.*

"Any idea what that means?" I asked.

"*Death is my reward.*"

I shivered. "What is it?"

"Copied from a cemetery gate nearby. St. Olave's. The place is crammed with corpses from one of London's plagues."

The date carved below the skulls read *1656.*

"What does it mean, *death is my reward?*"

"It's the motto of those who worship Adonis, Horseman of Death. They worship Thanatos."

My fingers tightened around the bottle. "His true name."

"How did you know that?"

"I heard it somewhere," I mumbled.

"I think he's working with Baleros."

A long, long sip of the whiskey. "He's on your kill list, right? I saw it."

"He is. And his kin."

Slow, steady breaths. "Why didn't you ever go back for him, to kill him? The Horseman of Death?"

"I needed two things to kill him. Stones from the Old Gods, and an immortal army to help me capture him. I have the stones already. As soon as I kill Baleros, I'll have my immortal army." Ruadan crossed his arms. "We might meet him soon."

"What makes you say that?"

"Like I said, he's the one with the power to spread the Plague. And what's more, the skeleton mural was a favorite of the death cultists. St. Olave's Cemetery was one of their meeting spots."

I sucked a steadying breath. "Baleros would never allow his followers to worship anyone but him. If I had to guess, he's simply forming his own death cult. He's the god. That's how it always is with him."

Ruadan stared at me for an uncomfortably long time, and I felt as if his gaze were seeing right into my soul.

Then, he turned and started pulling a cloak off one of the bodies. "We'll go disguised as Adonis's followers. We'll find Baleros's generals. They'll lead us to him."

CHAPTER 9

$\mathcal{D}$ressed in stolen cloaks, we arrived at St. Olave's Cemetery. Dread twisted through me at the sight of the cemetery entrance. Fog swept in front of the old stone archway. Spikes jutted out above the ancient gate. A total of five skulls stared out at us from the top of the arch, three of them arranged just like the carving in the pub. Here, again, we found the Latin inscription—*Death is my reward.*

Worshipers of the Horseman of Death.

Ruadan leaned down to whisper in my ear. "First, we gather information. We need to learn exactly what's going on here. Maybe we'll find out about Adonis. Don't draw blood until we need to. Understood?"

"Got it."

I was starting to notice that Ruadan often felt the need to tell me, "Don't start killing people right away."

From the gated churchyard, deep and rhythmic chanting floated through the air. A gust of cold wind rushed into my cloak, and the iron gate creaked open, welcoming us like a beckoning hand. We crossed through the archway, hoods over our heads.

Just as Boradrion had said, a meeting was taking place here. A crowd of men in cloaks stood in the center of the old churchyard, holding torches aloft and chanting. I distinctly caught the word *Thanatos.*

Would he be here? The Horseman of Death himself?

Inside the gates, the grassy ground was several feet higher than street level, and it took me a moment to realize why this was. Layers upon layers of bodies lay below us—the perfect place to worship Thanatos. Among the grass and trees, graves jutted from the ground.

No one seemed to notice us as we blended into the cloaked crowd.

At the far end of the churchyard stood a broad-shouldered man, over six feet tall. A tendril of fear coiled through me. Could that be him—the Horseman of Death, standing before us?

The crowd chanted his name, voices rising.

Their leader reached for his cowl, and my heart clenched. But when he slipped off the hood, I caught a glimpse of red horns. I let out a long, slow breath. Torchlight danced over a demon's sinewy features, and magic rippled off him, humming and buzzing over my body. Not the Horseman of Death.

I sniffed the air. From what I could tell, everyone else besides the horned demon was human.

Glowing with magic, the leader lifted his arms above his head and bellowed into the air, "We gather here to worship Thanatos!"

Gods almighty.

"Lord Gamigin, our leader!" the crowd chanted. "We gather here to worship the Lord of Death, Thanatos!"

Lord Gamigin spread out his arms. "We gather here to offer a sacrifice."

Please tell me it's not a virgin, unless it's one of Boradrion's friends....

From the shadows, a goat bleated. A human hunched over, leading the goat into the cemetery. The goat bucked, and the man struggled for control of its neck.

Lord Gamigin tutted. "Honestly, Gerard. Get control of that thing. Thanatos demands his blood sacrifices."

Gerard grunted as the goat kicked itself free, then barreled head-first into one of the cultists, knocking him over. The crowd parted as the goat sprinted out of the churchyard, onto the street.

Silence fell over the churchyard once more.

Gerard held up his hands. "Sorry, everyone. Bit of a difficult goat, that one. I'll sedate him next time."

"Never mind," Lord Gamigin's voice boomed. "For centuries, the Horseman of Death has filled this cemetery with corpses. The Romans knew him as Dis Pater. Others know him as Adonis. We know him as Thanatos. He has left behind his legacy. The weak fear mortality; the powerful worship it. Only through death do mortal lives have meaning! Only through death are you granted a release from the torments of this world. All gods seek to rule the dominion of death. Only Thanatos does. Death is our reward!"

A voice in the back of my mind whispered, *Monster....*

Damp, frigid magic snaked over my skin, and I hugged myself under my cloak. The chanting was stirring something inside me, a magic old as death.

"Thanatos! Thanatos!"

At the sounds of their chants, a pit opened in my chest. His name—the true name of Death—rang in my skull.

"I don't think this is a good idea," I murmured to Ruadan.

"Why not?"

I could hardly breathe. "This magic is dangerous."

"Are you joking?" Acid laced his tone.

"Thanatos! Thanatos!"

How could I tell him the truth?

As the cultists chanted, dark magic blossomed in my body.

I will steal your food and your breath.

"Thanatos! Thanatos!"

I am the seeping darkness that bleeds over long grasses....

A strange tingling sensation shot down my shoulder blades, a power yearning to break free.

"Thanatos! Thanatos!"

I wanted to take to the skies, to unleash a magic that would ripple across the horizon like an atomic blast.

"Thanatos! Thanatos! Thanatos!"

I am the rot in your bones. I am the hunter, stalking you while you chatter.

Power simmered in me, responding to their chants. But I had to stay in control here. My fingernails pierced my palms so hard I nearly drew blood.

"Thanatos! Thanatos! Thanatos!"

Around us, the humans were chanting louder and louder, the rhythmic sounds stoking my blood to a fever pitch.

I am your final thought when the breath leaves your lungs. I am the sound of teeth hitting porcelain. I conquer all.

As they chanted, cold rage slid through my bones. Ruadan had begun carelessly unearthing everything I'd tried to bury.

"Thanatos! Thanatos!"

They were chanting his true name.

My father's true name.

I wanted to destroy it all.

As a child, I'd been a tomboy. Knees covered in mud and scrapes. When my pale, blond hair started darkening to a girlish lavender as I'd gotten older, I'd cut it short and covered it with a hat.

I am the tear in your heart, splitting open.

At the time, when Ruadan had invaded our world with his fae cohort, I'd looked very much like a boy. That simple fact was probably the only reason Ruadan hadn't tried to kill me yet. The only reason Ruadan hadn't already pieced it all together. Demigods—especially male demigods—were so damned sure of themselves.

He should die for his arrogance. He should kneel before me. They would all kneel before me in the end.

I am the rattle in your throat.

It had all been Ruadan's fault. If he'd never come, I'd be ignorant and happy. I'd still be there in the woods, baking pies with my mum, probably married off to some handsome fae bloke.

My gaze flicked to Ruadan's perfect features. The moonlight gilded the masculine planes of his face and sparked in his pale, violet eyes. He was the true destroyer, and a buried lust for vengeance stirred in me.

I could turn him purple, make his limbs rot. I could make the blood run from his beautiful lips.

When you're not looking, I enshroud you from the toes up.

My shoulder blades wanted to unleash my power.

Bow before me.

Ruadan's magic snaked over my skin, feeling strangely invasive. "What is wrong with you?" he whispered. "I can hear your heartbeat."

I whirled, my lip curling, rage carving through my belly like a knife.

I'm a creature who should never walk the earth. A monstrosity. An abomination. I'm on your kill list.

Ruadan had never seen my true monstrous side—nor I his. Would it come out now? Could I kill him before he killed me?

"Thanatos! Thanatos! Thanatos!"

The chanting grew louder, but my gaze was still locked on Ruadan, his on mine. Frigid wind swept past us, and the air seemed to darken around him.

He leaned in again, his pine scent surrounding me. His magic licked at my skin, slow and dangerous. "Blend in, Arianna." An unyielding command from the Grand Master.

Not my real name, demon. My real name is Liora.

The demonic general raised his hands to the night sky. "Without death, there is no pleasure!"

"Oh, great Lord Gamigin!" the crowd chanted in unison. "Without death, there is no pleasure!"

My heart was a wild beast. *Thanatos!* The chants roiled my blood.

Ruadan's eyes bored into me. "Get control of yourself," he said in a low voice. The shadows around him sucked in all the light.

I am death. I fought the impulse to clamp my hand around his throat and squeeze. "You need to stop messing with my mind." My voice sounded strange even to myself. "You don't know what you're toying with, demon. There are powers even you can't fight."

Night fell in his eyes, and he took a step closer, until I could feel his raw power thrumming over my skin. "You are here on a mission."

"And tonight," the demon boomed, "we celebrate pleasure!"

Out of the corner of my eye, I glimpsed shifting cloaks, skin bared in the moonlight. It was the first time I realized the crowd wasn't entirely made up of men. Women lurked among them, too—women who were opening up their cloaks, ready to celebrate pleasure with the men. Breasts and penises all over the place.

The sight was so startling and ridiculous that it snapped me right out of my spiraling death rage. The instinct I'd been fighting—to clamp my hand around Ruadan's throat—simply disappeared.

I took a deep breath. I had a bad feeling it would come back, but I was in the clear for now. They wouldn't get a death angel here tonight.

I stared as a woman leaned up against a wall, her back to her partner. He grabbed her hips from behind, hands running over her breasts.

Honestly. Some people.

What had Melusine said about the Great Mortality? Half the people were flogging themselves, the other half banging in the shrubs.

I guess we'd found the fun ones.

We were supposed to blend in, weren't we? I wasn't about to take off my cloak, but maybe we could look a little fun.

I took a step closer to Ruadan, then ran my hand up his chest. He stiffened. Then, I wrapped my arms around his neck and pressed my hips into him, my breasts brushing against him. I stood on my tiptoes.

Pure black had slammed into his irises, and he stared at me with an intensity that rivaled my own. He gripped my waist hard with one hand, the other sliding into my hair. Then, he whispered, "We've blended in long enough." Tension rippled off him, and he pulled away from me with what seemed to be a great deal of effort. "I'll trap Lord Gamigin. You question him."

At the head of the churchyard, the demon lord still chanted in Angelic.

I surveyed the revelers, the men and women writhing against each other. I couldn't say I was shocked to see Uncle Darrell standing in a corner on his own, desecrating a shrub. Of course he was here. If there was a public trouser-dropping opportunity to be had in the great city of London, Uncle Darrell would find it.

The Wraith took a step closer to Lord Gamigin, shadows billowing around him.

My fingers twitched. I really wanted to hurt the people working for Baleros.

The temperature around us plummeted, ice spreading over the ground and graves. My breath clouded in front of my face.

Just as Lord Gamigin's dark eyes landed on Ruadan, ropes of dark magic spun out from Ruadan's hands, snaking around the demonic lord.

The humans began screaming, already fleeing. With a dark smile curling my lips, I shadow-leapt over to Lord Gamigin and jumped down hard behind him. I whipped my iron knife from its sheath, and I plunged it into his shoulder blade.

He grunted with pain, trying to rip himself free of the magical constraints.

"You worship death, do you?" I began. "It could be your lucky night. A release from the torments of this world. Tonight, I saw my friend rip a man in two with just a flick of his wrist. Would you like that? Give your life a bit of meaning?"

"What do you want?" he grunted.

"I want to know where Baleros is," I said. "And Queen Macha."

His own magic was working against Ruadan's, but the iron in my dagger had already weakened him. "I don't know where Baleros is," he said through gritted teeth.

I pulled the dagger from his shoulder and held it to his throat, nicking the skin just a little. "You're one of his generals, aren't you?"

"I'm not telling you anything."

I pressed the blade in deeper. "You worship death because you fear it. Tell me what I need to know, and I might let you live."

"I don't know where Baleros is. I'm the lowest-ranking general."

Godsdamn it. "Where do we find Queen Macha?"

He shook his head, his horns glinting in the moonlight. "I don't know."

"Tell me what you do know, demon, or I'll sacrifice you to Thanatos, since the goat didn't work out."

"I don't know where to find him, but there's a fae king. He of the fiery hair. He keeps Macha underground. Under the water."

Pressing the blade a little deeper, I demanded, "Where underground?"

"One of Baleros's generals, King Locrinus, is guarding Queen Macha. Beneath the wolf's grave. You'll never get to Locrinus. He's protected by the bean nighe and the Caoranach."

I had no idea what half of this meant.

The demon looked around, frantically. "But I will never tell his name. I'll die before I tell you his name!" he screamed valiantly into the skies.

"You already said Baleros's name, knob-end," I said. "What else do you know?"

"That's all we need," said Ruadan. "You might want to step away from the demon."

I jumped away from Lord Gamigin, and as I did, Ruadan's magic constricted, slicing through the demon's body. Just enough time for a final scream, then a gurgle. Ruadan had ripped him apart completely.

My lip curled. "I could have just used the knife. I honestly didn't know you had this brutal side."

Ruadan's back was already turned as he strode for the exit.

"Can you tell me where we're going?" I called out. "What's this about a wolf?"

"Whitechapel."

Jack the Ripper, hipster bars, imprisoned fae queens. Did anything good ever happen in Whitechapel?

My heart thumped in my chest like a war drum, and I stared at Ruadan, the man who'd destroyed my world, the one who wanted to kill me. My fingers twitched on my knife's hilt.

The day Ruadan had come into our world was the day everything had changed. We'd led a boring, domestic life, hidden in our own little realm with a small village of fae. We baked pies, played in the woods. I thought my dad was fae like the rest of us.

Then, my whole world had ended. My father—god of death—had killed everyone but me. How was it that he'd spared me? Was I so similar to him, a death angel myself?

I had a feeling Whitechapel's grim history wasn't about to get any rosier tonight.

CHAPTER 10

Our footsteps echoed off the pavement as we moved north through the city. Nineteen hours till death hit the city.

Ruadan's fear magic was still with me, and my mind flashed with images of my mother's blood in the soil, droplets of crimson on the bluebells, red hair spread out—

"I can still hear your heart," said Ruadan.

His heart might not be racing, but he looked just as tense as I felt, each of his muscles taut, shadows seeping into the air around him.

I smiled sweetly. "How about I stop my heart from beating so it won't bother you?"

He shot me a sharp look.

"I don't suppose your heart ever beats too hard, does it?" I said. "You might as well not have one."

Ruadan, demigod of darkness, of icy control. So many things about him terrified me, and I couldn't bring myself to actually voice any of the thoughts in my head.

"What's bothering you?" he asked at last.

My heart sped up. *You've healed me. You destroyed my world. You've saved my life. You want to kill me. Someday, the truth will come out, and one of us will have to draw blood first. One of us will die. Someday, the truth will come out, and I'll have to face—*

Nausea welled in my gut, and I hunched over, dry heaving. There was nothing left in my stomach, and I retched over the gutter. Eventually, I mumbled, "Until death us do part."

"What did you say?"

"I said, what's a wood-poppet? Is that a real thing?"

"No."

Ahhh. Ruadan's sense of humor, then. I wiped my mouth, hand shaking. "Your magic doesn't sit well with me. The spell you used back in the pub."

"Someday, you'll have to face yourself."

I froze in my tracks. "Please tell me you can't hear my thoughts."

"I can't. But I know guilt when I see it."

"I don't have anything to feel guilty about." I said it a little too sharply. I stood tall, staring him in the eyes. "Do you ever lose control, Ruadan, or have you been perfecting your icy resolve for seven hundred years? Has it ever cracked?"

"I'm half incubus. What do you think?"

"Boradrion said something about what happens when an incubus loses control." Incubi were rare. Apart from Ruadan and his half-brother, I'd never met any. "What happens then?"

Ruadan was already walking again, pulling his favorite "not answering" move.

I hurried after him. Scary as it would be, some part of me desperately wanted to see the incubus come out. The *real* Ruadan.

"How does it come about, your incubus side?" I asked. "What happens when it does?"

Baleros's first law of power: Get in your enemy's head. Knowledge gives you control over a person.

After another beat, he finally answered. "Fear brings it out, sometimes sex. My primal side takes over and it's hard for me to gain control again."

The way he answered so succinctly gave me the impression that he was answering with a mental bullet-point list rather than giving me insight into an ancient and terrifying psychological process. "Your primal side takes over?"

More silence, a thickening of shadows.

I couldn't imagine Ruadan often found himself afraid, but the impending Black Death certainly had him a bit rattled.

"So, do I need to know about what we're about to face underground?" I asked.

"When you saw King Locrinus in the hall, he was with a female. The one in the red dress made of human skin. That's the Caoranach."

"The serpent woman. I see. She and I had a little run-in down by The Spread Eagle."

"A run-in?"

"We tried to kill each other."

He stopped walking for a moment, then stared at me. The air thinned, a dangerous silence. "She tried to kill you, and you lived? How is that possible?"

Panic flickered through my thoughts. I'd lived only because of my death powers. Maybe no other creature could have withstood her.

"If she wanted to kill you," he added, walking again, "you'd have died. You and me both need to stay as far away from her as possible."

I bit my lip. "I didn't realize her dress was made of human skin."

"She lurks in underground rivers and transforms into a serpent. She's four thousand years old. Some say she's not even fae."

"What is she, then?"

"One of the Old Gods, maybe. Grown from the earth itself. She drains her enemies, fills the rivers with their blood. She's loyal to anyone who will feed her with pain. King Locrinus does just that. But we can avoid her if we stay quiet. She's drawn by loud noises. As long as we're quiet, we can slip past her unnoticed."

"That might be a bit difficult." I frowned. I'd never met a bean nighe, but I knew mostly that they were demented washerwomen who screwed with your mind. "Am I right in thinking that bean nighe tend to scream?"

"Only if someone is about to die. Or if they want to alert the Caoranach, in which case people definitely die."

"So how do we avoid death, exactly? How do we stop them from screaming?" I frowned. "If the bean nighe scream, we die because the Caoranach comes for us. But they also scream *because* we're going to die…. I'm having a hard time working out the causal relationship when creatures can both predict and influence future events. Do you have any thoughts about this?"

"Cakes."

Leave it to Ruadan to cryptically answer a very complex question by just throwing out a random baked good with no other explanation.

"Did you just say *cakes?*"

"The bean nighe are fomoire. They feed off death and agony. But they also feed off cakes. And legend says, once you satiate them with cakes, they are forever in your debt."

"Are you messing with me again?"

"No."

I blinked. "I see. And you're carrying cakes on you, are you?"

"No." A gust of wind rippled over us, and he seemed to be done talking. After another moment, he added, "You are."

I frowned. "Have you been rifling through my bag?"

"I can smell the jam and sugar from here."

"Right." With any luck, these primordial harbingers of death could be bribed with a half a packet of Jaffa Cakes and the fondant fancy I'd picked up at Costcutter in lieu of feeding off our misery. "Well, hopefully they're not choosy."

CHAPTER 11

When we reached the Aldgate pump, Ruadan stopped walking. It was an old, derelict water fountain. A silver wolf's head gleamed over a grate in the pavement.

"What is this, exactly?"

"This is where the last wolf in the city of London died. The wolf's head marks the spot. Once, Londoners drank this water." Ruadan leaned over, pulling off the grate. "Until they realized the streams were fed by London's cemeteries, poisoning their water with diseases."

"So King Locrinus, Carver of Enemies, Ruler of Elfame, is hiding out in corpse-water. Charming. What happens after we bribe the bean nighe and slip past the Caoranach?"

He met my gaze. "We move silently—in the shadows. Our primary goal is to find Queen Macha. She's likely to have information that can lead us to Baleros. It's a rescue mission, not a kill mission." He gestured at the opened grate.

I leapt in first, splashing down in the dark water. The river nearly reached my knees, the cold water chilling me. Ruadan jumped down next, silent as he landed. He flicked his wrist, calling up a ball of dim silver light to illuminate our path.

I breathed in deeply, taking in a rich mineral scent in the air. It took me a moment to figure out that the chalky odor was calcium, and another second to put together that this smell came from human bones. Tonight's missions were taking us to London's grimmest locations, all those full of ancient bodies. I tried not to think about the bone particles rushing over my legs. I'd had enough of human bits this evening.

We moved deeper into the tunnel, water rushing around my calves. I moved as quietly as I could, acutely aware that any noises would draw the Caoranach.

As we moved in deeper, a heavier scent floated through the air—the smell of death.

Most people said the bean nighe were simple harbingers of death. If they screamed, you could bet someone was going to die, and that it would probably be you. But there was more to it than that. They stirred up your darkest thoughts before they killed you, and they fed off the pain.

Long ago, they had lingered unseen over childbirth beds, washing the rags of the dying women and babies, drinking up their agony. I imagined modern medicine had started to screw things up for them, but the world had more than enough pain to go around.

A mournful, keening voice wended through the tunnel. Then, over the melody, the frantic sound of a flapping bird's wings. The bean nighe's song wasn't the frantic screech that heralded death, but it set my teeth on edge anyway. Whatever the truth was about bean nighe, they tended to screw with people's minds, and my mind had taken about all the screwing it could take tonight.

I leaned in, grabbing Ruadan's arm to pull him down and whisper, "Can you do your little body-ripping trick?"

He shook his head, then whispered in my ear. "My powers don't work on fomoire."

"They don't? Why not?"

No answer, but he was still standing close to me, not pulling his head away.

My lip twitched. "I think I'm going to consider this our first date."

So quiet I wasn't sure if he'd even heard it. We'd have a few dates in cemeteries and bone water, then we'd try to kill each other when the truth came out. A perfect relationship for me, really.

Instead of responding, he pulled away, walking silently through the water again. The truth was, even if I was angry at Ruadan, I wanted him so badly my ribs ached.

He'd ruined my life, and part of me still wanted more from him. Not just sex, but I wanted his secrets and his confidence and his trust. I wanted late-night conversations, my head resting on his chest to hear his heart, his arms encircling me. Gods help me, some part of me actually wanted to take *care* of this nightmarish demigod. I was on his kill list, and he'd told me relationships were forbidden anyway. Was I losing my mind completely? I sighed, a hollow opening in my chest.

As we walked forward, narrower tunnels branched off on either side of us, curving away into darkness. Escape routes if we needed them.

Ruadan sniffed the air, then turned to me. He placed a finger over his lips. I hadn't even been talking, and he wanted me to be quiet. The Caoranach was here.

Still, the bean nighe's singing grew louder, along with the rhythmic sound of beating wings. I gritted my teeth, willing my heartbeat to slow. Ruadan flicked his wrist, and the ball of silver light brightened.

As we moved deeper into the tunnel, another pearly light glowed up ahead of us. In the gloom of a dank cemetery tunnel, a single bean nighe shone like the moon in the night. She wore a silver gown, black hair cascading over pale shoulders, and she scrubbed at a cloth. I hadn't expected the bean nighe to be so beautiful, and she drew me closer, like the moon drawing in the tides. A sheathed sword glinted on her back. I didn't suppose we could trade the cakes for their weapons as well?

From the shadows skulked two more armed bean nighe, their dark eyes wide. All three were singing, their voices mingling harmoniously, echoing off the tunnel walls. Each of them scrubbed a scrap of crimson cloth, and droplets of blood dripped into the river.

If three beautiful washerwomen didn't seem like much of a protective force, that was only because they hadn't launched into the real shit yet. Fortunately, we'd come armed with baked goods.

"Cakes," said Ruadan under his breath.

"I know what I'm doing," I mouthed.

I slid my backpack off my shoulders and reached for the Jaffa Cakes, shoving aside a change of clothes and a few crumpled Tube maps.

The bean nighe fell silent as we drew closer, eyes turning to us. They gripped their blood-soaked cloths.

I held out the Jaffa Cakes in front of me as we approached the closest woman. She cocked her head, eyes wide as she stared at the treat.

"Will you let us pass?" I whispered, pointing at the cakes. "If we give you these fine cakes, will you let us pass?"

The only response was that eerie sound of beating wings, like an invisible bird flapping all around us. The closest bean nighe cocked her head sharply—an eerie, reptilian movement.

I took a step closer. Maybe they hadn't heard me. "They're actually limited-edition *strawberry* Jaffa Cakes. They're not the ordinary orange kind. They're quite... delectable."

A grin spread over her face. Despite the sharpened teeth she revealed, my shoulders began to relax.

The serving wench rolls an eighteen for her charisma check, and we are getting somewhere.

"If you let us pass, the Jaffa Cakes are yours." I shrugged. "I might even throw in a package of fondant fancies. Multicolored frosting. Unopened. Especially if we can borrow your swords for a bit."

Still grinning, the bean nighe nodded enthusiastically. Then, she dropped her bloodied cloth and snatched the box from my hand. The three washerwomen descended on the Jaffa Cakes, ripping them out of the cardboard and plastic, shoving them into their mouths. Crumbs rained down into the river.

When they finished, they ran their long tongues over their bony fingers, looking at me hopefully for more.

"You'll give me the swords, right?" I mouthed, pointing at their weapons.

All three nodded.

I reached into my bag, pulling out the fondant fancies—bright pink, yellow, and purple cakes, drizzled with chocolate. The bean nighe crowded around them, elbowing each other and snatching the cakes, mashing them into their mouths, grunting.

I crossed my arms, satisfied with my work. They'd agreed to the deal. They'd taken the cakes, and that meant our safe passage had been secured—swords and all. We'd already passed the first hurdle.

"Well," I whispered. "We'll just be on our way, then."

I took a step forward through the cold water, ready to brush past the three bean nighe.

As I did, the washerwomen dropped their glamour. They transformed, hair whitening and growing tangled. Blood streamed from their eyes, and their singing rose to a keening fever pitch. The sight of their gaping, dark eyes hit me like a gale-force wind, knocking me back. What the hells?

The first bean nighe opened her mouth, and she shrieked, the otherworldly sound curdling my blood.

I clamped my hands over my ears, trying to block it out. Someone was about to die. But was it them or us?

CHAPTER 12

*S*o much for the legends about cakes.

I shot a glance at Ruadan, and he gave me a quick nod, which I interpreted to mean "kill them now." Gripping the knife, I began to rush forward, well aware that I'd brought a knife to a sword fight.

But as I moved forward, a wall of darkness slammed into my skull.

I stopped running and looked back at the clearing with a growing sense of horror. I stared at the red hair spread out over the soil, at the fae bodies rotting before us. My father stood over my mum, black wings swooping from his shoulders, his expression haunted.

He'd killed her. His wings of death had come out and disease had spread over the village. Fae wilted like flowers in the sun. I'd heard rumors of the Angel of Death. I'd never known he was my father.

I turned and ran again, desperate for the portal. I needed to put as much distance as I could between myself and the Angel of Death.

He'd killed everyone.

Hadn't he?

Fury exploded. I ripped myself free from the vision until I found myself in the tunnel again. As I'd been reliving my past, some primal part of my brain had taken over. Somehow, I'd managed to avoid the bean nighe's sword, shadow-leaping around the tunnel.

I held my knife out in front of me, slashing it as a bean nighe moved closer. Her sharp teeth were bared, fury contorting her features. Swinging for her, battle fury blazed. I thrust the iron blade between her ribs, and her skin began to crumble and crack, the fissures of flesh weeping blood. *One down.*

Out of the corner of my eye, a flash of red hair.

Ruby's hair.

My heart leapt. I whirled. As I stared at the woman before me, the ground tilted beneath my feet.

Crimson cascaded over a white dress, eyes a pistachio green.

My chest tightened. "Mum?" I stammered.

Still alive. What's she doing here?

She reached for me. My legs shook, and I took another step closer, stretching out to touch her hand.

Ruadan shifted from the shadows and clamped his hand around my mum's head, snapping her neck. I felt the break as sharply as if it had been my own. Then, he tore her head off her body.

My screams echoed off the tunnel walls. A hollow opened in my stomach, and I blinked away the tears. "Why did you do that?"

He stared at me. "Why did I kill the bean nighe?"

I shook my head. Of course. I knew the bean nighe screwed with your mind. As I looked around me, I realized Ruadan had killed the other one, also. They were all dead.

"She looked like my mother," I muttered, before a jolt of panic pierced me. Had I just given away my identity to Ruadan? Had he seen Ruby, too?

His violet eyes gleamed in the darkness. "That wasn't your mother. It was a bean nighe glamour, harvested from our own memories. She looked like someone else to me."

"Who?"

Darkness bled around him. "My wife."

I swallowed hard. "You said there was a legend about cakes. If we fed them cakes, they'd be in our debt."

"Legends aren't always accurate. If they were, we'd call them facts."

"Legends aren't always accurate," I repeated for emphasis.

Like the legend about how Adonis had created the Black Death. That one wasn't a fact, was it?

I gripped my knife, searching through the gloom for our next threat. "I don't understand. Did the bean nighe scream because *they* were going to die? It seems like a poor evolutionary trait, since the screaming caused their deaths…." My thoughts were getting tangled again.

Ruadan's attention was on the water below us. "Does it matter now?" He reached down, swiping his fingertips through the shallow river. The silver light from his orb illuminated blood dripping from his fingertips into the stream.

My bones chilled. All this blood wasn't just from the bean nighe— the river itself had turned to blood.

My gaze trailed up and down the underground river, and I could see nothing but blood all around us. This was the doing of the Caoranach, lured by the noise.

Ruadan snuffed out his light, and I felt a finger over my mouth, signaling silence. After another moment, I felt the hilt of a sword in my hand as he handed me one of the bean nighe's weapons. My muscles had frozen completely.

A rough, raspy sound carried through the tunnel, raising goose-bumps on my skin.

Ruadan touched my cheek, then whispered, "Jump."

I clutched the lumen stone at my throat, summoning the cold, electrical magic.

I leapt—just as an explosion rocked the tunnel. Midair, I slammed into a hailstorm of oncoming rocks. Chunks of stone caught me in the shoulder and the hip, knocking me arse-backward into the blood river. I scrambled to my feet, gagging on the blood that had trickled into my mouth. Somehow, I'd managed to hold onto the sword.

From behind us, a snake's hiss rippled over the water. Ruadan hadn't been kidding. The Caoranach was bloody terrifying.

Ruadan grabbed me by the arm, pulling me up from the river.

Then, he practically threw me into a tunnel that branched off the main one. In here, darkness consumed us completely.

"Jump," he said again—unnecessarily, since at this point I had very much internalized the concept of *run from the snake woman.*

Another loud explosion, and rocks rained down around us. How was she making these tunnels collapse? I blocked my head with my forearms as debris slammed onto my arms. I grunted with pain, falling to my knees and dropping my sword.

When the explosion had finished, I forced myself up again, grasping around until I found the sword. Ruadan reached for me, and he pulled me close against his powerful, damp chest. His muscled arm clamped around me, and I could hear the sound of his heart beating hard. I'd wanted to hear his heart. Just ... not like this.

I wasn't sure where the Caoranach was now. Could she hear us if I asked him a question? My arms screamed where the rocks had slammed into them.

I stood on my tiptoes to get closer to Ruadan's ear, my body sliding against his. "How is she smashing the tunnels?"

His breath warmed my ear as he whispered. "Her tail. She's slipping around the tunnels, trapping us by collapsing walls."

I breathed in deeply. I hadn't understood exactly how *large* she could get.

Okay. So the great avoidance plan wasn't working. We'd have to kill the bitch.

Was it even possible to kill one of the Old Gods? Probably not, given that Ruadan was one of the most powerful creatures I'd ever met, and he was hiding in a hole to avoid her.

Down here, total darkness enveloped us, and the dank tunnel air felt oppressive. If it hadn't been for Ruadan's body warming mine through our wet clothing, I could almost imagine myself in the musty underground cage Baleros had kept me in. I'd grown used to being trapped underground, but being hunted by a snake woman was an unwelcome addition to the usual scenario.

Ruadan had said that she hunted through sound—especially loud noises. Right now, I could hear only his breath and mine. Was that enough to draw her closer?

As I pressed against Ruadan, her hissing grew louder, along with the raspy sound of scales rubbing against stone.

Shit, shit, shit.

Ruadan's arm loosened on me. I stepped away from him, tightening my fingers on the sword's hilt. The sound of my own breathing made my muscles tighten. I couldn't see a bloody thing in the damn tunnel. Ruadan, demigod of night, probably knew exactly what was going on, but it wasn't like he could tell me.

The coppery scent of blood grew stronger around us.

The Caoranach hissed again, and the sound slithered over my skin, raising bile in my throat. Then, when her body began to glow with faint golden light, all the breath left my lungs.

The serpentine lower half of her body practically filled the tunnel. She'd transformed into something different than she'd been before. Her face looked half-woman, half-monster: pale skin with two slitted nostrils; tiny, dark eyes and a wide mouth that showcased her fangs. Her eyes transfixed me, and I could hardly remember what I was supposed to do. Were we here to fight?

A dark, forked tongue flicked out of her mouth, and even in my mental fog, a survival instinct spurred me on to fight back. With a lightning-fast reflex, I slashed for her tongue. I cut into it just a little before she really hit me with it.

But before I could take another breath, she licked at us again. Ruadan swung for her, but her tongue hit his arm, then lashed at me. She caught me in the side, just below my ribs. I clutched the wound, already feeling the toxin spreading through me. The poison wound its way around my muscles, freezing me up. I dropped the sword into the blood river. Around me, the water was rising.

This was not a good situation. Ruadan and I were *both* about to be immobilized.

I gaped as the Caoranach transformed, her reptilian body contracting. No longer was there a giant serpent standing before us, but a woman clad in red leather, grinning at us. She had a tiny leather satchel at her waist—one that actually *did* look like it was made of human skin. I wanted to smash that grin right off her face.

Fear slid through my veins. I couldn't get out of this the same way I had before, not without potentially revealing my true nature in front of Ruadan. When he saw the death magic pulsing out of me, he might know. My blood roared in my ears. I willed my body to move. Still, I couldn't move a single muscle.

Ruadan had been hit, but he was still wielding his sword. He lunged forward, swinging for the Caoranach, but she dodged. Another lash from her tongue caught him in the side, and his body went still, a deep red gash showing through his clothing.

Panic began spiraling through me. The blood river was rising higher around us, at my waist now. Although I couldn't move my body of my own volition, my teeth chattered involuntarily.

When Ruadan dropped his sword into the rising blood, my stomach sank.

I could feel the ancient winds of death whispering through me.

Fae, demons, the unholy beasts who scrabble over the earth ... I will steal your breath.

Not my own voice. The voice of an Angelic horde, echoing off my skull.

The Caoranach smiled. "Now. Isn't this lovely? I have you both where I want you."

CHAPTER 13

$\mathcal{P}$ale blue light from her body glowed over the tunnel, gleaming over the rising river of blood. It had reached my hipbones, now, the smell of blood overpowering.

The Caoranach began shivering, teeth chattering. Apparently, the cold bothered her, too, and Ruadan was delivering heavy doses of ice. Frowning, she reached into her skin satchel and pulled out a thermos, followed by a teacup.

With her talons clacking against the metallic thermos, she unscrewed the top, then poured herself a cup of steaming tea, one taloned pinky extended. She stared at us over the rim of her teacup as she took a sip. Steam curled around her.

"Ahhhh…."

I hadn't admired her before, but now I had to admit the woman was genius. I'd never thought to pack hot tea in my bug-out bag. Assuming we got out of this situation, that was the first thing on my agenda.

The Caoranach drifted closer to Ruadan, and she took another sip of her tea. "I've been here since before the angels. Before the fae. I am one of the Old Gods. Did you know that?"

Frozen in place, I caught a whiff of her tea. I didn't know what was in it, but it smelled like death.

She took another sip from her cup, the curls of steam winding around her head. "Mmmmm." She closed her eyes as she drank. "Do you know how I make this tea? I squeeze my victims to death, gut them, and then dry their organs. The agony they felt when I crush them continues to feed me after their lives have ended."

Gross. I still admired the thermos, but mine would not contain organ tea.

She knocked back the rest of her cup, then threw it against a wall. The porcelain shattered against the rock. Now, her body glowed even brighter with that pale blue light.

"You know me, Prince Ruadan. You remember me, don't you? I was there when you were just a young boy. I'm older than language," she went on, "and I will be here after all of your race dies. Demons. Fae. The lot of you."

With an iron will, I forced my eyes to move, to look at him.

The Caoranach was only inches from him now, her cheeks pink, eyes half-lidded. Her sights were locked on Ruadan, her expression starved. She carved one long, silver talon down his chest, ripping open his clothing.

"Can you stop making it so bloody cold?" she snapped.

Good luck with that, woman.

Ruadan looked like he was shifting—eyes darkening, the ghost of dark wings cascading down his back.

The temperature plummeted, the river growing so cold it was a shock to my body. My breath misted in front of my face. Immobilized, I shivered uncontrollably. Snake Lady shivered, too.

"I remember you, too, Prince Ruadan, demigod of the night," she hissed. "You were only a child when he brought you to me. You hadn't become powerful yet. Hadn't developed those fine muscles I see before me now."

So they *did* have a history. I'd thought as much when I'd first seen them together. No wonder Ruadan's rage was turning this place into the inner circle of hell.

An infuriating smile curled her lips, and she inched closer, sloshing through the blood. It was up to our ribs now, and freezing. "Your master, Baleros, used to feed you to me. Down in that bloody cave, just like this one. Do you remember how many times I froze you? And I cut your body?" She tutted. "Don't get so angry. It was all part of your training. It made you strong, didn't it? Look at the man you are today. And it was such a wonderfully delicious sustenance for me. Your pain was finer than that tea."

My stomach twisted. She'd been his torturer.

He couldn't move, but I felt his primordial magic snaking over me all the same.

The World Key glowed on his bared chest—a stunning gold among all the gloom. But Ruadan didn't quite look like himself anymore. His skin had taken on a silvery hue, and phantom wings swept out behind him. And as his skin changed, it looked as if he were pushing the toxins out of his body. She didn't seem to notice. What would happen if he shifted fully? I was starting to think we might have a chance, here, even without my death powers.

The Caoranach slashed a talon across his chest, and blood poured from the wound. "Baleros feeds me. He always has. The least I could do is give him this little bit of skin from your chest." Her gaze flicked to me. "Has she told you what she really is, yet? She's not fully fae. Anyone can tell that. So what sort of demon is she? A demigod like you?"

My mind screamed. I didn't want to dwell on this particular topic.

She hugged herself, shivering. "I don't like the cold."

Her tongue shot out again—this time, stroking up his body. She didn't break the skin. Rather, the movement was distinctly sexual. Rage erupted inside me.

My angelic side was threatening to come out to play, but if I unleashed the terror of the gods, my secret would be known.

"A demigod," she purred, a taloned hand groping his chest. Her lips had turned blue, teeth chattering. Ice formed around her body. "What a wonderful gift Baleros has given me. You can come so close to death. I could torment you to the point that your mind would break over and over again. But you never died. Such a wonderful ... gift...." Her teeth were now chattering so hard she could hardly form words, and her eyes lost focus.

At that moment, Ruadan roared. He gripped her neck and twisted, the snap of bone echoing off the walls.

But she wasn't dead yet. With her neck disturbingly crooked, the lower half of her body began shifting. A scaled tail erupted from where her legs had been. Her serpentine form filled the tunnel, tail thrashing. Ruadan reached down into the rising blood and snatched his sword. He swung for her, hacking into her bent neck. Her shrieks pierced the air. Her body thrashed, tail booming against the tunnel walls as he cut off her head.

Except her tail just kept going on its own.

Light debris rained down on us, and I desperately wished I could cover my head with my arms to shield my skull.

Ruadan turned to me, his skin an eerie silver. How exactly had he broken free—just his sheer demigod strength?

I didn't have much time to contemplate it. The walls around us were shaking, and so was my body.

With Ruadan's rage freezing the air, the blood river chilled me to the marrow, and chunks of ice floated around us. Great mounds of rubble blocked our paths.

Ruadan lifted me into his arms, then carried me up to the top of the rubble. With his warm body pressed against me, I tried moving a muscle. I managed just one tiny movement—a twitching of my pinky finger as we reached the top of the rubble. That was it.

Holding me tightly, he carried my frozen body down the rubble on the other side.

The walls boomed again, large chunks of rock raining down around us. We were going to be buried alive in here, entombed by that creature's disembodied tail. As we plunged back into the river, the blood froze my body, rising higher, up to my breasts. Ice crystallized around us.

The loudest boom of all, and my heart slammed against my ribs. Ruadan pulled me tighter against him.

I clamped my eyes shut and braced myself for the collapse of the walls around us, for rocks battering my flesh, slamming into my skull—but I felt only Ruadan's powerful arms around me, his breath on my neck. Why hadn't the rocks slammed down on us?

I looked up at Ruadan's eyes, but I found only darkness. But behind his shoulders, a glimmer of starlight.

What in the hells…?

It took me a moment to realize what had protected us from the debris. Ruadan had unveiled his incubus wings, and they spread above us like a shield. The black, leathery wings gleamed with silver flecks like tiny stars. Faint light beamed from them over my skin and glinted off the icy blood river.

Right now, Ruadan had gone into his primal mode. Was this it? Was this him fully shifted? And if so—was this a bad situation?

His primal side had taken over, and I could barely move. Not to mention the fact that I was close to freezing to death, and Ruadan didn't seem to be able to control his ice rage. The only mercy at this point was that the blood river seemed to be receding.

Still, I was pretty sure that the way he'd spread out his wings, he was protecting me. Even in his demonic form, he was shielding me.

"Ruadan," I tried to whisper, but my muscles still wouldn't move the way I wanted them to. My teeth were chattering so hard I thought I might involuntarily bite my own tongue off.

He cocked his head, the movement pure animal. A low growl rumbled from his throat, trembling through my gut. Right now, I was completely reliant on Ruadan. But was the fae I'd come to know in there at all? Or was this some hellish demon from the shadow void, about to tear my throat out if I annoyed him?

His dark, preternatural gaze trailed over my damp chest, then he lowered his head to my throat. One powerful arm held me close to his hard body. Right now, I had a hard time reconciling this creature with the controlled, distant fae who ran the Institute.

He opened his mouth, and my pulse began racing out of control. His canines had lengthened completely. In fact, they looked like vampiric fangs….

His fingers clutched my waist so hard I was certain he was going to leave marks. I stared into his dark eyes. This wasn't the Ruadan I knew, but a bestial creature of the void. And right now, he seemed fixated on my throat.

My heart beat harder, and I fought to move my lips, my vocal chords. My attempt to say his name only came out as a moan. Godsdamn it, I wanted to move. How had *he* managed to break free?

Powerful shivers wracked my body again. Ruadan unleashed a long, slow growl, his dark magic snaking over my skin. His hard body pressed against me, warming me. My neck arched, and his eyes were locked on the vein in my neck, the pulsing blood. His tightly coiled muscles gave the impression of an animal about to strike. My heart pounded like a drum.

Incubi didn't drink blood. Did they?

Then, to my horror, he moved. His fangs pierced my throat—a sharp, delicious pain.

CHAPTER 14

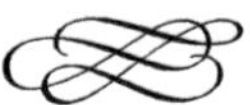

*E*cstasy bloomed in my body. Ruadan's tongue flicked against my skin, and my mind burst with images of the night sky, like an explosion of stars. My eyes fluttered closed, and I melted into him, muscles softening. My toes curled with white-hot pleasure, and I moaned. I'd never let anything bite me before.

No, no, no. Was he going to drain me? Was he even in there, under the demonic exterior? What the fuck was going on?

"Ruadan," I groaned. It took me a moment to realize that this time, I could say his name.

My fingers twitched, then my arm. I moved my hips a little, brushing against Ruadan's warm body—which seemed to have become even larger.

Ruadan pulled his mouth from my neck, and I reached up to touch his face.

I could move again. I blinked up at him. How had that happened?

He licked a droplet of blood off his fangs.

I ran my tongue over my lips, finding that I had control over my mouth once more. Now, the river's surface had lowered, back down to my hips once more.

Ruadan was still holding on tightly to me, and I slid my arms around his neck.

"Did you suck the toxins out of my blood on purpose?"

"Why else would I be sucking blood from your neck?" His voice sounded different—deeper, and otherworldly. In his clipped tones, I had the sense of barely restrained anger.

"Why would you be sucking my blood? Because you've fully transformed into a terrifying demon with giant leathery wings. With stars embedded in them." I reached up and touched his wing, running my fingertips over the apex.

He shuddered, and each one of his muscles tensed. He gripped me so hard now that it started to become painful. "I'm not fully transformed," he said. The tips of his claws pierced my skin.

Wait.

"You have claws?" The chattering of my teeth echoed in the small space. "Never mind. How did you free yourself from that woman's toxins? And how were you able to suck them out of my throat without poisoning yourself?"

"She imprisoned me for decades, feeding off me. I built up a tolerance to her toxins. I never let her know."

I stroked the side of his face. I wanted to wrap him up and keep him warm by a fireplace forever. "Can we get out of here? The blood river is full of ice. I'm about to freeze to death."

Ruadan flexed his wings, and rock rained down from them. Apart from the silver flecks in his wings, almost total darkness enshrouded us.

He straightened, finally releasing me. I surveyed the dim space, lit only by the faint light from Ruadan's wings.

The wall of debris blocked one side of the tunnel—the side we'd just come from. Dust clouded the air, and I coughed. "I guess we have nowhere to go but forward," I said.

I desperately wanted out of here. When Ruadan created another ball of silver light, I looked down at the river again. The blood was gone, and clear water rushed around us. The Caoranach, it seemed, had left us.

Still, red streaked my white dress, and my lip curled in disgust. "Godsdamn it, Ruadan. Can you turn off the ice?"

He ignored me, plowing on. I had the sense he didn't have much control over the temperature, and in his partially shifted form, he certainly had no desire to explain it.

After a few minutes, we came to another pile of rubble, and it nearly reached the ceiling. At the base of the rubble, Ruadan turned to me, his features cold as marble. Then, he lunged forward and grabbed me around the ribs. He hoisted me up as if I weighed nothing, dropping me farther up the pile. His partially shifted incubus side was irritatingly dominating.

"I can move on my own," I snapped through chattering teeth.

Truthfully, although Ruadan had sucked the toxins out of me, my body still wasn't working as it should. It felt as if ice had flooded my own blood, and every one of my muscles had gone rigid. As I climbed up the rocks, I was shivering out of control.

At the top of the rubble, we had only a few feet of space to crawl through, and it seemed to go on for a few yards. Walls had collapsed around us, and darkness yawned on either side, but most of the ceiling remained intact. As I crawled through the gap, the broken stone bit into my palms and my knees.

When I reached the end of the gap, the broken rock sloped downward into the river. Here, the water smelled clear, and it was only about a foot deep. As we reached the bottom of the rubble, the silver flecks on Ruadan's wings illuminated the dark water.

Up ahead, a beam of moonlight streamed into the tunnel, pouring in from a grate or something above. I hugged myself as I walked through the cold water. At this point, I'd mostly gone numb.

I breathed in again, taking in a floral scent. In the dim light, it took me a moment to realize there were vines growing on the walls down here, all of them flowering with white blossoms. Moonflowers, in fact. I hadn't expected to find beauty down in the sewers, but here it was. As Ruadan walked past the flowers, frost spread over their leaves, and the petals crystallized with ice. The moody bastard was killing everything.

"Ruadan," I said sharply. "Stop it with the damned ice. She really got to you, didn't she? She used to feed off your pain. She tortured you, and she's a monster. But you're the one who told me to master my emotions."

He whirled around, his expression unreadable.

I understood, even without him explaining. Baleros had sacrificed a young fae to that tea-drinking, skin-flaying monster.

I stepped closer to Ruadan. "I know how it would have happened. Baleros would have told you that he was doing you a favor. He was making you strong, you see. He was making you into a powerful warrior. But he had an ulterior motive. He wanted to curry favor with one of the Old Gods, and so you were a sacrificial victim. He'd torture you while convincing you he had your best interests in mind."

Violet magic sparked up and down his body, glinting off the edge of his wings. *That* was his incubus lust magic, but he was keeping it contained. He was protecting himself. Just a stony expression, eyes black as night. It seemed like his incubus form protected him so that he didn't have to feel anything. All his emotions were on the outside, making the air cold. With his wings out, claws sharpened, nothing could hurt him.

The survivor in me told me I had to do the same in my own way, that I had to protect myself. If I got close to him, if I let myself care for him, I wasn't sure I could take it when he learned the truth about me. I couldn't let myself love him and then watch darkness slam into his eyes when he realized who I really was.

The betrayal would kill me before the sword ever did.

Still, I needed him to get control of his emotions right now, or I'd freeze to death. I had the strange sense that if he could say it out loud, it might help. I moved closer to him, until I was within touching distance. His transformed appearance sent shudders through my bones, but he transfixed me all the same. Shadows bloomed around him—a miasma of darkness. His face betrayed nothing, his beautiful features like cold marble.

I pressed my palm flat against his cheek, trying to warm him. I held his gaze steadily. "What did she do to you? What did she and Baleros do?"

I brushed my thumb over his cheek, softly, and a chink of light flickered in his dark eyes.

He stared at me for what seemed like ages. At last, he spoke. "When I was a child, she kept me in a river of blood. Severity is the way of the Shadow Fae of Emain. It's how we grow strong. But her ways were extreme even for us. She carved my flesh from my bones, over and over. She'd bring me near death and feed off the torment. She grew strong off me."

Rage shot through me, hot and red. I'd save it for Baleros—this pure destruction trapped inside me. I'd keep it locked in my chest until it was time to unleash its full force.

"I cannot die," Ruadan went on in his emotionless voice. "At least, she could not kill me. Few know how to kill a demigod. It was as you said. Baleros told me the torture would make me stronger. It was part of my training. I was in and out of there for years until I reached adulthood. And then, I was of age. I was married. I was free."

I pulled my hand from his cheek. Impulsively, I reached out and stroked the top of his wing, and his sharp intake of breath echoed off the walls.

"Baleros was lying to us when he told us he'd make us strong," I said. "But here's what he never envisioned: that we *would* become strong, and we would come for him."

Ruadan's dark eyes surveyed me. Blood from the river streaked his bare chest. We'd gone right into his worst memories—the river of blood, the Caoranach. We'd practically relived it. No wonder he hated being trapped in places.

"I'm getting this blood off you," I declared. "I know you think you don't care right now, because you're an incubus and you don't feel normal emotions, but it will help to bring the real Ruadan back. Then maybe you can ease up on all the ice."

I reached down to the freezing river and scooped up the clear water, then splashed it over his chest. He stared down at me, unmoving. As I washed off his skin, violet magic pulsed from his body over mine.

Did he realize he was dosing me with little waves of his lust magic? As I cleaned the blood off him, a shiver of pleasure washed over me, and my skin heated. Being this close to Ruadan in his incubus state was a dangerous game, one that made my breasts feel tight against my damp dress. He stared down at me, impassive, and another wave of his magic rippled over my body.

This was very dangerous territory indeed.

CHAPTER 15

I brushed his bare skin with my fingertips, licking my lips. Water mixed with blood, turning pink.

"There," I said, my voice husky. "You'll feel better."

Till death us do part. I shoved the phrase out of my mind, and I watched the rivulets of pink streaming off him. Breath clouded around my face.

For some reason, I'd expected that, once cleaned of blood, he'd return to his usual form. Instead, he still loomed over me, wings spread. Not Ruadan anymore—just an ancient predator, looking at me like I was prey. A low, slow growl rose from his chest, rippling over my body. What exactly was happening?

Chunks of ice floated around my legs, and I was pretty sure my lips and skin had turned blue at this point. As much as I wanted to feel the warmth of his body, I took a step away from him, suddenly unsure of myself.

Ruadan cocked his head, gaze sweeping over me. Then, a glimmer of violet returned to his dark eyes. "You're freezing," he said. The dark wings behind him had started to fade—only phantom wings once more.

"Yes, thank you." I threw my hands up. "I've said that repeatedly for the past twenty minutes."

He reached for me, then pulled me close to his hard body. His warmth caressed my skin, and I leaned into him. My muscles began to relax. His body crackled with violet light, his magic warming me from the inside out. Still, I couldn't linger too long against him. I couldn't keep letting myself feel close to someone who was clearly my enemy.

A powerful hand stroked up my spine, and the air around us began warming. I started to forget about the whole enemy thing as my pulse began racing.

The water around us, too, began warming, ice melting. I met Ruadan's gaze, and he looked down at me, then gripped the top of my stained dress.

"Blood." A simple statement of fact, but his hand was gripping my dress so hard that the fabric cut into my skin. Frost tinged the air once more, and his wings spread out behind him—thick and gleaming with silver chinks.

I'd been right. The blood had bothered him. It reminded him of *her*.

With a great deal of force, I pulled his hand from my dress. "Calm down. I'll get it off me."

I had another dress stuffed into my bug-out bag. I slipped the bag off my shoulder, then I crossed to one of the walls. I hung the bag from a jagged outcrop.

I looked down at my dress, feeling uncharacteristically self-conscious. There was something about unbuttoning the dress in front of Ruadan that felt like a sensual performance. My cheeks heated as I undid the top, exposing my bra. Normally I'd just tear the thing off and toss it away, leaving the other person to process the awkwardness of my nudity. But this felt different, the air so charged that I couldn't meet his gaze. I couldn't even think about touching him or I was sure he'd pick up on my desire.

I could feel his eyes on me—Incubus Ruadan did not look away from bared skin. I wanted him to see me, all of me. At the same time, I felt like if I looked up at him, the world would combust.

I unbuttoned it down to my navel, and a raw, sexual energy skimmed and buzzed over my chest. My breasts seemed to strain against my bra, nipples peaking. Still, I kept my eyes down, just feeling the charge of his gaze stroking over every inch of my naked skin. Goosebumps rose on my bare flesh, and I unbuttoned the dress down to my hips.

My chest flushed, and at last, I dared to look up at him just a little, only raising my eyes as high as his torso. His body looked taut, tightly coiled. His violet magic crackled in the air, and lust pulsed across my naked skin.

He took a step closer, and my eyes swept over his muscled chest. His magic licked at my skin, warming me in places I badly wanted to feel him, a silky touch that heated my neck, my breasts, between my legs…. Molten heat swept through my core. I was wildly turned on, and Incubus Ruadan was feeding from my desire. Fueling it, too.

At last, I looked all the way up into his eyes, and blazing lust lit me up.

I unbuttoned the final button. The dress fell away, and I stood before him in my black bra and knickers, my pulse racing out of control. A muscle twitched in his jaw, his eyes black as the void again.

Violet-tinged light flickered around him, and my body ached for him. His attention was on me and me alone.

The corner of my lip twitched in a seductive smile.

That was all it took for him to move for me—a blur of black and violet, and he dropped all his restraint. He grasped me, pushing me against a wall, and the stone bit into my back. His powerful body pressed into me. I gasped, my legs opening wider. My neck arched, and I stared up at him. His muscled body pressed hard against me, and his eyes seared me.

He leaned down to kiss me. After the rough start, I expected something desperate, animal. But he was holding back. His lips moved sensually over mine—surprisingly gentle, stroking mine. I swept in my tongue, deepening the kiss, and he responded to it. His hands gripped my bare waist, then moved up my ribs, the pressure from his powerful fingers leaving a trail of heat on my body.

He pulled away from the kiss, and I nearly moaned. Then, his mouth moved over my neck, leaving a trail of searing hot kisses. My entire world right now was just his mouth, his hands, his heat. He caressed my body as he kissed me, until his thumbs traced the hollows of my hipbones, dipping under the hem of my knickers.

I moved my hips closer to him, encouraging his touch. His thumbs slid down further, skimming my skin and teasing me until, at last, one of his thumbs swept gently between my legs, the touch so painfully light I wanted to scream. I grasped his face in my hands, kissing him urgently, demanding that he move faster, harder. Another devastatingly light sweep of his thumb, and I groaned, moving harder against him, grinding myself onto his hand. I wanted him to let go completely.

I wrapped my arms around him, pulling him closer, and his kiss grew wilder with uncontrolled need. Then, his restraint seemed to snap. With a low snarl, he drew a long, silvery claw through the center of my bra, ripping it open. The tip of his nail grazed my skin, and the black lace fell away, revealing my breasts.

He kissed me again, claws just barely piercing my skin until I felt their sharp points retract. I writhed against him. As he kissed me— hard, this time—I moaned into his mouth, my body pure fire. I needed more from him, and the hot ache between my legs was driving me mad. My bare skin brushed against his, smooth and hot. I thrust my hips closer to him, nipples brushing his chest. I felt like I'd never get enough of him, and I needed him inside me now.

His hand slid down my back, firm pressure and hot skin, until it dipped into the back of my silky knickers. His touch singed me. I gasped, breath coming faster. I ached for him. Liquid fire flowed through me as he slid down my panties, and the tunnel air whispered over my naked skin.

For just a moment, I pushed him away. I wanted him to look at me —really look at me.

His slow, predatory gaze swept up and down my body—moving down past my breasts, my belly, lingering between my legs, the intent gaze of a hunter.... This time, I didn't lower my eyes. His magic lashed the air around him, and the power of his eyes on me ignited me. Dark wings swept behind him. A god of darkness, laser-focused on me.

Then, I reached for him, grabbing him by the waist of his trousers. I pulled them down, and within moments, he was lifting me up against the wall, hands gripping my bum. I wrapped my legs around him and thrust my fingers into his hair.

He whispered my name, his breath warming the side of my face. He was bringing out the wild beast in me, and I raked my fingertips down the front of his chest. He released a low growl. When he claimed my mouth, his kiss had grown savage. Both of us had lost all sense of restraint. He slid between my thighs, filling me. I felt my teeth on his neck, tasted the salt on his skin, and I groaned.

* * *

WITH MY LEGS still wrapped around Ruadan, I leaned into him, and the scent of pine enveloped me. I breathed deeply.

It took me a moment to realize that his wings had disappeared completely.

I cupped my hand against the side of his face. Now, the air felt warm—humid, almost. "The incubus is gone."

This was the real Ruadan. Unfortunately, this was also the Ruadan who wanted to kill me.

All at once, the horror of that thought slammed into my skull. I disentangled my body from his, sliding down his naked skin into the cold water once more. I didn't look him in the eye as I reached for my bug-out bag.

I tuned out the fact that Ruadan was saying my name, and I kept my gaze down. I pulled out my spare knickers and a simple black dress.

"Arianna," he said again.

That's not my name. My name is Liora.

Who would win in a fight between us? My father—the Angel of Death—hadn't been able to kill him. I had to think tactically, here, if I didn't want to die.

I tried to keep the tremor out of my voice as I asked, "How can Baleros kill you if you're immortal? You said almost no one knows how to kill demigods." I turned my back to him as I slipped on the new pair of knickers, like we were strangers again.

"There are two ways to kill a demigod," he said, his velvety voice rumbling over my skin. "One involves an Angelic spell—"

"Stop." I whirled and moved for him, covering his mouth with my hand. "I don't want to know."

The survivor in me was doing a shitty job right now. Maybe it was because I still wanted to feel Ruadan holding me close to his body, his heart beating against me.

"I've heard you speak Angelic," he murmured. "I'm not worried."

He had a point. My language abilities were nearly nonexistent, even if Angelic was my father's native language.

He kissed my cheek, so softly that I ached for him anew. "Are you worried you might lose your temper and slaughter me some day?"

Basically, yes. That was exactly what I was worried about.

I took a deep breath, not meeting his eyes. I pulled away from him, my body suddenly cold in his absence. "Look, what we just did was obviously a mistake. You said no lovers at the Institute, and that's a good idea. We're supposed to be working together, right? Let's not let it happen again, okay?"

As soon as the words were out of my mouth, ice frosted the air again.

I dared to look at him, and for just a brief, horrible moment I caught a glimmer of a wounded look. Then, his gaze shuttered again, and he fell silent. Ice skimmed over the river.

Emptiness yawned between my ribs, and I gritted my teeth, eager to change the subject. I stepped over a jagged bit of rubble. "Any idea where we're going?"

He sniffed the air. "Wyverns."

CHAPTER 16

"What, now?" I said. "Wyverns?"

"I smell them. We need to move in their direction. They're used as guards."

I breathed in deeply, scenting the air. A musky scent hit my nose, tinged with cedar embers. I'd never seen one of the reptilian creatures. I only knew they were enormous and muscular, and they breathed fire. "So that's what a wyvern smells like. Always wondered." I tried to keep my voice steady and light, forcing myself to ignore the dark truth that followed behind us like a stalker—that Ruadan and I were fated to be enemies.

Still, my voice came out sounding unnatural. I had no doubt that Ruadan had noticed. He noticed everything—my heart beating faster, my cheeks reddening. A man who saw everything and betrayed nothing.

"You think they're guarding Queen Macha?" I asked. And there was that unsteady tone in my voice again.

"Yes. Once we find her, we can use a portal to get out of there."

Unfortunately, we couldn't use a portal to get in without knowing where, exactly, she was.

Silence fell, broken only by the sound of our legs sloshing through the icy water. Our passionate moment had been just a temporary thaw, but as soon as I'd told him it was a mistake, we were back to wintry temperatures.

Still, I'd done the right thing by putting a stop to it, hadn't I? I was too much of a survivor to rush headfirst into something that would kill me.

Now, the silence felt worse than before—sharp and dangerous. I let out a long, slow breath.

Where was my life headed, exactly? I couldn't stick around the Institute forever—not while I was on Ruadan's kill list. But I couldn't quite bring myself to leave, either. Not yet. Bizarrely, the Institute was starting to feel like my home.

I had to say something to Ruadan, to smooth things over and to warm the place up again. Something that would probably start with, *About what just happened....*

But instead, I cleared my throat, my blood roaring. "Wyverns smell like musk. Bit like an old man's cologne."

Nope. That was not what I'd been going for.

"I, um...." I tried again. "The thing is.... Did you know that palm trees are actually a type of grass?"

Shit. Turned out, I was terrible at relationship talks.

Ruadan's eyes stayed straight ahead, his mouth closed in a firm line.

"How are we going to fight the wyverns, anyway?" I went on.

"Stab them through their eyes, pierce their brains."

I nodded at his sword. "We only have one of those, I notice."

He handed it to me, and I gripped the hilt tightly. It was a relief to have a proper weapon in my hand. Now, I could think about killing instead of the deeply uncomfortable topic of emotions.

As we reached a fork in the tunnels, the scent of musk grew overpowering. A low growl reverberated through the stony passages. I held my breath as we turned a corner.

The tunnel opened up into an enormous cave of turquoise water, its surface glimmering under Ruadan's silver light.

"How long can you hold your breath?" asked Ruadan.

"I guess we'll find out." I frowned. "You think your mother is being held below the water?"

"I can smell the wyverns all over the walls here." His gaze flicked upward at the enclosed ceiling. "And there's no other way out."

"And your mother can breathe underwater?"

"No. There must be a watertight chamber down there. We just have to get to it."

Ruadan dove under the surface, and his silver orb plunged into the water after him. I took a minute to suck in a long breath, filling my lungs. Then, I went in after him, kicking my legs hard to catch up. As I swam, the sword felt heavy in my hand, slowing me down a little.

Ruadan's sphere cast a dull, pearly light in the water. My lungs felt heavier the deeper we went, and after about thirty seconds, I started fantasizing about air. Sweet, sweet air in my lungs. It seemed to be endless turquoise water down here, tinged with the silver streaks of light.

Air.

Gods below, please don't make me endure the humiliation of having to give in and swim up for air.

At last, the silver light glowed over contours—something concrete lay before us. Rough stone, stairs…. A palace of sorts?

My lungs burned, but I focused on the structure taking shape before me. Ruadan's sphere of light grew brighter, another floating high above. They cast silver light over a rough, crumbling stone staircase, and an archway with a tower that rose into the dark waters above. The stern, carved face of a river god glowered from the tower, and carvings of octopus arms snaked over imposing columns. A marble man stood with his arms outstretched to the river's surface, as if worshiping the air above…. *Air. Sweet, sweet air.*

Maybe I couldn't die, but I sure as shit could feel pain.

What the hells was this place? I was starting to feel lightheaded, and I focused on tightening my grip on my sword's hilt. If I dropped my weapon, it'd all be over.

I'd been in many dangerous situations before, often with the odds stacked against me. But an underwater fight with giant reptiles was a bit beyond even my skillset. I could only hope the fight would happen once we breached the airtight chamber, and not while I was about to pass out under icy water.

I started to grow frantic for a breath, and I kicked my legs faster, now, urging Ruadan to increase his pace with me.

I mentally made a note that, in addition to a thermos of tea, my bug-out bag needed scuba-diving equipment.

We swam through the archway, then followed the trail of crumbling stairs up to an open door to the temple. Ruadan pushed on the door, and it shifted over a stone floor. His pale hair floated in the water around him. He squeezed inside the door, and I went in after him into a hall.

Statues with broken arms lined either side of us, their eyes gaping, noses missing. My throat was starting to spasm, now. What would happen if I drowned down here? Would my father bring me back to life again this time?

And how many times could I die in front of Ruadan before he pieced it all together? That little boy had been a girl—one who'd escaped, and who'd grown into a woman with purple hair.

A burst of fire shot out in the murky water, startling me.

Ah. We'd reached a wyvern—and, unfortunately, I still hadn't reached the air.

My heart stuttered as the enormous creature swam out from behind a corner. The wyvern's scales shone in the dull underwater light, and it opened its mouth to breathe fire. A small burst of flames shot from its mouth, dulled by the cold water. I swam closer, sword ready. Ruadan reached him first.

Ruadan reared his fist back, then punched it hard into the creature's eye. With his arm thrust into the wyvern's head, he jerked it around a bit. I stared as he gripped hard onto what I could only imagine was the wyvern's brain. The wyvern's scream floated through the water, and a dull flame burst out of its mouth before dying out again. The sight of Ruadan hand-lobotomizing the wyvern had been so gruesome, I nearly forgot about the oppressive pain in my lungs. Blood spilled into the water around them, snaking through the darkness.

Good. That's over.

No sooner had the thought crossed my mind than a hot blast seared my back, and I whirled to find another wyvern behind me. At this point, darkness was swirling in my mind, but my survival instincts began to take over.

The thing lunged for me, jaw opened. I thrust my sword at its eye, but with the friction underwater—not to mention the oxygen deprivation— the movement was off. The wyvern snapped for my arm, sinking its sharp teeth into my skin. Blood stained the turquoise water.

Darkness bloomed in my lungs, a sharp pain that threatened to eat me alive from the inside out. My throat spasmed. *Air. Air. Air.*

The wyvern tore at my arm.

I am the twilight shadow that creeps over long grasses....

The death angel in me was taking over. I just couldn't let it take over completely—couldn't let the real Liora come out.

I am the hunter who sneaks up behind you when you're trying to find the right words. I stalk in your shadows as you search to fill the silence, skirting away from the dark truth.

No—not now. My heart was a hunted animal.

I tried to shove the death instinct deeper inside of myself. I needed Arianna to fight this battle. Not Liora.

When you look away, I enshroud your body, creeping up from your feet to claim your life.

I knew how it would end. Ruadan would see what I really was, and he'd come for me. The betrayal would take the fight out of me.

Something tingled at my back, a hot rush where wings might grow.

No!

I had to finish this without shifting here.

With one final act of iron will, I forced the death instinct under the surface, and I thrust my sword into the wyvern's eye. Clouds of blood bloomed around us. I twisted it sharply, and the wyvern's body spasmed and twitched.

If I didn't take a breath within the next few seconds, the death angel would come out for good, and it would all be over.

CHAPTER 17

I whirled, catching a glimpse of Ruadan slaughtering another wyvern with his bare hands. Blood muddied the water around him. He pulled his arm out of the wyvern's head, then turned to look at me.

Through the flash of panic in his eyes, I had a hint of how I must look to him. I hadn't transformed into my angel form, but blood flowed from my arm, pooling in the water around it—red tendrils, curling around me like ribbons. I was certain my eyes were bulging, and the look of sheer terror on my face was probably unnerving.

He moved for me, a blur of black through the water. In the next moment, his mouth was on mine. I opened my lips, and he breathed into my lungs.

Air, thank the gods.

I don't think I'd ever loved him more than I did at that moment.

I turned from him, and I frantically searched the space around us for a way in. There didn't seem to be any doors....

It took me a moment before I spotted the entrance just above us— a hatch with a wheel, embedded in the top of the arch. And that was our way into a tower that hopefully contained a whole lot of air.

My lungs seared me from the inside out. I gripped the metal and began turning the wheel with all the strength I had left. At last, the hatch opened, a stone door sliding to the side. Desperate, I hoisted myself up into a dark chamber, and I sucked in a deep, glorious breath as soon as my head breached the surface. I flopped over onto a stone floor. Ruadan came in after me.

His silver sphere bobbed in the air above us, illuminating broken statues that jutted from the towering walls. I gasped for breath and surveyed the space around us. Stony rib vaults arched high above us, like a medieval cathedral. Engraved oak doors were inset into the wall.

Gods below, that had been a close call. If my dark angel had come out, Ruadan would be trying to kill me right now.

I sucked in another long breath, and Ruadan turned to look at me. Droplets of water peaked his lashes.

He pulled a lever on the floor, and the sound of shifting stone filled the chamber. The bottom of the hatch closed.

I peered down at myself, at the blood dripping off my body.

"You're injured," said Ruadan.

"Was it all the blood that tipped you off?" I gasped. "You look a bit winded."

An arched eyebrow. "*I* look a bit winded?" Ruadan knelt by my side.

As soon as I looked down at my own arm, the pain from the wounds came roaring into my consciousness, and I gasped. It looked worse than I realized. "I'm so glad we can just portal out of this place."

Already, his healing magic was snaking over my skin, shimmering violet that began healing the ragged injury. He traced his fingertips over the wounds as he healed me, and his magic tingled up my arm.

"Are you nervous?" I asked. We'd come to save his mother. What sort of state would she be in after years of captivity, under Baleros's care?

"About what?"

"About seeing your mum after she's been imprisoned for fifteen years. Seems kind of like a big moment."

He shot me a surprised look, then focused on my arm again. "I hadn't thought about what we might find. I've been unwilling to expect that she might really be alive."

"You haven't thought about her because you don't want to be disappointed." I knew a thing or two about protecting your heart.

"She's the one who gave me over to Baleros when I was three. We never had a warm relationship, but I used to think she was a literal goddess." A line furrowed between his eyebrows, and he seemed lost in his own thoughts. "I made her wreaths out of apple blossoms and clover, threaded with silk ribbons. They were my offerings to her."

My lips twitched in a smile, warmth pooling in my chest. "Did she wear them?"

"No." His magic caressed my skin.

I *really* wanted to see Ruadan making a wreath out of flowers. "If you made me one, I'd wear it."

A smile played over his lips for just a moment. "Do you actually want one?"

"Of course."

He met my gaze for a moment, his expression guarded, then focused on my arm again. At last, all the skin had healed.

As much as I'd thought about protecting my heart, I needed him close just for another moment. I wrapped my arms around his neck, pulling him in for a tight hug. I indulged for a second in his smell, in the feel of his skin against me. For an instant, his hand found the small of my back.

Then, he pulled away from me.

I crossed my arms, still catching my breath. "Do you think we'll find any more wyverns on the other side?" I asked.

I pressed my ear to the oak door, listening. It took only a moment before I realized the sheer pointlessness of trying to hear through a stone, airtight chamber wall.

Ruadan sniffed the air. "I have no idea. If it's anything we can't kill, I'll create a portal to get out of here."

He pushed on the oak door, and it groaned open, sliding against the rough floor. Ruadan's silver sphere shot into the room, but the darkness swallowed it up.

I took a tentative step inside after him. The air smelled of damp sediment, a hint of sulfur, and brine. A harsh sound rasped in the air around us, and a dank breeze lifted my hair.

How, exactly, was there a breeze in an airtight chamber?

The air whispered around me, and I was certain I heard the word *repent* in it, but I could see fuck-all. I gripped my sword tighter, totally unsure what to do in this situation. I was starting to feel nostalgic for my gladiator days. Granted, I had lived in a cage, but at least I'd got to fight monsters I could see in the open air.

From behind, a slimy limb snaked over my chest, and I whirled, swinging my sword. It sliced through the air, hitting nothing.

So, this is how it would be. We'd be fighting intangible wraiths in the dark.

Long, bony fingers tore at my hair. I pivoted again, but my sword slashed only air.

Then, from behind, a slithering hand covered my mouth, my nose, pinning me in place. Wet lips at my ear whispered, "Liora."

My heart skipped a beat. I couldn't let Ruadan hear my real name. I jabbed wildly behind me with my elbow, but my blows helplessly hit the air.

"Liora," the creature whispered again. What the fuck was this thing made of? Just disembodied arms and a wet mouth? "Liora," she whispered, a cold tongue licking at my ear. "You're far from home. You've lost your way, haven't you?"

Rage simmered under the surface, a roiling volcano ready to erupt.

The creature jammed her clammy fingers into my mouth, gagging me. They tasted of salty sediment and moss. Choking, I bit down hard on them, but she didn't seem to care, and she thrust her arm further into my throat. I couldn't breathe, and her moist flesh was invading me, stealing my air. A long, cold tongue licked up my neck, and I feared I'd vomit with her hand in my mouth. I wanted to rip her to pieces, but I couldn't grasp anything. She shoved her hand in farther, and I could feel the bile rising in my throat, threatening to explode.

"You know the truth, don't you, Liora?" Her voice was rising, my name loud on her tongue. What the hells was Ruadan doing right now? "You know what really happened that day, don't you?"

An image burst in my mind of red hair, blood streaming over pale skin—a trickle from red lips.

Rage erupted in a flash of white light, and in the next moment, I'd ripped her arms off of me. Now, my fist was hitting real flesh, fast as a storm wind. I pounded the creature, breaking bones, breaking skin. Then, I swung for her with my sword, the blade carving bone, carving flesh.

She kept whispering my name, over and over, until, at last … she went silent. Something heavy and wet fell to the floor.

Ruadan's silver sphere bloomed in the air again, casting its light over my attacker. I was surprised to see that she looked beautiful—a pale little waif with silver hair. The only thing animal about her was her long claws. She wore a long, green gown, and waxy limbs lay across the stone floor. I'd battered the shit out of her. Had that delicate little thing nearly killed me?

I glanced up at Ruadan. Two waifs lay at his feet, their eyes gaping. His kills had been cleaner—two simple snapped necks, jaws hanging open.

I caught my breath. "Did you hear any of that?" I asked.

"Any of what?" His voice sounded sharp. Something had definitely rattled him.

The bit about my name being Liora. "What she said to me. Did you hear it?"

He shook his head, his skin paler than normal. Whatever they'd said to him had unnerved him.

Clack, clack, clack.... A new sound echoed from the shadows. It sounded like bones tapping against each other. I tightened my grip on the sword, my palm slicked with blood from the waif.

A chill danced up the back of my neck as I stepped farther into the hall.

Ruadan whispered a spell, calling up another orb of silver light— larger this time. It floated further into the hall, until it cast its eerie light over a tall figure.

A throned woman sat before us—a silver cloak, a crown of black horns, dark feathers that swooped up from her collar. She held a silver scepter, its top crowned with an opalescent dome. Her eyes had the same opalescent sheen.

From one hand, her long, black nails clacked against the throne's stone arms. Her skin looked like marble, and ravens fluttered around her head.

I swallowed hard. Was this Ruadan's mum? No wonder he used to think she was a goddess. *I* believed she was a goddess, and I'd only just seen her for the first time. I could not imagine this woman being thrilled by a gift of floral wreaths from a little boy, and the thought of tiny Ruadan trying to impress her made me want to wrap my arms around him again.

"Mother," said Ruadan.

CHAPTER 18

She arched a thin, white eyebrow. "Ruadan. Fifteen years." Her voice sounded angry and calm at the same time, strangely dissonant. "It took you fifteen years to find me."

"I didn't know you were alive. Baleros staged your death."

Clack ... clack.... Her nails beat out a steady rhythm. She sniffed. "It's almost as if you learned nothing from him." The ravens fluttered about her head.

How old was this woman? She wasn't an ordinary fae, but seemed old as time itself. I felt like she'd been on earth long enough that she'd started to meld with it. She seemed a force of nature more than an individual. This was not a woman with ordinary feelings and desires.

Her head swiveled, a birdlike movement. When her pale eyes landed on me, I had to force myself to hold my ground instead of scuttling back. She sniffed the air again, her expression darkening. "What did you bring with you, Ruadan?"

Force of nature or not, I wasn't sure I liked the woman's tone.

I cocked a hip. "It's *who*. Not what. In the English language, when you're talking about a person, you say *who*."

A heavy silence fell over the hall.

"My name is Arianna," I said.

"Knight of the Shadow Fae," added Ruadan.

Queen Macha cocked her head, studying me like a bird of prey studies a mouse. "But that's not her real name, is it?"

My heart sputtered. *Oh, bloody hells.* Not only had I stumbled into the weirdest godsdamned family reunion since Edward IV drowned his brother in a bucket of Malmsey wine, but this queen was about to unveil my secrets.

Ruadan cut me a sharp look. "Not your real name," he repeated, a hint of steel in his tone.

Now, I had two ancient, terrifying fae staring at me and waiting for an explanation. I swallowed hard, my mouth dry. How much did she know? And *how* did she know anything about me?

"What makes you say that?" I asked in a voice so soft I could hardly hear it myself.

Clack, clack, clack.... "It's quite simple. I always know when someone is lying. You, little thing, are lying to my son."

My stomach dropped. Still, she didn't know much.

I stole a quick glance back at Ruadan, whose violet eyes pierced me to the core. Was that betrayal I read in them?

"Why are we talking about me? Shouldn't you two hug or something? I mean, it's been a while." I made my voice sound jovial. "Yay! You've got the gang back together."

Two sets of immortal eyes trained on me, the only sound the flapping of the ravens' wings.

I cleared my throat. "Or not. Whatever. I mean, I have a weird relationship with my—" *parents.* I let the word die on my tongue. No reason to dredge that up right now. "You know what? Never mind. I like your ravens, Queen Macha. I'm thinking of getting some of my own."

The birds swooped before her face as she stared at me, still as her throne.

"We should probably leave here," I offered. "Before something comes to kill us. I think that's the most important thing right now. And then we have some very important questions to ask about Baleros."

Queen Macha rose from her throne. The woman was only about five feet tall, but somehow, she managed to loom over us. "Yes. Son, open a portal before the wyverns return."

As if on cue, a wyvern's screech rumbled off the stone.

Ruadan touched his throat, and his World Key began glowing with pale gold. Already, the floor began trembling, until fissures opened in the dark stone. The flagstones crumbled and fractured. Dark, star-flecked waters burst from the floor, rushing in a whirlpool.

I leapt in with the others, plunging into frigid water once more.

* * *

IN THE INSTITUTE'S throne room, I hugged myself tightly, trying to warm up. Aengus tossed me a towel.

"Is no one going to ask the queen how she's doing?" I asked.

All eyes in the hall turned to me—Aengus, Ruadan, and the queen.

Clack, clack.... The queen sat in Ruadan's stone throne, and she tapped her claws on the arm.

"Queen Macha," I began, "given that you were imprisoned by a maniac for the past fifteen years, how are you feeling?"

She blinked. "Hungry."

I turned to Aengus. "See? It helps to ask these questions. Maybe we can get some sort of food."

"It's not that sort of hunger," said Ruadan.

Did I want to know? "What do you mean?"

Queen Macha lifted her chin. "I feast on the spirits of my defeated enemies, those fallen in battle. I feast on victory in war. The blood of the fallen nourishes me like a mother's milk. It's been a long time since I've ripped an enemy's filthy head from his body and drank from his demise. I long to choke Baleros with his own entrails. I would like to ram his skull up his own arse, and feed from his humiliating subjugation."

My jaw dropped for a moment. So *this* was Ruadan's mum.

I scrubbed a hand over my mouth. "We will work on that. Maybe after a regular snack of cheese and crackers or something to take the edge off?"

Ruadan was pacing the room, arms folded. His shadows claimed the air around him, and the room felt as cold as it had in the tunnels. It seemed as if a reunion with his long-lost mother hadn't done much to calm his nerves. "Queen Macha, we need information about where to find Baleros. We have nothing to go on, and we're running out of time."

She sighed. "He kept me alone in a room by myself for fifteen years. Underwater. He came to see me only twice."

"And what can you tell us?" Ruadan prodded.

"He came once to tell me that he was going to kill you, and another time to try to mate with me. I divested him of his entrails, and he did not make that mistake a second time. Unfortunately, Emerazel, flaming gutter-bitch of the fire hell, revived him after I slaughtered him."

Ruadan's magic whipped the air around him. "I know you learned something from his visits."

"Yes. He smelled of yews."

Ruadan's head snapped up, as if this was meaningful. "Yews."

"The tree?" I asked. What in the world…?

It was at this point that I noticed Melusine had crossed into the room. She stumbled into the center of the hall, her blue hair tangled over her shoulders. She held up a hand, like she was in class waiting to be called on. "I know this one," she blurted. "Yews. The sacred tree of Arubian."

"Arubian," I repeated, adding nothing helpful whatsoever to the discussion.

Melusine raised her hand again. "Yeah, I can actually field this one, too. I've been doing my research on the fomoire. I hear the name Arubian, I know he's fomoire. Death fae. Fomoire feed off unpleasant things, right?"

A spark of understanding lit in my mind. "Unpleasant things like the spirits of the defeated?" I turned to the queen. "*You're* fomoire as well?"

A dark smile curled Queen Macha's lips. "You didn't realize that my son was fomoire?" Harsh laughter burst from her throat. "Silly cow."

My pulse sped up.

Darkness rushed from Ruadan's body, slamming across the room. Silence fell again as the shadows dissipated. "Baleros." His voice as cold as ice. "We need to know about Baleros. You think he's working with Arubian?"

We were here to talk about Baleros, but the question lingered in my mind—what did Ruadan feed from? Seemed like we were both keeping secrets.

Queen Macha tapped the throne with her long fingernails. "Arubian has a fortress in East London. It's glamoured. An old cemetery, an abandoned church. A bunch of filthy human hoboes sit outside the glamour. If you can find your way through the glamour, you can find the palace. Baleros has a tendency to feed fomoire with human sacrifices. The fomoire become dependent on him for supplies, then loyal to him. I suspect Arubian is one of his generals, yes."

"What else do we need to know about him?" I asked.

"Arubian hunts the night skies, feasting off dread," said Ruadan.

I shrugged. "I mean, he sounds fun, I guess. Sounds like your kind of people. Since you're all fomoire."

Ruadan cut me a sharp look.

Melusine raised her hand again. "I got this one, too. One, he's got a whole pack of dogs, takes 'em right through the night sky. Two, he hates fire. He sees flames, he gets scared. Three, you're gonna need a strong fire demon to get through his glamour. Burn a hole right in it with the flames of Emerazel. Problem is, you're all Shadow Fae. Fire's not really your thing. Am I right?"

Ciara. We needed Ciara for this. I raked a hand through my hair. "Okay. We have to access some fire magic."

It was nearly dawn, and I desperately wanted to go to sleep, but there wasn't enough time to take a break.

"We don't have time to find a fire demon," said Ruadan.

Queen Macha cocked her head. "What exactly is the rush? What aren't you telling me?"

"I'll get you up to speed," I said. "Baleros nailed a hand to the door with a note, and it said we have a day to deliver Ruadan to him, or he'll unleash a plague. To prove he's serious, he already unleashed a small one. He also killed Grand Master Savus and stole the mist army. Your son is the new Grand Master, minus an army. Baleros has acquired a whole bunch of human soldiers who think they're dead, and they have a terrible habit of blowing themselves up."

"He's been a very naughty boy," said the queen. "How did he unleash the Plague, exactly? I know of no creature who can do that except the Angel of Death. And Adonis is locked in another realm. Or did he escape?"

Ruadan stepped forward. "It's possible Adonis was able to get out of his locked world, or that he slipped through the portal after my attack. Both are my enemies, both on my kill list. They may have formed an alliance."

Darkness swarmed in my mind, and the scent of myrrh pooled around me. My father's scent.

Maybe I'd be seeing him soon.

CHAPTER 19

*N*o. It couldn't be happening—they couldn't be working together.

"We have no idea how Baleros plans to do it," I said a little too sharply. "Just that he does. It could be a magical spell for all we know. He used magic to create the jackdaws."

"The strategy is simple," said Queen Macha. "Baleros is a traitor to the Shadow Fae and an enemy of Emain. We must amass an army of all the world's Shadow Fae and surround Arubian's palace." Her cheeks reddened, eyes gleaming. "We crush our enemies. Drag Baleros out, bring him to me so I may tear out his spine and whip his arse with it. I will need to feast on his ignominious defeat!"

Her shouts rang off the stone walls. I wasn't entirely sure she was thinking clearly right now.

Ruadan shook his head. "That's not a good idea. Baleros has a lumen stone. If he sees us coming with an entire army behind us, he'll be gone within a heartbeat. We have to go in silently, move in the shadows."

"We don't even know that he's there for certain," said Aengus. "If we keep hidden, we might be able to find out more information."

Queen Macha's lips curled back from her teeth. "I. Am. Hungry."

This time, her voice came out like a low hiss. I had the distinct impression that she couldn't think clearly when she was hungry.

"Fire magic," I said again. "I know where we can get a demon."

Aengus glared at me. "How will we summon this demon?"

"Mobile phone. Get the portal ready, Ruadan. This is happening."

* * *

Aengus, Ruadan, and I stood under an oak tree, bodies dripping wet. I shuddered, hugging myself. I *really* wanted some fae technomancer to create a type of portal that did not involve icy water, so we could arrive somewhere dry for once. But that was a problem for another day—a day when we were not facing an apocalyptic event within the next sixteen hours.

A pale flash of movement caught my attention through the trees, a glimpse of ginger hair.

I smiled as Ciara crossed to us, her feet crunching over the leaves. I wrapped my arms around her, then she cast a wary look at the two other Shadow Fae.

"It's okay, Ciara," I said. "We're all allies here. No one is arresting anyone, anyway."

"Well, in that case, it's good to see you all. How's the palace? I've been living under a car. I'm not complaining, but I have been living literally underneath a car. Not even in it. I can't get the doors open, so I just crawl between the tires. This morning I had to fight a pigeon for a chicken bone. So that was my day. But I bet the palace is real nice. Real beds. Right? You all sleep in real beds? Do you have to fight diseased scavenger birds for your food, or can you just eat it right off the plate?"

"Is there a point to this?" asked Aengus. "I thought you said she was a fire demon."

"We'll get you some food when we're done with this," I promised. "Unlike Ruadan, Ciara feeds on actual food."

I didn't know why that had come out so angrily. What was I doing getting mad at Ruadan for keeping secrets? I had plenty of my own.

Ruadan kept his eyes on Ciara, ignoring me completely. "The Shadow Fae are promising you immunity from your transgressions if you will aid us in our mission."

She nodded. "Yeah, sure. But I hope you're serious about the food."

"And a bed," I offered.

"In a locked room," Ruadan added. "We can't have fire demons roaming around the Institute."

"Locked room is better than living under a car," she muttered. "What's the job?"

"We need to get through the glamour outside the palace," said Ruadan. "And we need your fire magic for that."

She scratched a freckled cheek. "I don't really have great control over it, per se."

"Look," said Aengus. "We know literally no other fire demons, or we would have asked them. You'll just have to do your best."

"To be honest, the only time I used it was when Baleros had captured me."

I thought I understood where she was going with this. "You thought you were about to die then, right?" Exactly how my death powers worked.

Her brow furrowed. "I did, yeah. Obviously we can't make that—"

"Ruadan can make it happen," I interrupted.

"If I know that he's faking it, I won't really believe I'm about to die."

"Trust me," I said. "He will dredge up your worst fears and just shove them down your throat until your mind is about to break. It's one of his favorite pastimes."

Did he feed off fear, like Arubian?

"When we get through the glamour," said Ruadan, "we will find ourselves in the grounds that surround Arubian's palace. I don't know what to expect, except that Baleros supplies him with humans to feed off. We may find Baleros within these grounds, or we can interrogate Arubian until he tells us more."

Aengus's green eyes pierced the dark. "Once we get through the glamour, we'll need to be discreet and blend in with whatever is going on around us."

"And while you're blending in," added Ruadan, "I'll dash around the palace, searching for Baleros."

Ciara crossed her arms, beaming. "If there is one thing I'm good at, it's being a normal human. I believed I was a normal human for years, didn't know any different till I blew up in the Tower. I spent years doing normal human things like drawing my friends on the wall and hosting pimento cheese parties."

The two Shadow Fae nodded, and I didn't alert them to the fact that even when Ciara had believed she was human, literally no one had thought she was normal. They had no idea.

"See?" I said. "She'll be fine. Totally normal human."

"Let's go." Ruadan took off into the forest. Since we were supposed to be discreet, we had no orb of silver light to lead our way here. In any case, dawn would be breaking soon.

"Why do you always carry that bag with you?" asked Aengus.

"Because, Aengus. For eight years, I had nothing, and now I carry my own sweets with me."

"Sweets," he snorted.

I pulled one of the straps off my shoulder and shoved my hand into the bag. I snatched a cherry lollipop and handed it to him. As we walked in the forest, he unwrapped it and frowned at it. It became clear to me that Aengus had never had a lollipop before.

"You lick it, Aengus."

He waggled an eyebrow at me like I'd said something completely obscene, which I suppose was understandable. Then, he stuck out his tongue and licked the lollipop. Quite frankly, it *did* look completely obscene the way he did it, and I suppressed a smile.

Ciara held out a hand, and I gave her a butterscotch lollipop.

Around us, thick tree roots covered the path, and dark shapes lined either side of our way. As the first ruddy rays of dawn began to brighten the sky, I started to make out the shapes more clearly. We were walking past old, Victorian graves—crooked statues, broken crosses lining our path. At one point, this must have been a stately cemetery, well-tended. But over the years, the trees and shrubs had started to break the stones apart, shift the bodies out of place. Time had run riot around here, the ground bulging and disturbing the dead.

The plants here looked unfamiliar—their stems thick and tough, spiked. I had the sense that they grew only over places of death—fomoire in their own way, feasting off misery.

We skirted the edge of a clearing, where a man sat smoking a pipe. The pink glow of dawn illuminated his scruffy face, and he was singing a Beyoncé song to himself. He didn't notice us at all.

Just on the other side of the clearing stood an abandoned church. When had it last been used? World War II, maybe? The windows had been smashed and boarded up, probably bombed in the war.

I was about to move on when Ruadan stopped, tracing his fingertips over the air. "We're here. The glamour."

My mother had been an expert in glamour, but that magical gene had passed me by. I couldn't even see it.

Ruadan turned, surveying the brightening forest around us.

"Anyone around?" I asked.

He narrowed his eyes. "Just the drunk human we passed. We're fine." He turned his attention to Ciara. "We'll need your fire to get through this."

She popped her lollipop out of her mouth. "You gonna hit me with your scare magic?"

Aengus and I took a few paces back—then a few more, to avoid the intensity of Ruadan's magic. I wanted to get hit with neither fire nor terror right now.

When I was about twenty feet away from them, darkness bloomed around Ruadan, the shadows tinged with faint glimmers of stars.

Ciara started to shake, her jaw dropping. She clamped a trembling hand over her mouth and screamed into it. Then, flames erupted from her body. Ruadan shifted away.

A burst of fire climbed twelve feet in the air, a wall of flames. The air hissed and sizzled. Through the inferno, a gap opened up in the glamour, large enough to drive a train through.

"Now!" said Ruadan. "Get through!"

Ciara was still screaming into her hand.

I ran toward the gap and pushed her in, wincing as her body seared my palms a little. We rushed through the opening into a vast, grassy field. A carpet of wood-sorrel and yellow archangels grew among the tall grasses.

And at the far end of the field loomed a palace of white stone.

CHAPTER 20

let out a long, slow breath. I'd never had any idea that this was here.

"Nice work, Ciara," I said. Then, I leaned in and whispered, "What did Ruadan make you see?"

She licked her lips. "Fox in a wedding dress, walking on her hind legs through the forest. Her true love left her at the altar, and she wanted revenge. She carried a bouquet of dried lilies."

I frowned, unsettled. "That's very ... specific."

"She wanted to carve my eyes straight out of my head with a whittling knife," she trilled, trying to sound cheerful. "Like my grandaddy did to that fox I caught in a trap. He wanted to teach me a lesson. Golly, have you ever heard a fox scream?"

"Let's not talk about this anymore." Inside Ciara's head was a very dark place, and I didn't want to spend much time in there.

Up ahead, a small crowd of people were stumbling over the grass under the rose and violet sky. I could hear their laughter from here.

Were they having *fun*? Considering Arubian fed off terror, I had expected to find horror here, not laughter.

They moved around each other, laughter growing louder. The only thing strange about them was an oddly lumbering gait, as if they had weights attached to their feet.

As we moved closer, I started to make out their clothing—tiny shorts, sparkly tops, flashes of rainbow, striped socks pulled up to their knees. It took me a little while to piece together what was going on here.

What in the world…?

Arms whirling, they moved over the grass, giggling.

Ruadan leaned down, whispering close to my ear. "Can you help me interpret this? I don't understand."

"Rollerskating," I whispered. "I think we may be going to a roller disco."

I bit my lip, imagining Ruadan in a pair of tiny striped shorts and rollerskates. I tried so hard to suppress the laughter that I snorted.

He shot me a sharp look. "What's wrong with you?"

I shook my head. "I'm just really looking forward to this blending in part. But we're going to need to steal their clothes, so can you put them to sleep?"

No sooner were the words out of my mouth than violet-tinged magic spiraled out of Ruadan's chest. It snaked over the grass and swept around the humans. Instantly, his sleep magic began to take effect. Their arms windmilled around for a few moments until they toppled over into the grass.

When we reached them, I surveyed their prone bodies and their tight roller disco clothes. I looked up at Ruadan and Aengus. "I don't think any of this will fit you two."

"These clothes are ridiculous," muttered Ruadan.

I started stripping the shorts off one of the girls. I did my best to shield my body and hers as I traded my drenched black dress for her sparkly halter top and shorts. Then, I slid out of my shoes and pulled on her rollerskates. I was vaguely aware of Ruadan rifling through my bug-out bag, but I kept my attention focused on trying to keep my nipples hidden while I slipped into the halter top.

When I looked up again, Ciara had dressed herself in a red bikini top and glittery blue shorts, along with a pair of rollerskates. Already, she looked like a proper expert, shaking her hips to a distant beat as she rolled over the grass.

Ruadan and Aengus had simply ripped the wheel sets off two pairs of skates, and secured them to their shoes with the duct tape from my bag.

I frowned at them. They were still dressed like fae. We needed a hipster rollerskating look here.

I pulled an elastic band off my wrist, then crossed to Ruadan. "Lean down."

"What?"

"Just do it, Ruadan. Trust me."

He leaned down a bit, as if bowing, and I gathered his soft blond hair up into a messy man bun. I took a step back to survey it. That was all it took to make him look like a hipster.

"Good," I said. "Perfect."

He growled low. He wasn't sure what I'd done to him or why, but he didn't like it.

I opened up my bug-out bag for a quick review of my weapons before we went into battle. A few daggers, aerosolized deodorant, and a lighter.

When I looked up again, I found Ciara hacking away at Aengus's trousers to create a pair of short shorts. He glowered at her as she worked.

I took a deep breath, my pulse already racing in anticipation of our encounter with Arubian. I had to come to this thing sword-free. That was the problem with covert missions—you could never bring your favorite weapons, and you had to rely on a backpack full of knives and deodorant.

"Let's go," said Ruadan.

I rolled over the grass, using my arms to steady myself a bit. It took me a few minutes before I was moving smoothly, and then I started to get into it. I could have used these things in the gladiator ring.

Charcoal-grey clouds began gathering on the horizon, blotting out the rising sun. They seemed to be moving unnaturally fast, roiling and writhing like a living thing.

I glanced over at Ruadan, who was already ripping the wheels off the bottom of his shoes. I should've known that wouldn't last long.

"What about your disguise?" I asked.

"I'm the Wraith," he said. "I don't need a disguise. No one can see me, and I'll be mostly sneaking around the palace unseen."

Fair enough.

Aengus looked furious, stumbling over the grass in his rollerskates and tiny shorts. Ciara had also forced his enormous chest into a rainbow halter top.

A flash of white lightning cracked the darkening sky, followed by a boom of thunder. The air felt charged, heavy.

As we moved closer to the palace, another flash speared the sky—horizontal this time, slashing the dark clouds open with its light.

"Heat lightning," said Ciara.

I frowned. "It's not even that hot."

I rolled over the bumpy terrain, and pale flashes of light streaked faster across the sky. The hair on my nape stood on end.

By the time we reached the palace itself, the lightning had picked up pace, pulsing in the clouds as fast as a heartbeat, fast as neuronal connections. The palace itself looked completely undefended—no moat, no gate, just a gaping open archway that led into a courtyard. Through the archway, I could hear the deep, throbbing bass of a disco song. The sound of the Bee Gees seemed an odd contrast to the grotesque, humanoid gargoyles looming over the archway. They jutted from the ancient palace walls. Men with gaping leers, grinning as they pulled open their mouths or ripped out their own hearts.

"Ummm..." said Ciara. "I'm not really sure what's going on here."

"Neither am I," I said. "That's why we're in disguise. We blend in, make ourselves look like weak humans until we can figure out ... what the hells is happening."

Warm candlelight flickered in some of the palace windows. Was Baleros in one of those rooms? I was tempted to rush into the palace and tear the place apart until we found him, but like Ruadan had said, he could never see us coming. We had to know exactly where he was before we attacked.

Just before we crossed under the arch, the sound of baying hounds turned my head. I held my breath. Above us, a glowing figure streaked beneath the clouds, lightning flashing around him. He wore a dark cloak, and his eyes burned orange, like Mars—so bright I could see them even from here. Enormous, white phantom hounds pounded the sky, pulling his chariot and leaving streaks of pearly white in their wake.

I exhaled slowly. This fomoire was definitely not an ordinary fae.

"Is that Arubian?" I whispered.

"That's him," said Ruadan.

His path began to arc above the palace, a wide, graceful swoop.

"You three blend in," said Ruadan. "I'm going to search the palace. Don't do anything until I come back." Ruadan's enormous form grew indistinct, dark mist whirling around him.

My muscles tensed completely as we moved toward the courtyard. Arubian had covered the entire courtyard with a hardwood floor, and lights flashed over the rink. Partygoers skated around, laughing with each other. The Bee Gees song "Massachusetts" blared over a speaker, echoing off the palace's stone walls. On the outskirts of the parquet floor, lanterns jutted from the earth, at least six feet high, flashing with pink, green, blue....

I glanced at the palace walls, which formed a square around the rink. Was Baleros in one of those wings?

A blond woman with pigtails glided over the floor, ducking down low and sticking out a leg in a move I thought might be called "shoot the duck."

We rolled onto the disco floor—all of us except Ruadan, who I could no longer see.

The partygoers were singing along to the Bee Gees, something about the lights going out in Massachusetts. I thought Arubian fed off dread? Where was the dread? These people were having fun.

Aengus rolled headfirst into the crowd, having absolutely no control over the skates. He plowed into a group of laughing women, who helped him up, shrieking with delight. One of them grabbed him by the arms and swung him around in a circle, arm over arm. She was laughing uproariously, while he had a look of terror on his face. The Bee Gees warbled on.

Ciara grabbed my arm, and we took off over the floor. I had the sense that she'd spent her American youth on a pair of skates, because she was soon slipping away from me to roll backward like an expert, singing along to the disco, arms outstretched.

Bits of hail began raining down, catching in the colored lights of the rink like disco sequins falling from the sky. It was summer. Why was it hailing? I didn't care, because it was beautiful. I had a strange, giddy feeling, and I wanted to stay here all night, laughing with my new friends.

I tried a turn, skating backwards to the sounds of falsetto singing.

But when Arubian cut over the cloudy sky again—a ghostly flash of white—my nerves juddered. What exactly did he do with these people?

But the music seemed to mesmerize me, and I quickly forgot about him again. I tried a twirl on my skates, gripping onto the straps of my backpack.

Another flash of white—swooping closer this time—and my throat tightened. The melodious singing of the Bee Gees floated over the crowd, and Arubian's hounds began to descend. None of the humans seemed to notice the mood shifting, the air thinning. They didn't seem to notice the music changing and growing more dissonant.

It was only at that point that I noticed the streaks of red on the parquet floor—smears of blood among the melting hail. A severed finger. My stomach flipped.

Still, around me, the skaters danced on, smiling. I rolled closer to Ciara, then grabbed her arm.

"Ciara," I whispered. "Get ready for some disturbing shit."

"What do we do?" she asked.

"Nothing until Ruadan gets back. We stay alive, and that's about it."

A man with a potbelly and a yellow T-shirt skated past us. He twirled before us, smiling at his own prowess, then he looked me up and down. He grabbed his crotch, expertly skating backward. "Can I show you a little skating move I like to call the slap and tickle?"

I blocked him out completely, eyes flicking to the skies again as I caught a glimpse of Arubian charging for him. The Bee Gees sounded darker now, and my pulse began to race faster. The hounds were heading for the creepy man who'd just been leering at us, and he didn't seem to notice.

I grabbed Ciara's arm, and we skated away from him, blending into the crowd. I stole a quick look back at the man.

My jaw dropped as one of the hounds tore into his leg, and his heavy body slammed onto the parquet floor.

Now, a few people in the crowd began shrieking, finally noticing that something was amiss.

I gritted my teeth, willing myself not to jump into the fray. I was here to gain information about Baleros, and I wouldn't get anything if I tried to save every random, dickhead human.

The hounds backed away from the man, but they growled at him as he tried to stand.

Arubian swooped lower, and I caught a glimpse of his face—his skin the color of bone, features a beautiful mask of death.

CHAPTER 21

The crowd's screams trembled over my skin, and I mingled among the humans, watching from a distance as Arubian touched down on the parquet floor. A dark grin twisted his features, and he reached out a long, bony hand toward the man. The man's screams ripped through the air, and he scrambled up to his skates. With his damaged leg, he was off balance, now, and he kept stumbling as he tried to roll away. He left a shiny trail of blood behind him.

Arubian flicked his wrist, and one of the hounds snarled, lunging for the human again. The dog ripped at the man's arm, tearing into his flesh. The human went down hard.

Then, the hound transformed into a lean but muscled two-legged form—with pointed dog ears and sharp canines. As long claws grew from his fingertips, the shifter stalked his prey. The man was crawling backward like a crab.

Arubian glowed with silver light, his face a picture of ecstasy. Here was a fomoire, feeding in his natural habitat. It was repulsive, frankly.

The hound shifter lunged, striking his claws across the man's belly, opening him up. Bile rose in my throat, and I turned away from the sound of the screaming.

I'd seen my fair share of carnage in my days—hells, I'd delivered my fair share of carnage. But this seemed particularly cruel and drawn out. I'd hacked through necks, stopped hearts. I'd poisoned people with my mind. So why did I feel a sense of superiority? I guess my kills were fast, and I never relished my enemies' torment, never drew out their pain or their horror just for the fun of it. I was practical—Arubian was a sadist.

Was Ruadan? What the hells did he get up to in his free time? Did he have an underground nightclub somewhere, complete with a disco ball, where he tortured people to death on Saturday nights?

Despite the horror on the parquet floor, no one was leaving the roller disco. Another fae trick—trapping the victims in the rink just by screwing with their minds.

The white hounds circled the roller parquet floor, teeth bared. Were the Bee Gees still playing? Gods help us all, this was disturbing.

I rolled on, pretending like I had no idea what was happening.

I cast a quick glance back to Arubian, who now stood hunched over the dying man, lovingly stroking a bony fingertip over the human's lips like a mother hushing a baby. There was hardly anything left of the poor guy, and yet no one was delivering a mercy stroke. Blood pooled below him on the shiny floor.

I couldn't say I was learning much here. Had Ruadan found anything? Because we were running out of time, and I wasn't getting us any closer to Baleros.

As if hearing my thoughts, a dark form flickered by my side, and Ruadan's piney scent curled around me.

His breath warmed my ear. "Baleros isn't here. We need to interrogate the fomoire. Take out the dogs first. Then we go for Arubian."

I nodded, slipping my backpack off my shoulders. Good. I got to kill again.

Arubian was lost in his dark ecstasy, his body glowing. He didn't notice when I reached into my backpack, grabbing onto a sheathed knife. He didn't notice when I pulled out my tool belt and wrapped it around my waist, or when I shoved the dagger in it. I pulled out a lighter and a can of deodorant, slipping them into my belt, too.

I scanned the crowd, watching as they tried to scatter. Half the skaters were crying, terrified, and the other half were still laughing and oblivious.

The rest of the hounds began transforming, bodies elongating until they were shaped like men—only with snouts and long ears.

After what I'd just seen, I was hungry for their blood, and a smile already curled my own lips. *You like hunting the weak, don't you? You like to torment those who can't fight back. Let's see how you like messing with me.*

I didn't have to choose which shifter to go for, because one of them already had his sights set on me. Smiling, I skated away from him, luring him closer and swaying my hips. I moved fluidly over the floor, weaving between the crowd. This was a strange sort of seduction, one that would end in his death.

He prowled closer, then shifted back into his hound form to run, lighting-fast. As he leapt for me, I pulled out the lighter and can of deodorant. I flicked the lighter, sprayed the can, and flames burst into the air.

He yelped, jumping back, and burst back into his humanoid form. On the floor, he snarled, holding his face. I circled him on my skates, reaching for my dagger.

I hadn't quite pulled it out when his claws raked through my chest. Pain pierced me.

Fucker was *fast,* and he had much longer arms. I'd have to keep blasting him with fire. Gritting my teeth, I unleashed another burst of flame, igniting his white hair. While he was busy covering his skull, I lunged in with my iron dagger. I plunged it between two of his ribs, then pulled it out again to thrust it up his rib cage, tilting it toward his heart.

He slumped to the ground, dead.

And *that's* how you kill someone, civilized-like. No need to draw it out.

Already, another shifter was charging for me in his hound form. I gripped the blood-soaked knife and tossed it at the oncoming hound.

Unfortunately, he managed to shift just a bit at the last moment, and the dagger caught him in the shoulder instead of in his chest. I hadn't even slowed him down.

Shit.

I needed a *sword,* godsdamn it. I gripped the deodorant and blasted him with fire, but he wasn't dumb enough to come close when I had my makeshift flamethrower. It wouldn't kill him.

Baleros's fifteenth law of power: Always use your surroundings.

My gaze darted to the colorful lanterns that lined the rink, and I sped over to one of them. I gripped it with both hands, ripping it from the ground.

I grinned at the sight of its pointed tip, but my joy was short-lived. Powerful, white arms gripped me from behind, knocking me off balance, claws digging into the bare skin at my sides. I slammed onto my back, just barely managing to hang onto my makeshift weapon.

Two on one—they didn't care for fair fights.

How many people had they tortured to death? How many women —just like me, only weaker? The hound shifters liked to dominate.

From the ground, I gripped the metal lantern stake and swung for the legs of the closest shifter. I took him down, then leapt up to my skates—nearly falling off balance, as I'd forgotten about the wheels. I whirled, slamming the stake into the next shifter's head. He faltered, but the shifters were strong, and I didn't take him down. Clutching my new weapon, I began skating away until I could even out my odds a little bit. Just out of range, I turned and hurled the stake like a spear. It slammed into one of the shifters, and he fell back hard to the ground.

My gaze flicked to Aengus, who was fighting with his dagger. He'd ripped the wheels off his shoes, and he pivoted to drive his blade into one of the shifters.

I didn't even know where the hells Ruadan was, but the trail of shifter corpses told me he was racking up a body count somewhere around here.

I snatched another lantern from the earth, and when one of the shifters came for me, I snarled and drove the tip into his heart before he could even reach me.

The hounds were closing in—some shaped like men, some like

animals. Their snarls echoed all around me, and I turned in a circle to find that I'd been surrounded.

I am the twilight shadow that creeps over long grasses....

My death instinct began whispering through me, shoulder blades tingling.

I am the hunter who creeps up behind you.

One of the shifters lunged from behind, knocking me to the ground, face-down. Climbing all over me like I was the damn spoils of war, his teeth pierced the flesh at my throat. Pain screamed through my body. He was pawing at me, scoring my skin with his claws, and rage began to rise.

I'm not your prize. I will steal your food and your breath.

From the ground, I brought up my elbow hard into his ribs, cracking them so hard I must have broken them. Another slam from my elbow and he started to slide off me. When I stood again, I was gripping hard to the lantern. The shifters started to move in on me, eyes glowing.

I'm your last rasping breath.

I swung the lantern, carving its pointed tip through lungs, hearts, bellies—my body moving so fast my mind could hardly keep up. It wasn't me anymore; it was the dark angel. The euphoria of battle ignited me, and I felt my shoulder blades tingle.

I'm the darkness swaying beneath your feet.

CHAPTER 22

The pointed tip of the lantern found its way into a shifter's white neck, dark metal piercing ivory. With a roar, I ripped it free again, ready to take on the next shifter, my body buzzing. But when I scanned my surroundings, I found that the shifters were all dead.

I took in the rink. Arubian stood in the center of the floor, watching me. Ciara was hiding somewhere, I thought. Aengus was fighting off two hounds. By the archway, a shadow appeared to rip a shifter's heart out of his chest. That would be Ruadan.

I looked down at myself, and some of the death instinct slipped away from my body. Dark blood soaked my glittery disco clothes and my skates.

I was calming myself, now, but I felt rattled by the sense that my death instinct was growing stronger, desperate to break free. Maybe that's what happened when you spent too much energy trying to suppress something. Whatever you were trying to keep down would just ram you hard in the ribs until it got control again.

Shit.

Now, the humans were skating around the wounded bodies, some slipping on the blood. Most of them were crying, heaving for breath. And yet, it still seemed that they couldn't bring themselves to leave.

Arubian's eyes were locked on me and me alone.

I waited until I caught a glimpse of Ciara, red hair streaming behind her, before moving toward Arubian. As a fire demon, Ciara was supposed to be our real muscle here.

I gripped the lantern as I began to skate over to him, while Aengus and Ruadan moved behind him.

"You killed my hounds," he said quietly. Up close, I could smell the scent of yews.

Out of the shadows, Ruadan appeared, his violet eyes blazing. "Baleros. Where is he?"

Arubian pulled down his cowl to reveal dark hair slicked back on his head. His expression was much more amused than I'd expect from a man who'd just watched his henchmen massacred in his home.

"We're looking for Baleros," Aengus added. "Has he been feeding you these humans?"

"Where is he?" Ruadan asked, the air around him chilling.

"Ah. Baleros." Arubian was positively glowing with pearly light, beautiful as the moon itself.

Turning, he surveyed his domain. A few hunched servants had rushed out to mop up the gore with an efficiency that suggested they did this all the time. Arubian gestured at the remaining skaters, who were now clinging to each other, rolling past the carnage. "It's true, Baleros brings me these wonderful presents. These humans who keep me company, who stop me from starving."

Ciara stepped forward, holding up her hands to the sky. "I am a fire demon," she declared.

"Congratulations." Arubian didn't look particularly impressed, so the information about his fire fears might have been a bit misleading. He pulled a packet of cigarettes from his cloak and tapped them in his palm a few times. Then, he slid one from the pack, holding it out to Ciara. "Care to light this for me?"

She wrinkled her nose. "I don't really do that kind of thing."

This conversation had taken an unexpected turn, and I wasn't entirely clear how to get control again or how to instill the sort of terror we needed. Sighing, I pulled out a lighter from my tool belt, then lit his cigarette. Even the smoke smelled of yews.

As I tried to think of what to say, Ruadan disappeared into the shadows again.

Might as well get to the point. "Look, Arubian, can you tell us where to find him, or do we have to torture you with fire and lanterns? Those are your options."

"Not a giant fan of torture." Arubian shrugged. "And I *am* on a bit of a high from all the death." He blew a smoke ring into the air. "Fine, you didn't hear it from me, but I've heard a rumor that he's taken up residence in the old home built for Nan and Burly Hal. You know, before the awkward breakup."

"Who the fuck are Nan and Burly Hal?" I asked in my usual diplomatic tone.

Arubian's orange eyes burned into me, and they reminded me of dying stars. Why was he staring at me so intently? I wasn't the interesting one here. Ruadan was the half-fomoire demigod.

"Baleros has given me soldiers. Did you know that?" The red tip of Arubian's cigarette danced in the gloomy light as he gesticulated. "I can't say they've come in useful. They have been busy, after all, framing the Shadow Fae for their attacks. And they're protecting him in his palace. You'll never get past his army. You won't get within ten feet of him before they close in on you and blow you to pieces with iron shrapnel." He blew another smoke ring into the air. "I might see if I can turn up to watch the show. Sometimes, I can feed off fae." Arubian shrugged. "I know fear. Know it as intimately as I do my own hands."

Of course the weirdo was intimate with his hands.

I took a step closer, waving the lantern. "Who are Burly Nan and whatever?"

A thin shrug from Arubian. "It doesn't matter if I tell you. You won't be in this world much longer, you know. Baleros gets more control every day. Fear is the easiest way to control humans. You were once their protectors. Not anymore. How quickly they're turning on you. Maybe you're immortals, but how long do you think you'll stay in your comfortable palace when the savage mob of millions turn on you? You'll be forced to wander the earth, tortured outcasts. I'll help them make the guillotines myself."

"Ciara, get your fire ready," I said. "Did you know it took humans an average of forty-five minutes to burn to death on medieval pyres? Our librarian told me that. Wonder what it takes for a fae."

For just a second, I saw fear flash in Arubian's eyes. So it *had* been good information.

Arubian's hand started shaking. "I see the hounds got you with their claws." He cocked his head. "You know, I could see death whispering around you when you fought," he said. "I'm very in tune with death."

Shit. I needed to shut him up.

And that's when Ruadan decided to reappear, solid as a brick building, right by my side. *Now* this conversation had his full interest.

I furrowed my brow, doing my best "get a load of this weirdo" face. "I have no idea what you're talking about," I said. "Death whispering around me? Sounds like some bad poetry."

He shook his head, eyes burning. "No. Not poetry. I feed off death fears. You instill them. I feel positively radiant around you."

My pulse started racing.

Ruadan took a step closer to him. "What are you talking about?"

"Surely you must see it," said Arubian. "She's not a normal fae."

"Is that all you have to tell me?" Ruadan's eyes slid to me. "She's not a normal fae. Anyone who meets … whatever her name is … can tell that right away."

So that's how it was. We'd gone from our romantic moment in the sewers to *whatever her name is.*

Arubian's smile was pure poison. "You want to know what she is, don't you? You want to know if you can trust her. Has her pretty body been confusing you, distracting you from the truth?"

"This is…" I sputtered, trying to block out the pain from my deep wounds so I could think clearly. "This is stupid. Honestly, are you going to listen to a man who spends his free time massacring people in his own personal roller disco? He's weird as shit." Every one of my muscles had tensed, my nerve endings igniting with a fight-or-flight instinct.

This is it. This is when they learn the truth.

$\mathcal{A}$rubian's orange eyes were on me. "You can't be more than a few decades old, but you instill death like an ancient being. If it hadn't been so delicious to feed from the fear you created in my hounds, I might be in a very bad mood indeed. As it is, I feel glorious. Perhaps we should spend more time together. We're alike, you and I."

"Fuck off." Why was it that the creepiest people kept telling me we were alike, like I was a long-lost sister to all the earth's monsters? I was going to develop a complex about it. "Who are Nan and Hal? Where's their gaff?"

Arubian cocked his head, his interest intense. A smile cracked his pale features. "Ahhh…. Can it really be?" He tapped his fingertips together, his features delighted. "Did *he* have a girl? I didn't know it was possible, and yet I see the evidence before me."

He *knew*. I had to stop him.

"Where is the house?" I demanded, my voice rising as I lost control. I tightened my grip on the lantern, panic cutting through my chest.

He pointed a long, bony finger at me. "Ruadan, I can tell you exactly who this one is. She's—"

The lantern was out of my hand before he could get another word out, the tip piercing his throat, ripping it open. Arubian fell back, his body slamming hard on the parquet floor. The pole had impaled his neck, ripping his vocal cords apart. As an ancient fae, the steel wouldn't kill him, but I'd managed to silence him for now.

A cold sweat rose on my skin, my heart hammering. We hadn't finished interrogating Arubian, and I'd completely screwed up the mission. Still, it wasn't like I'd had a choice. Arubian had nearly told the truth about me.

I stared at his body. Shock held me still for a moment as I tried to process what had just happened. The jagged wounds all around my torso ached, and I gripped my bleeding side. My heart was pumping hard, and blood poured from my neck, my sides—the claw and teeth marks all over my body. The damned shifters had shredded me to ribbons. With the pain and the shock roiling in my mind, it took me a moment to realize that Aengus was yelling at me.

"What the hells was that?" he was shouting. "We still don't know where Baleros is. You killed our only source of information before we'd got any real answers—all so you could hide the truth from us."

Nausea curdled my gut. The silence that fell was cold and damp as wet soil. I racked my mind to think of an explanation.

This did not look good for me. It was clear, now, that I had a secret I'd be willing to do almost anything to keep, and that didn't exactly mark me as trustworthy. Ruadan's eyes had shifted to black, and he was looking at me like I was his enemy.

Blocking out the pain from my wounds, I folded my arms, my gaze darting between the two Knights of the Shadow Fae. "Arubian was wasting our time. He told us where to find Baleros. Nan and Burly Hal's place. We need to go now. Can you please open the portal?"

Aengus took a step closer, fury etched in his features. "Who the fuck are Nan and Burly Hal? Do you happen to know?"

"I thought you'd know." It sounded lame, even to me. I shot Ciara a pointed look, one that I hoped conveyed *help me here.*

"Yeah. Nan and Burly Hal," she added. "I've heard of them. Hackney, maybe? Or Islington by the tube station, near that kebab place?" She was terrible at bluffing.

Aengus growled, canines flashing. "This was all for nothing. All we've learned is that we're working with someone we can't trust at all. No—scratch that. We already knew that, considering you stabbed our Grand Master and left him to bleed. All you've done is confirm that you can't be trusted. Can we get rid of her now?"

My chest clenched. Our fragile alliance was falling apart fast.

Ruadan had gone so still, so quiet, it sent a cold thread of fear wending through my body. I could hardly see him, now, his body blending into the night. When I'd first met him, he'd seemed so ephemeral—a fleeting night wind, whispering over my skin. Then, I'd come to know him well enough that his violet eyes stood out like a neon sign to me, even when he was in his Wraith mode. But right now, he seemed to be slipping away from me, shadows blending into darkness. I couldn't see him anymore, couldn't grasp him. It seemed like there was something intentional about it.

The thought of losing him so fast opened a hollow pit in my chest.

I didn't even see Ruadan as he moved for me, had no idea where he was until I felt his finger on my arm, his touch feather-light. He leaned down to whisper in my ear so that only I could hear him. "This looks bad. And I don't know why, but I trust you implicitly and completely."

His words warmed me from the inside out. I wanted to throw my arms around him, but I knew it would look bad in front of Aengus. In fact, if Aengus saw us embracing, he'd assume Ruadan's mind was clouded by lust.

Was it?

Guilt twisted through me. I was hiding something important from Ruadan, and it should be obvious to him, now. I'd ruined the mission just to keep my secret.

"Of course you can trust me." The words tasted bitter in my mouth.

"What the hells is going on? Is she working with Baleros?" barked Aengus.

"Gods below, Aengus," I protested. "You have to know that I want him dead. I want him dead, and I want us to stay alive. That's what matters, isn't it?" This, at least, was the truth.

"She's telling the truth." Ruadan's tone brooked no argument. "I know she is."

At that moment, mist began pooling around us, and a shiver rippled up my spine. It whirled in unnatural eddies.

"Looks like Arubian's mist soldiers are finally arriving. We're out of time here."

Without another word, Ruadan turned and walked away. A sharp tendril of pain wound through me as he did. He trusted me for now, but he'd learn the truth at some point. And when he did, the trust would dissolve. We'd be enemies.

As he started speaking in Angelic, the parquet floor began rumbling.

All around us, the mist army materialized, fog twisting around their weapons. Then, from the shadows, the jackdaws began moving, running for us.

"We need to go *now*," I said.

Cracks began to widen in the ground, sparkly water gleaming in the chasms.

My heart skipped a beat at the sight of a jackdaw running for us at full speed. My jaw dropped at the sight of the bomb strapped to his waist.

"Jump!" I yelled. "Now!"

Ciara jumped in, then Aengus.

The blast went off, searing the skin on my right side just as Ruadan was pulling me in. The icy water soothed my burnt skin. As soon as we drifted deeper, Ruadan let go of my wrist.

I sank into the dark water. I hadn't felt this alone since Baleros had first thrown me in an empty, underground cage.

* * *

THE MISSION HAD BEEN a complete disaster, one that made me look as if I were working against the Institute. Why would Ruadan still trust me at this point?

Lungs burning, body burned and ripped, I climbed out of the

portal. I was surprised to find that Ruadan had opened the portal into his own bedroom.

As I climbed out onto his flagstone floor, blood poured off my body. I flopped onto my back next to the portal, gasping for breath, wincing at my injuries. My mind whirled, the floor seeming to tilt beneath my back. I was in rough shape here.

From the floor, I heard Ruadan issue an order—Aengus was supposed to get Ciara settled in somewhere, an upgrade from her home under a car.

I gritted my teeth, closing my eyes. Did I even have any skin left on the right side of my body?

Gentle hands pulled my backpack from me, slipping off the straps of my bug-out bag. A powerful pair of arms scooped me up, and I opened my eyes to look up at Ruadan.

"Sorry," I said.

"For lying?"

My throat tightened. "Sorry for killing Arubian prematurely."

He lay me down on the bed, and I grimaced.

"My skin hurts."

"Shhhh."

My eyes closed again, and I felt Ruadan's magic skimming over me, his fingertips tracing lightly around the ragged neck wound before moving down toward my side. Sleep was threatening to overwhelm me, but I fought to stay awake.

"You haven't told me everything, either," I said defensively. "You didn't tell me you were fomoire."

"Shhhh. Rest."

"You haven't told me what you feed off of."

His magic wrapped around me like a caress. "We only have fifteen hours," he said. "We'll address our precise natures after we kill Baleros."

He was right, of course, but I could tell that the distance between us bothered him as much as it bothered me. He wasn't meeting my eyes as he worked. I reached up and touched his cheek, and for just a moment, his gaze slid to me. I'd never seen him look so vulnerable before. Then, the spell was broken, and he ripped his attention away, concentrating completely on the claw marks on my side and the burns.

His magic was like a divine silk over my body. Still, I couldn't quite relax.

You and I are the same.

Blood still covered my skin, and my little roller disco clothes were sticking to me. I wanted those clothes off me before I fell asleep.

I forced my eyes open and pushed myself up onto my elbows. "I'm not going to sleep covered in blood," I muttered.

"You need rest."

I wasn't a monster. I didn't want to look like one. "I'll just be a minute. Don't go anywhere."

Half asleep, I stumbled to my feet and began peeling off my bloodied clothes, discarding them on Ruadan's bare floor. I crossed into the bathroom, where his bath of hot, bubbling spring water called to me. I slipped into it, my mind racing with images: death spreading out from my body like a miasma; Ruadan as a boy, threading a wreath of wildflowers for a mum who wouldn't wear them. After a minute, I stepped out of the tub and toweled off.

Wearing only a towel, I crossed back into his room.

I found the room empty, and my heart clenched. I couldn't explain it, but closeness to him was starting to feel like some basic, primal drive, as instinctive as the need to eat or sleep. I had a brief, overwhelming urge to run naked through the halls until I could find him and drag him back here and wrap my naked body around his, to force his lips to mine.

Tears stung my eyes. I'd let these fantasies trail on far enough. We could never be together, and there was no point obsessing over it. Morning sunlight streamed in through the window.

The survival instinct in me told me what I needed now more than anything else: sleep.

I crawled into Ruadan's bed and pulled the covers up around me, slipping fast into a dreamless sleep.

I awoke to the tawny evening sun.

I had the strangest feeling that a boom had sounded, but I couldn't tell if it had been in my dream or real life. In fact, considering I'd been healed and rested, I felt oddly delirious. I blinked, trying to clear my mind, but the edges of everything around me seemed hazy.

"Ruadan," I whispered.

It took me a moment to realize the bed was empty. Where had Ruadan gone? And why was the world tilting back and forth like I was on a boat?

My mouth felt like cotton, and I licked my lips, trying to get up to speed mentally.

Let's see … roller disco, hounds…. Oh, and we had a time limit before Baleros unleashed the Black Death and told everyone I was Adonis's daughter. And I'd just spent many hours sleeping. Why hadn't anyone woken me? And what the hells was wrong with my head?

I rolled to my side. Plaster and stone dust covered the sheets. What the hells?

BOOM. The walls shook, and more dust rained down on top of me, the bed trembling.

What in the world was going on?

I sat bolt upright. When the sheets fell off me, I realized I was still naked. My clothes from yesterday still lay on the floor—shredded, wet, and blood-soaked. Every other time I'd woken in the Institute, I'd found fresh clothes left by someone or other, and the room tidied.

Dizzy, I rose and crossed to Ruadan's dresser. Off-balance, I stumbled, then rested for a moment on the wood. I pulled on my underwear and boots, but the rest of my clothes had been shredded the night before.

I pulled a drawer open, then picked out one of Ruadan's shirts—a black one with buttons. I pulled it on, and the hem reached halfway down my thighs.

What time was it? Surely, we only had a few hours left. I should never have slept so long. What was I doing? Confusion clouded my mind.

BOOM!

My heart shuddered. Were we under attack? Off-balance, I crossed to the windows. I touched the glass, staring outside. From here, I had a view of the courtyard and the inner ring of connected towers. Somewhere beyond the outer wall, dark smoke curled into the air. I sniffed—gasoline and a strong chemical scent floated on the wind, along with burning wood and stone. Jackdaws bombing us again?

My limbs were too heavy. I looked down at my wrists. For just a moment, I caught the faint shimmer of magic pulsing through my veins. Something was happening to me.

Frantically, I snatched my bug-out bag off the floor. It had almost dried after the last trip through the portal. As I stumbled, I shoved my hand into the bag, picking out a soggy Galaxy chocolate bar. My stomach rumbled, and I tore it open as I walked, gnawing into it.

I pushed through the door into the courtyard, squinting at the blazing afternoon light. The sun dazzled me, and I shielded my eyes with my arm.

BOOM.

Instinctively, I ducked, covering my head as the earth shook. From inside the fortress walls, I still couldn't see a damn thing—just the smoke rising above the towers.

Then, I forced myself up, holding out my arms to steady myself. I broke into a jog, rushing into the Cailleach Tower.

As I moved, voices whispered around me. The colors seemed too bright today—garish, almost.

In the Tower, I gripped the banister hard to get myself up the stairs.

At last, I reached the throne room.

Melusine was on the floor, hunched over a book, with a tall stack of volumes by her side. Aengus sat slumped against one of the columns. He looked dazed, his jaw slack. His mouth opened and closed mutely. What was he doing just sitting there?

"What's happening?" I swayed on my feet. "I don't feel right. And you don't look right."

Aengus stared at the ground. "Poi—poi ... porcu-pie."

"Poison," said Melusine. "We think. I'm amazed you're up at all. Aengus isn't doing so well."

"Poison from what?" Was it connected to the bombs blowing up our Tower?

"I've been working on it for hours," said Melusine from the floor. "Aengus and Ruadan have both been delirious all day, though Aengus took a sharp turn for the worse about an hour ago."

"And you're fine?" I slurred.

She nodded. "We think it came from Arubian's palace. At least, that's what I think. Ruadan and Aengus aren't doing much thinking at all."

I glanced at Aengus again. For just a moment, a vicious look in his eyes sent ice through my blood, and his face seemed to transform, dark veins streaking his skin. Then, his jaw went slack again, eyes unfocused. My blood surged.

Was I hallucinating?

Focus. "Where is everyone?"

"All the other knights are still out searching for Baleros. Searching for something to do with Nan and Hal. Quite frankly, we don't really know what we're doing right now."

"Don't trust," said Aengus. "Don't trust Arianna. Parry … honor…."

My lip curled, fingers tightening into fists. *I come from the Horseman of Death, and I will end you.* Aengus was making me angry, using what seemed to be the last of his dwindling brain power to cast doubt on me. I wanted to shut him up.

Aengus managed to point at me. "Who … are your parents?"

The death instinct swooped through my skull, threatening to erupt. Phantom wings tingled on my shoulder blades. *It's time to let you know the truth about myself.* I lunged for Aengus, then slammed my fist hard into his jaw.

I reared back my hand to hit him again, but a piercing scream stopped me.

I whirled to find Melusine staring at us, gripping the book. "Stop! Both of you!" she shouted. "Look, I see two people under the effects of the poison getting angry, I think maybe the poison is at fault. That's just me."

I unclenched my fist, still staring at Aengus. Guilt flooded me. The guy was near death, and I'd just bashed him in the skull.

"Sorry," I muttered. "I'm not thinking. I'm sorry. Sorry. Sorry." I couldn't stop saying the word.

"Shhhh," said Melusine. "Just stay away from him. You two both need to keep a distance."

Melusine was talking sense, as usual.

"Right," I conceded. "Where is Ruadan? Out searching with the other knights?"

She flipped a page in the book, and the gesture looked angry. I'd annoyed her. "No, Ruadan and Aengus never made it out, because of the poison. Ruadan is doing better than Aengus, on account of Ruadan being a demigod and Aengus being just your average, every-day, run-of-the-mill fae." She cocked her head. "Doesn't explain why you're doing better than Aengus. I guess we'll get to that later. Right now, we have to stop Aengus from dying, because the poison is eating his brain at an alarming rate. Ruadan and his mum went outside to try to kill humans."

"That doesn't sound good," I drawled. "And the booms?"

Melusine cleared her throat. "Humans have made makeshift nail bombs. Full of scraps of iron that can kill fae. They're lobbing them through the hole in the moat."

My skin grew cold, and my mind cleared for a moment. "Ruadan is out there, delirious, in the middle of nail bombs?"

Melusine shrugged. "Queen Macha is with him, feeding off their deaths."

I pinched the bridge of my nose. I needed to caution them about something—there was an added danger there, if I could just put my finger on it. Thoughts wafted through my mind like dandelion seeds in the wind, and I reached out to snatch one.

"Wait. Wait. Arubian was right. If the humans see Ruadan killing them, they'll turn on us. We can't fight them all. This is bad PR. Very bad."

Even in my fog of confusion, I was beginning to understand that we were screwed. We had only a few hours left till the Plague hit. Humans were attacking us. Oh, and we'd been poisoned.

Baleros was about to win again—because, of course, he always did.

Aengus's skin was shot through with dark veins once more, and his head lolled. Just moments ago, I had been ready to batter him to death. Now, panic gripped me at the sight of him withering before my eyes. The only one still functioning here was Melusine.

"What have you found in your books?" I demanded.

She scratched her cheek. "I found in the literature references to a legendary unicorn named Nan. That's about it."

I winced. "I don't suppose the unicorn is a promising lead?"

"No." She pulled out another book. "And I haven't been able to spend long on that. I'm trying to figure out the poisons first. One thing at a time, you know what I mean?" She cracked the book open.

Whispers sounded around my head, breath on my neck. I leaned against a column to steady myself, and dread tightened my chest. "We're running out of time." I had a bad feeling that as time dwindled,

Ruadan would simply give himself over to Baleros. He'd stand in front of the gate in iron cuffs.

I bit my lip hard. I shouldn't have killed Arubian so fast.

From the floor, Aengus was trying to say the word "unicorn."

I crossed my arms, gripping my own biceps hard to try to clear my thoughts.

Nan ... Nan ... Nan....

Queen Nan....

The pain of my own grip helped me clear my head a little to think. There was something familiar about the name Nan, if I could only grasp onto it.

Nan ... Queen Nan's lace....

"I know the name Nan." I started pacing, closing my eyes. "You should have woken me up earlier. I could have figured this out."

I was mentally ticking over the name Nan. It was such a plain, solid, unsexy name, that it had stuck in my brain....

"Nan," I said at last. "Nan Bullen."

Melusine looked up from her book. "Who?"

"The demoness queen I saved from one of the hell worlds. Her name is Nan Bullen. Queen. She lives in one of the empty rooms here. Didn't know what else to do with her after I saved her." Melusine and Aengus just stared at me as I swayed on my feet. "It's worth a shot, isn't it?"

CHAPTER 25

$\mathcal{D}$ressed in her green gown, Queen Nan Bullen swanned into the throne room, a golden crown gleaming on her dark hair. In her six-fingered hand, she held a long, thin cigarette.

She took a puff, the smoke curling around her. "You called for a queen?"

Might as well get right to the point. "Do the names Nan and Burly Hal mean anything to you?"

She strode up to the empty throne like she owned it, then draped herself in the chair, letting her legs dangle over the edge. She chuckled darkly. "Nan and Burly Hal. How could you not know? Forgotten so quickly, time fleeth before us like a hind through the wood."

Oh, please get to the point. I wasn't sure I could keep myself standing much longer.

It was at that point that Ruadan strode into the room, his dark clothing glistening with blood. He looked a lot steadier than I felt, but his eyes were pure black.

"Who is this?" he asked.

"This is Queen Nan," I slurred. "Did you fix the problem outside?"

"No."

The queen cocked her head at Ruadan, smiling coquettishly. "Have you come to praise my beauty? I'll accept a poem."

Dark magic whirled around her, and in it, I saw wolves and stags forming. She tapped her cigarette holder, and ash dropped onto the floor in a neat little pile before the throne.

Ruadan's magic iced the room. "Do you know who Burly Hal is?"

Queen Nan's sigh was a delicate thing. "Do you know I didn't even feel it when they cut off my head? He brought in a French swordsman. That, at least, was a nice gesture. If I'd made a spectacle of myself like the Countess of Salisbury, running around with chunks out of my flesh as the axeman chased me, I'd have never lived it down in my hell world. Not that they gave me much respect, anyway." She pointed at a tall, peaked window. "My death spot was just over there. My blood stained the stones, dripping through the wooden scaffold. Noble blood, not that it spared my life."

At last, even with the fog in my mind, I started to piece it together.

And apparently, Ruadan had, too, because he said, "Queen Anne Boleyn."

She lifted her hand. "Didn't have six fingers when I was alive. The gods gave me an extra one in the hell world. Bastards."

She looked at me, her dark eyes enchanting.

"You want Burly Hal? He was my husband, Henry VIII. You killed his demon form in the hell world. Thank you for that. He was a deeply unpleasant person."

"What was the home built for you?" Ruadan was rubbing a knot in his forehead. "We need to know, now."

Another delicate sigh. "He had the whole place engraved with our initials, intertwined. True love, it was. Until he moved on—"

"The home," Ruadan barked. "A palace?"

Those dandelion seeds of thoughts wafted through my mind…. A Tudor palace … pearls and silk.

I scowled at Ruadan. "Weren't you alive when it was built? You should know this."

"I hardly paid attention to human affairs," he shot back. "Humans are alive one instant and dead the next. There's not much point in learning their names."

"Quite true in my case," said Nan, her smile electrifying. She seemed to be enjoying the attention so much, I had a feeling she wouldn't let it escape her grasp so quickly. She'd cling to it like a drowning woman clung to a branch. "I'll accept a love poem as payment."

I glanced at Melusine, who was still flipping furiously through a book about poison.

Ruadan stared at Nan, his whole body tensed, a lion about to strike. I had the impression he was fighting his natural impulse to simply attack and terrify her until she gave him what he wanted, but some gentlemanly part of him reined it in. He stood there, shadows cutting the air around him.

"He'd be really bad at poetry even on the best of days. No good," I said. "He barely speaks, and when he does, it's usually about death. But he has the nicest muscles." I giggled.

Shit. Had I said that out loud?

Nan blinked her long eyelashes. "A song, then, from the muscled gentleman! Compose me a song, dedicated to my beauty."

"It's not going to happen," I shouted, losing patience. "If you want romance, Aengus can sort of paw at you. He's lonely and he has soft hands since he never worked a real day in his life."

She flashed me a look of pure, hot rage. Right. So it wasn't lust she was after, but actual courtly love or whatever. Something I honestly didn't understand.

I turned to Ruadan, grabbing his arm. "Can you make her one of your floral wreaths?"

Ruadan cut me a sharp look, and I knew he was still considering violence. He'd be producing neither a crown, nor a poem, nor a song. See, men never had to be flexible in that way. He could just stand there, rigid as a rock, and say *this is who I am, and I'll be fucked if I'm changing.* Women—like me and Queen Nan here—we were used to being mutable. I could be flirtatious when the situation called for it, or aggressive when I needed someone to fear me. I could be funny or flattering, or I could take charge. I didn't necessarily do it all well, but I was used to adapting.

Perhaps I had to field this one.

I stepped forward, struggling to keep my balance.

"Beautiful queen." I stumbled over my words. "Your beauty is like a moon, and also like jewels, and like ... dew on the grass. And your eyes are like—" I let out a long breath. "A lovely pair of beetles. No. Those dark volcanic stones, and like the black heart at the center of Queen Nan's lace. Cheeks like ... pink flowery petals made of skin." I winced. "Breasts like two fleshy flotation devices."

Well, I'd done my best.

She nodded, satisfied. "Fair enough. Hampton Court—"

"Hampton Court Palace!" Melusine shouted, hand raised. "I just remembered."

"Thanks Melusine," I said. "Very helpful."

Queen Nan leaned back in the throne. "It's not fortified like this place is. No tower walls to keep it in. Has your enemy got a powerful army, by any chance, to defend him?"

"Yes," I sighed. Somehow, Queen Nan had become part of our strategic planning process, since she was one of the few here who could think straight. "And we haven't got an army."

"I'll go into the palace on my own," said Ruadan. "I'm leaving now."

"How?" I asked. "Night hasn't fully fallen yet. You won't be able to shadow-leap around."

"I can create night." He looked dazed. "We can't waste any more time."

"Wait." My jaw dropped. "You can *create night?*"

A flicker of night darkness swirled around his powerful body. "It's a temporary, artificial night. The sun seems to disappear, the stars come out." Ruadan scrubbed his hand over his jaw, eyes on the floor as he thought. "But the only problem is ... the only problem is...."

Ruadan was struggling to finish his thought. I, too, understood there was something wrong with this plan, but I couldn't put my finger on it.

Melusine raised her hand. "It would instantly alert Baleros that you were there."

BOOM. The walls shook. Apparently, the humans weren't done hurling their grenades at us. I held onto a column to stabilize myself, woozy as hell.

"Not to mention," Melusine added, "you've all been poisoned. Am I right? You wouldn't be able to create night that easily."

Ruadan paced the room, not answering. "Night will fall in two and a half hours," he eventually said. "That leaves us only a half hour after darkness falls...." His dark gaze went unfocused again.

Three hours left. When I closed my eyes, my mind filled with images of rotting bodies in the street. I gasped, opening my eyes again.

I bit my lip hard to clear my thoughts, then began pacing furiously across the floor. "You can't attack him like this. Even if we find the palace, you'll be dead within moments unless you're completely sharp. He'll be ready for you," I muttered.

"We have to be prepared for the fact that Adonis might be there," said Ruadan.

I closed my eyes, and my father's image flashed in my mind like a lightning bolt. Blue eyes, golden skin, black hair. Once we achieved our objectives—once Ruadan killed Baleros, my father was next on his list. Then me. Would this happen tonight?

At every moment, I was moving closer to the execution block—my father and me, moving up together. My blood would drip through the scaffold onto the stones below.

Not if I got the mist army first. Whoever killed Baleros got his army. Ruadan had said he needed the immortal army to kill Adonis. Maybe he needed it to kill me, too.

I bit my lip so hard I pierced the skin. Blood pooled in my mouth, and I forced those thoughts out of my mind.

I had to go with him. I had to kill Baleros before he did.

"I'll go with you," I blurted. "Once darkness falls completely, you can distill your Wraith magic. That thing that makes it so hard to see you. Give me that, too." I held up a hand, wiggling my fingers. "Look. You can put it in a ring, and I'll slip in with you. I can wear the lumen crystal. I'll zoom around the palace, all silent, until I find him. Until I find Adonis." I shook my head. *Not Adonis.* "Baleros. Until I find Baleros."

Ruadan was rubbing his forehead again. "I need to be the one to kill Baleros. I need to restrain him and take him through the portal. Only I can do that. I just can't think...."

BOOM.

I gritted my teeth at the explosion. The humans were really starting to piss me off at this point.

"I'll send ravens out," said Ruadan. "They'll swoop over Hampton Court Palace now, and they'll report back if anything seems unusual. Fortifications, guards, weapons, anything. In the meantime, I'm calling back all the knights from the search for Baleros. We need them on top of every gate, patrolling every outer wall."

"Except we can't just kill them," I said. What would Baleros do? "We need the humans on our side. Create a tyrant."

Ruadan's lip twitched. "One who oppresses the masses."

"Execute him publicly," I added.

"I'm afraid I'm a bit lost here," said Melusine. "Anyone care to fill me in?"

"Turning the tables on Baleros," said Ruadan. "Framing him for the killing we're about to do."

"Fighting back against the humans while making it clear Baleros is behind all this," I said. "Let them think he's in power here."

Melusine frowned. "And how are we supposed to convince Londoners that Baleros has taken over the Institute within the next few hours?"

"We fly his flag over the tower," said Ruadan. "Create the impression that he's invaded."

Aengus groaned from the floor. "My head. My head. Headddd."

Oh, right. Aengus was about to die from poison. "Have you found anything useful yet, Melusine?" I snapped. "We're about to lose one of our knights here."

"Give me a minute," shouted Melusine, flipping another page. "It's not as simple as— Oh, hang on. This is it! The poison. It's from

Arubian's hounds. All you need is a skilled fae mage to reverse it, one who knows potions from the Old Gods. If you don't, it says here in the literature that immediate death follows a period of delirium and decreasing mental acuity. The brain literally turns to liquid. So that's unpleasant."

Shit.

"Good," said Ruadan, absentmindedly. "But we have no mages skilled in the magic of the Old Gods. Not since Esther got into a fight with the gorta and starved to death in the grass moat."

"Kill me," said Aengus weakly.

Mum. My mother had known the magic of the Old Gods. She'd know what to do.

If only I'd paid attention to her lessons before she died….

CHAPTER 26

I swallowed hard, tiredness creeping up on me, stirring up my thoughts. My mother had known about the Old Gods —she'd known all about them. *She'd* be able to cure us all. A dark laugh escaped me, echoing off the stone.

My father had killed the person who could save us now.

My confusion had sharp edges, a dark delirium. I'd died once. Iron sword right through my heart. I'd drifted into the afterworld, and my father had caught me. I clamped my eyes shut, the possibilities swarming in my mind.

Would Adonis be there tonight when we invaded Hampton Court Palace? Would I find my father again?

My shoulders had tensed so much they hurt. When I closed my eyelids, I saw my father's face again: his golden skin, the gray-blue eyes. I never knew him as the Angel of Death—not until the end. I knew him as the man who brought me warm milk at night and read me Greek myths in bed by candlelight.

I'd see him soon, wouldn't I? I felt his presence around me, and his rich scent of myrrh, the warmth of his hug. A phantom angel feather brushed my cheek.

That day, when Ruadan had invaded, my father had lost control.

He'd killed everyone with his fear, waves of death rippling out from his body.

What had the shock done to him once he realized he'd killed my mum? When he'd seen her bleeding from the mouth? What if the trauma had warped him, turning him into a vengeful creature—one who wanted to spread death? One who'd be willing to work with Baleros?

The whispers grew louder around me, and now, I could hear what they were saying. They were repeating Ruadan's thoughts.

Creatures like you were never meant to walk the earth.

Pivoting, I turned to pace the floor again. I wasn't a proper horseman of death like my father was. I didn't have the power that he did. I'd killed a few fae when they'd ganged up on me, but that was it. Only Adonis—Thanatos himself—could slaughter an entire city at once.

I couldn't do that. I wasn't like him. I wasn't a monster.

When I opened my eyes again, I realized I was gripping my own hair, and Ruadan was staring at me.

"Something weighing heavily on your soul?" asked Ruadan.

"No," I said sharply. "It's just the poison. And I don't know a mage skilled in the powers of the Old Gods."

"I know of one," said Ruadan. "But she doesn't trust men anymore, and she's unlikely to help me. How much time do we have, Melusine?"

"It says here that once language abilities deteriorate, uhh … you got about a half hour before Aengus kicks it," she replied. "Maybe a bit more."

I sucked in a sharp breath. We couldn't let Aengus die. "Lead me to this woman, Ruadan. We'll go together. I'll do my best to charm her."

Ruadan nodded. "Fine. I'll summon the other knights to secure the fortress. Melusine, you make Baleros's flag. A bundle of sticks. Raise it as soon as you can. I'll try to get the antidote, along with Arianna or whatever her name is."

"Bunch of sticks with an axe blade." Melusine pushed up her glasses. "I know. You don't worry about a thing, Grand Master Ruadan. I'll get the flag flying faster than you can say … an epic poem of some kind. Something that would take about twenty-three minutes to say. In other words, it will take about twenty-three minutes for me to make it."

BOOM.

I clamped my hands over my ears. Was it the delirium, or were these explosions growing louder?

"Where exactly are we going?" I asked as the ground rumbled beneath my feet.

The World Key at Ruadan's neck glowed, and dark magic snapped around him. "Emain."

The floor cracked and opened up under me, and I plunged into the cold water.

* * *

An hour and thirty minutes left.

I pulled myself up out of the portal, and freezing water poured from my body onto damp, mossy soil. Ruadan was already standing in the forest. Oak boughs arched over him, and the air smelled heavy with earth and musk and … apples? I breathed in again, closing my eyes. This was the land of my dreams.

I still felt confused, but here, the delirium had taken on a lighter feel, no longer as dark and sharp.

Ruadan nodded, his black clothing sculpting his perfect body, pale hair down his back. I pulled myself out and stood, my body dripping water.

Ruadan had gone still, tuning into something. It took me a moment to hear the distant sound of drums trembling over the earth.

"Why do those drums sound familiar?" I asked.

"Because you heard them in one of my memories. It's the Wrenne Festival. The night of the sacred hunt." Late sunlight sparkled through the tree branches, and Ruadan squinted in the honeyed light. "Nyxobas, god of night, will be covering this land at any moment, turning day into night. He draws down night, here, because he is worshiped."

"What do you mean?"

"I mean night will fall any moment here, just for the festival. Nyxobas does that."

"Could you call in a favor with your granddad and ask him to kill Baleros on our behalf?"

"He doesn't do favors like that. He doesn't care if I live or die. He only cares if he's worshiped."

I blinked. "He sounds charming." I twisted the hem of my dress, wringing out the cold water onto the earth. "Where's this friend of yours who hates men?"

"She'll be at the festival." When I looked up, I realized how close I was standing to Ruadan. I let myself indulge for a moment in breathing in his piney scent. We could just stay here….

"I don't want the queen to know that we're here," Ruadan added.

Oh, right. The mission. "Any reason?"

"My sister will want a formal audience. She'll want to know about our mother, what condition she's in, what's happened to her. Why we've been poisoned. She'll want to know what my plans are, what my mother's plans are, how I'll capture Baleros, and so on. It will take hours that we don't have."

"How do we stay hidden?"

Ruadan stroked a hand down his chest. "Wrenne is a festival of disguises. We dress ourselves from the bounty of the forest and hide our faces."

"So what exactly do we wear? Leaves?"

"Hemlock boughs, oak leaves, animal skins, furs, antlers."

Was this his confusion, or did he really think we were about to rustle up some animal skins and antlers right now?

I looked up at the sun slanting lower on the horizon. Mauve and pumpkin stained a sapphire sky—Nyxobas's unnatural sunset, starting already.

I toyed with the fabric of my wet dress. Once again, I seemed to have moved closer to Ruadan, as if drawn by an invisible thread. Now, I was only inches from him, and I felt an electrical pulse moving between us. My eyes lingered over his lips, and I remembered how it had felt when he'd pressed them against mine, how my body had lit up when he'd touched me.

"I'm getting distracted," I muttered.

"Wrenne does that to people. Not to mention, our minds...." He trailed off. He'd gone completely still, but his magic pulsed onto my body, hot strokes up my neck, up my thighs.

I could have sworn I felt his magic licking between my legs, and I gasped. Was he doing that on purpose?

"We don't have a lot of time," he added. His voice stroked over my skin, an intoxicating caress.

Still, he wasn't moving, and his eyes pierced me, taking me apart piece by piece.

What had I said to him after our moment in the sewer? That it had been a mistake, and it could never happen again. I'd already let myself get deep enough into this. I'd let myself care too much.

"Like you said." My voice came out husky. "We have a time limit. Pressed for time."

His eyes stayed locked on me as if he were mesmerized. "The drums."

"The drums," I repeated. I could feel their rhythm pulsing through my blood like a heartbeat. I forced myself to step back from Ruadan, and I glanced at the sky again. "We need that antidote."

Between the leaves, the mauve hues had deepened to a dark blue, and the moon seemed to hang over us. I could still feel Ruadan's heat radiating around me, his magic tingling over my skin.

When I looked down from the darkening sky, Ruadan had disappeared, and I was completely on my own.

I was utterly losing it. "Ruadan?"

CHAPTER 27

*I*t took a minute before he answered.

Then, at last, his voice floated from the shadows: "You need a disguise."

I took a deep breath, then bit my lip again to master my thoughts. I understood dressing like a human, wearing the appropriate outfits for nightclubs and bars, but clothing myself in leaves was a bit unfamiliar.

I crossed to an oak, its trunk wrapped with ivy, and pulled a knife from my thigh holster. I cut through the ropes of vines until I'd formed a large pile of them on the earth.

Then, I knelt on the ground and rifled through my bug-out bag until I found a plastic mini stapler. I smiled. How anyone got through life without a bug-out bag was beyond me.

I stood and began stripping off my clothes, starting with my wet shirt. The crisp forest air slid over my bare skin as I pulled off my bra, and my breasts peaked in the breeze. I slid off my knickers next. For just a moment, I lingered there, thinking of Ruadan, wishing he'd come back.

Focus on the mission.

I crouched, naked, on the earth. The forest breeze whispered over my bare skin, raising goosebumps. My mind turned back to Ruadan's delicious magic, his mouth. I had to stop myself from hunting him down right now. Licking my lips, I shoved the shirt, my underwear, and my boots into the bag.

With the drums pounding in my belly, I wasn't sure I could keep my hands off Ruadan. Even without him here, liquid desire was lighting me up. I lifted the ivy off the ground and stood.

Focus, Liora. We're here on a mission. Put on your damn leaf clothes.

I clenched my jaw, forcing my attention to the ivy. I began wrapping it around myself, and it skimmed over my skin, the leaves soft as silk. I stapled the leaves and stems together over my chest. Then, I tied the vines around my lower half, creating a short shirt.

When I'd just about covered up my bum, I turned to find Ruadan staring at me. "How long have you been standing there?"

Given the darkness in his eyes, I was guessing he'd been there for a while. He didn't speak, reverting into his eerie animal stillness, and the forest wind whisked over us.

His chest was bare, now, and he wore a kilt of animal skins and a pair of antlers. A cluster of leaves covered the World Key at his throat.

"Where did you get all that?" I asked.

His dark gaze drank me in, sliding slowly down my breasts, my bare waist, my hips....

Then, abruptly, he turned to the oak next to him. He ripped a bunch of leaves from a bough. Frowning, he worked at them for a minute until he'd created two masks of oak leaves, each with eye holes and a strap around the back, made of the stems.

That was ... impressive.

He handed me one of the masks, and I slid it over my head, smiling at him.

Then, I snatched my bag from the ground, slipping it over my shoulders.

We started walking in step, moving to the rhythm of the drum. The setting sunlight streamed through the tree branches, and night began to claim Emain's forest.

Ahead of us, someone raced through the oaks: a woman wearing a scrap of animal skin, flowers over her breasts. She wore a floral wreath on her head, and ribbons streamed behind her, tangled in her ginger hair. Just a few paces behind her, a man ran past, antlers on his head.

I frowned. "So is this basically a festival where men wear antlers and chase women around in the woods and try to have sex with them?"

"Yes."

Well, there it was. It was remarkably similar to what Uncle Darrell and his humans attempted in Richmond Park, except I assumed in Emain people here actually got laid. "And that's it?"

"Sometimes the women chase the men," he added. "There are bonfires, music. We sacrifice sixteen prisoners in a bonfire, and we eat things made with apples, like pies—"

"Wait," I held up a hand. "Did you just slip in a bit about burning people to death?"

"The prisoners, yes. In the bonfire. Then we have pies made from—"

"I understand how pies work. That part doesn't need that much explaining. I'm stuck on the burning people to death part."

"Oh?"

"I mean, at the very least, don't the tormented screams of the damned kind of kill the sexy vibe you're all going for?"

He frowned, tracing a hand over his bare chest. "How so?"

My stomach dropped. "You know what? This is probably one of those things it's better if we don't talk about. Let's just chalk this up to a cultural difference, and we will not talk about it, because I'm starting to think problems between people are better when you don't talk about them." I might have been babbling a little.

"You should really sleep more."

I scowled at him. "It's the poison making me confused."

"In general, you should sleep more. In a bed, not on the floor."

"In *your* bed?"

A wicked smile, just for a moment. "Perhaps."

I liked Ruadan when he let down his guard. Too bad this couldn't last.

An enormous bonfire gleamed in a clearing in the distance, roaring at least six feet high. Maybe that was where we burned the prisoners. I *really* hoped we'd be missing that part of the evening.

This time, when I glanced at the sky, it had darkened to a midnight purple. The moon beamed over the tree line—unnaturally large—and the drums rumbled in my belly. I closed my eyes, breathing in the heavy air, its scent mossy and sweet at the same time. The atmosphere somehow felt fertile here. I stole another glance at Ruadan's bare chest.

You'd think that a man in an animal-skin skirt, a leaf mask, and deer antlers would look a *bit* off. It's not a look you're likely to find in men fashion's blogs or on *GQ*'s best-dressed list. But somehow, it looked perfect on Ruadan. He looked like he'd emerged from the forest itself, a man hewn from its oaks and rocks, driven by wild, animal instincts. I found myself licking my lips. It took me a moment to realize Ruadan was staring at me, too, his eyes blazing at the sight of my tongue lingering on my lower lip.

When we reached the clearing, I surveyed the space around us. Here, revelers were dancing around the bonfire. Bare-chested men wore masks made of animal skins and feathers, faces blank, feature-less. They'd painted their bodies with white and blue symbols. Like me, many of the women wore nothing but leaves, so I didn't have to endure the *flaming forest fuck-party faux pas* of coming underdressed.

Across from me, a man in enormous antlers danced around the fire on oak stilts, his face covered in leather. Others wore what looked like burlap over their faces, the effect unnerving overall.

"Do you see her?" I asked in a loud whisper.

He sniffed the air, then shook his head. "She's not here yet."

"You know her by her smell?"

"Yes."

"How well do you know her, exactly? That you can just sniff the air and smell her body?"

Firelight danced over his masculine features, and he didn't answer. Classic Wraith move.

One of the masked dancers swooped closer to me, his head

surrounded by raven feathers. The dancers were chanting something in the ancient fae language. Was it something about making sweet, sweet love to the sound of prisoners burning to death? It was anyone's guess.

The fire blazed hot, dry heat wavering over my skin. I was at least twelve feet away from it, but it still drew beads of sweat on my forehead and the tops of my breasts.

I leaned closer to Ruadan. "We don't have to join in the dancing, do we?"

"No." He nodded at the forest path. "But if we stand here, we'll draw attention to ourselves. We should wait in the cover of the trees until she arrives."

I was only too happy to move away from the creepy masked dancers, and I stepped backward to the tree line. The fire heated my skin even from here.

The atmosphere intoxicated me, luring me away from my task. Thoughts flitted through my mind like fireflies. *Find the girl ... bring her back to the Institute ... kill Baleros....*

Worship Nyxobas ... worship the night ... hunt. Join the hunt here.

Death blooms in you like a seed. Make the most of life.

A few steps deeper into the forest's darkness, and it was just me and Ruadan. My body heated.

Worship the forest.

CHAPTER 28

hen I looked at Ruadan, I felt certain no one else in the world existed. I smiled at him, chest flushing. The drums pounded louder in my ears, the rhythms reverberating over my skin. As I studied Ruadan's body—thickly corded, built to kill—heat swooped through my core.

The forest wanted me to enjoy myself.

My fingers slipped into the top of my leaf skirt, and I tugged it down. Why was I wearing this? The night didn't want me to wear this. The night forest wanted me naked—wanted my palms and knees in the earth, hips up, legs wide on the ground underneath him.

The hunt was calling to me. I took another step back into the bosom of the forest, and my bare feet sank into the rich soil. Ruadan's eyes were locked on me, and he prowled closer. His gaze took in my mouth, then lowered to the curves of breasts. My nipples tightened under his stare.

I wanted the leaves off me, wanted my knees in the dirt, wanted to gasp along with him. Wanted to breathe in his heat, his musk and salt. Wanted to fill myself…. I was *hungry.* I ached with need. My teeth, my tongue, my mouth needed his body. My body needed his mouth, tongue on my thighs, between my legs.

Another step back into in the woods' embrace, and Ruadan was prowling after me, eyes gleaming with silver. He was a god of the hunt moving after his prey. I tugged down the leaves at my waist even more, showing him the curve of my hips. *This is what you need.* Ruadan's muscles tightened.

Lure him closer....

I turned away from him, facing a tree. I wanted to feel his fingers brushing between my legs, his hot mouth on my throat. My back arched, legs spreading in invitation.

It took only another heartbeat for Ruadan to find his way to me. His powerful body pressed against me, warming me. Then, he slid his hand over my belly, and he brushed it down slowly.

I want. I want. I want.

His fingers traced over the hollows of my hips. My back arched, hips grinding into him.

I felt the cold air skimming over my bare skin through the leaves. The drums were stoking something primal in me, something between a sex drive and bloodlust.

Get what you want.

I turned to face Ruadan, and I slid my hands up his chest, grazing my nails against his torso. I gripped his shoulders, then tried to push him to the ground. His enormous body didn't budge.

I pushed him hard in the chest. "On the ground."

I leapt on him, wrapping my legs around him, and he fell back to the earth.

With a coy smile, I leaned down. I straddled him, whispering in his ear. "I want you to see me. The *real* me." I wasn't quite sure what I was saying, but the words were just tumbling out.

He looked feral, canines flashing. How long would he let me be on top of him before he threw me to the earth and tried to dominate me? He gripped me hard by the waist, fingers possessive.

I pressed my mouth to his neck, giving him a little lick, a flick of my tongue over his skin. The hint of salt tasted delicious, and I rocked my hips over him. I licked again, reveling in the feel of his hands on me. I brushed light, sweet kisses over his throat, then moved lower over his collarbone, his chest.

His body was tense as a bow string, and with each kiss on his chest, I felt him twitch. His magic was skimming over me like silk, stroking my body in places I wanted to feel his hands.

I kissed him on the mouth again, rolling my hips into his. When I pulled away from the kiss, I caught his lower lip between my teeth.

He stroked a hand up into my hair, gripping it hard. The other hand was on my bum.

I kissed his neck slowly. I rocked my hips again, pleasure racing up my body from the apex of my thighs.

He reached for the leaves over my breasts, ready to tear them off.

I gripped his hand, stopping him. My body heated. "Wait."

I took in the perfect, masculine planes of his body, the scent of pine and apples. I ached for him so hard I could barely think of anything else. Still, I wanted something from him. I needed him to speak to me.

I leaned down, whispering in his ear. "I need you to tell me that you want me."

On top of Ruadan, I felt like a goddess. The intensity in his dark eyes made my body heat and swell. He was looking at me like he wanted to fling me to the ground—like he wanted to flip me over onto my hands and knees and claim me. He was resisting. Always resisting.

I tugged down the leaves just a little to reveal the swell of my breasts, and I moved my hips over him. "I want the truth from you. Say it to me."

"And what about your truth—?"

I clamped a hand over his mouth.

No. No. Not that. Not my truth.

My heart thundered. "I want to hear the truth about how you feel about me."

His eyes widened, swirling with black. I leaned forward, my nipples grazing his chest. Gently, I kissed his neck, flicking my tongue over it again. His body felt hard beneath mine, pure steel.

He gripped my hair, pulling my ear to his lips. His other hand flexed on my bum, his grip punishing. He whispered in my ear, "I want you as a lover, and I have from the moment I saw you. I want you naked in my bed, always. I want you to be mine."

"There it is." I licked his neck.

He ripped the leaves off my hips, and my breath sped up. I ripped his clothes off him, and we moved to the rhythm of the drum.

* * *

Naked and satiated, I fell back on the soil. My head felt *slightly* clearer for the moment, but I didn't think that would last long.

I wanted to stay here forever, just Ruadan, the forest, and me. I felt his hands brushing over my skin as he wrapped my body in leaves again. I opened my eyes to watch him work, and I brushed a strand of his blond hair out of his eyes.

Unfortunately, we couldn't stay here forever, and we needed that antidote before we lost our battle completely.

My muscles started to tense. We had a fae mage to bring home, and a psychopath to destroy. And we had just over an hour until that same psychopath unleashed a plague.

With a new set of leaves tied over my chest, I sat up.

"Can you smell her now?" I asked. "Your mage friend."

He turned to look at the bonfire through the trees, and his eyes narrowed. "She's here."

"Good." I pulled on my bug-out bag. "What does she look like? What's her name?"

"Aerwyn. She's short. Amber eyes. Pale, golden skin. Curvy."

We began walking, and the scent of burning cedar curled around me. Something about the description of her bothered me.

"She has purple hair," he added. "With a streak of blue."

I frowned. "So she looks exactly like me, but with a blue streak in her purple hair."

"I wouldn't say that, exactly."

"And you slept with her, right?"

"Slept?"

"You had sex with her."

"It was a long time ago," he said.

I clenched my teeth. It wasn't important. The important thing about my relationship with Ruadan was that he planned to kill me at some point, but he just didn't know it yet.

A hollow opened in my chest, and I breathed in deeply, trying to calm myself.

I stole a quick glance at Ruadan. Could I trust him well enough to tell him the truth? I didn't think so. Ruadan seemed to put duty above everything else.

As we reached the bonfire, a flash of purple hair caught my eye. Aerwyn was dancing around the fire, swaying her hips seductively, a slow, languid movement. She wore a mask of oak leaves and wildflowers.

I took a deep breath, swaying slightly. "Any tips on how I could convince her to help us? All I know about her is that she hates men."

"Use that."

Not super helpful, but okay.

I felt weird interrupting her dance, but I crossed to her anyway, the bonfire heating my skin. I needed to get her alone, and to do it in a way that wouldn't call too much attention to our conversation. I had to look like an ecstatic reveler.

I tried to sway my hips a little, too, as I sidled up to her. Up close, she didn't look exactly like me—her mouth was a bit smaller. I couldn't see her face completely under the mask, but she looked beautiful.

I grabbed her by the hand. I pulled her away from the fire, and she laughed, skipping along by my side as I led her from the clearing.

Once we'd moved deeper into the forest, I turned to her. She smiled at me, her cheeks pink. Giggling, she grabbed my waist, moving in for a kiss.

I held up a hand to gently stop her. "Okay, that's … you seem very nice, but that's not why I'm here."

"It's not?" She was still smiling. "I like you because you look like me." She had a lilting accent, and I thought her first language might be Fae. She tried to pull me closer again.

"Aerwyn. I need your help," I said.

She cocked her head, her smile disappearing. "How did you know my name?"

"I came here with someone you knew." What was my best angle? "Okay, here's the story. I've been poisoned by Arubian's hounds' claws, and so have my friends, and we heard you could help with that," I blurted. "Can you give us a potion or whatever?"

Behind her mask, I saw her amber eyes widen. "Arubian?"

"Yes."

"Sure. I can make a potion. If you don't get it, the toxins will eat your brain."

My chest tightened. "That sounds pretty bad."

She blinked at me. "I can tell you're telling the truth." She brushed a strand of hair out of my face. "But what did you mean *us*? Who did you come here with? I need the *whole* truth."

I didn't suppose I could just gloss over that bit and get back to the potions. "Umm...."

"Don't lie to me," she snapped. "I always know. And without my help, your brain will become liquid."

My throat had gone dry, but the truth had worked before. "I'm here with Ruadan, Prince of Emain. He's the Grand Master of the Institute we're protecting in London. You don't need to see him, you could just give us the potion. Please."

Fury flashed in her eyes, and she gripped my shoulders so hard I thought she was going to break something. "Ruadan?"

"He mentioned you might have a history...." I trailed off, my head woozy again. Which, I reminded myself, was my brain starting to liquidize. "If we could just get back to the potion."

"He broke my heart. Completely shattered me. He seduced me, made me fall in love with him. He made me depend on him. I *needed* him. And he left me." Her thumbs were digging into me. "He just left. He shattered me completely. He'll do the same to you."

The air around us thinned, breeze growing cold.

"The betrayal will kill you before the sword ever does."

CHAPTER 29

My heart skipped a beat. Had she actually said that last part—those words I so often said to myself? "Wait, what did you just say?"

"I said he shattered me completely."

I shook my head, still catching my breath. "I'm sorry."

"He *likes* breaking hearts," she hissed. "He feeds off it."

My chest hurt. He'd break my heart, too. It was as inevitable as death.

It took me a moment to put together the pieces completely. "He feeds off heartbreak? That's his fomoire drive."

She nodded. "Oh, yeah. Real charming."

That woman who'd been singing karaoke in the pub, mascara streaming down her face—Ruadan had seemed completely fascinated by her. Now, it all made perfect sense. He'd been feeding off her heartbreak.

A tendril of pain coiled through me. Had he said he wanted me in his bed? He'd feed off my pain, too.

Still, Ruadan's dark side was not my top concern right now. We needed the godsdamned antidote. Even with my liquidizing brain and the delirium of Wrenne, I had a ruthlessly practical side that could

579

take over when I really needed it—the survivor in me that had kept me alive.

I needed the poison out of me. I needed Baleros dead. My survival depended on it.

"I'm sorry about Ruadan," I said. "But I still need your help."

She crossed her arms. "Fine. But I'll need to punch Ruadan in the face."

"That's fine with me."

I took her by the hand again, leading her back to Ruadan, who stood in the shadows of the oak grove. He was holding something in his hand, but I didn't have a chance to see what it was.

As soon as we reached him, Aerwyn pulled her hand away from mine. She ran over to him and punched him hard in the jaw.

He hardly moved, just a sharp turn of his head. He managed to hold onto whatever was in his hand.

"Hi, Aerwyn."

Aerwyn clutched her fist, wincing from the pain. Then, she shoved a finger in Ruadan's face. "You are a bad, bad man." She pushed the mask up on her face and stared at me. Now, I could see we looked a bit different, her lashes and eyebrows lighter than mine. "What's your name?"

"Arianna."

"All right, Arianna. Give me a minute."

She disappeared into the shadows, and I turned to look at Ruadan.

"Is your face okay?" My voice came out sounding angry. I felt like he'd already broken my heart, even if he hadn't. He would, though. Of course he would.

"My face is fine." He held out his hand, and for the first time, I realized what he was holding. A wreath of leaves, threaded with bluebells. "I thought you might like this."

For just a moment, I forgot all about the fomoire issue, the impending heartbreak, the kill list. "You made me a crown."

"I thought you'd look beautiful wearing that." His voice skimmed over my body. "And nothing else."

Then, I remembered everything Aerwyn had told me, and it all came crashing back into my muddled mind—how he made people love him, then broke their hearts. How he wanted me dead but didn't know it yet. I turned away from him, clutching the wreath. How long until he realized the truth about me, before he put it all together?

When I turned back, fear slammed into me. Ruadan stood before me in his nightmarish form—black, star-flecked wings, dark eyes, a silver sheen on his skin. Fully transformed, dark horns gleamed on his head.

His lip curled, exposing his canines. "Creatures like you don't belong on earth," he snarled.

He was going to rip my heart out of my chest.

I had to kill him first, and my shoulder blades itched. I'd let my death magic wash over him. *Sever all emotional ties. Kill them all.*

I gasped, stumbling back from him, trying to hush the death instinct.

Then, as quickly as the image had arrived, it flitted away again. Ruadan's wings had disappeared, the horns gone.

A hallucination? I held my chest, gasping for breath.

He frowned at me. "Are you all right? You look terrified."

"It's the poison," I stammered. "I need that godsdamned antidote." I exhaled slowly.

Sever all emotional ties. This won't end well.

With a shaking hand, I laid the wreath on the ground. "That's sweet, but I'm not taking that with me. This won't end well."

Had I said that out loud?

When I looked up at him again—for just a moment—I saw a look of hurt in his eyes. It was gone again, so fast I couldn't be sure it had been real.

Just then, Aerwyn sashayed back through the shrubs holding a fistful of herbs and moss. "I've already blessed them with the power of the Old Gods. Just mash this up with rainwater, boil it, and let it cool. Once you drink it, it will counteract the effects of the poison. Will you be able to get it back safely?"

I nodded. I had Tupperware in my backpack that should keep it secure.

Ruadan looked at her. "Thank you for—"

"Go fuck yourself!" she shouted.

With that, she was off into the shrubs again. I shoved the handful of herbs and moss into my plastic container, then sealed it up tight.

Within moments, the cold waters of the portal were ripping open the ground.

* * *

I HELD a warm cloak around myself in the throne room, watching as Aengus drank the last bit of the antidote. *Less than an hour left.*

I'd already drunk mine, and within moments, my head had felt miraculously clear again.

Outside, the sun was dipping lower, growing redder. Real, this time, and not the work of Nyxobas. Any moment, now, we'd be able to make our way to Hampton Court Palace. But first, Ruadan wanted us to secure the Institute.

I strapped a sword and sheath to my waist. I wasn't exactly sure what the plan was yet, but I felt better when I wore it.

Melusine sidled up beside me. "What was the Wrenne festival like?"

"I'm just glad we missed the prisoner-burning," I muttered. Small mercies.

"What?"

"The burning of the sixteen prisoners at the bonfire."

She frowned. "They don't burn people. It's a fertility festival. The poison must have confused you."

I scowled. Ruadan's weird sense of humor again, I supposed.

Another explosion rocked the Institute, the sound nearly deafening. I clamped my hands over my ears. Who'd given them all the grenades? Bloody hells.

At that moment, Ruadan crossed into the room, weapons crammed under each of his enormous arms.

"We need to contain this, now," he said. "We have to defend the

Institute before they rip through the outer wall completely. Wear cowls to hide your identity. Shoot anyone attacking us."

I crossed to Ruadan, pulling a bow out of his arms and a quiver of arrows. I had a sword on me, but it wouldn't do much good from the Tower.

I pulled the quiver over my torso and held onto the wooden bow. It had been my mother's weapon of choice, and she'd taught me to use it for hunting deer. Never for hunting humans, but like I'd said … women could be adaptable.

"Queen Macha and the other knights are already on the battlements," said Ruadan.

I pulled a cowl over my head.

Ruadan rushed out of the hall—already on his way to slaughter the humans attacking us—and I followed close behind him.

I moved swiftly, running through the hall, the corridors, the courtyard under the blood-red sky, until I found my way to the parapet that loomed above the Thames. To my right, half a tower had crumbled to the pavement, dust clouding the air. Scorch marks darkened the stone.

Strangely enough, the idea of killing was a relief from my thoughts. Better to kill some attackers than to think about Ruadan—about that damned wreath, and the look on his face when I'd thrown it on the ground.

I couldn't even be sure that look had been real. I'd been dosed up on hallucinogenic toxins, and the truth was that he was a fomoire who wanted me dead. As I nocked an arrow, the thought hit me like a bullet. Of *course* he fed off heartbreak. The man was an incubus as well as a fomoire. On one side, he fed from love—the other, from love's destruction.

I stared as a man in a tracksuit below us reared back his arm, ready to hurl a grenade. I set my sights on him.

Seriously, *where* the fuck had they got grenades from? Baleros, probably.

I loosed the arrow, and it caught him in the chest. He fell to the ground, and the humans around him screamed. They looked so furi-ous, so enraged, that I wondered for a moment if Baleros had cast some sort of rage spell on them. But no—it was really just that they were terrified of us, and humans acted like sadists when they were scared.

A man in an Arsenal T-shirt gripped a Molotov cocktail. I nocked another arrow and released it. My shot caught him in the neck.

I didn't love killing humans. It seemed just a little too easy, and they were supposed to be our allies.

Maybe I could try another method of crowd control.

I crouched below the parapet and jammed my hand into my bug-out bag. I pulled out another arrow, along with tissues and a tiny plastic bottle of whiskey. I wrapped the tissues around the arrow's tip, then poured the whiskey on it. My gaze flicked to the sky.

Almost time to go.

I snatched my lighter from the bag, then lit the arrow's tip until a flame roared up in the dim light. Then, I aimed it just before the mob, and I let it fly. The humans started to scatter, pushing away from the flaming arrow. A few more fiery arrows, and they were scrambling over themselves to get away.

With the threat of flaming arrows raining down, the humans began to scatter at last.

CHAPTER 30

Thirty minutes left.

I glanced at the sky, which was darkening to a muddy purple over the Thames. As soon as the last of the sun rays fell behind the horizon, it was time to take on Baleros.

We'd never finalized our plan, and I had a bad feeling Ruadan planned to slip off on his own—that he'd be ready to simply give himself up if it didn't work out.

Baleros was always one step ahead, and he'd be ready for Ruadan. No way in hells was I letting the Grand Master play into Baleros's hands. Gripping my bow, I whirled. I needed to find Ruadan before he left, as the last of the orange light dropped behind London's skyline.

Where was he? From here, I could see the other knights on the battlements, and Baleros's flag flew proudly over us all. But everyone had their hoods on, and I couldn't tell which knight was Ruadan. I strained my eyes, trying to search for his dark magic.

I sniffed the air, searching for the scent of pine and apples.

Where was he?

As the sun disappeared, there were just enough shadows to use the lumen stone. It glowed around my neck. I touched the stone, feeling

585

the electric magic crackling through me. I stared at one of the inner walls, leaping to the walkway.

I landed hard on the stone, then peered over the wall, catching my breath. As I looked out over the courtyard, I gasped. Ruadan had already opened a portal in the middle of the grassy courtyard.

Worse, he'd already gone through it.

I swallowed hard as the portal began to close. Before I could waste another heartbeat, I shadow-leapt through the darkness, plunging into the icy waters. The portal closed above me.

* * *

I HELD my breath under the water, feeling my sword weighing me down. Light pierced the surface, cold rays cutting through the darkness. I kicked my legs hard, pushing myself up toward the light.

But something was wrong, and it took me a moment to figure out what it was. Why was there so much light? It was supposed to be night—that was the whole point.

Dread coiled through my chest, tightening my lungs. This wasn't right.

I reached the air, gasping. I had a moment of relief—night still covered the sky, stars gleaming above me. Ruadan had opened a portal right into the Thames itself, and the ruddy bricks of Hampton Court palace loomed over the river.

Although it was still night, the palace itself blazed with an unnatural, golden light.

I treaded water in the chilly Thames, staring up at the palace's grandeur over the grassy bank.

So, *this* was Baleros's plan—light up the palace from the inside out, use the goddess's fire magic to extinguish all the shadows. There was no way Ruadan could leap through the palace when it was lit up like a Christmas tree.

Where *was* he, though? I kicked in the water, swimming over to the river's edge. Catching my breath, I hoisted myself out onto the damp grass. With the bright light of the palace streaming over me, I felt exposed. Still, I didn't see any jackdaws roaming around, ready to blow me up.

A flicker of darkness caught my eye. Like a caged animal, Ruadan was pacing the riverside. His movements looked feral, and I didn't get the sense he was quite as controlled as he normally was.

Baleros unnerved Ruadan just as he did me. He warped our ability to act logically, to defend ourselves. That ruthlessly pragmatic side—the survivor in us—got lost in the haze of emotions when Baleros was involved.

I crossed to him, shoulders tensed. I had the uneasy feeling that he might turn on me like a wolf about to die. The fact that he didn't even notice me coming showed me how lost he was in his own fury. When I was only a few feet away from him, he turned sharply, his shadows devouring the golden light around him. From the darkness, his pale gaze seared me.

"What are you doing here?" he asked sharply.

I need to get the mist army before you do. "I wanted to make sure you didn't die or turn yourself in."

His magic slashed the air around him, a maelstrom of darkness. "What powers do you have that you could help a demigod? I'm not clear on that."

There was an edge of steel in his voice. A challenge. His dark magic rippled over me.

"We have twenty-five minutes until Baleros unleashes the Plague," Ruadan went on. "If I go into his palace, I'll likely end up dead. If I don't, half the city of London will die." He raked a hand through his hair. "Do you know what it's like when people die of the Plague? Flesh rotting with gangrene, swollen glands that split open and bleed—tokens of death. Lungs that stop working, vomiting blood—"

I clamped my hands over my ears. "I get it. Stop. I get that it's terrible. This isn't helping." My head was spinning. I hadn't been entirely familiar with the symptomology of the Black Death. Why would I have been? But this sounded … uncomfortably familiar. I'd seen this before. And, apparently, so had Ruadan. "How do you know so much about it?"

"It's how my wife died."

"I thought you said—" I nearly said *my father,* but I stopped myself. "I thought you said Adonis killed her."

He shot me a sharp look. "He did. I told you about the legend, and it's true. She died of the Plague—but I could see the dark magic on her. The magic had a certain scent to it, something Angelic."

"What did it smell like?"

"Myrrh."

The word set frost racing up my spine.

Myrrh. The scent of Adonis.

Some legends weren't true. Others were. I schooled my features to calm.

"That's why I think Adonis is working with Baleros," he went on. "He must have escaped his realm. He's not an ordinary angel. He's practically a god. Maybe he opened his world. Maybe he came through the portal after me."

I breathed in deeply. I could have sworn I smelled the scent of myrrh on the air here now.

My throat tightened. "But why would they work together?"

"It would make sense for them to form an alliance, wouldn't it?" He paced over the grass. "They both want me dead. Baleros wants the World Key. Adonis will be hell-bent on vengeance for causing the death of his wife. He'll want to stop me from killing him and his son. It's why the cult we found was worshiping Adonis. Feeding him."

Something cold and dark was cutting at me from within. "And you think only Adonis can cause the Black Plague." I was clinging to shreds of hope. "You don't think it could be a spell?"

"I think Adonis *is* the Plague." The air had chilled to a wintry cold. "The plagues of the fourteenth century, the seventeenth century, the plagues that wiped out half of Europe. That was Adonis losing control of himself—every time. I'm sure of it. When I invaded his world, he created a plague then, too. I saw them die before me. The same symptoms—the buboes, the purpling skin and rotting flesh. That's what I mean when I say he has to die. A creature like him is too dangerous for this world."

All the air had left my lungs. It was hard to argue with this point. I'd seen it happen myself. I remembered what my mum had looked like.

A creature who killed half of Europe just by getting emotional. Of *course* such a monster could no longer stay on Earth.

Ruadan could never know the truth about me. Maybe we'd shared a moment in the sewers, and another in the forest. Maybe he thought he trusted me. But once he found out who I really was, duty would compel him to kill me.

And maybe he wouldn't be wrong. What dark kernels of destruction were blooming in me, even now?

Sharp edges of pain pierced my chest, and I hated the fact that tears were starting to sting my eyes.

Ruadan was staring at me closely, like he'd read my expression but didn't know what to make of it. And worse—was his body *glowing?* The fucker was feeding off my broken heart already.

Anger ignited. I didn't think about it before I swung for his face, before my knuckles connected with his perfect jaw. The sting of bone meeting bone was a satisfying release.

He touched his cheek, staring at me with a shocked expression. Still glowing, the bastard.

"What's going on?" he asked sharply. "That's the second time a woman has punched me tonight."

"Nothing. What's going on is that we have about twenty minutes to get into that palace and try to kill Baleros. Because if we don't, every terrible thing you just described will happen to everyone we know. Melusine, Ciara, Aengus. Every human and everyone at the Institute will have their fingers rot off or whatever. And I'm not letting you give yourself over without a fight. That's it. That's final. We're in this together."

Ruadan stared at me for a long minute, and the breeze rushed over the Thames. "We probably won't come out of there."

"I know."

But a creature like me shouldn't be here in the first place, right?

Ruadan's jaw twitched. "Go back to the Institute. I'll do this alone. I'm the one he wants."

"No. We can work together. You can use your magic to make it dark in there, while I try to find Baleros. Maybe we don't get to capture him and take him through a portal, but at least I can hack him to pieces with an iron sword. I can slow this down, give us a few more days. And if Adonis—" My voice broke. "If Adonis is there, we can slow him down. Everyone can die, even the Horseman of Death. You have those magic stones or whatever, right? The ones that can kill him?"

"I'm ordering you to return." Steel laced his voice.

I'm done taking orders tonight. I turned, heading for the palace. "If you won't bring the darkness, I'll go in the light."

I marched over the grass toward the beaming palace. The faint scent of myrrh curled around me.

Dad?

"Arianna," Ruadan barked. He was moving after me.

I turned to face him. "There's nothing you can do to stop me from running into that palace. I get to choose when I die, not you. I don't care if you're the Grand Master. There's not an army on Earth that could drag me back through that portal right now. We're finding Baleros together. Now, we have less than twenty minutes. I need you to make it dark."

Ruadan's eyes were black as pitch. He turned to the palace. "At the first sign that your life is in danger, I'm giving myself up."

"That's sweet." Ruadan would have no idea why I sounded so bitter. *The fact is, my love, you're gonna be the first one to draw a sword on me when you find out the truth.*

Another hot tear spilled down my cheek, and I hated myself for it.

What I was not expecting was for Ruadan to pull me into his arms at that moment, to envelop me with his warmth in a gentle embrace.

For just a moment, I let myself rest my head against his chest. And for just a moment, I imagined that this was our reality—that we were just a normal couple who loved each other. That we weren't possibly rushing to our deaths, that we weren't keeping secrets from each other. For just that perfect moment, I pretended this wasn't the end. I listened to his heartbeat, and I breathed in the scent of pines and apples.

Then, I pulled away from him again. "I don't know anything about this palace, or any palaces, really. Where would we find Baleros in there?"

Ruadan sniffed the air. "We'll have to scent him out."

"Roses. Sickly sweet roses."

"I remember."

I closed my eyes, breathing deeply to pick through all the smells. After a moment, the faint scent of roses floated on the wind from one of the palace walls—inside one of the courtyards.

"I've got it," I whispered.

"Wait," said Ruadan. He pulled a silver ring off his finger, and his violet magic pulsed and sparked around it until the whole ring glowed with his magic. "This will help you move undetected. My Wraith magic, distilled."

He handed it to me, and I slipped it onto my thumb. His magic skimmed over my skin. There was something strangely intimate about using another person's magic. It was like sleeping in their bed or wearing one of their shirts over your bare skin—a strange closeness to another person's essence, a little spark of their soul.

We walked over the grasses, along the perimeter of Hampton Court Palace, moving closer to the scent of roses coming from the courtyard. We kept at enough of a distance that we weren't bathed in too much light, our forms indistinct with Ruadan's magic.

The silence that bloomed around us had thorns.

I couldn't admit the truth to Ruadan, but I couldn't hide it from myself anymore. The other truth. The part about how I'd fallen in love with him.

For such a complicated thing, it was as simple as that. I didn't have a choice in it, any more than the ocean had a choice about crashing against the shore. It just was.

CHAPTER 31

*H*is fingers brushed against mine as we walked, and an electrical charge passed between us.

"Why did you punch me?" he asked quietly.

"Why does anything happen?" I asked. "Why does the ocean crash against the shore?" There was that image in my mind again.

"Because of the wind and the moon's gravitational—"

"Okay, that was a bad example."

"Sometimes earthquakes, or—"

"I get it." I swallowed hard. In this day and age, it was hard to think of anything without a viable explanation.

"Whatever it was," he said, "it was an amazingly inadequate answer."

"Says the man who answered literally no questions for years."

At the entrance to the courtyard, the scent of roses grew stronger, and I peered around the corner. There was so much light blazing out of the palace windows that I couldn't see anything within them.

Ruadan's wraith magic flickered around us, disguising us. Golden light blazed over the court—so bright it looked like daylight. Through the archway, I could see a fountain. Dark red liquid flowed from its ornate spigots—either blood or wine, I couldn't tell.

"We have to go in there," I whispered. "Can you make it a little darker?"

The temperature dropped, and darkness swelled around Ruadan, his pale hair whipping in the wind. A frigid power rippled over the landscape, and the bright golden light dulled to a dusky purple.

Now, there were just enough shadows for me to leap into the courtyard, into the darkness beside the fountain. Ruadan followed behind me, touching down on the cobbles in the shadows.

The palace walls towered high above us. From here, I could smell the distinct scent of claret. But over that, Baleros's rosy smell bloomed on the wind. It was coming from an archway on the other side—just to the left, I thought. Now, I had a pretty good idea of where to leap next.

Ruadan was doing that *indistinct* thing, and I couldn't quite see him, but I could feel his power close to me. "Almost there," I whispered.

Just for a moment, I caught his gaze. Not the shadowy eyes of an incubus, but Ruadan's violet eyes—the real Ruadan.

I wanted to tell him that I loved him, but something stopped me. I think it was that pragmatic survivor in me. The survivor knew it would kill me if my confession was met with silence. I might have had only a few more minutes to live, here, and it might be best if I didn't spend them falling apart emotionally.

Golden light lit up some of the windows, and if I wanted to move around rapidly inside the palace, I'd need even more darkness.

A flicker of myrrh on the breeze, and my pulse quickened. I did not want to find my father here. "I don't feel Adonis's presence." My voice broke as I lied. I hated lying, but I wanted it to be the truth.

An ice-cold wind whipped over me.

"How would you know what his presence feels like?" Ruadan asked.

Shit. I shook my head. "I don't know. I just don't feel anything like angel magic."

A lie. It was all around me, pulsing over my skin. The scent of myrrh tinged the wind under the roses.

I had to stop my father. Stop Adonis. Get the mist army.

I had twenty minutes to do it. No, less now.

Ruadan kept staring at me until I gave his arm a little smack. "We don't have time for this. You need to bring the darkness, now. Cover this place completely in shadows. I've got my iron sword. Let's go."

"You've got three minutes before I announce my presence." He closed his eyes. His body seemed to grow, and a wave of pure, dark power washed over me—thrilling and dizzying at the same time, like standing at the edge of a chasm. The effort of creating night seemed to have consumed him completely, and when I stared at him, it was like looking into the void itself. His body was still as marble. Never had he looked more remote.

When I closed my eyes, stars whirled in my mind over a blanket of vibrant purples and midnight blues.

When I opened my eyes again, shadows had blanketed the entire palace. I couldn't even see Ruadan anymore.

"I need you to stay out here," I whispered. "Promise me you'll stay here. Keep it dark."

His only response was a silky stroke of his magic over my skin, and my spine straightened at the touch.

I turned, then shadow-leapt to the archway. I felt around in front of me, then pushed through a wooden door. An *unlocked* wooden door. For just a moment, I hesitated. Was that a little too convenient? My heart thundered, and I drew my sword as I stepped inside.

I had to act fast. It was dark as the shadow hell in here. I reached out to feel the room around me—the cold stone of a wall, the swoop of a stone banister up a stairwell. I sniffed the air again, tuning into Baleros's scent.

Tracing my fingertips along the cold stone banister, I swooped up the stairs, toward the rose smell. I landed at the top of a stairwell.

Fifteen minutes left.

I touched the lumen stone at my neck, focusing on the room's interior. Pure blackness, shadows thick as velvet. And yet, by the echoing sounds of my footfalls, I had the sense I was in an enormous hall—one with high ceilings. Just a bit more light would have come in useful right now.

I shadow-leapt farther into the hall, and the overpowering scent of roses hit me. I wanted to throw up. I reached out in front of me to feel for Baleros, certain I'd touch the rough wool of his clothes.

Instead, my fingers touched flowers, their petals soft and wilted.

Actual roses.

Fuck, fuck, fuck. That had been the scent we'd followed? A little less darkness would be helpful, but I couldn't communicate that to Ruadan now.

A footfall behind me turned my head, and my heart leapt into my throat. I cut my sword through the darkness, swinging for the sound of the movement. A grunt and a gargle as the blade went through flesh, through bone. I just had no idea who I was fighting. Another creak of the floor, and I pivoted, my blade hacking into someone's neck. Blood sprayed on my skin.

Who was I fighting? Around me, I could hear the sounds of more footsteps, more guards moving.

Either my eyes had begun to adjust to the darkness or Ruadan was letting up on the shadows, because now I could just about make out the contours of the furniture around me.

Unfortunately, I could also make out the glinting of metal on the people surrounding me.

My stomach leapt. Guards crowded this room, closing in on me. I whirled and ducked, fighting off my attackers. I had to shadow-leap away from them.

Gods below. Was Baleros even in here, or had I simply been lured in by the scent of damn flowers?

Ruadan pulled back a bit more of the darkness. Silver light beamed into the room from stained-glass windows high above us, and I got a better view of the fae around me.

Battle fury thrummed through my blood, and I whirled into action. I drove my sword into a guard, plunging it right into his heart. Magic tickled my shoulder-blades, my power threatening to erupt. Adrenaline surged, blood pounding.

I am the blackening of your skin. I am the silence of a closed throat.

I was a maelstrom of fury, blade meeting flesh, over and over; carving, hacking, destroying....

Bow before me.

Until not a single guard remained.

I stood, catching my breath.

I needed to shadow-leap out of here, to keep moving. Except—I wasn't sure where I needed to go.

I sniffed the air again. Roses. Myrrh.

Dad?

They were here, I was sure of it. Baleros and Adonis.

My heart stuttered at the sight of a large, male form in the corner of the room.

"Dad?" I whispered.

I took a step closer, but a shrill singing rooted me in place. The singing of a bean nighe. I clamped my hands over my ears.

A wall of black, pressing down on my mind. This was the third scent in the room. The chalky scent of calcium, human bones—the stench of death and riverbeds. The bean nighe.

I forced my hands away from my ears, gripping my sword. I was ready to kill.

"Arianna." Baleros's voice, familiar as a lover's touch.

He *was* here. My heart stopped. Where *was* he?

Channeling the magic of the lumen-stone, I shadow-leapt to the silhouette I'd seen. But I found no one there—just an empty corner of the room.

As I got ready to leap again, one of the bean nighe shrieked louder. Someone was about to die.

I whirled, searching the contours of the room for Baleros. Where was he? That stupid vase of roses was confusing me.

I tuned into the sound of the bean nighe instead. Then, I shadow-leapt, touching down behind one of them. She screamed, and I silenced her with a blade through her throat. Why had he brought the bean nighe here?

"Arianna," Baleros said again, this time in a singsong voice that melded with the bean nighe's wild song. "Not your real name, is it?"

Something dark and dangerous was stirring inside me. "No," I said.

I leapt again, landing behind a second bean nighe near the center of the hall. I carved through her with the blade.

"I'm Liora."

CHAPTER 32

*T*hree minutes left.

"Angel of death," said Baleros. "If you were as powerful as your father, I might actually be frightened."

"Where is he?" I demanded.

"Who?"

"Adonis. I can smell him."

A dark chuckle from the shadows. "Miss him, did you? Even after what he did to your family?"

The bean nighe's wails grew louder, echoing off the high ceiling. How many of them were there? At last, the screeching erupted into wild shrieks. Death on the horizon, all around us.

Just like it had in the sewers, a wall of darkness slammed into my skull.

The memory claimed my mind, and I stared at my mother's hair, spread out over the soil. My father, Horseman of Death, had killed them all.

Except ... that wasn't what happened....

I fought against the cage of this vision, desperate to break free.

My fingers shook, legs trembled. I wasn't in the palace anymore. Now, I was back home, crouching behind a mulberry bush. Heart thundering, I stared at the fae invaders. My father had told me to run, but I couldn't tear myself away yet. I pulled my cap lower over my head, shielding my eyes. I could hardly breathe. I didn't know how to fight. My father had told me to hide here, not to move. I wasn't sure I could move if I wanted to, not with fear freezing my muscles.

The invaders rode enormous horses, hair flowing behind them. Darkness pulsed around their powerful bodies. They'd come here to kill us all. They were only a few hundred yards away, now.

My father stood in the clearing, his sword drawn. He didn't look scared at all. Why did he seem so calm? Why wasn't he afraid of dying?

From my hiding spot, I caught a glimpse of red hair—my mother taking cover behind an oak across the clearing. She nocked an arrow, then loosed it. With perfect aim, it struck one of the fae invaders. One after another, she let the arrows fly. I'd seen her kill a deer before, but nothing like this, each arrow finding its mark perfectly.

But there were too many invaders, racing closer, swords drawn.

My father turned to me, spotting me. He shouted at me to run.

They were going to kill us all.

Shimmering midnight wings sprouted from my father's back, each shot through with silver.

My world tilted.

I'd never seen the wings before, and their otherworldly beauty almost shocked me out of the horror of what was happening, almost robbed me of the realization that my father was an angel of death.

That's why they'd come for us—to rid the earth of angels.

The invaders were upon us, now, blades gleaming in the sunlight. My shoulder blades tingled, a dark power threatening to unleash itself. Shadows clouded my mind. I closed my eyes.

This time, I remembered it all—the dark truth I'd been running from for years.

From deep within me, a hurricane of dark magic ripped through the forest, our home. This time, I felt it come from me, wilting the plants around me, stealing breath.

I'm the toxins in your blood, the red drop on your lips. I make your fingers curl, black as mold. I'm a mother eating her young, the skull in the soil. All fall before me.

Dark magic erupted from my ribs, from my gut, a maelstrom of death—suffocating, poisoning all life around me.

I opened my eyes again.

All the fae around us were falling to the earth like autumn leaves. Blood dripped from my mother's mouth onto the soil. Her skin had turned purple, fingers blackening….

It had been me. The plague.

I ran from the clearing. Death sang its dirge around me as I sprinted, crunching over the soil.

I am the stalker that creeps up behind you. I will steal your food and your breath.

I ran until my legs were ready to give way, until my lungs ached for air. I ran until I found the glimmering, star-flecked portal.

* * *

MY OWN SCREAMS rang in my ears as I snapped free from the memory. I wanted blood.

I am the stalker that creeps up behind you. I will steal your food and your breath.

At last, I understood.

My father hadn't killed everyone that day. It had been me. A sharp hollowness pierced me from the inside out. I'd killed my mother. I was as powerful as Adonis, and my magic had slaughtered the whole village.

Had my father been able to bring her back? I had to—

I blinked, looking around. The survivor in me needed me to focus on the present. *Take stock of your surroundings. Stay in the moment. Don't let Baleros distract you.*

I caught my breath, surveying the dark hall around me. Silver light streamed in from the stained-glass windows, washing over the tapestries and the piles of guards I'd killed. Moonlight bathed the roses wilting on all the banquet tables and silvered the two dead bean nighe bleeding on the wood floor.

Adonis wasn't in here. No one living was in here.

While I'd been reliving the worst day of my life, Baleros had slipped away, leaving me distracted.

I wasn't his target. Ruadan was the real target.

A deep voice boomed from outside. "I am Ruadan, Prince of Emain, son of Queen Macha."

My toes curled. *You idiot.*

He was giving up, trying to turn himself in.

With a ragged breath, I gripped my sword, racing down the stone steps.

When I flung open the door to the courtyard, I found Ruadan surrounded by Baleros's entire army—the mist soldiers, the jackdaws in their cloaks. Distantly, I heard the sound of someone chanting an Angelic spell.

My father was an expert in Angelic.

I sniffed the air. Roses—and myrrh.

Fog curled around the darkened courtyard. In the center of the mist army, shadows pooled around Ruadan. He was creating darkness—for me, so I could get away. I wasn't leaving him.

Tendrils of magic snaked through the air around him. His power seemed to be weakening, the star-flecked shimmer of his magic dulling. Why?

The sound of Angelic grew louder. With a jolt of horror, I understood what was happening. Ruadan had said one of the only ways to kill him was to use an Angelic spell—and Baleros, it seemed, knew the exact spell. Baleros was trying to make him mortal.

Panic punched me in the gut.

I sniffed the air, homing in on the roses until I found him. There. Baleros stood all the way on the other side of the courtyard—in the archway, holding a sword. He held something else, as well. Something that gleamed in the moonlight.

A lumen stone glowed around his neck. I couldn't give him the chance to leap away by letting him know I was coming.

I touched my lumen stone, then leapt into the air just before him. Fast as a hummingbird's breath, I swung the sword for his neck as I landed.

A precise arc, a hair's breadth away from his skin. I cut the lumen stone off him, and it fell to the brick.

He stared at me, the corner of his lip twitching. He was gripping a sword, but he couldn't move it. Not with me threatening to slice his jugular.

I steal your food and your breath, draw your ribs out from under your skin....

I pointed my sword at his throat. "Hi, Baleros."

He didn't look concerned. "Tick tock, Liora. I gave you a time limit. Three minutes till nine. I'll need the iron on Ruadan when he gives himself up. I'm sure you understand."

"Where is Adonis?" I asked through gritted teeth. The air smelled heavy with the scent of myrrh.

"I think he'll be disappointed with you."

With a jolt of horror, I realized that the rhythmic cadences of Angelic were still floating through the air, the spell carrying on where Baleros had left off. Dozens of voices chanted in unison. With the tip of my sword trained on Baleros's throat, I stole a quick look behind me. The jackdaws had simply picked up where Baleros had left off. They all knew the spell. They were going to kill Ruadan right here.

"Stop them," I said.

With a movement so fast I could hardly track it, he brought his sword to my neck. That look I'd stolen had cost me.

*Gods*damn *it. I should have just killed him instead of asking about Adonis.*

I stared into his eyes, which were lightly crinkled at the corners. The death angel in me longed for release, and my father's magic surrounded us. Where *was* he?

My heart boomed against my ribs, heavy footfalls of a dark beast.

I am the stalker that creeps up behind you when you're trying to find the right words.

A vision flashed in my mind—Ruadan threading flowers together for me.

I couldn't stand here while they killed Ruadan. I had to stop this.

I'm here when you're searching to fill the silence, fleeing the dark truth.

A voice in my mind. A thousand voices, mingling together, high and low, dissonant. Magic raced down my back, my shoulder blades blazing with power. The wind whipped around me, cold and unforgiving.

You hold up a landscape you painted; you grin at your gold; you buy a house on the hill overlooking the lake. You smile proudly. See this? you think. It will last forever. You don't see me looming behind you. I'm a long twilight shadow over cemetery grass. I enshroud your body from the toes up.

Dark ecstasy claimed my mind as wings erupted from my back. I lifted off the earth.

Sweet release, an embrace of the dark truth.

My midnight wings—streaked with gold—lifted me into the air, night wind racing over my skin, tearing at my hair.

I read the shock on Baleros's face.

Bow before me.

From above, I drove my sword into him, impaling him from the skull down, splitting him in two. For just a moment, blood poured out of him. Then, his body erupted into flames, the hot blast knocking me back.

His sword fell to the ground with a clang. And something else, too —a gleaming chalice.

What *was* that? The cup called to me with its own dark magic, and I yearned to pick it up. But it wasn't the time, and I needed to stay in the air. Baleros wasn't truly dead. The Fire Goddess would revive him. But I had his mist army, now, and it was time to deploy them.

My powerful wings lifted me higher over the crowd of jackdaws, and they still chanted.

I raised my sword, shouting my first command to my mist soldiers: "Attack the humans!"

A smile curled my lips, relief washing over me. Fog curled into the air as the mist soldiers whirled into action. Their swords began carving into the black cloaks.

All fall before me.

From the air, I glanced at Ruadan. My mist soldiers were attacking the jackdaws, but his power was fading fast, coils of star-flecked magic flitting away from his body like smoke on the wind. His eyes were closed, his body hunched as they turned him mortal. The sight of it bruised my heart.

I rob your memories, leave you with only a final glimmer of knowledge. I take that, too. I steal your food and your breath, draw your ribs out under your skin, carve your belly.

I shouted his name, but he couldn't hear me. It was like he was totally collapsing into himself—a black hole of magic. Shadows swallowed him.

The mist army was fighting the humans, but not fast enough. The jackdaws had no fear, and they weren't running. They were standing their ground, chanting. Stealing his immortality.

I'm the green smear on your mouth, the sallow in your skin, the swaying darkness under your feet and your last rasping breath. I'm the eternal darkness that awaits you at the end, and I have always been with you.

Death rippled out of my body like an atomic blast. Euphoria claimed my mind.

From the sky, I stared down at the courtyard to see the humans falling to the ground. Ruadan, too, had doubled over, his enormous form collapsing onto the stone.

In the end, you will all bow before me; you will all lay down your lives and worship at my altar.

Their bodies were a beautiful canvas of purple, red, and black, painted with my brush. My own landscape. Death was my creation.

Ecstasy lit me up as I completed the task I'd been born for. I'd killed them all. They rotted below, bleeding from the mouths, the streaks of red. The Plague was a beautiful mixture of cold hues and warm, purple skin—

The Plague.

The scent of myrrh was overpowering. It was Adonis's scent, but mine, too.

Baleros was winning. Nine o'clock. I was spreading the Plague myself, and the wave of death I'd unleashed was still rippling over the city. My heart was ready to explode. I should be thinking about all of them, about the city of London itself, but only one thought crystallized in my mind.

Was Ruadan still immortal, or had I killed him?

My wings pounded the air like a heartbeat as I swooped to hover over where he lay on the stone.

When I met Ruadan's violet eyes, relief flooded me. But only for a moment. The truth was out now, and he was staring at me in my real form.

With what looked like great effort, he forced himself to stand. Wrath etched his features, and something cold split me in two.

Here I am, Ruadan. A creature never meant to walk the earth. The monster who spreads the Plague.

From the air, I looked out over the horizon, at the midnight magic rippling toward London. I needed to stop the death from spreading. *Could* I stop it?

When I closed my eyes, I saw her again—my mother. This time she looked alive, her body blazing with light. I didn't come from Adonis alone—I'd come from my mother, Ruby, too, a being of light. I could remember her light touch on my skin, the gold in her eyes, her kisses on my cheek when she thought I was asleep.

The waves of death seeped back into me, drawn back from the horizon. I pulled my magic back into myself.

My enormous wings beat the air, and I lowered myself to the ground to face Ruadan—my lover and my enemy.

For the first time since I'd met him, I found him shifted completely. Black leather wings spread out behind him, his eyes swirling with darkness. Two dark horns gleamed on his head. He looked like my nightmarish hallucination—the one where I'd envisioned him trying to kill me.

He was holding something aloft—the gleaming chalice. Dark magic wafted off it. It smelled of myrrh....

The sight of him fully shifted sent ice streaming through my veins and left me breathless. A low growl trembled over my skin, then deepened and rumbled through my gut. The incubus in him had come out completely, and he wanted blood. Violet magic crackled over his muscled body.

Ruadan as an incubus was a strangely beautiful nightmare. Part of my brain was screaming at me to run. But his magic was skimming over my body, and the other half of my brain wanted to take a step closer to him, to bask in his eerie beauty, feel his breath on my neck. Ruadan was dangerous as hells—a hunter who could lure you to your own death.

His body glowed as he fed off my pain.

My finger twitched at the hilt of my sword. Everyone had to die sometime.

CHAPTER 33

The mist army spread out behind me, awaiting my next order. Tendrils of fog curled off their bodies, twining in the river's breeze.

Another flash of the death instinct rattled along my bones, spurring me on to kill the enemy before me. My wings thumped the air, feet lifting off the ground just a little. Maybe … just maybe, if my magic was powerful enough, I could kill even a demigod—Angelic spell or not.

Death, the conqueror, reigns supreme. All fall before me.

My fists tightened, nails piercing my palms. *Rein it in, Liora. Stay in control.*

In the end, all bow to me—even the gods.

The look he was giving me was glacial, eyes black, body unmoving. I gripped my sword as I landed before him. His wings spread out behind him. Long, black claws had grown from his fingertips, and I stared at the unyielding, otherworldly face of a predator.

Gripping the chalice, he stared at Death—his ancient enemy.

Kneel, demigod, or I'll rip the life from your body.

I gritted my teeth, my mind flashing with the image of a wreath made of wildflowers and leaves, the one I'd left in Emain. Emptiness ate at my chest. Half of me wanted to sneak off into the shadows, to curl up like an animal crawling off to die. The other half—the survivor in me—wanted to destroy, wanted to leave this man bleeding on the stone before me.

His cold, lethal stare cut me to the quick.

I'd known that the betrayal would kill me before the sword ever did, and at that moment … the way Ruadan was looking at me, it felt like a battle I was losing.

I felt my wings fold and shrink into my shoulder blades as the death instinct flitted away on the wind.

I tried to read Ruadan's expression, but I found nothing there. Just the icy stare of a void demon. I knew how he moved. If he wanted to, he could rip my heart out before I had the chance to see the first twitch of his muscles.

This painful, jagged silence broke my heart. My chest felt like it was being cleaved in two, and Ruadan's body glowed as he fed from my heartbreak.

I glanced at the chalice he was holding, breathed in the scent of my father. Only then did I understand—distilled magic. My father had never been here at all.

I wasn't the Angel of Death anymore. I wasn't Arianna. I was just Liora, and I'd never felt so alone in my life.

Ruadan's power strengthened as he fed off my pain.

"Adonis didn't have a son," I said. "He had a daughter who dressed like a boy. That was me." I tightened my grip on the sword. "My name is Liora. Half fae, half death angel. I saw your kill list. I'm on it."

Silence pressed down on us, interrupted only by the sound of the wind rushing over the river.

I didn't see Ruadan move—just a dark sweep of wind, then I felt his body behind me, his warmth pressing against me. He traced a clawed fingertip over my collarbone, and something dangerous and electrical raced through my blood. It felt like a caress, one tinged with sharpness. It was a warning, too. My head would be gone before I had a chance to react.

My heart beat so hard I was sure Ruadan could hear it.

"Did he send you?" asked Ruadan.

I could hardly think straight, confusion clouding my mind. "Who? Baleros?" We'd been over this. I already told him the truth.

"Adonis."

Anger roiled. "I haven't seen him since the day you came to kill us. He's not working with Baleros. He never was. That chalice you're holding there is my father's magic distilled. Just like you distilled yours in the ring I'm wearing."

"The Unholy Grail," said Ruadan, his voice pure ice. "Some legends are true. It's a magic that doesn't belong on Earth. The destroyer of worlds."

"Speaking of not belonging, you should never have come for us." Rage laced my voice, an anger I didn't know I'd been sheltering. If Ruadan hadn't invaded that day, I wouldn't be here. "You didn't belong in our world. We were fine until you came."

I stole a glance behind me, at his powerful body looming over me. In the V of his dark shirt, the World Key glowed with gold. Those few inches of skin were the root of all this chaos. Anger snapped through my nerve endings, ready to explode.

"From where I'm standing, you're the destroyer of worlds." The fury in my voice surprised even me. "We weren't hurting anyone where we were. We were locked in our own world. You crushed it." I elbowed him hard in the chest, but he hardly moved. "What do you expect when you invade a place? You think you can come to kill people and they won't fight back? Guess what, Ruadan? It wasn't my father who killed everyone. It was me. I killed your cohort. I killed your brothers. I killed my mum, too. That was me. I didn't know it until the bean nighe made me relive it just now. I'm powerful, just like my father. Now you know. I'm on your list. So what are you going to do?"

I stole another look behind me. Darkness swathed him, mist and shadows curling around him in wild whorls. Silence cloaked the courtyard, coldness danced up my spine. Any moment now, he'd rip my head off like I'd seen him do to his enemies.

The tip of his claw traced over my neck. This wasn't Ruadan—this was the incubus.

Or was it the same thing? I told myself that the Angel of Death wasn't me. I told myself I was just Liora, and that was all there was to it. But maybe we couldn't carve ourselves up that way, into neat little parts. Death was a part of me—just like this cold, predatory demon was a part of Ruadan. We all had our own ways of protecting ourselves. This was Ruadan's.

I reached up, and I ran my fingertips along the inside of his wrist, the vulnerable part. Then, I kissed his skin.

His arm stiffened. Then, an almost inaudible exhale—a hint of relief.

At last, he spoke. "I need the mist army to defend the Institute." His voice was like dark velvet skimming over my body, so smooth I nearly forgot the threat he was delivering.

"There's only one way to get it." It was a dangerous dare, but I needed to see what he would do. My heart slammed against my ribs. I could still do it. If I needed to, I could let the death angel come out.

I pulled his arm from me and stepped away over the cobbles, and he didn't stop me. I turned to face him. Those dark, otherworldly wings still swooped behind him.

He took a step closer to me, and my heart nearly stopped. Then, he simply walked past me, stalking off into the shadows by the Thames.

Emptiness cut me open. In this world, Ruadan and Baleros were the only ones who knew the truth about me, and both reviled me.

A hot tear spilled down my cheek, and I wiped it away. "I can still help you," I called out. "I'll help you defend the Institute."

No response. Only the dark, heavy quiet of the river.

CHAPTER 34

Mist curled around my new room, fogging up the window. I swiped my palm over the cold pane. From here, I had a distant view of the Institute, and the mist army patrolling it—*my* mist army, as I was quickly coming to think of them.

For the past two days, my mist soldiers' eerie presence had been enough to deter the human terrorists from trying to mob the Tower. And while the mist soldiers had helped defend it, the Tower's mages had rebuilt the golden moat.

I had no idea what Ruadan had done with the Unholy Grail, or what he planned to do with it. We hadn't spoken in days.

As I stared out the window, Ciara sidled up to me, crossing her arms. "Aren't you feeling a bit cooped up in here?" she asked. "You haven't left in two days."

I hadn't wanted to take my eyes off the Institute. It had been my home. Maybe I was no longer a Shadow Fae, but I couldn't stop thinking about it.

"I'm fine," I said. "Just keeping an eye on things. What did you hear when you went out today? Did our ruse work?"

"*Our* ruse?" she said. A not-so-subtle reminder that I was no longer a knight. "You mean the Shadow Fae plan to pin the blame on

Baleros? *The Sun* already published an article about Baleros, right after a story about two soap stars who were falling out of their bikinis. They're calling Baleros the Trenchcoat Terrorist."

I smiled. "Good. Perfect."

"Things seem to have calmed down a bit since you killed all the jackdaws," she added.

"Any sign of Baleros out there?" I asked.

"I haven't heard anything. Don't you have your mist soldiers looking for him?"

I loosed a long sigh, turning back into the center of the room. Three of the mist soldiers sat on the floor, staring into space. They were here to protect us and occasionally buy snacks. The rest I'd sent out on missions—hunting for Baleros, protecting the Institute. Only, it was hard to get information from them, seeing as they didn't speak. I'd simply sent them out with the instructions to find a man who smelled of roses and wore the mark of Emerazel on his shoulder.

"They haven't turned anything up yet. One of them came back with a handful of roses, and I thought maybe he was trying to give me a message about having found Baleros, but after a while, it became clear that he'd been confused about the mission and thought I wanted roses."

"Well, I need some air," said Ciara. "I'm going out for Kit-Kats."

"At this hour? Just send one of the mist guys."

She shook her head. "I can't sleep if I don't move around some. Anyway, you don't need to worry about me anymore, on account of me being a fire demon."

"Fine. But take a mist guy with you."

"Whatever."

One of the soldiers rose from the floor, fog billowing around him. He followed Ciara out the door.

I stared at the other two, now, wishing they could speak. I didn't like the silence anymore. It felt like I'd been buried alive.

I had hardly anything in the room to distract me. It was a step up from living under a car, like Ciara had, but it was basically an empty apartment. A bare, unheated living room with woodchip walls and an empty fireplace. An adjoining kitchen with a broken washer-dryer and a fridge that didn't work. No furniture.

I hadn't spoken to Ruadan in days. I wasn't a knight anymore, apparently, but he hadn't tried to kill me. Had my mist soldiers gotten me off the kill list? Or had they moved me up it, since Ruadan wanted to control them?

I had no idea what my current status was. Right now, I was in limbo.

I stared out the window at the Institute again. This was beginning to feel a bit sad, frankly—my life on the outside, still obsessed with the palace.

A pile of pillows and blankets lay in a corner of the room, and I crossed to them. I lay down, pulling one of the wool blankets on top of me. In this limbo world of mine, distinctions between daytime clothing and pajamas had no meaning. I just slept in the jeans and T-shirt I was already wearing.

I frowned at the mist soldiers. "Can you guard outside the door? I can't sleep with you staring at me there."

Once they left the room, I pulled off my bra and lay down on the blankets. I lay flat on my back, arms over my head, and I closed my eyes. As I drifted off, I thought of Ruadan's fingertip stroking along my collarbone, sending an electric thrill pounding through my blood. I imagined his skin, the faint taste of salt on his neck. I licked my lips and reached under my T-shirt. My hands brushed over my hardening nipples.

My skin heated, and my eyes opened. And when they did, my heart started to gallop out of my chest.

Ruadan was there—standing above me, his pale violet eyes piercing the darkness. I pulled my hands out from under my shirt.

"Are you here to kill me?" I asked breathlessly.

"No."

Good. Because I wouldn't want to have to unleash my dark side again. "Were you watching me while I slept?" I snapped. "Creep."

"I'm half-incubus. Creepily looming over people while they sleep is part of my nature."

"Have you come to ask me back to the Institute?"

He shook his head, and my heart sank. "No."

"Then why are you here?" That rage erupted in my tone again. I couldn't help how I'd been born.

"The Unholy Grail. The Plague, contained in a chalice. It's the ultimate bargaining chip."

"Okay. And?"

"Its existence is a threat to every living creature on Earth. But only one person can destroy it. The person who made it."

I shook my head. "My father. Why would he have made a chalice like that?"

"I guess we'll find out."

Warmth flickered between my ribs. Was I going home? "So, you don't want to kill him anymore."

"Destroying the Unholy Grail is our priority."

Cold. Clinical. An icy demon of the void.

"You want to open the world again. The portal to my home," I said quietly.

My chest tightened. What would we find there? My father, alone? Left with no one but the people I'd killed all those years ago? Nothing but the bodies surrounding him?

My father, the fallen angel, left in a world on his own, surrounded by death. I shouldn't have left him there.

I moved for Ruadan, so fast I didn't know what I was doing. I gripped his forearms, fingernails digging into his flesh. "You have to take me to him, Ruadan." It was the voice of my death angel, the voice of many.

His calm, soothing magic whispered over me. "I need to be able to trust you."

"And I need to trust you."

No reply. Classic Ruadan.

He plucked my hands off his arms. Then, with a furrow between his eyebrows, he reached into his cloak. He pulled out a wreath—one made of oak leaves and threaded with honeysuckle.

He handed it to me.

Shocked, I took it from him. "What does this mean?" I asked.

He looked as confused as I was. I wasn't sure I'd ever seen him look confused before. "I don't know."

He rose, heading for the door.

"Tomorrow, we find Adonis."

The door closed behind him.

I turned to watch out the window until I saw the blur of dark wind through the night—Ruadan heading back to the Institute.

The Grand Master might not like it, but he needed me. He needed my mist army. He needed me to speak to Adonis.

I lifted the wreath to my head.

COURT OF DREAMS

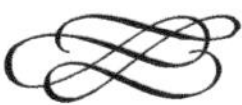

SHADOW FAE—BOOK FOUR

CHAPTER 1

Any minute now, Maddan would realize that I was standing about two feet away from him, watching as he pretended to do hot yoga.

Right now, he was sliding his hand down his leg and sticking his bum out in a half-arsed stretch. It was clear he was deriving no inner peace from this class, nor improved flexibility. Based on the angle of his gaze and the revolting bulge in his shorts, his real goal here was to stare at women's bums.

The sight before me was basically a living nightmare, and there were few things I'd rather do less than watch the Prince of Elfame sweat into terrycloth bands while sporting a semi. I may have survived years in the gladiator ring, but there was only so much horror one woman could handle in a lifetime.

Sadly, I didn't have a choice. Maddan had crucial information, and I needed to beat it out of him as soon as he stepped out of the yoga studio door.

Here was my current situation: I'd become a fugitive from the Institute, an enemy of the Shadow Fae. The knights now knew I was an angel of death. They understood that I'd hidden my true nature from them, and that I was a bit dangerous. Like, I could kill most of the earth's population if I lost my temper. It seemed these facts vexed them.

As a fugitive, I hadn't slept in weeks. I'd been moving from one flat to another, snoozing only for a few minutes at a time. See, if I dreamt, they could find me.

But even in my fevered state, I'd come up with a brilliant plan.

I needed to prove I was one of the Shadow Fae, that I belonged in the Institute, and that they shouldn't kill me. If I used Maddan to gather key information about the Institute's enemies, I could demonstrate that I was still on their side. That I was still meant to fight alongside them.

And then, I could sleep.

I blinked, fighting fatigue. Maddan hunched over in a sad approximation of downward dog.

Let the monster out to play....

I bit my lip, trying to clear my thoughts. I was at the point of delirium where I'd actually started hearing voices—particularly the mocking voice of my old gladiator master, Baleros. If I figured out how to kill him, not only could I get back in the Institute's good graces, but maybe I could silence his presence in my mind. Maddan could lead me to him, and I'd kill him. It all made perfect sense.

My heart hammered against my ribs as I weighed my options. When I attacked the prince, I wouldn't have any magic to work with. Not unless I wanted to unleash a set of black feathered wings and an outbreak of plague that would kill all of London.

I stared at the ginger prince. I had only one weapon with me: a dagger strapped to my waist, just under my jersey. Maddan, on the other hand, had proper magical weapons. For one thing, he wore a lumen stone around his neck. That meant that if he got outside, into the darkness, he'd be able to leap away from me through the shadows.

As I studied him closer, I got a better read on his magical defenses. His body shimmered with a second kind of magic—the glimmering red agony kind. If I tried to trap him in this room, around all these humans, the Prince of Elfame would take out every person in here—including a sweet-looking elderly woman in a cat T-shirt.

Our blond teacher lifted her arms over her head. "And take a deep breath in through your nose."

As she spoke, my attention was still on Maddan. I'd attack him in the stairwell away from the humans, before he opened the door to the street outside. The fluorescent lights in the stairwell would stop him from leaping away.

"And let yourself roll down, one vertebra at a time." The instructor's soothing voice filled the room. "And move down to your hands."

Maddan's gaze was fixed straight ahead, intent on a tight pair of leggings—violet, like Ruadan's magic.

At the thought of him, a hollow pain opened in my chest. I hadn't heard a word from him in weeks. He'd given me a pretty wreath, then he'd disappeared like a puff of mist in the night.

If he wanted me dead, I couldn't run from him forever. *No one* could run from the Wraith. I'd tried it once. I'd traveled miles through icy rivers. I'd woken to find Ruadan looming over me, weapons glinting. As a god of the night, sleep was his dominion. He could track me through my dreams.

We'd had our moments, sure. He'd healed me, brought me into his bed when I'd been sleeping on the floor. We'd protected each other numerous times. We'd shagged in a sewer. But the fact was, I was half death angel, and Ruadan had sworn to kill my kind.

The abrupt loss of him from my life felt like a jagged ravine in my chest, but I was a survivor. I could outsmart him. If I didn't dream, he couldn't find me. Ha! I was perfectly safe, as long as I allowed myself to slowly go insane. A brilliant plan, really, apart from the hallucinations, confusion, and complete inability to regulate my emotions.

My little monster.... Baleros's voice purred in the darkest hollows of my mind. *Scrambling in the dirt.*

Another piercing bite of my lip, and my attention snapped back to the yoga class.

"Exhaling out through your mouth, and let the relaxation fill your muscles." The teacher's voice re-centered me. "Arms into prayer pose, and ... did you guys hear about the people who got the Plague?"

Okay. This particular yoga teacher needed to work a bit on her relaxing patter. Guilt coiled through my gut at the mention of the Plague. Where the hells had it come from? I'd let out some of my death magic when I'd tried to save Ruadan at Hampton Court Palace, but I had thought it was only a tiny bit.

"Arms over your head, and breathe out." She smiled. "Really horrific. And I've heard it's going to get worse. Like, death everywhere, all over London's streets. And moving down gently into child's pose, take a deep relaxing breath. But yeah, it's, like, people bleeding from swollen glands in their necks."

A monster like you shouldn't be on earth, should you? said Baleros's voice.

I gritted my teeth, then whispered under my breath, "Shut up, Baleros. Get out of my head."

"Okay, and now let your head hang, rolling down slowly," the teacher chirped. "And some people are saying it can make your skin rot."

I sucked in a sharp breath at this vivid description, my body now vibrating with tension.

Should have kept you in your cage under the earth.

"Get out of my head!" I failed to keep my voice down that time.

Bollocks.

Maddan's attention shot to me, and the shock of understanding shone on his pale features. He pivoted, rushing through the class toward the front of the room.

A smile curled my lips. *That's right, bitch. I'm here for you.*

I sprinted after him, weaving between the yoga students. I slammed through the door into the stairwell. Only a few moments to catch him before I lost him.

Adrenaline sparked through my veins as the prince thundered down the stairs of the old Victorian building. I pulled my dagger from its sheath, its blade pure iron.

Death magic beat in my chest like a raven's wings, and I shot down the stairs right after him. He was getting too close to the exit, nearly at the door.

Just as he reached for the handle, I snatched the back of his shirt, clenching it in a death grip.

I braced myself for a blast of his red pain magic. It took only a moment for the shimmering magic to explode from his body, and agony ripped through my bones and muscles. Still, I held onto his shirt tight, forcing myself to maintain my concentration with an iron will. Then, I slammed him against the wall, face-first. Lightning-fast, I rammed the iron dagger into his shoulder blade. The iron in the knife would stop him from summoning any more red magic. His scream echoed off the high ceiling.

Pressing him firmly against the wall, I stood on my tiptoes. "Stop screaming or I'll cut your tongue out."

"You're a sadist," he whimpered.

"I'm a monster, and you tortured me too, so I'm less inclined to go easy. Now keep your voice down."

"What do you want?" he stammered.

"I want to know where Baleros is. He's an enemy of the Institute."

"So are you."

My stomach dropped. Even Maddan knew about my fugitive status? "What?" He'd caught me totally off guard.

"You're not part of the Institute anymore," he grunted. "So why do you care?"

I felt unmoored, completely lost. He was getting me sidetracked, and I pressed the blade in further. "Stop distracting me. I want to know about Baleros. I know your father is working with him. Tell me where to find him or the pain will get worse."

Maddan groaned, thrashing to get away from me.

I twisted the blade, eliciting another scream. "I said where is he, you worm!"

"I don't know!" he whined. "Baleros doesn't trust me to know his location."

I narrowed my eyes. This was actually a believable claim. Baleros was many things, but stupid wasn't one of them. "Tell me what you do know. What's he planning?"

He groaned. "Baleros is not happy that you took the mist army from him. In fact, he's furious with you."

"And?"

"Plague…" he groaned.

"What about it?" Ruadan had captured the Unholy Grail—the artifact that held my father's death magic. The Institute had been keeping it safe. So how could anyone spread the Plague when the magic could only come from my dad or me?

Maddan groaned. "Ruadan, all the Shadow Fae. They've got the Plague. They'll be dead within days."

At his words, that jagged ravine in my chest cut a little deeper.

CHAPTER 2

My blood roared in my ears. "What are you talking about? How is Baleros spreading the Plague?"

"The Unholy Grail is in the Tower."

"I know that, worm." I dug my fingernails into his shoulder. "That means it's safe."

"Except that someone in the Tower knows how to unleash its magic," he said. "Baleros's agent infected the Shadow Fae. They don't know there's a traitor among them, and he's still there."

My mind screamed with panic and a sense of vindication at the same time. So this *had* been a good idea.

"The knights don't know someone in the Institute has turned on them?" I asked in disbelief.

He grunted from the pain. "They're not even looking for a traitor. All Shadow Fae think you spread the Plague. I'm surprised you're still alive. Why haven't they killed you?"

Another brief flash of vindication. I'd been *right* to be paranoid, to refuse sleep, to move from place to place.

Then, the reality of the situation hit me. The knights were all dying, and they definitely wanted to kill me.

"*Who* is working for Baleros? Which knight?" I hissed. "I need a name!"

"I don't know that!" he screeched. "And what difference does it make? It's too late to save them."

My knees went weak. "What do you mean too late?"

His face was mashed against the wall. "No one can reverse the Plague. No one except Adonis, and you don't know where he is, do you?"

Now Maddan was trying to get information from me. I wasn't about to give it to him.

In any case, I could find my father, maybe. If I could get Ruadan to open the portal and send me through into my old home.

"A name," I said icily.

"I swear to the gods I don't know that. I just know the Plague is already spreading, and you're too late. Baleros wants to create chaos. He wants Ruadan dead so he can get the World Key. The Plague is supposed to weaken the Wraith. Then, Baleros's agent will kill him as soon as he gets the chance. He'll cut the key off his corpse."

A wild surge of protectiveness rippled through me. Maybe the Shadow Fae wanted me dead, but I had to warn Ruadan about the truth. I just needed more details.

I pushed Maddan hard against the wall. "Tell me anything you know about the traitor. Anything at all."

"I don't know. I don't—"

A scream from the stairs cut through the interrogation. I glanced at the elderly woman in the cat T-shirt.

"Murderer!" she shrieked. In her panic, she dropped the yoga mat from under her arm.

Bloody hells. I couldn't imagine why I'd liked her earlier.

"Stay where you are!" I shouted at her.

I couldn't deal with both of these screaming people at once. I had to keep Maddan pinned or he'd slip away into the shadows outside.

Cat Lady was still screaming, her shrieks deafening me.

Let the monster out....

My breath sped up as I started losing control. "What's his entire plan, Maddan?" I shouted.

"I told you. Spread the Plague. Get the World Key. Take over the Institute."

"Why is he so hells-bent on doing this?"

"Because!" Maddan shouted impatiently. "If he can open and control the worlds, he can use his power to control the demons trapped within them. He can conscript them to join his army, offering them freedom in return for their swords. He wants to rule the world. It's not complicated."

Dread slid through my bones. "What else do you know?"

"He won't fail. Now, he has a powerful ally on his side."

"The person in the Institute? Who?" I barked.

"Someone you know very well—"

The creaking of the door made my heart skip a beat. Cat Lady had slipped past us and opened it. Maddan craned his head to look outside, into the shadows.

It was enough. I felt the electrical rush of shadow magic from his lumen stone, the whoosh of air as he leapt past me. The knife in his shoulder blade had torn his flesh when he'd jumped. I held nothing but the gore-soaked weapon now.

I stepped outside, onto the main road. Cat Lady was running down the pavement, screaming into her mobile phone. Maddan was nowhere to be found. Six of my mist soldiers milled around the sidewalk, but they hadn't been able to stop Maddan's leap.

I loosed a sigh, rubbing a knot in my forehead. My muscles burned and dizziness clouded my thoughts.

The Shadow Fae were all dying of the Plague—and they thought it was my fault.

My days were numbered—but so were those of all the Shadow Fae. If I could get to Ruadan and speak to him, maybe I could convince him of the truth. We could find my dad together. It was the only way to move forward.

* * *

Ciara sat next to a human on a white leather sofa. His name was Jared.

I paced in front of them, wringing my hands as I did. My body buzzed with nervous energy. I'd sent a message to the Institute, explaining clearly that I had crucial information they needed to hear. Now, I only had to wait to hear back from them.

Jared let out a sigh, staring at me dreamily. "Amazing to have real supernaturals here." A blond wig was draped over his wool sweater, and a set of plastic ears poked through the hair. The whole enormous room smelled of stale cigarettes, incense, and sweat. "Legally, I'm not allowed to be in a room with women unsupervised, but I don't think the rules apply to your kind."

I pivoted, turning the other way. "Good to know."

Jared was one of those humans who had a total hard-on for the fae. He believed he was meant to be one of us, but the gods had messed it up. He was thrilled to let Ciara and me stay in his luxurious but stinking apartment for a night. Embarrassingly, he actually knew more of the Ancient Fae language than I did, and he'd started teaching me the few commands I needed to really control the mist army.

Apart from the stench, Jared's flat was a perfect hideout. It offered a balcony view of the Institute's gatehouse—just on the other side of the stone courtyard. We were so close that the golden glow of the moat beamed onto his hardwood floors through his balcony windows.

I turned to the balcony windows again, staring out. The Institute's battlements seemed to rise from a cloud of fog, and the moat's golden light streamed through the mist in perfect rays.

My throat tightened as I thought of what was going on behind those Tower walls: Shadow Fae dying in the Institute, cursing me with their final breaths.

A sharp crack of pain pierced my chest. I'd only unleashed my death angel side to save Ruadan—I never would have tried to hurt him. I wouldn't harm the other Shadow Fae, either.

It stung that Ruadan believed I'd poison them on purpose. Is that what he thought of me? That I was some sort of a—

A monster like you....

"Shut up, Baleros," I muttered.

The betrayal was eating at me like a cancer. In the depths of my mind, Ruadan's perfect features began to merge with Baleros's rugged face.

"I need to talk to Ruadan right away." I slid the balcony door open, and the chilly wind rushed over my skin. Mist floated in on the breeze and coiled around me.

"Liora."

I turned to find Jared lifting his wine.

"Ye mighty faestress! Please partake in mead with me as we dine together, we fae." He looked at me hopefully, eyebrows raised.

I scowled, grabbing a bottle of whiskey off his marble countertop. "First of all, you don't have mead. Second of all, faestress is not a word. Next of all, mead is gross, and I would never drink it. What number were we on? It doesn't matter. The point is, please stop talking, because I'm busy thinking about death and betrayal."

He raised his arms. "O wild spiritess of the oaks—"

My lip curled, and I growled at him, letting my canines show.

He fell completely silent, paling. Mist skimmed over his floor and his sofa.

Ciara frowned at me. "Stop scaring the rich human. And stop worrying. Once the note gets to Ruadan, he'll get right back to you. He knows you wouldn't hurt him. You'll be back in the Institute in no time. What can you see out there?"

"Whole lot of fog." That was the problem with the mist soldiers. You could never see shit.

I could beckon them to me at any moment by whispering a particular spell, but I tried to stay patient. They had to get the message to Ruadan. I'd included just enough details that he'd understand the urgency of the situation, but not so many that they could fall into the wrong hands.

I turned back to the balcony, hovering in the doorway. How sick was Ruadan? I could only hope his demigod nature gave him added protection. After all, that's how he'd survived my blast of death magic, years ago.

But any amount of weakness could provide an assassination opportunity to the traitor.

The great, ancient fae warrior was vulnerable in the Institute, and I had to keep him safe.

CHAPTER 3

"Forsooth, thine friend speaks the truth." Jared leaned back on his sofa, spreading out his arms. "Thou will be back within ye old stone walls within no time."

Had there been a time when I'd been nice to humans? Back when I'd donated a bottle of hand lotion every week to the woman in my squat, or when I'd tolerated Uncle Darrell's stories about sticking his dick in the forest soil. Those days felt like centuries ago. Now, I felt the monster inside rattling the bars of its cage, straining at the leash. Human deaths would feed my strength.

Once, I could spend a Friday night drinking cheap beer with humans, listening to Taylor Swift. Now, death fluttered between my ribs like dark moths, and I yearned to taste the blood of mortals.

Never meant to walk the earth....

"Faestress, can I touch your skin?" asked Jared.

"Quiet, mortal," I snarled. He'd be so easy to kill....

When in my life had I ever uttered the phrase *quiet, mortal*? Sometime after I'd let my angel wings out, phrases like that had just started rolling off the tongue.

Darkness spilled into my mind like ink. I pivoted, pacing again.

How had my father managed to control this power for thousands of years? Oh—that was right. He hadn't controlled the power. That's how Ruadan's wife had died. And also half of Europe.

A monster like you....

I stepped out onto the balcony, goosebumps rising on my skin in the damp air. The briny scent of the river floated over me, and I strained to see through all the fog. Were my soldiers at the gate now?

I took a long sip of whiskey, hoping for a brief bubble of inner peace. Could the whiskey drown out Baleros's voice in my head?

Should never have been born. An abomination.

Jared was still prattling on behind me. "We will celebrate the Old Gods by drinking of their bounteous gifts!"

I'll turn your body to ash, Jared. How about that?

Although I couldn't see the base of the gatehouse, I was sure that the mist soldiers would have delivered the message by now. They should be moving through the ancient doors and over the moat of light, into the Institute itself. With any luck, Ruadan would see that I told the truth. He'd know that I'd never tried to hurt him.

At least, not since the time I stabbed him.

"They've got to get back here soon, right?" asked Ciara.

"I don't know. Ruadan has sort of ghosted me recently."

Loneliness corroded me. I'd never told him how I really felt. Was it too late now? The weight of unspoken words pressed on me like a ton of craggy rocks. The assassin might have already killed him, and I'd never told him the truth.

I hugged myself, staring at the fortress. It's not like I could just barge in there. I wouldn't be able to get beyond that bloody golden moat without an invitation.

Fatigue seeped into my brain like a toxin, and I wavered on my feet.

With one hand, I gripped the balcony rail to steady myself. I studied the Tower until something caught my eye. It wasn't the mist soldiers, though. No, my blood thundered at the sight of a powerful fae male on the Tower walls, gilded by the light of the moat, his silver crown gleaming. The wind whipped at his cloak, and a few tendrils of fog snaked around him. Strands of pale, blond hair lifted in the breeze.

My blood warmed, cheeks heating at the sight of him. He was all right.

Ruadan. I'm going to see you soon.

I clutched the balcony rail so hard I was at risk of breaking it.

But as I stared at Ruadan across the stony courtyard, the shadows seemed to consume him—a midnight darkness flecked with stars, tinged with moonlight. For a moment, he looked like a god of night, as if he'd been sewn from a starry cloth. Then, he just disappeared into the darkness as if he'd never been there at all.

My heart was beating out of control, and I wondered if I'd just hallucinated him. In the tiny iron box where Baleros had kept me— those times I'd angered him—I'd had plenty of hallucinations. Sometimes I even thought I'd gotten out.

And now that I'd been avoiding dreams, maybe they were creeping into my waking life.

At last, the distinct silhouettes of soldiers became clearer in the misty courtyard below us. My body vibrated with tension. Was one of them holding a note?

"Arianna," said Ciara.

The name irritated me. I wasn't Arianna—not anymore. The death fluttering in my chest did not belong to an Arianna. Arianna lived in a cage and scrambled over the floor for sweets. She was nearly as pathetic as Jared in his plastic ears.

Liora was vengeance incarnate.

With my free hand, I still gripped the balcony rail. My shoulder blades began to tingle, wings ready to erupt. "My name is Liora."

"Liora," Ciara corrected herself from behind me. "Sometimes you can be a bit … intense about things. I think this might be one of those times. I can kind of see it in the way you look like you're about to break the railing."

"What?"

She rose from the sofa. "Look, I sense something bad coming up. My Aunt Starlene always told me that I had a knack for predicting the future. She once put a rattlesnake in her pants when someone offered her five dollars, and I *said* it would end badly because I just had like a sick sense about it—"

"Sixth sense. But not now, Ciara. I need silence."

"Her swelling never went down," she continued. "So as you can see, I was right. And my point is, when you get this message back, I don't want you doing anything crazy, because my sick sense tells me something crazy might be the first thing on your agenda."

"Sixth."

"The first thing," she repeated more sternly.

I slid the whiskey back onto the table. "Never mind. Look, the Shadow Fae are dying in there," I said. "Someone in there is going to assassinate Ruadan. They think I'm to blame, and I'm running out of options."

Jared's door opened. Plumes of fog billowed into the room, and my blood pounded as the mist soldiers marched in. Anticipation lit my nerves on fire as one of the soldiers held out the paper to me.

Now, I'd find out what I'd been waiting for.

I'd expected to find a note of some kind. Instead, someone had just marked my own letter with a red X over the words I'd written. It looked like someone had actually just slashed blood over the page. What the hells...?

You know, they could have at least explained:

You're not wanted.

No death angels allowed.

Will probably kill you, k thx bye.

Any of those things would be preferable to this godsdamned silence. Then again, what if the mist soldiers had given the letter right to the traitor? I needed a new plan.

I gripped the paper hard, my emotions roiling.

Then, I whirled. I snatched my bug-out bag off the ground. I rifled through it for my weapons, and I strapped myself with knives—one holstered around each thigh. I jammed my headlamp on my head.

"I mean, this is exactly what I was talking about," said Ciara. "You have a murdery look, and now you're strapping weapons to your body."

I will crawl up the throats of my enemies and steal their final breaths.

Death pounded in my blood, and I willed my mind to calm. I had to keep that monster in its cage, but I could feel it growing stronger, darkness seeping from my pores.

My foes will choke on their own blood. "Maybe I should kill everyone," I muttered.

Had I said that out loud?

Ciara wrinkled her nose. "Or just a nap, maybe, before you do anything rash? I could get you some of those cheesy crackers you like...?"

I snatched the whiskey off the table and flicked on my headlamp. "I'm going to speak to the Grand Master of the Institute."

"Now how the hells do you think you're going to get into that Tower?" Ciara chided.

Without replying, I marched past her, into the hall. I was done waiting to find out if Ruadan was okay or not. The walls, the moat of light—they were for lesser beings, not the angel of death.

Not Liora.

CHAPTER 4

On the winding, ancient road, darkness spilled through my veins.

They thought I was a monster, and I wasn't about to prove them right.

With another long sip of whiskey, I grew a little bit bolder. A little thing like a magical moat couldn't keep me out.

I dimmed my headlamp a bit, accidentally sloshing a little whiskey onto my own face. Maybe I'd been drinking a *bit* too fast, but at least the buzz was helping to calm my death angel side. I was no longer thinking things like *the death of mortals feeds my soul.*

Good, good. If I could permanently stay *just* the right amount drunk, I might not lay waste to life on Earth.

As the death drive dissipated, mental images of Ruadan replaced it: the gentle curve of his lips, the way he wrapped his hand around my neck when he kissed me, the spark of hurt in his eyes when I told him nothing could happen between us. I could almost feel the soothing stroke of his magic licking at my throat.

Desire roared in my chest, so fierce my body trembled.

The wind rushed over my skin, and my purple hair whipped into my face.

If you loved someone, you did everything within your power to keep them safe. If I found Ruadan dead when I broke into the Tower, I wasn't sure what I would do. I wasn't sure if anyone would survive my fury—

Another slug of whiskey to calm the monster within. *Take it easy, Liora. Keep the dark angel locked away before she kills the whole world.*

Somewhere under the roaring river of my thoughts, I had a vague sense of losing control. A drowning voice was saying *that the drunk stumbling through the streets with a crooked headlamp and a rage problem might not be living her best life right now.*

Still, I kept walking. I crossed under a bridge, where pigeons and sparrows roosted above me. They stopped cooing as death approached, flapping away, frantic. I had the sense that the grass and dandelions were wilting around me, that I was a toxic thing.

I am ashen skin, the blood in your lungs.

What I needed was a slightly stronger buzz.

All creatures fear me. All life crumbles to dust before me.

I hiccupped, taking another sip.

Across the street, a group of men laughed raucously over their pints. Didn't they know death itself was near?

Watching them, I stumbled, nearly falling before I righted myself again.

"Hello, darling!" It was one of the men across the street—one wearing a white T-shirt with the cross of St. George. "I like your pretty little headlamp. Give us a smile, darling."

I smiled, then added. "How about I engrave a permanent smile on your face with one of my knives?"

"Ooh, she's a feisty one, isn't she? Come on over here, love. I'd like to tussle with you." He seemed to think I was joking about the knives, although they were clearly strapped to my legs, and I was clearly a monster. Idiot. He pointed to his crotch. "Come on. It's not going to suck itself, is it?"

His friends burst into raucous laughter. I understood how this worked. Not about seduction, was it? Just a performance for the benefit of his friends.

Cold fury simmered, burning away my drunken clumsiness.

I held out my hands to either side, a smile curling my lips. "All right, lads. You want a show? I'll give you a show."

The one in the St. George's cross T-shirt stumbled across the street toward me. "That's a good girl. Give us a show, then."

In a flash of an instant, I was by his side. I touched his cheek, letting the death magic spill out of my fingertips, charcoal gray like smoke. Images flickered in my mind: the bare bones of trees, a cathedral of thin stones arching above, the ribs of a spare skeleton.

"When I'm done with you, you human beast, your skin will curl off your body and your guts will blacken and liquefy. Your life has no meaning. After you putrefy, no one will remember your name."

The full force of my anger terrified even me, and I stumbled back from him. *Shit, shit, shit.*

The human gaped at me, fear freezing him.

"Nope," I held up my hands. "Nope, I'm good. I'm in control. No liquefying organs tonight. Everything is *lovely.* Nice to meet you, fine sirs." I jabbed St. George's Cross in the chest. "But do not harass any more women or I really will peel your skin off. Not even joking."

Nausea crept into my gut as I moved away from them. I'd nearly let the death angel take over completely. If it had, I could have hit the Institute with another dose of the Plague. I could have finished them off before I even got to warn them.

My whiskey buzz had grown richer and deeper, and I nearly didn't notice the tingle of magic down my shoulder blades as I walked away from the humans.

Thing was, I needed to let the monster out just a little in order to get into the Tower.

I will rot your food until your cheeks hollow out, and bony fingers stuff your gullet with grass.

Feathered wings erupted from my back in a burst of euphoria. The scent of myrrh enveloped me. In a wave of ecstasy, I lifted into the air.

Ahhh, this is what I was meant for.

The river wind rushed over my skin. My wings were a rhythmic heartbeat as I lifted into the air. I was born for this—flight in the skies.

As my angelic form took over, I could only regret all the years I'd spent tethering myself to the earth, living like a caged beast.

What a waste. A goddess locked in a cage.

Kings and beggars, queens and strumpets. All fall at my feet.

Fifty feet in the air, I skimmed over the stony courtyard. I'd nearly reached the Tower gate.

The Tower: forbidding and silent, secrets locked inside. The fortress and its Grand Master were two peas in a pod.

"Two peas in a fucking pod," I yelled at no one. Apparently, I still had a very good whiskey buzz going, even in my angel form.

The Tower's stone walls failed to respond to my comment. Not a flicker of light, not a twitch of a curtain. The golden moat loomed far below. Still flying, I corked the whiskey bottle. There was a bit left, and I didn't want it spilling.

My wings beat the air, lifting me higher. The Shadow Fae hadn't thought about angels when they'd designed their magical moat. They thought we were all gone. Fools. I giggled as I soared higher.

I flew parallel to the magical barrier, feeling it tingle on my skin. I raced up toward the heavens, wind tearing at my hair.

A moat would keep out the demons, yes, but demons couldn't fly as high as angels. We were meant for the heavens, creatures of the celestial realm. Laughter kept bubbling up, and the dark night winds kissed my skin as I raced higher.

Who needed sleep, anyway? I could do this forever, just me and the sky. Up here, I didn't hear Baleros's voice.

When the air began to thin, and the clouds spread out far below me, the power of the barrier seemed to fade. At last, it glimmered away to nothing.

I'd made it above the protections.

I circled over a moment, looking down at the Tower. I couldn't even see it from here, but I was certain I just had to fly straight down.

I angled my wings, then pressed them flat against my back. I dove in a wild free fall. The rush of the flight was burning away some of my whiskey buzz, and my thoughts started to grow slightly clearer.

I'll admit that at this point the plan didn't seem like the *best* of ideas, but I was already committed to it.

I plummeted, swooping lower and lower, diving, exhilarated. Then, when I could see the stone rings of the Tower below me, I spread my wings out to either side, slowing my descent.

I knew what I was up against. If the Shadow Fae were healthy enough to defend the fortress, I was about to face iron arrows. They'd pierce my flesh, knock me out of my flight, and sap my magic.

I knew they'd hurt, but could iron arrows kill me? Iron didn't hurt angels, but it did hurt the fae. And if my life was in danger, I'd have to fight back with my knives. Granted, throwing knives at the knights wouldn't entirely help the legitimacy of my *look, we're all on the same side here* argument.

As I dove lower, I needed to position myself as close as possible to the entrance of the Cailleach Tower. I hoped to find Ruadan there on his throne, although who knew where he was. I wasn't even entirely sure what time of night it was.

Now, I was only a hundred feet above it. Something whooshed past my head. Another shot skimmed my thigh.

Ah. So the Shadow Fae were healthy enough to shoot. In a way, that was good—

Another arrow zipped past me, and adrenaline surged. I altered my flight path a bit, zig-zagging to make myself hard to hit.

Under attack, the worst part of me longed to unleash the full force of my death magic. I wanted to let it burst from my chest like a plume of black smoke.

I was hurtling for the ground, faster and faster, starting to wonder if I could nail the landing. I mean, flying came naturally to me, but *landing?* I had no idea. I'd never done this before. Still, I had to stay laser-focused right now on one thing, one person.

Ruadan.

And oh, gods, the earth is coming for me fast.

BAM. The force of the fall rattled my bones. I landed hard in the tall grasses outside the Cailleach Tower, grunting as I rolled. The Tower's bells tolled, signaling danger. The impact dazed me, and I scrambled to think of my next move.

Hide, Liora. I hunched down, as if that would somehow make the giant black wings inconspicuous.

Nothing to see here, folks. Just the angel of death invading your fortress, drunk as shit.

Another arrow slammed down in the ground by my side, shouts ringing out. Then another, piercing my thigh. This was getting real. The pain ripped through me, sharp as a hot razor. It definitely felt like iron arrows could kill me, angel or not.

I whirled, scanning the battlements. A flicker of movement on one of the Tower walls—a Shadow Fae readying another arrow. My mind whirred with the calculations, my vision suddenly focused. I could disable him before he shot me, not risk another arrow while I ran for the Tower doors.

As he nocked his arrow, I unleashed my knife, and it sped through the air. The blade found its mark right in the Shadow Fae's wrist.

Before another Shadow Fae got the chance, I pivoted and sprinted into the Cailleach Tower. With the arrow in my leg, I stumbled on the stairs. The weight of my wings threw me off a bit, too. I didn't know how to get rid of them, or if I had any control over that at all.

Nausea was still rising in my gut—either from the whiskey or the iron, or the realization that I'd decided to take on an entire fortress of knights who wanted me dead. I had a terrible feeling I could end up puking in the throne room as soon as I saw Ruadan, and I wanted to avoid that as much as possible. I was here to state my case—that I was a rational person with helpful information, and not just a crazy drunk with an arrow in her leg and wings she couldn't control.

At last, I reached the top of the stairs, and I kicked through the oak doors.

There, I found Ruadan, slumped on the throne, his eyes dark and lifeless. Shadows writhed around him. He wasn't moving. In fact, I saw not a single sign of life apart from the movement of his magic.

Panic thundered through my blood. Had the Plague taken the demigod already?

I couldn't breathe.

CHAPTER 5

"*R*uadan?" My voice echoed off the high stone ceiling. I took a nervous step closer.

Even now, his otherworldly beauty stole my breath—the cheekbones sharp as blades, pale hair cascading over powerful shoulders. His stillness sent shivers dancing up my spine.

My legs shook. "Ruadan—"

Something slammed into my back, and pain blazed from the rear of my shoulder. An iron arrow in my back had knocked me forward, hard, onto my hands and knees.

The whiskey bottle shattered, broken glass cutting my palms. Then, my wings retracted into my body. Already, I was growing weaker from the iron. Whatever happened next, I wouldn't be able to put up much of a fight.

I reached for another one of my knives and looked behind me. Aengus was pointing an arrow at me. Blood poured from his wrist, a wound that had been ripped right open. So *that's* who I'd hit with the knife.

Was he the traitor? I had no idea.

Gripping my knife, I glared at him. "What happened to Ruadan?" I rasped. "Did you do this to him?"

Aengus cocked his head. "Do what to him?"

"Why is he slumped over like that?"

"He's fine, since no one threw a knife at him and the Plague hasn't touched him yet." He let out a cough. "Can't say the same for myself."

"Hmm. I would apologize for the knife, but you did shoot me with arrows."

"Oh, did I? How uncouth of me. I guess I was a bit peeved that you poisoned us with death magic and then staged a terrifying armed invasion of the fortress. Next time, I'll use a sword."

"The way you phrase it really puts a negative spin on it, you know that?" The pain from the arrows in my back and thigh shot through my bones.

Aengus towered over me, green eyes boring into me. I couldn't find the slightest hint of warmth in his expression.

"I came here to deliver a message."

An arched eyebrow. "Oh? From your master, Baleros?"

Wanker. "Baleros is not my master. I did not spread the Plague." I didn't trust Aengus right now, and I wanted to speak to no one except Ruadan. If Aengus was the traitor, I didn't want to pass on information to him. "What's wrong with Ruadan?"

Aengus raised the arrow again, ready to shoot. He didn't look like he was going to answer my question.

The gravity of the situation hit me like a fist to the throat. I could report to Aengus or to no one. I was dependent on him.

"I have information," I said. "But it's for Ruadan." I'd intentionally left the traitor bit out of my letter in case it had fallen into the wrong hands. I'd said only that Ruadan faced a threat, and I needed to explain it to him directly.

Aengus narrowed his eyes. His sickly pallor suggested he really did have the Plague. "You're drunk. I thought you'd invade, but I didn't expect you to be drunk. Though, on second thought, I'm not sure why that would surprise me."

"I'm not that drunk. The buzz wore off quite a bit with the second arrow. Why is Ruadan unconscious? You're sure he doesn't have the Plague?"

"Yes. He's the only one unaffected."

My chest unclenched. "So tell me what's wrong with him."

"I'm not telling you anything. I'm deciding at what point I should kill you and how to do it."

"Wait, wait!" I shouted, my voice echoing off the vaulted ceiling. "Did someone put him under a spell or something?"

"No. Ruadan did that to himself, and he's not available to speak to you right now. As you can see." Blood poured from Aengus's wrist onto the stone floor as he aimed his arrow at me. "You have two seconds to pass on your valuable information before I plant an iron arrow in your eye socket. Will it kill you? I'm not sure. It will definitely sting."

My heart was a frightened rabbit. I didn't have a lot of options. And somehow, I didn't believe Aengus was the traitor. He could be an arsehole, but he'd always been completely loyal to Ruadan. He was trying to protect him even now, in his own obnoxious way.

I held up my hands, dropping the knife. "Fine. I'm not the source of the Plague. I tortured Maddan to get information from him. There's a traitor in here. Someone is using the Unholy Grail to spread the Plague, and he's being commanded by Baleros. When the traitor gets the chance, he's going to kill Ruadan." I nodded at the Grand Master. "So whatever is going on with him, you need to assign a guard or several at all times."

"I guard him."

"Good. Keep doing that. And I'm not done. Baleros's plan is to weaken the Shadow Fae, steal the World Key, and harvest an army of demons from other realms to take over the world. He will thrive as the Plague spreads. He will use the chaos to make the world his own."

Aengus's bowstring was completely taut.

My gaze flicked to Ruadan, who didn't appear to be registering any of this, his eyes empty.

"You need to protect him." I could hardly think clearly with the pain shooting through my limbs. "Someone in here wants him dead, and he looks vulnerable. Tell me what's going on with him."

"No." Aengus loosed his arrow, and it caught me in the chest. I fell hard to the ground, my mind now registering only the pain.

* * *

When I woke, my mouth tasted toxic, and my throat felt like I'd swallowed shards of broken glass. I coughed, and agony shot through my chest. I'd been shot once in the back, in the thigh, and once through the collarbone. The iron from the arrows had seeped into my blood. If I weren't half angel, I'd probably be dead by now.

Someone had been kind enough to pull the arrows out of me before they'd shoved me into the Palatial Room—the tiniest cell in the Tower's dungeons. The air was heavy down here, rich with the scent of decay. And … piss. My own, in fact, given the dampness of my trousers.

Yep, this was definitely a low point in my life.

I licked my parched lips. For just a moment, I gripped the bars. The brief touch burned my fingers, reminding me that they were made of iron.

"Barry wants a friend!" A nasal, high-pitched voice rose from the darkness and rattled around my skull.

"What the fuck," I muttered under my breath. I couldn't see much in the gloom, but apparently I'd been stuck down here with another prisoner. One with a voice like nails over a chalkboard.

"Barry wants to know your name! One, two, threeeeeeee!" The shrill voice pierced my eardrums, and I clamped my hands over my ears.

Somehow, I could still hear his voice through my palms.

"Barry likes to eat jam off his fingers. One, two, threeeeeeee!"

Shut the fuck up. Shut the fuck up.

I opened my eyes, still keeping my hands pressed over my ears. After a moment, my eyes began to adjust to the dim light. Somewhere to my left, a torch flickered over the dark cells.

The warm light wavered over Barry—a hairy creature crouched in the cell across from me. Rags hung off his thin frame, and he sat hunched over, pawing at the ground. Despite his wretched state, he had a lumen stone glowing around his neck. How did he get *that?* And why didn't he simply shadow-leap out of here if he had a lumen stone? Maybe I could trick him into giving it to me.

He grinned at me, his teeth long and filthy. "Barry likes to sing. One, two, threeeeeeee!" he whined in a voice that penetrated my skull, piercing my very soul.

"Barry!" I shouted. "If you don't shut up, I will have to kill you."

He thrust out his lower lip. "Barry sad."

I leaned forward, grabbing the iron bars. I didn't even care about the pain from the bars any more. "I don't give a fuck if you're sad, Barry. I need quiet. I have been poisoned by iron."

"Liora needs soft hug," he shrieked, the nasal voice curling my toes. "Barry's flesh is soft like a wheel of cheese. One, two, threeeeeeee!"

I cocked my head. How did this wretch know my name?

He glared at me from beneath his enormous eyebrows. He looked like some sort of caveman. What the hells was he?

"Barry," I said. "How do you know my name?"

"Barry eats flesh from sheeps in pies. Barry puts peeled oranges in pants. Barry—" A coughing fit interrupted him. When he recovered, I could hear the rasping in his breathing.

Another plague victim. Good. Maybe he'd be unconscious soon.

"Since you know so much," I began, "can you tell me what happened to the Grand Master?"

"Barry want a friend!"

I gritted my teeth. "I'll be your friend if you give me your necklace."

A look of panic crossed his features, and he tucked it into his shirt. "Barry wants to love you."

I couldn't take this anymore. I was retreating to my happy place. I pressed my shaking palms over my ears once more, doing my best to block out his shrill yammering.

I leaned back against the craggy rocks of the Palatial Room, trying to will myself back to sleep.

CHAPTER 6

I completely failed to sleep, and instead was forced to listen to Barry the Caveman shriek about all the types of food he liked, and reiterate his previously established desire for friendship, hugs, and peeled oranges in his pants. He was worse than the iron wounds eating at my body.

At last, footfalls tapped farther down the hall, then the sound of a coughing fit filled the dank dungeon. Another plague victim coming for us.

Please. Please, I just need anyone else to talk to.

By this point, I had no idea how much time had passed. It felt like about eight years. But in non-Barry measurement, where the time passed normally, it was probably something like six hours.

"Barry likes to feel potatoes! Potatoes have the gentle curves of a woman. One, two, threeeeeeee!"

Nausea rose in my gut, and I waited eagerly for the new visitor.

To my shock, Barry stood up in the cell across from me. He dusted off his clothes, and he waved. "Oh, heya, Niall."

I blinked. Barry's voice had become completely normal—soft and deep and ordinary-sounding.

"Hi, Barry." Niall—one of the Shadow Fae—crossed into view and carefully handed Barry a thermos through the iron bars.

"Cheers, mate," said Barry, sounding like a perfectly normal person. He took a sip. "Oh, you've sweetened it as well, that's lovely. Two sugars? That's exactly how I like it. You know, I was catching a bit of a chill down here. Bit damp. Not great for the ol' plague symptoms, if I'm honest," he grumbled.

Niall shot me a furious look, and he pointed at me. "We've got her to thank for that."

At this point, I was thoroughly confused. I gaped as one of Barry's eyebrows drooped off his face.

"Whoopsy-daisy." Barry pressed the eyebrow back on again.

He was wearing fake eyebrows?

"Anyone care to tell me what's going on?" I asked.

Niall glared at me. "You infected everyone with the Plague, invaded the Institute, and you will likely be exalted in the morning when the Grand Master gives us permission."

Exalted, unfortunately, was the ancient fae word for a torturous death. Evisceration, if I remembered correctly.

Niall pivoted, walking away. No tea for me, I supposed.

"Wait, Niall. I need to speak to Ruadan." My voice echoed off the stone walls. Niall did not reply.

And then, it was just Barry and me again.

I glanced at him. He leaned against the wall, sipping his tea. He patted his false eyebrow.

"Who are you, and why have you been tormenting me with that shrill voice?" I asked.

"Ahh, well, I am in fact Barry." He coughed again. "Got a bit of the Plague from your death magic, so I'm feeling a little poorly. I'm a new recruit, hoping to be a Shadow Fae. Apparently, there was an opening since you turned out to be a...." He scratched his cheek. "Repulsive abomination or whatever they call it."

"They're calling me a *what?*"

"Ruadan, the new Grand Master, disapproved of traditional torture methods, so he asked us to get creative. This what I came up with. I workshopped it for a few days with the other lads. Aengus said you'd end up in here when we caught you, and we should test it out before your execution. It's good, right?"

"You've got to be kidding me." Even with all the iron in my blood, there was a chance I could still kill him and everyone else in the Institute if I wanted to. Only the fact that I cared about the Institute stopped me from trying. "And they already gave you a lumen stone?"

"Guess so. What did you think of the 'one, two, threeeee' bit? Niall wasn't sure—" He cleared his throat. "Sorry, I'm not really supposed to break the fourth wall like this. Do you mind if I just...."

He took a sip of tea, then returned to his crouching position, hunching over and pawing at the dirt.

"Barry pretends his hand belongs to a beautiful woman. One, two, *threeeeee!*"

Death beats in my breast like raven wings. Their bodies will feed the soil.

* * *

ANOTHER SIX HOURS or perhaps four hundred years passed before Aengus arrived, his loud cough heralding his arrival.

"Heya, Aengus," said Barry, cheerfully, dropping character.

"Good work, Barry." Aengus's injured hand had been bandaged, and he glowered at me. "Did you get any information out of her?"

Barry blinked at him. "I wasn't really ... I didn't actually know there was a purpose to this, as it were."

It seemed like ages since I'd had a sip of water, and my mouth was so dry I could hardly wet my lips enough to speak.

"Aengus," I rasped.

He cocked his head and stared down at me. "Your time has come."

My heart sank. "What time has come?"

"The Grand Master has awakened."

This was better news. "Awakened from what?"

"He was communing with the void." Aengus started coughing again and wiped the sweat off his forehead. "This illness you spread is deeply unpleasant. I feel that I am rotting from the inside out."

"It wasn't me, fuckwit." I closed my eyes, marshaling my patience. "You're letting the real threat swan around the Institute. You're not even protecting Ruadan right now, because you're letting Baleros trick you. Look, can you get back to the part about Ruadan communing with the void? What does that mean, and why is he doing that when he clearly has better things to do?"

"Everyone in the Institute wanted you dead, since you're a terrorist and an abomination."

Any icy shard of rage. *Before I kill you, you will watch your own teeth rot and fall from your mouth like October leaves. Your blood will spatter on your porcelain sink.*

I slowed my breathing, trying to behave like a normal fae. "I do not feel that *abomination* is an accurate description of my nature."

Or did I?

"You know what?" Aengus shot back. "I don't actually feel the need to explain this to you. You're coming with me now."

"Care to share where we're going?"

"Not particularly," said Aengus. He unlocked the iron bars, and the door creaked open. With all the iron in my blood, I couldn't make a break for it even if I'd wanted to.

I gripped the jagged rocks, trying to pull myself up, but my body was weak from the iron poisoning. Halfway up, I grew dizzy and fell back into the rough walls. Then, with an iron will, I righted myself.

As I stepped into the hall, Aengus gripped me hard by the elbow, yanking me out. The sudden movement stirred a wave of nausea, and I turned away from him to vomit back into the Palatial Room. From the burning, I was pretty sure it was mostly the whiskey from the day before. I wiped a shaking hand across my mouth.

If things went really poorly, I'd probably be executed in a horrific manner. If things went well, I'd probably end up sitting in that pile of my vomit. That was a *best*-case scenario.

"Are you quite finished?" asked Aengus.

I straightened as best I could, then leaned into him. "I'm realizing, now, I made a mistake when I aimed in the other direction."

"You smell disgusting," he said.

I smiled at him, pleased he had to deal with my stench. "Do I offend your delicate sensibilities? At one point, I thought you were a warrior. Silly me. You really ought to leave here and form a knitting club."

"Are you scared of dying?" asked Aengus.

A flash of fury lit me up, the death angel straining on her tether. "I want you to know I'm acting with a great deal of restraint right now, Aengus."

Choke on bile.

Aengus's sallow cheeks paled even further.

I'd known the risks when I'd come in here, that I'd probably be hit with arrows. I'd never imagined that Ruadan would allow my death.

Of all the things Ruadan could have been doing—fortifying the castle, finding Baleros—instead, he'd spent these weeks floating around in the shadow void?

When you loved someone, you did anything in your power to save them. Meanwhile, he'd slipped off to the shadow void.

Betrayal pressed down hard on my broken body. "Killing me won't solve your problem. Baleros is coming for Ruadan whether I'm here or not."

We reached the top of the stairs, and Aengus unlocked another iron gate. When he pushed through the next set of doors into a hall, sunlight streaming through the peaked windows blinded me. So, it was daytime.

Wincing, I held up a hand to shield my eyes. A wave of dizziness washed over me, and I leaned into Aengus again while darkness claimed my mind.

CHAPTER 7

shock of cold woke me—icy water trickling down my hair, my shoulders.

I lay flat on my back on the flagstones, staring up at Aengus and Niall. Barry stood just behind them, one of his false eyebrows drooping.

"There," said Aengus. "She's awake again. Pity the ice water didn't wash the stench away."

He held out his hand to help me up, but at this point, I'd walk on my own two feet if it killed me.

With a great deal of effort, I forced myself up onto my elbows. Grimacing, I rolled to my side, then pushed myself up to a sitting position. On shaking legs, I stood slowly.

When I'd straightened as much as I could, I felt magic whispering down my shoulder blades.

I shot a ferocious look to Aengus. *Cross me, fae, and your body will wither and rot like a blighted plant.* I stared into his bloodshot eyes, and the urge to unleash death nearly overwhelmed me.

Shaking, I turned from him to face the throne room.

When I hobbled into the hall, I tuned out everything else except Ruadan before me. I forgot about my filthy appearance, the piss on my trousers, the fake caveman trailing behind me. I forgot how much I hated Aengus, and the pain wracking my body. I barely registered the other Shadow Fae lined up in the hall on either side of me, gaping at me.

My eyes were locked only on Ruadan, and his on mine. His piney scent hit me, tinged with apples. And for that moment, the death angel drifted away from me.

Ruadan looked as electrified as I felt. He straightened when he saw me, his entire body tense. Darkness swirled in his eyes, and shadows writhed in the air around him. As our gazes met, the temperature in the room plummeted about twenty degrees. The flames on top of the torches wavered in the blast of cold air, some of them snuffing out.

My gaze swept over him, taking in his powerful body, the thickly corded muscles and savage tattoos that covered his forearms—the silver crown that gleamed on his head. He was a vision of pure, dark power. Aengus had been right. The Plague hadn't touched him.

I may not have looked like it from the outside, but a dark power lived within me, too—my own destructive monster, tethered in its cage. They'd threatened to eviscerate me. I should be unleashing that power now, letting it tear through every living creature in here. But some primal, instinctive power compelled me to protect Ruadan, even now.

Was it the same for him? As he stared at me, he gripped the arms of his throne so tight it looked like he could crack the stone, his obsidian eyes piercing me.

In his view, I was a threat to the Institute. I'd infected them and taken their mist army. Logic dictated that I needed to die for the good of the Shadow Fae.

Logic also dictated that I should kill all of them before they had the chance.

You will sicken—

A rocky barrier rose in my mind, slamming right into my death thoughts. What was that about?

"Liora," said Ruadan. The sound of my real name on his tongue wrapped around my body like silk. The sensual voice of an incubus, as deadly as his wrath.

"Grand Master Ruadan," I said.

"The Shadow Fae here believe you are part of Baleros's plans to weaken our defenses. They believe you spread the Plague."

I held my breath. If Ruadan lost faith in me, I wouldn't be able to take it. The betrayal would be a sword in my heart.

"You transformed into your angelic form," he went on. "You broke into the Institute, armed."

A coughing fit erupted in the hall, echoing off the high ceiling. I glanced at the other fae around me. Melusine stood huddled against a pillar, her eyes glassy. Apart from Ruadan, demigod that he was, everyone in the room looked sick—pale skin, dry lips, shadows beneath their eyes.

"I broke in here to give you a message," I said. "There is a traitor in here, and he is the one who spread the Plague."

Aengus folded his hands in front of him. "The traitor is obviously you. No one else doubts that, right?"

"It is obvious," said Niall. "And if nothing else, she is a child of the apocalypse. It is our mission to destroy her kind."

"And by the way." Anger laced my voice. "While you were floating in a giant black hole for the past few weeks, we could have been teaming up to kill Baleros. I mean kill him for good."

Ruadan's head tilted back, and he stared at me, challenging.

Aengus stepped into the center of the room. "Let's get back to the execution."

Melusine cleared her throat. "If I may speak? Grand Master? It seems to me that we know the Old Gods chose Liora. They knew what she was, and they chose her anyway. We saw what happened to Grand Master Savus when he tried to defy their will."

I was pretty sure I heard Aengus mutter something about how the Old Gods were wrong.

Ruadan's dark magic whipped at the air around him. "The Old Gods approve of her. And now, her guilt or innocence will be determined by another of the earthly gods."

Tension crackled in the air.

"Why are we giving her this chance?" Niall protested. "It's obvious she spread the Plague here in the Institute."

"I have been in the void for weeks." Ruadan's tone brooked no argument. "This is what Nyxobas has instructed me to do. He will put her on trial in the void. As you know, he does not lie. He will inhabit my body, and we will hear from Nyxobas directly. After all, it is not for us to decide. It is for the gods to decide. Do any of you have any further arguments?"

Cold silence filled the room, and Ruadan's gaze slid over all the Shadow Fae.

Before anyone could utter another word, the room started to change, darkening. A shadowy form rose up behind Ruadan, looming over the hall, silvery eyes burning like stars. Horns loomed above his head in a crescent shape.

I shivered at the vision of the god of night. His presence was dizzying, and I felt like I was standing on the edge of a precipice. I stared ahead of me as the shadow god slipped into Ruadan's body. Star-tinged darkness shimmered around him, and his eyes blazed with silver starlight. Ruadan's tattoos began snaking over his powerful forearms, resembling living creatures.

Dread trembled over my skin. Imbued with the essence of Nyxobas, shadows breathed around Ruadan, and he loomed over the hall.

I felt tiny before him. Broken, too.

A glacial coldness took over the room. I shivered, hugging myself. Was the trial beginning already? I wasn't ready.

The voice that Ruadan used to speak was not his own, but seemed to come from the iciest depths of Hell. "Chaos reigns in the Institute."

His pale gaze fell on me. Despite my primal instinct to flee from an earthly god, I forced myself to stay still. Looking at a god was like facing a wild animal. If I showed fear, he'd eat me alive. With an iron will, I straightened my spine.

"Half angel," said Nyxobas. "Celestial harbinger of death. Half fae, of the Old Gods. Her presence here sows discord. A traitor lives among you, spreading plague. Only a death angel can fix it. Did the deathling cause this, or another? Each of you will prove your loyalty by leaping into the void. In the vast shadows, you will prove your purity. Once I have found the traitor, the portal will seal over."

The shadows faded around Ruadan, and the godlike enormity slipped away.

I let out the long breath I'd been holding.

So this was Ruadan's ploy to maintain control within the Institute—bring in the big guns. Almost no one wanted me here, but they wouldn't argue with Nyxobas.

Aengus looked furious. "All of us are to be tested? You know the risks of leaping into the void."

I didn't, as it happened. "What are they, exactly?"

Melusine raised her hand and immediately began speaking. "I know this one. Time can pass differently in the void. And if you spend too long there, you will return as a demon."

Ruadan still gripped the armrests of his throne. "Nyxobas's decision is clear. You all go into the shadow hell. Succeed, and you join us again. Fail, and it means you are a traitor to the Institute. Nyxobas will seal the portal and claim your soul."

So *that's* what Nyxobas got out of this. The man loved claiming souls.

I stared at the Grand Master, shadows still pooling in his eyes. Was this all an elaborate way of getting me off the Institute's kill list?

"Grand Master—" Aengus began.

One withering look from Ruadan silenced him. "You are all dismissed. All of you apart from Liora."

Around me, the other Shadow Fae turned and began marching out of the room. Fury etched their features, and at least two of them made rude gestures at me.

When they'd all left, the heavy oak door closed behind them, leaving me alone with the Grand Master.

He rose from his throne and crossed to me, moving swiftly. "Your attack on the Tower was not a good idea."

"It wasn't an attack. I was trying to speak to you about the traitor's threat." My mouth and throat felt like sandpaper.

Ruadan scooped me up as if I weighed no more than a sparrow, and I leaned into his chest. I closed my eyes, listening to his heart as he carried me.

"Why did you slip away to the void for weeks? We could have been doing something more useful, like teaming up to kill Baleros."

He held me tight, walking with me in his arms. "I killed him before I went into the void. I hunted him down and sliced Emerazel's sigil off his body. Then I cut off his head."

I opened my eyes, my heart leaping. "You did? So he's dead?"

His features darkened. "Cutting off the sigil didn't work like we thought it would. He returned. Emerazel brought him back."

Nausea curdled my stomach. "You mean we can't kill him?"

"Everything can be killed. I just don't know how, yet."

I leaned into his chest again as he carried me down the stairs. "Where exactly are we going?"

"To fix you before your trial. Nyxobas could return at any point, but I don't want you going into the shadow hell broken like this." His seductive voice held an edge I couldn't ignore.

Already, his soothing magic was whispering over me.

"Speaking of running out of time, we need to keep you safe. Baleros's agent could attack at any moment."

"Shhh," he said. His grasp on me was impossibly gentle, like he was afraid of breaking me.

And yet, when I looked up at his face, I could see a cold, hard rage written there, and the Wraith's perfect features blazed with the ancient wrath of an unforgiving god.

CHAPTER 8

*R*uadan lay me gently by his burbling stone bath. Outside, the sun was setting, and vibrant pumpkin rays streamed through the warped window glass. The light washed over the beautiful planes of Ruadan's face, giving him a warmth that contrasted with his cold expression.

I couldn't feel the pain in my chest anymore, but I felt weak as a withering dandelion.

I blinked, trying to focus. The iron was not only messing with my body, but it had started to screw with my mind, too.

"I'm going to undress you."

"Fine." My mouth tasted like a dry riverbed, and clouds had gathered in my mind. "Wait, why?"

"The water will help to clean your wounds, and the angelica and lavender in the bath will help me to heal you. They will slow the spread of the iron in your system while I pull it out with my healing magic."

Someone had turned my throat into gravel. "I need something to drink."

I lay against the stony bath while Ruadan crossed back into his room. He returned a moment later with a tall glass of water. I took it from him and drank it down. Water had never tasted so delicious and pure before.

While I slaked my thirst, Ruadan crouched by my side. I put the glass down on the stone, and nodded at Ruadan, signaling that I was ready for him to undress me. I probably could have managed it myself, but I didn't want to move any more than I absolutely had to.

Ruadan reached for me, and he unbuttoned the top of my dress, fingers brushing against my skin. Powerful, cold anger rippled off him. Given how gentle his movements were, his rage didn't fit.

When I looked at him this closely, I saw the full force of it—the angry set of his jaw, the eyes black as gleaming jet. Icy mist clouded the air, and a frigid breeze rushed over the stone floor. For a moment, I almost wondered if Nyxobas had returned. But no—it was just Ruadan, furious as hells.

Why was he so mad at me?

My own fury started simmering. We should be on the same side, but he was rejecting me just because I'd had the misfortune to be born as a death angel. When it came down to it, I had been loyal to him. When I'd unleashed the death angel, I'd been trying to save him. Did he not care about that?

He was still unbuttoning my dress, and my helplessness before him only added to my anger.

I sort of wanted to punch him in the jaw and tell him to piss off with his trial. I'd make a speech on my way out. Something about how we are defined by our actions and not our births, and anyway he was a heartbreaking monster, too, so who was he to judge.

I narrowed my eyes at him, still working on my speech. *Oh, and by the way, Breaker of Hearts, I'm sorry your brothers died, but you ruined my life, too, when you invaded that day, and don't fuck with death angels if you don't want people to die. That's how it works.*

Still, I thought maybe it was better to wait until after he'd healed me before I launched into it. Like, it might be more effective when I could stand independently.

He'd unbuttoned my dress down to my navel, his eyes deeply

intent on my wounds. Each one of his muscles was tightly bound, and he looked like a coiled animal ready to strike.

Anger rippled through me, so hot I was pretty sure I snarled. He'd come into my world and ripped it apart. If he'd never come, I wouldn't have killed everyone in the first place.

I will scatter your ashes to the—

A barrier of black rock slammed into my mind. Then, an acrid wave of nausea rose in my gut, interrupting my thought.

I was starting to understand. When it came to Ruadan, my death instinct felt as wrong as the iron in my blood. Deep inside, my death magic warred with an insane, animal sense of protectiveness over him.

Why had I taken arrows for him to get in here? What the hells was wrong with me?

I let out a long breath, then closed my eyes. Mentally, I was drifting. Ruadan had ruined my old life, and right now, it was coming back to me so vividly. I hardly ever allowed myself to think of Eden, because when I did, a sharp tendril of pain curled through me. Now, visions of my home burbled into my mind like spring water: swimming in the clear creek with my mum, the tiny gemstones gleaming in her forehead. My dad used to call me Bug. I couldn't remember why. I think it had started as Lovebug and just got shortened. Once, he'd engraved my nickname on the mantle over the hearth, then etched a crescent moon around it.

"Are you still with me?" asked Ruadan. His healing magic was already starting to brush over my body.

"Yup," I said, but my mind was still in Eden.

I opened my eyes again, meeting his furious, dark gaze with my own anger.

"So," I began. "You feed off heartbreak. How's that going?"

Right now, he was probably feasting off me. He paused his hands by my navel and stared into my eyes. His own eyes were pure black, and I could read nothing in them except wrath.

Ruadan, breaker of hearts, ruiner of lives.

"That's right, lover boy," I crooned. I smiled at him, even though

I'm sure there was no joy in it. "We both have our monstrous secrets, and I know yours."

He didn't know I'd been in on that secret, and he went completely still. His healing magic ebbed.

With all the strength I had in me, I leaned forward. "How many hearts have you broken over the centuries? Thousands, I'd imagine. A man looking as nice as you, with those muscles and that perfect face. It must come naturally to an incubus and a fomoire. An incubus stirs up lust. You get people to love you. And a fomoire like you can just drink up their pain."

It enraged me that he could feel *my* heartbreak, and that it was strengthening him right now. If I'd had the energy, I would have smashed everything in the room.

Ruadan didn't answer me, because of course he didn't. Still, I felt the temperature drop even further, until the flagstones beneath me were blocks of ice. An eternity of silence and frost passed between us.

His eyes were on mine—pure and cold as an arctic night sky. To my surprise, he leaned even closer, his face close to mine. He pressed his hands on either side of my hips, so close I could practically kiss him.

"You're hurt that I didn't protect you," he said.

"What?" I stared at him. "That is not at all what's happening."

"I failed to protect you."

I blinked. He felt my heartbreak, but he'd completely misunderstood it. "That is not even close, Ruadan. I don't need your protection. I'm hurt that you left me—twice. Once at Hampton Court Palace, and then again for the past several weeks. You abandoned me when you found out what I was."

His face brushed softly against my cheek. "You should have trusted me." His voice—soft as silk, but edged with a sharp blade underneath. "You kept your true nature from me because you feared me."

"You kept yours from me."

"Not because I thought you would kill me for it. You should have known I wouldn't kill you, after everything we went through together."

My heart twisted, anger still roiling. "I was on your kill list for years. My dad is on your kill list. I slaughtered your brothers." The room was frigid, and I started shivering. Ruadan's anger was always palpable. "You're angry that I couldn't read your soul. You feel that I should understand you implicitly without you ever having to speak. My powers are amazing, but that's not one of them."

Ruadan pulled my bloodied dress off my shoulders, his fingertips brushing my skin. I stank like the bottom of a sewer, but it didn't seem to register with him.

"Just to be clear," I said, "I'm not on your kill list?"

His fierce expression made me catch my breath. "Of course you're not. You should never have doubted me. I protect those I love. What sort of a person do you think I am?" His gaze flicked to the festering wound at my shoulder, and he winced. Ice shot through the air. "At least, I try to protect those I love."

And at those words, a buried ember ignited in my heart.

CHAPTER 9

*R*uadan might be Prince of Emain, Grand Master of the Institute, but he had a primitive side. Love meant protection to him. The fact that I'd doubted him had made him feel like he'd failed me. And the fact that I'd shown up in his throne room ravaged by iron wounds made him feel like a failure again.

I was usually really good at being strong and holding my feelings back, but the second I felt safe with someone, the tears would start to flow. And right now, they were stinging my eyes, making my vision even blurry. It was enraging, because I wasn't done being mad.

A tear spilled down my cheek, infuriating me. I wiped it off with the back of my hand. "You should never have come to Eden."

"I know."

"And after we found the Unholy Grail, you left me without saying a word. You looked at me—saw me in my true form—and then just left. Then you came to my room and left me a wreath. You said we needed to get the Unholy Grail together. And after that, you disappeared for weeks. I thought I might be back on the kill list. I had no idea what was happening, because you don't tell me. Your vow of silence made things easy for you, didn't it? You didn't have to speak for all those years. It's a beautiful cop-out. You can avoid communicating with anyone while appearing noble."

He scrubbed his hand over his jaw. "I'm sorry. I'm still out of practice when it comes to talking." The darkness in his eyes faded to violet. "I wanted you here at the Institute, but I couldn't get to you during the past few weeks."

"Why exactly did you disappear into the void?"

"The Shadow Fae were mutinying, with Aengus leading the rebellion. They wanted you dead immediately, and I was worried they'd defy my orders. They agreed to wait to act until we heard from Nyxobas. In order to retain control over the Institute, the Shadow Fae needed to hear from him directly. So I went into the void to contact him. But sometimes time passes strangely there. It felt like just a moment, but I was in the void for weeks." He nodded at the steaming bath. "Can you get in? We need to finish healing you."

I unhooked my bra, letting it fall off me, goosebumps rising over my skin. Then, I grabbed Ruadan's arm. He helped me to stand, and I leaned against his powerful body.

"What happens next?" I asked.

"Nyxobas will arrive when he chooses. He will open the void for you, and you will enter. When you return from the shadow hell, with Nyxobas's approval, you and I are going to find your father. He will help us remove the Plague from the Institute. Then, we find Baleros, and we imprison him forever. You and I, together."

"And you're not going to kill my father?"

"It's no longer my top priority."

"So that's a no, or…?" I winced as I bent over to pull off my knickers, my bones screaming.

"That's a no. We need him."

"Good. So can you make any predictions for when I go through this void?"

"I don't know exactly what will happen." He held onto my arm to help steady me. "Nyxobas isn't particularly communicative."

"Sounds familiar." Then I stepped into the bath, lowering myself into the warm, bubbling water. Steam curled around me as I slid down. I leaned back in the bath, meeting Ruadan's gaze.

He reached out, stroking my throat, then traced his fingertips around the jagged wound on my collarbone. It had gone black and rotten around the edges—disgusting, really. Deep, purplish blood leaked from the wound, and I grimaced at the sight of broken bone protruding from my skin. The veins around the wound pulsed with dark blood.

As Ruadan touched the healthy skin around it, his magic slipped over my body like a balm. With his magic intensifying, the purple in my veins began to fade, the pain ebbing. Deep relaxation spread through my body, and my eyes started to drift closed again. I had absolutely no desire to go into the void. I wanted to stay here forever.

Another memory rose in my mind—this one more recent. I was in the forest, handing Ruadan the crown he'd made for me. A brief look of hurt flashed in his eyes.

A sigh escaped me. "I'm sorry I gave the crown back."

"I'll make you another." His hand moved lower over my ribs, and my skin pulsed with the euphoria of his magic. Already, my body was stirring with arousal at his touch. I breathed in the scent of the herbs in the bath, the air heavy with their perfume.

When I opened my eyes again to look down at my collarbone, I was stunned to find that it had almost completely healed. The skin had closed over, and it looked like a pale, indented scar.

Ruadan's violet eyes never left my face, his expression so intent it looked like he wanted to devour me. Sometimes when I looked at him, the sheer power of him hit me like a gale-force wind.

"Why exactly were you so angry with me when I first came into the Institute?" I asked. "Was it because I'd invaded or because I'd hidden what I really was from you?"

Apart from the hand brushing over my body, most of Ruadan had gone completely still—a strange silence found only among the ancient fae. "I wasn't angry with you." His soft voice caressed my naked skin, a dark temptation. "I was angry with myself, because my men threw you in the prisons."

I arched an eyebrow. "You need to stop thinking that you have to protect me." The arrogance on this one. Darkness roiled between my ribs. I needed no protector. The corner of my mouth twitched anyway. I liked his sentiment, even if it made no sense. "I'm an angel of death. I don't need protecting."

"Well, maybe the other Shadow Fae will pay."

"Pay? How?"

He traced a fingertip lazily in the burbling bath, his magic washing over me, doing its healing work. "Sometimes, in the shadow void, Nyxobas punishes spirits by forcing them to confront the wrongs they've committed on earth. Sometimes to relive them. He forces you to confront your past."

I paled. "And you're sending me into the shadow void."

"Right."

"I have killed *hundreds* of people in the arena, and I slaughtered my entire village. So … it might not be a good time for me there."

"It might not happen for you."

"Good."

I leaned back in the bath. It was then that I realized that not only was his magic healing my body, it was actually making me feel rested. I'd barely slept in weeks, and yet I no longer felt quite as insane. I was starting to feel … energetic. Gods bless Ruadan and his magic.

As I sucked in a deep breath, the curves of my breasts floated above the steamy water's surface. Ruadan's gaze dipped to them, and his shadowy magic lashed the air around him.

I grabbed a bar of soap from the rocky bath's edge and started to lather myself up, watching his eyes follow my hand's movements. I made the strokes slow and sensual, moving over the tops of my breasts. His desire licked the air around him. Mesmerized, he wrapped one of his hands over mine, lacing my fingers with his. His hand slid over my skin with mine. Heat raced through my body.

A drop of water slid down my throat, and he followed it with his eyes. Then, one of his hands moved away from mine. His fingers brushed down the front of my chest and my waist, and molten heat rushed through my core. An ache began to build in me at his light touch.

It wasn't just his beauty or his touch that stoked my heat. It was knowing that he loved me.

His violet eyes were locked on me, and he began tracing slow circles, moving lower—now in the hollow of my hips. Tingling heat radiated out from his touch. His incubus side was coming out, and he was toying with me.

He drank me in with his gaze, and the look he was giving me promised pure, sensual pleasure. My thighs clenched.

"I know it doesn't make sense to protect you," he said. "It's my instinct, as powerful as my will to live. I want to keep you safe and close by my side."

I wanted to grow claws and sink them into his skin to bind him close to me. I had the same primal instinct to keep him safe—not free from hurt, because he could take a little pain, just like I could. But I wanted to keep him close to me.

My chest flushed, pulse racing. This close to his savage beauty, it was hard to think straight. I only knew I wanted to feel his tongue on my neck, his hands on my breasts, his mouth between my thighs.

As he traced circles over my hip bones, my knees started to fall open, and my breath hitched. Liquid heat flowed through me, and a hot, pulsing ache pounded between my thighs.

I straightened, and my nipples floated just above the warm water. They hardened in the cool air. "You want me close by your side?"

His eyes seared me for a moment, then he leaned closer. "By my side, in my bed," he whispered, his breath warming the shell of my ear. "Naked and wrapped around me forever."

His fingers went to the inside of my left thigh. Despite the heat of the bath, I shivered. I wanted to feel his hand all the way down at the apex of my thighs, but he was moving with the infuriating slowness of an incubus, enjoying his control. He traced light circles on my inner thigh with his fingertips. I shuddered with desire.

I opened my legs wider, desperately aching for him. I wanted him inside me now. "Are you going to come in here?" I didn't like the way it had come out as a desperate plea.

His magic thrummed over my skin, fingers moving just a little higher. With his other hand, he brushed his thumb over my lips. I caught his thumb in my mouth, and I rolled my tongue over it. Now, I burned for him so deeply I could almost moan. In fact, I think I *did* moan.

A low, animal growl rose from Ruadan's throat. I moved my hips until I was grinding myself against his hand. I still needed more.

"Come in here with me," I said in something between a command and a plea.

His fingertips were still teasing me, stoking my lust to an insane ache. A slow smile curved his beautiful lips. "I won't fit, will I?"

Wild hunger blazed in my body. "We'll make you fit."

He dipped his fingers into me, and I writhed against him. *More, more.* That sharp, pounding desire built inside me, until I could think of nothing else but the word *more.*

Dark heat enveloped me. I moved against him, desperate for release. At last, I managed, "Get into the bath with me. Now. No more arguing."

He rose and pulled off his black shirt, exposing his muscled body. He was pure perfection, built like a god. Which made sense, since he *was* part god.

And I was about to have my fill of him.

CHAPTER 10

My gaze roamed over every inch of him. My stomach swooped at the network of tattoos on his body, snaking savagely over his powerful warrior's thighs. As I stared at him hungrily, I almost didn't realize that my own hand had found its way between my thighs to replace his. My breath raced.

At last, he stepped into the bath and kneeled between my legs. He leaned against me. "I'm going to keep you close to me. You're a death angel, but you're *my* death angel, and I keep you safe from now on."

"Then you're my fomoire monster." I wrapped my arms around his neck.

He kissed me sensually, his tongue sliding against mine. Another growl from Ruadan, and his hand gripped my hair, his body stiffening. The slow sensuality was now transformed into raw animal desire. He pulled me hard against him. He was done teasing me now, burning from hunger like I was, claiming my mouth with his wild kiss. I wrapped my legs around him.

Then, with one savage stroke, he buried himself inside me. I gasped, waves of pleasure lighting me up.

There was nothing now except me and Ruadan, and the heat of our bodies merging deeper with each glorious stroke.

Pleasure washed over me, wild ecstasy where our bodies joined. I could only feel the movement of our slick skin together, my tongue on his neck, teeth in his throat. I ran my fingernails down his back as he thrust deeper. The world around me dimmed, and it was just Ruadan and me.

He whispered into my ear, repeating his promise. "From now on, I keep you safe."

It was those words that sent me over the edge, and my cries echoed off the stone walls.

* * *

WITH DAMP HAIR, I lay on Ruadan's chest in the tub. The warm water burbled around us, steam curling about our bodies. The air around him had darkened with shadows, his magic whipping at the air. He brushed his hand over my neck.

The torch flickered in its sconce, and a chill fell over the room. Then, the hot, burbling water turned glacial.

"Ruadan! Gods below. Stop it."

No sooner were the words out of my mouth than I realized that Ruadan's tattoos had begun sliding all over his body again.

I froze, my heart thumping wildly. So *this* was the moment Nyxobas chose to return and to inhabit his grandson's body. While we were lying naked in a tub together, my legs wrapped around him.

He rose from the bath, his eyes shimmering with silver-tinged starlight. I crossed my legs, and I crossed my arms over my chest.

He looked at me impassively, completely uninterested in my nudity. "The time has come for your trial."

As I stared up at him, I had that strange, dizzying feeling that I was standing on the edge of a precipice, and that I wanted to jump. "Right here?"

He shook his head. "You will complete your trial outside. I've opened a portal in the Tower Green."

"Okay. Sure. So, I'm naked and this is a little awkward." Still, I couldn't stay in the freezing bath any longer. "Is there a towel you could hand me?"

A vortex of shadows whirled around him, and his silvery eyes transfixed me. He did not answer.

Of course he didn't; he was Ruadan's grandfather.

Unable to take the icy bath any longer, I stood, my teeth chattering. Maybe it was Nyxobas's complete lack of interest in my nudity, but I quickly stopped feeling self-conscious in front of him.

"Just give me a second to get dressed," I said, plucking Ruadan's shirt off the ground.

"Travelers into my portals may not sully the waters with clothing."

I cast my mind back to the enormous demon named Bael, who'd arrived in the Tower completely naked. He'd said basically the same thing.

"Sure, that makes sense," I muttered. *Weirdo.*

Well, it wasn't like I had my own clean clothes here, and I wasn't going to put the filthy, piss-stinking jersey on again.

"But if we're going outside," I said, "I'm going to at least wrap something around myself. I don't need Barry leering at me."

I strode into Ruadan's bedroom and pulled one of his sheets off the bed. When I turned back to Nyxobas, he'd vanished.

With the sheet wrapped around me, I crossed to the window. The sun had set completely now, and darkness had fallen over London. The moon seemed startlingly bright, a jewel hanging over the courtyard, and the stars cast silvery light over a transformed courtyard. Where wildflowers had been just moments before was now a gaping chasm, about twenty feet across, filled with dark water.

I swallowed hard as I looked out at it. I was supposed to jump into that abyss, and I had no idea what I'd find when I did.

Ruadan said I'd be facing the sins of my past—but I had too many to count.

* * *

Wrapped in Ruadan's bed sheet, I stood at the edge of the portal, where the grass and soil simply gave way to dark waters. I had to journey into one of the hells, but at least I felt rested. Sleep deprivation was its own sort of hell, and one that I'd escaped.

Nyxobas—inhabiting my lover's completely naked body—stood nearby, horns gleaming over his head, tattoos slithering around him.

The rest of the Shadow Fae had joined us, wrapped warmly in their cloaks. Fever flushed most of their faces, and beads of sweat dotted their brows. I had to get this over with as fast as possible so we could find my father. It was the only way to heal them all. What did they plan to do if I turned out to be the traitor, as they imagined? They thought they could petition for my father's help after they threw me into the shadow hell? Aengus and the others hadn't thought this through at all.

If the portal sealed over me, it would at least relieve them from a harrowing trial in the shadow hell. Sick as they were, I couldn't imagine they wanted to jump into freezing waters to face possible torture. But didn't they realize they needed my help to rid themselves of the death magic? Right now, they could hardly see beyond their own misery.

I stared into the portal, dreading my own imminent trial. In my heart, fear twined with an insane desire to leap in.

Aengus cleared his throat, then gestured to urge me on. The movement was interrupted by a coughing fit.

I glanced at Nyxobas, who looked like some sort of combination of Ruadan and the god of night—Ruadan with paler skin, darker hair, and phantom horns. He loomed over the edge of the portal, tattoos slithering over his powerful body. He looked beautiful and remote at the same time—strangely alluring despite his otherworldliness. This time, when I looked down at the waters, the urge to jump in was overwhelming.

And this was the essence of shadow magic, wasn't it? The shadow creatures: vampires, incubi, succubi, fomoires of heartbreak.... These creatures possessed the kind of magic that lured and seduced you to your own death.

I took a step closer to the portal, nearly ready to drop the sheet when I remembered everyone was looking on.

I shot Aengus a sharp look. "Turn around. All of you."

Aengus nodded at the other Shadow Fae. Melusine gave me an encouraging nod before she turned away.

As the rest of the Shadow Fae turned away from me, I stared into Nyxobas's silvery eyes. I took one long breath, steadying myself.

Then, I leapt into the portal—but I didn't hit the water. Instead, I plummeted farther down, dropping into pure darkness. My arms lifted above my head, cold air racing over my bare skin.

Then, I could no longer feel my body at all. It was just me and the darkness. I had no sense of up or down, no sense of horizon. Had I ever existed at all?

Emptiness began to poison my thoughts. If I'd never been alive, then I'd never loved…. It had always been this way—just me and the darkness.

No, no. Had I been alive once?

It didn't matter. I wasn't alive now. I didn't exist now. And now was all that mattered.

Wisps and fragments of thoughts floated in the wind like dandelion seeds.

Love dies when we die….

I never loved.

The pain of this thought hit me so intensely I was sure my mind would shatter, and the portal would close me inside forever.

CHAPTER 11

$\mathcal{I}$t was at that point that a new thought struck me. I could feel pain.

I could feel. If I could feel, it meant I existed.

I exist.

Feeling started to return to my body, to my limbs and my fingertips and the tips of my toes. I touched my own throat, my fingers warm against my skin.

"I exist," I said out loud, the sound of my own voice a strange and illicit thrill, vibrations rumbling against my hand. A stony floor materialized beneath my feet, and I sighed with relief at the feeling of stability. Something solid underneath me.

Then, a thin, silver light, like the light of the stars, washed over the space around me.

I wasn't naked anymore. I'd been dressed in a long, silvery gown, the fabric pure gossamer. My purple hair cascaded over bare shoulders.

I wasn't wearing shoes. As I walked forward, a world began to take shape around me, the contours oddly familiar. A gray cottage of rough-hewn wood, a narrow village road. Buildings wrapped in flowering vines.

Just on the edge of the village, beyond this clearing, dark forests yawned on either side. I didn't want to look into those woods.... It wasn't safe there. They'd always seemed so alive to me, the trees breathing and moving, but now their trunks stood like stone sentinels ready to kill me.

It was only safe here, in civilization. The darkness in the forests was just a little *too* dark, too savage.

Why was it so empty here?

It took me a little while to realize what I was looking at. Then, the shock of familiarity hit me.

This was Eden—where I'd lived with my mum and dad long ago, before Ruadan had come. This was the village they'd created—the wooden homes, the elaborate stone temples, overgrown with honeysuckle and moonflowers. The perfect melding of the wild and the divine. This beautiful world was the only one I'd known in those days, before I'd leapt through the portal to London.

Sadness pierced me as I was forced to face the truth.

I'd killed all of them, hadn't I? And this was my reckoning.

That's why the buildings were empty. Gods, I just wanted to see another living person, someone with a beating heart. Here, the loneliness was crushing.

The sound of footfalls pattered behind me, and I whirled.

"Hello?" I called out.

Silence greeted me. I exhaled, walking again.

I wasn't sure I wanted to see my old house, the one where my mum had tried to teach me to dance, where my dad had read me books in his lap. I didn't want to see it empty and dead like these buildings. These were the carcasses of my past life.

Footfalls again, and I turned. This time I caught a flash of pale skin, a glimpse of purple—

My heartbeat raced. "Hello?"

Whoever it was had disappeared around the corner of a house, and I picked up my pace to follow.

"Who's there?" I needed to find them. I couldn't be alone here.

When I rounded the next corner, I saw her—the little girl with the amber eyes; the short, purple hair that she'd cut herself. A white dress short enough to show off her skinned, dirty knees. Her mother had wanted her to wear it. She hated dresses, the way you were supposed to keep them clean and unwrinkled, and she wanted to run through the woods and pretend to hunt.

I swallowed hard. "Liora," I whispered.

She giggled, then ran off into the gloom of the forest.

"Wait!"

I chased after her, my bare feet pounding the dirt. How could a little girl run so fast? My blood turned cold as I ran deeper into the forest. Blossoming hawthorn trees surrounded us, but their branches looked oddly sharp and spiked—half tree, half medieval weapon.

She ran on the narrow path, and I tried to keep up with her. The branches scraped my skin, drawing blood like claws.

My pulse pounded in my ears. I had to chase her. I had to tell her to be careful—that a fae cohort would come here today. A fomoire would ruin her world, and she had to be ready. I broke into a sprint.

How the hells was she so fast?

"Stop!" I yelled.

Abruptly, the little girl stopped and turned to see me.

She gaped at me, her eyes black and empty. "You don't exist. You never did. You never loved."

My legs started shaking, and I felt the ground giving way beneath my feet again. A seed of understanding began to bloom in my mind. "I'm onto you." I gritted my teeth. "You're not a little girl. You're not me. You're a demon of the void."

At my words, her body began to shift, limbs elongating. A tall, pale demon appeared before me.

No longer a little girl, the demon loomed over me. Silver horns jutted out from his blond hair, and his canines glinted. He wore a blue T-shirt and jeans, which seemed a bit weird for a demon.

"Liora," he chanted in a singsong voice. "Liora. Liora, Liora. Death poisons her aura."

Anger tightened my lungs, my fists clenching. As he sang, that old image rose in my mind—the one of my mum lying flat on her back, the skin around her neck discolored to a bruise purple.

The demon's form flickered away again. "She killed her mum, she killed her friends, and they won't come back anymore-a."

Rage ignited, and I ripped a spiked branch off a tree. "That doesn't even rhyme properly, you stupid twat!" I shrieked.

"Liora, Liora…." He continued on with his enraging chant. He kept flickering between the tree trunks—just glimpses of his tall, pale body.

This was a trial, wasn't it? That meant I probably had to kill him. Good. I *really* wanted to kill him.

But the more I chased him, the farther away he seemed to slip. The ground looked purple here, discolored and rotten. The color of bruises, of rotting flesh … blood stained the soil.

If I didn't kill this demon, I'd be trapped here forever, forced to relive my worst memories. Forced to tread on my mother's neck.

That's what Hell was, wasn't it? Nyxobas, you fucker. Was this really necessary?

Baleros's twentieth law of power: Bring your enemy to you.

I stopped in my tracks, closing my eyes, catching my breath.

Silence yawned around me. Then, the icy stroke of the demon's fingertips up my spine sent a sharp pang of loneliness shooting through me.

You never loved….

I spun around, driving the spiked branch right into the demon's heart. His hazel eyes widened with shock. There was something familiar about them….

Dark blood poured from his chest. Then, he disintegrated like dust, and particles of his demon body floated away on the wind.

I sighed. There. Alone again.

I looked around me, waiting for the portal to open once more. I'd swim out of the portal water and drag Ruadan back to bed before we went off in search of my dad.

But no portal was opening in the earth. Instead, the forest around me began to shift, the sharp lines of the trees growing softer. Then, the godsdamned blond demon appeared again, farther along down the winding forest path. He walked toward me, his smile mocking. I was sure he was about to start singing again.

"How many times do I have to kill you?" I shouted.

I gripped my head, my mind whirling. Maybe I'd approached this wrong. Since joining the Institute, there had been a few trials where I *wasn't* supposed to kill someone. The gorta, the creepy banshee in that East London shop....

It would be nice if someone would lay out the ground rules ahead of time, given that my first instinct was always to kill.

I let out a long, slow breath, studying the creature before me. The closer I looked, the less it looked like he was mocking me. In fact, his strangely familiar hazel eyes looked haunted. By his pointed ears, I could tell that he wasn't just a demon. He was at least part fae.

"What do I know you from?" I asked.

His mouth opened and closed mutely, and the stricken look on his face filled me with guilt.

Then, he spoke again. "I ... a darkness. I ... a darkness. Dick."

I scratched my cheek. "Okay, friend. What am I supposed to do here?"

"Amgggr pentagra bus hole."

"Yeah, I'm going to need something a little clearer." I scrunched my nose as a seed of understanding began to bloom in my mind. "Did you used to be a fae? Have you been trapped in the demon world, slowly turning into a demon?"

He nodded. "Stank rubs."

"How long have you been here?"

He gripped me hard by the shoulders, his lip trembling. "Eternity."

"Literal eternity or...?"

His fingers tightened even more. "Since you killed me."

I felt the world tilting beneath me, time slowing down. My mouth went dry. "I killed you. In the gladiator ring?"

He stared down at me, the planes of his face growing more familiar.

"Who are you?" I stammered.

"Liora," he whispered, his expression desperate, pleading.

"No. What's your name?"

"Darkness. Mike."

Panic gripped me. Mike—Mike from Eden. The boy I'd chased through the forest.

"What are you doing here?"

"I … a darkness…."

I swallowed hard. "Right. I killed you."

He nodded, his grip loosening a little on my shoulders. "Nesting locks of dark. Throglint oak." His eyes went wide, then he whispered in my ear, "Dick."

I swore to the gods that before he'd been in the shadow hells, he'd made sense. This place had warped him completely. Nausea rose in my gut. I'd done this to him. I'd sent him here, and he'd completely lost his mind.

"Okay, Mike. It hasn't been an eternity. More like a decade. I know it feels like an eternity." I frowned. "I want to get you out of here." I looked around the dark wood, searching for a way out. I didn't see one.

Nyxobas hadn't sealed me in here, had he?

"Any clues about how to get out?"

"Infestations demon Tznaia Amman roots, deathling open door. Darkness." He was speaking a pidgin demon language. Gibberish.

Or was it gibberish?

"Please." He kept his hands on my shoulders. "Miracle. Deathling."

Deathling open door.

"Where is the door?" I asked.

"Deathling," he repeated.

The gods of death had dominion over the dead. I could *open* the door.

I'd already seen that my own thoughts could influence the space around me. The less empty I felt, the more power I had. I closed my eyes, thinking of Ruadan and the floral crown he'd given me in Emain. This time, I rewrote the script, imagining that I'd taken the wreath from him. In this version of the story, I put the wreath on my head.

Warmth spread through my chest, and I stepped away from Demented Mike.

When I opened my eyes again, I felt Ruadan's electrifying presence around me, and I smelled the scent of pine. I felt loved.

Then, I willed the ground before me to cleave open. Dark, churning waters rose from the forest soil, and a portal ripped open the forest floor.

I grabbed Demented Mike around the waist, and I pulled him into the water with me.

CHAPTER 12

Catching my breath in the air, I hoisted myself out of the freezing portal. I clawed my way onto the grass, then frantically turned to reach into the cold water for one of Mike's long limbs. I grasped his arm, clutching on tight, and I dragged him out of the portal. He gasped, holding onto the portal's grassy rim. Mike's dark eyes were wide with wonder at the stars above us.

I tried to ignore the fact that I was completely starkers once more, and that all the male Shadow Fae were staring at me right now. I sat on the grass and folded my knees to my chest, wrapping my arms around them.

Aengus frowned at me, folding his arms. "Okay. Okay. So Nyxobas let you back. You're not the traitor. Now, who the hells have you brought back with you? And must you always bring back these wretches from the hell worlds?"

"He's an old and dear friend," I said, conveniently omitting the part about that time I'd killed him and sent him to the shadow hell. I hugged my legs tightly to my chest.

From behind, I felt a sheet wrap around my body, and I looked up at Ruadan. It was him again, his eyes violet. The god of night had left us for now.

"Well," said Aengus, "that's the first one over."

I glared at him. "Are you going to admit that you were wrong about me being a traitor and that you owe me an apology?"

Aengus rolled his eyes. "Fine." His tone was exasperated. "I'm sorry I said you were a traitor and that we should rip out your entrails in a painful execution. You're still an abomination, though, and I make no apologies for that view." His forehead wrinkled with consternation. "Is it just me, or are the youth of today particularly *sensitive* about things? Snowflakes, the lot of you."

With every interaction, I was starting to grow more certain that Aengus was the traitor. I fought the urge to just push him right into the portal and watch Nyxobas claim his soul.

Barry raised his hand. "Just to clarify, we don't all need to go in, do we? I'm only a recruit, so obviously I'm not a part of this."

"Everyone in the Institute," said Aengus. "Until we find our traitor."

Barry paled. It was, after all, a terrifying prospect to leap into a hell world where we were forced to reckon with past sins. Barry would probably be subject to a torturous Neanderthal routine.

I stood, holding the sheet tight around myself, and started to cross to Ruadan.

But as I took a step toward him, pale light began beaming from his eyes once more, and his tattoos slid over his powerful forearms, his chest, his muscled thighs. I tried not to think about how sexy he looked right now. The world of magic was always strange, but lusting after your lover while his grandfather's spirit inhabited his body crossed some sort of line even for me.

Nyxobas-Ruadan shadow-leapt over to Aengus. The god grasped the knight by his throat and lifted him high in the air. Aengus's clothes burned away from his body, leaving him completely naked.

Then, Nyxobas threw Aengus into the portal. Dark water splashed high into the air, shimmering with flecks of silver.

I stared as the watery surface calmed. Now, the moon and stars shone off its glassy surface.

I glanced at Mike, who was also nude, regretting that I didn't have a sheet for him. Not that he seemed to mind. His hands were on his hips, proud as could be, and he strode through the flowers, whistling.

I looked at the portal again. It didn't seem to be closing over with grass like I'd expected, trapping Aengus inside. I leaned over and skimmed my fingertips along the cold, glassy surface. It was black ice, and as I touched it, steam curled off.

Then, the ice cracked with a booming sound. Another enormous crack, and Aengus's fist broke through the surface. Frantic, he grasped for the edge of the portal with one hand, punching another hole in the ice with the other.

I glanced at Ruadan. Nyxobas still imbued his body, and he seemed unmoved by this struggle. We weren't supposed to help him, were we?

At last, he punched a hole big enough for his head and shoulders. His lips had gone blue, and he gasped for breath. Manically, he clawed and scrambled over the ice, until he flopped, naked, onto the grass.

He curled into the fetal position, hugging his knees to his chest. He was whispering something that sounded like *trapped in the stone room*, the same words over and over again. Then, "Shot through with iron arrows...."

I crossed my arms, looking down at him. I *really* wanted to gloat, but gloating about the misfortunes of someone already dying of the Plague seemed a bit tacky.

Barry gaped at him, pale as milk.

When I looked around at the other Shadow Fae, they looked just as terrified. But they looked ill, too. Most were too weak to stand, and sweat dampened their brows. Melusine's throat bulged with swollen glands, and her eyes were closed.

My throat tightened. Would they survive a brutal trip into the void? Fever and disease were eating them alive.

Ruadan loomed over the portal—no longer filled with Nyxobas's power, but still exuding dark magic. "As you see, Nyxobas has returned both Aengus and Liora. They are not our traitors. The god of night has left us for now, but he will return to test the rest of you when he sees fit. In the meantime, no one leaves the Institute."

Niall's teeth were chattering, and he coughed into his arm. "So what now? We just wait for Nyxobas to return while we die of the Plague?"

I crossed to Ruadan, my bed sheet dragging over the wet grass. "No. Now we find my father, the angel of death, and he's going to cure all of you." I glanced at Ruadan. "But we should probably put some clothes on before I introduce you to my family for the first time."

Melusine rubbed a swollen gland in her neck, wincing as if in pain. "If your father can cure us, why can't you? You're right here."

I shook my head. "I don't know how. My father will."

She coughed. "You could at least try. You have the same powers as your father, and you're right here. What if we have to go through the trials while fever is killing us? Look at Aengus."

Tension vibrated through my body. She simply didn't understand how badly this could backfire. "I could make it worse. If I try to use my death angel powers, you could end up sicker. Trust me. Look, I promise we'll be back quickly. We just need to get some clothing on, and we will be back within a few minutes with my dad."

So why was it that I didn't quite believe the words coming out of my own mouth?

"Liora is right," said Ruadan. "It won't take long. Asking Liora to experiment with her powers should be a last resort, undertaken only if we cannot find the Horseman or compel him to help us."

Dread crawled up my neck. Why would we not be able to find him? Of course we'd find him. He'd be in Eden where I'd left him.

And yet ... something about my time in the shadow void had seemed like a premonition. Those empty houses, standing like carcasses. Demented Mike had been trapped there. How many others had I consigned to one of the hells?

I locked the cage on my thoughts, refusing to dwell too long on my worst fears.

For the first time in over ten years, Ruadan was going to open a portal to my old home, and I'd see them again. My heart was ready to burst.

I could hardly breathe with the anticipation. When we broke

through into Eden, my dad would be waiting for me. He'd pull me into a hug and call me Bug and tell me it wasn't my fault. And that he'd brought my mother back, and that everything was fine.

Then we'd return to London together. As a team—as a family—we'd figure out how to rid the world of Baleros's malignant presence. This would happen.

Right?

I wouldn't let myself think about the nightmarish vision of my old home in the shadow hell. I refused to entertain the idea that I might find everyone dead. That I'd be standing over a grave for my mum, or that my father had lost his mind. I would definitely not think of him mad with grief, his shoulders slumped, dark wings drooping behind him as everyone he ever loved abandoned him—

My legs felt weak.

"Clothing," I blurted at Ruadan. "We need clothes." I gestured at the Tower walls. "My entire mist army will stay here to guard the Tower. I'll command them to surround the Institute."

Ruadan nodded. "Tell them that if they see anything amiss, they should report to Aengus."

"Yes. Sure. Can we go now?"

I needed to go before the terrifying images claimed my mind. Before I lost my nerve completely.

* * *

IN RUADAN'S ROOM, I pulled a shirt on over my bare chest.

"Are you all right?" Ruadan asked.

"I'm fine. Almost ready."

As if it had traveled with me from the shadow void, sharp emptiness spread between my ribs—a chasm that could eat me alive. I took a deep breath as I slipped into a pair of black leather trousers. My hands shook a bit as I buttoned them.

Fully dressed now, Ruadan closed the distance between us. His healing magic brushed over my skin, soothing my fears. He leaned in and pressed his forehead to mine. Silky magic kissed my skin. "I can go first," he said. "I can see what it's like before you join me."

I closed my eyes, marshaling my resolve. He understood I was afraid of what I'd find there. He'd be returning to the place where he saw his brothers die—but he was thinking of me.

"You can't go alone," I said. "If Adonis is there, you might not make it out alive. If anyone should go alone, it would make more sense for it to be me. I'm the one who can convince him."

Still pressing his forehead against mine, he shook his head *no*. "It's better if I go with you. Eden has been sealed for ten years. I don't know what we will find there."

"I'll be fine. Death angel, remember? I'm very hard to kill."

He straightened. "I don't think that you need me to survive. I just think I should be with you."

I nodded. So maybe he wanted to protect my heart. Maybe he was imagining the same things I was—a landscape of dust and gravestones.

I sucked in a sharp breath. "Mike, the demented fae I brought back, was from my village. I killed him, and he's been in the shadow void this whole time. I think I must have put our whole village in the hells."

Ruadan brushed his knuckles over my shoulder. "He can reverse death magic. He can reverse the Plague. That's why we're going to find him. Maybe that ability was strong enough to bring some of them back. We could be returning to a thriving village in Eden."

My chest unclenched. Ruadan was right. I should not underestimate Adonis. I smiled at him. "Okay. You're right. Let's do this." I glanced at the sword slung around his waist. "Do you really think we should go in armed? It's a family reunion, and it might take a moment for them to recognize me. Going in with weapons might send the wrong message."

"I'll keep it sheathed."

"Fine. And let me walk in front." Then, I pulled on my headlamp. I had no reason to bring the headlamp or the bag, but I just felt better with them. I felt like myself. "Right," I said. "Open the portal before I lose my nerve."

Without another word, the floor opened up in front of us, a watery fissure in the stone that widened.

Ruadan took my hand, his violet gaze on mine. I nodded at him, and we leapt in.

CHAPTER 13

The freezing vortex pulled us under. I clutched Ruadan's hand as we sank deeper into complete darkness. I found a brief moment of peace in here, a respite of purity in the blackness.

After a few moments, moonlight pierced the water. *Eden.*

I was home. Still holding hands, we started to kick our way to the top. By the time we reached the surface, I felt like my heart was about to explode.

We pulled ourselves out at the same time, and I gaped at the world around me—the dark forest, silvered in the moonlight. The clearing just a hundred feet away. With my head out of the water, I gasped for air. Clutching the portal's mossy edge, I stared at the silent oaks around me. We'd emerged in the woods.

I pulled myself out, and I sloshed onto the rich earth. I breathed in, taking in the smells of moss and ancient trees, the faint aroma of honeysuckle and blackberries—the ones I used to pick with Mike. *Home.*

Ruadan rose, too, and his hand instinctively hovered by his sword. His muscles were tensed, and he looked ready to kill.

"Simmer down, Ruadan," I said. "It's a family reunion, remember?"

"I know." He motioned for me to go on toward the village itself.

The silence here felt heavy as a grave, broken only by the groaning of the wind through the tree branches. It wasn't that late at night, was it? Maybe nine?

The wind rushed through the trees, making the boughs creak above us. Among the oaks and rowans, I squeezed out my wet hair, then started walking toward the forest's edge. Except there were no lights like there should have been. The village should have been lit up at this time of night, but we had only the moonlight lighting our way.

Here, the trees' boughs seemed to arch protectively above us. I glanced at a gnarled oak—just by the spot where I'd hidden the day Ruadan had invaded.

I reached for Ruadan's hand, taking comfort in its warmth. The breeze toyed with his pale hair. An ancient fae prince like him belonged in the forest. Just not this forest. The image in my mind of his invasion felt so vivid here. He'd been *terrifying.* A god of war.

At the forest's edge, my heart was racing out of control. Dark buildings all around, not a sign of life anywhere. "There should be lights," I whispered.

I swallowed hard. Through the trees, I had a view of Eden. Timber-frame houses crowded narrow roads, just as they always had. A temple to the Old Gods stood in the center of the village, and I could see its elegant stone roof from here, the tallest building in Eden. Everything was just as it should be.

Except life was completely absent from this place. I couldn't even sense a blackbird's heartbeat. Chilly wind whipped over my skin and hair.

As we stepped into the clearing, a heavy weight pressed on my chest, and I stared at the darkness before me. I released Ruadan's hand and broke into a run for the nearest building, just on the village's edge.

A thin layer of dust coated wooden shutters. I unhooked the shutters, then pulled them open. They creaked apart to reveal dark windows. I cupped my hands to peer inside the glass. This had been the bakery once, but now dust and cobwebs coated the furniture. My throat went dry.

"There's no one here," I said to Ruadan.

"But Adonis will be here. Even Adonis couldn't get out of a locked world."

He had a point. But what sort of state would I find him in?

I turned to survey the dirt road that wound into the center of Eden, where the temple stood. Just like in the shadow void, the buildings were dark and shuttered.

Ruadan's fingers twitched at his hilt, and he sniffed the air. "Something isn't right here."

I swallowed hard. "Yeah. Well, I mean, I did kill everyone, so that is probably the thing that feels a bit wrong."

He shook his head. "No. I feel magic here. I just don't know where it's coming from."

"What kind of magic?"

His brow furrowed. "Fae magic, I think."

Hope lit in my chest. Fae magic. My mother had powerful fae magic. Was she still around somewhere?

Quietly, we followed the path deeper into the village, and I gripped Ruadan's hand hard. The dirt path wound around the buildings, toward the village green. The temple stood on a gently rolling hill.

And before the temple, I found piles of rocks—silvery light streamed over dozens of them, in little crooked pyramids. Dried floral wreaths rested on top of the piles. The sight of them was a punch to my gut. These were fae grave markers.

One of the wreaths caught my eye—dried honeysuckle and crimson anemones. My parents' favorite flowers, intertwined. My legs felt weak, and I gripped Ruadan's arm to steady myself.

Where was my dad? Someone had buried the dead, which meant he couldn't be among them. Not to mention the fact that my powers wouldn't kill him.

"Where would we be most likely to find him?" asked Ruadan, trying to keep me focused.

The tremors in my hands had returned. "We should look in my old house."

I let go of Ruadan again, and I broke into a run, feet pounding on the dirt road. My parents' home wasn't far from the green, near the burbling brook. I was nearly there—nearly to my dad.

I turned off the path, running in the tall grasses outside my old home, where wildflowers dappled the ground.

It was too dark. Just like the others, it looked like an empty vessel. I ground to a halt, investigating it. Vines covered the house's exterior like nature was trying to suffocate it, and moonflowers blossomed all over them. Where the hells could my father have gone if he wasn't here?

Our house didn't have shutters, and I cupped my hands to peer through the dusty glass window. I couldn't see much beyond the grime—but the Angel of Death did not live in grime. Clearly, Adonis was not here. Still, maybe I could find a clue of some kind that would tell me what had happened to him.

"I'm going in," I said.

I shivered as I pushed through the door into the darkened cottage. Behind me, Ruadan chanted in Ancient Fae, and he called up a sphere of golden light that cast a warm glow over my house.

The orb floated into the old living room, casting a dull amber glow over the dust. I coughed, my gaze sweeping over the table where we'd eaten dinner, and the chaise lounge where I'd sat in my mum's lap for stories.

With a lump in my throat, I crossed to the ornately carved mantle. Among the carvings of leaves and flowers, I was searching for the moon and the word "Bug."

But when I drew closer, my heart constricted. The moon carving was there—but my nickname wasn't. No "Bug." I frowned at it, tracing over it with my fingertips. Everything was just as it had been, except that one little detail.

The shock of it disoriented me, and it felt like I'd been erased from history. Now, the ground no longer felt quite so solid beneath my feet. Had I somehow imagined that detail of my life?

Dizzy, I felt as if my spirit were curling into the air like fog. I wasn't sure what was real anymore. The fae, the gladiator, the death angel—all the different Lioras vying for control, none of them stable, none rooted to the earth. Which one was real? I closed my eyes, overcome by the feeling that I was watching myself from the outside. Here was a woman who'd probably lost her mind long ago.

For one wild, dizzying moment, I had the horrifying thought that I'd never left Baleros's cage—that this was all something I'd dreamt up to make myself into a hero. It was the escape route of a broken spirit.

My breath heaved in my chest. No, it had ended even earlier than that. Maybe I'd died that day, when Ruadan had come, that day I'd killed everyone else—

"Liora?"

Ruadan's deep voice called me back to reality.

His violet eyes surveyed me with concern. He must have read the sheer terror and confusion in my eyes, because he touched the side of my face, painfully gently. His magic snaked down my body—a firm touch that warmed me and seemed to fuse itself to the floor, steadying me. Tendrils of his magic wrapped around my ankles and feet.

I'm here.

"Thanks."

His magic had grounded me, and somehow he'd known to do it instinctively.

With his magic helping to stabilize me, I looked up at him—at those violet eyes that were sometimes so cold. "I don't understand what's happening," I said. "My dad engraved my nickname into that mantle a long time ago. I remember it really clearly. It should say 'Bug.'"

"While you were inspecting that, I was trying to get a read on the magic here. There is magic all around us."

I frowned at the mantle, then cocked my head. "Are you sure you took us to the right place?" I asked. "What if it's a replica?"

He shot me a disbelieving look. "Of course I took us to the right place."

I ran my fingertips over that moon carving. "Is it possible this place is glamoured? That the real world is hidden somewhere under this one?"

"It's possible. But it would take someone extremely skilled at fae glamour to pull it off."

"That's why I asked. My mother was brilliant with glamour. Unfortunately, I didn't inherit her skills." I bit my lip. "Shit. Whatever is happening, Adonis isn't here. And I promised the Shadow Fae I'd be fast. We may not have a ton of time until they succumb to the Plague."

"I think you could heal them."

I shook my head, still staring at the mantle. I frowned at it. I hadn't noticed it at first, but on the lower ridge of the mantle, a line cut through the wood—nearly imperceptible at first among the intricate carvings of leaves and berries.

I gripped the top and bottom of the mantle, jaw dropping as I slid a section away to reveal a hollow alcove. "This is new."

Inside the alcove lay a small, folded piece of paper. As Ruadan looked on, I unfolded it, my heart stuttering.

Find Aenor.

Was it my mother's cursive handwriting? I think it was. And that meant she was alive.

"What does it say?" asked Ruadan.

"Find Aenor." I met his gaze. "Any idea who or what Aenor is?"

He pulled the paper from my hands, frowning at it. "Aenor. Flayer of Skins, Scourge of the Wicked."

"She sounds … nice. They want me to find her? Any idea why? Or where she might be?"

"We can find out."

"How do you know her name?"

"She's on our kill list, but she wasn't a priority."

"Of course. She has useful magical powers, which means you want to kill her."

"We don't know that they're useful."

"If my parents are sending us to her, she has useful powers. My parents knew that I'd check the mantle to see my name. They didn't want anyone else to find this, but they wanted me to see it."

"You sound certain that your mother is alive."

I smiled, a weight lifting off me. "I think it's her handwriting. I think my father brought her back."

"Let's search the rest of the house and the rest of Eden as fast as we can. If we sniff for your father's scent and shadow-leap, we can cover a lot of ground fast."

I nodded, though I already felt in my bones they weren't here. I shadow-leapt through the house, finding it nearly exactly as I'd left it. Then, we whooshed through the abandoned town, through the homes and the cemetery on the green, through the woods and the temple. And as we searched, I clutched that piece of paper in my hand. Wind rushed over me as we moved swiftly around Eden.

This was turning into a much more complicated recovery mission than I'd hoped.

Once we'd sniffed out every building and scoured the forest, we were certain that Adonis wasn't here. And I was sure this wasn't the real Eden anymore.

Near the cemetery green, Ruadan opened another portal. We were returning to the Institute empty-handed, and nothing had changed yet.

But now, I had a tiny shred of evidence my mother could be alive.

CHAPTER 14

*S*odden with portal water, we crawled onto the Institute's Tower Green. A canopy of night still arched above us; the moon shone bright with Nyxobas's power.

As I stood, the air began to chill around us, the moon burning brighter in the sky. I turned to look at Ruadan.

Except he was no longer Ruadan. Now, Nyxobas's crescent of silver horns beamed from his skull. His body had grown, and night magic billowed around him like smoke from a bellows.

I pushed my damp hair out of my eyes. "Hey, Nyxobas. Any chance you can turn up the temperature on your portal water? The knights are dying."

No response—just those eerie, silver eyes. A whorl of shadows consumed Ruadan.

Beneath my feet, the earth rumbled. What the hells was happening now? We had to find Aenor. I desperately wanted to get to my parents as soon as I could, but Nyxobas was interfering.

"You're a god," I grumbled. "You could just tell us who the traitor is."

In the center of the courtyard, the grassy earth cracked open, and I held out my arms to balance myself as the void gaped open before us. I backed away from it, not eager for another trip into a hell world.

When I looked up again, Nyxobas had shifted. He now stood at the edge of the portal, holding Niall by the neck. In his other hand, he gripped a Shadow Fae named Turi. Both of them had pale lips, and they were barely able to keep their eyes open. They looked at me expectantly, hoping I'd brought back a cure for them. I just shook my head with a pang of guilt.

The chokehold Nyxobas had on them probably wasn't helping the situation. He really was an arsehole. These knights were his servants. They had dedicated their souls to him, and he treated them like this.

Nyxobas threw both of them into the portal, and they sank deep into the darkness. The surface smoothed over once more, turning to ice.

Nyxobas turned to me, his glacial gaze boring into me.

I didn't want to be with the remote god of the void right now. I wanted Ruadan back, and I wanted to find my parents. I was still clutching the tiny piece of paper that had held Aenor's name, but the portal water had washed my mother's handwriting away.

I vaguely registered the other knights arriving as I stared down at the ruined paper.

A touch on my arm called my attention away from it, and I looked up at Melusine's sickly face. Her lips were parched, and dark circles hung beneath her eyes. She smelled faintly of vomit.

"Where's your dad?" she asked.

I shook my head. "I'm sorry. We didn't find him. We have a lead, though. Someone named Aenor, Flayer of Skins. Does that ring any bells?"

Her expression looked dejected, and she held up her hands, addressing the rest of them. "No death angel. I see no death angel, no father, and I put two and two together. We're screwed. We're all gonna die—"

"Shhh…" I cut in. "That's not good for morale. I'm working on it."

She pulled her cloak around herself more tightly. "Who's in the void?"

"Turi and Niall."

"I need to lie down and get some rest before he throws me in."

As she stumbled away, Nyxobas stalked toward me. I eyed him with surprise. Why was he studying me so closely? Even if he was in my lover's body, he unnerved me completely. I gave him my best *back off* glare.

The look did absolutely nothing to put him off, which I suppose made sense, since he was a night god who'd fallen from the heavens and lived tens of thousands of years in Hell. My narrowed eyes were not going to strike fear into his heart.

When he was just a foot away, he stared down at me. "Life and death mingle within you," he said, his voice the oddly dissonant sound of young and old people speaking at once. "The beginning and the end. Seeds growing from the ashes."

What do you say to that? "Okay. Thanks." This wasn't helpful information. But maybe he *could* help with something. "Do you know anyone called the Flayer of Skins, by any chance?"

His attention darted back to the portal, where the ice began to crack.

Of course he didn't provide any useful information. The gods never did.

A fist hammered at the ice—then another. Both Niall and Turi were fighting their way out. I would stay just long enough to see their heads breach the surface.

My fists tightened. "Is there a less grueling way you would test the knights? They're very sick."

His attention remained on the cracking portal. "It refreshes me to feel your spirits in the void."

"But they're dying. They're your servants."

"Fix it, then." His voice seemed to come from a million miles away.

Simple as that. Just—fix it. "How?"

He whirled, then he cupped my face with his icy hand. Emptiness spun through my body as I stared into his glacial, silvery eyes and took in his stark beauty.

He leaned in and whispered, "You know how this ends, don't you?"

"It ends with us imprisoning Baleros."

His breath was a frigid breeze on the shell of my ear. "It ends with Ruadan's death."

The words crashed into me like a wave. Ruadan had said that Nyxobas didn't lie. He knew the future, and he spoke the truth.

"If you know so much, why don't you help us?" My fingers tightened into fists. "It's not going to happen. I won't let it." My promise felt like a lie. What control did I have over any of this? "He's your grandson," I added, although I knew he didn't care.

Shadows writhed around him, obscuring his face.

I backed away from him, surveying the other Shadow Fae again. Barry looked like he was going to be sick. He held a hand over his mouth, hunching over while the two knights fought to break out of the ice.

At last, a booming crack filled the air, and a large fissure split the ice.

I tried not to think about Nyxobas's prediction, but I felt like the world had been pulled out from under my feet.

At last, a hand slammed through the ice, piercing it completely. Within moments, Turi was hauling himself out, and he rolled onto the grass. On his hands and knees, he vomited up blood, and I winced. Niall was out a moment later, heaving for breath, his body convulsing as he scrambled to find purchase on the ice.

I rushed over to him and grabbed his arms, pulling him out of the shattered ice. As soon as his legs were clear, the ice melted away, steam rising into the air.

Nyxobas was already scanning the knights for his next victim.

I wasn't doing much good here, watching this. And if Ruadan wasn't available to help me learn about Aenor, I'd have to try to discover this information on my own.

Behind me, another knight whimpered as Nyxobas gripped him by the throat, ready to slam him into the cold.

Where else could I find out about Aenor? If my parents knew her, perhaps she'd been in Eden, too. Or maybe she'd visited before the worlds had closed for good.

I started pacing, the cogs in my mind turning.

There was only one other person in the Institute who'd lived in Eden. And while he might be mad, Demented Mike could have some answers buried in his addled brain. He'd been there when our world ended, and he'd been there before.

I shadow-leapt over to Melusine, who lay on the grass, and I gently tapped her shoulder to wake her. She blinked, her dark eyes taking a moment to focus.

"Melusine?" I asked softly. "Do you know anything about a potion or tonic that could help clear someone's addled mind?"

"Of course I know something like that." She started to stand.

I stopped her with a gentle hand. "Just tell me how to make it, then go back to sleep."

"In the herbarium, you'll find mandrake, dragon's blood, a gryphon's saliva, and Earl Grey tea."

I blinked. "Earl Grey?"

"I know, it's disgusting, but it's a necessary part of the spell. Boil it all together into a tonic, and it will clear the patient's head." Her eyes were heavy-lidded, and they started to close again.

"Wait, Melusine?"

"Yes?"

"If Nyxobas leaves Ruadan's body any time soon, tell him I went to find Demented Mike."

"Sure thing."

A smile curled my lips. If this tonic worked, it would bring about my first meaningful conversation with someone from Eden in over ten years.

CHAPTER 15

I clutched the warm brew and hurried down the hall toward Demented Mike's room. In Eden, he'd been one of my best friends. Two years older than me, but tolerant of me following him around. He'd wanted to be human, for some bizarre reason, and he used to teach me all the dirty words he knew.

In the hallway, moonlight streamed through the peaked windows onto the floor, and I glanced for a moment at the trials going on outside. With any luck, they'd all be over soon.

I pushed open the door to his room, and light beamed in from the hallway. He lay flat on his stomach in the dark, his palms pressed against the flagstones. His cheeks had the pinkish hue of fever, and sweat beaded on his face.

Shit. The plague magic was still pulsing around the Institute, infecting people. And Mike had caught it.

He turned to look at me, his eyes wide, and he snarled. "I Gmm, the Noe I Ainml I called Nma please…" he hissed from the floor.

He was speaking fragments of a demon tongue he must've picked up in the shadow void. I had no idea what he was saying.

"So, I brought you some hot tea." I left the steaming mug on the floor, and he scuttled over to it on his hands and knees. "I think it might help things a bit."

He lapped tea from the cup like a cat. Then, he looked up at me, his eyes wide. "Here I kad Amman roots ktzsnc embers shhhh krditzsmtz I demon mrrnkg aisa hee cnhnma miracle."

I sat on the edge of his bed, and light from the moon beamed into the dark room. "Okay, so, I would love to reconnect with you, Mike, but I think we have a little work to do to get you back to your old form."

He slurped the tea. "Darkness…."

"I know. It was bad in the void. I'm sorry." I closed my eyes, trying not to think of what might've happened to the others I'd killed. I had to keep it together right now, long enough to save the Institute. "Mike, does the name Aenor ring a bell?"

He sat up now, and he stared at me. He took another long sip of his tea, his clouded expression clearing a little. I waited with him in silence while he slurped it.

"I have some questions to ask you, when you're ready."

"I … a darkness." He cocked his head, looking suddenly more alert. "There were no other fae in the void. Just me. I heard people speaking to me, even though you weren't there. I heard you speaking to me sometimes. The gods are hungry for souls, and they care for nothing else. They think the souls of others will fill the emptiness … but it never does. One god, split into seven, tormented ever since. In the hell worlds, we feel the pain of the gods."

He stared at the floor, lost in his thoughts.

"I met some other demons after a while." Another sip of tea. "They kept me company. I learned bits of their languages. Then, after an eternity passed, I saw you."

"I'm sorry." Guilt twisted inside me. How did I explain this to him? "Thing is, it turns out I'm a death angel, and I didn't know. And when the fae army invaded, um … a whole bunch of death magic exploded from me and killed everyone by accident. I'm not yet sure what happened to the others, and I'm just trying to put together the pieces and find my dad to help me."

He drank another sip. "I know what happened. The voices told me in the void. It's okay. You weren't in control of it. I understand. The gods are in control. They're always in control. And the gods will have their souls."

We were getting somewhere. Coming to Demented Mike was the best idea I'd had in a while.

"Do you know what happened to everyone else?" I asked.

He nodded. "Of course. Your father brought them back from the dead."

My heart leapt. The first good news I'd had in ages. "My mum, too?"

"Everyone but me. He could never find me. I fell in too deep. I started turning demon fast, machalail grumm slut puppet." He closed his eyes, taking another sip of the tea. "Only you could find me. Your powers are like his, but maybe stronger. Both of you can lift this illness I have. This death magic. And as long as you both live, you can raise each other from the grave."

Alive. Despite everything happening, I beamed with joy. "Okay. This is good. This is helpful. Do you know why Eden is empty? We opened the portal and we found only graves."

He shook his head.

"Do you know where my father is?" I pressed, desperate now.

"Eden."

"I couldn't find him there."

Hope bubbled in my chest anyway. My mum was alive. Everyone I'd killed in Eden was alive again. I'd find my family again. I was certain we could get my dad to help us cure the Shadow Fae—and to imprison Baleros forever.

"Mike, have you ever heard the name Aenor?" I asked. "When I went into Eden, I couldn't find my parents. But I did find a note from them that said to find Aenor. I think she must be someone who can help me. Then I can get you back to your family."

He traced the rim of his teacup with his fingertip. "Aenor. Aenor. Aenor," he muttered. "Flayer of Skins, Scourge of the Wicked."

"Yes! That's her. How do you know her?"

"She visited your father sometimes. Before the worlds closed for good."

"Where would I find her?"

He frowned. "I don't remember what she looked like. Just that she smelled of honey and soil. And lemony flowers, and mossy limestone. And she gave me a human finger bone. She sells them, I think."

Aenor, Flayer of Skins, who reeked of honey and dirt and sold human bones. She sounded lovely.

"I'm tired. Noe I Ainml." Mike closed his eyes once more and curled up on the floor, muttering to himself in Demonic. His teeth chattered.

I pulled the soft wool blanket off the bed and covered his shivering body with it. I crossed to his window. From here, I had a view of the Tower Green, and Nyxobas was gripping another knight by the throat. I couldn't even see who it was. Melusine, maybe? He hurled them into the void and another brutal trial began.

I turned to rush outside. I had a few more facts to go on now, but I needed help interpreting what they meant.

CHAPTER 16

I crossed out onto the Tower Green once more, and the sound of shrieking pierced the night calm. Nyxobas stood before Barry, whose face had gone completely white, his body rigid. Barry opened and closed his mouth a few times as if he were trying to speak. His lumen stone glowed faintly under his shirt.

"Do you have something to say?" Nyxobas's voice sent a chill snaking up my spine.

"Had no control," Barry stammered. "You know. You know. You *know*. I had no control. Baleros controls me."

Nyxobas grabbed him by the throat, and Barry started to choke. He was still trying to speak, and he was able to get out the words "necklace" and "control."

I caught my breath. That necklace around his throat—the one I'd seen in the dungeon—had Baleros given it to him?

Before Barry could utter another word, Nyxobas hurled him into the portal.

Barry's body sank beneath the watery surface, and the necklace along with him. Cold magic rushed over my body like an icy wind. Then, I stared as the earth began to close again, the ground trembling. Grass and soil shifted and sealed over the portal.

So. That was our traitor.

An interrogation would have been useful, but that was not how Nyxobas operated.

When the portal had sealed over completely, I glanced at Nyxobas —still the pale, gleaming eyes of the god and tattoos that shifted over his forearms.

His pale eyes were locked on me, and my chest hollowed out. Then, the violet in Ruadan's eyes returned, and I let out a breath as the real Grand Master returned. The other knights were sitting around the sealed portal, shaking in their cloaks.

Melusine clutched a hot cup of tea, her hair drenched. "Good. That's over. Barry was the traitor, and we can all move on with our lives."

"Our very short lives," said Aengus through chattering teeth, "considering we are about a day away from death. Where is the Horseman?"

I shook my head. "I don't know yet. I'm still working—"

"Then you have to try to help us!" shouted Aengus. "At least try."

"And if I make it worse?" I asked.

"Don't make it worse," said Aengus.

Ruadan's body had gone completely still, and his violet eyes burned in the gloom. "I know that you have the power within you, but you might not be ready just yet. It's your choice, Liora. We can still try to find Adonis."

I rubbed a knot in my forehead. "I'll try. I just think I'll need alcohol." Then, I stared at the grass in the courtyard. Something wasn't sitting right with me. Something besides my upcoming task. "But, I'm not quite ready to move on from the Barry situation yet. I mean, don't you think Baleros could have sent someone more competent than Barry?"

"He was talking about his necklace," Melusine added from over her tea. "Something about control. Like it wasn't his fault."

I glanced at Ruadan. "So you didn't give him that lumen stone? I saw it on him in prison. Just for a moment."

Ruadan shook his head. "That necklace didn't come from us. Charmed, probably, with powers of mind control. Barry was a pawn."

"The necklace was beaming with shadow magic." I ran my fingers through my hair. "I just don't feel like this is the whole answer. Maddan said the traitor was someone I knew. He said that Baleros had a powerful ally. Barry was neither of those things."

The night wind toyed with Ruadan's hair. "I'm sure that wasn't the entirety of Baleros's plans. Everyone will remain on high alert until we've locked Baleros in our dungeons forever, chained with iron."

I breathed in deeply. "When Nyxobas is in your body, do you remember what he says?"

"Most of it." Then he frowned, his body still. "But he said something to you, and it's a blank. I can't remember it at all. What was it?"

When I thought of Nyxobas's prophecy, I just wanted to wrap my arms around Ruadan and keep him close. I wanted him in that hot bath with me forever, locked away safely in his room. And most of all, like a lioness, my instinct was to destroy anyone who would come near him. I longed to tear their flesh off their bones, to turn their bodies to dust. I even wanted to destroy Nyxobas for what he'd said.

My love for Ruadan was a raging fire.

Darkness coiled around him. "What did he say to you?" he pressed.

It didn't matter, because I wasn't going to let him die, no matter what the prophecy said. "He just said that we faced danger. Nothing we don't already know." After Ruadan's insistence that I trust him, the lie tasted like poison in my mouth.

But the thing was, Ruadan had a tendency to try to sacrifice himself—just like he had at Hampton Court Palace, when he'd tried to give himself over to Baleros. If Ruadan thought this was the ending— that he was destined to die—he might rush into it. I saw no reason to hasten that option.

"Look." I gestured at the knights, who were sitting on the grass, most of them shivering and sweating at the same time. "Let's get them all inside to the hall. I'll have a bit of whiskey to calm my death instinct, and I'll see what I can do."

"Now, please," said Aengus. "We don't have time for you to fruitlessly search the world for your father. My fingers are about to rot off. I think the tips of my toes have started to go necrotic."

I glanced around at the Shadow Fae, all of them silent, staring at me. A painful-looking lump had formed on Aengus's neck, and a red rash had climbed over Niall's face.

Already, I could feel the wings at my shoulder blades aching to come out.

So I was supposed to cure them, but I had no idea how. Right now, I felt about as competent as a dog sitting at a desk with a pencil to complete his income tax returns.

Would instinct take over and show me the way, or would I simply kill everyone in the city?

I guess we were about to find out.

* * *

In the Great Hall, the knights sat at tables over steaming cups of tea, looking at me expectantly. I'd had enough whiskey to give me a good buzz, and I now felt much more confident about the situation. I was a death angel, and I could do this.

Ruadan touched my arm. "Are you sure you're ready to try?"

"I think so. I'm feeling better about it. And Demented Mike said I was as powerful as my dad."

"Demented Mike?"

I bit my lip. "Granted, his nickname probably doesn't inspire much confidence in his pronouncements. Anyway, he's the demon-fae I pulled from the shadow void. He thinks I can do it."

Ruadan nodded, then stepped away from me. I closed my eyes, trying to summon my angel side. Someone's coughs echoed off the high, stone ceiling. I waited for my wings to burst out of me.

Nothing was happening, and I could practically feel the frustration of everyone around me. How did I make this happen?

Someone—Aengus, probably—let out a dramatic, exasperated sigh.

I opened one of my eyes to see what was happening. Just the

knights, glaring at me from their wool blankets, steam from tea curling around them.

"Just give me a minute," I muttered.

The last times I'd transformed, I'd been panicking: when Ruadan had invaded Eden, when I'd thought he was going to die at Hampton Court Palace, when I thought he might be dying within the Tower. So, I just had to channel that sense of panic, that primal flame of protectiveness.

I glanced at Ruadan and the World Key glowing at his neck. Nyxobas said this ended with Ruadan's death. Baleros planned to slaughter my lover, to cut the skin off his body. Wild, protective fury roiled in my chest as I looked at him. I wanted to rip Baleros limb from limb, to spread his bones and flesh to the far corners of the earth so I could keep my love safe.

That flame in my heart ignited, and electric power shot down my shoulder blades. My shoulders flung back, arms stiffening.

I'll bury your bodies in long-forgotten graves. The yews will feed from your flesh.

Euphoria ripped through me, and wings erupted from my back, lifting me higher, toward the rib-vaulted ceiling. Why did death feel so glorious?

Now, I simply needed to control the death magic, to pull it away from the Shadow Fae. Except, I didn't really feel in control. In fact—

The Great Hall below me seemed to fall away, and I was no longer in the Institute, but back in my cage, covered in dirt. Ciara snored by my side, and Baleros stood above me, grinning down at me. "Let's let the little monster out of her cage, shall we?"

The gate creaked open, setting me free to do the one thing I was good at. The one thing the monster had been born for.

Killing.

When I'd crossed into the ring that day, sword at my waist, I'd been expecting the usual opponents: a cyclops, a demon, a horde of vampires. Instead, I found a scrawny teenage boy. With his peach fuzz mustache, acne, and terrified expression, he looked oddly human.

But Baleros had trained me well. I knew never to underestimate my opponent, no matter how weak he looked. I knew that survival meant striking first. *Baleros's seventh law of power: Kill or be killed.* Hesitation meant death. The scrawny boy before me was likely a shapeshifter, disguising himself as an innocent.

It wasn't until my blade went through his neck, when I saw the blood and the bone and the piss staining his jeans, that I'd understood the real situation. He was just as he'd appeared—a terrified human boy.

As the crowd stared at me in stunned silence, their expressions told me everything I needed to know. This had been a different sort of lesson from Baleros. The lesson here was not one of survival.

The lesson was that I was a monster.

And monsters belonged in cages, didn't they?

Someone was calling my name now—screaming it, in fact.

The image of the arena thinned, until I found myself in the Great Hall once more, hovering above the knights. Now, the only sound was my wings beating the air.

"Liora!" It was Ruadan. "Stop."

I looked down at the Shadow Fae, my gaze roaming over Melusine, Aengus, Turi…. To my horror, they looked *worse.* Melusine's skin had taken on a greenish hue, and her eyes had closed. The glands in her neck were purplish with swelling. Aengus lay sleeping, his chest still rising and falling.

Only Ruadan was still standing.

My wings retracted, shooting back into my body. I fell *hard* to the stone floor.

This had been a terrible idea. I was made only to kill, not to heal. They never should have counted on me.

I pushed myself up to my feet, dusting off my body. My failure was crushing, and I felt it like a pain in my chest. "I'm sorry. I don't know how to control this power."

"You haven't had time to learn," said Ruadan.

If Baleros didn't live in my mind, would it have worked?

Melusine groaned, her eyelids heavy. "Fix this."

I gripped my purple hair, ready to pull it out. "I will. I will. I just need to get to my dad."

Ruadan touched my shoulder. "We'll find Aenor. We will get to your father. We can search the Tower's records for references to her whereabouts."

"Searching records sounds slightly time-consuming. Okay, tell me if this means anything to you. Any idea where we would find someone who sold human finger bones and smelled of soil, honey, lemony flowers, and limestone?"

"Black elder tree. They have lemon-scented flowers."

"You are full of amazing facts."

He scrubbed a hand over his mouth. "Black elder trees and limestones—the London Wall, by Barbican. She's underground, perhaps, because of the soil and the fact that you're generally not allowed to sell bones above ground."

I gripped him by the shoulders. "Good. Good. We have a location. I'm getting my lumen stone and my bug-out bag, and we're going to find this bone-selling freak."

And it *had* to work, because the Shadow Fae wouldn't survive much longer.

CHAPTER 17

I gripped my bug-out bag, trying to push out thoughts of my failure and of the knights dying in the Great Hall. I still had a bit of a buzz from the whiskey, but it wasn't enough to lift my dark mood.

This time, we'd come armed. I had no idea what we were going to find when we met Aenor, Flayer of Skins, but everything I'd learned about her so far led me to believe she was a complete psycho. And if I *really* needed to, I could always beckon the mist army to me.

We'd shadow-leapt to Barbican in only a few minutes. Here, moonlight and the distant glow of streetlights illuminated the crumbling old Roman wall. Empty windows in the wall gaped like dark wounds. Once, it had protected the city from barbarians. Now, it was just an ancient fragment, a testament to a forgotten London that intersected with a serene canal.

We were sniffing the air, trying to home in on the scent of lemony blossoms and human bones. The damp breeze skimmed my skin. I had the sense that in this ancient part of London, we were walking over layers of lives, centuries of souls that now still clung to the crumbling rock wall.

Ruadan inhaled deeply. "Honey," he said. "That's the one scent not native to this place. It must belong to Aenor. We're in the right place."

At last, we were getting somewhere, and my pulse raced with anticipation. I sniffed the air too, and after a moment, I got a faint whiff of honey.

To our right, modern apartments loomed over a placid canal, but Ruadan had thought Aenor might be underground. Now, I tuned into a powerful magic that thrummed through the air. It felt like the music of string instruments vibrating over my skin. Was that Aenor?

Ruadan pointed at a squat tower inset into the Roman wall. "The scent of honey is coming from there."

He led me around the corner to a dark alcove within the wall—a hollowed-out tower, one side of it collapsed. The dark canal flowed serenely by its side. I couldn't see much in the darkness—just grass and the crumbling tower, overgrown with plants.

"Honey and lemony blossoms," I whispered.

Ruadan caught my eye. "When we meet her, be cautious. We don't really know what the note meant."

I frowned. "I suppose." A terrible thought twisted in my skull. "You don't think this could be a trick played by Baleros, do you?"

Ruadan shook his head. "Baleros had no way to get into Eden. But we should be careful anyway. Things could have changed since your mother wrote that note. Just don't announce who you are right away, until we learn more about her."

"Okay, fair enough."

Ruadan crouched down. "She's here." He reared back his arm, then rammed his fist into the earth, all the way up to his elbow. He moved his arm around for a moment, seemingly grasping something.

Then, with a groaning sound, he pulled up a wooden hatch door. And as he did, the faint smell of honey and lemon hit me—along with the metallic scent of blood.

Aenor.

But before we could leap in, the sound of hissing echoed off the stone behind us. My pulse racing, I whirled.

A small horde of vampires was moving for us. There were at least twelve of them—large, ancient vampires, their movements swift and precise, fangs bared, armed with swords. Odd. Vampires usually just used their teeth and hands.

My blade was already out, and Ruadan drew his sword, ready to take them on.

A dark smile curled my lips. It had been far too long since I'd killed anything, and bloodlust pounded through my veins. The angel of death in me was stirring once more. Gods, there were a lot of them. They must've been lying in wait.

I will slake my thirst on your blood.

I let my body fill with the ancient shadow magic of the lumen stone, and I leapt closer to the vampires, touching down on the stones with a swing of my sword. My blade hacked through the first vampire's neck, slicing off his head. The winds of battle rushed through me, and I pivoted, attacking another vamp.

My sword clashed with his, sparking in the night. Soon, I was moving like a storm wind, whirling and ducking as we fought.

Ruadan fought by my side, gracefully attacking. Clouds of ash darkened the air around us as we killed the vampires. My wings ached to emerge, but I fought hard to keep them down. The last appearance of my angelic side had not gone well.

Pivot, strike, carve.... I drove my sword through the heart of a female vampire, then through her neck. Her body dissolved into ash so thick I coughed.

My blood thundered as more vamps crawled from the shadows. Why did they keep coming for us, when they saw death awaited them? Maybe we were outnumbered, but they were on suicide missions.

I rip open your veins. I cover your eyes, fill your mouth with soil.

The tip of a blade swiped me from behind, but I danced away from it, nearly losing my balance.

The vamps were all around us—too many for this to be a coincidence. It was at this point that I noticed the gleaming magical necklaces around their throats.

Baleros was controlling them, just like he'd controlled Barry. They were mindlessly following his orders.

Pivot, strike, carve.

Ash rained around us as the vampires met their final deaths. I stole a quick glance at Ruadan. His savage grace, brutal and controlled, took my breath away.

Pivot, strike, carve.

I inhaled clouds of cinders. Where the hells were they all coming from?

Somehow, Baleros had been watching us closely.

Death kissed my skin as I moved among them, ushering them to their final graves.

I will end you all.

From shadows all over the courtyard, crawling from behind the Roman wall, through its gaping windows—more and more vamps were coming for us. Now, a sharp coil of panic curled around my heart.

Each one of them wore a glowing, magic necklace—and they all wanted to slaughter Ruadan. Baleros had been watching us, either through spies or a scrying mirror, and he'd sent his entire army here to slaughter us.

I took a step back toward the Roman wall, quickly getting backed into a corner. My pulse was racing out of control, but I didn't want to unleash the monster now.

We needed help.

As I swung my sword in increasingly wild arcs, I whispered the spell for the mist soldiers. *"Mogidellior deusaman."*

As soon as the spell was out of my mouth, a thick fog curled around the vampiric mob, until I could hardly see them.

I leapt up to one of the crumbling tower walls, crouching on a stony outcrop. From there, I used the few fae commands I knew to control the mist soldiers. I changed the shapes of the soldiers, transforming them into beasts that ripped the vampires apart.

"Aerouant dispennior."

A group of mist soldiers melded together into a dragon with enormous teeth, and the creature roared. It slashed at the vampires with its talons, its ethereal body tinged with moonlight.

"Diaoull lazannior."

Beastly creatures formed from the mist with talons the length of swords, teeth sharp as iron spikes, tails like thorny maces that crushed the vampires' limbs.

"Evell dispennior."

Birds as large as pterodactyls formed from fog swooped down, plucking up the vampires, carrying them away.

My monstrous mist soldiers picked off one vampire after another, tearing them to shreds, dragging them away until we had only a small crowd left. Then, I leapt back down into the fray—not far from Ruadan. He was still fighting viciously, unfatigued, and I started fighting alongside him.

I drove my blade through the heart of another vamp. His body started to slump, and I gripped his hand. A tattoo marked his skin— the bundle of sticks. Baleros's symbol. No surprises there.

I let him fall to the ground, then I severed his head. With only a few vampires remaining, it was time to get some information before they were all dead.

"Ruadan!" I shouted, fending off another attacker. "Cover me. I need to torture someone."

A statuesque, brunette vamp lunged for me, her sword raised. I gripped the hilt of my own sword, blood pumping hard. Behind me, I could hear Ruadan's blade clashing with our attackers. I had no doubt he could hold his own with these numbers.

I felt as if sharpened claws were stroking down my shoulder blades, making me shiver. My wings ached to emerge, but I kept in control.

"I am the beginning and the end." I spoke the words quietly, but they echoed off the stone around us. *I am your broken spirit as pain eats your body. I am the insects that make their home in your flesh.*

The vamp looked startled, her eyes widening as her attacks grew slower. I was holding back, unwilling to unleash my death magic— and yet the force of my presence struck fear into her. Fog coiled around her in thick tendrils.

Good. I seemed to terrify her so much I didn't actually need to torture her.

I took a step closer. She started shaking, frozen in place.

My fingers twitched. "Stay here and tell me what I want to know, vampire, and I'll let you live."

I gripped her by the throat, lifting her into the air. I could read the terror on her features—the silent, abject horror of her final death.

My wings were desperate to emerge, but I couldn't lose control completely again. "Do you understand what I'm saying, vampire?"

She nodded mutely.

"Do you work for Baleros?" I asked.

She nodded again.

"Where is he?"

"A … a church. I think. We're not supposed to know which one." She was struggling to speak—possibly because I was nearly crushing her throat, but I didn't want to let her go.

"Which church?"

"I don't know the name." Her body trembled. "But I can tell you something else! He gave something to the god of night. A ring. Some kind of magic ring. A cage. It had—"

Her eyes bulged wide, and a gagging sound rose from her throat. Then, her eyes went dull and dead.

Had I broken her?

But when I looked down at the vampire, I saw that it wasn't me who'd killed her. No, the tip of a long, iron knife protruded from her chest. Before my eyes, her body crumbled into a pile of dust, the iron knife clanging beside it.

What the hells?

I looked up, and my heart skipped a beat. There—another angel in the sky, his wings thumping the air like a war drum. The moon haloed his head, making it hard to see his face.

My breath left my lungs. Dad?

He was holding another knife—one aimed right at me. My chest constricted, and time seemed to slow down, the night wind rushing over me. Why did he look like he wanted to kill me?

When he threw the knife, I dodged. It narrowly missed my chest.

I breathed out. Not Adonis, then. My father would not have missed.

Ruadan's low growl rumbled over the stone, his eyes on the angel as well. Piles of ash lay around us. It was only at this point that I realized my thoughts had been confused, muddled by my desperation to see my dad. Sometimes demons had feathered wings, and that was what this was.

Ruadan's icy magic whipped through the air as we stared up at the haloed demon, my lungs tight as a drum.

As the demon pulled another iron knife from a sheath, I got a glimpse of a purple amulet at his throat—a glowing lumen stone. Then, as he shifted away from the moon, a glimpse of red hair.

"Maddan," said Ruadan.

I took a step closer, gaping at him. "Maddan? Who gave you *wings?*"

CHAPTER 18

He threw another knife, but I leapt forward and caught the hilt in midair.

"Good reflexes," he said. "You must be jealous that I can fly without creating an apocalypse."

I crossed my arms. "Um, actually, I can do it fine as long as I'm perpetually drunk." My mist soldiers still stood around me, waiting for my next orders. I could command them to tear Maddan to pieces, but I had so many questions for him before he died. "Okay, prince, how is it that you're flying, and how did you end up here?"

His wings beat the air. "Baleros asked me to keep an eye on you. He trusts me, now that I'm powerful. And as soon as I saw all the mist so far away from the Tower, I knew I'd found you. That's the problem with the mist armies, isn't it? Not very discreet. I flew toward the fog, and I thought, *there's my girl, torturing someone for information.* Again. And now I can tell Baleros where you are. He will make me one of his generals in no time."

"He already knows where we are." Ruadan gestured at all the dusty piles. "He sent his army after us. The army died. You are completely useless."

Maddan's lip curled. "Right, well, I killed one of them before she gave you any valuable information. As I said. I'm an important asset."

I gaped at him. "Can we get back to the wings? Because what the hells?"

A bright blast of shadow magic crackled along Maddan's arm. "Mmmm, no. How about I kill you instead?"

A bone-shattering burst of shadow magic slammed me back into the stone wall. The magic seemed to freeze me from the inside out. Glacial emptiness pooled in my ribs, eating at me. My mind flickered with images of the shadow void—the skeletal trees, the jagged isolation.

Grunting, I rolled onto my hands and knees, muscles locking with the cold. The blast had knocked Ruadan back a bit, too. But since shadow magic was an intrinsic part of him, he absorbed it better.

From the rocky ground, I looked up at Maddan, who hovered like a dark angel before the moon. Violet shadow magic crackled over his body, icy cold. How had he acquired all this magic?

Wisps of magic curled off Ruadan, too. He summoned a ball of shadow magic in his palm, and he hurled it at Maddan.

Maddan rocketed back, but he recovered quickly. Within moments, bolts of shadow magic ignited the sky between them, flashing like lightning. As they fought each other, shadow magic elec-trified the air.

"Evell dispennior," I said, and my mist soldiers melded together into an enormous bird. The creature swooped for him—but just before his beak clamped down on Maddan's head, the winged fae prince shadow-leapt away. The mist bird swirled and twisted back down to earth—silent sentinels once more, awaiting my commands.

Ruadan turned to me, his powerful body still crackling with magic. His eyes had darkened to pure black.

My muscles groaned, and I rubbed my shoulder. "I'm going to need a theory about what just happened, because that was bizarre. You got any ideas about how Maddan got wings?"

"Somehow, he's been in the void for a long time. The shadow void transformed him into a demon. The Maddan we just saw there is not the same as the Maddan you last knew."

"I have so many questions, I don't even know where to start." I rubbed my eyes. "Okay, I have one. I just saw him two days ago, minus the wings. How could it be that he's been in the void for a long time?"

"Time can pass differently there. Two days here could have been decades there. I doubt he went in willingly. His father probably forced him into the void in the hopes of getting a more useful son."

"Right. Okay, second of all, did Nyxobas make this happen?"

"Yes."

I really hated Ruadan's grandfather at this point. "Why would he give that walking cold sore more power?"

Ruadan cocked his head. "Have you wondered why Baleros has vampires working for him?"

I hugged myself, still cold from the shadow magic. "He always had vampires in the arena, but it *is* odd, considering he had committed his soul to Emerazel. The goddess of fire and the god of night are ancient enemies. They're not usually working on the same side."

"And yet, somehow, he's amassing shadow creatures on his side. For whatever reason, Nyxobas is doing him favors. Nyxobas turned Maddan into a demon."

Demented Mike's words rang in my head. *The gods are hungry for souls, and they care for nothing else.*

I glanced at the moon. "The vampire I just interrogated said something about a ring. And a cage. Baleros gave Nyxobas a magic ring. Does that mean anything to you? A ring cage?"

Ruadan stared at me, eyes dark as jet. "A soul cage."

"What?"

"It's an object—like a ring or a stone—that's full of thousands of souls. They're extremely rare. They're the most powerful currency when bargaining with a god. With a soul cage, you can get a powerful ally. At least for a time."

The gods only care about one thing.... "Bloody hells. We don't even know what favors he's asked for. We have no idea what to expect." I thrust my fingers into my hair. "Maddan said that Baleros had a powerful ally on his side. I guess now we know who it is." My stomach was still in knots.

"What else did the vampires say?" asked Ruadan.

I nodded at one of the piles of ash, though I had no idea who was who at this point. "She said Baleros is in a church."

"Good. Okay. It's a start. But there are almost fifty churches within the square mile in the City, and several hundred in London as a whole."

We'd have to find Baleros later. Aenor came first. "You know what? Let's get this Skin Flayer woman first, and we will narrow down the churches later. We still need to get to my dad, or we won't have any Shadow Fae left to help us capture Baleros." I turned to my mist army, and I dismissed them with a single fae word. *"Distronnor."*

They wafted away, light puffs of smoke in the night. The Institute was vulnerable and needed the protection more than I did right now.

"Are you ready?" asked Ruadan.

I nodded, and we shadow-leapt over to the trap door Ruadan had opened. From there, we peered down into the tunnel. A faint, golden glow lit earthen walls. Ruadan was the first to jump into the trap door, his sword still drawn. He landed hard on the dirt floor, then beckoned for me to follow.

I scooted over the edge and jumped in after him, turning to face the source of light. We couldn't see much from here, and particles of dirt hung in the air. A cackling noise filled the dank tunnel, and the sound sent a shiver up my spine. Gripping our weapons, we marched toward the source of the light until the tunnel opened into a cavernous, earthen room.

On the far side, a woman with white hair sat in front of an aged television set, laughing. Two black cats dozed in her lap.

I had a feeling *this* wasn't Aenor. She smelled faintly of mold and soil, and little else. My first instinct was that these were guards of some kind—demonic creatures in disguise.

My hands started to sweat, paranoia spiking as I surveyed the room. *Calm yourself, Liora.* I was ready to stab this lady just because Baleros had trained me to kill first and ask questions later. I risked killing not only an innocent woman, but the person who could tell us where to find Aenor.

I loosened my grip on my sword. I was free from Baleros's influence now. I cocked my head, studying the woman.

She'd fashioned her nightgown into a sort of bowl, out of which she was eating sugar cereal mixed with what looked like small finger bones. Apart from the cats, the television, and an old pair of clogs on the floor, the room was just earth walls and floor.

Behind her ragged armchair, an aged door stood set into the wood. Like she was guarding it.

I cleared my throat. "Excuse me, do you know—"

She grunted, then pointed a bony finger at the television. "Don't interrupt my stories."

"We're looking for Aenor, Flayer of Skins," said Ruadan.

She popped a finger bone in her mouth. "Not me. I'm Karen, Watcher of Television. And you're interrupting the best parts."

After the night we'd had, I was all out of patience. "My name is Liora, Eviscerator of Those Who Don't Answer My Bloody Questions."

Ruadan put a steadying hand on my arm, and I felt soothing magic skim up my bicep. I narrowed my eyes at him. *Don't try to calm my anger. It's my oldest friend.*

Then, I let out a steadying breath. I wasn't Baleros's pawn anymore.

Ruadan's magic snaked over the room, almost as a warning. "You're Aenor's guard."

"Got that right." She crunched the cereal. "No one gets past me."

My fingers twitched on my hilt, and I glanced at the door just behind her. But it was Ruadan who spoke as he drew his sword from its sheath. Thick, dark vampire blood dripped off the blade onto the floor, and the cats began to stir in her lap, hackles raised.

"We're running out of time," said Ruadan, his voice laced with steel. "And we need to speak to Aenor, now. I don't want to have to hurt you."

This time, it was my turn to put a hand on Ruadan's arm, stilling his fury. "Wait," I whispered. What if she was just a frail old human woman with her cats?

She narrowed her eyes at the television. "No one's speaking to Aenor tonight," she grumbled. "Get out of here before I get cranky."

Ruadan shot me a furious glare. I'd interrupted his terrifying demigod flow. "I will kill you if I have to," he added.

"You can stop grandstanding and showing off!" she barked. "You're about to forfeit your souls."

Oh, *shit*. What?

Her jaw unhinged, dropping open to reveal a chasm. The sound of a thousand tormented screams rose from her gullet, vibrating around my skull, then the room went silent once more. Her dark eyes were wide with fury.

The scream had transfixed me in place. Already, I could feel my body hollowing out, emptiness carving through me.

Bloody hells, Karen.

CHAPTER 19

*J*ust then, the door creaked open, and a voice called out, "Karen! I told you to send them through."

Karen snorted. "These two monsters?"

"Yes," the female voice said from the other room. "I've been waiting for them."

The TV reception crackled and sputtered. Karen reached down to throw a clog at the television set. She burst into laughter again, stuffing her mouth with sugar cereal and finger bones.

I turned to see what was so hilarious, disturbed to find that it was a PSA about drug addiction, featuring a man convulsing on the floor with a syringe sticking out of his arm.

She giggled. Then, without taking her gaze from the screen, she said, "Aenor's through there. Waiting, apparently. You can go on."

I stepped around the bits of cereal and bones on the floor to get to the door, and I squeezed past her armchair.

I pulled open the door to reveal a shop filled with shelves of herbs, shrunken heads, and other unsettling curiosities. A rough-hewn counter stood by the far wall, its surface cluttered with bell jars of taxidermy animals and gnarled trinkets. But my eye was really drawn to the girl standing in the center of the shop.

Her pale blue hair draped over narrow shoulders and a tank top. She was hula-hooping in jean shorts and high heels. With her large, dark eyes and heart-shaped face, she seemed far too innocent for the eerie-looking tattoos all over her body. Her hips moved rhythmically to a crackling Elvis record. *Suspicious Minds*, specifically. Not what I'd been expecting. Gorgeous, tan skin, like a tiny goddess.

"We're looking for Aenor, Flayer of Skins," I began. "Scourge of the Wicked," I added, though it was probably not necessary. How many Aenor Skin Flayers could there be?

She blew an enormous pink chewing-gum bubble and popped it. The hula-hooping continued. "That's me."

I shot a quick look at Ruadan, but I could hardly see him. He was pulling his indistinct trick, coming in unnoticed.

"You're Aenor?" I asked.

"Yeah. I thought I saw you coming in one of my scrying mirrors. As it happens, I need to cut a deal with the Shadow Fae. Karen was supposed to let you past. She gets confused when she's watching her stories."

I'd been so fixated on Aenor that I nearly hadn't noticed the hearts nailed to the wall—desiccated, each one with a nail through the center. By their size, some looked human, and others looked demon or fae.

I bit my lip. "You sell hearts?"

"Yeah. *Men's* hearts." Just like that. Like it needed no other explanation beyond their gender. *Nothing untoward here. The owners of these organs had Y chromosomes, so obviously it's all above board.*

As she hula-hooped, she toyed with a silver locket around her neck.

"Right. Great. So—" I glanced at Ruadan again, hoping to convey with the arching of a single eyebrow that he needed to let me handle this, because this chick was crazy, and she hated blokes. I had no idea if he understood the gesture, since I couldn't see his face.

"Who are you?" she asked. Her accent was American.

I cleared my throat, now even more certain that I should disguise my identity until I knew more. What was a normal-sounding, believable pseudonym?

"My name," I began, "is … Dr. Margery T. Beaglehole."

Nope. Not that. Frustrated, I pinched the bridge of my nose, and I was pretty sure I could hear Ruadan sighing behind me.

"Yeah, that's not your name," said Aenor. "Adonis might have killed loads of people with his mind, but he'd never be cruel enough to name his kid Margery Beaglehole."

I stared at her. So, the jig was up. "How did you know I'm related to him?"

She finally stopped hula-hooping, letting the plastic ring drop to the floor. "Where's the guy you were with? The big demi-fae shadow demon? I saw him in the scrying mirror."

"Here." Ruadan chose that moment to appear, his eyes obsidian black, muscles tensed.

"Holy crap." Her pupils dilated for a moment, chest flushing so fast it was nearly imperceptible. Then, her gaze shuttered, and her lip curled in a sneer. She actually *snarled* at him like a wild animal.

I stepped in front of him protectively. "You can't have his heart. It's staying in his chest."

"He's a heartbreaker." She looked rattled, and she crossed behind the counter. "Do you know that?"

"We have been over that. So, back to the task at hand—how did you know I was Adonis's daughter?"

"You look like him. He's an old friend." She looked the same age as me, but she was obviously much older.

"I'm looking for him," I said, still giving away as little as I could. "Do you know anything?"

She touched the locket around her neck again. "I'm not real good with men, you know?"

I glanced at the dried hearts. "Is that so?"

"Most men are selfish, abusive, murderous assholes. Adonis was different. I mean, sure, he was the Horseman of Death." Another pink bubble popped. "But he didn't mean to kill people. He actually cared about people. He saved my life, once. And after that, we stayed friends.

He actually listened to me. Sometimes it was really trivial shit. 'Oh, I had a hard time breaking a bone demon's ribs to get his heart out today.' Other times it was, like, existential dread. You know? Anyway, he's a good listener."

"Right. I remember. Vaguely." My instincts told me she was telling the truth.

"When the apocalypse started kicking off and all the other horsemen showed up," she went on, "I started to get worried about him. That's why he gave me this locket." She opened it up, but the glass inside appeared murky. "I could see him in it, just to make sure he was okay. That way, I'd know his curse hadn't taken effect, and I'd check on him when he was in Eden—just little glimpses of him. But a couple of weeks ago, he just disappeared from my locket. I don't know what happened to him."

My stomach fell. "How could he be gone? The worlds have been closed. He was locked in Eden. Only someone with a World Key can open the worlds. Baleros doesn't have a World Key."

"Baleros?"

"The man who's been spreading disease," I replied. "Rotten to the core. A festering sore on London's arse. He's—"

Ruadan touched my arm. "She gets the idea."

I inhaled deeply through my nose. "He's a bad man. Former slave master and would-be tyrant. He's after the World Key on Ruadan's chest. He spread plague to the knights of the Institute using the Unholy Grail. Now we need my dad to help cure them."

She cocked her head. "If you're his daughter, you must have some of his powers."

I nodded. "Right, but they kill people. Anyway, how could my father disappear from a locked world? He had no way out."

"I'm sure he's still there," she said. "But something happened to him to make him ... unseeable. I have no idea what." She leaned over the counter, her eyes suddenly intense, and she gripped my arms. "He can't die, can he? He once told me he can't die. Unless your mom kills him."

I bit my lip. "I doubt she did that."

She pointed at Ruadan. "He's a seneschal from the Institute. He has a World Key. Why can't he get you into Eden?"

"We did go, and we found no one. Just graves. But I'm pretty sure it was glamoured," I said. "It was like a facade. There was just one tiny detail that was different. And under that detail, I found the note to come find you."

She nodded slowly. "Ah. Good. Well, I can help you get through glamour. That's probably why he sent you to me. I'm desperate to know where your dad is, and I've been wanting to strike a deal with the Shadow Fae."

"Good." Ruadan's icy presence filled the room. "That's settled. We'll go now."

She narrowed her eyes at him. "You know it's after midnight, right? I mean, I'm a night owl, but why does this need to happen right now?"

I leaned on the countertop, urgency tensing my muscles. I stared into her dark eyes. "It needs to happen right now, Aenor, because there's a plague spreading in the city of London. The person who is causing all this wants to take over the world with an army full of demons. And the knights of the Institute have to stop him. Except they've got the Plague, and they're about to die."

She arched an eyebrow. "I'm not really a fan of the Institute, is the thing. I used to have a shop above ground like a normal heart-selling fae. Since the Institute took control, I've literally had to go underground. I live in constant fear that one of you will kill me. I'm not saying I want them to die, but...." She shrugged.

Ruadan's dark magic thickened. "You said you wanted something from the Shadow Fae in return for your help. Is that what you're building up to?"

She blew a strand of pale blue hair out of her eyes. "Yeah. I want protection. If I help you, I want to live freely in London. I don't want any Shadow Fae stabbing me with iron just because I'm not in a locked realm like a good little girl."

"Agreed," said Ruadan. "But you know that if the current knights die, they'll be replaced by new knights. And those knights won't honor this agreement. So we need Adonis to heal them now."

She smacked her hand on the countertop. "Then I guess we'd better find him." Without taking her eyes off me, she bellowed, "Cora! Get your butt out here. We've got some witchery to do."

A minute later, a girl with peach-colored hair stumbled into the room through a beaded curtain, rubbing her eyes. Like Aenor, tattoos covered her pale skin. "Are you kidding me, Aenor? This had better be important. In my dream, I was *just* about to kiss this super hot incubus. I think he was a demigod—" She blinked, staring at Ruadan, then me. "Who are these people?"

Aenor pointed at Ruadan. "Well, he's an incubus, for one thing. And I think possibly a demigod."

Cora stared at him. "I was just joking. I hate incubi. I mean, I find you repulsive." Then she looked away, muttering something that sounded like, "Too much."

"He has a World Key," added Aenor. "And he is promising us amnesty from the Shadow Fae in return for our help."

"The both of you, then," said Ruadan.

Aenor straightened. "The both of us require amnesty. Permanently."

"Fine."

Cora was staring at his chest, where the World Key glowed. "Bloody hells." She rubbed the sleep out of her eyes. "Just so I'm clear, we don't need to attack the Shadow Fae?"

"No." Aenor drummed her fingernails on the countertop. "I know her dad. They need our help."

"At this hour?" said Cora. "Why?"

I met her gaze. "At the risk of sounding dramatic, you're going to help us save the world."

"And more importantly," added Aenor, "that whole bit about amnesty."

Cora heaved a sigh. "Fine. What do we need to do?"

Aenor turned away from the counter. "We need to travel to

another world and disintegrate its magical defenses. Let's get our things together, shall we?"

CHAPTER 20

It was only a few more minutes before we were deep in the watery portal, swimming our way to the surface.

I climbed out of the portal, then whirled around to help Aenor and Cora out. I gripped their arms, hauling them up. Both of them had their own bug-out bags now, full of their own witchy stuff. Probably waterlogged hearts of men.

Aenor dropped her sodden bag on the earth, catching her breath, and Cora hunched over with her hands on her knees as she recovered.

Ruadan called up a ball of silver light that illuminated the clearing a bit more. While the two witches caught their breath, I surveyed the woods around me.

It looked so much like the home I remembered. Moonlight streamed between the leaves, and the wind rushed over groaning boughs of ancient oaks. To my left, outside the wood's edge, were the village homes, silent and still as graves.

I wrapped my arms around myself, shivering. I knew the desolation of this landscape was just an illusion, but the forest's quiet felt wrong. The only sound here was the low song of the wind through the trees. It was like I was standing in the hollow carapace of my former home.

I glanced at Aenor, who'd started pulling things out of her witch bag to lay on the moss. So far, she'd yanked out a demon heart, a few bones, wax candles, a jar of salt, and a few jars of herbs.

"Can I help?" I asked.

"No," said Aenor. "Just stay out of the way while Cora collects a crow."

I glanced at Cora, who was making a cooing sound, holding her hands up to the tree branches. I stared as a dark bird fluttered onto her finger. Cora held onto its body, whispering into its ear. The crow's eyes closed as it relaxed. Then, she released the bird above us. It flapped over our heads, the sound of its wings oddly loud.

As she did that, Aenor poured the salt in a circle around us, muttering quietly in Angelic. She placed four candles in the center of the circle, then snapped her fingers to light the candles.

Aenor looked at me and curled a finger to beckon me to her. "Everyone come closer. Join hands with us."

"We need all the power we can get," added Cora.

Aenor's blue hair—and mine, too—wafted in the air. The hair on the back of my arms was also standing on end as the air charged with magic.

Cora's peach hair snaked around her head as if she were underwater. She closed her eyes. "This glamour is powerful. Can you feel it?"

Ruadan stepped into the circle of magic, his pale hair lifting in the breeze. He traced his finger through the air, leaving a trail of dark magic that glimmered faintly. "It's not just fae magic. There's night magic here, too."

What on earth? "How? Neither of my parents could use night magic. We had no night demons in Eden. Are you sure?"

He shot me a sharp look, which I quickly interpreted as *I am a demigod of the night; do not question my knowledge of night magic.*

Aenor held out her hands to either side. "I guess we'll find out when we break through the glamour."

My entire body felt taut as a bowstring, buzzing with tension. Nothing about this seemed right—the night magic, my father's mysterious disappearance from Aenor's locket. I couldn't escape the feeling that something terrible had happened.

"Hang on," said Cora, pulling her hands away from the circle. "I was a little sleepy before, but now that the ice water portal has woken me up, please explain again why we're about to open a world with the Horseman of Death in it. Is it just me, or is a Horseman of Death someone you're better off leaving alone?"

I glared at her. "It's just you. He's not dangerous."

"Explain," she shot back.

"Okay," I said. "The horsemen were all born with a curse. It was an Angelic spell known as a seal. If the seals were opened, the horsemen turned evil. If my father's seal had opened, he would have carried out his true purpose—to kill nearly everyone on earth using his death magic. But his seal was never opened. The curse never took effect."

"Liora's mother took the spell off him completely," added Aenor. "She used her magic to do it. She had some kind of insanely powerful fae magic at her fingertips. And that's why we're going to need all the power we can get to break through the magical protections she put up."

"Okay." Cora held out her hands to either side, signaling that we were supposed to start.

I grasped Cora's hand in one of mine, and Ruadan's in the other.

"Wait." Cora jerked her hand away, and she stared at Aenor. "You said he disappeared from your locket, right? What if he changed? Maybe the curse took hold after all. Don't you know the prophecy of the gods?" Her hair whipped wildly around her head, and a ferocious wind rushed through the forest. *"I looked, and behold, an ashen horse."* Leaves blew off the tree branches, rushing around us in a vortex. *"And he who rode it had the name Death, and Hell followed him."*

As she spoke, my skin went cold, and my shoulder blades ached to release their wings.

"We get the idea, Cora," said Aenor.

But Cora wasn't finished. She closed her eyes. *"And power was given to them—to kill with sword, and with hunger, and with death, and with the beasts of the earth."*

I felt like my soul was rising from the grave. As she spoke, I felt overwhelmed by the urge to unleash death all over the world, followed by the urge to dull my rage with whiskey. But I was fresh out. My gaze flicked to the moon. Red tinged its surface, as if thick blood were spilling across its surface. Then, the illusion disappeared again.

"Why are you quoting this ancient prophecy?" Ruadan's eyes had darkened, the temperature chilling around us.

Death magic still whispered over my skin. *As I walk the earth, grass and wheat turns to ash before me....*

"Because the prophecy hasn't yet come to pass," said Cora. "But it will. The gods always make good on their prophecies. And they always have their way. We're just their pawns."

Nyxobas's words knelled in my mind: *Ruadan dies at the end of all this.*

"Bollocks," I said. "Gods' prophecies are a load of shite. They don't always come true." I had nothing logical or factual to back up my argument—just my own iron will.

Cora made a sign warding off blasphemy.

"We don't have time for a theological argument right now," said Ruadan. "You have heard about the Plague spreading, right? It has spread beyond the Tower walls, and it will get worse. If the Institute falls, and if Baleros gets his hands on the World Key, he will conscript armies of demons to serve him. Then, death will truly stalk the earth."

"That's the thing about prophecies," I said. "They're vague. Could be anything. We still have free will." Despite my rising fears, I tried to be logical. "Are you going to help us or not?"

"She'll help us," Aenor said, cutting in. "She's a religious nut, but she mostly just wants the opportunity to say 'I told you so' if she happens to be right."

"Opportunity granted," I said testily. "Let's begin."

We held hands once more. Cora and Aenor began chanting. Above our heads, the crow cawed loudly, flapping its wings. The candle flames rose higher, casting wavering golden light over the oak grove.

The prophecy Cora quoted rang in my mind. *Hell followed him....*

Around us, magic whipped along with the breeze, rushing and tingling over my skin. Ruadan's energy blended with the spell's magic, and his power felt cold and silky on my body.

I am the dark rot that starts in your fingertips....

Above us, the crow cawed, and the winds picked up, blowing fallen leaves in a vortex around us. The candle flames rose to the height of our chests now. Something had to be working. At any moment, I could be rushing into the real Eden, embracing my parents.

A powerful magic erupted around us. Then, I stared as the world around us shimmered and the glamour fell away. A few lights burned in the village windows. *Home.*

My heart leapt, cheeks warming. "We're here," I whispered.

I pulled away from the circle, taking a step toward the village.

"Be cautious, Liora," said Ruadan.

It was like I felt his voice inside me instead of hearing it out loud, and I paused to turn back to him. His eyes were on me, his warm protectiveness washing over me. He looked at me like he'd been cursed and I was his salvation. He was right. How could I have ever doubted him?

I turned away from him, heading back to my old home. I broke into a run once more, tearing down the path for my house. Warm lights beamed from windows onto the dirt roads. My feet pounded over the ground, and I sprinted past the crooked homes, the temple, the grassy common—beautifully, wonderfully free from grave markers, not a stone in sight.

Then, I careened toward my old home, where a light burned in the kitchen window.

Mum. Dad....

I screeched to a halt before their door, jolted by the awareness that barging into their home might alarm them.

I caught my breath, and my heart slammed against my ribs. Then, I knocked gently on the door. When there was no answer after a few moments, I rapped again, a little louder. Silence greeted me.

I turned, looking across the town green, where I could see the witches walking cautiously.

I shifted to the window, cupping my hands to peer inside. Light burned in a lantern, and a few plates were set out in the kitchen. Signs of life. Where were my parents, though?

I couldn't wait any longer, and I decided to try the door. My parents *never* locked the house. Why would they? We knew everyone in Eden.

I turned the knob, and the door creaked open.

Lanterns, lit with oil, hung from the ceiling, bathing the room in gold. I rushed over to the fireplace, where I found the word *Bug* engraved, just as it should be. I ran my fingertips over it, unable to control the shaking.

"Dad?" I called out, my voice catching.

More silence greeted me.

I took in the space around me, trying to rein in my wild emotions.

Our living room was combined with the kitchen—a stove and fireplace on one side, sofas and a rug on the other. A hall at the back led to the bedrooms and the library and bath upstairs. They could be upstairs, I supposed.

"Dad?" I asked again, quietly. Apprehension danced up my spine. Something was wrong here, and it took me a few moments to figure out what it was.

Why had my parents left the lanterns on at this hour? It was the middle of the night, and they didn't leave them on when they were upstairs sleeping.

I sniffed the air. The room smelled musty. No, worse than musty. It smelled *rotten*.

My heart skipped a beat. Something was definitely wrong in Eden.

CHAPTER 21

I turned to find Ruadan behind me, sniffing the air as well. He frowned.

I was about to scream at him to get out of here—that if my dad found him, everyone would die. Except my dad didn't seem to be here.

"Something's wrong," he said. "The scent of fae is too faint. I smell you, and the two witches … the rest of it is faint. And the smell of rotten food is powerful." He peered out the window. "Cora and Aenor are checking on some houses across the way."

My chest clenched. "I know. Let me just look upstairs."

"Perhaps you should do that alone."

He spoke the truth. If Ruadan burst into my parents' bedroom while they were sleeping, the wave of death my father would unleash would kill anyone within a fifty-mile radius.

"Yeah, you might want to search discreetly outside, doing your invisible Wraith thing. I can handle my empty house."

"Call to me if you need me." Ruadan disappeared in a blur of dark magic.

I drew my sword, stepping into the hallway. The floor creaked as I walked down its length, my heart thundering. I swallowed hard, standing outside my old room. The door was closed, and I turned the knob, inching it open. I caught my breath.

My parents had kept it *exactly* as I'd left it. The stuffed rabbit I'd loved—who I'd creatively named *Mr. Rabbit*—lay on my green velvet pillow. I was thirteen when I'd left, too old for soft toys, but I still slept with Mr. Rabbit every night until the day the world had ended.

An old pair of shorts and a shirt lay strewn across the floor where I'd left them. A baseball cap, my T-shirts, my trousers in a ball in the corner. The room was preserved like a museum of misery. While the rest of the house had been clean, a thick layer of dust covered the surfaces in this room. My parents hadn't touched a thing in here, like they could distill my essence just by leaving it untouched.

While I'd thought every day about how much I missed them, I'd never thought about how much they must have missed me. I hadn't been imagining what they'd gone through.

With stinging eyes, I crossed back into the hall, heading for the stairwell. I moved swiftly up the stairs, heading for their bedroom. The door was open a few inches, but it looked dark inside.

Holding my breath, I inched it open. Then, my chest constricted at the sight of another empty bedroom. Moonlight streamed over a tidy double bed and sleek furniture.

While my room had been preserved, this one looked different. A portrait of me, as I was at age twelve, hung on the wall. Short purple hair, my eyes wide open with an innocence I'd long since lost. The bed had been made, and I picked up one of the pillows. I smelled the myrrh scent of my father's magic, but it was faint.

A single, midnight feather lay on the floor by the bed.

I crouched down to pick it up. I twirled it between my fingers, and the silver streaks in the feather caught in the moonlight streaming through the window. Breathtakingly beautiful, just like he was. I shoved the feather into my pocket as a keepsake.

My blood roaring, I rushed to the closet door, and hope began to bloom. Clothes from both my parents hung on hangers—my mum's shimmering dresses, my father's sober black clothes. They looked new. They'd been here recently, I was sure.

I turned back to the bed, blood pumping hard. I crawled onto the mattress, straining my eyes in the faint light. A single strand of cherry-red hair lay across the pillow.

"Mum." I plucked the hair off the pillow, feeling slightly like a weirdo. But it was my one tenuous connection to her now.

Maybe they'd run to hide because they'd seen us coming? I glanced back at the short-haired, wide-eyed, full-cheeked girl in the portrait. They'd hardly recognize me now. A gladiator, covered in scars.

I felt completely uneasy in here. The hair on my nape stood on end. I had the strangest feeling that I was being watched—a primal part of my brain warning me of danger.

But who was watching me? There didn't seem to be anyone here.

I searched one room after another—the library, bathroom, the guest room. Apart from my room, everything looked a bit changed—new furniture, new clothes. And no people. No matter what, my parents were just out of my reach, elusive. I felt like I was chasing smoke.

I gazed out one of the windows that overlooked my parents' garden. For just a moment, I thought I saw a pair of pale eyes glaring at me from the shrubs. In the next moment, they were gone again.

Adrenaline pounded through my blood. Who was out there?

I rushed back down to the kitchen, skin tingling again as the faintly rotten smell hit my nostrils. A clean set of plates lay on the wood table, along with bowls and spoons. A corked bottle of wine stood on the table, too.

I crossed to it and uncorked it, sniffing. It didn't smell terrible. When I drank it, it tasted acidic. If I had to guess, it was a few weeks old.

I crossed to the fireplace, where a lidded pot hung. It smelled stronger here. I pulled the copper lid off the pot, and an acrid smell hit me—burnt, rotten meat. I couldn't even tell what it had been originally, but it was now a charred mess, and it looked as if it had been left there for weeks. I retched.

So they had been about to eat dinner, and then they'd just disappeared, letting the food char? How was this possible?

I rushed out of the house, into the cool night air. "Ruadan!" I called out. I wasn't trying to be quiet anymore. Now, I was certain my parents were gone from Eden.

Ruadan flitted over to me in a whirlwind of shadow magic.

A few houses down, Aenor and Cora crossed out of a home. Aenor shrugged.

"There's no one here," said Ruadan. "Anywhere in Eden."

"We just found a load of half-eaten, rotten food and clothes left out," said Cora.

"Everywhere, it looks like the people who lived here just disappeared, mid-dinner."

I shook my head. "How is this possible? The worlds were locked. Only a seneschal like Ruadan could open them."

"Or…." Ruadan's dark magic lashed the air around him. "Or a god. It's the gods' power that we drew on to create the locked worlds. A god could toy with it now." Ruadan traced his fingertips through the air, and shimmering night magic followed in the wake of his stroke. "Perhaps Nyxobas toyed with this world."

"The night magic…" said Cora. "Why would Nyxobas open this world?"

"Godsdamn it!" I started pacing. "This is one of the favors that Nyxobas is doing for Baleros. We think that Baleros gave him a soul cage. A magic ring."

"A soul cage," Aenor repeated. "You could have mentioned we were up against someone with a soul cage before we came in here."

Ruadan met my gaze steadily, and I could feel the rage curling off him like smoke. "The gods only care about one thing."

"Souls," Cora finished his thought. "And the gods always win."

Ruadan swore under his breath.

I threaded my fingers through my hair. Anger flooded me. "What if Baleros found a way to…." What if he'd killed everyone? I could hardly finish the thought. I was pacing furiously now, my mind racing. "No," I reassured myself, "Baleros wouldn't kill them. All those fae lives. Too wasteful." I was muttering to myself now, desperately trying to read into Baleros's thought processes. "No, that would be a waste. He's not a sadist just for fun, he finds a way to use people, doesn't he? Leverage, slavery … living creatures have intrinsic value as long as he can use them…."

"Are you okay?" Aenor was looking at me with concern.

"I'm just trying to figure out what Baleros has done with my parents." I heaved a sigh. "And everyone else. I don't suppose you know any tracking spells?"

Aenor cocked her hip. "Yes, but I need something from the person, like a fingernail or a—"

"A feather?" I pulled the feather from my father's wing out of my pocket. It glinted silver in the moonlight.

"Exactly," said Aenor. "We'll need a few more things for the spell."

"Blood from a succubus," added Cora. "Ashes from a phoenix."

"And I'll have to burn the feather as part of the spell," said Aenor.

"I've got a strand of hair from my mum as well." My gaze darted between them defensively. "What? I missed them."

"They'll do, but we want to get out of this world before using them," said Ruadan. "I'll open the portal, and we can return to their bone shop."

Good. I didn't like it here anymore, and I couldn't escape the eerie feeling that I was being watched, that the primal part of my brain was warning me that something was amiss.

Ruadan backed away from us, then summoned his violet magic. His body glowed with gold.

I frowned at him. His gold and violet magic whipped the air around him, and the World Key glowed so brightly on his chest that it was beaming through his black shirt. Tension rippled off him, and violet magic crackled over the earth by his feet. Shadow magic, I thought.

I shivered. "Something wrong?" Normally, he'd just rip open a hole between the worlds without a second thought.

He opened his eyes, and shadows slid through them. "Yes. The portal isn't opening."

CHAPTER 22

Dread coiled around my heart.

"If Baleros can get a god to open a world…" said Ruadan in a voice that chilled me.

"He can close it, too," Aenor finished his sentence. "Like a prison."

I clenched my fists so tight my fingernails pierced my palm.

"Stand back," said Ruadan.

I beckoned to the two witches. "Let's get far away from him. His magic is powerful."

As we walked away, Ruadan shadow-leapt across the green. Not far from the temple, his body glowed brightly with shadow magic and the gold of the World Key on his chest.

Then, a wave of magic erupted from his body, tearing along the earth and ripping up grass on the green. The force of it knocked me *hard* to the ground, and I grunted, rolling over. I coughed at the dirt clouding the air. I rose, dusting myself off. By my side, Aenor helped up Cora, muttering angrily as she did. Dirt and particles of leaves and glass clouded the air.

"Please tell me that opened the portal," I said, coughing into my arm.

"It did not open the portal," was Ruadan's somber response.

As the dust cleared, I could see magic crackling over the ripped-up soil and roots, but the ground was still closed over. I coughed into my arm again.

"Since Nyxobas used shadow magic to seal this," said Ruadan, "my own shadow magic is only adding to the shield. I think I just made it stronger."

"So we are just trapped here now," said Aenor.

Cora's pinkish hair snaked around her head, electrified by the shadow magic in the air. "Not to be a jerk, but this is what I meant when I said the gods always win. We live in their world, we play by their rules, and they don't give a single divine fuck about us. They always win, and we always lose."

"You're a right ray of sunshine, aren't you?" I said.

She narrowed her eyes. "Trust me on this."

"What about the one we came through? Will that still be open?"

Ruadan shook his head. "I can't feel it anymore. I think it closed up after we came through here."

"Let's check," said Aenor, already taking off, her pale blue hair trailing behind her tiny body.

I clenched my fists as I hurried after her. "So what is happening now? Baleros has a god doing his bidding permanently? He won't even need the World Key with that sort of power. He can just have Nyxobas do the work for him."

Ruadan shook his head as he stalked toward the forest's edge. "No. In return for thousands of souls, Nyxobas will do a favor or two for him. For a short time. He won't give him a World Key, and he won't be permanently doing his bidding. Baleros wants to be able to open the worlds in order to harvest his armies, right?"

I nodded. "So he started with this world, because…." I bit my lip. "Well I don't know, exactly, but it must be linked to my father. We know Baleros is obsessed with spreading the plague. My father could do it if he feels enough emotional pain." Panic clawed at my heart. "What if Baleros wants to kill my mum, or torture her until my dad breaks? What if he—"

Ruadan touched my arm, brushing his knuckles over my bicep. His calming magic snaked over my body like a balm. "We don't know exactly what Baleros is thinking, and we may not figure it out until we find him. We have to take this one step at a time. The next step is getting out of here. Then we find your father using the tracking spell. We'll get through this."

"Right. Right." I wrung my hands. "One step at a time."

"Baleros has made one mistake," said Ruadan. "He's playing two gods against each other, making promises to both Nyxobas and Emerazel. I'm not sure how it will end, but it probably won't go well for him. You cannot serve two masters."

We walked in gloomy silence, slipping beyond the line of creaking oaks until we reached the forest portal—or, at least, the mossy soil where it had been. My stomach fell.

"Gone," said Ruadan. He traced his fingertips thorough the air, and violet shadow magic shimmered. Then, his pale eyes shifted to the two fae witches. "What gods do you serve?"

Aenor cocked her head. "What does that matter?"

That's when the feeling returned to me—the eyes on my back, watching us. Ruadan sensed it too, and he whirled, drawing his sword.

"You feel that, too?" I whispered, drawing my own sword. "The eyes watching us?"

"Yes," he said.

"I thought no one was here," Aenor said in a hushed voice. Blue magic swirled and crackled down her arm.

Ruadan nodded back to the forest's edge, signaling that we should move toward it. We walked quietly, looking all around us for the source of the threat. I tried to scent what we might be dealing with, but I only smelled the electrical scent of shadow magic among the forest's usual smells.

Ruadan sniffed the air again, and a low growl rumbled from his chest. The air grew colder around us. Glacial, even, and icy mist frosted in front of my face.

A growing sense of dread tightened my gut. We were trapped in Eden, and the one thing I knew for certain was that Baleros wanted Ruadan dead so he could rip the skin off his chest.

Baleros had trapped us here to die.

A flicker of movement caught my eye, and my fingers tightened on the hilt of my sword. We paused within the shadows of the forest's edge.

Across the clearing, near the rows of houses, a creature crawled out of one of the homes. He crept low to the ground with elongated movements. He looked vaguely human, except his body was emaciated, ribs sticking out, and his fingers were long and sharply pointed. His face had a slightly elongated, skeletal snout, and ivory antlers jutted from his head.

"What the hells?" I breathed.

"Shadow demons," Ruadan whispered. So *that's* why we couldn't smell them—they just smelled like all the other shadow magic around here.

More pale, gray eyes appeared from the shadows—dozens of them, and my legs started to shake with anticipation. The demons howled; a lonely, desolate sound that opened a pit in my stomach.

This was what I was made for—killing. This was where I felt comfortable. My wings tingled at my shoulder blades, and a dark smile curled my lips. *Come at me, you animals.*

As they started to run for us, I broke into a sprint to meet them, my sword ready.

I'll bury all of you in the earth. I'll rip your hearts from your bodies.

Magic flashed around me as Cora and Aenor began hurling their spells, blue and green igniting the air around us. When the magic struck the demons, they screamed—the sound was disturbingly human, agonized.

I reached the nearest demon, and I swung for him. I struck him through the neck, severing his spine. Battle fury surged in my bones, and I whirled.

Pivot, strike, carve.

I was moving fast enough that I kept them off me with the tip of my blade, swinging it in controlled arcs around me.

I glanced at Ruadan. His movements were breathtaking. Never was his divine nature more apparent than when he was fighting. Me?

Not so graceful. I grunted, sweating, snarling—half animal. But I was delivering just as much death.

I scanned the surroundings. More gray eyes closing in on us. An army of them. My pulse roared.

So we were trapped in a locked world with an entire bloody legion of bestial demons hells-bent on killing us.

Bloodlust charged my body, increasing my speed as I fought them. But they were moving fast, too. A demon's claws raked at my back, drawing blood. They were all around me now, closing in. Another claw pierced my flesh, and it sparked something in me—a wild hunger. I wanted to taste blood.

A demon hand grabbed me from behind, claws digging into my throat.

"Grmmel margrr numen," one of them whispered in my ear. A demon tongue.

I grabbed him by the arm and flipped him over my shoulder, slamming him down on the earth. Then, I drove my sword through his neck.

Now, the world around me started to seem a little indistinct, the edges hazy. Still, I fought to keep my focus. I swung again, trying to keep up my speed. My swings were a little off now. What was happening to me?

Sparks danced before my eyes, and with each swing of the sword, silver trailed through the air.

This was not good.

I saw a gap in the demons around me, and I frantically cut my way through it, trying to fight my way out. I made a break for it and started sprinting. I was fighting to keep up my speed, but some kind of toxin seemed to be poisoning me.

Poison in the demons' claws.

I didn't make it far before they cornered me, isolating me from the others. I couldn't see Ruadan anymore, or the flashes of blue and green magic from the two witches.

As I tried to make my retreat, I realized I'd ended up near the rows of houses—only the buildings looked different now, like they were made of bone.

To my horror, the demons' faces began to shift. They were no longer the skeletal, elongated snouts of beasts—they were transforming into fae faces. Distinctly familiar faces that made my heart wither.

CHAPTER 23

Dozens of Baleroses surrounded me, smirking at me while I stumbled away from them. Now, the air smelled of roses, that sickeningly sweet smell.

"Losing control, are you?" said one of the demons, an infuriating smile curling his lips.

I staggered closer to him, swinging for him with my sword. I missed.

The laughter of a dozen Baleroses rang around me. I was dizzy now, and the slave masters were toying with me.

I fell back through a door, landing hard on a wood floor. Was I back in my parents' house?

A Baleros leapt for me—his face was that of my old master, but his hands sharpened into lethal claws. Metal clanged on wood, and I knew I'd lost my sword.

Baleros smiled above me, controlled and lethal. "You were born evil, Liora, angel of death. Born to kill. Flowers wilt around you, grass turns to ash. Your breath is a toxin that poisons the earth. Sparrows fall from the sky and the trees turn to bone. You are an abomination on this earth; a festering, rotting monster, repugnant under your skin.

You would kill your own kin." Claws raked down the front of my chest, drawing blood. "You kill those you love."

I punched him hard, again and again in the jaw. He unleashed that scream again—the one that sounded half human, half beast. His clawed hands gripped my throat, squeezing, piercing the flesh.

More poison.

"A monster like you," he whispered, "should stay in its cage."

Darkness slammed into me. I wanted blood, flesh, bones. I wanted to crush them into the earth.

And I would.

My voice came out choked. "A monster like me should stay in its cage." Rage flared hot though my muscles, and I punched him hard in the face again, cracking his jaw, breaking bones. "But I got out."

Fury burned through my body—and with it, strength. I was a hurricane of vengeance, and my enemies were all around me.

I punched him again, hard, and the creature fell off me. I snatched my sword off the floor. That dark, cold euphoria snaked through my body as I grabbed the hilt.

The demons were right—I was born to kill.

Flowers wilt before me.

Bollocks. I needed some alcohol to stop myself from murdering my allies.

Instinctively, my demonic attackers were already backing away as death magic started to snake off my body. My beautiful, dark wings erupted from my shoulder blades. As they did, I snatched the wine off my parents' table, chugging it down, ignoring the sharp vinegary taste.

I dropped the empty wine bottle and gripped my sword with both hands.

Despite my buzz, I felt steady on my feet as I moved around the room, slaughtering one demon after another. My sword cut through their spines, severing their lives instantly. I no longer felt dizzy or off-balance.

Their deaths filled me with power, my body growing gloriously strong.

I was a fomoire in my own way. Ruadan fed off heartbreak; I fed off death. And right now, I felt positively glowing.

Pivot, strike, carve.

Demon blood and gore stained my parents' floor. In the back of my mind, I knew my mum would be furious. But I kept slaughtering, kept hammering them with my blade.

I moved in a maelstrom of brutality until every creature—every freakish, Baleros-headed demon in my parents' home—lay broken on the floor. I stood over them, catching my breath. It was at that point I realized the illusion had faded. They no longer looked like my old gladiator master—just ordinary freakish demons.

In any case, my childhood home had become a mausoleum of my enemies. Right now, I liked it that way.

Sword in hand, I crossed to the door and stalked outside.

I will take more lives tonight. Their heads will rot on spikes. I will create a garden of death.

Colored magic sparked in the air across Eden, electrifying it with blue and green, the air tinged with the scent of brine. My lips tasted of salt.

Ecstasy lit me up as my wings lifted me into the air, moonlight washing over me as my flight carried me closer to the mob of demons. I dodged the sparks of blue and green magic as I flew. The demons had surrounded the fae witches.

I'll feed the soil with their blood.

I angled my wings, flying lower. Blood dripped from my sword. I attacked from above, cutting through necks, their skulls. I'd fertilize this beautiful fae earth with the gore from their bodies.

Fools sacrifice to the earthly gods. Death is the greatest power of them all. I landed on the soil and whirled into action. *Break their bodies—feed the earth. All fall before me.*

As death power filled me, imbuing every muscle with strength, I became insatiable. I wanted to drive every living creature into the earth, crush each of them to dust. Around me, I no longer saw the demons' faces, only their beating hearts. Life I needed to crush. Hearts that must stop. With every ruptured aorta, another wild thrill of power rippled through my chest.

Now, I'd snuffed so many lives out that there were hardly any left. Gods, I wanted *more*. More still lungs, more severed heads. More blood on my blade.

There—a most beautiful heart beating, so large and healthy. I needed to rip the thing in half. All beautiful things must die. I'd crush it like a rose in my fist.

A name pierced the fog of my bloodlust, and my movements stilled. Death magic started to ripple along my arms, down my fingertips, and I yearned to unleash it, to slaughter every living creature. How glorious it would feel to kill them all … every last moth and hummingbird. I'd crush the sparrows in my fist and wring the blood from their bodies, grind their bones to dust.

"Death is my name," I snarled. "All fall before me."

"Liora!" That beautiful, rich, deep voice stroked my skin, calming me. Silky magic brushed over my body. My body was shaking, legs trembling, but that soothing magic warmed me from the inside out.

The heart—the one I'd longed to stop with my powers—still beat. And now, I became aware of the body around it. The powerful fae body, the one marked with savage tattoos. The arms that would always protect me—violet eyes and pale gold hair.

"Ruadan," I breathed.

All the death power rushed out of my body like a wild river and nausea replaced it. I hunched over on the ground, on my hands and knees. Dark blood soaked the soil from all the demons I'd just killed.

I choked down my urge to vomit, mastering control of myself once more. Then, I lifted my eyes to search the battleground around me.

But the battle was over. Only Ruadan remained, and the two fae witches, peeking out from behind the trunks of oak trees. Their brightly colored magic still electrified their bodies.

Aenor stepped out from behind the oak, her dark eyes wide. "That was … interesting."

Ruadan leaned down. Holding my elbow, he helped me rise to my feet, his magic still soothing me. As it whispered over my skin, it took some of the shaking out of my limbs, the cramping out of my muscles. My wings had disappeared, and strangely, their absence felt like a loss.

I surveyed the land around me. Broken bodies littered the ground —severed spines, streams of demon blood seeping into the earth.

"You're a formidable ally," said Ruadan. "Dangerous, but formidable."

I pointed at his heart, catching my breath. "Sorry about the, um— I almost killed you."

Tentatively, Cora stepped out from behind the tree. "So *that's* what people mean by 'orgy of violence.' I'd never had the visual before. I could have done without it in my brain, honestly."

I gripped my stomach. "Are you really judging me? One of you goes by the nickname *Flayer of Skins.*"

Aenor shrugged. "I do keep things tidy, though." Then, she crouched down and pulled out a knife. She started to carve out one of the demon's hearts. "This will fetch a pretty penny."

"Who do you plan on selling it to?" asked Cora. "The corpses of the other demons? There's no one else here, and we remain trapped."

I looked at Ruadan. "Any ideas how to open the world beyond what we've tried?"

He scrubbed a hand over his mouth. "My magic only strengthened the barrier between the worlds. It melded with my grandfather's. Our magic is one and the same. We need the magic of other gods to break through it. And it has to be powerful."

Aenor gripped the bleeding demon heart. "Good thing you have us, then. I serve Dagon, the sea god."

Cora raised a hand. "Storm god."

"I can chant the Angelic spell to open the world," said Ruadan, "but I'll need your magic to break its bonds."

Apprehension tingled over my skin once more, the hair rising on my nape, and I glanced at the forest's edge. Ice slid through my bones. There, between the trunks, thousands of pale eyes gleamed with shadow magic. A legion of demons surrounded us, ready to strike again.

I swallowed hard. "You might want to do that now, ladies."

Aenor looked into the woods, her pupils dilating. "Oh, dear."

"I'm not going to be able to kill them all," I said. A deep fatigue had spread through my bones. "I'll do what I can while you work your magic."

"Careful, Liora." Ruadan's voice, again like balm around my body.

Sword in my hand, I stalked toward the forest's edge. "Just open the portal as fast as you can."

From behind me, Ruadan's Angelic chants filled the air. The air ignited with storm and sea magic—salt and the scent of brine floated on the breeze. Lightning cracked the sky, clouds roiling overhead. A heavy rain started to fall. The two witches were strange creatures, but I'd quickly come to love them and their magic.

The first line of demons rushed for me, tearing through the forest, snarling. Luckily, there weren't many yet. This time, I knew better than to let them get their claws into me. The tip of my sword kept them at bay. Adrenaline sapped away the weakness in my bones.

The ground trembled, thundering with the sound of the oncoming horde of demons. A few favors, Ruadan had said. But Nyxobas had transformed the entire landscape. My former home, overtaken by these miserable creatures.

Come on, witches. Open that portal.

Thousands of pale eyes, running for us over the gnarled forest roots.

A blast of powerful magic rippled out over the earth, vibrating through my bones. I fell to the ground, and Ruadan screamed my name.

I pushed myself up from the earth, gripping my sword hard. When I rose, I caught a glimpse of the portal gleaming behind me. It glowed with the blue and gray of seas and storms, and lightning struck its surface.

The two witches jumped in, but Ruadan was waiting for me at the portal's edge, holding out his hand to me.

I charged for it as fast as I could, and when I reached it, I slammed into his body, knocking him into the portal with me.

We sank deep beneath the salty water.

CHAPTER 24

$\mathcal{I}$ climbed out of the portal and into Aenor's shop. The portal's opening was narrow, but it still filled most of the space. Aenor and Cora had already slipped behind the counter. Next to me, Ruadan hoisted himself out, seawater dripping off his muscled body.

Aenor turned and nailed the waterlogged demon heart to the wall.

Exhaustion had sapped my strength, but I now felt more frantic than ever to find my parents. Now I knew Baleros had gotten to them.

In the center of the room, the portal closed, and I steadied myself against the wall, still catching my breath. "What do we need to do now? You said we needed something for this tracking spell. Some kind of blood—what else?" I realized I was shouting, and I probably shouldn't be yelling at the people who were helping us, but my panic was starting to dissolve my patience.

"We've got most of it here," said Aenor.

"But we don't have everything," added Cora.

"We need a...." Aenor blushed, and her gaze flitted nervously to Ruadan. "A satyr's ... you know."

"What?" said Ruadan, irritated.

"His *manhood*," Aenor whispered.

"His penis?" I blurted, baffled.

Aenor's cheeks were now as bright as Cora's hair.

I held up my hands. "I'm sorry. You go by the name Flayer of Skins, Scourge of the Wicked. And you live in a shop with hearts nailed to the wall, one of which I just saw you carve out of a demon's chest. You're covered in blood, which you seem fine with. And you can't say the word 'penis?'"

"I was born in a different time," she said defensively.

I blew out a long breath. "Well, my bag of satyr dicks is fresh out, so does anyone have any ideas?" Again, I found myself yelling at the people helping me. Maybe my little death-angel stint in Eden had brought out my unpleasant side.

Cora rubbed her eyes. "I should probably add that we've literally never found a satyr penis. They don't give them up very easily. They have a thing about wanting to keep them attached."

"Can't imagine why," I said.

"I know where we can get one," said Ruadan.

The room fell silent, and I blinked at him. "I'm not sure I even want to know."

Ruadan frowned. "Is it a problem if it's attached to the satyr, or do we need it severed?"

"We just need it to stir with," said Aenor.

Cora's brow furrowed as she considered Ruadan's proposal. "I mean, I suppose he could just sort of … stick it in the potion and give it a good stir." She gyrated her hips, then cleared her throat. "Please forget that I just made those hip movements."

Ruadan shrugged. "It will be easier to convince a satyr to lend us his penis if we don't have to remove it."

I clapped my hands together. "Good, okay. Where do we find a satyr?"

"The Carnival of Secrets," said Ruadan. "All we need is a coin from the ringmaster to gain entrance."

I gripped his arm. "I'm not even really understanding the words you're saying right now. Just tell me the rest when we get there. Let's get on this now." I nodded at Aenor. "You two—get the potion ready, and we'll bring you the dick."

* * *

THIS TIME, the portal opened into what looked like a darkened city park, and Ruadan led me to a forlorn-looking circus tent. The tattered fabric looked as if it had been here for a century, and it flapped in the wind. It was a tiny thing, and it looked completely abandoned.

"We'll find a satyr in there?" I whispered.

"I think so. I haven't seen him since the worlds closed. It looks … smaller now."

At this point, I knew better than to sheathe my sword going into any new dark place. There was a good chance I'd be killing at least one person in there, especially since we were covered in seawater and blood and looked terrifying.

Side by side, we moved closer to the tent. Ruadan lifted the canvas flap, and it yawned open into complete darkness. For a moment, I felt the dizzy sense of standing on the edge of a void—that the tiny, ragged exterior belied the vastness within here.

Then, a light sparked—a silver sphere from Ruadan that floated in the air. It illuminated a faded, checkered floor and a man who stood before us wearing a mask of a horse's head. And behind him, striped curtains—no, not curtains. As the light rose, I saw that it was an impossibly tall woman, her skirts blocking our way. Blond mermaid hair waved over her shoulders, and she smiled down at us.

As we walked closer, she lifted her skirts, allowing us to walk between her legs.

I cleared my throat, finding all of this a bit awkward, and I resisted the weird impulse to look up between her legs as we crossed between them into a long, dimly lit hall. The length of this hall didn't seem possible, given the size of the tent outside, and yet here we were, walking toward a gold-framed door at the far end. A glass case on a stand stood by the side of the door.

As we drew closer, the gold door swung open, and a small, white-eyed man stepped out wearing a top hat. Then, the door slammed closed behind him, and a golden lock slid shut with a loud click.

Ruadan looked at me. "Let me handle this." He turned to the man and said, "We bring love in exchange for coin."

The little man reached into his pocket and pulled out a gold coin. He tossed the coin high into the air, and Ruadan caught it.

Ruadan turned to the glass case. For the first time, I had a good view of it. Inside sat a red-lipped wooden doll with bulging eyes, dressed in a sailor costume. Ruadan slid the coin into a slot below the doll, and a mechanical whirring noise started ticking, the doll's body jerking around.

Then, its head snapped toward me, eyes locked on mine. The doll's wooden mouth opened and closed. "Liora." He broke into high-pitched, disconcerting laughter, tinged with the sound of cranking gears.

My gaze flicked to Ruadan. *This satyr penis better be worth it.*

The doll creaked and jerked, shifting position. Its wooden mouth opened and closed. "To enter here, you must answer this question." More high-pitched laughter. "Liora. How did Nyxobas prophesy this would all end?"

Ice slid through my blood. I'd hidden the truth from Ruadan—again, and I knew how much he hated that. Could I get off on a technicality?

"Badly."

The doll twitched. "What did he say?" he barked.

"You have to be more specific, Liora," Ruadan prompted. "It's the only way to open the lock."

Anger roiled in my chest. Cora's words—the ones about the gods always winning, always controlling everything—were starting to get to me. I hated nothing more than feeling powerless. I glanced at the golden lock on the door. Could I hack through it with my sword? With enough strength, could I just smash the thing?

Then, I swallowed hard. If Ruadan said it was the only way in, then it was the only way in. Gods knew he had enough strength of his own, so brute force wasn't gaining us entry.

I stole another quick glance at Ruadan, and I steadied my breath. I clutched the hilt of my sword. "He said that this all ends with Ruadan dying, but I think it's bollocks so I didn't bother passing it on."

"Lie!" said the doll. A peal of shrieking, mechanical laughter.

I hated this little wooden bastard. "It's what he said. You asked what he said, and I told you."

"But you know Nyxobas doesn't lie," said the doll. More earsplitting laughter.

Dread fluttered in my skull. Whatever else happened, I didn't want to live in a world that Ruadan wasn't in.

I smacked the glass. "I answered your question. Let us through."

The doll went still, jerking to a halt.

I glanced at the door, and the lock slid open. The little man shifted out of the way.

Ruadan's eyes had darkened, like they did whenever he sensed a threat, whenever his life was at risk. Despite my assurances about Nyxobas's prophecy being bollocks, Ruadan believed it. "Why did you lie to me again?"

"Because I don't want it to be true!" I hissed. "I don't want to live in a world that you're not in. You and I belong together. I am Death, but you give me life. Your loss would stop time and blacken the skies. Your death would be *my* apocalypse."

The mechanical doll groaned, emitting another cackle.

I pointed at it. "If you died, my soul would die, too, and I'd turn into that fucking thing. A creaking, empty, dead-eyed husk devoid of real life. Do you understand? So it won't happen, because it can't. I'm Death, and I say when the apocalypse happens. Fuck your grandpa. That's it. End of story. Now let's move on from that wooden weirdo, and have a normal, focused mission procuring a satyr cock, shall we?"

Ruadan was staring at me, so intently and deeply that I felt as if he were seeing into my very soul. His magic skimmed and snaked over my skin like a caress, and he reached up to cup my cheek.

His touch was painfully light. The gentleness of it was like a knife to my heart, because it felt like a goodbye. I didn't want this now. This felt like the end. *This* was why I hadn't told him.

Before I could say another word, the door groaned open. I pulled away from Ruadan, not accepting his goodbye, and I took a step into the doorway. Flashing, colored lights pulsed over a tent crowded with people and swaths of bright silks in scarlet and cobalt.

Truthfully, the biggest draw to my eye were all the breasts. In the crowded tent, the women were hardly dressed. Many of them were in sequined corsets that exposed them from the nipples up. Others wore thigh-high stockings and the tiniest of knickers. Many of the men were shirtless, their muscled bodies oiled, mustaches waxed into curls.

Brightly colored lanterns hung from the top of a peaked circus tent, casting lurid lights over half-naked acrobats above us, and a tightrope walker who wore only a bowtie, high heels, and a feathered bustier. A luxurious white lion prowled around the edge of the circus, and a naked woman with long blond hair rode a horse like Lady Godiva.

I tried to keep my eyes off all the writhing bodies around us—the thrusting and groping and gyrating hips. It was less of a circus and more of an orgy designed by a Victorian pervert.

I narrowed my eyes. "What did you say you used to come here for?"

I already knew how he was going to respond—with something vague and evasive like. "I didn't say, actually." To my surprise, he met my gaze evenly and said, "I'm an incubus. I came here to feed off lust, so I could gain strength."

"Oh. Right." He made it all sound so reasonable when he put it that way.

His gaze slowly made its way down my body. As it did, I looked down at myself, shocked to see that my own clothing had transformed. My leather trousers had changed into a tiny skirt, short enough that I was pretty sure my bum was peeking out the back. Thigh-high fishnet stockings covered my legs, and a tiny striped top stretched over my breasts—enough, at least, to cover the nipples. My bra had disappeared entirely. I yanked the tube top up higher, readjusting it.

Most annoyingly, my sword had vanished. "What the hells?"

"The circus master is the satyr. This is his magic."

I looked up at Ruadan, whose clothing had changed into a cloak that covered his entire body. Only his pale violet eyes shone out from beneath his cowl. That gaze now swept over my body, lingering over my curves, my breasts, my hips, and I could feel his magic licking at my body.

He gripped me by the waist, his touch again agonizingly light.

"Not now," I whispered into his neck. "Save that for later. *After* we save the world."

After we save the world—and you are still alive because I won't let you die.

His quiet growl trembled over my exposed skin.

"Now, where do we find this satyr?" I asked.

Ruadan tore his eyes away from me and looked around the circus tent.

A woman in a sheer bra and knickers walked up behind him and stroked his back, brushing a kiss over his neck. She was gripping a bottle of whiskey. "Been a long time since I've seen you, fae prince," she giggled.

I arched an eyebrow at her. With her attention focused on Ruadan, I reached for the whiskey bottle in her hand. I might be needing this at some point. "Do you mind if I just…?"

She didn't notice as I pulled it from her grip.

Ruadan quirked a smile. "Celeste. Do you know where I can find Andre?"

"No time for me tonight?" She pouted.

"Not tonight, love," I said. "We need Andre. We need his penis, more precisely."

She let out a long sigh. "Don't we all?"

"Not like that— Never mind. Where is he?"

She pointed across the tent. "You'll find him there, watching the glitter wrestling."

We started weaving through all the lovers, the contortionists, and the wandering bears who were wearing more clothing than most of the women.

At last, we reached a particular ring. There, we found a golden satyr, standing proud. For a man with goat legs, he really wasn't bad-looking, his face model-perfect, hair golden and wavy. Curled horns swooped back from his head, and the fur on his legs was the same beautiful amber as his hair. I tried not to look at his enormous erection, though I was fully aware it would be coming into play later this evening.

Ruadan sped up his gait, and I tried to keep up with him.

As we approached, the satyr turned to us, arching his eyebrows in surprise. "Ruadan! It's been yonks!" Then, his expression darkened. "Wait a moment. I forgot you were with the Institute. You are, aren't you? Bloody fascists. Assassinating everyone. I was doing wonderful business in London before you forced us all into this closed world. I need fresh blood in here, you know?" He licked his lips, and he swept his gaze down my body. "Like this pretty little thing. Saucy minx you got here. Can I *have* her?"

I resisted the urge to tell him this saucy minx was death personified, though the idea of wilting his raging boner was appealing. Instead, I smiled, playing nice. We needed his help.

"I'm taking you back to London, Andre," said Ruadan. "You can recruit for fresh blood there until it's time to return to your world."

His eyes widened. "Why would you do me this favor?"

"We're going to need your penis," I said.

He smirked, purring, "Don't they all?"

"No, I mean we need it to save the world," I added.

"Of course you do." He put his hands on his hips, beaming. "I've been waiting for this moment all my life."

The grim look on Aenor's face when we returned to her shop immediately told me something was wrong. As Ruadan helped Andre out of the portal, Aenor pulled me behind the counter, her nails digging into my skin.

"What's happening?" I hissed.

"I am here to save the world!" Andre proclaimed.

Aenor's dark eyes were on me alone. "Okay, good job on … *that*, but I have bad news."

"What?"

"One of my little sparrow spies was watching the Institute. And it seems that while you were fetching the satyr, Baleros came for your mist army. He destroyed them."

My stomach fell. "How is that possible?"

Ruadan cursed in Fae. "They're unprotected now."

Aenor shook her head, frowning. "He used powerful fire magic. He dissolved the mist army with flames. They're gone. Evaporated."

"This fucker has two gods working for him!" I shouted.

"This won't end well for him," Ruadan said again. But since I had no idea of the specifics on how that would backfire, it wasn't terribly comforting. "And we can get the mist army back, I think. Just not right now."

Cora stepped forward and tugged on my arm. "Let's get the spell done, at least. Once your father cures the knights, the Institute won't be quite as vulnerable."

I followed Cora, and we all crammed into Aenor's tiny, bone-decorated bedroom. Aenor stood against the wall, shielding her eyes as Ruadan directed Andre to the sea-green potion on the ground.

I did my best to not to watch Andre thrusting himself into the bubbling potion, and I was *definitely* pretending not to hear the unsettling sighing noises he was making. The news about the mist army had already nauseated me enough.

"Okay!" I shouted. "I think that's quite enough stirring, Andre. Am I right, Aenor?"

"I'm sure it's fine," she called out from under her hands.

"All right, Andre," said Ruadan in a weary tone that suggested he'd had to stage this kind of intervention before. "You have done the world an immeasurable service."

Andre rose, grinning from ear to ear. "My glorious priapism will be praised in hymns and ballads from now until the end of time."

I nodded. "That's right. Lots of ballads. Now move along. Go around the portal to get to the door, and say hi to Karen on your way out."

The floor creaked as he crossed out of the room.

Aenor's features brightened as soon as he was gone. "Okay. Good. Let's find your dad, shall we?" She crossed to the bubbling potion on the ground. "Cora, I'll need your help." Green magic sparked along her arm and charged down the end of her fingertips.

Cora stepped out of the corner of the room and summoned her own magic—a beautiful gray-blue that flickered around her hand. A phantom wind billowed through the room, lifting our hair, whipping at our skin. I had the strangest sensation of flying, that a salty tempest was buffeting us in this cramped room.

Their colored magic mingled above the potion, a stunning turquoise. My heart slammed hard against my ribs like a battle drum.

At last, I'd find out where my parents were. I'd wrap my arms around my mum for the first time since I was a little girl.

The cloud of shimmering blue-green magic bloomed and pulsed above us. Then, an image began to take shape within the swirls of magic—stone arches, wood pews, stained glass windows—an ancient-looking church with a vaulted ceiling.

The vampire had said something about an old church. Baleros was in one, wasn't he?

"St. Bartholomew's," said Ruadan. "It's not far from here."

I stared at it, starting to believe it at last. I was about to find my parents.

Aenor dropped my mother's cherry-red hair into the cauldron next. The cloud of magic swirled a bit, then reformed to look like the same church. They were *both* there.

"They're together," I breathed.

But what the hells were they doing in that church?

They were in trouble, somehow. Baleros had trapped them. There was simply no other explanation.

I snatched my bag off the floor, now with a fresh stock of whiskey. "Let's go get my parents."

* * *

THE SUN WAS STARTING to rise by the time we neared Smithfield, tingeing the city with coral. Even after I'd left the circus world, I'd remained in this stupid tiny outfit, and I tugged up my little striped tube top to cover my nipples. We'd borrowed swords from Aenor, but her clothes were too small for me.

Ruadan's gaze slid to me. "What do you expect to see when we find your father?"

"I have no idea. But I imagine we're…." I was about to say *rescuing him*, but then I felt stupid. He was the bloody Horseman of Death. He didn't need saving. "I don't know."

If he was okay, why hadn't he come to find me once Nyxobas had let him out of Eden? Finding his daughter should have been the first thing on his agenda. Adonis. Thanatos. Death himself. What in the heavens and hells would stop him from hunting his only child down at his first chance?

"Aenor said his curse had never taken hold," Ruadan added. "What if Baleros figured out how to reverse that?"

"You're being kind of a downer right now, Ruadan." I refused to give credence to this theory. "Let's cross that bridge when we come to it."

We moved swiftly along the narrow alleyways. No portals for us this time, since ripping a watery hole in the earth tended to attract a fair bit of attention.

Despite what Ruadan had said, I couldn't entertain the idea that my father's seal had been opened, unleashing his curse.

I breathed in Ruadan's smell: the apple and pine scent that had started to seem like home to me. As I did, I felt a fierce desire to protect him. And that meant acknowledging when threats might be real. My soul felt like it was ripped open as I imagined a deadly show-down between my father and my favorite demigod.

"I can't die from his death powers," I said quietly. "You can, if they're powerful enough."

My throat went dry at the thought of Ruadan growing sick with the Plague. Somewhere inside me, I had the power to stop this death magic, except that I had no idea how to control it.

I touched his arm. "Look, I have no idea what will happen. But you have your own way of gaining strength if you need it." I flashed him a sad smile. "All you have to do is tell me you don't ever want to see me again." All he had to do was break my heart.

The look he gave me pierced me to the core. He opened his mouth to reply, but before he could get a word out, a shadow crossed over us. Something above had blotted out the sun for just a moment.

My blood roared as I glanced up at the heavens.

My stomach clenched at the sight of two winged creatures swooping above us—dark angels, wings outstretched, one much larger than the other. No—demons, probably. Silhouetted against the rising sun, their features were obscure. My heart slammed like a war drum. They both had bows and quivers slung over their backs, and their aerial position was a huge advantage.

Here, in the sunlight, Ruadan and I wouldn't be able to move through the shadows the way we could at night.

I sucked in a sharp breath. "Can you see who that is?"

"Maddan." Ruadan squinted into the sunlight as they swooped overhead. "The smaller one is Maddan. The other ... I don't know yet."

I didn't like the way they were swooping above the alley, like vultures eying up their prey.

Then, Maddan nocked an arrow, aiming it directly at us.

Bollocks.

I readied my sword, but when Maddan unleashed his arrow, Ruadan reached up, deflecting it with his sword.

"We're going to need to run, but they can hit us easily from their vantage point. We'll just have to go fast." The air frosted as Ruadan summoned a blast of shadow magic to hurl at our celestial attackers. Then he shouted something in Ancient Fae that I was pretty sure was a vile swear. "They're absorbing the shadow magic. Are you ready?"

"Wait." Running through an alley left us vulnerable, and we'd just get hammered from above. Tingles raced down my spine, and I could feel the death angel ready to erupt out of my body. Good. We actually needed her, now, to slaughter the demons above us. "Not yet, Ruadan," I said. "Cover me for a second. I have another idea."

Just had to make sure I didn't lose control completely.

Ruadan yanked me by the waist, pushing me against the wall just under a gutter overhang in the alley that shielded us a bit. I reached into my bug-out bag and yanked out the whiskey I'd taken from Celeste. I took a long, glorious sip. Then another.

Above, the larger demon started screeching in a high-pitched voice. I couldn't quite hear what he was saying, but there was something oddly familiar about it. How did I know that voice?

Ruadan pulled me tight against him, the arrows coming faster now. I could feel the air start to cool with his dark magic.

As I drank deeply from my bottle, Ruadan gaped at me. "We're waiting here just so you can drink whiskey?" he asked incredulously.

I drained the last drop. At last, I felt the comfortable buzz that I needed not to slaughter the whole world. "I need to drink whiskey so I can fly."

"What?" he barked. "You have to drink whiskey to fly? That's a shit superpower."

I'd had no idea that Ruadan used words like *superpower*. There were a lot of things I still had to learn about him, which meant we had to get out of here alive.

"I'll distract them from above, and you run away."

"I'm not taking part in a plan that involves the phrase 'you run away.'"

"Look, there are literally no good options here, so don't act like there's a better plan." I glanced at the mouth of the alley, and my pulse raced as I saw a flicker of movement. Demons were waiting for us to come out. When Ruadan got to the end, they'd trap him and cut the World Key right off his chest.

"Let's go," said Ruadan.

"Wait!" I grabbed his arm. "They're waiting for us at the other end. It's an ambush."

CHAPTER 26

The thought that there was still so much I didn't know about Ruadan occurred to me a second time. We had to get out of here so I could learn every single thing about him, about every moment of his long life.

Arrows were slamming into the wall next to us.

But right now, I had one crucial question. "Ruadan, can you fly?" I shouted. "Winged creatures can fly." *Thunk.* "Except chickens, penguins. Ostrich." *Shit, shit. Focus, Liora.* "My point is, now would be a good time to fly."

Thunk. Thunk. Arrows hit the wall on the other side of us, and we pressed into each other as tightly as possible.

"I can only fly when my incubus side comes out. And that only happens when I'm threatened."

"Are you fucking kidding me?" It came out like a screech, melding with the screeching of the demon above. The arrogance of a demigod. We were trapped in an alley, hammered with arrows by demons from above. On either side of the alley, more demons were waiting to kill us. But Ruadan didn't feel threatened. No, this was just an ordinary morning, apparently.

I'd only seen him transform twice. Once with me; the other time had been in the tunnels, when his old childhood tormentor—the serpentine Caoranach—had nearly killed him. She had been the one who *really* got to him.

I pulled him tight against me. "I'm sorry."

"For what?"

"For what's about to happen."

Then, I grabbed his throat as tight as I could, and I felt his body go rigid. I stood on my tiptoes, getting as close to his ear as I could.

I mimicked the lilting fae accent and deep voice of the Caoranach. "I've been here since before the angels," I said, in a voice that sounded exactly like hers. "Before the fae. I am one of the Old Gods. Your pain was finer sustenance than my tea."

Then, I bit his neck as hard as I could, drawing blood.

Black, leathery wings swooped down behind him, blocking out the sun above us. Star-flecked darkness swirled in his eyes and two dark horns gleamed on his head; a hand at my throat, black claws piercing my neck. For just a moment, I wondered if this was the worst idea I'd ever had, born from the whiskey I'd just chugged. Then, my breathing slowed again. My beautiful nightmare, a god dredged from primordial depths.

I might be death incarnate, but Ruadan still had the ability to send a shiver of primal fear up my spine. A voice in the ancient part of my brain told me to run, but I knew better. Even his monstrous side wouldn't hurt me.

"There you are," I said. "I love you. Even your ill-tempered side."

I'd never told him I loved him before. Now that it was out of my mouth, the terrible weight of those unspoken words had lifted off my chest. Now, I never wanted to stop saying it.

An arrow slammed against his wings, bouncing off—a useful shield. Snarling, he pulled his hand away from my throat. Now, his gaze was sliding down my body, taking in the tube top that had slid down, one of my nipples peeking out. He growled quietly, then grabbed me by the waist, holding his sword in the other hand.

He'd gone from primal demigod of wrath to a lust monster. His magic stroked my skin like a dangerous caress. As arousal stirred in my own body, I could see him feeding from it, and his dark magic bloomed from his body.

Ruadan's wings had formed a shield around us, protecting us from the oncoming hail of arrows. Thin veins of silver shone in his wings, and light shone through the membranes. They looked thin, but they were protecting us.

I reached up to touch his black wing, and he sucked in a sharp breath, muscles tensing. His lust magic stroked over my bare skin, and his body glowed.

"Are your wings indestructible?" I asked.

His eyes had swept down to my breasts, and he cupped one of them, thumb stroking over my nipple. "Not quite. Nothing is indestructible."

My breasts peaked under the full, intense stare of an incubus.

And this was the problem with Incubus Ruadan. He might have wings, but his focus wasn't necessarily in the right place. Even with his powerful wings forming a dome around us, we couldn't stay here forever. The demons waiting for us at the mouths of the alley were about to trap us in here, and his wings wouldn't shield us for long.

Footfalls echoed off the alley walls, and Ruadan's head whipped to the right. The air turned to ice. The demons had decided to come for us.

"We need to get out of here," Ruadan snarled.

"I know. That's what I've been saying. Now. You need to use those big wings right now. And I need to use mine."

I will crush my enemies into the realm of the dead.

Ruadan grabbed me around the waist, and his powerful wings began thumping the air, lifting us out of the alley, into the coral morning sun rays. I gripped my sword in one hand and looped the other around his neck.

I will ensnare your bodies in chains of darkness.

A volley of arrows slammed into us, most of them hitting Ruadan's wings—but one of them pierced his leg.

I breathed in Ruadan's piney scent, then I whispered, "Let go."

My wings weren't out yet, and to my surprise, he trusted me

enough to drop his grip on me anyway. For just a moment, I plummeted. My bug-out bag dropped to the ground, but I clung tightly to the sword.

I am the beginning and the end.

Then, dark euphoria spiraled through me as my own wings burst from my shoulder blades. Cool morning air whipped over my body. I'd been meant for the skies, and up here, I felt clear-headed.

I started flying in an erratic path, trying to make myself harder to hit. The pace of incoming arrows now suggested to me that they were running out. Ruadan's leather wings were carrying him toward Maddan, and I started to head for the other demon.

The sun blinded me, and it took a moment before I could focus on the second attacker—the larger one, whose screeching pierced my eardrums.

He was nocking another arrow. I finally recognized what he was saying.

"One, two, threeeeeeee!"

"Barry?" The bloody caveman? Was there anyone Nyxobas hadn't transformed in the shadow hell?

Barry loosed his arrow, and I blocked it with my sword.

I enshroud your body with rot.

I angled my wings, flying faster for Barry. Up close, Barry looked quite a bit different than the hunched little Neanderthal I'd found in the dungeons. This Barry was enormous and muscled, his body covered in brown hair. His teeth were long and yellow, pointed at the ends, and pale eyes burned with hatred. Fresh out of arrows, he screeched and pulled a sword from his sheath.

Battle fury crackled up my spine as I reached him.

I swung for him, and he managed to deflect it. On the second slash, I sliced the quiver off his back, the tip of my blade carving into his skin.

"One, two, threeeeeee!" A nasal screech, straight from the depths of hell.

Our blades clashed, sparking in the ruddy morning light. His stench was unbearable. Did showers not exist in the void? Whatever the case, Nyxobas had dutifully transformed him into a powerful warrior.

At this point, I wanted to slaughter Nyxobas myself.

Death has dominion over all gods.

For someone who looked like a winged caveman, Barry moved swiftly, his swordsmanship sophisticated. Our position had shifted, no longer over the little alley but in the skies above Smithfield. Centuries ago, these streets had run with the blood from butchered cows and executed traitors, or from victims burned by fanatical queens for heresy. Today, they'd run red with the blood of demons if I could help it.

"Barry lonely in the void!" he yelped.

His plaintive voice was worse than his attack, and the whining tone threw me off. Still, I was driving him back, controlling the fight and dominating him.

My gaze flicked back to Ruadan. To my horror, I realized he was no longer fighting Maddan alone—an entire horde of shadow demons had flocked to him. He moved in a blur, an explosion of dark, shadowy magic that froze the air. But there were so many of them, descending like a plague of locusts.

"Bollocks!" Barry had been acting as a distraction, pulling me away from Ruadan when I needed to keep him safe. Ruadan, of course, was the real target. I needed to act as his guard.

Now, several shadow demons were flying closer, still in the distance but moving for him. Had Baleros managed to transform each and every one of these demons in the void?

No, he probably hadn't needed to. All demons hated the Shadow Fae, since we tended to assassinate them. All Baleros had to do was get the word out across the earth to the demons hiding in the shadows, underground, afraid for their lives—an uprising was beginning: *The Great Rebellion starts in London. Live free; kill the Shadow Fae.*

It was a wonder the Institute had lasted as long as it already had.

I had to end this little skirmish now and get over to Ruadan.

CHAPTER 27

I positioned myself just above Barry's dark wings.

He opened his mouth. "One, two, threee—"

"Shut up, Barry!" I bellowed. I brought my sword down hard into his wings, carving through bone and muscle.

He yelped like an animal, then spiraled out of the skies, falling hard into Smithfield Square.

I glanced at Ruadan. The man was terrifying, a vortex of dark magic and icy air. Blood covered his body, but his sword hung at his waist. This savage version of Ruadan was ripping one of Maddan's wings off using his bare hands. No *wonder* Ruadan kept his brutal side under tight wraps.

Like a sadistic child toying with a fly, Ruadan ripped the second wing off Maddan. The bloodied, wingless creature began to fall to earth.

I swooped lower, racing for Maddan as he fell, nearly free-falling myself.

Death to the Prince of Elfhame. Death to Baleros's allies.

I swung. My blade sliced through his neck, carving his head from his body.

I shot Ruadan an irritated glare, as if to say *that's how you kill, a perfectly civilized decapitation the way the gods and nature intended*, but he completely missed the look because another winged demon was moving closer now. And at any moment, more would be upon us.

My wings thumped the air. The thrill of destroying Maddan was short-lived—a high-pitched scream turned my head.

"One, two, *threeeeeeee!*"

Barry's bloody wing had *already* healed, and he flew for me again—this time clutching sharpened iron stakes. Demon Barry was a lot sturdier than Maddan. And where the hells had he got the iron stakes from?

He hurled one at me. But just before it reached me, I snatched it in midair. The iron burned my palm, but I twirled it around and hurled it at Barry, catching him in the wing.

Death to the allies of Baleros.

The iron spike ripped his wing a second time.

"Threeeeeeeee!" he shrieked. He tumbled to the pavement, blood streaming from his body.

I'd finish him off for good later. Right now, I needed to help protect Ruadan from the legions of shadow demons surrounding him. We were drastically outnumbered, and cold rage spurred me on faster, the wind whipping over me as I flew closer to Ruadan.

Of course Baleros waited until the sun rose to stage his real attack. In the light, we couldn't leap away.

I'll be a blight on the earth.

I longed to just unleash my death magic, but if it was powerful enough, I'd take Ruadan down with it and finish the knights for certain. Instead, I joined the fray. My sword was a tornado of steel, hacking into wings, carving off horns and limbs. Ruadan moved swiftly and gracefully, like a night storm. *Strike, thrust, hack.*

The blood of our enemies rained over Smithfield. Demons, their wings decimated, plummeted to the pavement.

Protect the one I love.

I fought with the fierceness of a king protecting his fortress, every inch of me now moving precisely.

But more demons kept coming, some of them flying behind me. I couldn't whirl fast enough to take them all on.

From behind, a sword cut into my wings.

I'd been stabbed many times, cut with swords and knives. A fire demon had singed my entire left leg once. But I'd never experienced the exquisite pain of a wing injury, an agony that seemed to rip me apart from the inside out. It spread through my body and set up camp inside my skull.

Then, the swoosh of air around me as I fell.

I slammed down hard on the concrete, body cracking with the fall. Was I screaming? Pretty sure I was.

From my cleaved wing, sharp pain ripped through me. I rolled onto my hands and knees. I'd lost my sword in the fall, and I desperately scanned the pavement for it.

"One, two, *threeeeeeeeeee!*" My head whipped to the side to see if Barry was coming for me. He wasn't. Instead, he was gripping iron spikes and slamming them into the ground with a disturbing sort of glee. His wings may have been ripped, but he didn't seem to mind, so intent was he on stabbing the pavement with iron spikes. What was he doing? He was obviously completely mental now, but his physical strength was truly stunning.

I had no time to contemplate that further, because another demon was moving for me, his body a vortex of darkness with two burning white eyes. His form flickered in and out, but I got glimpses of a lithe, leathery demon with long claws.

Shit. He moved like the Wraith, and I'd lost my weapon.

I pushed myself to my feet, wishing my wings would retract like they normally did. Apparently, that didn't happen when one of them had been ripped.

As the leathery demon reached me, I burst into action using only my body. I hammered his desiccated face with my fist, and I kicked him hard in the chest. He was moving just as fast, but I managed to dominate, landing one punch after another.

A primal instinct in the back of my mind, an invisible thread that connected me to Ruadan alerted me that something was wrong. I glanced up at the skies. My heart stuttered at the sight of Ruadan careening for the earth, his wings ripped, bleeding.

"No," I whispered.

It was just enough of a distraction that I lost the advantage. In the next moment, the demon's clawed fingers were around my throat, piercing my neck.

Baleros's second law of power: Caring for others makes you weak.

I kicked him hard in the crotch, and he dropped his grip on me. My victory was short-lived. Already, another creature was ripping at my wings from behind. Pain screamed through my body.

I was surrounded, but my survival instincts were still keeping me focused. I kicked a demon so hard in the throat that he dropped his sword, and I snatched it as it fell. I swung it in wild arcs, trying to keep the demons at bay. I had to kill them all to get to Ruadan.

Where the hells was Baleros? I could almost feel his corrupted presence tainting the air.

I swung at the demons around me. Then, an iron arrow from above pierced my chest. I fell back onto the pavement.

Pinned to the ground by half a dozen demon hands, my wings and spine splintered with pain. Someone kicked the sword away from me. I bucked and thrashed, trying to break free.

Panic stole my breath as I spied a glimpse of Ruadan on the other side of Smithfield. I caught just a fleeting instant, but it was enough to know what was happening. Enough to rob my mind of all sense for one horrible, quiet moment.

The demons had surrounded him, and they were driving iron spikes into the ground through his wings.

My world tilted.

They wanted to pin him there like a butterfly, then carve the World Key off his chest.

He could have made a portal to get out of here. Why the hells hadn't he made a portal to escape?

I searched for a shadow I could leap to, but in the bright morning light, they were few and far between, and the demons kept hitting me. I growled, fighting wildly against the demons gripping my arms.

That's when a thought struck me with the sharpness of an arrow to my skull. Ruadan was staying because of *me*. He'd promised to stay by my side and to keep me safe. He'd promised he wouldn't run away. And he wasn't breaking that promise now. Even if he *really* should be.

A blow to the side of my head dizzied me for a moment. My death magic threatened to burst out of me.

If it weren't for me, Ruadan would be out of here by now.

And if it weren't for Ruadan, I'd probably be spilling my death magic into every living creature around me right now. I'd kill all of London in one glorious death spasm and free myself from the attackers beating the living shite out of me.

Instead, I was grappling here with a demon horde.

Caring for others makes you weak.

Ruadan needed strength, and I needed a real weapon again.

A demon kicked me in the head, and I fell forward. Where was that sword?

Focus, Liora. Get to Ruadan.

I ripped a loose cobble from the ground—a possible weapon. I started to stand, ready to kill with it. But before I could use it, another arrow pierced me from behind, and I fell to my knees again. Where had that sword gone?

Get up, Liora. Get to Ruadan before someone robs the world of the fae prince—the boy who made his mother a crown of flowers, who grew up to be a warrior.

The world needed him, and so did I.

I rose again, fury igniting me with a pure clarity, and my gaze locked on my newest attacker—a winged demon with enormous fangs. The cobble was out of my hand in a fraction of a heartbeat, and it slammed into his skull, cracking it. I snatched his sword from him before he hit the ground.

My desperation to get to Ruadan burned the fear from my body. There was nothing now except my sword and the wounds of my enemies.

Snarling like a savage thing, I hacked my way out of the crowd of attackers, running for Ruadan. I needed to tell him to open the portal —*could* he open the portal with that iron pulsing through his blood?

Probably not.

And I was no longer strong enough to get him out of here unless I went full angel.

CHAPTER 28

I ran for him anyway, sprinting across the square, but I was still in the stupid satyr heels. I shadow-leapt to a shady tree not far from him—but there was just so much godsdamned light around. It must have been magically created.

From behind, a demon grabbed at my hair and my wings, slowing me down. I whirled, swinging my sword to sever the creature's body in two.

When I turned back to face Ruadan, panic slammed into me. A cloaked figure stood above him, knife glinting. Bright magic lights blazed above him, eliminating shadows. I couldn't leap any further.

Even with the cloak, I knew it was Baleros. I broke into a run again, my mind screaming. *Stop him.* Baleros brought the knife up above Ruadan, ready to skin him.

A furious roar from Ruadan shook the stones beneath my feet. My spirit leapt as Ruadan ripped himself free from his iron pinions, tearing at his wings. The pain must have been unbearable, shredding his leathery wings. Ruadan caught Baleros's hand before the knife could plunge into his chest. Then, Ruadan twisted his arm, breaking it.

I was almost at him now, my sword ready. Baleros's dark eyes shifted to me. For the first time, I knew he was afraid of me.

I drove the blade into his neck, severing his spine and throat in an instant. His body burst into flames, knocking me back with the heat. I coughed as the scent of charred flesh filled the air.

A temporary victory—nothing more. The fire goddess had claimed his body. Ash wafted into the air around us. He could come back at any moment, revived by the goddess he served. And worse, the demons were still surrounding us, intent on our deaths.

Ruadan wrapped his arms around my waist. His leather wings were forming a barrier once more, but they wouldn't last forever. The rips in his wings made my chest tight.

"They're after me," he whispered into my ear. He lifted one of his arms over my shoulders and carefully cupped my head in the cocoon of his wings. "They're after the World Key, not you. I can cover you while you get out of here."

"I'm not leaving you here, you moron," I whispered back. "Make a portal."

"I can't. There's too much iron in my blood." He loosened his hold on me. "When I open my wings—"

I locked my arms tightly around him. I wasn't letting him go. I wasn't letting Baleros get his hands on the Prince of Emain again.

"Fine," I said. "Open your wings."

Light poured in as Ruadan's wings parted, but I kept my grip tight on his waist, squeezing him to my body.

I am the alpha and the omega.

With an iron will, my broken wings lifted us into the air with all the strength I had left. "Hold on to me," I said as we rose above Smithfield.

He weighed roughly as much as a truck, and pain screamed through my shoulder blades. He gripped onto me, too, holding me tightly around the waist with his powerful arms. His wings were beating the air slowly, but they'd been damaged more than mine. I didn't think he could fly on his own.

"What the hells are you doing?" he said. "I told you to run."

"Was that an order?"

"*Yes.* I'm the Grand Master. Have you forgotten?"

"Almost there." I grunted with the effort. My grip on him was ferocious. Only a few feet to the churchyard.

My father was supposed to be in that church. Would we find him there?

I was barely holding on, unable to think clearly.

Two arrows *thunked* off Ruadan's wings. He snarled, tightening his grip on me.

We finally reached the gated churchyard, and I tried to move slower for a gentle landing, but my strength was giving out.

Good enough.

I let go of Ruadan, and he jumped to the ground, landing hard on a raised patch of grass between tombstones. I landed just after him, the impact shooting up my calves and thighs.

I searched the church for signs of my dad, but I didn't see him. I could *smell* him, the dark scent of myrrh. A sheen of shadow magic glimmered over the church, protecting it like a shield.

A loud *thud* from behind me turned my head. Already, a demon with an axe was trying to hack through the wooden door at the gate.

I ran for the ancient church doors, but as I touched the metal doorknob, a blast of electric shadow magic knocked me back. I just barely managed to stop myself from falling back flat onto my broken wings.

"Dad?" I shouted at the church, like an idiot.

The church did not respond.

To our left, a demon with an arrow was aiming it over the iron gate. There really wasn't much cover here, and we needed a portal immediately. In the church's ancient, arched doorway, Ruadan began shielding me again with his wings. His powerful body pressed against mine, wings splayed open to keep me safe.

I turned to him. "You need to heal," I said, hoping the ferocity in my voice would convey my meaning.

If he wanted to gain strength, all he needed to do was tell me he didn't love me. He just had to say he never wanted to see me again. The power of that heartbreak would feed him with the strength of a thousand armies.

You're a monster, Liora, and you never should have been let out of your cage. That's what he needed to say to me—the truth that I carried with me at all times. That was all. The pain of a perfect betrayal would feed his broken body, and he could open a portal.

Instead, he was cupping my face.

"Do it," I whispered.

I couldn't entirely spell it out. If I said, *"Tell me you don't love me,"* and he repeated it like a puppet, I wouldn't believe his words. My heart wouldn't break enough. He had to crush my spirit in his own words. Why did he not get this?

"I love you," I prompted him. *Don't you get it? Feed, fomoire.*

He pulled me against his powerful chest, kissing my neck. "I love you, too," he murmured. "That's why we will keep each other safe."

Warmth spread through my belly. "You idiot. If you broke my heart, we could be getting out of here right now."

His dark, fierce gaze bored into me, then stroked down my body. He slid his hands down to my waist, gripping me possessively. "That's not the only way I grow strong." Dark seduction laced his voice.

Could I really give him the strength he needed right here, with the demons closing in on us?

I supposed lust wasn't the *worst* idea.

I pressed myself against him, standing on my tiptoes to kiss him. From my waist, his hands slid lower, cupping my bum under my barely existent skirt. He was teasing me just enough to make my blood roar.

For a fraction of a moment, I prayed to the gods that my dad wasn't in the church right now. Then, I forgot about him entirely, my attention completely focused on Ruadan's hands on my body and the silky feel of his tongue against mine. I hoisted myself up, wrapping my legs around his waist.

Ruadan pulled away from the kiss, then whispered in my ear, "Get ready for this."

That was all the warning I had before the ground opened up in the stone beneath us and I plunged into the cold waters. As the portal churned around me, I thought my wings would rip right off my back.

CHAPTER 29

asping for breath, I lay flat on my stomach on a bed of the softest moss I'd ever felt. The air smelled heavy and damp with honeysuckle and ferns. A river burbled nearby. Morning sunlight streamed through towering oaks, flecking the emerald earth with chinks of amber.

I inhaled again, catching the faint scent of apples on the breeze. So Ruadan had taken me back to his childhood home once more—back to Emain. This was home to him, the first place in his mind he'd imagine when he thought of safety.

Gods, I wanted to stay here with him forever, just living in the forest. Clean water, meals of mushrooms and honey, fish from the river. Just basically eating and sleeping and kissing Ruadan whenever I wanted.

Except that would mean leaving the Institute and possibly most of London to die a horrible death.

I felt as if every bone in my wings had been broken and poorly sealed back together again with duct tape. Turned out that wings were *fabulous,* and they could make you feel euphoric. They made you feel like a god. But the flip side was that they made you vulnerable and could leave you a crumpled and broken heap on a forest floor.

"Wings are like love," I muttered into the moss.

"What?" Ruadan asked.

"Nothing."

I turned my head to look at him. Shirtless, he was crouching, pulling up clumps of moss from the earth. What was he doing? And more importantly, how was he moving? I supposed he'd probably been managing the pain of wing injuries for centuries, while this was a whole new world to me.

"What are you doing with the moss?" I asked.

"I need to fix your wings," he said. "You won't be able to transform to your normal form while they're broken like that."

"What about yours?" I asked.

"We'll heal my wings after."

My cheeks heated as I thought of what sort of healing that would entail.

He shifted closer to me. "This might hurt a bit at first," he said.

I held my breath, and I winced at the feeling of pressure on my right wing, but the moss was cool against it.

"This isn't ordinary moss," Ruadan murmured. "It's enchanted, from the Emain forest. With this and my magic, you'll heal fast."

Along with the moss, his magic slid over my wings, soothing all the pain. I breathed in and out deeply, taking in the rich forest air. Already, I could feel my wings growing stronger. Healing magic spiraled over my feathers, stroking each one, straightening their quills and down.

It occurred to me that Ruadan was perfectly savage and perfectly serene at the same time. He was a beast, comfortable with himself. And when I was with him, my mind felt tranquil. He excited my body with a wild intensity, and yet he was the only one who could calm the raging waters of my mind. He was the only one who could subdue Baleros's voice. My old master lived in the darkest hollows of my skull, whispering *monster,* and Ruadan was there to silence him.

Ruadan—god of sleep—had the power to make me feel normal and whole. And that was amazing magic indeed.

His fingertips brushed down my wings, stroking my delicate

feathers, and I shivered at his touch. The tips of my feathers were immensely sensitive, and at that moment, I knew I never wanted anyone but Ruadan to touch them. I trusted no one like I trusted him.

His magic whispered over them, a healing balm that felt like it was made for me. I breathed in the charged, enchanted air of the Emain forest.

At last, when my wings felt completely strong once more, they retracted into my shoulder blades. I sighed and rolled over onto my back.

My little top had slid down somewhat, and bits of moss and soil stuck to the top of my breasts. I brushed them off, wondering precisely how many demons I'd exposed myself to when I'd been fighting in the ridiculous satyr-inspired outfit. Then, I pushed myself up to my feet.

Despite the gentleness of Ruadan's healing, I still had a monster before me. This was Ruadan the Incubus, not Ruadan the sophisticated Grand Master.

His dark gaze was as bestial and ferocious as ever. He looked *hungry* for me, his intensity charging the air around us. In the underground river, when I'd taken off my clothes in front of him, I'd been unable to meet his gaze—certain that if I had, the world would combust around us. Now, I could feel his eyes on me, and I wanted to burn in that inferno.

"Now you," I said.

With a sly smile, I tugged down my tube top until my breasts popped out, and I slid the top all the way down over my belly and hips, the curve of my arse, until I stepped out of it completely.

When I stood up again, Ruadan stared as my nipples hardened in the forest air. Goosebumps rose on my skin with the anticipation of his touch, and a pale flush spread over my chest.

Arching an eyebrow, I backed up against the rough bark of an oak. The feel of his silky magic on me was a sexual promise that made my toes curl, and I tugged up the hem of my short skirt.

His body had gone completely rigid, and a feral growl rumbled out of his chest. His wild magic skittered along my breasts and belly, and it stroked my thighs. We hadn't even touched yet, but he was looking at me like he wanted to devour me, and already, a molten hot ache was building between my legs. I wanted to feel his hands there, his tongue thrusting.

He made a low and bestial sound, and he started to move for me. I held up one finger, signaling for him to stop right where he was. Violet magic flared out from his body. He looked as if he were ready to rip this forest apart to get to me.

He'd get to me soon enough, but stoking desire was all about *just* the right amount of denial.

And right now, Ruadan's body was already responding to my desire. His muscles beamed with violet light as he fed off my lust, and his body was taut with anticipation. By the tightly coiled look of his muscles, he was using every inch of his restraint not to attack me right now. He took a step closer even though I'd told him not to, eyes coal-black. A muscle twitched in his jaw.

With his gaze penetrating me, I reached under my skirt, hooking my thumbs into the hem of my tiny knickers, and I pulled those off, too, down to my ankles. The breeze—along with Ruadan's magic— kissed my bare thighs. Despite its coolness, my skin was hot. A strand of my lavender hair stuck to my cheek.

I left the tiny skirt on, but nothing else. Already, I was so turned on I couldn't think straight. I beckoned Ruadan closer, wildly aching for him. My thighs clenched as he took a step closer, and liquid heat arced through me.

Snarling, he moved for me like a beast let out of his cage. He gripped my wrists, pinning them over my head. My pulse pounded hard and fast, and my breathing sped up. My nipples brushed against his chest painfully lightly. His other hand was on my hip, his grip fierce.

I'd made him wait, and now he was in complete control. He kissed me slowly, savoring it.

I groaned, trying to move against him. Gods, I needed him now. I pulled away from the kiss for a moment, catching my breath, and I pulled my wrists from his grasp. I unbuttoned his trousers, staring into his dark eyes as I did. He gasped as my fingertips brushed against him.

"Tell me how you feel about me." The ultimate aphrodisiac.

With his free hand, he caressed my face. "You're perfect for me, as if the gods made us for each other. Even if you're flawed, the whole of you is perfect. If I lost you, I'd never sleep again." Now, his hand stroked down my body, palming one of my breasts. "Enough talking."

His mouth was hot on my neck, tongue flicking over my skin. At the apex of my thighs, a fiery, slick ache built so intensely I wanted to groan. Lust pounded through my blood, pulsing hot. One of his fingers stroked me, and I almost lost my mind. I'd made him wait before, and now I was on the verge of begging him.

"Ruadan." His name came out like a moan, pleading. I reached up for his wing, brushing my fingertip over the top. His body stiffened, fingers tightening on my arse.

I hooked my leg around one of his, and I ran my foot up the back of his leg, my little skirt riding up even higher. His gaze swept down between my thighs.

At that, he reached down and ripped the little skirt off me. My desire was almost unbearable as he lowered me to the ground, deftly managing to cup the back of my head. He was still being too gentle, too careful with me, the ache in my core demanding that he move faster.

I let my legs fall open, and he moved between them. I gripped him hard around his back, pulling him into me.

He slid into me, and I moaned his name. Our bodies merged as he filled me deeply. Everything left my mind except the feel of his slow, powerful stroke. He claimed my mouth with his, kissing me deeply as he thrust into me. My legs wrapped around him, and I thrust my fingers into his hair, trying to pull him closer as my hips moved against him.

It was like we'd been made for each other—my lover, perfect in his flaws, the one who made me feel safe and calmed the wild waters of my mind. We melded with each other, intertwined like flower stems in a wreath—no end and no beginning between us.

"I love you," I breathed into his neck.

As he whispered it back, ecstatic release rippled through my body, and I shuddered around him.

CHAPTER 30

Still naked, I curled around Ruadan's body on the soft, mossy earth. Completely satiated, he glowed with powerful shadow magic. He'd healed completely, and his wings, no longer broken, slid back into his body.

He stroked his hand down my back slowly. We couldn't stay here much longer. The Shadow Fae needed Adonis's power, and we had to return to London. But I needed just another moment here with him before we took on our enemies.

"Why this particular part of the forest?" I asked into his chest. "You were in immense pain. You nearly died. And in your panic, you took us to this particular part of Emain. Why here?"

He stroked my hair. "This is where I used to play as a very young boy. Before I joined the Shadow Fae and before Baleros trained me. Before I laid eyes on the Caoranach. I used to play here with my half-brothers."

I sucked in a sharp breath. His brothers had died when I'd unleashed my magic. "What were their names?"

"Mochan and Nuallan. Both were older than me. They hunted boar here. They were brilliant hunters. We'd roast the meat over a fire at the end of the hunt. They let me drink their beer sometimes."

I smiled at his memories. Then, I lifted my head from his chest. "There are boar here?"

Ruadan kissed my neck. "They only come out at night. I carved my own spear from a branch. I didn't kill a single boar. I just liked being with Mochan and Nuallan. Before Baleros trained me, I wasn't suited to killing. I didn't like seeing the boars hurt. Obviously, I got better at it."

"Let's not talk about Baleros."

His hand stilled on the back of my hair. "But we do have to go capture him now."

I groaned. "I know. We need a plan," I said, willing my mind to clear from the haze of pleasure.

"We return to London. We find your father to heal the Shadow Fae, and we imprison Baleros in the Tower."

I cupped his face in my hands and stared directly into his eyes. "And then after we kill Baleros, you will give me a crown of wildflowers, and I will marry you."

Silence fell. For a moment, my heart stuttered, unsure of how he would respond. Then, an expression I'd never seen on Ruadan's face before—a completely unguarded smile. "Where I come from, females don't propose marriages."

"Pretty sure that's everywhere."

"But it's fitting that you would ask me. And how could I refuse?"

Smiling, I shrugged. "I mean, I wasn't even really asking, I was just telling you what's going to happen. And I'm death incarnate. So you really *can't* refuse."

His hand stroked down my back, and he leaned in for another kiss.

I felt as if the mossy earth were reaching up to keep me here with soft forest hands. Was this place enchanted, or was I overcome by the seductive magic of being with Ruadan?

In either case, Ruadan broke the spell by pulling away. "We have to get back to London."

I knew what he meant without him spelling it out. By this point, the Shadow Fae could be dead.

I sighed and sat up, frustrated to find that my only viable piece of clothing had been ripped in two. "I don't suppose there are any stray nymphs around here we could steal clothing from? I'd rather not reunite with my long-lost family with my fanny on display."

He rose. "So particular. I may have to rethink our marriage plans if you're that high-maintenance about everything."

The smile on his lips stopped me from throwing a clump of moss at him.

"I'll be back in a minute with some clothes for you," he said. "And while I'm off, we need to figure out how to discreetly approach the church. We know that the demons are waiting for us there. As soon as we return, they'll try to rip us apart again. If we portal in, they could be waiting for us with swords before we even breach the surface. We need to enter discreetly. Then, we have to get past the shadow demons and break through the bonds of shadow magic to get to your father without anyone knowing, in the broad daylight."

"You make it sound hard or something." I stood, slipping into my underwear. I'd wear a stolen dress, but stolen knickers were a bridge too far.

I closed my eyes, envisioning the layout of Smithfield Square. Any portal we opened nearby would be an obvious red flag. We might as well arrive with flashing lights, screaming *Hey demons! Come rip our wings off again! Fresh World Key skin for you!*

Unless there were something else for them to focus on....

I bit my lip. In the daylight, everything was a million times harder. There were a few shadows cast by the buildings and trees, but we'd have to be fast as lightning if we wanted to go undetected. I'd had a hard time finding the shadows in the chaos earlier. That meant knowing exactly where to jump ahead of time, with no time for scanning the horizon.

I chewed my lip, trying to visualize Smithfield Square. I was pretty sure there was concrete on one side, like a building of some kind....

The crunching of leaves pulled me away from my thoughts, and I looked up to find Ruadan crossing toward me with a black dress in his hand.

"You didn't have to kill anyone, did you?" I stood, pulling it from his hand.

"No," he shrugged, still glowing wildly. "I'm an incubus. It's not that hard to charm a dress off a nymph."

I glared at him.

"What?" he said. "I got you the dress you asked for."

"Fine." I pulled it over my head. "I had some thoughts about our plan. We need to create a distraction while one of us shadow-leaps over to the doors undetected and breaks through the shadow magic."

He scrubbed a hand over his mouth. "That's what I was thinking. I'll draw their attention toward me, and I can teach you how to break the bonds of shadow magic."

I crossed my arms. "How can you be the distraction? You're the one they want. They'll just surround you and Neanderthal Barry will rip you to shreds with iron spikes again."

"*Again?* That never happened."

"It nearly happened. The point stands. You're the target. They'll come right for you."

He shook his head. "I won't look like me."

"How? Neither of us have powers of glamour."

"With enough concentration and my newly recharged magic, there's one form I can take. At least for a few minutes, long enough to create a distraction that will terrify all of them."

I frowned. "What would terrify Baleros? He can't die. He just keeps coming back like a plague of locusts."

"With enough power, I can take on the form of my grandfather. Baleros won't know why Nyxobas has arrived, but a god showing up on your doorstep is never a welcome sight. No one tries to kill a god. You just have to move quickly, because I won't be able to hold his form forever."

"Okay. So we open up a portal at a safe distance, probably in a nearby building where they can't see us. You come out into Smithfield Square, you do your terrifying god thing. Meanwhile, I shadow-leap toward the church as fast as I can, and hopefully no one is looking at me because they're all focused on the terrifying god of the void."

"You have the lumen stone, so you'll be able to whisk through completely undetected. You have the shadow route mapped out in your mind, right?" he asked. "Because you won't have time to pause and scan for them."

I blinked. "Shadow route?"

"Where all the shadows would be falling at the time we arrive."

"I … was there a tree?"

He stared at me, probably trying to ascertain if I was joking.

"I know there was a building of some kind," I added. "Probably several. Look, I was in the middle of being beaten to death by demons, so I failed to stand around memorizing shadow placements for possible future use. My mistake."

"Okay. We'll work on that. I'll open a portal into a building on Cock Lane."

I smirked at that, then hoped Ruadan hadn't seen the twitch of my lips. A thousand-year-old fae prince probably didn't titter at the word "cock."

"Do you know the Golden Boy of Pye Corner?"

I opened one of my eyes. "Is this a nursery rhyme?"

"There's a statue on the corner of that building—a chubby little boy made of gold that the humans stuck there because they foolishly believed the great fire of 1666 was a punishment for gluttony and not the result of one of Emerazel's temper tantrums. Close your eyes."

I did as he said. He touched my temple, and the image of the golden boy statue blazed in my mind. Now, I could remember seeing it. I could picture the whole street corner—the brick and stone and the fat golden statue. "Okay. I've got it now."

"We'll open the door of that corner building, below the statue. The sun will be casting shadows on the left side of Giltspur Street. From there, you'll shadow-leap toward the square."

With his hand on my temple, he talked me through each shadow— each tree, every dark corner beside the ancient hospital, and the shadows cast by the tombs in the churchyard.

Now, I had a clear shadow route in my mind, and I'd be able to traverse it almost instantly.

I opened my eyes. "And once I get to the church door? How do I break through the shadow magic?"

"You need to use the power of a god and meld with the magic."

"Good. Okay. How do I use the power of a god?"

He slid a silver ring off his pinky and slipped it onto my finger. As soon as he did, his magic spilled into me. I shivered at the intimate feel of a god's power in my body.

"My magic is imbued in this ring. Freshly charged, linked to Nyxobas. He's the one who created the barrier on the church. I could feel it. When you get to the shield, you have to meld with the magic there. You'll slip into the void for just a moment as you do. Make sure you stay grounded. Focus on your feet."

"On my feet?"

He nodded. "Focus on their connection to the ground. It will keep you in our world. It should only take a moment. A fraction of an instant. Envision the barrier breaking apart."

Even with Ruadan's soothing magic billowing around me and racing through my body, my shoulders were growing tenser. Everything hinged on what happened after we opened that door into Smithfield.

Everything.

And the truth was, I had no idea what I'd find once I opened those church doors. I'd been imagining throwing the doors open to find my father locked in a cage. I imagined that he needed us to simply free him, and he'd burst forth from the church and save us all.

But who the hells knew what we were really up against? What if it was more than Nyxobas's magic trapping Adonis in the church? Gruesome, disturbing possibilities were spiraling through my mind.

Ruadan brushed a strand of my lavender hair out of my eyes. "What are you thinking, love?"

That we've been pursuing my dad this whole time, and what if he's not the answer we've been hoping for?

I filled my lungs with the forest air. "That I will rip the throat out of anyone who tries to hurt you. Anyone." I blew out a long breath. "Also, that I've sobered up, and I'm all out of whiskey."

"You don't need it."

"Except, without it, I might kill everyone if I have to let the death angel out."

"You won't."

"That's sweet." I pulled him toward me in a hug, and I murmured into his chest, "But you just think that because you're blinded by love." I twisted his magic-imbued ring around my thumb. "Since you agreed to marry me, I'll just consider this our engagement ring."

He leaned down and picked a dandelion from behind me. "No, I'll make one."

"A wreath of wildflowers. Of course." I plucked it from his hand, then twirled the dandelion stem between my fingertips. I brushed the soft yellow tip against his nose. "Give it to me once we've chained Baleros in iron."

CHAPTER 31

Dripping with icy portal water, we stood in an old stone building at one of the corners near Smithfield. The gods' magic from the ring electrified me.

Ruadan looked back at me. "I'm going to cloak myself in the form of the night god now. In his true form, Nyxobas has a dizzying effect on people. Like vertigo. You might want to avert your eyes. I'll stride into the square, and then you need to leap into the shadow route directly after me. Do you remember it?"

"Yes. I remember it exactly."

"Good. Look away as I transform."

I stared at the floor as the temperature plummeted in the room, and tendrils of shimmering dark magic snaked in whorls and eddies around us. He'd told me not to look, but I stole a quick glance at the form before me—a black cloak, perfect features pale as moonlight, hair coal-black, eyes gleaming with silver. Shivers rippled over my body, and I was overcome by a disturbing sense of trespassing. The real face of Nyxobas was something I was never meant to see. Looking directly at him was a violation of a kind—and a strangely addictive one.

Ruadan was right—I did feel as if I were standing at the edge of a cliff, and that I wanted to throw myself over the edge, to lose myself in a vast nothingness. I forced myself to tear my eyes away from him, and he swept out the door.

Now, Liora.

It was time. Everything hinged on the next few minutes, and my pulse raced out of control.

I resisted the urge to stare at Nyxobas's strange, star-cloaked beauty again, and I stared at the shadow across the street—my target.

My pulse roared in my ears. Cold shadow magic whispered through my blood, made more powerful by the ring Ruadan had given me. I mentally melded with the shadow by the old hospital walls, and I leapt.

From there, I was already on to my next target—a shadow beside a tree within the square—then the next—the darkness at the exact spot where the Scottish rebel William Wallace had been eviscerated nearly a thousand years ago. I refused to let myself look at Ruadan, but I was vaguely aware that shadow demons were *literally* crawling from their hiding spots, prostrating themselves before their god.

With the demons' attention occupied, I leapt to the gate before the church, peering through the hole to the churchyard. Then, my final leap—to the shadows in the arched doorway of the ancient church. My heart was a wild beast as I made the final leap to the church door, where shadow magic glistened in dark waves. I stepped into the barrier, melding with it—just as Ruadan had told me to.

And just as he'd said, vertigo dizzied me. For a moment, I felt myself plummeting into the depths of the void.

Questions spiraled in my mind. Was I really here at all, a superhero with a stunningly hot lover? A girl who thought she was destined to save the world? Was that *actually* realistic—or was it more likely that I'd gone mad on the dirt floor of Baleros's cage after all his mind games?

It was obvious now. I'd imagined it all.

When Baleros had locked me in the dark iron box, I lived a million fantasy lives. This was just one of them.

How stupid to think I'd ever leave the iron box. And Ruadan was so perfect, the only explanation was that I'd dreamt him up. I was here again, trapped in an iron box. I'd be here forever.

Now that the fantasy world had been ripped away from me, the weight of my grief was so crushing I could hardly move. I was frozen, unable to move a finger or a toe.

There had been no Ruadan, no Institute, no special powers, no love, no mission to save the world. I could see nothing now except the inside of the iron box, and it burned my skin. I was here always and forever, Baleros's discarded toy.

I felt my soul ripping in two.

No. No. No.

It had to be real—I had to be real. Focus on my feet. My aching feet in the stupid high heels that came from the satyr and his stupid giant dick—

My consciousness ripped back out of the void, and I was standing in the church entryway again, certain that almost no time had passed at all. Just a hummingbird heartbeat. Merged with the shadow magic, I envisioned the shield shattering—and it did, like dark glass around me.

Gods below. That had nearly been a complete disaster.

Dangerous to give such a damaged person this much power. And that was the problem with me, wasn't it?

Still, I had to press on right now, before Ruadan lost the ability to cloak himself. I could hardly breathe as I touched the door handle. I turned the knob, and the door swung open into darkness.

I breathed in the scent of myrrh, my legs shaking wildly, knees weak. "Dad?"

Candles alit in their sconces and torches burst with golden light, illuminating the vaulted stone ceilings, the peaked arches and columns around the church. A trumpet song—a dirge—rang out, and my blood froze. Somehow I knew it heralded death. Then, the clopping of hooves echoed off the ceiling.

On his ashen horse, Adonis rode into the nave. Wings spread out, he loomed over this place of worship like a god. I stared into his pale eyes, flecked with gold, and his cold power hit me like a fist. His midnight wings swooped majestically behind him, the feathers shot through with silver, just as I remembered them.

I wanted so badly for him to call me "Bug," but this wasn't right.

I couldn't breathe. This wasn't the father I expected. This wasn't the man who'd held me in his lap and told me stories about birds who were bullied by larger birds and then made friends with kittens. This was not the man who'd wiped my runny nose or brought me water in the night. Not the man who'd stroked my hair and told me that monsters weren't real, even though he knew better than anyone what a lie that was.

No, this was Thanatos. This was my father as the Horseman. He rode his ashen horse into battle—his companion in the end of the world.

A powerful ally.... One that you know well.

It wasn't Nyxobas. My *father* was Baleros's ally.

I stared at the Horseman of Death. I knew just by looking at him, by the cold look in his eyes, that my father's seal had broken open. His curse had been released, the real Adonis lost forever.

I felt my heart breaking right there, and I wasn't sure it would ever heal.

Thick, red blood began streaming down the ancient flagstones beneath the horse's hooves.

Before me stood an ashen horse. Its rider was named Death, and Hell followed close behind him.

The wavering light gilded his coldly beautiful features, glinting in his eyes. He looked familiar and alien at the same time, and the contemptuous look on his face stopped me where I stood. A powerful sword hung at his waist, and he unsheathed it, hardly looking at me.

Sword in hand, he looked straight ahead, staring out the church doors. My heart felt like it was about to burst.

"Dad?"

My first thought was that this couldn't be him. My dad wouldn't just ignore me like this. But I could feel the death magic spiraling off him, and I could smell the myrrh. And worse, I could see the dark magic writhing around his throat—just over the necklace of red rose petals encased in amber that he always wore.

I wanted to throw up. The curse had overtaken him—the seal had opened, and the Horseman of Death had arrived. And he didn't even seem to know me.

Cora's words returned to me: the prophecy of the gods. *I looked, and behold, an ashen horse; and he who rode it had the name Death; and Hell followed him.*

As I stared at him, the monster inside me ached for release. My wings were ready to burst forth from my shoulder blades. He was here to kill, and I had the strongest urge to join him—to just give in to what I really was and to level the whole city.

I gritted my teeth, and I focused again on my feet on the ground, trying to root myself in the reality of the situation. If the seal of Death had been opened, and if his curse had taken hold, was there actually any hope at all?

To my horror, I smelled something else in the ancient church, something besides the dark myrrh of my father. The sickly-sweet scent of roses. Baleros had been here. Baleros and the Horseman, working together.

"Dad?" I called out more desperately, hoping this time to get through to him. "Why are you here?"

He looked at me but didn't quite seem to see me, and he slowly guided his horse past me over the worn church flagstones. "Authority was given to me." His voice boomed off the ancient stone vaults. "To kill with sword and with famine and with pestilence and by the wild beasts of the earth."

A sob caught in my throat. This was not the reunion I'd been hoping for. What the hells was I supposed to do now? Our entire plan had hinged on finding my father, and finding him *sane.*

My pulse thundered through my veins. We were out of time.

My dad kicked his horse, galloping from the church, and the sound of clopping hooves echoed off the stone walls.

The breath left my lungs.

Ruadan. I didn't have any other plan right now except getting to

Ruadan and keeping him safe. His disguise would wear off soon. Everything else would have to wait.

I charged into the churchyard after my father, then shadow-leapt backward on the route I'd mapped earlier.

There, in the center of Smithfield, was the god Nyxobas. Or at least, Ruadan disguised as Nyxobas. His body seemed to suck up light like a black hole, and the world darkened around him. Only his silver eyes gleamed from the vortex of magic. I leapt into the pool of shadows surrounding Ruadan, taking cover in the billowing darkness.

I tried not to look up at him, worried I'd lose my mind if I did. Instead, I closed my eyes and touched his cheek. "I found my dad, but the seal of death has been opened. He's cursed. I need you to leave here now—"

His hand was on the small of my back, pulling me into the vortex of darkness. I was dizzy again, overcome by the feeling that I'd imagined it all. I forced myself to focus on the high heels.

"I'm not leaving you with Baleros," he said. "We fight him together."

"He's not here. I'll try to deal with my father. But you need to—"

The smell of roses made my stomach twist, and I whirled around to see Baleros. His body trembled, but he was approaching the god all the same. He wore his usual clothing—the baggy wool getup of a Victorian showman.

"God of night." His dark eyes twinkled. "When my Angel of Death slaughters half the city, I will be sure to dedicate the souls to you, Nyxobas." He bowed with a strange flourish.

A surge of wild protectiveness shot through me like flame. I stepped out of Nyxobas's shadows. Baleros wanted to use my father to kill—and he'd be sure to count Ruadan among the dead.

There was no running from the Angel of Death if Baleros had him as an ally. One way or another, we had to end this now.

A ferocious fire burned in my heart, and my will to protect Ruadan hardened like volcanic rock. Dark magic flitted down my shoulder blades, sharp and smooth as a knife's edge. My wings burst out of me.

"Liora," Ruadan said from behind me. The shadows around him disappeared. He'd dropped the guise of Nyxobas.

Now there was nothing between Baleros and him but me.

I had no whiskey, now, to quell my most savage thoughts, but Ruadan's serene magic brushed over my skin. I simply had no other options. I had to end this.

She had the name of Death, and Hell followed her.

My gaze flicked to the skies. My father was circling above, midnight wings resplendent as clouds gathered beyond him. I felt an overwhelming longing to follow him up there, to unleash destruction over the city.

My fingers twitched.

Baleros's eyes widened at the sight of me. A vision burst in my mind—the tip of my blade carving a horizontal slash across his chest, a vibrant splash of crimson, then a downward slash.

Then, the burst of flame that would revive him again.

"What did you do to my father?" I growled.

Baleros stared at me. "He's simply doing what he was born to do. The gods gave us all roles, didn't they? The monsters of death, the breakers of hearts."

"And what are you?" I asked.

"Me? I'm just here to put on a good show."

I drew my sword, desperate to slice him.

Kill by sword, famine, and plague, and by the wild beasts of the earth.

My death magic was ready to shoot from my ribs like hundreds of praying mantises bursting from an egg.

Woe to the people who dwell on this earth.

My father—cursed—swooped beneath the darkening skies overhead. Baleros was so close to getting what he wanted, but I'd never seen him looking so unsure before.

How do you threaten a man who revives himself? "Where's my mother?" I asked.

Baleros shrugged. "Your mother, your entire village from Eden. I have them all. As long as you step away from the fomoire you're shielding, I'll return them all to you. Completely safe." He shoved his hands in his pockets, attempting to look composed, but I could see the sweat beading on his forehead. "And you'll have your father back, too. All I need is the World Key."

I tightened my grip on the hilt of my sword. "You're not getting Ruadan. I don't care how many times I have to kill you. I'm prepared to kill you over and over in increasingly creative ways, until the end of time. In fact, I've been looking for a hobby."

Ruadan stepped out from behind me, his sword glinting in the sunlight. "This sounds like leisure time we could both enjoy."

Baleros looked up at the skies again, eyes locking on my father, and nausea rose in my gut.

The beast climbs from a bottomless pit.

Baleros's dark eyes glistened. "Then you've made your choice. And of course you choose death. You're a monster, just like him." A mocking half-smile. Then, a subtle gesture—just a flick of his eyes up to the death god above. "I never should have let you out of—"

Ruadan lunged forward, driving his sword into Baleros's chest, ripping his body apart with brutally efficient violence.

I tore my gaze from Baleros's shattered body to look at my father. Had Baleros signaled to him?

The necklace—the red flowers around my father's neck—glowed with magic.

Trumpets blared, and darkness spilled out from his body.

CHAPTER 32

A *star named Wormwood fell from the sky, poisoning the rivers. Hail, fire, and blood rain down on the earth, and the mountains crumble into the sea.*

My toes curl with ecstasy and sulfur blasts from my mouth.

The explosion of death magic that hit me was a disturbingly pleasurable rush, perfect power trembling through my bones. Sulfur, blood, and ash clouded the air around me, and an overpowering scent of myrrh. Then, the smell of charring of flesh.

When the magic departed my blood, I was left with the taste of dust in my mouth, my limbs shaking with euphoria.

Even before the air cleared, I could feel it around me—the absence of life, the stillness of the hearts and blood. Leaves withering on their branches, grass wilting to a dry gray.

And most of all, grave silence.

Death reigned.

A small fire burned before me—the charred remains of Baleros's body. He'd rise again, a repulsive, corrupted phoenix from the ashes. No one else would.

I didn't want to look to my left. Ruadan lay there, his heart no longer beating. I already felt his death—the absence of his magic in

805

the air suffocated me. It was like someone had sucked the oxygen from the world. I felt like my soul had died with him.

My whole body had gone cold, fingers twitching.

I glanced up at the skies, where my father carved a vicious arc above London, feathers gleaming.

Then, slowly, I forced myself to turn my head.

Ruadan's perfect body lay curled like a child sleeping, his skin gray, chest no longer moving. His sword had fallen from his hand, glistening with gore. His pale hair hung in his face, and a cluster of wilted dandelions lay by one of his hands.

The sight of him broke me, and a strange quiet overtook my mind, silent and still as the dead lying around me. I wanted to lie down with them, and my body no longer wanted to move.

Nothing could kill my dad except my mum. I didn't really understand it except that she had some kind of magic from the Old Gods.

That meant I did, too. Right?

The angel—the creature once my father—circled overhead like a bird of prey. He wasn't my father now. He was the Horseman of Death.

I pulled a bow off one of the demons, and I ripped his quiver off him. I plucked an arrow out. The iron stung my fingers, but I pierced the tip of my finger with the arrowhead anyway. I'd poison it with my blood.

Then, I nocked the arrow, training the tip right on my father's heart.

Pure, heavy silence in my skull, dark as the clouds of ash above me. Only then did my hands stop shaking.

I loosed the arrow, and it shot through the air, finding its mark in his chest.

One shot, and the arrow tip—coated in my blood—pierced his heart. The shot jolted him, and his wings seemed to carry him for a few moments. Then, he spiraled down to earth. A sharp chasm of grief split my chest, but my mind was too quiet to make sense of it. Something had broken in me; I'd moved into a place without language or meaning. Now, only instinct drove me.

I surveyed the ground around me, and a glint of metal on one of the demons' bodies caught my eye. I crossed to him, and I plucked a knife off his body. Then, from another fallen demon, I pulled an iron mace. Its heaviness felt perfect in my grip. That was what I needed for what would come next.

I scanned the ashy air around me.

Now, I needed the scent of roses.

Baleros was coming back, and he wouldn't stray far from the World Key. Some fierce, animal part of me wanted to protect Ruadan's body with all the fight I had left.

I sniffed the air, mentally sifting past the scents of myrrh, sulfur, blood, and decay. After a few moments, I found what I was searching for. The sickly-sweet rose petal scent among all the death.

The church again.

My powerful, black wings beat the air, carrying me toward the medieval church. The sooty wind tore at my hair as I flew, and it stung my eyes. But within moments, I was at the church doors.

I gripped the hilt of the knife as I crossed into the church. In the nave—where, just minutes before, I'd seen the Horseman of Death—I now found Baleros brushing ash off his clothes.

His head snapped up as I stalked toward him.

Vaguely, my brain recognized the look of terror on Baleros's face and that he'd gone pale as milk.

Only a heartbeat until I was before him.

First, I had to break his bones. That's where the mace came in. Crouching, I swung it into his knees—the right one, the left. I vaguely registered his screams, that he was falling to the stone. I whirled, smashing into his ribs. I crushed his arms next.

Baleros was the one who'd taught me to use a mace—the brutal and precise swings, the blunt force.

When he lay crumpled and broken, bleeding onto the flagstones, I pulled out the knife. As if from a distance, I heard myself say, "You made me think I was a monster. But there's a difference between being a monster and a survivor. And that's what I am—a survivor."

Until now, I'd never really escaped that dirt cage—not completely.

Because the rusted bars and crushing sense of worthlessness had lived on in my mind. All Baleros's lessons—the laws of power, my true nature—had lived in me. I'd carried the one central truth he'd imparted to me—that I was a monster. I'd never freed myself from that prison.

I'd always known that I'd never rid my mind of his voice until his heart stopped forever. And that was why he had to die.

The thing about Baleros was that he kept coming back. But the thing about the gods was they wanted nothing more than the souls that were due to them.

Whatever Baleros was screaming at me, I tuned it out. I'd broken most of his bones, and he wasn't going anywhere as I carved the symbol in his chest—the sigil of Nyxobas. Three pointed arrows, the moon, and a circle. Blood streamed down his chest.

When I'd finished making the mark of Nyxobas, I straddled him at the waist. I brought the knife down hard, sliding it just under his ribs to stop his heart.

A flicker of euphoria in my own chest. Then, I leapt off his carcass.

I stared as a white light bloomed from his body like smoke—his soul leaving his corpse.

I took a few more steps back as the gods appeared.

To my left, Emerazel's charcoal body appeared in the church in a blaze of flames, her skin cracked with fissures of lava. And to the right, the vortex of starry shadows, the icy eyes of the night god. Two ancient enemies, one miserable little soul.

The gods hardly noticed me, this angel of death in their midst. I took another step back and stared as the two gods grasped for Baleros's soul, greedy as children fighting over a piece of cake.

They ripped his worthless soul in two, tearing it down the middle like an old rag. My old gladiator master, forever shredded, never again to be whole.

I kept the knife from Baleros's chest, my own little macabre trophy, and I rolled it between my fingers. The weight of Baleros's lessons evaporated off my body like a lifted curse.

The smell of rot filled the air, and I frowned. More death—here in the church?

I traced my fingertips over the stone walls as I followed the scent of death out of the church, the smell drawing me like a candle flame draws a moth.

I stalked out of the church, an angel of death covered in the blood of her old master. I crossed under the vaulted arches to the cloisters. I pushed through the door, and the scent of death hit me like a fist.

That's where I found them—the inhabitants of Eden. They lay in piles on the cloister floor, iron chains around their bodies.

It took me a few moments to find my mother's vibrant red hair, covering her purpled face. Her body was hunched over on the stones. All this was Baleros's work. His masterpiece—his greatest show.

Too bad there was no one left to watch it.

Still, that eerie silence in my skull, quiet as a pile of bones….

I still held tight to that knife, slick with Baleros's blood.

With my wings cascading behind me, I crossed out of the church. Out here, the ashen landscape of death mirrored my state of mind. I wanted to join the dead.

That's when the grief slammed into me, a knife-sharp split in my chest, the pain so intense I could hardly think. It was like my heart had been hewn from my chest. My ribs had turned to iron spikes. My body was punishing me for continuing to breathe while Ruadan didn't. Ruadan's secrets would die along with him. His childhood in Emain, the memories of his brothers—all dead with him.

With that acrid burst of death magic from my father, I had no doubt that the knights of the Tower were lying dead now, too. Bodies rotting in their cowls.

London was a mass grave.

My own death magic was ready to burst out of me and rain all over the earth, just as my father's had done—

It took a few moments for the words to come back into my mind so I could understand things again. Red hair, my mother's slumped body. This was the second time I'd seen my mother dead—both times from the Plague. That particular death magic that my father and I possessed.

Dead twice.

Now, my thoughts were roaring in my skull, the noise deafening. That tiny, red ember lit in my heart again.

But Baleros's voice wasn't there in the din. Just mine, now.

Red hair, spread out over the dirt.

My father had brought my mother back, hadn't he? He'd brought them all back from the shadow hell after they died of plague. I had my father's powers. We could reverse this magic. Both of us could reverse it.

Fix it, then.

My wings lifted me into the air. The hollowness of my chest had knife-sharp edges. I needed to fill it with something. I swooped over Ruadan's body, taking in the wilted flowers in his fist. The sight of him ripped me apart once more.

I needed to fix it, just as Nyxobas had said.

My chest was an empty vessel as I hovered above him.

The name Liora—it meant *my light.* They'd called me that because I had my mother's light, and now a fiery light began to burn brighter, deep inside me.

I let a vision dance in my mind of Ruadan threading together dandelion wreaths, of him hunting in the forest with a spear he'd made for himself. I could almost feel our fingers entwining once more.

His essence—that savage serenity—poured into the hollowness in my chest. It curled around my ribs, easing some of that sharpness, warming me. As Ruadan's essence filled me, so too did the death magic all around me. I was pulling it into me, feeding from it. My back arched, and I drew the magic out of the dead around me.

I let the toxins fill me with spirals of dark power. Then, my wings lifted me higher in the cloudy, sulfurous skies.

My father's myrrh-scented magic whirled into me, filling the void between my ribs. Power infused my limbs and wings, spreading out from my heart, down my shoulder blades, snapping through my bones. It shot down my arms, my legs, until it reached the ends of my toes and my fingertips. My chest swelled as the deaths of everything around me flowed into me.

The deaths of all those around me—the demons, the fae, the knights in the Tower—they all poured into me.

I could feel life slowly returning around me—the withered leaves turning green again, faint pulses starting to beat in veins. Tiny puffs of breath filled still lungs, and skin began to warm.

Ruadan.

I soared down once more. My eyes were on Ruadan's body as the color returned to him and one of his fingers twitched.

A low, almost inaudible beat—the pulse of blood. A heart's pumping. Then, Ruadan's electrical magic crackled in the air.

All around me, life stirred. The lungs of demons filled with air. Somewhere, I was certain my mother was stirring among the bodies in the cloister, pushing her red hair out of her eyes once more.

But right now, I was angling my flight towards Ruadan. And I wouldn't feel whole again until our limbs were intertwined, chests pressed together, hearts beating in unison. I threaded my fingers into his hair, and I pressed my lips to his. This was where I was meant to be.

My wings slid back into my body, and I pulled away from the kiss to look at Ruadan.

He stared at me, stunned, irises black as pitch. "You brought me back."

"Baleros is dead. For good," I murmured into his neck. "And we're never again going to part."

CHAPTER 33

I knelt by my mum, and we stared at each other. She looked exactly the same—same pistachio-green eyes, porcelain skin. Same cherry-red hair. I'd changed drastically, but she'd been preserved like a perfect blossom in amber. She was even wearing one of her glamorous dresses: gold beads and gossamer threads. Tiny blue gemstones gleamed from her forehead.

She cocked her head, frowning as if unwilling to believe I was real. Then, light beamed from her features, and her eyes glistened. She touched my cheek. "Liora?"

I didn't know what to say. How did we recap everything that had happened? *So, I killed you, then ran away to become enslaved, and then a Knight of the Shadow Fae arrived and we had to find a satyr's penis and....* Instead, I just said, "Yeah."

She grabbed onto me so tight I thought my ribs would crack, and I thought, for a moment, her claws had come out. Her loud sobs echoed off the walls, and her tears wet my shoulder. Around me, I heard the sound of chains breaking as Ruadan freed the other fae.

I wrapped my arms around her. She was smaller than me now. How had that happened? The last time I saw her, I could still fit in her lap and rest my head on her shoulder when I was upset. Now, I felt like I could break her. Her hug was ferocious. Mine was gentle.

Through her sniffles, she let out a long breath. "When did you get so big?"

I pressed my face into her neck. "Some time in the past dozen years, I guess."

Her fingertips brushed over my upper arm. "How did you get this scar?"

Oh, Mum. That was one of dozens. "Long story."

She pulled away, narrowing her eyes at me. "Did anyone try to hurt you after you left Eden?" The fierceness in her voice actually made me jolt.

I just shrugged. "I'm fine."

She nodded. "Right. I want you to tell me everything that happened since I last saw you. Everything. Every day and every hour."

"I will. I promise. In a bit. Are you okay, though? You were just … dead."

"You killed me again, didn't you?"

I wiped a tear off my cheek. "Oh, I see. Just coming right out with the murder accusations thirty seconds into our reunion?"

"It's the second time you've hit me with your death magic. Your father's going to have to teach you to control it."

That sharp fissure of grief started to open in my chest again as I realized she didn't know about Adonis, and I was going to have to tell her.

"It wasn't me," I said. "This time, I mean. It was Dad. Or, rather, the Horseman of Death. I brought you all back, just like he did when I killed you."

She went still, her body rigid. "What?"

"His seal has been opened. He turned into the Horseman of Death. I had to kill him. His body is in Smithfield, outside."

She arched an eyebrow at me, the look a mum gave when she thought you were full of shit but didn't want to say so. A long sigh. "Oh, Liora." The disappointment in her voice made me feel terrible.

She gripped my shoulders so hard I was certain she'd leave bruises. "None of what you're saying makes sense."

"I know what I'm talking about," I said defensively, feeling suddenly like a child who'd just reported a monster under my bed. "I just did a whole death angel thing and brought everyone back from the dead."

Gripping my hand hard, she pulled me toward the churchyard. I shot a helpless look at Ruadan, following her lead.

"First of all," my mum said, "I pulled the curse off him long ago. He can't be cursed."

We'd only just become reunited, and I already wanted to argue with my mum. "He killed everyone, Mum. I saw him in the church, and he said some creepy stuff about killing with swords and beasts. He barely looked at me, then he flew out into the skies. The air smelled of sulfur and blood, and then he unleashed his death magic. That's how you died."

"Second of all," she went on, ignoring my airtight arguments, "you can't kill him. Only I can."

Granted, I was less certain of this one. The blood thing had been a guess. "I thought maybe my blood would kill him, because you can kill him, and I came from you."

She shook her head, practically dragging me into Smithfield. "It's not my blood that could kill him. It's the magic in these." She pointed at the tiny gemstones in her forehead. "I'm sure you did some damage, Liora, but you didn't kill him. He'll be fine."

I frowned. "Okay, fine. But he had *definitely* turned evil."

"Evil, yes. Cursed, no." She beamed at me. "Liora, what have you been doing all this time? I can't believe how big you are."

My throat was tight. "We can go over that later. How did you end up in the cloisters?"

"Nyxobas found his way through the glamour. He knocked out our entire village with his sleep magic a few weeks ago. I woke up chained and soaking wet in the cloisters, and your father was gone. That's all I know. I've hardly eaten anything in weeks."

We drew closer to my father, who lay flat on his back in the square. The arrow I'd shot him with protruded from his chest. Blood streamed from it. He'd gone completely still.

My mum looked back at me with pride. "Did you shoot him down from the air? Well done, Liora. You weren't that good with a bow and arrow last time I saw you. You'd hardly used one."

I blinked at her. What was even real right now? "Um, I feel you might not be taking this situation as seriously as you should be."

She fixed her green eyes on mine. "Your father can't die unless I kill him. And even if that happened, you could bring him back, just like he brought you back weeks ago. You have that power over each other." She took another step closer, inspecting me carefully. "That's why I always knew you were okay. At least until a few weeks ago, when someone killed you. Your father had to bring you back. What happened then, exactly?"

I swallowed hard. "His name was Baleros, and he was a monster." I gestured around me. "He's responsible for all this. For Nyxobas taking you out of Eden. For whatever happened to Dad. A whole bunch of shit. But he's dead now."

"You killed him?"

I nodded. "For good this time."

That pride shone from her face again, along with the gleaming of the gemstones in her forehead. Despite everything I'd been through, I felt as proud as she looked.

My mum knelt next to my father's body. His wings spread out beneath him—the darkest blue, feathers shot through with strands of silver.

"But like I said," my mum added, "you didn't kill him."

Something I hadn't noticed before now caught my eye—the faintest hint of shadow magic glowed around the necklace he wore, the one with a flower encased in amber. I knelt by his side, staring at the necklace. It was so faint I could hardly see it, but it was there—a vague midnight glimmer of shadow magic. Just like Baleros had used on Barry. Baleros had used his magic to control the both of them.

"I think I found the problem." I reached around his throat and unclasped the necklace. I lifted it into the air, the crimson flower glinting in the sunlight.

Soft footsteps sounded behind me, and I smelled Ruadan's piney approach, felt his magic curling around me. He leaned down and plucked the necklace from my hand, then rolled it over between his fingertips. "Nyxobas charmed this."

My mum stared at Ruadan, eyes hard as flint. "Who's this ancient fae, exactly?"

I cleared my throat. "That's a long story, really…. There are a lot of … really just a lot of misunderstandings over the years—"

My mum looked like she was about to go feral. "He's too old for you."

My mouth opened and closed, and I considered pointing out that the Horseman of Death lying before us was several thousand years older than she was.

Ruadan looked her directly in the eye. "I'm Ruadan, Prince of Emain, Grand Master of the Shadow Fae Institute. I saw you years ago when I—"

"I have an idea," I said, interrupting this reminiscence before he got to the *tried to kill your husband* part. Ruadan had many beautiful qualities, but tact wasn't his strong suit. "How about we get the arrow out of my dad's chest, and then we can chat about all the fun memories later."

Ruadan cocked his head, then nodded. "Yes."

I looked down at my dad's perfect face, the dark sweep of lashes and straight black eyebrows. Already, I could tell my mother was right. The arrow had stopped his heart, but there was still life in him. His skin still had a healthy glow.

I gripped the iron shaft, then yanked it from his chest. With his eyes still closed, he took a deep breath. Then, his eyes opened, and I leaned over him to look into them—the sapphire and gold of my memory.

A little crease formed between his dark eyebrows.

"Dad. I'm sorry I…." I swallowed hard. "Shot you out of the sky." I bit my lip. "Although you were killing everyone, so…."

He beamed at me, drawing me close into his arms. "Bug."

I breathed in the scent of myrrh. He wasn't a monster—and neither was I.

CHAPTER 34

On top of one of the Institute's towers, I sat on a blanket between my mum and my dad. We were drinking wine out of silver goblets, and we stared up at the spray of stars across the sky. Their bodies warmed mine, and I plucked another strawberry from the bowl before us.

"And that's how I became the amazing sword fighter I am today." The pride in my voice was evident.

After several hours, I'd finally finished telling them about what I'd been doing since I'd last seen them.

"A *gladiator?*" The rage in my father's voice ruined the serenity of the moment. "A *slave?*"

"It wasn't that bad," I lied. "I made a good friend. Ciara. And then I got out." I left out the iron box and the sweets. I was done with that part of my life, now, and there was no need to keep reliving it.

A few clouds began gathering on the horizon, covering the moon.

"I want to raise Baleros from the dead and kill him again," said my dad.

"Can you do that?" I asked.

"No," he admitted.

"Tell me again why we're not supposed to kill Ruadan," said my mum. "He came into Eden to kill us. He took you away from us."

I heaved a sigh. "I already told you. He didn't take me away. I ran through the portal because I thought Dad had killed everyone, since you'd never before told me he was an angel. And Ruadan didn't know what he was getting into, either, when he came to Eden. He thought he was coming for an angel, and that was it. Not the Horseman. And moreover, I love him, and he loves me."

Silence fell, broken only by the sound of the wind rushing over the parapet.

"I feel safe with him," I added.

We could have argued, I supposed, about whose fault it was that the worlds closed at all—was it the Institute's? Was it my father's? Instead, they let my last words hang in the air for another minute.

My mum watched me pull another strawberry from the bowl. "Since when did you start eating strawberries?"

I took a bite. "What?"

"You don't eat strawberries," my father added. "You hardly eat any fruit."

"Or meat," my mum added.

"Just bread and butter," said my dad. "If you weren't immortal, I'd worry about your health."

"And milk," my mum added. "You always need milk at night at three in the morning."

It was quickly becoming clear that their image of me would be stuck in the distant past, at least for a while. I might look completely different, but in their minds, I was still a child. I was still young enough to wake them up at night with nightmares.

And for just a few minutes, I liked it that way.

There was still time for them to get used to me—the adult me, the one who could take care of herself. We were immortals, and we'd get around to it. But for this night, I was just their daughter again.

They'd have to return to their own world at some point, but with Ruadan at my side, I'd be able to see them whenever I wanted. I'd have my family back.

* * *

I LAY ALONE in the bed I shared with Ruadan, wrapped in our silky sheets. Three months had passed since I'd found my parents again, since I'd pulled the death magic off Ruadan and the Knights.

Three months of pure bliss.

Through his magic, Ruadan had lured me into sleeping in an actual bed, like a civilized person.

Outside, the setting sun cast ginger rays over periwinkle clouds. Night would fall over the Institute's ancient riverside towers soon.

I closed my eyes, thinking of the moment I'd brought him back from the dead.

The truth was, caring for other people could make you vulnerable, but it could make you strong, too—like the mums who suddenly develop the strength of a superhero to lift a car off their toddlers. My love for Ruadan had turned me into someone who could heal, not just kill.

A knock sounded on the door, and I wrapped a bed sheet around myself. Then, I crossed to the door.

I pulled it open to find Ruadan there. He was dressed in his finest black clothes, and they fitted beautifully over his powerful body. Light from the setting sun washed him in hues of gold.

He held out a flowered wreath to me.

"What's this?"

"Moonflowers for the night realm, columbines for faithfulness, myrtle for love, and yew leaves for death. I couldn't ignore the monstrous side that I love."

I took it from him, smiling. Something ivory flashed in the wreath. My nose wrinkled. "Did you put bones in this?"

"Bits of tusk from an Emain boar."

"Right. And what is that about?"

He frowned. "They're just large feral pigs, basically."

I blinked at him, and it took me a moment to remember that Ruadan had an extremely dry and extremely strange sense of humor sometimes.

Then, a smile danced over his lips. "They represent your ferocity and mine."

So he thought of me a *bit* like a feral pig. Ruadan was not the best with tact, but I loved him anyway. "Well, it's strange and perfect."

His gaze swept over me. "You're not dressed."

"It's a good thing I'm not. It's bad luck to see a bride in her dress before the wedding. How much time do we have?"

"The sun will set in about twenty minutes."

"Best leave me to get dressed, then. I'll meet you outside, when I'm making you my husband."

Of course, only a moonlight wedding would do for the Shadow Fae.

I glanced at the dress hanging on the wall. My mum had made it, of course. Dresses were more her thing than mine. It was the thinnest of materials, ephemeral and gorgeous, with tiny flecks of glittering, pale blue gems, just like the ones in her forehead.

I pulled it on and inched it down over my hips. The silky material fitted me perfectly—tight around the hips, but with enough room that I could move my legs—and the lace sleeves showed off my strong arms. My mum had done well. Even the high-heeled shoes matched the dress perfectly, though I could hardly walk in them.

I lifted the crown of flowers to my head, then turned to look at myself in the mirror. I smiled. No one did glamour like my mum, and I looked perfect. I couldn't wait to see the look on Ruadan's face, although I knew he liked me well enough in tattered, bloodied clothes anyway.

A last ray of amber light caught my eyes before the sun slipped behind the horizon completely.

"I … a darkness. Dick." A deep voice turned my head. Demented Mike stood in the door holding a flower out to me—a red anemone, just like the ones that grew on the riverbank in Eden. "For you." He smiled. "Happy."

I crossed to him and plucked it from his hand, smiling. "Thanks, Mike. We need to get you some more of that magic tea."

He shoved his hands in his pockets and turned, sauntering down the hallway, whistling. It was weirdly good to see him again, even if we still needed to work on his language skills.

I turned back to the mirror and threaded the red flower into my crown. It was only another moment before more footsteps sounded down the hall and Melusine poked her head in the door.

Then, just beside her, Ciara's freckled face, grinning.

"You guys can come in," I said. "For a minute." I peered out the window at the chairs arranged on the Tower Green in two rows of semicircles. Guests were already starting to arrive and fill them, their jewels gleaming in the twilight.

Ciara lay on my bed. She wore a pink dress with puffy sleeves and sequins, and I had no idea where she had found it, but it looked several decades old and distinctly human. She propped herself up on her elbows, staring at me dreamily. "You look beauuuuutiful. I could just light you on fire. Grrrrrrr, why does beauty make me feel aggressive?"

I wrinkled my nose. "Please don't light me on fire." Ruadan was letting her live here at the Institute with us—and so far, a little fire magic had come in handy among the Shadow Fae.

Melusine held a long bit of gossamer fabric in her hands. "I see a wedding dress, I think the wedding is about to start. I put two and two together. But you need your veil."

"I'm glad I have you here, then," I said.

I faced the window while Melusine pinned the veil to my floral crown. "What's this made out of?" I asked.

"Spider silk, woven by the dungeon spiders."

"I did not know we had dungeon spiders." I still had so much to learn about this ancient fortress....

I stared through the aged glass panes at Ruadan, who drank from a silver cup. For once, he was the one who seemed to be fortifying himself with alcohol instead of me.

My parents were out there—standing as far as they could from Ruadan's mother, Queen Macha. Gods, she still scared the shite out of me. My mother-in-law for the rest of eternity, a woman who fed off the violent subjugation of her enemies.

Well, maybe we could just avoid her.

It was at this point I realized that I had no idea how this wedding ceremony was going to work. I assumed I'd just walk down an aisle with flowers or something, but the chairs in semicircles were throwing me off. "What exactly is going to happen at this wedding, Melusine?" If anyone would know the details, it would be Melusine.

"That's right. You weren't raised among the fae nobility," Melusine pointed out. "So you have no idea. It starts with the music. Then there's the twining. Then the spirits of the fallen return to pay their respects. Then there's the dancing, eating, and more dancing for seven days, during which time everyone calls you 'queen.' That does not continue after the seven days, so don't get used to it."

I cleared my throat. "Sorry, what's the *twining?*"

"Oh, well, you'll find out soon." She nodded at the window. "The moon is out. Time to start."

I took a deep breath. All of a sudden, I was more nervous than I'd been before my gladiator matches. Gods, give me a sword and a mace and someone to kill and I knew exactly what I needed to do. A wedding ceremony surrounded by fae nobility—and a literal queen— had me trembling as I walked.

At the base of the Tower, I pulled open the door to the green.

Ciara and Melusine pushed past me, then ran frantically through the grass to get to their seats. I heaved a deep breath, trying to find Ruadan through the dim light. I couldn't see him there, and I still had no real sense of what I was supposed to do.

I took one step, then another, feeling wobbly in my high heels. Frowning, I decided I needed to ditch the heels. They weren't me. I kicked them off, hiked the dress up a bit so I could walk more freely, and just started strutting toward the center of the circle, hoping everything would work out—the confident gait of a warrior. I was meeting Ruadan there, and that was all that mattered.

As I walked, the strange fae music swelled—strings and drums that vibrated over my skin.

Everyone was watching me—my dad, my mum, Aengus, and Aenor and Cora, who were gripping each other's arms and grinning like giddy children. Queen Macha in her gleaming crown was smoking a *cigar*, blowing smoke rings and glaring at me. I had not seen that one coming.

I saw Ruadan just as the moonlight hit his perfect features, and he beamed at me, radiant and perfect as the night sky. The love in his eyes was pure magic.

Apparently, we had seven days of music, eating, and dancing ahead of us, but I would make it my mission to drag Ruadan back to our room as much as I could, and to wrap myself around him. My mind whirled with visions of our future—fighting side by side, sleeping in the same bed. Maybe children. Had we talked about children? We hadn't. Did he want children? Did I want children? I thought I did, but how would I fight demons with a giant pregnant stomach? So many questions.

But as soon as I reached him, that soothing magic whispered over my skin, and the chaos in my mind began to calm and still. Ruadan wrapped his arms around me and whispered into my ear that he loved me.

As he did, shadow magic twined around us, binding us together. Then, ropes of vines sprouted from the earth and encircled our bodies, rooting us to the earth and to each other. The plants wound firmly around us. So *this* was the twining, I supposed.

I had no idea what I was meant to do, so I pushed up onto my tiptoes and kissed Ruadan on the mouth. We were two broken monsters, now healed.

If I was a raging ocean wave, he was the dark quiet underneath. And we were perfect for each other.

* * *

THANK you for reading The Shadow Fae Books.

Please pick up the next series of books for the continuation of the story in the Sea Fae, which follows the story of Aenor.

DEMONS OF FIRE AND NIGHT: BOOKS 16-18
SEA
FAE
C.N. CRAWFORD

www.ingramcontent.com/pod-product-compliance
Lightning Source LLC
Chambersburg PA
CBHW070828020826
48982CB00015B/808